The Stirling / South Carolina Edition of James Hogg

General Editors: Douglas S. Mack and Gillian Hughes

Reviews

Chastity, carnality, carnage and carnivorousness are among his favourite subjects, and dance together in his writings to the music of a divided life. [...] The later eighteenth century was a time when [Scotland] had taken to producing writers and thinkers of world consequence. One of these–though long disregarded as such, long unimaginable as such–was Hogg.

(Karl Miller, *TLS*)

Simple congratulations are in order at the outset, to the editors and publisher of these first three handsome volumes of the projected *Collected Works* of James Hogg. It has taken a long time for Hogg to be recognised as one of the most notable Scottish writers, and it can fairly be said that the process of getting him into full and clear focus is still far from complete. That process is immeasurably helped by the provision of proper and unbowdlerised texts (in many cases for the first time), and in this the ongoing *Collected Works* will be a milestone. [...] There can be little doubt that in the prose and verse of these three volumes we have an author of unique interest, force, and originality.

(Edwin Morgan, *Scottish Literary Journal*)

Edinburgh University Press are also to be praised for the elegant presentation of the books. It is wonderful that at last we are going to have a collected edition of this important author without bowdlerisation or linguistic interference. [...] The stories [of *Tales of the Wars of Montrose*] are certainly entertaining and their history is described by the editor Gillian Hughes who has also provided notes, a glossary, an introduction, and guidance on the historical period. These books of Hogg have been wonderfully presented and edited. Hogg's own idiosyncratic style has been left untouched.

(Iain Crichton Smith, *Studies in Scottish Literature*)

[*Winter Evening Tales*] is the 11th volume in the ground-breaking Stirling / South Carolina research edition of Hogg's works, a project which has time   ew insights into his uneven (ion and exceptional editing b   ists

D1439610

Reviews of the Stirling / South Carolina Edition
(continued)

some of Hogg's best work—the macabre story 'The Long Pack', the wierdly brilliant 'Connel of Dee' [...] glints of his sophistication and capacity for burlesque; and a radical double-take on his rival Scott's novels.

(**SB Kelly**, *Scotland on Sunday*)

As Ian Duncan observes in his astute introduction, 'Far from being naive, Hogg's "simplicity" is the effect of a subtle art' [...] Nor is the subtle art confined to the narration of the individual tales: the collection works collectively, each piece contrasting, and yet oddly consistent, with its neighbours. Like an intricate pattern, threads appear in one tale, to disappear and be picked up again in different company later on. To read the stories in sequence is to enjoy both a series of beautifully crafted, strongly textured tales and a more complicated work in which individual pieces comment on each other, sometimes confirming, sometimes ironising the truths that have become evident so far. [...] Gratitude galore is therefore due to Ian Duncan and to the general editors, Douglas Mack and Gillian Hughes, for enabling readers to appreciate Hogg's extraordinary collection of tales once more, in this finely-produced, beautifully-edited addition to *The Collected Works of James Hogg*.

(**Fiona Stafford**, *Studies in Hogg and his World*)

While [Hogg's] great longer stories and novels remain mysterious and challenging, these tales, often more successful and widely-read in his lifetime, present more immediate puzzles which, as the title of one of these collections suggests, can engage the reader in a single evening (of whatever season). *Winter Evening Tales* is a marvellously inventive collection, full of interest and diversity. [...] In an edition that is continually uncovering, or recovering, works of real interest and real readerly enjoyment, *Winter Evening Tales* stands out on both counts.

(**Penny Fielding**, *Scottish Studies Review*)

JAMES HOGG

Winter Evening Tales

Edited by
Ian Duncan

With a Chronology
by Gillian Hughes

EDINBURGH UNIVERSITY PRESS
2004

© Edinburgh University Press, 2004

Edinburgh University Press
22 George Square
Edinburgh
EH8 9LF

Typeset at the University of Stirling
Printed and bound in Wales by Creative Print & Design, Ebbw Vale

ISBN 0 7486 2086 9

A CIP record for this book is available from the British Library

The publisher acknowledges support from

 Scottish
Arts Council

towards the publication of this volume

Hogg Rediscovered
A New Edition of a Major Writer

This book forms part of a series of paperback reprints of selected volumes from the Stirling / South Carolina Research Edition of the Collected Works of James Hogg (S/SC Edition). Published by Edinburgh University Press, the S/SC Edition (when completed) will run to some thirty-four volumes. The existence of this large-scale international scholarly project is a confirmation of the current consensus that James Hogg (1770–1835) is one of Scotland's major writers.

The high regard in which Hogg is now held is a comparatively recent development. In his own lifetime, he was regarded as one of the leading writers of the day, but the nature of his fame was influenced by the fact that, as a young man, he had been a self-educated shepherd. The second edition (1813) of his long poem *The Queen's Wake* contains an 'Advertisement' which begins as follows.

> The Publisher having been favoured with letters from gentlemen in various parts of the United Kingdom respecting the Author of the *Queen's Wake*, and most of them expressing doubts of his being a Scotch Shepherd; he takes this opportunity of assuring the Public, that *The Queen's Wake* is really and truly the production of *James Hogg*, a common shepherd, bred among the mountains of Ettrick Forest, who went to service when only seven years of age; and since that period has never received any education whatever.

This 'Advertisement' is redolent of a class prejudice also reflected in the various early reviews of *The Private Memoirs and Confessions of a Justified Sinner*, the book by which Hogg is now best known. This novel appeared anonymously in 1824, but many of the early reviews identify Hogg as the author, and see the *Justified Sinner* as presenting 'an incongruous mixture of the strongest powers with the strongest absurdities'. The Scotch Shepherd was regarded as a man of powerful and original talent, but it was felt that his lack of education caused his work to be marred by frequent failures in discretion, in expression, and in knowledge of the world. Worst of all was Hogg's lack of what was called 'delicacy', a failing which caused him to deal in his writings with subjects (such as prostitution) that were felt to be unsuitable for mention in polite literature. Hogg was regarded by these reviewers, and by his contemporaries in general, as a man of undoubted genius, but his genius was felt to be seriously flawed.

A posthumous collected edition of Hogg was published in the late 1830s. As was perhaps natural in all the circumstances, the publishers (Blackie & Son of Glasgow) took pains to smooth away what they took to be the rough edges of Hogg's writing, and to remove his numerous 'indelicacies'. This process was taken even further in the 1860s, when the Rev. Thomas Thomson prepared a revised edition of Hogg's *Works* for publication by Blackie. These Blackie editions present a bland and lifeless version of Hogg's writings. It was in this version that Hogg was read by the Victorians, and, unsurprisingly, he came to be regarded as a minor figure, of no great importance or interest. Indeed, by the first half of the twentieth century Hogg's reputation had dwindled to such an extent that he was widely dismissed as a vain, talent-free, and oafish peasant.

Nevertheless, the latter part of the twentieth century saw a substantial revival of Hogg's reputation. This revival was sparked by the republication in 1947 of an unbowdlerised edition of the *Justified Sinner*, with an enthusiastic Introduction by André Gide. During the second half of the twentieth century Hogg's rehabilitation continued, thanks to the republication of some of his texts in new editions. This process entered a new phase when the first three volumes of the S/SC Edition appeared in 1995, and the S/SC Edition as it proceeds is revealing a hitherto unsuspected range and depth in Hogg's achievement. It is no longer possible to regard him as a one-book wonder.

Some of the books that are being published in the S/SC Edition had been out of print for more than a century and a half, while others, still less fortunate, had never been published at all in their original, unbowdlerised condition. Hogg is now being revealed as a major writer whose true stature was not recognised in his own lifetime because his social origins led to his being smothered in genteel condescension; and whose true stature has not been recognised since, because of a lack of adequate editions. The poet Douglas Dunn wrote of Hogg in the *Glasgow Herald* in September 1988: 'I can't help but think that in almost any other country of Europe a complete, modern edition of a comparable author would have been available long ago'. The Stirling / South Carolina Research Edition of James Hogg, from which the present paperback is reprinted, seeks to fill the gap identified by Douglas Dunn.

Douglas S. Mack

General Editors' Acknowledgements

The research for the first volumes of the Stirling / South Carolina Edition of James Hogg has been sustained by funding and other support generously made available by the University of Stirling and by the University of South Carolina. Valuable grants or donations have also been received from the Carnegie Trust for the Universities of Scotland, from the Modern Humanities Research Association, from the Association for Scottish Literary Studies, and from the James Hogg Society. We also record with gratitude the fact that the contributions of Dr Gillian Hughes and Dr Janette Currie to the present volume (see Volume Editor's Acknowledgements) were made possible by a major research grant awarded by the United Kingdom's Arts and Humanities Research Board to the Stirling/South Carolina Edition. The work of the Edition could not have been carried on without the support of these bodies. The General Editor for this volume was Gill Hughes.

Volume Editor's Acknowledgements

I have incurred many debts in the preparation of this edition of *Winter Evening Tales*, above all to the General Editors of the Stirling/ South Carolina Edition, Douglas Mack and Gillian Hughes. Their knowledge of Hogg, his world, and the lore of scholarly editing is exceeded only by their generosity and patience. Gill Hughes ought really to be listed as a co-editor of this volume—she kept me supplied with wise advice and vital information, weeded out many errors, and cheered me up along the way. I shall miss our working together.

I am also grateful to my research assistant at Berkeley, Nick Nace, for the diligence, accuracy, and good humour he brought to the final stages of preparation; and to Audrey Healy, at Yale, who transcribed the second volume. I owe a great deal to the community of scholars of Hogg and Scottish Romanticism, much of which will be evident in these pages. Among those who responded to my calls for help, Peter Garside, Suzanne Gilbert and Ann Rowland were especially generous with their time and expertise. Jenni Calder, Hugh Cheape, Penny Fielding, Caroline Jackson-Houlston, Tony Inglis, Wilma Mack, Donald Mackenzie, Jean Moffat, the late Jill Rubenstein and Olena Turnbull also assisted with inquiries. Janette Currie deserves special thanks for supplying me with information about early magazine printings of 'The Long Pack', incorporated into this paperback edition.

I thank the Trustees of the National Library of Scotland, the Houghton Library at Harvard University, the Beinecke Rare Book and Manuscript Library at Yale University, and the John Murray Archive for permission to use and cite manuscript materials in their holdings. And I thank the librarians and staff of the National Library of Scotland, the Yale University Libraries, the Knight Library at the University of Oregon, the Alexander Turnbull Library at the National Library of New Zealand, the Stirling University Library, the University of British Columbia Library, and the Bancroft and Doe Libraries at Berkeley. Material assistance was provided at various stages by the Whitney Humanities Center at Yale University, the Barbara and Carlisle Moore endowment at the University of Oregon Department of English, and the Committee on Research of the Academic Senate at the University of California, Berkeley.

Ian Duncan
University of California,
Berkeley

Contents

Introduction

Winter Evening Tales (1820) belongs to the era of cultural innovation and experimentation we call 'Romanticism'. Nothing like it had been published before; nothing quite like it would follow. *Winter Evening Tales* was also James Hogg's most successful work of prose fiction in his lifetime. Widely and favourably reviewed, it sold well enough for the publishers to bring out a second edition, corrected by the author, a distinction achieved by none of Hogg's other prose fiction titles. Several editions of *Winter Evening Tales* appeared in the U.S.A., and a selection from it was translated into German.

Winter Evening Tales also had the most complicated genesis of any of Hogg's works. Its different stages of composition, publication and revision span the whole of his career. Despite a claim that he wrote most of the tales in his shepherding youth and 'altered nothing', many of them had already appeared in print, notably in Hogg's weekly periodical *The Spy* (1810–11), and were revised for *Winter Evening Tales*, in some cases substantially. In the decade following *The Spy* Hogg offered his stock of 'rural and traditionary tales' to several Edinburgh publishers, including Constable and Blackwood, before Oliver and Boyd brought out *Winter Evening Tales* in the spring of 1820. In the last years of his life Hogg negotiated with a series of publishers to reissue his collected fiction under the generic title of *Winter Evening Tales*. However *Tales and Sketches of the Ettrick Shepherd*, as the collected edition was eventually called, published posthumously and reissued throughout the nineteenth century, omitted several pieces that had appeared in *Winter Evening Tales*, including one of the very best, and abridged and bowdlerised some of those it did keep.

In effect, then, despite its early success, *Winter Evening Tales* disappeared after Hogg's death, as it was broken up and diluted in the posthumous edition of his works. Restoration of the original collection enlarges our view not only of Hogg's achievement but of British Romantic fiction as a whole. The outstanding example of a 'national' genre pioneered by Hogg, the miscellaneous collection of regional popular narratives, *Winter Evening Tales* poses a vibrant demotic alternative to the culturally and commercially dominant form of the historical novel established in 1814 by Walter Scott. Hogg's experimental medley of stories, novellas, anecdotes, poems and sketches contains some of his most engaging (as well as some of his strangest) inventions: terse masterpieces of mystery and the uncanny ('Adam Bell', 'The Long Pack'), virtuoso improvisations on folktale themes ('John Gray o' Middleholm'), moving renditions of vernacular storytelling ('An Old Soldier's Tale', 'Tibby Johnston's Wraith'), an alternately pathetic and ludicrous historical romance ('The Bridal of Polmood') and–the collection's highlights–two brilliant autobiographical novellas, 'The Renowned Adventures of Basil Lee' and 'Love Adventures of Mr George Cochrane'.

1. Production

Hogg's 'Memoir of the Author's Life' (1821) offers a romanticised account of the production of *Winter Evening Tales*:

> The greater part of these Tales was written in early life, when I was serving as a shepherd lad among the mountains, and on looking them over, I saw well enough that there was a blunt rusticity about them; but I liked them the better for it, and altered nothing. To me they appeared not only more characteristic of the life that I then led, but also of the manners that I was describing.[1]

In fact the book's gestation involved several stages of publication and quite a lot of textual alteration. Eleven of the tales had appeared a decade earlier, in Hogg's periodical *The Spy*. While some of the slighter pieces were reprinted without revision, Hogg worked up others into more ambitious narratives, in two cases ('The Renowned Adventures of Basil Lee', 'Love Adventures of Mr George Cochrane') developing loose sketches into fully-realised novellas. *Winter Evening Tales* included several other pieces designed for publication elsewhere. First printed in magazines in 1809–10, 'The Long Pack' enjoyed a lively chapbook circulation before Hogg revised it for *Winter Evening Tales*. A version of 'King Gregory' had been printed in the *Edinburgh Annual Register for 1812* (1814). 'Connel of Dee' had been written in 1814 for an unpublished volume of poems called *Midsummer Night Dreams*. A version of 'Halbert of Lyne' had appeared in a book by Hogg's friend R. P. Gillies, *Illustrations of a Poetical Character* (1816); Hogg and Gillies may have collaborated on the poem. The 'Shepherd's Calendar' sketches had appeared in 1817 and 1819 in *Blackwood's Edinburgh Magazine*. 'An Old Soldier's Tale', rejected by Blackwood, appeared in the *Clydesdale Magazine* in 1818. 'The Bridal of Polmood' (the longest piece in the collection) and three shorter tales made up the set.[2]

Hogg's account of the genesis of *Winter Evening Tales* was part of the new material he wrote to update his 'Memoir' for the second edition of *The Mountain Bard*, the work with which he had first won a measure of literary fame in 1807. In *The Mountain Bard* Hogg assumed the title of 'The Ettrick Shepherd', an untutored rustic genius, and the 'Memoir' is accordingly more concerned with promoting this pastoral-bardic persona than with literal accuracy about *Winter Evening Tales*. Nevertheless, we need not doubt Hogg's claim that much of *Winter Evening Tales* was 'written in early life', if we cultivate a flexible enough sense of what he might have meant by 'writing'. Recent scholarship has challenged the idea of a strict demarcation between cultural practices of orality and literacy; in transitional states of modernisation, especially, 'literary' and 'oral' acts of invention, improvisation, memorisation, compilation, transcription and revision are mixed together in the work of composition.[3] In an early bid to interest a publisher in his collection of tales, Hogg described his creative process as a reflexive relation between 'collecting' and 'writing over': 'I have for many years been collecting the rural and traditionary tales of Scotland and I have of late been writing them over again and new-modelling them'.[4] Collecting, writing over, new-modelling: the terms characterise a writing practice in which invention and transcription, supposed to undergo a functional separation in modern culture, remain fused, fluid. Just as some of Hogg's songs flowed in and out of 'folk' tradition, or local cultures of oral peformance, so some of the stories in *Winter Evening Tales* circulated in the anonymous popular print media of chapbook and weekly miscellany. Authorship is a variable, not fixed, function in these cultural circumstances, and Hogg's tales mix oral- and print-cultural conventions as promiscuously as they mix genres. In 'John Gray o' Middleholm' Hogg shows off his virtuosity as an interpreter of tradition, ringing variations on a widely-diffused yet regionally specific folk tale—even incorporating a narrative twist from St Luke's gospel. Elsewhere he represents himself as recording the narratives of local informants in their own words; it is not possible for us to make a distinction between invention and reportage. In the case of 'The Long Pack' the author performs as a sort of auto-collector, reclaiming his own chapbook rendition of an apocryphal item of local 'news'. 'The Bridal of Polmood' stages a subversion of history, the official written record of books and archives, by a blatant 'invention of tradition'.

Hogg was forty years old when he committed himself to a full-time literary career. After a decade or so contributing occasional poems and letters to periodicals, he had made enough money from *The Mountain Bard* to lease and stock two farms in Dumfriesshire. Both investments failed: 'in February 1810, in utter desperation, I took my plaid about my shoulders, and marched away to Edinburgh, determined, since no better could be, to push my fortune as a literary man'.[5] Hogg attempted to take the metropolis by storm—editing a weekly periodical called *The Spy*, the greater part of which he also wrote himself. It was in *The Spy*, according to its modern editor, that 'Hogg made the transition from occasional author to professional literary man'—a transition marked by the shepherd-poet's '[discovery of] his creative voice in prose'.[6] Hogg's tales and sketches, many of them experimenting with popular narrative voices, are the most original component of *The Spy*, making it—in Robert Crawford's words —'one of the places the modern short story was born'.[7] But polite readers, offended by the sexual content of some of the stories, cancelled their subscriptions, and *The Spy* folded at the end of August 1811, exactly a year after its first issue.

Undeterred, Hogg kept up his new-found aptitude for prose fiction. In October he describes himself 'scribbling away every day' in a letter to his friend Eliza Izet: 'I have finished a highland tale lately and some smaller pieces'.[8] Eighteen months later, in the spring of 1813, he made the first of several attempts to launch a book-length collection of prose tales drawing on material from *The Spy*. No doubt the completion of his most ambitious work to date, a volume of original ballads in a historical-romantic frame called *The Queen's Wake*, set an encouraging precedent. On 23 March he informed Mrs Izet of his intention to publish 'two volumes of Scottish rural tales sometime this year', preferably 'in London and under a feigned name', and solicited her advice as to 'which of those in the Spy I should select'.[9] On 3 April he wrote to his first patron and mentor, Walter Scott:

> I would fain publish 2 vol[s] 8vo. close print of *Scottish Rural Tales* anonymous in prose I have one will make about 200 pages alone[.] some of the others you have seen in the Spy &c. Some people say they are original and interesting.[10]

(The longer tale is most likely 'The Bridal of Polmood', which alludes to the lawsuit over the Hunter inheritance ongoing in 1813.) Hogg decided to give first refusal of the prose tales to Archibald Constable—the most prestigious of the Edinburgh booksellers, the publisher of the *Edinburgh Review* and Scott's poetry, as well as Hogg's earlier ballad and song collections *The Mountain Bard* and *The Forest Minstrel*. Constable however had been cool about *The Queen's Wake*, and Hogg had taken it to another publisher. Hogg's decision to approach him again, on the crest of that work's success, shows a certain audacity. It is unlikely that the idea came from Scott, who was at that moment engaged in delicate negotations with Constable on his own behalf. Although Scott had broken off business relations with Constable in 1809, the desperate state of affairs at his own firm of Ballantyne & Co., exacerbated by a crisis in the national money-market, drove him to sign a new agreement with the publisher on 18 May 1813.[11]

Hogg sent in his proposal to Constable just two days later. Perhaps he had got wind of Scott's arrangement, and thought he might try his luck there too. Hogg explains that the prose tales will be a new departure for him:

> I have for many years been collecting the rural and traditionary tales of Scotland and I have of late been writing them over again and new-modelling them, and have the vanity to suppose they will form a most interesting work[.] They will fill two large vols 8vo price £1 or 4 vols 12mo price the same[.] But as I think the Ettrick Shepherd is rather become a hackneyed name, and imagine that having gained a character as a bard is perhaps no commendation to a writer of prose tales I am determined to publish them under a fictitious title. The title page will consequently be to this purpose. *The Rural and Traditionary Tales of Scotland* by J. H. Craig of Douglas Esq[.]
>
> With regard to pecuniary concerns I am not at all greedy that way and have not the least doubt of our agreement only I should like to bargain so that the work or at least the edition should belong exclusively to the publisher that so he may have an interest in furthering it to the utmost of his power. As I really do intend to conceal the real author that the critics may not suppose it is the work of a book-maker and as no one in Edin. knows of it save Mr. J. Grieve you will easily see the propriety my dear sir of concealing this from all living[.][12]

Hogg's desire to mask his authorship, for reasons of literary decorum as well as commercial advantage, looks forward to the 'anonymity game' soon to be played with a world-wide public by Scott. But Constable was not interested, not even when Hogg wrote to him again in July proposing the issue of a single volume to test the waters.[13] Fiction was not in Constable's line—until the following year, when he consented to publish a novel called *Waverley*.[14] In any case, as part of the May 1813 agreement signed with Scott, Constable had just taken over a large portion of unprofitable Ballantyne inventory, including several volumes of *Popular Tales* and *Tales of the East* edited by Henry Weber, another Scott protégé. No doubt the acquisition fortified his reluctance to speculate on four volumes of tales by James Hogg.

The unprecedented success of the Waverley Novels guaranteed a predominance of prose fiction in Scottish publishing in the decade after Waterloo, and a corresponding decline of the wartime genre of the long metrical romance. With Scott's example before him, it was natural that Hogg should try again to sell his rural tales. Four years after the approach to Constable, he took the proposal to an ambitious rival bookseller named William Blackwood, who had begun to rise in the trade thanks largely to his position as Scottish agent of the London publisher John Murray. Blackwood took over *The Queen's Wake* when its original publisher, George Goldie, went out of business, and he was bringing out two more volumes of Hogg's verse romances. In 1816 he acquired—but subsequently lost—Scott's *Tales of My Landlord*, a series of Scottish historical novels with regional settings. On 4 January 1817 Hogg wrote to Blackwood, 'My "Cottage Winter Nights" is ready for the press':

> The work consists of "The Rural and Traditionary Tales of Scotland"[.] They are simple carelessly and badly written but said to be very interesting[.] The Bridal of Polmood which you read is the longest tale, not the best, but a fair specimen[.][15]

Hogg asked Blackwood for a copyright fee of £63 7s. per volume of 300 pages. In his 'Memoir' Hogg says he showed Blackwood the manuscript of 'two tales I wished to publish', 'The Bridal of Polmood' and 'The Brownie of Bodsbeck'. Blackwood accepted 'The Brownie' but 'would have nothing to do' with 'The Bridal of Polmood'. Hogg replaced it with 'The Wool-gatherer', revised from *The Spy* (where it had appeared as 'The Country Laird', February 1811), and a new tale, 'The Hunt of Eildon', to make up a two-volume set.[16] If the set sold well, another two volumes would follow. In December Hogg wrote to Mrs Izet: 'My Cottage tales in prose will be published in the spring two or four volumes as my friends shall advise after they have seen the first two[.]'[17] In the New Year he sent Blackwood the text of an advertisement:

> In the press and speedily will be published Vol's 1 and 2
> of Mr Hogg's *Cottage Tales* containing *The Brownie of Bodsbeck*
> and *The Wool-Gatherer*. These tales have been selected by him
> among the Shepherds and peasantry of Scotland and are ar-
> ranged so as to delineate the manners and superstitions of
> that class in ancient and modern times &c &c[18]

It thus seems clear, as Douglas Mack has suggested, that the two
volumes published by Blackwood in May, 1818–*The Brownie of
Bodsbeck; and Other Tales*–were drawn from the stock of 'rural and
traditionary tales' Hogg had offered Constable five years earlier.[19]

Sales of *The Brownie of Bodsbeck* were disappointing, however, and
Blackwood declined the remaining two volumes of 'Cottage Tales'.
In 1819 Hogg offered them to another Edinburgh firm, Oliver and
Boyd, who were printing his song collection *Jacobite Relics of Scotland*
for Blackwood. Hogg had been acquainted with George Oliver since
at least 1804, when the latter ('then one of the best singers in Scotland') sang his patriotic song 'Donald M'Donald' at a 'great ma-
sonic meeting' in Edinburgh.[20] The suggestion to approach Oliver
and Boyd seems to have come from Blackwood, who would also
help Hogg secure Longmans for his novel in progress, *The Perilous
Castle* (*The Three Perils of Man*). Afterwards, Blackwood complained
that Hogg had led him to believe that *Winter Evening Tales* would
consist only of reprinted pieces from *The Spy* (in other words, the
material left over from *The Brownie of Bodsbeck*), edited by Hogg's
nephew, Robert Hogg; and that, as in Hogg's original proposal for
'Cottage Winter Nights', the collection would appear anonymously.
Blackwood's complaint casts an interesting light on the tightly-knit
Edinburgh publishing world, with its volatile mixture of hearty
collegiality and fierce rivalry. Writing several months after the work's
publication, in the course of a rather complicated disagreement between author and publisher, Blackwood charges Hogg with having
abused his confidence:

> It was on this principle when you first talked to me of your
> Tales, that I advised you to give the book to Boyd *because it
> was to be anonymous* you told me. To my great disgust and
> astonishment however a few months afterwards it was ad-
> vertised with your name. How this happened I never en-
> quired at you, for I supposed that Boyd, to serve his own
> interest, had prevailed upon you to agree to this, and that
> then you found yourself obliged to write new matter and

make the Book a good deal different from what you at first
told me it was to be a collection of Tales from the Spy Magazines &c collected and published by your Nephew.[21]

While Blackwood had refused to publish more of Hogg's tales, evidently he still regarded his name as a valuable property. Indeed the
use of that name by other authors in *Blackwood's Edinburgh Magazine*
was one of the grounds of the present quarrel.[22]

Hogg signed an agreement with Oliver and Boyd on 2 August
1819 for an edition of 1500 copies of the new work, for which he
would receive £100, payable in two promissory notes. Oliver and
Boyd sold half of the edition to their London associates, G. & W. B.
Whittaker, for the same fee.[23] Peter Garside characterises Hogg's
new publishers:

> Oliver & Boyd had only published two novels to date (both
> in 1819), but were to manage a good handful in the new
> decade. Their choice of partners was also felicitous. Rela-
> tively new to the scene, Whittakers were soon to become
> major publishers of fiction in the 1820s (responsible [...] for
> 49 works or 7.4 per cent of production). With a list made up
> of Scott imitations and domestic moral tales, they were not
> obtrusively 'evangelical' nor specialists in 'silver fork' fic-
> tion. Oliver & Boyd were equally pragmatists, claimed good
> connexions with the wholesale trade, and were more than
> willing to offer 'liberal' terms to shift stock fast. Such factors
> help explain the moderate but real success achieved by *Win-
> ter Evening Tales*.[24]

Announced as forthcoming (in the *Edinburgh Weekly Journal*) as early
as 25 August 1819, *Winter Evening Tales* stalled at the press for eight
months: 'I am really sorry that work has been so long in the press
but we have both been partly to blame', Hogg wrote to Boyd on 8
March 1820. No doubt the publication of *Jacobite Relics* contributed
to the delay; the publishers' correspondence with Whittaker also
comments that 'the Authors being 40 Miles from this has retarded
us much'.[25] Hogg may have found himself obliged to produce more
copy than he had originally calculated. According to the terms of the
agreement, the new work was to consist of two volumes, each containing 'not less than 350 pages'—a standard format.[26] However, the
printers set Hogg's text in such a small, cramped typeface that he
had to supply them with the equivalent of nearly four volumes' worth
of copy to make up the set. *Winter Evening Tales* was advertised in the
New Year and published, at last, in two volumes duodecimo, price

fourteen shillings, on 19 April 1820.

Three months later, George Boyd wrote to Hogg informing him that the *Tales* were 'selling well'; Whittaker reported lively business in London.[27] Encouraged by the news, Hogg contemplated making Oliver and Boyd 'not only my publishers but my principal ones', promising them a new edition of *The Mountain Bard* and even *The Brownie of Bodsbeck*.[28] By October author and publishers were negotiating over a second edition of 1000 copies. Boyd urged Hogg to be 'as moderate as possible' so that they would be able to offer 'liberal terms' to Whittakers and the wholesale trade. Hogg requested and received £116 13s. 4d.; the agreement was signed on 26 March 1821.[29] In asking for this sum, one sixth of the calculated retail profits of the edition, Hogg seems to have been following advice given to him by Scott in 1818.[30] Garside speculates that the exorbitance of the demand provoked Oliver and Boyd to turn down Hogg's next work of fiction.[31] Yet they agreed to his terms readily enough; Scott's career was at its zenith, and publishers were happy to invest large sums in Scottish fiction. Perhaps Hogg was not being altogether unreasonable when he complained of having been 'manifestly taken in the last edition'—especially since he had provided four volumes' worth of work for the price of two.[32] While nobody could expect to match the copyright fees earned by Scott, first-time author Robert Mudie had received £200 from Oliver and Boyd for his satiric national tale *Glenfergus*, published concurrently with *Winter Evening Tales* and advertised alongside it—riding on the more famous, but worse paid, author's coat-tails. (Indeed, the strategy appears to have persuaded people that *Glenfergus* must also be by Hogg.)[33]

The second edition of *Winter Evening Tales* featured corrections by the author—limited to the first volume, since the second, apparently, did not need them. (Hogg's revisions are discussed in the 'Note on the Text' to this edition.) The edition sold slowly, however, and Oliver and Boyd turned down Hogg's 'Border romance', *The Three Perils of Man. Winter Evening Tales* did remarkably well in the U.S.A., although the absence of an international copyright agreement meant that Hogg never made a penny from American sales. Two competing editions appeared in 1820 in New York (from Campbell, Duyckinck, Collins, Long and Bliss; and from Kirk & Mercein, Wiley & Halstead, W. B. Gilley, and Haly & Thomas). Leavitt and Allen republished it in the 1830s, and again in the 1850s; while editions appeared in Philadelphia in 1836 (Walker), and in Hartford in 1847 and 1851 (Silas Andrus—a reprint of the New York Leavitt and Allen edition.) A German translation of selected Tales, *Die Wanderer im*

Hochlande: Winter-Abend-Erzählungen, charmingly ascribed to 'Sir James Hogg' and with a preface by Sophie Man, was published in Berlin in 1822 and again in Vienna in 1826.[34] An 1823 instalment of the 'Noctes Ambrosianae' has Hogg gloating, 'how they translate me in Germany[!]'[35]

The relative success of *Winter Evening Tales* gave it a leading role in Hogg's later ambitions for his prose fiction. In October 1822, complaining to Boyd about the sluggish sales of the second edition, he announced: 'I want the Brownie &c as I was telling you and all published in a set as *Winter Evening Tales* and either a continuation in other two vols or not as you please'.[36] Hogg had always thought of *The Brownie* as belonging to the series that he variously called 'Rural and Traditionary Tales', 'Cottage Winter Nights' and 'Winter Evening Tales', and he recurred to the idea throughout the remainder of his career. Vexed by financial troubles in 1826, he wrote to Blackwood, 'I think the whole of my select Scottish tales should be published in Numbers one every month with the Magazine to be packed with it and a part of the first No sent gratis to some of your principal readers'. This was an idea some years ahead of its time. Hogg followed up with a more conventional proposal for 'an edition of my Scottish tales revised in four close printed volumes and the Shepherd's Callander in two'.[37] He tried again in 1829, provoked by the appearance of the first volumes of Scott's 'Magnum Opus'. This time Blackwood replied cautiously that he might be interested, if Lockhart were to edit the collection; but Lockhart privately informed Blackwood he would have nothing to do with it, and Blackwood dragged his feet.[38] As late as June 1831 Hogg was still discussing the possibility of Blackwood's reissuing his tales in twelve monthly numbers; and in December he had not given up hope that Lockhart would write a preface for 'Winter Evening Tales *a new series*' or 'The Tales of Altrive' and see it through the press.[39] Relations between Hogg and Blackwood broke down later that month, and Hogg turned to a new publisher, James Cochrane in London. The collection began to appear, at last, the following year, under the title of *Altrive Tales: Collected Among the Peasantry of Scotland, and from Foreign Adventurers*. This was to be a twelve-volume set, 'printed uniformly with the Waverley Novels'; volumes four through seven were to be made up of stories from *The Shepherd's Calendar* and *Winter Evening Tales*. Unfortunately, Cochrane went bankrupt after the appearance of the first volume, and no more were published.

The project was finally taken up in 1833 by John Blackie, a Glasgow publisher specialising in works of devotion and 'useful knowl-

edge' rather than fiction. It was Blackie who realised Hogg's idea
that his tales be reissued in monthly numbers. Evidence recently
brought to light by Gillian Hughes and Peter Garside indicates that
Hogg's tales were printed in gatherings suitable for issue in shilling
parts before being bound into volumes, although it appears that they
were actually published in monthly volumes at five shillings each.[40]
The cheap reissue format in parts and volumes, originally projected
by Constable as a vehicle for gaining new classes of readers in an
era of unprecedented demographic expansion, had been pioneered
after the publisher's death by his former partner Robert Cadell in
Constable's Miscellany (1826–35) and the 'Magnum Opus' edition of
the Waverley Novels (1829–33). The success of 'Magnum Opus'
inspired a number of avowed imitations and supplements, such as
Murray's *Works of Lord Byron* (1832–33) and Colburn and Bentley's
Standard Novels (1831–55). Hogg's early enthusiasm for the format
suggests (contrary to the stereotype of the unworldly Shepherd) that
he was keenly attuned to new developments in the publishing trade
as well as to the circumstances of his public. He claims, interest-
ingly, 'that I am by far most popular in England', and that 'next to
Scott's Tales' the new edition 'will be the most popular circulating
Library work in Scotland'.[41] The double boast reflects a desire to
reach different classes of readers: if 'circulating library' suggests a
middle-class public, most of the expanding population of literate
artisans and tradesmen was to be found now in England. (Rather
touchingly, Hogg also urges Blackie to make sure that the tales are
printed in a large typeface, 'for old people are fondest of them'.[42])
Nor was Hogg's sense of his readers misguided. Garside has found
records of *The Brownie of Bodsbeck* and *Winter Evening Tales*–Hogg's
original sets of 'rural and traditionary tales'–in libraries of the newly
founded Mechanics Institutes in England and Scotland, as well as in
circulating libraries.[43] The American popularity of *Winter Evening
Tales* indicates a public less bothered by the charges of 'coarseness'
levelled against Hogg by his British reviewers, who were busy forg-
ing a Victorian standard of middle-class taste.

In the last decade of his life, then, Hogg envisaged a collected
edition of his prose tales that would compete with the Waverley
Novels, Scott's 'official' set of national historical novels dedicated to
King George IV, by offering an alternative model of Scottish fiction.
This arming of commercial imitation with formal and ideological
critique had become Hogg's characteristic strategy for following
Scott's lead in the literary marketplace. Instead of the stately proces-
sion of historical romances, Hogg's tales and sketches reiterate their

miscellaneous, popular origins and resist absorption into a larger, synthetic, uniform genre—a 'Waverley novel'. It thus makes little sense to assimilate Hogg's conception of a 'collected works' to the canonical formation of the author's *œuvre* that Scott translated to the novel from the high genres of drama and poetry. 'Winter Evening Tales', like 'Rural and Traditionary Tales' or 'Cottage Tales' or 'Altrive Tales', is the generic title for a loose, capacious, fluid stock of narratives that Hogg drew upon, reworked and recombined throughout his career as opportunity arose. Now he insisted, once again, on restoring *The Brownie of Bodsbeck* to the set. This along with some new material would make up 'The Ettrick Shepherd's + *Winter Evening Tales* + A new edition + Greatly enlarged and improved + *The Brownie of Bodsbeck* to constitute the first numbers of the series + New tales the second &c &c'.[44]

Hogg died at the end of 1835. The Blackie edition, called *Tales and Sketches, by the Ettrick Shepherd*, appeared in six monthly volumes from December 1836, in an identical format ('small octavo', i.e. 18mo, volumes retailing at 5s. each) to the Scott 'Magnum Opus' edition. *Tales and Sketches* included two hitherto unpublished pieces in the reshuffled gathering of reprinted (and re-edited) tales, novels and extracts. Nine of the original *Winter Evening Tales* are omitted, however, including one of the set's highlights, 'Love Adventures of Mr. George Cochrane'—presumably judged too racy for what was by now a Victorian public. *Tales and Sketches* also excludes 'Highland Adventures', 'Dreadful Story of Macpherson', 'Maria's Tale', 'A Singular Dream', and (another of the highlights) 'John Gray o' Middleholm', along with the three poems; 'Connell of Dee' appears, however, in the companion set of *Poetical Works of the Ettrick Shepherd*. *Tales and Sketches* also features the author's 'final corrections', some of which are drastic, although scholars have decided that few of them (a notable exception being *The Brownie of Bodsbeck*) were made by Hogg. This was the version in which Victorian and modern readers encountered what was left of *Winter Evening Tales*.

2. The Literary Context

In his 1813 proposal to Constable, Hogg seeks to detach the new project from his established persona as 'The Ettrick Shepherd':

> I have for many years been collecting the rural and traditionary tales of Scotland and I have of late been writing them over again and new-modelling them [...] But as I think

the Ettrick Shepherd is rather become a hackneyed name,
and imagine that having gained a character as a bard is perhaps no commendations [*sic*] to a writer of prose tales I am
determined to publish them under a fictitious title[.] The title
page will consequently be to this purpose. *The Rural and
Traditionary Tales of Scotland* by J. H. Craig of Douglas Esq.[45]

Hogg recognises that different genres may require different types of
author. The distinction between 'bard' and 'writer of prose tales'
follows the Scottish Enlightenment history of cultural forms, according to which poetry originates in primitive societies close to nature,
while prose is a later, commercial development.[46] Hogg proposes
(in Schiller's useful terminology) to exchange the guise of 'naive
poet', the mouthpiece of an organic community, for that of a 'sentimental' author, interpreting that community–his own alienated origins–to modern readers. The bardic role of Ettrick Shepherd had
committed Hogg to a highly problematic cultural ethos of 'authenticity'–problematic in that it turned out to rely, as Hogg's critics kept
reminding him, upon a radical separation of his poetic powers from
modern, polite society and manners. In *The Spy* Hogg had experi-
mented with an avowedly modern and urban editorial persona, able
to represent metropolitan life through a metamorphic fluidity of style.
But Mr Spy proved too volatile–too alienated–for the Edinburgh
cultural establishment, and (as Hogg complained) it shut him down.
The new persona proposed in the letter to Constable, 'J. H. Craig
of Douglas Esq.', offers a more solid, reputable mediation between
rustic and polite cultural identities, in the figure–made canonical by
Scott, Border Sheriff and Laird–of a local landowner.

Elaine Petrie has offered the ingenious and plausible suggestion
that 'J. H. Craig of Douglas' is a cipher for 'J[ames] H[ogg] [writing
from] Craig of Douglas', the name of a hill on the farm of Blackhouse
overlooking the confluence of the Douglas Burn and Yarrow Water.[47] This was the heartland of the great Border ballads, and Hogg
had worked here as a shepherd in the 1790s, as we read in one of
the sketches included in *Winter Evening Tales*. The pseudonym allows
Hogg, then, to combine both kinds of Romantic cultural authority,
absorbing the 'naive' function of shepherd-bard within the 'sentimental' role of antiquarian laird, collecting the traditions of the country. Hogg's persona reverses the social trajectory of Scott's–Edinburgh lawyer turned Border laird on the strength of a sentimental
investment in his ancestry. Here the hireling shepherd turned Edinburgh man of letters has come back again, as proprietor of the
ground: reckoned as an imaginary domain, a literary tradition.

Hogg's proposal is thus an especially sophisticated example of what Mary Louise Pratt has called 'autoethnography'—the self-authorising discourse with which writers from cultural peripheries 'undertake to represent themselves in ways that engage with the [metropolis's] own terms'.[48] Hogg would end up using the 'J. H. Craig of Douglas' pseudonym for another generic experiment, his 'Dramatic Tale' *The Hunting of Badlewe* (1814). His sets of rural tales, when they came out, proudly announced themselves as written by 'James Hogg, Author of "The Queen's Wake"'—no longer a persona but an author, buoyant with the success of a major poem. The autoethnographic function remains legible, meanwhile, in the subtitle: *Collected among the Cottagers in the South of Scotland.*

Hogg's was not the only proposal for a work of Scottish fiction submitted to Constable in 1813. Others came from John Galt, with an early version of *Annals of the Parish*, and John Gibson Lockhart; all three authors would be pillars of the house of Blackwood in the following decade. Among the thriving genres of wartime were the metrical romance or ballad-epic on national, historical and legendary themes, represented by Scott's *Lay of the Last Minstrel* (1805) and its successors, including Hogg's own romantic miscellany *The Queen's Wake*; and the prose 'National Tale', dominated by Irish authors such as Maria Edgeworth (*Castle Rackrent*, 1800; *Tales of Fashionable Life*, 1809–12) and Sydney Owenson (*The Wild Irish Girl*, 1806). It is hardly surprising that several authors should have thought of adapting the conventions of the national tale to a Scottish setting before the appearance of *Waverley* in 1814.[49]

National tales offered their middle-class readers a regionally specific representation of the manners and traditions of rural communities, located in one of the ancient nations absorbed into the British state at the successive Acts of Union. The typical national tale narrates the discovery of this local way of life by a visiting stranger, a gentleman from the metropolis, who may be an absentee landlord or simply a tourist. The visit yields a dialectic of education and improvement (the stranger learns to sympathise with the community and helps modernise its economy) and an alliance between metropolitan and regional elites (sealed with the stranger's marriage to an Irish heiress). The visitor's point of view secures the formal dominance of a polite, imperial English discourse and a unified teleological plot, even when that plot requires the reformation of the visitor as well as of 'backward' local customs. Popular voices may lend authenticity to the gentry alliance, in the comic or elegiac interjections of faithful retainers, but their concerns are kept subordinate in plot and style. The tenantry, in short, plays a supporting role in the narrative of nationalist reformation of the gentry. Even when 'cottagers' are included in the narrative of improvement, it is as human resources in schemes determined by their betters—or else as representatives of a residual, pre-modern class of peasantry, mired in a variously sordid or glamorous cultural past.

A Scottish variant of the national tale, Elizabeth Hamilton's *The Cottagers of Glenburnie; A Tale for the Farmer's Ingle-Nook*, had already appeared in 1808. The titles Hogg projected for his collection—'Cottage Tales', 'Cottage Winter Nights', 'Collected among the cottagers of the South of Scotland'—echo Hamilton's, as does the title of the poem from which Hogg takes his epigraph, Robert Fergusson's 'The Farmer's Ingle'. The books themselves, however, could scarcely be less alike. *Cottagers of Glenburnie* relates the moral, economic and (above all) hygienic improvement of the eponymous clachan by a virtuous settler, securing the middle-class and missionary point of view in a relentless equation of village life with *dirt*. (The most frequently recurring Scots word in Hamilton's text must be 'clarty'.) *Winter Evening Tales* defies the national-tale convention—developed and complicated in Scott's historical novels—of an enlightened English narration that admits the voices of the peasantry only to clean them up and put them in their place. The title-page citation of 'The Farmer's Ingle' looks forward to undoing Hamilton's sanitising exclusion of a modern Scots tradition of vernacular writing, in verse rather than prose, that represents popular life in something like its own terms, enunciated from within a local community. Hogg's choice of the reprobate Fergusson over his usual favourite, Burns, seems deliberately to reject the associations of the more famous poem inspired by Fergusson's, 'The Cotter's Saturday Night'—in which Burns puts the domestic virtues of the tenantry on show for gentle readers.

In *Winter Evening Tales*, then, Hogg attempts something like a prose equivalent of the achievements in Scots verse of Fergusson, or of Burns in such poems as 'The Holy Fair' and 'Death and Dr Hornbook': rather than following the full-scale novelisation of regional life perfected by Scott in his early series of *Tales of My Landlord* (1816–19). Hogg's strategy involves not only the representation of popular voices telling their stories in their own words, as opposed to their absorption into a polite master narrative, but also the refusal of an extensive, complex, unifying plot, with its assimilation of local episodes to a general (national and historical) purpose. (In this Hogg also departs from Edgeworth's mimicry of an Irish servant narrator in *Castle Rackrent*, whose account is folded ironically into a larger historical scheme.) Hogg offers his readers something more like the ethnographic raw material of the national tale, not yet ideologically and aesthetically processed, with all its gaps left open, its unevennesses intact. In this respect, *Winter Evening Tales* also resembles the great Enlightenment ballad collections, such as Scott's *Minstrelsy of the Scottish Border* (1802–03) or Hogg's own *Mountain Bard*: except that the prose medium abolishes the distancing, archaising effects of verse, and brings its material into a relation of contemporaneity and rough equality with the modern reader. To evoke another Romantic analogue, we might think of *Winter Evening Tales* as a prose equivalent of *Lyrical Ballads*. Again, though, Hogg writes from within the idiom and perspective of 'common life', while Wordsworth and Coleridge, as surely as (if more cryptically than) Scott and Edgeworth, write from outside it. Faithful to its partial origins in *The Spy*, Hogg's miscellany (which includes verse narratives) insists on an incongruous variety of form, voice, register, style and texture. In this formal insistence *Winter Evening Tales* presents itself as constituting not simply a lack in relation to the novel—something imperfect or unfinished—but an alternative, non-novelistic genre of national fiction, close to its roots in popular print media (miscellanies, chapbooks) as well as in oral storytelling.

Collections of prose tales, often set in elaborate narrative frameworks, mark the beginnings of vernacular literary fiction in early modern Europe, from Renaissance examples such as Boccaccio's *Decameron* to the volumes of 'Arabian Nights' Entertainments' translated throughout the eighteenth century. More recently, the genre had been eclipsed by the book-length forms of the novel, even as short stories and sketches were beginning to proliferate in periodical miscellanies such as *The Spy*. Collections of short fiction did not begin to appear in significant numbers until after *Winter Evening Tales*, in the 1820s, when 'Tale' became one of the generic titles most favoured in Romantic-era fiction publishing.[50] A reviewer posed the question in 1815:

> What is the difference between a Tale and a Novel? Is it that a tale is supposed to be a shorter and less laboured production than a novel; that a tale is designed to relate the natural occurrences and simple incidents of life; while a novel sets real life and probability at defiance, and demands, as its essential features, a heroine, a lover, a plot, and a catastrophe?[51]

In this restatement of the conventional distinction between 'novel' and 'romance', a predominance of form, as plot, defines the novel, while 'nature' and 'real life'—pure content—mark the tale. Despite the reviewer's preference, it was the artificial and fashionable medium of the novel that drew the middle-class public, while the very artlessness of the tale betrayed its place at the margins of polite literacy. Book-length collections of tales were often didactic, aimed at lower-class or youthful readers, as in Edgeworth's own *Moral Tales* (1801) and *Popular Tales* (1804), setting themselves above the trash of chapbooks. At the same time, up-market designations such as 'National Tale', *Tales of Fashionable Life* and *Tales of My Landlord* show novelists exploiting the genre's associations with nature, simplicity and 'common life' in order to signal their own formal and ideological innovations.[52] (The ironic discord between 'tale' and 'fashionable life' in Edgeworth's title is probably no longer audible today.) In short, then, the term 'tale' signified both a popular, 'naive' kind of fiction and its sophisticated, 'sentimental' appropriation in the years that Hogg was writing *Winter Evening Tales*.

Hogg's title aligns his book with other naive compilations, such as Maria Hack's *Winter Evenings; or, Tales of Travellers* (London, 1819), and—cashing in on the American popularity of his own collection—a book of stories for children by Samuel Goodrich called *Peter Parley's Winter Evening Tales* (Philadelphia, 1829). At the same time, the echo of a Shakespearean precedent, *The Winter's Tale*, situates Hogg's enterprise in a genealogy of sophisticated literary meditations on the 'primitive' conditions and effects of storytelling.[53] 'A sad tale's best for winter', says the doomed prince Mamilius, promising to indulge his audience with 'sprites and goblins' (II. 1). The end of the play invokes the thaumaturgic power of a wonder come adrift from belief, barely residual in 'old tales': 'This news, which is call'd true, is so like an old tale, that the verity of it is in strong suspicion. [...] Like an old tale still, which will have matter to rehearse, though credit be asleep and not an ear open' (V. 2); 'That she is living, / Were it but told you, should be hooted at, / Like an old tale' (V. 3). Old tales may bear a vital imaginative principle which urbane cultures, relegating them to childhood and to a superseded cultural past, are in danger of forgetting.

The Winter's Tale itself is more like a Scott novel (more like *Guy Mannering*) than it is like *Winter Evening Tales*, which rather resembles the mass of chapbook tales and broadside ballads disgorged from the pedlar Autolycus's pack in the fourth act of Shakespeare's play. One of Hogg's tales, 'The Long Pack', had circulated as a chapbook previous to its appearance in *Winter Evening Tales* (and would continue to circulate afterwards, as would another selection, 'Duncan Campbell').[54] 'The Long Pack' reflects cryptically on its own low origins in a demotic print culture that may seem occult, even menacing, to the view of propertied-class literacy, especially after the war against revolutionary France and domestic repression of radical Corresponding Societies. What kind of parable of the printed word can we read in a chapbook tale smuggled between the respectable covers of a book, which takes for its theme the dangerous contents of a pedlar's pack? In Hogg's tale the pack, introduced into a rich household, turns out to contain a malign double of Autolycus, hidden there for purposes of robbery and murder; the plot is foiled when a servant fires his gun at the suspiciously stirring object. All that remains, after an exciting nocturnal battle, is the unclaimed, obstinately nameless dead body of the intruder. Perhaps the neighbouring gentry have set up the robbery attempt—perhaps not; the question is raised but left open. The spectre of popular subversion, Hogg's tale seems to suggest, may be a paranoid figment, the projection of an internecine struggle among the landlords themselves—a thought that thickens rather than dispels the atmosphere of paranoia. Meanwhile the tale has focused on the experience of the faithful servants, who come out of this adventure with flying colours. Their role in the action is ethically clear and accountable; its larger social and historical meaning remains shrouded in obscurity.[55]

Elsewhere, culture rather than class constitutes the field of difference opened in Hogg's tales. 'Adam Bell' invokes both superstitious and rational explanations for its mysterious sequence of events—a laird disappears from his estate, his wraith is seen, a man is killed in a duel, rumours swirl—but in order to suspend both categories. The fiction lays claim instead to an uncanny epistemological zone, a debateable land between traditional and modern modes of knowledge, marked by one of Hogg's favourite terms, 'unaccountable'. Recounting the unaccountable, storytelling affirms its own logic, taking from reason and faith without being subject to either.

Most of Hogg's tales, however, concern themselves with representing modes of experience and feeling in Scottish Border communities, rather than with metafictional or allegorical reflection. This applies to ghost stories like 'Tibby Johnston's Wraith' (a gravely delicate study of bereavement) as well as to the ethnographic reportage of 'A Peasant's Funeral' or 'The Shepherd's Calendar'. Nearly all of the tales maintain a Border viewpoint, whether the narrator be a veteran of military campaigns in the Adirondacks or the Grampians ('Basil Lee', 'An Old Soldier's Tale') or the reciter of an ethnic joke about Highland emigrants in Canada ('Story of Two Highlanders'). Most of them are embedded in particular Border regions, evoked through suggestive detail, from Annandale and Eskdale ('Love Adventures of Mr George Cochrane', 'The Wife of Lochmaben') through Ettrick ('The Shepherd's Calendar') to Berwickshire ('Basil Lee'). 'Love Adventures of Mr George Cochrane', the comic masterpiece of the collection, displays Hogg's virtuosity in rendering different local dialects. 'The Bridal of Polmood', set during the reign of James IV, caresses the hills and burns of Tweedsmuir even as it roughs up the historical record. Many of the tales affirm an autobiographical as well as a local vein of reference. The extended narratives of 'Basil Lee' and 'George Cochrane' play a set of scandalous fictional variations on Hogg's own early manhood, while sketches such as 'Storms' (in 'The Shepherd's Calendar') affect a documentary style of memoir. Several tales devolve into narrations by local informants, some of whom seem to be real persons known to Hogg ('An Old Soldier's Tale', 'John Gray o' Middleholm', 'The Shepherd's Calendar', 'Tibby Johnston's Wraith'). Others simulate the improvisatory charm of oral storytelling. 'Duncan Campbell' pays an idyllic visit to the author's childhood before veering into a lost-heir romance. 'John Gray o' Middleholm' concocts an effervescent synthesis of traditional narratives from folkloric and biblical sources.

Experimentation with genre is overt in the metrical tales, all of which were written for publication elsewhere. 'Halbert of Lyne' begins as a polemically 'fashionable' exercise in blank-verse soliloquy, associated here with Edinburgh literary and blue-stocking salons, before it settles into a shaggy-dog story about choosing a bride. 'King Gregory' decants legendary Caledonian history into a formal imitation of the Border ballad. 'Connel of Dee' stretches the pseudo-archaic spelling and diction of Hogg's 'antique style' around a Gothic sexual fantasia, to create a bizarre hybrid of makar's dream-vision and *Blackwood's* terror-tale. In what now reads like a burlesque of Freud *avant la lettre*, the hero undergoes a grotesque, escalating sequence of castrations: catching his wicked-fairy wife in bed with one of her lovers, watching as she chops off a previous husband's head with a domestic guillotine, remaining sentient while he drowns in a river and slimy coiling eels devour his private parts. The poem, one of Hogg's fascinatingly bad performances, marks the extreme, phobic exhibit in a gallery of cautionary meditations on marriage in *Winter Evening Tales*: from the tragic futile jealousy of the laird of Polmood through George Cochrane's misadventures in courtship to Basil Lee's deliverance by an angelic former prostitute (with a great deal in between). Hogg married Margaret Phillips (happily, as it turned out), whom he had known for ten years, between the first and second editions of *Winter Evening Tales*.

'Basil Lee' shows off Hogg's genre-switching bravura at its most accomplished. Admired by early reviewers for its recreation of the plain style of Defoe, 'Basil Lee' inaugurates a tradition of nineteenth-century revivals or imitations of eighteenth-century anti-heroic picaresque, the best known example of which is probably Thackeray's *Barry Lyndon*. (In its affective range, opening up unexpected depths and delicacies alongside the humour and violence, 'Basil Lee' effortlessly surpasses the programmatic cynicism of *Barry Lyndon*.) Far from being archaic or retrograde, the Defoism of 'Basil Lee' elaborates a condition of radical modernity in the sheer mobility and contingency of its narrative subject, who rushes between a Berwickshire farming community, the revolutionary war in America, supernatural encounters on the Isle of Lewis, and the Edinburgh marriage-market. In other words, Hogg boldly recasts what was (and remains) 'modern' about Defoe: the sense of narration taking place within the very breach of modernity, made world-historically vivid here in the jump from a minutely local Border countryside to the transatlantic wilds of empire—in short, eschewing a 'national' for a colonial geography. The tale is also remarkable for its internal reproduction of the formal principle of Hogg's collection, the narrative anthology or miscellany. As Basil shifts across professions and territories, his tale recklessly shifts genres. And if we recall the contemporary narrative horizon of the national tale and historical novel, we can watch Hogg's tale performing a critical decomposition of them into their constituent parts: the absence of a formal synthesis expressing a thoroughgoing ideological refusal rather than a 'naive' inadvertence.

Hogg's refusal is most scandalous in the love plot. The on-and-off affair between Basil and Clifford ruthlessly parodies the national-historical novel convention that secures the role of the maiden as donor (bringing cultural authenticity to the hero) by splitting her into 'fair' and 'dark' avatars. Here the trickster-whore turns out—wonderfully, shockingly—to be the same as the bountiful fairy who saves the protagonist by giving herself to him, and the combination shatters a polite morality. Nor does the liaison represent a cultural solution to questions of history or national identity—questions that the tale hardly bothers to ask, even as it has begun by announcing the theme of a linked 'instability' of character and career. Basil may resemble Scott's wavering Waverley-hero, not only in finding himself astray in the arena of world-historical conflict, but in the sheer unwittingness with which he stumbles through heroic action—except that Basil's outburst of military prowess savagely inverts the conduct of Waverley at Prestonpans, hastening about the battlefield to rescue enemy officers. The historical event itself (the American revolutionary war, no less) remains senseless, as pointlessly episodic as Basil's ghost-hunting adventures on the primitive isle of Lewis. 'Basil Lee' resolutely ignores, finally, the plot of moral and psychological development—*Bildung*—with which historical progress and national reformation are integrated in Scott and Edgeworth. The ex-prostitute Clifford alone personifies a quasi-magical or providential power of spiritual direction in the narrative, but her interventions highlight its absence anywhere else.

Readers may find some of Hogg's other experiments less satisfying. The novella-length tale that opened the second volume of *Winter Evening Tales*, 'The Bridal of Polmood', lurches between a rude burlesque of Scott's 'school of chivalry'[56] and a moral anatomy of the disasters of a rash marriage. Hogg writes a parody of history from below, in which popular tradition, of a flagrantly 'invented' kind, tramples uproariously upon antiquarian authority and the fictions it supports. Paroxysms of pathos and violence alternate with bedroom farce, exposing the boorishness of Scotland's flower of chivalry on the eve of Flodden. Hogg effectively capsizes the decorum of historical romance, but—in contrast to 'Basil Lee'—finds nothing very interesting to put in its place. (*The Three Perils of Man*, the 'Border romance' published hard on the heels of *Winter Evening Tales*, revisits this territory with far richer inventiveness.) Here, in contrast to *Basil Lee*, we find a sheerly negative critique of the aesthetic horizon provided by a certain genre; the tale depends for its own intelligibility on our awareness of that horizon.

Readers may also lose patience with the long ghost story 'Welldean Hall'. After a sprightly beginning—Hogg's haunted library would give M. R. James the idea for one of the best of his *Ghost Stories of an Antiquary*—the tale bogs down in perfunctory plot complications and funny-talk routines. Yet the presence even of failed or half-baked experiments contributes to the vitality of a collection which everywhere finds energy in unevenness. This energy or vitality, for which there is no satisfactory technical designation, precedes any resolution of Hogg's tales into the modern, 'artistic' genre of the short story, with its high degree of formal closure and stylistic unity. *Winter Evening Tales* thus compels us to rethink the relation between literary form and literary history. The life of the collection lies in its resistance to available models even as it mines them, refusing to settle into new generic moulds.

3. Reception

Winter Evening Tales was widely and on the whole warmly reviewed. Its reception, more consistently favourable than for any of Hogg's other works of prose fiction, reiterated the high tide-mark of the author's reputation, reached in 1813 with *The Queen's Wake* but sustained only intermittently since then. Hogg would find it increasingly difficult to publish his subsequent book-length works of prose fiction, and their critical reception was correspondingly less sympathetic.

In a pattern typical of the response to Hogg throughout his career, almost all the reviews of *Winter Evening Tales* praise the truth and vivacity of the author's depiction of rural life while deploring his vein of 'coarseness'. Both praise and blame tend to lock Hogg back into the role of peasant poet, a gifted witness of his social origins but blundering when he ventures into higher circles. There are, however, one or two subtler appraisals, and we see that Hogg's persona could serve various interests.

The Scotsman, for example, the newspaper of record of the Edinburgh Whigs, fired off its laudatory notice ('unquestionably the work of a man of genius') as the opening salvo in a renewed campaign to rescue Hogg from the mohawks of *Blackwood's*. It even ventured a favourable comparison with the Tory potentate Scott:

> [Hogg] has presented us with a most faithful picture of the religion, the sense, the humour, the weaknesses of our border and pastoral countrymen; and although his tales may not always be equally amusing, they are more interesting to a philosopher, and to all who enjoy deep or strong feelings, than those of his still more illustrious countryman.[57]

The stock phrase is repeatedly used to characterise Hogg's achievement: he has drawn 'a faithful picture of the manners and characters of the peasantry, and the middle orders, of the south of Scotland'.[58] John Wilson, writing in *Blackwood's Edinburgh Magazine*, draws his own romantic picture of the author as naive storyteller:

> Of the treasures accumulated during all his wanderings, he has now laid a portion before us in these unvarnished tales.

They are written, as we have said, with the utmost simplicity—they breathe the very spirit of the man that tells them—
and they reveal so many new and delightful particulars concerning the domestic economy of our peasantry, that we are
sure they will be read by every one that has any love for
Scotland, or any curiosity respecting the manners of her children—with an interest different, indeed, in kind, but scarcely
inferior in degree, to that with which they have all read the
sketches of homely Scottish life in the works of the Ettrick
Shepherd's best friend and patron, the author of Waverley.[59]

Now the comparison with Scott marks the limits of Hogg's achievement. While he addresses himself to 'the peasantry of Scotland',
writes the *British Critic*, 'his pictures are admirable'; when he attempts
to depict polite society, or draw upon 'the resources of his own invention', his powers fail.[60]

At its most generous, such criticism credits Hogg with an art that
conceals art, rather than a kind of *idiot-savant* flair for transcription.
His tales are 'brought to life without the usual artifices of literary
midwifery', nods the *Monthly Review*, comparing him to Defoe (p.
264). The *London Magazine* admired an 'exquisite delicacy of thought,
and light grace of manner', offsetting the regrettable 'vulgarity and
nonsense'.[61] Perhaps the most perceptive appreciation came in the
Newcastle Magazine, which found that Hogg's tales cast their spell in
re-reading rather than at first impression:

> There is a charm about them which we cannot describe. We
> did not like them at first. We thought them childish, not fit
> for the age, carelessly written, sometimes vulgar, and, in
> short, not to live long in public estimation. But we have
> changed our opinion; because, after a re-perusal of some of
> the tales, they have pleased us more and more with their
> simplicity—their Arabian-night sort of running on, by which
> we get half through a volume before we know where we
> are, and wish, when we get to the end, that another volume
> was yet to come.[62]

Far from being naive, in other words, Hogg's 'simplicity' is the effect of a subtle art.

While appraisals of individual works vary, the long tales that open
each volume attracted particular notice. In an exact inversion of
twentieth-century critical preferences, contemporary reviewers
tended to admire 'The Bridal of Polmood' as the most ambitious,
'artistic' piece in *Winter Evening Tales*, and deplore 'Basil Lee' as the

prime example of Hogg's coarseness.[63] 'Basil Lee' provoked a remarkable variety of attempts to define this objectionable quality. *The Scotsman* singles out the story as 'absurd and written in very bad taste', but more because of its kinship with the fantastic mock-autobiographies of *Blackwood's* satire than because of the 'want of refinement' or 'occasional coarseness' that the reviewer lists among Hogg's general faults. The *Newcastle Magazine* actually approves of the tale's moral tendency, but suggests that 'it would have been more considerate to female readers to have kept the intercourse of Basil and Miss Mackay a little more in the background' (p. 125; in the circumstances, this was a remarkably tolerant demurral).

The distinction is amplified in the most extensive, and most revealing, of these complaints, in the *British Critic*. 'The reader is perpetually introduced to characters, whom it is a shame even to talk about, and such as never can be, and never ought to be represented, without shame and disgust'. Depictions of 'prostitutes and blackguard gentlemen' must not be allowed to fall into the hands of 'our wives and daughters'—since, in certain cases, 'it is better to be ignorant of vice, than even to detest it'. Yet Hogg's own principles are judged to be 'unexceptionable'. 'What we complain of in him is the want of common refinement; it is the coarseness of his language that we dislike, rather than any impropriety; and the absence of all delicacy, that we are offended with, rather than with any positive immorality' (pp. 623–24). The critique is remarkable for its forthright, if tortuous, attempt to locate an emerging middle-class standard of taste in a domestic style of manners and language, defined by the selection of topics that may be properly 'introduced' to wives and daughters, rather than in a public domain of ethical or political values. Wilson, in *Blackwood's*, puts the case more succinctly: 'Mr Hogg is as moral a man as ever lived, and as moral a writer; but he is too fond of calling some things by their plain names, which would be better expressed by circumlocution; and now and then he betrays what we shall at once call, *vulgarity*'.[64] In other words, the issue is linguistic standardisation according to middle-class usage. This proto-Victorian cultural standard, in the process of being forged in these same periodicals, would hobble Hogg's reputation for the next hundred years.[65]

Hogg's response to these complaints, in the 1821 'Memoir', shows him well aware of their hypocrisy. 'Indelicacy' is the invention of bourgeois prurience and censoriousness:

> As to the indelicacies hinted at by some reviewers, I do declare that such a thought never entered into my mind, so that

the public are indebted for these indelicacies to the acuteness of the discoverers. Wo be to that reader who goes over a simple and interesting tale fishing for indelicacies, without calculating on what is natural for the characters with whom he is conversing; a practice, however, too common among people of the present age, especially if the author be not a blue-stocking. All that I can say for myself in general is, that I am certain I never intentionally meant ill, and that I hope to be forgiven, both by God and man, for every line that I have written injurious to the cause of religion, of virtue, or of good manners. On the other hand, I am so ignorant of the world, that it can scarcely be expected I should steer clear of all inadvertencies.[66]

The irony becomes overt in the last sentence. Hogg's defensiveness suggests that he is remembering the objections heaped ten years earlier on *The Spy*–objections which took the form of a disastrous withdrawal of subscribers. Yet in *Winter Evening Tales* Hogg not only reprinted but revised and expanded the kind of material–notably, the original version of 'Basil Lee'–that had got him into trouble in *The Spy*. Hogg's sensitivity to these charges is reflected, as I argue in detail in my 'Note on the Text', in the corrections he made for the second edition of 1821, in which phrases that were likely to have caused offence were softened or removed. Other details were allowed to stand, however, and Hogg did not make any large-scale revisions. The most offensive feature of the whole collection, the unashamed treatment of the liaison between the protagonist and the harlot in 'Basil Lee', remains intact.

Despite its early success, *Winter Evening Tales* sank almost out of sight in the twentieth century, no doubt because of the collection's fragmentation in the posthumous 'corrected' editions of Hogg's fiction. Like most of his other works, it languished in the shadow of *The Private Memoirs and Confessions of a Justified Sinner* following that work's modernist revival. Louis Simpson's 1962 critical survey cites *Winter Evening Tales* to exemplify the unevenness of Hogg's achievement. Simpson inaugurates the modern reversal of the judgements of Hogg's contemporaries by condemning the plot and style of 'The Bridal of Polmood' and praising 'Basil Lee', both for the 'strong effects' achieved by Hogg's 'flat' style and for its heroine: 'Hogg's most complicated and convincing female character, an immoral good fairy seen in flashes, never entire'.[67]

The more recent scholarly attention to Hogg's experiments with longer narrative forms, in *The Brownie of Bodsbeck*, *The Three Perils of*

Man and *The Three Perils of Woman*, reflects a continued preference for the novel as the exemplary genre of modernity over mere 'tales'. Douglas Gifford is one of the few critics to have offered any detailed consideration of *Winter Evening Tales*, which he judges to be 'Hogg's only really successful collection of fiction'.[68] Gifford discusses 'Basil Lee' and 'The Bridal of Polmood' as contrasting experiments in the representation of an anti-heroic, morbid psychology later perfected by Hogg in the *Confessions of a Justified Sinner*, although farcical interpolations spoil 'Polmood'. 'Basil Lee' receives an extensive and sympathetic appreciation. In 'its anti-hypocrisy and honesty, and in the freshness of style, in its brevity, its simple language, its swift action', Hogg's novella offers a healthy corrective to the proto-Victorian style promoted by his peers in *Blackwood's Edinburgh Magazine*.[69]

David Groves, in another critical monograph, reads Hogg's fiction through an allegorical scheme of psychic alienation derived from Northrop Frye. '"Connel of Dee" is an extended metaphor to describe the poet's descent into the unconscious', while the hero of 'Love Adventures of Mr George Cochrane' endures a 'descent into the purely physical' that separates him from 'the one very simple essential truth that might lead to harmony and fulfilment'.[70] Three articles published in *Studies in Hogg and his World*, the journal of the James Hogg Society, address particular features of *Winter Evening Tales*, although no extensive consideration of the collection has appeared to date in its pages. Peter Garside analyses the publication of *Winter Evening Tales* in 'Three Perils in Publishing: Hogg and the Popular Novel'; the present editor briefly discusses the cultural-historical thematics of the 'unaccountable' in 'Adam Bell' and 'Basil Lee', in 'The Upright Corpse: Hogg, National Literature and the Uncanny'; and Kate McGrail argues that 'Connel of Dee' is based on a poem by Dunbar, in 'Re-making the Fire: James Hogg and the Makars'.[71]

Notes

1. James Hogg, *Memoir of the Author's Life* and *Familiar Anecdotes of Sir Walter Scott*, ed. by Douglas S. Mack (Edinburgh: Scottish Academic Press, 1972), p. 50. Mack reprints the 1832 *Altrive Tales* version of the 'Memoir', but the present passage dates from the 1821 reissue of *The Mountain Bard*. See also *Altrive Tales*, ed. by Gillian Hughes (S/SC, 2004), pp. 50, 243.
2. For details of the sources and revisions of particular tales see the explanatory Notes to this edition.
3. See Penny Fielding, *Writing and Orality: Nationality, Culture, and Nineteenth-Century Scottish Fiction* (Oxford: Clarendon Press, 1996).

4. James Hogg to Archibald Constable, 20 May 1813, in National Library of Scotland (hereafter NLS) MS 7200, fol. 203.

5. Hogg, *Memoir*, p. 18.

6. James Hogg, *The Spy*, ed. by Gillian Hughes (Edinburgh: Edinburgh University Press, 2000), pp. xl–xli.

7. Robert Crawford, 'Bad Shepherd', *London Review of Books*, 5 April 2001, pp. 28–29 (p. 29).

8. Hogg to Eliza Izet, 15 October 1811, in the James Hogg Collection, Beinecke Rare Book and Manuscript Library, Yale University: General MSS 61, Box 1, Folder 13. The 'highland tale' may refer to 'An Old Soldier's Tale', offered to *Blackwood's Edinburgh Magazine* at the end of 1817.

9. Hogg to Eliza Izet, 23 March 1813, in the James Hogg Collection, Beinecke Rare Book and Manuscript Library, Yale University: General MSS 61, Box 1, Folder 13.

10. NLS MS 3884, fol. 122.

11. See J. G. Lockhart, *Memoirs of the Life of Sir Walter Scott, Bart.*, 10 vols (Edinburgh: Cadell, 1839), IV, 77–78, and *The Letters of Sir Walter Scott*, ed. by H. J. C. Grierson, 12 vols (London: Constable, 1932–37), I, 422–27, and III, 264–72.

12. NLS MS 7200, fol. 203.

13. Hogg to Constable, 12 July 1813, NLS MS 7200, fols 205–06. 'Anonymity game' is Jane Millgate's term in *Walter Scott: The Making of the Novelist* (Edinburgh: Edinburgh University Press, 1985), p. 107.

14. Peter Garside notes that *Waverley* was the first novel to be published by Constable, whose firm brought out only seven fiction titles besides Scott's—see 'Three Perils in Publishing: Hogg and the Popular Novel', *Studies in Hogg and his World*, 2 (1991), 45–63 (p. 50).

15. NLS MS 4002, fol. 155.

16. See *Memoir*, p. 45, where Hogg says that both the substitutions were newly written.

17. To E. [Eliza Izet], 14 December 1817, in the James Hogg Collection, Beinecke Rare Book and Manuscript Library, Yale University: General MSS 61, Box 1, Folder 38.

18. Letter dated 13 January 1818, in NLS MS 4003, fol. 86.

19. James Hogg, *The Brownie of Bodsbeck*, ed. by Douglas S. Mack (Edinburgh: Scottish Academic Press, 1976), pp. xvi–xvii.

20. Hogg, *Memoir*, p. 14.

21. NLS MS 30,002, fol. 15 (Blackwood to Hogg, 25 November 1820). The major bone of contention between Hogg and Blackwood was the reissue of *The Mountain Bard*. Robert Hogg was helping out his uncle as amanuensis; Hogg had asked Blackwood to find a situation for the lad, and the suggestion that he edit a collection of tales from *The Spy* may well have come from that request. See Hogg to Blackwood, 27 October 1819, in NLS MS 4004, fol. 152.

22. In his letter to Blackwood of 20 November 1820, to which Blackwood's letter just cited is the reply, Hogg had complained: 'I am almost ruing the day that I ever saw you. [...] No one has any right to publish aught in my name without consulting me' (NLS MS 4005, fol. 169). The use of Hogg's identity by others would become full-blown in the 'Noctes Ambrosianae' series in *Blackwood's* from 1822.

23. See the Oliver and Boyd Letter Book I: Agreements, in NLS Acc. 5000 / 140, and Copyright Ledger, in Acc. 5000 / 1, pp. 137–38.

24. Garside, 'Three Perils in Publishing', p. 55.

25. Hogg to George Boyd, 9 February 1820, in NLS Acc. 5000 / 188. Oliver and Boyd's statement of account to Whittaker of 21 December 1819 is in Acc. 5000 / 189. The Edinburgh printers all seem to have been overstretched at this time, with a shortage in the paper-supply contributing to delays; the publication of Scott's *Ivanhoe* was also held up in the autumn of 1819. See Graham Tulloch's 'Essay on the Text' in the Edinburgh Edition of *Ivanhoe* (Edinburgh: Edinburgh University Press, 1998), pp. 412–14.

26. Hogg to Boyd, 2 August 1819, in NLS Acc. 5000/140, p. 56 (Letter Book I: Agreements).

27. Boyd to Hogg, 24 July 1820, in NLS Acc. 5000 / 140, p. 58, and 5000 / 189.

28. Hogg to Boyd, 20 November 1820, in NLS Acc. 5000 / 188.

29. Boyd to Hogg, 26 March 1831, in NLS MS 2245, fol. 50, and the Oliver and Boyd Copyright Ledger in NLS Acc. 5000/1, p. 137.

30. 'Oliver and Boyd gave me one fifth in bills over the whole editions. Sir W. Scott long ago told me always to stick by that rule for that if the edition were above 2000 and sold the author's moiety of the profits always amounted to nearly one fifth but if the impression was below that to one sixth and I have always stuck by that rule.'–see Hogg to Blackie, 11 February 1833, in NLS MS 807, fols 18–19. Since Hogg is negotiating with a publisher there may be some rhetorical exaggeration.

31. Garside, 'Three Perils in Publishing', pp. 55–56.

32. Hogg to Boyd, 6 November 1820, in NLS Acc. 5000 / 188.

33. Lady Louisa Stuart wrote to Scott on 16 January 1820: 'And do I guess right when I pitch upon a book called Glenfergus, not yet come out, always announced along with a work of Hogg's (but never said to be by him) & published by Whitaker & Boyd? I have asked what it was and whose, and people always answer–'Oh of course that is to be Hogg's also''–but the *of course* does not seem evident to me. If I am not seeing into a millstone, there is some mystery under that manner of advertising the two together': *Letters of Sir Walter Scott*, VI, 116 n. Astute as she was, Lady Louisa seems to have thought that *Glenfergus* might be by Scott.

34. The German translation includes versions of 'Basil Lee', 'Duncan Campbell', 'The Long Pack', 'King Gregory' (in prose), 'A Highland Ghost Story', 'Cousin Mattie', 'Major Macpherson', 'Duty and Passion' (*Pflicht und Leidenschaft*), and 'The Wedding of the Laird of Palmood' [*sic*]. In a ludicrous metamorphosis of Hogg's characters, the introduction to the second volume features a dialogue between 'Lord Cochrane und Sir Basil Lee.'

35. 'Noctes Ambrosianae, No. VIII', *Blackwood's Edinburgh Magazine*, 13 (May 1823), 592–611 (p. 609). 'Renowned Adventures of Basil Lee' has recently been translated into Italian by Marina Rullo as *Le celebri avventure di Basil Lee* (Milan: Giovanni Tranchida, 1997).

36. Hogg to George Boyd, 17 October 1822, in NLS Acc. 5000 / 188.

37. On 19 March 1826 Hogg wrote to Blackwood: 'I think it is high time you were beginning some publication of mine to liquidate all or part of my debt and I think the whole of my select Scottish tales should be published in Numbers one every month with the Magazine to be packed with it and a part of the first No sent gratis to some of your principal readers' (NLS MS 4017, fol. 138). His letter of 12 September 1826 stated, 'I therefore wish that at all events you and Davis would publish an edition of my Scottish tales revised in four close printed volumes and the Shepherd's Callander in two There could be no risk in losing at 1000 copies as I should be satisfied with a moiety of the profits or an acknowledgement to the probable amount. I should like above all things that my nephew Robt took the charge of the

edition but there are many large curtailments that I only can manage but if you think it would answer better to have it printed in London that can easily be managed'. (NLS MS 4017, fols 139–40.)

38. Hogg, *Memoir*, p. 60. On 26 May 1830 Hogg wrote to Blackwood: '[Another idea] is to publish all my tales in numbers like Sir W Scott's to re-write and sub-divide them [...] But as my good taste has been watched with a jealous eye by the literati I would have the work published under the sanction of Lockhart' (NLS MS 4036, fol. 102).

39. Hogg to Blackwood, 25 June 1831, in NLS MS 4029, fol. 255. Hogg to Lockhart, 14 December 1831, in NLS MS 924, fol. 67.

40. 5 February 1833, in NLS MS. 807, fol. 17. Hughes and Garside have recently discovered records of the printing of Hogg's tales in numbers in the Blackie archives, and are preparing a full account of the matter.

41. 9 February 1833, in NLS MS 807, fols 18–19.

42. 5 February 1833, in NLS MS 807, fol. 17.

43. Garside, 'Three Perils in Publishing', p. 60.

44. Hogg to Blackie, 11 November 1833, in NLS MS 807, fol. 20.

45. Hogg to Constable, 20 May 1813, in NLS MS 7200, fol. 203.

46. See, for instance, Adam Smith, *Lectures on Rhetoric and Belles Lettres*, ed. by J. C. Bryce (Oxford: Oxford University Press, 1983), pp. 136–37, and Hugh Blair, 'A Critical Dissertation on the Poems of Ossian', in *The Poems of Ossian and Related Works*, ed. by Howard Gaskill (Edinburgh: Edinburgh University Press, 1996), pp. 345–46.

47. I thank Douglas Mack for bringing Elaine Petrie's suggestion to my attention.

48. Mary Louise Pratt, *Imperial Eyes: Travel Writing and Transculturation* (London: Routledge, 1992), p. 7.

49. For the wartime vogue for verse romance and epic, see Stuart Curran, *Poetic Form and British Romanticism* (New York: Oxford University Press, 1986), pp. 128–79. For the national tale see Katie Trumpener, *Bardic Nationalism: The Romantic Novel and the British Empire* (Princeton: Princeton University Press, 1997), pp. 128–57.

50. As many as 34.3% of new fiction titles published in the 1820s designated themselves as 'Tale/s', a striking increase from 14.3% in the 1800s; see Peter Garside, 'The English Novel in the Romantic Era: Consolidation and Dispersal', in *The English Novel 1770–1829: A Bibliographical Survey of Prose Fiction Published in the British Isles*, ed. by P. D. Garside and Rainer Schöwerling, 2 vols (Oxford: Oxford University Press, 2000), II, 15–103 (pp. 34–35, 50–51). See also Tim Killick, 'The Rise of the Tale: A Preliminary Checklist of Collections of Short Fiction Published 1820-29 in the Corvey Collection', *Cardiff Corvey: Reading the Romantic Text*, 7 (December 2001), <http://www.cf.ac.uk/encap/corvey/articles/cc07_n04.html>.

51. See the review of Jane Taylor's *Display: A Tale for Young People* in *Eclectic Review*, new series, 4 (August 1815), p. 158, cited by Gary Kelly, *English Fiction of the Romantic Period 1789–1830* (London: Longman, 1987), p. 73.

52. See Kelly, *English Fiction of the Romantic Period* (pp. 64–65, 72–73, 98–99) for a discussion of some of the varieties of fiction claiming the designation of 'tale' in the period. Hogg's dedication to *The Mountain Bard* (1807) had referred to the book's contents as 'TALES'.

53. The generic rubric is older than Shakespeare. George Peele's *The Old Wives' Tale* (1595) characterises itself as 'a winter's tale to drive away the time'. More recently titles such as Isaak Dinesen's *Winter's Tales* (1942) and Italo

Calvino's *Se una notte d'inverno un viaggiatore* (*If on a winter's night a traveller*, 1979) strike the same note of an unfettered story-telling.

54. William Harvey comments, no doubt hyperbolically, on the popularity of the chapbook versions of Hogg's tales. 'They were printed by the thousand, and editions came from almost every press in the country': *Scottish Chapbook Literature* (Paisley: Alexander Gardner, 1903), p. 103. For Hogg's manuscript and early versions of 'The Long Pack', see the Appendix to this edition.

55. Harvey comments: 'The concealment of a robber in a pedlar's pack was a thing that concerned the everyday life of the people, and many a later chapman who had the good fortune to possess a large stack of goods would be looked upon with suspicious eyes until he opened his bundle and proved that there was no robber where no robber should be': *Scottish Chapbook Literature*, p. 105.

56. See the exchange between Hogg and Scott recorded in *Familiar Anecdotes of Sir Walter Scott*: 'Dear Sir Walter ye can never suppose that I belang to your school o' chivalry? Ye are the king o' that school but I'm the king o' the mountain an' fairy school which is a far higher ane nor yours'—*Anecdotes of Scott*, ed. by Jill Rubenstein (Edinburgh: Edinburgh University Press, 1999), p. 61. Hogg refers to Scott's metrical romances, especially *Marmion* (like 'The Bridal of Polmood' set in the reign of James IV), rather than his novels—*Ivanhoe* is contemporary with *Winter Evening Tales*.

57. See *The Scotsman*, 29 April 1820, p. 143. The article of 11 November 1820, 'Mr Hogg and Blackwood's Magazine', marks the high point of the campaign to rescue Hogg from the Tories: 'His name is taken as a cover for malignity of which he is incapable [...] coupling the name of a man of genius with puerility and nonsense. [...] In the black catalogue of offences committed by this worthless gang against decency and principle, there is perhaps nothing so atrocious as their conduct to Mr Hogg' (p. 367).

58. See *Monthly Review, or Literary Journal*, new series, 93 (November 1820), 263–67 (p. 264).

59. 'Hogg's Tales, &c.', *Blackwood's Edinburgh Magazine*, 7 (May 1820), 148–54 (p. 148).

60. *British Critic*, new series, 13 (June 1820), 622–31 (p. 622).

61. *London Magazine*, 1 (June 1820), 666–71 (p. 668). See also 'Hogg's Tales, &c.', *Blackwood's Edinburgh Magazine*, 7 (May 1820), 148–54 (pp. 149, 154).

62. *Newcastle Magazine*, 1 (November 1820), 122–36 (p. 129).

63. The notable exception is Wilson, who approves, on the whole, of 'Basil Lee', and praises 'Love Adventures of Mr George Cochrane' as 'by far the best of the Tales': *Blackwood's Edinburgh Magazine*, 7 (May 1820), 148–54 (p. 149).

64. *Blackwood's Edinburgh Magazine*, 7 (May 1820), 148–54 (p. 154).

65. A few other judgements may conveniently be given here. The *Monthly Review*, new series, 93 (November 1820), 263–67 (p. 264) thought that nothing in *Winter Evening Tales* was 'offensive to modesty' save 'Basil Lee', 'the worst in the collection; yet it is easy and flowing'. The *Gentleman's Magazine*, 90, Supplement (1820), 611–13 (p. 611) found that 'though some of [the tales] are unpardonably vulgar (but not indelicate) in their language, others are extremely pathetic, and some of them possess even fine writing'. The *Monthly Magazine; or, British Register*, 49 (July 1820), 555–56 grumbles that the tales are 'thrown together in rather a crude and undigested shape, and though they contain much humour, it is in general of a very coarse nature'.

66. Hogg, *Memoir*, p. 50.
67. Louis Simpson, *James Hogg: A Critical Study* (Edinburgh and London: Oliver and Boyd, 1962), p. 141.
68. Douglas Gifford, *James Hogg* (Edinburgh: Ramsay Head Press, 1976), p. 71.
69. Gifford, pp. 91–92, 98.
70. David Groves, *James Hogg: The Growth of a Writer* (Edinburgh: Scottish Academic Press, 1988), pp. 65, 98.
71. See *Studies in Hogg and his World*, 2 (1991), 45–63, 5 (1994), 29–54, and 7 (1996), 26–36 respectively.

Research Additions

Since the first publication of this edition of *Winter Evening Tales* Janette Currie has provided me with information about early magazine printings of 'The Long Pack', and Gillian Hughes has identified the first publication of 'An Old Soldier's Tale' in the *Clydesdale Magazine*. This new information is incorporated in the explanatory notes of the present edition and in a revised editorial note to the Appendix, 'Hogg's Manuscript of "The Long Pack"'. I thank Dr Currie and Dr Hughes for bringing these sources to my attention.

Select Bibliography

Editions of *Winter Evening Tales*

Winter Evening Tales was first published in Edinburgh by the firm of Oliver & Boyd in April 1820, and a second edition with some authorial revision brought out by the same firm the following year. The posthumous six-volume *Tales and Sketches by the Ettrick Shepherd* (1836–37) of the Glasgow firm of Blackie and Son includes a number of the component tales of *Winter Evening Tales* but omits several of the best and obliterates Hogg's design for his collection. A number of American reprintings, however, signify the continuing popularity of *Winter Evening Tales* in the United States. An edition was produced in the year of first publication by Kirk and Mercein, Wiley and Halsted, W. B. Gilley, and Haly and Thomas in New York, and a second New York edition of 1820 published by S. Campbell, E. Duyckinck, Collins, G. Long, and E. Bliss. Walker of Philadelphia published an edition in 1836, and Silas Andrus of Hartford two editions of 1844 and *c.* 1850. The New York firm of Leavitt & Allen subsequently published editions of *Winter Evening Tales* in 1850, 1871, and 1873 respectively. A German translation, with a preface by Sophie Man, *Die Wanderer im Hochlande. Winter-Abend-Erzählungen. Nach der dritten Englischen Original-Ausgabe des Sir James Hogg* was published in Berlin in 1822 and reprinted in Vienna in 1826. The only modern edition of *Winter Evening Tales* is the volume of the Stirling /South Carolina Research Edition of the Collected Works of James Hogg upon which this paperback is based, edited by Ian Duncan and published by Edinburgh University Press in 2002.

Collected Editions

The Stirling /South Carolina Research Edition of the Collected Works of James Hogg (Edinburgh: Edinburgh University Press, 1995–), now underway but not yet complete, is a modern scholarly edition. Previous editions which are useful but bowdlerised are *Tales and Sketches by the Ettrick Shepherd*, 6 vols (Glasgow: Blackie and Son, 1836–37), *The Poetical Works of the Ettrick Shepherd*, 5 vols (Glasgow: Blackie and Son, 1838–40), and *The Works of the Ettrick Shepherd*, ed. by Thomas Thomson, 2 vols (Glasgow: Blackie and Son, 1865).

Bibliography

Edith C. Batho's Bibliography in *The Ettrick Shepherd* (Cambridge: Cambridge University Press, 1927), is still useful, together with her supplementary 'Notes on the Bibliography of James Hogg, the Ettrick Shepherd', in *The Library*, 16 (1935–36), 309–26. Two more modern and reader-friendly bibliographies are Douglas S. Mack, *Hogg's Prose: An Annotated Listing* (Stirling: The James Hogg Society, 1985), and Gillian Hughes, *Hogg's Verse and Drama: A Chronological Listing* (Stirling: The James Hogg Society, 1990). Subsequent information about recently-discovered Hogg items may be gleaned from various articles in *The Bibliotheck* and *Studies in Hogg and his World*.

Biography

Gillian Hughes is currently writing a modern Hogg biography: her *James Hogg: A Life* will be published by Edinburgh University Press. Karl Miller's *Electric Shepherd: A Likeness of James Hogg* (London: Faber and Faber, 2003) is a fascinating interpretation of Hogg's life as well as his works. Hogg's life up to 1825 is covered by Alan Lang Strout's *The Life and Letters of James Hogg, The Ettrick Shepherd Volume 1 (1770–1825)*, Texas Technological College Research Publications, 15 (Lubbock, Texas: Texas Technological College, 1946). Much valuable information may be obtained from Mrs M. G. Garden's memoir of her father, *Memorials of James Hogg, the Ettrick Shepherd* (London: Alexander Gardner, 1885), and from Mrs Norah Parr's account of Hogg's domestic life in *James Hogg at Home* (Dollar: Douglas S. Mack, 1980). Also useful are Sir George Douglas, *James Hogg*, Famous Scots Series (Edinburgh: Oliphant Anderson & Ferrier, 1899), and Henry Thew Stephenson's *The Ettrick Shepherd: A Biography*, Indiana University Studies, 54 (Bloomington, Indiana: Indiana University, 1922).

General Criticism

Edith C. Batho, *The Ettrick Shepherd* (Cambridge: Cambridge University Press, 1927)

Louis Simpson, *James Hogg: A Critical Study* (Edinburgh and London: Oliver & Boyd, 1962)

Douglas Gifford, *James Hogg* (Edinburgh: The Ramsay Head Press, 1976)

Nelson C. Smith, *James Hogg*, Twayne's English Authors Series (Boston: Twayne Publishers, 1980)

David Groves, *James Hogg: The Growth of a Writer* (Edinburgh: Scottish Academic Press, 1988)

Thomas Crawford, 'James Hogg: The Play of Region and Nation', in *The History of Scottish Literature: Volume 3 Nineteenth Century*, ed. by Douglas Gifford (Aberdeen: Aberdeen University Press,

1988), pp. 89–105

Silvia Mergenthal, *James Hogg: Selbstbild und Bild*, Publications of the Scottish Studies Centre of the Johannes Gutenberg Universität Mainz in Germersheim, 9 (Frankfurt-am-Main: Peter Lang, 1990)

Penny Fielding, *Writing and Orality: Nationality, Culture, and Nineteenth-Century Scottish Fiction* (Oxford: Clarendon Press, 1996)

Karl Miller, *Electric Shepherd: A Likeness of James Hogg* (London: Faber and Faber, 2003)

Criticism on *Winter Evening Tales*

Douglas Gifford, 'The Basil Lee Figure in James Hogg's Fiction', *Newsletter of the James Hogg Society*, 4 (1985), 16–27

P. D. Garside, 'Three Perils in Publishing: Hogg and the Popular Novel', *Studies in Hogg and his World*, 2 (1991), 45–63

Ian Duncan, 'The Upright Corpse: Hogg, National Literature and the Uncanny', *Studies in Hogg and his World*, 5 (1994), 29–54

Kate McGrail, 'Re-making the Fire: James Hogg and the Makars', *Studies in Hogg and his World*, 7 (1996), 26–36

Ian Duncan, 'Walter Scott, James Hogg, and Scottish Gothic', in *A Companion to the Gothic*, ed. by David Punter (Oxford: Blackwell, 2000), pp. 70–80

Roger Leitch, 'Hogg, Pedlars, and the Tale of "The Long Pack"', *Studies in Hogg and his World*, 12 (2001), 139–42

John Barrell, 'Putting Down the Rising', in *Scotland and the Borders of Romanticism*, ed. by Leith Davis, Ian Duncan, and Janet Sorensen (Cambridge: Cambridge University Press, 2004), pp. 130–38

Chronology of James Hogg

1770 On 9 December James Hogg is baptised in Ettrick Church, Selkirkshire, the date of his birth going unrecorded. His father, Robert Hogg (*c*.1729–1820), a former shepherd, was then tenant of Ettrickhall, a modest farm almost within sight of the church. His mother, Margaret Laidlaw (1730–1813), belonged to a local family noted for their athleticism and also for their stock of ballads and other traditional lore. Hogg's parents married in Ettrick on 27 May 1765, and had four sons, William (b.1767), James (b.1770), David (b.1773), and Robert (b.1776).

1775–76 Hogg attends the parish school kept by John Beattie for a few months before his formal education is abruptly terminated by his father's bankruptcy as a stock-farmer and sheep-dealer and the family's consequent destitution. Their possessions are sold by auction, but a compassionate neighbour, Walter Bryden of Crosslee, takes a lease of the farm of Ettrickhouse and places Robert Hogg there as his shepherd.

1776–85 Due to his family's poverty Hogg is employed as a farm servant throughout his childhood, beginning with the job of herding a few cows in the summer and progressing as his strength increases to general farmwork and acting as a shepherd's assistant. He learns the Metrical Psalms and other parts of the Bible, listens eagerly to the legends of his mother and her brother William (*c*.1735–1829), of itinerants who visit the parish, and of the old men he is engaged with on the lightest and least demanding farm-work.

1778 Death on 17 September of Hogg's maternal grandfather, William Laidlaw, 'the far-famed Will o' Phaup', a noted athlete and reputedly the last man in the district to have spoken with the fairies.

c. 1784 Having saved five shillings from his wages, at the age of fourteen Hogg purchases an old fiddle and teaches himself to play it at the end of his day's work.

1785 Hogg serves a year from Martinmas (11 November) with Mr Scott, the tenant-farmer of Singlee, at 'working with horses, threshing, &c.'

1786 Hogg serves eighteen months from Martinmas with Mr Laidlaw at Elibank, 'the most quiet and sequestered place in Scotland'.

1788 The father of Mr Laidlaw of Elibank, who farms at Willenslee, gives Hogg his first engagement as a shepherd from Whitsunday (15 May); here he stays for two years and begins to read while tending the ewes. His master's wife lends him newspapers and theological works, and he also reads Allan Ramsay's *The Gentle Shepherd* and William Hamilton of Gilbertfield's paraphrase of Blind Harry's *The Life and Adventures of William Wallace.*

1790 Hogg begins a ten-years' service from Whitsunday as shepherd to James Laidlaw of Blackhouse farm, whose kindness he later described as 'much more like that of a father than a master'. Hogg reads his master's books, as well as those of Mr Elder's Peebles circulating library, and begins to compose songs for the local lasses to sing. He makes a congenial and life-long friend in his master's eldest son, William Laidlaw (1779–1845), and with his elder brother William and a number of cousins forms a literary society of shepherds. Alexander Laidlaw, shepherd at Bowerhope in Yarrow, is also an intimate friend who shares Hogg's efforts at self-improvement. 'The Mistakes of a Night', a Scots poem, is published in the *Scots Magazine* for October 1794, and in 1797 Hogg first hears of Robert Burns (1759–96) when a half-daft man named Jock Scott recites 'Tam o' Shanter' to him on the hillside. Towards the end of this period Hogg composes plays and pastorals as well as songs. His journeying as a drover of sheep stimulates an interest in the Highlands of Scotland, and initiates a series of exploratory tours taken in the summer over a succession of years.

1800 At Whitsunday Hogg leaves Blackhouse to look after his ageing parents at Ettrickhouse. Going into Edinburgh in the autumn to sell sheep he decides to print his poems: his *Scottish Pastorals* is published early in the following year and receives favourable attention in the *Scots Magazine* for 1801. More popular still is his patriotic song of 'Donald Macdonald' also composed at about this time, in fear of a French invasion.

1802 Hogg is recruited by William Laidlaw in the spring as a ballad-collector for Scott's *Minstrelsy of the Scottish Border*, and meets Walter Scott himself (1771–1832) later in the year. He begins to contribute to the *Edinburgh Magazine*, and keeps a journal of his Highland Tour in July and August that is eventually published in the *Scots Magazine.*

1803 The lease of Ettrickhouse expires at Whitsunday and Hogg uses his savings to lease a Highland sheep farm, signing a five-year lease for Shelibost in Harris on 13 July, to begin from Whitsunday 1804. On his journey home he stops at Greenock where he meets the future novelist John Galt (1779–1839) and his friend James Park. He is now a regular contributor to the *Scots Magazine*, and also earns prizes from the Highland Society of Scotland for his essays on sheep.

1804 Hogg loses his money and fails to gain possession of Shelibost through a legal complication, retiring into England for the summer. On his return home he fails to find employment, but occupies himself in writing ballad-imitations for the collection published in 1807 as *The Mountain Bard*.

1805–1806 Hogg is engaged from Whitsunday 1805 as a shepherd at Mitchelslacks farm in Closeburn parish, Dumfriesshire: his master Mr Harkness belongs to a local family famous for their support of the Covenanters. He is visited on the hillside by the young Allan Cunningham (1784–1842), and becomes friendly with the whole talented Cunningham family. Around Halloween 1806 (31 October) he becomes the lover of Catherine Henderson. Towards the end of the year Hogg signs leases on two farms in Dumfriesshire, Corfardin and Locherben, to begin from Whitsunday 1807.

1807 *The Mountain Bard* is published by Archibald Constable (1774–1827) in Edinburgh in February. At Whitsunday Hogg moves to Corfardin farm in Tynron parish. *The Shepherd's Guide*, a sheep-farming and veterinary manual, is published in June. Hogg acknowledges paternity of Catherine Henderson's baby, born towards the end of the summer and baptised Catherine Hogg on 13 December.

1808–09 As a result of trips to Edinburgh Hogg becomes acquainted with James Gray (1770–1830), classics master of the Edinburgh High School and his future brother-in-law. He also meets a number of literary women, including Mary Peacock, Jessie Stuart, Mary Brunton, and Eliza Izett. After the death of his sheep in a storm Hogg moves to Locherben farm and tries to earn a living by grazing sheep for other farmers. His debts escalate, he becomes increasingly reckless, and around Whitsunday 1809 becomes the lover of Margaret Beattie. In the autumn Hogg absconds from Locherben and his creditors, returning to Ettrick where he is considered to be disgraced and unemployable.

1810 In February Hogg moves to Edinburgh in an attempt to pursue a career as a professional literary man. In Dumfries-shire Margaret Beattie's daughter is born on 13 March, and her birth is recorded retrospectively as Elizabeth Hogg in June, Hogg presumably having acknowledged paternity. Later that year Hogg meets his future wife, Margaret Phillips (1789–1870), while she is paying a visit to her brother-in-law James Gray in Edinburgh. He explores the cultural life of Edinburgh, and is supported by the generosity of an Ettrick friend, John Grieve (1781–1836), now a prosperous Edinburgh hatter. A song-collection entitled *The Forest Minstrel* is published in August. On 1 September the first number of Hogg's own weekly periodical *The Spy* appears, which in spite of its perceived improprieties, continues for a whole year.

1811–12 During the winter of 1810–11 Hogg becomes an active member of the Forum, a public debating society, eventually being appointed Secretary. This brings him into contact with John M'Diarmid (1792–1852), later to become a noted Scottish journalist, and the reforming mental health specialist Dr Andrew Duncan (1744–1828). With Grieve's encouragement Hogg takes rural lodgings at Deanhaugh on the outskirts of Edinburgh and plans a long narrative poem centred on a poetical contest at the court of Mary, Queen of Scots.

1813 Hogg becomes a literary celebrity in Edinburgh when *The Queen's Wake* is published at the end of January, and makes new friends in R. P. Gillies (1788–1858) and John Wilson (1785–1854), his correspondence widening to include Lord Byron (1788–1824) early the following year. Hogg's mother dies in the course of the summer. Hogg tries to interest Constable in a series of Scottish Rural Tales, and also takes advice from various literary friends on the suitability of his play, *The Hunting of Badlewe*, for the stage. In the autumn during his customary Highland Tour he is detained at Kinnaird House near Dunkeld by a cold and begins a poem in the Spenserian stanza, eventually to become *Mador of the Moor*.

1814 Hogg intervenes successfully to secure publication of the work of other writers such as R. P. Gillies, James Gray, and William Nicholson (1782–1849). George Goldie publishes *The Hunting of Badlewe* in April, as the Allies enter Paris and the end of the long war with France seems imminent. During the summer Hogg meets William Wordsworth (1770–1850) in Edinburgh, and visits him and other poets in an excursion to the Lake District. He proposes a poetical repository, and obtains several promises of contributions from important contemporary poets, though the project leads to a serious quarrel with Scott in the autumn. The bankruptcy of George Goldie halts sales of *The Queen's Wake*, but introduces Hogg to the publisher William Blackwood (1776–1834). Having offered Constable *Mador of the Moor* in February, Hogg is persuaded by James Park to publish *The Pilgrims of the Sun* first: the poem is brought out by John Murray (1778–1843) and William Blackwood in Edinburgh in December. Towards the end of the year Hogg and his young Edinburgh friends form the Right and Wrong Club which meets nightly and where heavy drinking takes place.

1815 Hogg begins the year with a serious illness, but at the end of January is better and learns that the Duke of Buccleuch has granted him the small farm of Eltrive Moss effectively rent-free for his lifetime. He takes possession at Whitsunday, but as the house there is barely habitable continues to spend much of his time in Edinburgh. He writes songs for the Scottish collector George Thomson (1757–1851). Scott's publication of a poem celebrating the ending of the Napoleonic Wars with the battle of Waterloo on 18 June prompts Hogg to write 'The Field of Waterloo'. Hogg also writes 'To the Ancient Banner of Buccleuch' for the local contest at football at Carterhaugh on 4 December.

1816 Hogg contributes songs to John Clarke-Whitfeld's *Twelve Vocal Melodies*, and plans a collected edition of his own poetry. *Mador of the Moor* is published in April. Despairing of the success of his poetical repository Hogg turns it into a collection of his own parodies, published in October as *The Poetic Mirror*. The volume is unusually successful, a second edition being published in December. The Edinburgh musician Alexander Campbell visits Hogg in Yarrow, enlisting his help with the song-collection *Albyn's Anthology* (1816–18). William Blackwood moves into Princes Street, signalling his intention to become one of Edinburgh's foremost publishers.

1817 Blackwood begins an *Edinburgh Monthly Magazine* in April, with Hogg's support, but with Thomas Pringle and James Cleghorn as editors it is a lacklustre publication and a breach between publisher and editors ensues. Hogg, holding by Blackwood, sends him a draft of the notorious 'Chaldee Manuscript', the scandal surrounding which ensures the success of the re-launched *Blackwood's Edinburgh Magazine*. Hogg's two-volume

Dramatic Tales are published in May. Hogg spends much of the summer at his farm of Altrive, writing songs for *Hebrew Melodies*, a Byron-inspired collection proposed by the composer W. E. Heather. In October George Thomson receives a proposal from the Highland Society of London for a collection of Jacobite Songs, a commission which he passes on to Hogg.

1818 *The Brownie of Bodsbeck; and Other Tales* is published by Blackwood in March, by which time Hogg is busily working on *Jacobite Relics*, his major preoccupation this year. A modern stone-built cottage is built at Altrive, the cost of which Hogg hopes to defray in part by a new one guinea subscription edition of *The Queen's Wake*, which is at press in October though publication did not occur until early the following year.

1819 On a visit to Edinburgh towards the end of February Hogg meets again with Margaret Phillips; his courtship of her becomes more intense, and he proposes marriage. Hogg's song-collection *A Border Garland* is published in May, and in August Hogg signs a contract with Oliver and Boyd for the publication of *Winter Evening Tales*, also working on a long Border Romance. The first volume of *Jacobite Relics* is published in December.

1820 During the spring Hogg is working on the second volume of his *Jacobite Relics* and also on a revised edition of *The Mountain Bard*, as well as planning his marriage to Margaret Phillips, which takes place on 28 April. His second work of fiction, *Winter Evening Tales,* is published at the end of April. Very little literary work is accomplished during the autumn: the Hoggs make their wedding visits in Dumfriesshire during September, and then on 24 October Hogg's old father dies at Altrive.

1821 The second volume of *Jacobite Relics* is published in February and a third (enlarged) edition of *The Mountain Bard* in March. The inclusion in the latter of an updated 'Memoir of the Author's Life' raises an immediate outcry. Hogg's son, James Robert Hogg, is born in Edinburgh on 18 March and baptised on the couple's first wedding anniversary. Serious long-term financial troubles begin for Hogg with the signing of a nine-year lease from Whitsunday of the large farm of Mount Benger in Yarrow, part of the estates of the Duke of Buccleuch—Hogg having insufficient capital for such an ambitious venture. In June Oliver and Boyd's refusal to publish Hogg's

Border Romance, *The Three Perils of Man*, leads to a breach with the firm. Hogg also breaks temporarily with Blackwood in August when a savage review of his 'Memoir of the Author's Life' appears in *Blackwood's Edinburgh Magazine*, and begins again to write for Constable's less lively *Edinburgh Magazine*. In September there is a measles epidemic in Yarrow, and Hogg becomes extremely ill with the disease. By the end of the year Hogg is negotiating with the Constable firm for an edition of his collected poems in four volumes.

1822 The first of the 'Noctes Ambrosianae' appears in the March issue of *Blackwood's Edinburgh Magazine*: Hogg is portrayed in this long-running series as the Shepherd, a 'boozing buffoon'. June sees the publication of Hogg's four-volume *Poetical Works* by Constable, and Longmans publish his novel *The Three Perils of Man*. There is great excitement in Edinburgh surrounding the visit of George IV to the city in August, and Hogg marks the occasion with the publication of his Scottish masque, *The Royal Jubilee*. A neighbouring landowner in Ettrick Forest, Captain Napier of Thirlestane, publishes *A Treatise on Practical Store-Farming* in October, with help from Hogg and his friend Alexander Laidlaw of Bowerhope. James Gray leaves Edinburgh to become Rector of Belfast Academy.

1823 In debt to William Blackwood Hogg sets about retrieving his finances with a series of tales for *Blackwood's Edinburgh Magazine* under the title of 'The Shepherd's Calendar'. His daughter Janet Phillips Hogg ('Jessie') is born on 23 April. That summer a suicide is exhumed in Yarrow, and Hogg writes an account for *Blackwood's*. *The Three Perils of Woman*, another novel, is published in August, and Hogg subsequently plans to publish an eight-volume collection of his Scottish tales.

1824 Hogg is working on his epic poem *Queen Hynde* during the spring when his attention is distracted by family troubles. His once prosperous father-in-law is in need of a home, so Hogg moves his own family to the old thatched farmhouse of Mount Benger leaving his new cottage at Altrive for the old couple. *The Private Memoirs and Confessions of a Justified Sinner*, written at Altrive during the preceding months, is published in June. Hogg contributes to the *Literary Souvenir* for 1825, this signalling the opening of a new and lucrative market for his work in Literary Annuals. In November a major conflagration destroys part of Edinburgh's Old Town. *Queen Hynde* is published early in December.

1825 Another daughter is born to the Hoggs on 18 January and named Margaret Laidlaw Hogg ('Maggie'). Hogg turns his attention to a new work of prose fiction, 'Lives of Eminent Men', the precursor of his *Tales of the Wars of Montrose*. In December John Gibson Lockhart (1794–1854), Scott's son-in-law and a leading light of *Blackwood's*, moves to London to take up the post of editor of the *Quarterly Review*, accompanied by Hogg's nephew and literary assistant Robert Hogg.

1826 Hogg is in arrears with his rent for Mount Benger at a time which sees the failure of the Constable publishing firm, involving Sir Walter Scott and also Hogg's friend John Aitken. By July Hogg himself is threatened with arrestment for debt, while the Edinburgh book trade is in a state of near-stagnation. James Gray is also in debt and leaves Belfast for India, leaving his two daughters, Janet and Mary, in the care of Hogg and his wife.

1827 Hogg's financial affairs are in crisis at the beginning of the year when the Buccleuch estate managers order him to pay his arrears of rent at Whitsunday or relinquish the Mount Benger farm. However, 'The Shepherd's Calendar' stories are appearing regularly in *Blackwood's Edinburgh Magazine* and Hogg is confident of earning a decent income by his pen as applications for contributions to Annuals and other periodicals increase. The death of his father-in-law Peter Phillips in May relieves him from the expense of supporting two households. Hogg founds the St Ronan's Border Club, the first sporting meeting of which takes place at Innerleithen in September. The year ends quietly for the Hoggs, who are both convalescent—Margaret from the birth of the couple's third daughter, Harriet Sidney Hogg, on 18 December, and Hogg from the lameness resulting from having been struck by a horse.

1828 Although a more productive year for Hogg than the last, with the publication of his *Select and Rare Scotish Melodies* in London in the autumn and the signing of a contract with Robert Purdie for a new edition of his *Border Garland*, the book-trade is still at a comparative standstill. Hogg's daughter Harriet is discovered to have a deformed foot that may render her lame. A new weekly periodical entitled the *Edinburgh Literary Journal* is started in Edinburgh by Hogg's young friend, Henry Glassford Bell (1803–74).

1829 Hogg continues to write songs and to make contributions to Annuals and other periodicals, while the spring sees the pub-

lication of *The Shepherd's Calendar* in book form. Hogg continues to relish shooting during the autumn months and the country sports of the St Ronan's Border Club.

1830 Hogg's lease of the Mount Benger farm is not renewed, and
the family return to Altrive at Whitsunday. Inspired by the
success of Scott's *magnum opus* edition of the Waverley Novels,
Hogg pushes for the publication of his own tales in monthly
numbers. Blackwood agrees to publish a small volume of
Hogg's best songs, and Hogg finds a new outlet for his work
with the foundation in February of *Fraser's Magazine*. Towards
the end of September Hogg meets with Scott for the last time.

1831 *Songs by the Ettrick Shepherd* is published at the start of the year,
and a companion volume of ballads, *A Queer Book*, is printed,
though publication is held up by Blackwood, who argues that
the political agitation surrounding the Reform Bill is hurtful
to his trade. He is also increasingly reluctant to print Hogg's
work in his magazine. Hogg's youngest child, Mary Gray
Hogg, is born on 21 August. Early in December Hogg quar-
rels openly with Blackwood and resolves to start the publication of his collected prose tales in London. After a short stay
in Edinburgh he departs by sea and arrives in London on the
last day of the year.

1832 From January to March Hogg enjoys being a literary lion in
London while he forwards the publication of his collected prose
tales. Within a few weeks of his arrival he publishes a devotional manual for children entitled *A Father's New Year's Gift*,
and also works on the first volume of his *Altrive Tales*, published in April after his return to Altrive. Blackwood, no doubt
aware of Hogg's metropolitan celebrity, finally publishes *A
Queer Book* in April too. The Glasgow publisher Archibald
Fullarton offers Hogg a substantial fee for producing a new
edition of the works of Robert Burns with a memoir of the
poet. The financial failure of Hogg's London publisher, James
Cochrane, stops the sale and production of *Altrive Tales* soon
after the publication of the first (and only) volume. Sir Walter
Scott dies on 21 September, and Hogg reflects on the subject
of a Scott biography. In October Hogg is invited to contribute
to a new cheap paper, *Chambers's Edinburgh Journal*.

1833 During a January visit to Edinburgh Hogg falls through the
ice while out curling and a serious illness results. In February
he tries to interest the numbers publisher Blackie and Son of
Glasgow in a continuation of his collected prose tales. He tries

to mend the breach with Blackwood, who for his part is seriously offended by Hogg's allusions to their financial dealings in the 'Memoir' prefacing *Altrive Tales*. Hogg sends a collection of anecdotes about Scott for publication in London but withdraws them in deference to Lockhart as Scott's son-in-law, forwarding a rewritten version to America in June for publication there. He offers Cochrane, now back in business as a publisher, some tales about the wars of Montrose, and by November has reached an agreement with Blackie and Son. The young Duke of Buccleuch grants Hogg a 99-year lease for the house at Altrive and a fragment of the land, a measure designed to secure a vote for him in elections but which also ensures a small financial provision for Hogg's young family after his death.

1834 Hogg's nephew and literary assistant Robert Hogg dies of consumption on 9 January, aged thirty-one. Hogg revises his work on the edition of Burns, now with William Motherwell as a co-editor. His *Lay Sermons* is published in April, and the same month sees the publication of his *Familiar Anecdotes of Sir Walter Scott* in America. When a pirated version comes out in Glasgow in June Lockhart breaks off all friendly relations with Hogg. The breach with William Blackwood is mended in May, but Blackwood's death on 16 November loosens Hogg's connection both with the publishing firm and *Blackwood's Edinburgh Magazine*.

1835 *Tales of the Wars of Montrose* is published in March. Hogg seems healthy enough in June, when his wife and daughter, Harriet, leave him at Altrive while paying a visit to Edinburgh. Even in August he is well enough to go out shooting on the moors as usual and to take what proves to be a last look at Blackhouse and other scenes of his youth. Soon afterwards, however, his normally excellent constitution begins to fail and by October he is confined first to the house and then to his bed. He dies on 21 November, and is buried among his relations in Ettrick kirkyard a short distance from the place of his birth.

Winter Evening Tales

WINTER EVENING TALES,

COLLECTED AMONG

THE COTTAGERS

IN THE

South of Scotland.

By JAMES HOGG,

AUTHOR OF " THE QUEEN'S WAKE," &c. &c.

IN TWO VOLUMES.

VOL. I.

" In rangles round afore the ingle's lowe,
  Frae Gudame's mouth auld-warld Tales they hear,
O' Warlocks loupin' round the Wirrikow,
  O' Ghaists that won in glen and kirk-yard drear,
Whilk touzles a' their tap, an' gars them shake wi' fear."—*Fergusson.*

EDINBURGH:

PRINTED FOR OLIVER & BOYD, HIGH-STREET; AND
G. & W. B. WHITTAKER, AVE-MARIA-LANE,
LONDON.

1820.

Winter Evening Tales

The Renowned Adventures
of
Basil Lee*

I HAVE for these twenty years been convinced of the truth of the proverb, that a fool can best teach a wise man wit; and that it is, in fact, on the egregious misconduct of the thoughtless and foolish part of mankind that the wise and prudent calculate for their success, and from these that they take their lessons of perseverance and good management. It is on this principle that the following sheets are indited, that others may be warned from the rock on which I have split; I therefore conceal nothing, but relate uniformly the simple truth, though manifestly to my disadvantage. I have not written my life as a model to be copied, but as one to be avoided, and may those who laugh at my inconsistences learn from them to steer a different course.

There is one great evil under the sun, from which, if youth is not warned, their success in life will be frustrated, and their old age without comfort and without respect. From it my misfortunes are all to be traced, and from it I am suffering at this day. I look back on the days that are past, and am grieved. I can now see all my incongruities, and wonder at my inadvertency in not being able to correct them.

The evil that I complain of, by which all my views in life have been frustrated, and by which thousands as well as myself have

---

* The original of this extraordinary journal was lodged in my hands in the summer of 1810, by an old man, having the appearance of a decayed gentleman. It was when I commenced publishing THE SPY, that it was given in to me, for the purpose of being revised and published in that paper. A small portion of it was published, but, owing to the freedom with which the writer expressed himself, it gave offence, and was therefore cut short and discontinued. The writer, it is probable, had been offended at this, for I never saw him again; but I have since been informed, that his name is Basil Lee, and that he was alive in 1817. He never, in all these memoirs, mentions his family name, and it is evident that he wishes to conceal it. His friends will therefore excuse me for having sub-joined it, for the sake of giving interest to the narrative; and if he himself is still in life, I shall be glad to hear from him. The large portion that I have been obliged to cancel, it was surely better not to appear.

suffered, without attributing their disappointments to it, is neither more nor less than *instability of mind*–that youthful impatience, so notorious in every young and aspiring breast, which impels the possessor to fly from one study to another, and from one calling to another, without the chance of succeeding in any. This propensity to change, so inherent in young and volatile minds, I have often seen encouraged by parents, who would as frequently apply the sage remark, that "when one trade failed, they could, when they pleased, take up another." It is the worst principle on which any man can act, and I will prove it to all the world, first from reason, and afterwards from experience.

The mind of man, survey it from what point of view you please, bears a strong resemblance to a stream of water. I hate similes in general, but the fitness of this pleases me so much at first sight, that I must follow it out. The river when it first issues from its parent spring, is a trifling insignificant rill, and easily dammed or turned aside, either to the right hand or the left; but still as it advances, it gathers strength and power, and, unless by means the most elaborate, becomes irresistible. When it approaches the latter end of its course, it becomes steady and still, and at last moves heavily and laggingly along, till it mixes with the boundless ocean. The stream is human life, and the ocean is eternity; but the similarity betwixt these is so apparent, that the most simple can be at no loss to trace it.

If this stream, in any part of its course, is divided into two, each of these come far short of having half the strength and force of the original current; and if parted again, they still lose in endless gradation. The consequence of this is, that the oftener a stream is divided, it becomes the more easily subdivided again and again. A shoal, or any trivial impediment, that never could once have withstood its accumulated force, stops its diminished currents, and turns them whithersoever chance may direct–a smaller obstacle does it the next time, until the noble river ends in becoming a stagnant lake, or a cumberer of the adjacent grounds. So will it prove with man, if the energies of his soul are enfeebled by a variety of unconnected pursuits.

Again, let it be noted, that it is of little moment into what channel you turn this stream at first, provided you can confine it to that channel alone, for it will continue to deepen, and bank itself in by degrees, until that channel appear to the eyes of all the world as its natural course. So it is with the human mind, even in a more extensive degree; for if its course is bent towards *any one* object, it is ten to one that it obtains it. I hope this plausible theory is perfectly understood, for it is a pity it should be lost; but I think he must have a very thick head who does not comprehend it. And now, having finished the reasoning and reasonable part of my work, I will next prove my theory, by a history of my life, up to the day in which I finish the last page of this manuscript.

I was third son to a reputable farmer in the upper parts of Berwickshire, who occupied an extensive track of land, partly arable and partly pasture. At the parish school I received such an education as was generally bestowed on the sons of farmers in those days. I could read the Shorter Catechism and even the Bible with great fluency, though with a broad and uncouth pronunciation. I could write a fair and legible hand, and cast up accounts tolerably well, having gone through Cocker's Arithmetic as far as the Rule of Three. But when I came into Vulgar Fractions, the trick of dividing a single number into so many minute parts quite disgusted me; as I judged that thereby I was confusing myself with a multiplicity of figures, of which there was no end; so I gave it up.

At fourteen years of age, I was, by my own choice, bound apprentice to a joiner in the neighbourhood, with whom I was obliged to serve out my time, much against my will; for I deemed myself master of the craft, and much superior to my teacher, before half my time was expired. After I had struggled through it, I went home. My father hinted to me, that I ought to take the wages my late master offered me to continue with him, until something better should be found. But this I slighted with high disdain, declaring that I would go to London or America, before I accepted of less than double the sum proposed; and that, at any rate, was I never to learn any thing better than making a plough or cart-wheel?

No master could be found who would come up to my conditions, while the ease and indulgence that I experienced about my father's house, made me heartily wish that no such might ever be found; and this sentiment made me contrive some strong and unanswerable objections to every proposal of the kind, until the prospect of getting me advantageously engaged as a journeyman died somewhat away; and, that it might not too abruptly be renewed, I proposed to my father to hold one of his ploughs, a task, to which I assured him, I was completely adequate, and gave him some wise hints of keeping forward the work of the farm, by the influence which my presence would have upon the servants. My father, who was a good-natured worthy man, acquiesced, and I fell to work; and certainly for some weeks wrought with unusual vigilance. I had one principal motive for staying at home, which my father did not advert to; I was in love with Jessy, one of the servant maids, a little blooming arrogant gypsy, out of whose sight I could not be happy. I quarrelled with her daily, and agreed with her again, begging her pardon before night. I looked, simpered, and sighed; but all these delightful signals of love she received with seeming disdain. I was jealous of her beyond all bounds, and if I saw her smile upon any other young man, or talking apart with one, my bosom burnt with rage and revenge. I haunted her as if I had been her shadow, and though I did not know of any thing that I wanted with her, yet I neither could be happy out of her presence, nor contented when in it.

Though I believe my performance as a ploughman was of a very inferior species, I remember I soon became superciliously vain of it, which provoked my neighbour ploughmen to treat me with very little deference. I was not slack in telling them, that it arose all from envy, at seeing themselves so much outdone by me, in a business which they had practised all their lives, but had never understood. There was no standing of this from a novice, for the border hinds are an independent and high-spirited race of men, and matters went on any way but cordially between us. My partial father came over to my side, which made the breach still the wider; and at length they told him to my face, that they would no longer work along with me, for, that besides not keeping up my part, and leaving them all the drudgery, I took it upon me to direct them, while, at the same time, I knew no more of farm labour than a cat.

I said it was impossible for me to work longer with such boors, that I wrought nearly as much as them all put together; but that they wanted to be idle, and wished not for any such pattern. "Poor shilly shally shurf!" exclaimed one of them, in great indignation, "You haud a pleugh! ye maun eat a bowe o' meal an' lick a peck o' ashes first! deil hae't e'er I saw ye gude for yet, but rinnin' snipiltin' after the bits o' wenches." Knowing who was present, I threw off my coat in order to give the scoundrel a threshing, but my father ordered him to hold his peace and go about his business; and taking hold of me, he led me *by force* into the house, and there was no more of the matter.

Thus was I taken from the plough's tail, and sent to herd one of the parcels of sheep, the one that contained the smallest number, and required the least attendance of any on the farm. I entered upon this celebrated classical employment with raptures of delight. Never had a mortal such a charming prospect of true felicity. I rejoiced in the opportunity that it would afford me of reading so many delightful books, learning so many fine songs and tunes, of which I was passionately fond, and above all of kissing Jessy below the plaid. Every thing in the shepherd's life was bewitching, but this crowned them all. And that I might not want plenty of opportunities, I was resolved to be so careful, that I could not possibly get home to above one meal in the twenty-four hours, and of course as she was house-maid, she would be obliged to carry all my meat to me.

Such was the delicious picture I had sketched out to myself of the enjoyments of the pastoral life. But, alas! every pleasure in this im-perfect state of things has its concomitant evil attending it; and the shepherd's life did not at all come up to my expectations. I put all the above refined experiments in practice; I read a number of curi-ous books,–sung songs to the rocks and echoes,–blew on the german flute so violently, that my heart palpitated with exertion,–and, for once or twice, kissed Jessy below the plaid. But it seems this had been a freedom of which the little minx did not approve; for thence-forward, a raggamuffian of a boy was sent with my meat, which so altered the shepherd's views, that the nature of his flock was changed with them, and he got home for his victuals as well as any other shepherd in the country.

Moreover, by indulging in all these luxuries of fancy and imagi-nation, these dreams of love and soft delight, I neglected my sheep. They injudiciously scattered themselves over a great extent of coun-try, and got mixed among other flocks, from which I had no means of separating them. They were soon involved in inextricable confu-sion, while, at the same time, I was driven quite desperate; and though not naturally of a bad temper, I often lost myself so far as to get quite enraged at the innocent creatures, and used them very ill, because forsooth they went wrong, which it was my business to have prevented, and for which, certainly, they were blameless. However I wanted to be revenged on them.

There was another thing that mortified me a great deal; I found that so much depended on my dog, that all my exertions without his assistance, availed not a straw in keeping my flock right. I was in fact much more dependant on him than he was upon me, and of that circumstance the haughty brute appeared to be fully aware. He was a very sagacious animal, but as proud as Lucifer, and would not take an ill word off my hand. Whenever he was in the least degree irritated, or affronted, he never chose to understand what I wished him to do; and if he did ought at all, it was the contrary of what I wanted. I knew this to be mere affectation on his part, and done to answer some selfish end, or for the still worse motive of provoking his master; so I cursed and swore, and threw stones at him, which he took good care should never hit him; and out of the reach of all other offensive weapons he prudently kept, whenever he saw me in bad humour. In return for this treatment, he took his tail between his legs, and trotted his way home, without once deigning to look over his shoulder, either to listen to my flattering promises of kindness and good bits, or my most violent threatenings of retaliation. There was I left by the provoking rascal, almost duly every day, as helpless a creature as could be conceived. I shouted, halloo'd, and threw my hat at the lambs, until I often could shout and run no longer; yet all my efforts could never prevent them from straying off at one corner or another. I soon found that the nature of the colley is quite the opposite of that of a pointer or spaniel, and to be well served by him you must treat him as a friend; he will do nothing by force, but from kindness and affection he will do any thing. I was compelled to treat mine with proper deference and respect, and when I did so never had cause to rue it.

There was another evil that attended me; I was obliged to rise much too early in the morning; it did not suit my habits at all, and far less my inclination, for I felt that I was not half satisfied with sleep. The consequence of this was, that whenever I lay down to rest myself during the day, I sunk into the most profound slumbers imaginable, often not awaking for three or four hours, when I generally found my flocks all in utter confusion. I had not the skill to gather and separate them like a shepherd accustomed to the business, and these long sleeps in the fields embittered almost every day of my life. Neither did I much relish the wet clothes, that I was obliged to bear about on my body from morning until night, in rainy weather; it was highly uncomfortable, and a dark mist was the devil and all. I wondered how any man could keep his flocks together in a mist, or know where they were; for there were some days that, from beginning to end, I never knew where I was myself. Then there was the vile custom of smearing them with tar all over the bodies. How I did hate that intolerable operation! Next I was exposed to cold, to snow and rain, and all manner of hardships. In short, before the first half year had expired, I had fairly come to the conclusion, that the life of a shepherd, instead of being the most delightful and romantic, was the most dull and wretched state of existence; and I longed for a fair pretence for throwing up my charge, and the plaid and crook, for ever.

That pretence was not long wanting. Out of deference to my father, the neighbouring shepherds had patiently borne with my inexperience and neglect, and had often brought my scattered flocks back to me, in hopes that after a little experience I would grow better. But seeing that I grew still the more negligent, they combined in a body, and came to my father, and making an old man named Willie Beatie their spokesman, they represented me in such a light, for a lazy, insignificant being, as I never shall forget; and there was something which the old crabbed body said that day, that I found afterwards to be too true. "Ye'll get nae luck o' that callant, sir," said he, "gin he dinna haud his neb better to the grunstane. I wat weel, I hae naething to say ferrar nor what concerns the sheep, but I trow, gin ye dinna tie him til a job that he canna get quat o', he'll flee frae ae' falderall till anither a' the days o' his life; he'll be a plague amang the women too; an' a' thegither ye'll mak but little mence o' him."

My father did not much relish that piece of information, and which he gave the old man to know; but Crusty was not to be snubbed in that way, for his observations grew still more and more severe on my character. "Ey troth, gudeman, ye may just tak it as weel, or as ill as ye like, I carena the black afore my nail about it; a' that I said I'll stand to; I hae naething to do wi' nae honest man's bairn, only I ken this, gin I had sic a chap for a son, I wad either bind him to a sea captain, or gie him a penny in his pouch, an' strap him aff to the Indians—he'll get plenty o' women there as black as slaes; an' that will be better than to hae him rinnin' jinking after fouk's wives an' dochters here, an' bringin' disgrace baith to you an' ither fouk—gin *he* dinna' soon come afore the kirk, I hae tint my skill. But I hae nought to say to that—only, gin ye had to gather his sheep for him, as often as I hae done for this half year bygane, ye wadna be pleased at him mair nor me. When I see a young chap lying slubberin' an' sleepin' a' the day in a heather bush, I can guess what he has been about a' the night."

I never in my life would as gladly have been quit of any body as this old termagant, for I was afraid every moment that he would come out with something which, if my parents knew, would ruin me. My favourite Jessy had been lately married, which I did not much strive to prevent, having laid a plan with myself of seducing her affections afterwards. No sooner was the ceremony over, than I set about my laudable scheme, with all manner of despatch; but the little devil thought proper to inform her husband, and not being aware of this, on my return to see her, I had nearly paid very dear for my temerity. My character being now entirely at their mercy, I was in horrors lest they should expose me, and I feared that this old inveterate rascal had already got hold of the story and was coming out with it then. However I did not hear any more of it, and have taken good care ever since, how I paid my addresses to other men's wives. It may be a very pleasant thing to gain their affections; but when they tell, and put all out together, it comes to be a very disagreeable business.

In the appeal made by the shepherds, my father was obliged to acquiesce, and another lad was hired to my flock. It proved a great relief to me, and I now remained idle about my father's house. I played incessantly on the fiddle, to the great annoyance of the family, and soon became a considerable adept. Certainly my strains were not the sweetest in the world, for I paid no regard to sharps or flats; but I had a good bow-hand, and held on with great vigour, taking care never to stick a tune because I went wrong in it. I soon attained a high character as a musician, and heard some very flattering encomiums on my skill from country neighbours, who even went so far as to aver that "I needed not to be afraid to gang through a tune wi' auld Neil Gow himsel."

I soon observed that my parents were growing uneasy on my account, and dissatisfied that I should be thus trifling away the best of my time. I was terrified for the axe and long saw again, and began to cast about for some creditable business to which I might betake myself; for, now that I had lost Jessy, and all the delights I promised myself in her company, I had nothing of that nature to bind me to home. At length it was decided that I should set up as a grocer in the town of Kelso, which quite delighted me; and at the next term I set up business.

My father's circumstances being well known, I had plenty of credit; neither was I slack in accommodating others in the same way, so that my customers mutiplied exceedingly. My luxuries melted from my shop like the snow from the mountains, and new cargoes poured in like the northen blasts that supply these; but, in spite of my inclinations, and a natural aversion that I had to spirits of every description, I soon began to get dissipated. I was fond of music and song, which often gathered idle people about me, whose company, though I wished to decline, yet I could not resist; and by degrees I was led on till I took my glass as freely as any of them; so that oftentimes, when I came into the shop at night to wind up my affairs for the day and to balance my books, I was so drunk that I knew not one thing from another.

I committed a number of small mistakes in these degrees of elevation, which had nearly cost me a deal of trouble. I had once nearly lost a family of good customers, by selling them, instead of tea, a quarter of a pound of cut tobacco which did not agree with them. I likewise furnished an honest man with a quantity of snuff, instead of Jesuit barks. He drank it for the removal of some impediment about the stomach, but it had quite a different effect from that desired. To give people a dose of saltpetre instead of glauber salts was a frequent mistake with me; I never could know the one from the other, and had twice to give damages on that score. But the thing that frighted me worst of all, was the giving a glass of vitriol to a highlander over the counter instead of whisky. He drank it off, and went away without any remark, save that "she was te cood;" but when he left the shop I observed that his lips were primmed close together, and the tears were streaming over his cheeks. On examining the bottle I discovered my mistake, and had no doubt that the man would die instantly. I learned that he was driving highland cattle, and was seen with them about a mile beyond the town; but I thought he could not live, and expected every day to be apprehended for poisoning him. Day came after day, and no word arrived of the dead highland driver; till at length, about a month after, I was thunderstruck at seeing the same old man enter the shop, and again ask me to sell him "a glassfu' of te whisky." I could not believe my eyes; but he removed all my doubts by adding, "an it pe your vill, let her have te same tat she got fan she vas here pefore." I said I feared I had none of that now, but that some alleged it was not quite the thing. "Hech, man, she shoorly vas te cood!" replied he, "for hit no pe little tat mak auld Tonald pegh (pant), an py cot she vas mhait and trink to hersel for two wheeks."

What a tremendous stomach the old fellow must have had! but I was so overjoyed at seeing him again, that I gave him two or three glasses of the best spirits I had, for which I refused to take any payment. He took off his bonnet, bowed his grey-matted head, and thanked me; promising, at the same time, "always to pe my chustomer fan he came tat vay."

I continued in business only twenty months, and by the assistance of a steady old man, had kept my books perfectly regular; but at this time I committed a great blunder, by suffering a bill granted by me to a rival house to be protested, and still to lie over, on account of some temporary disappointment. Such a neglect is ruin to a man in business. He had better make any sacrifice. This, I know, that it knocked my business on the head, which, with a little more attention, could not have failed of doing well. My credit was ruined, and every debt that I owed was demanded up at once. Though I had stock, I had neither command of money nor securities; and being void of patience, and disgusted with the duns that came on me at every hour of the day, and the threats of prosecutions, I lost heart. Most unadvisedly I locked up the doors of my shop, and gave my books and keys over to my father, absconding, at the same time, till I saw how matters turned out. I was excessively cast down and dispirited at this time; and I remember of being greatly mortified at hearing what passed between two Kelso girls, whom I overtook on my way to Edinburgh. "Wha's that impudent chap?" said the one. "He's a broken merchant i' our town," replied the other. "What right has a creature like him to come an' keek intil fo'ks' faces that gate?" said the first. I felt myself terribly degraded, and was glad to get out of hearing; but their words did not go out of my head for a month.

My father craved time; which was granted. As soon as he had looked over the state of my affairs, he took the debts all upon himself, and gave securities for the whole at six and twelve months. He sold off the stock by public roup; and, though some of the goods were sold at a disadvantage, when all was settled, there was a reversion to me of £160 over and above the sum that he had advanced to me at first. Though he was pleased to find things terminate so well, he was grieved at my having given up a business that promised to turn out to such advantage, and expostulated with me in a very serious manner—a thing which he had never done before. I remember every word of one sentence that he said to me that day; it was very nearly as follows: "Ye're still but a young man yet, son, an' experience may noozle some wit intil ye; for it's o'er plain ye hae muckle need o't. I fear I may say to you, as the good auld man Jacob said to his son Reuben, 'that ye are unstable as water, and shall not excel. He that abideth not by the works of his hands, nor is satisfied with the lot that falleth unto him, shall lift up his voice by the wayside, and no man shall regard him; because he regarded not the voice of him that begat him, nor listened to the words of her that gave him birth.' Son, I hae likit a' my bairns weel; but I had the maist hope o' you. My heart was prooder o' ye aften than I loot on; but gin it be the Lord's will to poonish me for that, I maun e'en submit. I canna be lang wi' ye now. I maun soon leave ye, an' gang to my lang hame; but there's nought will bring my gray hairs sae soon to the grave, as to see the improodence o' my bairns: an' O I wad like weel to see you settled i' some creditable way; i' some way that ye might enjoy peace and quiet i' this life, an' hae time to prepare for a better. The days o' pleasure an' mirth will soon be o'er wi' ye, an' when ye come to my time o' day, there will be mony

actions that ye'll rue, an' this last will be ane amang the lave. Is it not
a strange thing! that you, who are sae clever at every thing, can yet
succeed in naithing?"

I resolved to do better; but I was Jack of all trades, and master of
none. I had now a small sum of my own, which I never had before;
and having never yet cost my father much money, the choice was
still left to myself what I would try next. When a young man gets his
own choice, he is very apt to fix on the profession that his father
followed, especially if he has been fortunate in it. So it was with me
at this time; when, as I conceived, I had learned to calculate matters
aright. I fixed on the life of a farmer, and resolved to be industrious,
virtuous, and sober. I even resolved to marry a wife—a rich one,
and be the first man in the country; and, as far as I can judge, from
my own experience, in every man's views of life that forms a principal part. My father approved of my plan, but at the same time gave
me many charges never again to think of changing that honest and
creditable profession for any other; "for I gie ye my word, son,"
said he, "that a rowin' stane never gathers ony fog; and ane had
better late thrive than never do weel." I promised steadiness, and
really meant to keep my word; and I do not think that ever any
person had higher hopes of happiness than I had at that time. I was
about to enter on that course of life which all men covet, from the
highest to the lowest. What did the merchant and manufacturer toil
for, but for a competence to enable them to retire to a farm in the
country?—What did the soldier and the professional man risk their
health and life for in foreign climes, but for the means to enable
them to retire to a farm in their native country? And this happy and
envied state I was about to enter into in the flower of my age, and
the prime of my life. I laid out all my plans of life in my farm-house;
they were perhaps a little too luxurious, but altogether they formed
an Eden of delight. I calculated on my crops so much an acre—on my
cattle so much a-head—the produce was immense!—quite sufficient
for the expenditure of a gentleman. I was so uplifted in my own
mind at my unexampled good fortune, that my words and actions
were quite eccentric. I hurried from one place to another, as if every
moment had been of the utmost importance; when on foot I ran, and
when on horseback I gallopped. I am sure the cautious and prudent
part of the community must have laughed at me, but I perceived it
not, and thought that every one admired me for my cleverness. The
farmers thereabouts are rather a well-bred class of people, and none
of them ever tried either to mortify or reprehend me, but suffered
me to take my own way. From the rugged freedom of the peasantry,

however, I got some severe rebuffs. I was one day riding into Dunse in fine style, having set off at the gallop, without being well aware of it; "hallo! stop!" cried a brown-looking peasant, with a spade over his shoulder. I wheeled round my horse in the middle of his career. "What's wrang wi' ye, lad? Are ye a' weel eneugh at hame?" "To be sure we are, you dog; what do you mean?" said I. "O, gin ye be a' weel, that's eneugh. I thought ye war outher riding for the doctor or the houdy," (midwife,) said the horny-knuckled rascal, and chop'd on his way, gaping as he went.

At another time I was hiring a lad at a fair in Greenlaw, but parted with him about some trifle; thinking afterward that I was in the wrong, I called him to me as he passed, intending to give him all that he asked; but, not knowing his name, I accosted him thus—"Hallo, you fellow with the white stockings, come hither." He looked aside to me with the greatest contempt—"An' wha the deil was't made you a gentleman, and me a fellow?" said he; "the kail-wife o' Kelso, I fancy? Or was't the salts an' senny leaf?"—Another time at a wedding I chanced to dance a good deal with a pretty country maiden, named May Glendinning, and kept her sitting on my knee, being resolved, if possible, to set her home at night. Her sweetheart was grievously chagrined at this, but could not help it. "What's come o' May, Geordie?" inquired one; "I think ye hae tint May a' thegither the night." "I canna get her keepit a minute," said Geordie, "for that stickit shopkeeper."

A loud roar of laughter ensued, at which I was highly incensed, and resolved to be revenged on the clown. I kept May the whole night, and after many entreaties prevailed on her to suffer me to accompany her home. We went into her father's byre and sat down on some clean hay to court. I said a great many kind things to her, not one of which was true, and always between hands endeavoured to prejudice her against Geordie. I said he was a low ill-bred rascal, and no match for such a lovely and lady-looking maid as she; and many bitter things I uttered against him: among others, I vowed that if I saw such a dog as he touch but the palm of her hand, I would kick him. That moment I was rudely seized by the collar. "Come on, then, maister shopkeeper," said a rough voice, in the dark, at my side. "Here's Geordie at your service; an' I think he can hardly deserve his brikfast better frae you than ye do frae him." I seized him in the same manner, and in that violent way we led one another out. Being burning for revenge, I meant to give him a merciless drubbing. On getting fairly out we struggled hard; but, by bad luck, I fell undermost, and that just in the vile quagmire at the root of the dunghill. There the wretch held me down until the wheezing liquid abomination actually met above my breast; then, giving me two or three bashes on the face, he left me with a loud laugh of scorn, saying, as he struggled through the mud, "It's no ilka chapman that maun try to lick the butter aff Geordie Bailley's bread." The dog was of the race of the gypsies. I went home in a miserable plight.

Having expended the greatest part of the money that my father advanced to me in stocking my farm and furnishing my house, I saw that I would soon want money, and determined on having a wife with a fortune instantly. Accordingly I set out a-wooing to one Miss Jane Armstrong, daughter to a wealthy and respectable farmer. I proved a very awkward lover; and though nothing ever pleased me so much as courting the servant girls, when courting a woman that I really esteemed, I felt as if performing a very disagreeable task. I did not know what to say, for it was a new kind of courting that I neither understood nor relished—it was too systematic and ceremonious for me; however, I thought, that on getting her for my wife all that kind of flummery would be over, and I persisted in my suit, till at length matters came to be understood between us, and nothing remained to do but to name the day. I rather esteemed than loved Miss Armstrong, and went about the whole business rather as a matter of duty than in consequence of a fond attachment.

About this time I chanced to be over in Teviotdale on some business, where I met with a Miss Currie, with whom I was quite captivated. She was handsome, lively, and full of frolic and humour, and I never was so charmed with any lady in my life. I visited her every week, and still became more and more enamoured of her. She treated me so kindly, and with so little reserve, that for three months I never went to see Jane Armstrong but once. The Armstrongs took this heinously amiss, and, all at once, without giving me any notice, the lady was married to a cousin of her own—a baker in Coldstream. I was not even invited to the wedding.

I felt this as a great weight taken off my shoulders, and plied my suit to Magdalene Currie: but to my mortification I soon afterward learned, that the reason why she received me with so much ease was, because she did not care a farthing about me, having all the while been engaged to another, with whom she was joined in wedlock a short time after. I looked exceedingly sheepish, and did not know what to do. I could no more set out my head among the ladies, so I went home and courted my own housekeeper.

This was a delightful amusement, but it was a most imprudent and dear-bought one. From the time that I began toying with this girl, I found that I was no more master of my own house. She did what she pleased, and the rest of the servants followed her example. If a man wishes for either honour, credit, or success in life, let him keep among females of his own rank—above it if he will, but not lower.

I was, moreover, always of an ostentatious and liberal turn of mind, and here I kept a good table, and plenty of French brandy, in my house, which then cost only 1s. 6d. per Scots pint. My neighbours discovered this; and though I never invited any of them, for, in truth, I did not want them, yet there was seldom a day passed on which I did not receive a visit from some of them. One came to hear such and such a tune, which he wanted to learn; another a song of mine that he could not get out of his mind; and a third merely to get a crack, and a glass of brandy and water with me. Though I always left my farming and joined them with reluctance, yet after drinking a glass or two with them, these ill humours all vanished, and I drank on—sung, and played my best tunes—and we never failed to part in great glee, and the most intimate friends in the world. This proved a great source of uneasiness to me, as well as expense, which I could ill afford. I was grieved at it, yet could not put an end to it. The same scenes of noise and riot recurred once or twice, if not six times every week. The servants joined in the same laxity and mirth; and leaving the door half open, they danced to my tunes in the kitchen. This drew my elevated friends away from me to join them, after which, a scene of wrestling and screaming ensued, and all that I could do, I lost the command of my house and family.

My familiarity with my lovely housekeeper still continued, and for a whole year I was like a man going out away with his eyes tied up, who might have seen well enough would he have suffered himself to look. Such a man, though he were sensible that he was going astray, would not think of taking away the bandage, and looking about him to see again where the right path lay, but thinking it capital sport would continue the frolic and run on. It is not easy to conceive such a fool, but exactly such a one was I.

I soon had some pregnant proofs that the days of my housekeeping were drawing towards a conclusion. The failure of my crops, and the insurmountable indolence of my servants without doors, not to mention the extended prospect within, all announced to me, that of my hopeful household there must necessarily be a dispersion. I judged it a far easier and more convenient mode of breaking up the concern, for me to go and leave them, than to be making my delightful housekeeper and all her irregular, lazy, and impudent associates, pack up their baggage and leave me. I perceived before me a system of crying, whining, and obloquy; not to mention church anathemas, that I could in nowise encounter; so as the war was then raging in America, I determined on going there in person, to assist some of the people in killing their neighbours. I did not care much which of the parties, provided I got to a place where I should never see nor hear more of my drunken neighbours, profligate servants, lame horses, blighted crops, and unfathomable housekeeper.

I acquainted my brother with my resolution; and notwithstanding of his warmest remonstrances, I persisted in it. So he was obliged to take my farm, for fear I should give it to some other; and as he considered it a good bargain, he gave me a fair valuation of all my farm stocking. We settled every thing ourselves, and that as privately as possible. I applied at the War Office, and there being then a great demand for young men of spirit to go out to America, I found no difficulty in purchasing an ensign's commission in a regiment then lying in lower Canada. In the course of a few days I turned my back on my native place, and my face toward the western world, in search of something—I did not know what it was, but it was that which I could not find at home. Had I reflected aright, I would have found it was prudence; but I would not suffer myself to reflect, for my conduct at that time was not calculated, on a retrospection, to afford much consolation; but I hoped, in a life of danger and anxiety, to experience that sort of pleasure which is the result of hope and variety.

I do not intend here to give even the general outlines of our progress in America; my own private memoirs, which I am writing, are quite a different matter, and I fear will be found too much in unison with my former behaviour and general character. I have often thought that the more one suffers in mind from any misfortune, the more apt he is to fall again into the same improprieties that caused it. Moral philosophers may account for this; I cannot; but of this I am sure, that my whole life has been fraught with instances of it; and on taking a general review of the actions of men, I persuade myself that it prevails to a degree that no casualty can account for. I had no sooner made my escape, disgracefully enough, from a disagreeable dilemma with one girl, than I got into another much worse.

On my rout to America, I joined, at Cork, a Lieutenant Colin Frazer, who was conducting out two companies of recruits to join our transatlantic army, and of course I was a subordinate officer to him. I never liked him from the beginning; he was too selfish and conceited of himself, and pretended to be so much of a gentleman, (though he had never before been from the banks of Loch Ness in the Highlands,) that it was impossible to know how to speak to him. I could not speak English otherwise than in the broadest border dialect, while he delivered himself in a broken highland jargon, at which I could never contain my gravity. With all this we were obliged to be constantly together at mess, as well as other times; and from the moment that we first met, my nature seemed, even to myself, to have undergone a complete change. Perhaps the idea of being now a soldier contributed greatly to this; but from being a good natured, careless, roving, absurd fellow, I became all at once proud, positive, and obstreperous; and in keeping up these dignified pretensions, I daresay was as absurd as in the conducting of my mercantile and farming transactions. Still I cannot help thinking, it was this haughty overbearing Highland devil that stirred up these unnatural propensities in my breast. We never looked one another openly and frankly in the face, when we conversed together; if we did, it was with a kind of sneer; and our custom was to sit opposite one another, with averted eyes, and cut and snub one another all that we could, still pretending to be in good humour, yet all the while full of bitterness and gall.

This state of affairs was soon brought to a climax, by my spirit of gallantry. Among the few females that were in the ship, there was one Clifford Mackay, a most beautiful, angelic young lady from the Highlands. The moment that I saw her I was seized with a strong curiosity to know all about her, and what was her motive for going out to America; and that curiosity was mixed with the romantic passion of love. I saw that she and Frazer were acquainted, and indeed he appeared to be her only acquaintance on board; but he behaved to her with such reserve, and kept at such a distance from her in public, that I was altogether astonished how he could behave in such a manner to so sweet a creature, and marked him down in my mind as a cold hearted insensible vagabond of a fellow. This apparent neglect endeared the lady still more to me, and interested my heart so much in her, that I could scarcely ever keep from her company. There was no little kind office that lay in my power that I did not proffer, no attention that I did not pay, at which Frazer would often sneer in the most insulting way. "'Pon my wort Miss Mackay, put you'll pe ketting exhellent attensions," he would say; or at other times, "Shurely you'll pe unter fery much kreat oblighations to the worthy and callant ensign." I was so imprudent as one day, in an ill humour, to repeat one of these sayings in his own tone and dialect, in mockery. He gave his mouth a twist, curled up his nose, and turned round on his heel, saying at the same time, "You shall pe answering for this py and py, my prave fellow." "O that I will, I daresay," said I, as saucily as might be. In the meantime I plied the beautiful Clifford, until her heart was melted, and she told me her whole story, and a most interesting story it was; unluckily for me there happened not to be one word of it true, an inference which I would have been the last man in the world to have drawn. I proffered myself her friend and protector, in the most noble and disinterested manner; and though these were not frankly accepted, still they were by degrees admitted, until at last they terminated as all these generous and benevolent protections of the fair sex do. I was blessed beyond measure in the society of this adorable and delicate creature; and as Frazer now kept a shy distance from both of us, I had as much of her delightful company as I chose. I really felt exceedingly happy with this angel, and began to value myself highly on my personal accomplishments, that had thus gained me the affections of such a lady in so short a time.

She was going to live with her brother, a man of great consequence in upper Canada, under the care of Frazer, who was an acquaintance of her father's. I engaged to see her safely there, if he failed in the charge he had undertaken, or to assist him in it as far as lay in my power; and on reaching her brother's house, why, marriage was a thing to happen of course; but on that subject we did not talk much. As we neared to the shores of America, she still spoke less and less of her brother, who at one time was her sole discourse; and after coming to anchor in the St Lawrence, she never more mentioned his name, unless in answer to some question that I chanced to ask concerning him; and when our baggage was removed from the ship into boats, I observed that Frazer took no notice whatever of either her or her effects. I thought I likewise perceived a kind of despondency in my charmer's looks that quite overcame me, and I resolved to dedicate my life to her. I never durst look forward to the future, or calculate with myself what were to be the consequences of this amour; but these came upon me much sooner than I could have presumed.

We sailed for three days up the river, after quitting the vessel. Frazer, Clifford, and I were in the same boat, as were also an Irish and an English gentleman. Our noble lieutenant spoke next to nothing, but upon the whole did not behave uncivilly. We came at length to a village on the north side of the river, where we were obliged to land, and wait some days for the arrival of other troops and some waggons. Being now got fairly to land, and in a place where retirement was easy to be obtained, which hitherto had been impossible, Frazer had resolved to let me know what I was about. Accordingly, the next morning after our arrival, I was waited upon by the Irish gentleman who came with us, who presented me with a challenge from the Lieutenant. I never was so confounded in my life, and wist not what to do or say; but read the note over and over, I do not recollect how oft. Macrae, the Irishman, noticed my dilemma, which I daresay amused him, and then he calmly enquired, what answer he was to return to his friend. "The man's out of his judgment," said I.—"I do not see," said he, "how you can draw that inference from any thing that has passed on the present occasion. Certainly he could not do otherwise than demand satisfaction of you, for the gross manner in which you have insulted him, by seducing his ward and friend; and that avowedly, it being a transaction that was neither hid from the ship's crew, nor from the men he is destined to command." "The devil run away with him and his ward both," said I. Macrae burst out a laughing; and remarked that "that was no answer at all to send to a gentleman; and that as he had the greatest respect for his friend, he would not hear a repetition of such ribaldry; and that, after what he had seen and heard of my behaviour, he judged it more meet that I should be beaten like a dog before the men, and hooted from the king's service in disgrace." In my confusion of ideas, this had never occurred to me, that I was now obliged to fight a duel with any one who liked, or be disgraced for ever. So plucking up a momentary courage, I wrote a note in answer, accepting his challenge as soon as I could procure a friend to be my second. The English gentleman, Mr Dow, who had accompanied us from Britain, being lodged in the same house with me, I applied to him for advice, and stated the matter exactly to him. He said it was an ugly job, and he feared there was no alternative but fighting the gentleman, unless I chose to make every concession, and be disgraced. "As to either the grace or disgrace of the matter," said I, "I do not mind that a pin; but as I suspect the gentleman has been very shabbily used by me, I will rather make any concession he chooses to name, than fight with one I have wronged. I do not approve of fighting duels. My religious principles do not admit of it." He smiled and shook his head. "I believe," said he, "you are a very honest good fellow, but you are a simple man, and know nothing of the world. You must leave the matter entirely to me. I suspect you must fight him, but as he is the challenger you have the right of choosing your weapon. I will however wait upon him, and shall bring you off if I can." "For God's sake do," said I; "I will rather make any acknowledgment he likes, than kill the honest brave fellow, and have his blood on my head, after having offended him by hurting him in the tenderest part." "O that will never do," said he; "never talk of concessions, just in the outset of life; leave the matter wholly to me, and behave yourself like a man and a Scotsman, whatever be the issue." I promised that I would; and away he went to wait on Frazer, my insulted Lieutenant. How I did curse his hot Highland blood to myself, and wished him an hundred times at the bottom of Loch Ness, or on the top of the highest of his native hills, never to come down again till the day of judgment. I then cursed my own imprudence; but amid all my raving and execrations, I attached no blame to the lovely and gentle Clifford Mackay. The preference that she had given to me over Colin Frazer, her Highland friend, acted like a hidden charm in her behalf.

I now began to consult seriously with myself what weapons I should make choice of. I could in nowise bow my mind to pistols, for I found that I could not stand and be shot at. I accounted myself as good a marksman as any in Britain, but that I reckoned of no avail. What did I care for killing the man? I had no wish to kill him, farther than by so doing I might prevent him from killing me at the next fire, and on that ground I would have aimed as sickerly as possible. I would not have minded so much had I been sure of being shot dead at once, but to have a ball lodged inside of me, and have my nerves wrecked and teased by bungling American surgeons trying to extract it, was the thing that I was determined on no consideration to submit to. I would not have a doctor twisting and mangling my entrails, in search of a crabbed pistol bullet, for no man's caprice, nor woman's neither; so I determined not to fight with pistols.

I tried to discuss the merits of the small sword, but it was a vile insidious weapon, and worse than the other, if worse could be; a thing that came with a jerk by the wrist, as swift as lightning, and out through one's body in a moment. The blue holes they made through one were very unseemly, and not to be cured. There was something upon the whole very melancholy in the view of the issue of a duel with small swords; so I resolved to decline fighting with them.

The broad-sword? Why, it was a noble weapon; but to trust myself under the broad-sword of an enraged highlander, would be a piece of as desperate temerity as braving the bolt of heaven. Besides, I had never learned to fence. Still, however, a man had it in his power to defend himself against that weapon, and there was a great deal in that—he might use some very strenuous exertions for

that purpose; and if nothing else would do, an honourable retreat
was in his power. Upon the whole, though I did not approve of
trusting myself under such a weapon, in such hands, yet I rather
leaned to that than any other; or, on second thoughts, I judged that it
would be as good, and as genteel, to make choice of the swords that
we wore, which were neither broad nor small ones, but something
between the two, and not remarkable for their sharpness.

Mr Dow returned; and in the most calm and friendly way, informed me that he found it a very disagreeable business, much more
so than he thought meet to disclose to me, till he saw what would be
the issue. I asked if nothing but my life would satisfy the fellow? He
answered that he would not be satisfied with any concessions that a
gentleman could make; that if I kneeled before all the men, and
confessed that I had wronged him, and begged his pardon, he would
be satisfied, but with nothing less. "Why," says I, "since you think
the gentleman is so grossly wronged, I do not see why I should not
do this." "By the Lord, sir," said he, with great fervour, "if you do
you are lost for ever. Consider, that in so doing, you do not only
confess your error, but confess that you are a coward; and the next
thing that you must do is to hide your head from every human acquaintance. I have considered the case as my own, and conceive
that there is no other method of procedure, but to give the gentleman the satisfaction he desires, and on that ground I have appointed
the hour and the place of meeting. It is to be in a lane of the ajoining
wood, at seven o'clock in the evening; the choice of the weapons is
left to you."

"Why should it not be just now?" said I. "The sooner any disagreeable business is over the better; and as for the weapons, to give
him every advantage, since I have been the aggressor, I'll give him
the weapon for which his country is so much famed. We will decide
it with our swords. Does he think that men are mice?"

Dow gave me a slap on the shoulder, and, with a great oath, swore
that that was said like a man; "and I'll go and tell your opponent
that," added he, " which I trow will stunn him." I had now taken my
resolution, and went away with him to the place quite courageously,
though all the while I scarcely knew what I was doing, such a tremor
had taken hold of me. Dow's looks cleared up. He went away and
warned Frazer and his second of my mortal impatience for the combat, and then we two walked in the grove awaiting their arrival;
and, after all, they were not in any great hurry. When they arrived,
our seconds insisted on our shaking hands. To this I had no objections in the world, but I saw that Frazer would rather have shunned

it; he held out his in the most proud disdainful way, while I with great bluntness took hold of it, and gave it a hearty squeeze and a shake. "Captain, man," says I—and I fear the tear was standing in my eye—"Captain, man, I little thought it would ever come to this with us!" "You did not, did you?" replied he, "and fat te deol did you pe taking her to pe?" and with that he flung my hand from him.

"Well, well, captain, here's for you, then," says I, drawing out my sword and brandishing it in the air. "Pooh, pooh! te deol, tamnation, and haill!" ejaculated he; and, twisting his nose, and turning away his face as if he had found a stink, he drew out his sword, and, stretching out his arm, put its edge to mine, with such marks of disdain as never were before witnessed by any living creature. I struck with all my might, thinking to hit him a dreadful smash on the head or shoulder, and cleave him to the teeth, if not to the heart; but he warded the blow with the greatest indifference, and attacked me in return. I had now to defend myself with my utmost puissance, which I did instinctively, by keeping my arm at full stretch, crossing my sword before me, and making it ply up and down with the swiftness of lightning; and a most excellent mode of defence it is—one that I would recommend to any man in such circumstances as I then was. So effectual did it prove, that Frazer, with all his science, could not touch me. He still followed up his advantage, and pressed hard upon me, as he well might, for I had now no leisure again to strike at him, I was so strenuously intent on defending myself, and had so much ado with it. He came closer and closer on me; and in the meantime I fled backwards, backwards, till at length one of my heels coming in contact with the stump of a tree, I fell flat on my back. He rushed forward to disarm me, but, in my trepidation and confusion, I had no idea of any thing but resistance, and even in that awkward position I struck at him again. It seems that a highlandman does not know so well how to ward a stroke that comes upwards on him, as one that comes down, for with that stroke I wounded him both in the belly and the wrist. This so incensed the raggamuffian, that, placing his one foot on my sword arm, near the shoulder, and the other on my belly, he put his sword's point to my mouth. I roared out; but the savage that instant struck me in at the mouth, and pinned my head to the ground. I had never fought since I was at the school, and wrought merely as it were by random, or rather instinct. I had no conceptions remaining with me, but the boyish one of retaliation as long as that was in my power; so making a desperate effort, with a half-arm stab I wounded him in behind, sticking my sword directly in a part of his body which I do not choose to name. This made him spring forward and fall; and the whole of this catastrophe, from the time that I fell on my back, was transacted in two seconds, and before ever our friends had time to interfere; indeed I am never sure to this day but that they both viewed it as a piece of excellent sport. However, they now laid hold of us, and raised us up. I was choaked with blood, but did not feel very much pain. All that I particularly remember was that I was very angry at Frazer, and wanted to get at him to kill him. Instead of being afraid of him then, I would have given all that I had in the world to have had the chance of fighting him with pistols. He was as much incensed; for when Dow supported me away towards the river, I heard him lying groaning and swearing in broken English—"Cot's heverlasting tamn!" I heard him saying, " tat she shoult pe mhortally killed py such a crhaven of a lowlands bhaist! Such a treg of te chenerations of mans! phoor mhiserable crheature, tat she should pe putting her pike into te nershe of te shentlemans! hoh, hoh! pooh, pooh, pooh!"

There was no surgeon in the village save a farrier, that bled American horses, men, and women, alternately as occasion required, and he being first engaged by my adversary, there was no one to dress my wound, save Mr Dow and the unfortunate Clifford, who, poor soul, when she saw me all bathed in blood, and learned what had been the cause of it, burst into tears, and wept till I thought her heart would break. One of my jaw teeth was broken out, but otherwise the wound turned out to be of little consequence, the sword having gone merely through my cheek in a slanting direction, and out below the lap of the ear. It incommoded me very little; but it was otherwise with poor Colin Frazer; he was pronounced by all that saw him to be mortally wounded, though he himself affected to hold it light.

The other body of recruits and the baggage-carts at length arriving, we continued our march, Frazer causing himself to be carried in a litter at the head of the troop, until we arrived at Quebec. Here he had the advice of regular surgeons, who advised him not to proceed; but no cognizance was taken of the affair, farther than the examination of witnesses, whose depositions were taken down and signed. The head-quarters of the regiment which we were destined to join lying still a great way up the country, at a place called St Maurice, the command of the body of recruits devolved on me. The men that joined us last, at the village of Port Salmon, were mostly Irishmen, and commanded by a very young man named Ensign Odogherty. He was a youth according to my own heart, full of frolic and good humour; drank, sung, and lied without end; and I never was so much amused by any human being. The other Irishman, Macrea, remained at Quebec, but Dow still went on with us. I found he meant to join the army as a gentleman volunteer.

One night when we were enjoying ourselves over a glass, at a petty village, Dow chanced to mention my duel. I requested him not to proceed with the subject, for it was one that I did not wish ever to hear mentioned again as long as I lived. Odogherty, however, having merely learned that such an event had occurred, without hearing any of the particulars, insisted on hearing them from end to end; and Dow, nothing reluctant, recited them with the most minute punctuality. Odogherty's eyes gleamed with delight; and when the other came to the conclusion, he rose in silence, holding his sides, and keeping in his breath, till he reached a little flock bed, where, throwing himself down, he continued in a roar of laughter for a quarter of an hour, save that he sometimes lay quiet for about the space of a minute to gather his breath.

When he had again composed himself, a long silence ensued. After a storm comes a calm, they say; but it is as true, that after a calm comes a storm. Little did I ween what a storm this calm was brewing for me; but found it soon to my experience.

"Now, my dear friend," said Dow, "that you are past any danger from your wound, and I hope from all ill consequences of this rough and disagreeable affair; pray, may I ask if you know who this young lady is, or of what extract or respectability she is of, for whom you have ventured your life and honour, and whom you have thus attached to yourself?"

"I know that very well," replied I. "My Clifford is a young lady of the highest respectability of any in the shire of Inverness, though her father is not rich; but that is a common occurence with Highland gentleman, especially those that are generous and best beloved; besides, she is one of a numerous family, and named after an English countess, who is her godmother. Her father is Neil Mackay, Esq. of the town of Inverness; and she has a brother in Upper Canada, who holds the highest commission but one under government in all that country. It is to him that I am conducting her, and I hope to do it in safety."

"Not with safety to yourself I should think," rejoined he. "You should surely, my dear sir, re-consider this matter, else you will certainly have more duels to fight than one. Do you conceive it such a light thing to seduce a young lady of quality? Or how could you set up your face to her brother, a man of such rank, after the way that you have publicly lived with his sister?"

Never had such a thing entered my head as this; the thing most apparent, one would think, of any in the world. But, as I said before, I never durst trust myself to reflect on the consequences of this amour; these had all to come on me in course. I could not answer Mr Dow a word, but sat gaping and staring him in the face for a good while. At length I exclaimed with a deep sigh, " What the devil shall I do?"

"Why," said Odogherty, "I think the way that you should take is plain enough behind you, to look forward I mean. The young creature is ruined to all purposes and intents, and will never be a woman of credit at all at all, unless you marry her. On my conscience I would marry her this instant; that I would; and make her an honest woman to herself."

I looked at Dow, but he remained silent. I then said, that I thought our young friend's advice had a great deal of reason in it, and that to marry her was the best, if not the only thing I could do. Dow said, that at all events I might ask her, and hear what she said, and we would then consult what was best to be done after.

I posted away into the little miserable room where she sat, resolved to marry her that night or next morning. I found her sitting barefooted, and without her gown, which she was busily employed in mending. "My dear Clifford," said I, "why patch up that tawdry gown? If your money is run short, why not apply to me for some wherewith to replace these clothes that are wearing out? You know my purse is always at your service." She thanked me in the most affectionate terms, and said, that she feared she would be obliged to apply to me by and by; but as yet she had no need of any supply, my kindness and attention to her having superseded any such necessity.

"I am come, my dear young friend," said I, "at this moment, on an errand the most kind and honourable to you. We are now entering on the territory in which your relation holds a high command, and it is necessary, before we come to his presence, or even into the country over which he holds control, both for your honour and my own safety and advancement, that we be joined in the bands of wedlock. I therefore propose, that we be married instantly, either tonight or to-morrow morning."

"You will surely, at all events, ask my consent before you put your scheme in practice," returned she.

"Yes, most certainly," said I. "But after what has passed between us, I can have no doubt of the affections and consent of my lovely Clifford."

"You will however find yourself widely mistaken," replied she.

"Is it possible?" said I; "is it in nature or reason, that as circumstances now stand with us, you can refuse to give me your hand in marriage? Does my adored Clifford, for whom I have risked my life, my honour, my all, then not love me?"

"God knows whether I love you or not!" exclaimed she; "I think of that you can have little doubt. But as to marrying you that is a different matter; and I attest to you once for all, that nothing in the world shall ever induce me to comply with that."

"And is this indeed my answer?" said I.

"It is," said she; "and the only one ever you shall get from me to that question. I therefore request you never again to mention it."

I went back to my two companions hanging my head, and told them the success of my message, but neither of them would believe me. I then returned to Clifford, and taking her by the hand, I led her into the room beside them, barefooted and half naked as she was; and placing her on the wicker chair at the side of the fire, I stood up at her side in a bowing posture, and expressed myself as follows.

"My beloved, beautiful, and adorable Clifford; ever since we two met, you have been all to me that I could desire; kind, affectionate, and true. I have consulted my two friends, and before them, as witnesses of my sincerity, I proffer you my hand in wedlock, and by so doing to make you mine for ever. And here upon my knees, I beg and implore that you will not reject my suit."

"Rise up and behave like yourself," said she, with a demeanour I never before saw her assume. "You do not know what you ask. And once for all, before these gentlemen, as witnesses of *my* sincerity, I hereby declare that no power on earth shall either induce or compel me to accept of your proposal, and as I told you before, that is the only answer you shall ever get from me. Suffer me therefore to depart." And with that she hasted out of the room.

"By St Patrick!" cried Odogherty, "the girl has gone out of her senses, to be sure she has. On my conscience, if she has not dropt the reasoning faculty she has picked up a worse, and that by the powers I will prove it, that I will."

"On my soul, but I believe the creature has some honour after all!" exclaimed Dow, leaning his brow upon his hand.

"What do you mean, sir, by such an expression?" said I; "Whom do you term creature? Or whose honour do you call in question?"

"Hush!" said he; "no foolish heat. I beg your pardon. I am sure you cannot deem that I mean to give any offence. In the next place, I must inform you, that this lovely and adorable lady of quality, for whom you have ventured your life, and whom you have just now, on your knees, in vain implored to become your wife, is neither less nor more than a common street-walking girl from the town of Inverness."

My head sunk down till my face was below the level of the lamp, so as to be shaded in darkness. I bit my lip, and wrote upon the table with my finger.

"It is indeed true," said he; "I know all about it, and knew from the beginning; but I durst not inform you at that time, for fear of your honour as a soldier, which I saw stood in great jeopardy. Her father indeed is a Neil Mackay, of the city of Inverness, but instead of being a gentleman, is a mean wretched house-carpenter; a poor tippling insignificant being, who cares neither for himself nor his offspring. Her mother was indeed a woman of some character, but she died of a broken heart long ago, so that poor Clifford was thrown on the wide world while yet a child, and was seduced from the path of rectitude before she reached her fifteenth year. Lieutenant Colin Frazer your friend, being at Inverness on the recruiting service, chanced to fall in with her; and seeing her so beautiful, and elegant of form, and besides possessed of some natural good qualities, he tricked her out like a lady in the robes in which you first saw her, and brought her with him as a toy, wherewith to amuse himself in his long journey."

I could in nowise lift up my face, for I found that it burnt to the bone; but there I sat hanging my head, and writing on the table with my finger. Odogherty had by this time betaken himself to his old amusement, of lying on the flock bed, and holding his sides in a convulsion of laughter. Dow seemed half to enjoy the joke, and half to pity me. So, thinking the best thing I could do was to take myself off, I ran away to my bed without opening my lips.

Poor Clifford bathed and dressed my wound as usual, but we exchanged not a word all the while. She imagined that I was very angry and sullen, because I could not get her for my wife, and that I took it heinously amiss; and when she had done dressing my cheek she impressed a kiss upon it, and I felt one or two warm tears drop on my face very near my own eye. Duped as I was, I found my heart melted within me, and some feelings about it that whispered to me, she must be forgiven. If ever I had merit in any thing that I did in my life, it was in my tenderness to this poor unfortunate girl. I could not for the soul of me that night have mentioned Neil Mackay, Esq. of the city of Inverness, nor yet his excellency the deputy governor of upper Canada. I declare, that I never more mentioned the names of these two august personages in her hearing. I deemed that she had thrown herself entirely at my mercy, and I thought it was cruel to abuse my power.

Nevertheless, I spent a very restless night. If I recollect rightly, I never closed an eye, so dissatisfied was I with my conduct. There was I come out a desperate adventurer, going to join a gallant regiment commanded by a brave and reputable officer, with pay that would barely keep me from starving; yet I behoved to make my appearance at head quarters with a fine lady in my keeping, and that same fine lady a common town girl, picked up on the streets of Inverness, the daughter of a scandalous drunken cooper. My blood was heated, and my nerves irritated, by the brandy I had drunk the night before, and I felt very much inclined to hang myself up by the neck. In this feverish and disgraced state, I formed the resolution, before day, of deserting over to the Americans. I could not think of leaving the forlorn Clifford behind me, therefore I disclosed to her my whole design. She tried to dissuade me, but I remained obstinate, till at length she flatly told me that she would not accompany me, nor any man, in so dishonourable and disgraceful an enterprize; and that if I persisted in going away, she would instantly give intelligence of my flight, and have me retaken and punished.

"You ungrateful wretch!" said I; "Do you know what you are saying? Dare you take it upon you to dictate to me, and hold me under controul as I were a child?"

"No," replied she; "I never dictate to you; but I see you are dissatisfied with something, and unwell; and were you to take this rash step, I know you would repent it as long as you lived. I am not so far enslaved to you but that I must remain the mistress of my own will; and I shall never assent to any measure so fraught with danger as well as disgrace."

I was going to be exceedingly angry, and mention the cooper to her, and the deputy governor, and I do not know what all; but she, dreading that some violent outbreak was forthcoming, stopped me short by a proposal, that I would at least take eight and forty hours to consider of it, and if I remained of the same mind then, she would not only accompany me, but devise some means of escape safer than could be decided on all at once. I felt extremely mortified at being thus outdone, both in reason and honour, by a wench; however, I could not refuse my acquiescence in this scheme; and I confess, I am aware that to this poor girl I owed at that time my escape from utter infamy, and perhaps a disgraceful end.

On reaching St Maurice, we were all joined to General Frazer's

regiment, save seventeen men, who were sent with Mr Dow to supply a deficiency in a company of Colonel St Leger's regiment; and
the very day after our arrival, we set out on a forced march to oppose the Americans that were approaching to Montreal. Here I was
obliged to leave Clifford behind, who, with other retainers of the
camp, a much more motley train than I had any notion of, was to
come up afterwards with the baggage. Before taking my leave of
her, I clad her in a new gray frock, trimmed with blue ribbons, handsome laced boots, a bonnet and veil, and was not a little proud to
see how well she became them, and that there was in fact no lady
either in the camp or country that looked half so beautiful. Every
officer who chanced to pass by her was sure to turn and look after
her, and many stood still and gazed at her in astonishment. There is
something in the face of a lady that is a true Highlander, more majestic and dignified than is to be seen in any other of the inhabitants
of the British islands. This poor unfortunate girl had that look in a
very eminent degree. No one could look at her without thinking
that nature had meant her to occupy some other sphere than the
mean one in which she now moved.

I do not, as I said before, intend to describe this campaign. I hate
the very thoughts of it; but I cannot resist giving an account of the
first action that I was in. It took place at the foot of Lake Champlain,
immediately above Fort St John. The Americans were encamped in
some force on the height of a narrow fortified ridge of hills, from
which it was necessary to displace them. We marched out to the
attack early on a morning. The air was calm and still. In going up
the slaunting ground, our commander wisely led us by a rout which
was completely sheltered by a rising eminence from the effects of
their cannon. I soon perceived, that on reaching the summit of this
ridge, we would be exposed to a fire that I had no doubt would kill
us every man, while our enemies would fire in safety from behind
their trenches. What would I have given to have been off, on some
other service, or by some means, in going up that hill? The calls of
nature were very frequent with me. I am not sure but that I looked
for some opportunity of skulking, but the thing was impossible. It
was not even possible for me to fall down among the dead, for as
yet there was none fallen. I was in the front rank on the left wing,
and very near the outermost corner; and just before we came to the
verge of the ridge, I looked on each side to see how my associates
looked, and how they seemed affected. I thought they were all, to a
man, terribly affrighted, and expected a clean chase down the hill.
As soon as we set our heads over the verge we began a sharp fire,

and were saluted by a destructive one from their works: our men fell thick. The two next to me, on my right hand, both fell at the same time. I made ready for flight. A bullet struck up a divot of earth exactly between my feet; I gave a great jump in the air, and escaped unhurt. "The devil's in the men!" thought I, "are they not going to fly yet?" The reverse was the case. The word *quick march* was given, and we rushed rapidly forward into a kind of level ground between the two ridges. Here we halted and kept up a brisk fire, and I scarcely saw one of our men falling. It was the best conducted manœuvre of any I ever saw; but this I discovered from after-conversation and reflection, for at that time I did not know in the least what I was doing. We were by this time completely covered with smoke, and by hurrying us thus from the ridge into the hollow, the shot of the Americans past cleanly and innocently over our heads, while at the same time we could still perceive them bustling on the verge between us and the sky; and I believe our shot took effect in no ordinary degree. Their fire began to slacken, for they had taken shelter behind their trenches. We now received orders to scale the last steep, and force their trenches at the point of the bayonet. We had a company of pikemen on each flank, but no horse. The Americans had a small body of horse, about sixty on each wing. As we went up the hill I heard an old grim sergeant, who was near to me, saying, "It is utter madness! we are all sold to a man." The murmur ran along, "We are sold—we are sold;—to a certainty we are sold." My ears caught the sound.—For my part, I knew little either of selling or buying, except what I had seen in the market at Kelso; but I said aloud, "I think there can be little doubt of that;"—a shameful thing for an officer to say! and, looking round, I made as though I would turn again—No, devil a man of them would take the hint—they went the faster, and the old burly ill-natured sergeant, though assured that he was sold to destruction, and puffing and groaning with ill humour on that account, hurried on fastest of any.

The centre and right wing were engaged before us, and a terrible turmoil there seemed to be; but I did not see what was going on, till the Yankee horse in a moment came and attacked us in flank. We had been firing off at the right, and I believe they never got a shot of our fire until they were among us, threshing on with their sabres. One tremendous fellow came full drive upon me. I did not know in the least what I was doing; and chancing to have a hold of my flag-staff with both my hands, I struck at him with my colours, which, flapping round the horse's head, blindfolded him; and at the same moment the cavalier struck at me, but by good luck hit the flag-staff, which he cut in two not a foot from my hand. I ran for it, and left my colours about his horse's head or feet, I did not stay to examine which; but, owing to the pikes and bayonets of our men, I could only fly a very short way. When the old crusty sergeant saw the colours down and abandoned, he dashed forward with a terrible oath, and seized them, but was himself cut down that moment. The dragoon's horse that left the ranks, and came upon me, had been shot. I deemed that he had come in desperate valour to seize my standard, whereas his horse was running with him in the agonies of death, and knew not where he was going. There is something here that I do not perfectly recollect, else I declare I would set it down. I have forgot whether my joints failed me, and I fell in consequence; whether I threw myself down out of desperation; or if I was ridden down by the wounded horse; but the first thing I recollect was lying beneath the dying horse, face to face with the dragoon that cut my flag-staff in two, who was himself tangled in the same manner. Our troops had given way for a little, for the small troop of horse rode by us, over us they could not get, for the horse lying kicking with its four feet upmost. I thought I was in a woful scrape, and roared out for assistance, but none regarded me, save the Yankee dragoon, who d——d me for a brosey-mou'd beast. I liked his company very ill, for I saw that he would stick me the moment he could extricate himself; and, fairly desperate, I seized the sergeant's pike or halbert, that lay along side of me, and struck it into the horse's shoulder. The animal was not so far gone but he felt the wound, and made a flounce around, as if attempting to rise, and at that moment I got clear of him. The dragoon had very near got free likewise; but, luckily for me, his foot was fixed in the stirrup beneath the horse, and with all his exertions he could not get it out; but he laid hold of me, and tried to keep me down. I seized hold of the sergeant's halbert again—pulled it out of the horse's shoulder—and stabbed the Yankee through the heart. The blood sprung upon me from head to foot. His eyes turned round, and his countenance altered. At that moment I heard a loud voice, as at my ear, cry out, "The colours—the colours—secure the colours." This was the voice of an American officer, but I thought it was some of our people calling to me to bring my colours along with me, which I did instinctively, and without the most distant idea of valour or heroism in my mind. At that moment I cared not a pin for the colours, for, being quite raw to soldiership, I did not see the use of them, not having the least conception of what moment it could be to an army to have so many flaring clouts flapping in the air above them.

This onset of the Yankee horse was merely a dash, to throw our lines into confusion; they were now scouring away, fighting as they went, toward the centre, so that I joined our lines again, that were advancing rapidly, without any interruption. I had my demolished flag in one hand, the dead sergeant's long halbert in the other, and was bathed in the blood of man and horse over the whole body. An old English officer came running to meet me: "Well done, young Scot," cried he, and shook me by the hand: "by G——, sir, I say, well done! you have behaved like a hero!" "The devil I have," thought I to myself, and stared the old veteran in the face. I saw he was quite serious. "If that is the case," thought I, "it is more than I knew, or had any intentions of;" but I was quite delirious, and knew not what I was about, for I remember, that on the very evening of that day, the transactions of the morning remained with me only as a dream, half recollected. The old man's words raised my madness to the highest pitch. I swore dreadfully at the Yankees—threw down my colours, and began to strip off my coat, the first thing that a countryman of Scotland always does when he is going to fight with any of his neighbours. "No, no," said the old lieutenant, "you must not quit your colours after fighting so hardly for them; you must not throw them away because they have lost the pole. Here," continued he, and giving them a hasty roll up, he fixed them in my shoulder behind, between my coat and shirt, where they stuck like a large furled umbrella; and having then both my hands at liberty, I seized the long bloody halbert once more, and with my eyes gleaming madness and rage, and, as I was told, with my teeth clenched, and grinning like a mad dog, I rushed on in the front of the line to the combat. In a moment we had crossed bayonets with the enemy; but I had quite the advantage of their bayonets with my long pike, which was as sharp as a lance, and the best weapon that since that time I have ever had in my hand; and it seems I did most excellent service. I wounded every man that came within my reach, pricking them always in the face, about the eyes and nose, which they could not stand. Our division was the first that entered both the first and second trench. In about twelve minutes hard-fighting with swords and bayonets, we drove them from them all, and they fled. When once I got their backs turned towards me I was more bent on vengeance than ever, having learned by experience in my first combat to blood, that spitting a man in behind was good sure fighting. Many of the enemy shared the same fate of Colin Frazer.

At the fords of the river Champley, the Americans gaining the wood, were safe from the pursuit, and a full halt was ordered. No sooner had we formed, than my worthy old friend the English officer, whose name I then learned was Lieutenant George Willowby, came, and taking me by the hand, he led me up to the general, precisely as I was in the battle, with my colours fastened most awkwardly in my clothes, my long halbert in my hand, and literally covered with blood. "My honoured general," said he, "suffer me to present to you this young Scotch borderer, who has just newly joined the regiment, and who hath performed such deeds of valour this day as I never witnessed. I saw him, your honour, with my own eyes, when the American cavalry turned our flank, in the very rear of their army, down among his enemies fighting for his colours, and stabbing men and horse alternately like so many fish. And, do you see," continued he, pulling them out of my back, "he brought them safely off, after the staff was cut in two by the stroke of a sabre. And having them fixed in this manner, as your honour sees, he has led on the lines through the heat of the engagement, and actually opened the enemy's ranks again and again by the force of his own arm."

The general took me by the hand, and said he was proud to hear such a character of his own countryman—that he knew a Scot would always stand his own ground in any quarter of the world if he got fair play—that he did see the division, in which I was situated, the foremost in breaking in upon both lines, which it appeared had been solely owing to my gallant behaviour. He concluded by assuring me, that such intrepidity and heroic behaviour should not, and would not, go unrewarded. That same night, Odogherty, who cared not a fig for lying, took care to spread it through all the mess, and the army to boot, "that on my first landing in America, I had been challenged to single combat by a tremendous Highlander, the first swordsman in Britain, because I had chanced to kiss his sister, or used some little innocent familiarities with her; that I had accepted the challenge, met him, and fairly overcome him; and after running him twice through the body, had made him confess that he was quite satisfied, while I, as they saw, had only received a slight cut on the cheek."

I was regarded all at once as a prodigy of valour—and never were any honours less deserved. I believe I did fight most furiously after I went fairly mad. I had lost all sense of fear; but I was merely plying and exerting myself as a man does who has taken work by the piece, and toils to get through with it. I had some confused notion that these Americans were all to kill, and the sooner we could get that done the better; and besides, I was in great wrath at them, I suppose, for wanting to kill me.

This acquisition of honours gave a new turn to my character again. I determined to support it with my life, and was engaged early and late in perfecting myself in all warlike exercises. I was given to understand that I would be raised to the rank of lieutenant in the course of three weeks, and had small doubt of being soon at the head of the British forces. There was one principal resolution that I formed in my own mind in this my sudden elevation. It was the generous one of parting with Clifford Mackay. I thought it was base that there was no one to enjoy the emoluments and pride of my growing rank, but the daughter of a despicable Highland cooper—a wench brought up among girds and shavings, or perhaps in a herring barrel. The thing was quite incongruous, and would never do! so I began to cast about for a lady of great riches and rank, and made many knowing inquiries, but could not hear of any that was grand enough in all America. Odogherty thought proper to take advantage of this vain presumption, and brought me into some vile scrapes. In the mean time I longed exceedingly for the arrival of Clifford, from whom I had now been a long time separated; but it was principally that I might tell her my mind, and put her upon some plan of providing for herself. The baggage and ladies at length arrived at Montreal, escorted by Major Ker, and three companies of dragoons. The officers went down by lot to see their friends, and my turn came the last of any. I was rejoiced to find that our general himself, and the greater part of our officers, had acquaintances that stood in the same relation with them as Clifford did to me; and not a little proud to see them all outdone by her in beauty. It was rather a hard matter to part with so much beauty, sweetness, and affability; but, considering the great figure that I was to cut in life, it was absolutely necessary; so, just before we parted, I made up my mind to the task.

"Clifford," said I, with a most serious and important face, "I have a proposal to make to you, which I like very ill to make; but both for your sake and my own, I am obliged to do it."

"I am in the very same predicament with regard to you," replied she; "I had a proposal to make, which has been at the root of my tongue for these twelve hours, and could never find its way out, for there was something below it that always drew it back. But now that you have mentioned proposals, I find it is at liberty. Suffer me therefore to make my proposal first, and do you make yours afterwards. You must know then, that there is scarce an officer in your regiment who has not tried to seduce my affections from you, and some of them have made me very tempting offers. I have made a resolution, however, never to be either a mistress or wife to any one in the same regiment with you, and under your eye; but Major Ker of the dragoons has made me an offer, that will place me in affluence all the rest of my life. I am afraid that you will weary of me, for I will become burdensome and expensive to you, and your pay is small; and therefore I would not give him any answer until I asked at you whether I should suffer myself to be seduced by him or not."

I was thunderstruck with astonishment at the simplicity and candour manifested in this proposal, and stood gasping and staring at her a good while without having a word to answer. There is a great difference in giving up an object voluntarily, and having it wrested from you. "I am very much obliged, in faith," said I, "to Major Ker of the dragoons, as well as my brother officers! confound them for a set of dishonourable knaves! there is one, I am sure, that would not yield to be guilty of such a discreditable act, my friend and companion Ensign Odogherty."

"Bless your simple heart," said she; "Ensign Odogherty was the very first man among them who made the proposal, and what I refused to his blarney he was like to have taken by force. He is a perfect devil incarnate, that Odogherty."

"The young Irish dog!" exclaimed I, "I'll cut his throat for him."

"If you would presume to cut the throats of all who offend in that particular," replied she, "you may exercise your skill on every officer in the army. I never yet knew an officer in the British army, neither old nor young, and I am sorry that I speak from experience, who would not seduce his friend's mistress, or even his wife or sister, if he found it convenient."

"It is an abominable system!" exclaimed I, "and ought to be reprehended. I would not seduce the wife or sister, or mistress of a friend for—"

"Hush!" said she, laying her hand upon my mouth; "you might have left out the last. And do you ever, in the pursuit of your pleasures, consider, that among all our sex, who is she who is not wife, sister, or daughter, to somebody? But this is wide of the subject of my proposal, which you have not answered."

"Are you tired of me, my dearest Clifford?" said I, "and would you wish to leave me for another? If so, I will scorn to retain you by force. But you may well know that I would rather part with all the world than part with you. And as to wealth, take no thought of that, for I have large funds that I brought from home, which I have as yet scarcely touched; and moreover, I am already promoted to the rank of lieutenant, and expect to be a captain in a very short time. But if you should leave me, what would all these additions of wealth avail me?"

So much are we the children of caprice, I have often been ashamed on looking back to my actions, to see in what manner I have been swayed by the meanest of all motives. Every thing was soon made up between Clifford and me, and she continued living under my protection for three succeeding years. I never found it convenient to get a very rich wife, nor practicable to rise any higher in the army than a poor lieutenant. Indeed there was an incident occurred that had very near been the cause of my being again reduced to the ranks.

Ours was a most licentious army. The men were brave, but they had no other good quality. Gaming prevailed to a degree among the officers that can scarce be credited. No opportunity of intriguing with the ladies of the country was let slip; and though we were often almost starved to death for want of meat, we were generally drunk once in the twenty four hours, often for a considerable portion of that time at once. Moreover all of them had their mistresses, either hanging about the camp, or at no great distance from it, and for the whole of the two last winters that I remained there, our head quarters presented the most motley scene that can be conceived of dissoluteness and meagre want. We were obliged to depend mostly on the supplies from England for our sustenance; these became more and more uncertain; and though I valued myself on being able to bear these privations better than my associates, I often suffered so much from hunger, that I never saw meat but I coveted it, and took it if I could conveniently come by it.

The officers of our regiment were invited to dine with a gentleman, of great riches and high respectability, in the district of New York, not far from the place where we were then stationed. The entertainment was elegant and expensive, and we drank with great liberality. Gambling commenced, and was carried on with much noise, and little regularity, till after midnight. All the while there was a long table stood behind covered with viands, at which every man helped himself as he pleased. At length we went all off, a little before day, in a state of high elevation. Our path lay down a narrow valley by the side of the river Tortuse. Odogherty, and a Lieutenant Jardine from Annandale, were immediately before me, going arm in arm, and excessively drunk. I kept near them unperceived, for the sake of getting some sport, and soon saw, to my astonishment, that they made a dead halt. On drawing near, close behind them, I heard that they were consulting about the best means of getting over the river. I was amused beyond measure at this, and could not comprehend the meaning of it, for the path did not lead across the river, which was quite impassable on foot–the moon shone almost as bright as day–I stood at their backs and heard the following dialogue:

Odog. By the powers, and I believe we are come to the end of our journey, before we have got half way, that we have.

Jar. Od man, my head's no that clear, but I canna mind o' wading ony water as we came up. I fear we're gane wrang.

Odog. How the devil can that be? Have we not come straight up the path that goes down the side of the river? There is no other road but that, so we must either push on or turn back.

Jar. By my trouth, man, an' I think we had better turn back as drown oursel's, an' lippen to the man for quarters. He's a cannie discreet man.

Odog. By my shoul but I know better than to do any such thing. Don't you see that all the rest of the gentlemen have got over? There are none of them here.

Jar. It makes an unco rumbling noise, man. What will we do gin it tak us down?

Odog. Why, come up again, to be sure.

Jar. Weel, weel; gie's your arm. Here's wi' ye, Captain Odogherty– Gin Sandy Jardine dinna wade as deep as ony chap in a' Airland, deil that he gang down the gullots like a flowy peat. Here's wi' ye, Maister Odogherty.

Odog. Don't be in such a hurry, will you not, till I be ready before you?–Think you, I will spoil all my fine clothes?

Jar. Oh, ye're gaun to cast aff, are ye? Gude faith, Sandy Jardine will let his claes tak their chance, there's mae whar they cam frae.

Odogherty stripped off his stockings and shoes, and tied his buckskin breeches around his neck, and giving his arm to his inebriated companion, they set forward with undaunted resolution, either to stem the roaring stream, or to perish in the attempt. I had by this time squatted down with my face to the earth, and was almost dead with laughing, having discovered their grotesque mistake. The moon was shining bright on the road all the way, but at this place a group of tall trees, that rose between the path and the river, threw a shadow right across the road; and, hearing the rushing sound of the river behind the trees, they concluded that it was that which intercepted their way. Indeed I never witnessed a stronger deception; for the beams of the moon trembling through the leaves, looked exactly like the rippling of the stream. Jardine roared and laughed, when he found that they were wading through a shadow, till he made all the woods ring, but Odogherty was rather affronted.

I joined the train; and we went on laughing and making a noise, till we were interrupted by the rest of the officers all in a group. A most disagreeable business had occurred. The gentleman with whom we dined had sent two household servants on horses by a nearer path, to waylay us, who, addressing themselves to the senior captain, for neither General Frazer nor our Colonel were present, informed him, that their master had lost a valuable gold snuff-box set with diamonds, which he had been using all night at the table. The Captain rashly desired the men to begin by searching himself, and go on over all the company; and at the same time swore, that with whomsoever the box was found, he should suffer the most condign punishment.

The search was going on when we arrived, and we were instantly surrounded by those that had already undergone the fiery trial; but when the two Americans came to me, I refused to be searched. The Captain swore, that whoever refused to be searched should be drummed out of the regiment. I said I would refer that to a court martial, and not to him; and at the same time I swore an oath, that I would run the first man through the body who offered to seize on me, or put a hand in my pockets.–"Seize the dog; seize him, and down with him! We know with whom the snuff-box is now,"–burst from every mouth. I was forcibly seized and disarmed, but afterwards shaking myself loose, I dealt among them some lusty blows with my fists, and never perhaps did I fight with more inveterate desperation. It was to no purpose. I was pinioned fast by numbers, and searched. Wo be unto me!–The grinning American took out from one of my coat pockets, a roasted wild turkey deprived of a wing; and out of the other an immense black pudding. I was grievously mortified; and would rather have died on the spot.

When they came to search Odogherty, they found him bare-footed, and bare-legged, and without the *small clothes* (as the ladies now with great indelicacy term them): "How does this come about, sir?" said the Captain; "what is become of the rest of your dress?"

"O, plaise your honour, I have lost them."

"Lost them? have you lost your clothes off your body? The thing is impossible."

"To be sure, and I have. Look your honour, here are the shoes; and look you, here are the stockings; but the braiches, I fear, are quite gone."

"You must have *taken* them off for one purpose or another?"

"To be sure, and I did; and it was for fear of wetting them too: for your honour, they cost me a pound all to nothing, so I would not be after wetting them; so I put them round my neck, your honour."

"Ensign, this is the most absurd story I ever heard, and argues very little in your favour. How the devil could you wet your clothes, when there is neither rain nor dew?"

"Bless your honour, there is another way of wetting braiches besides all these, and that there is; and now when I remember, it was to wade the water that I stripped them off, and tied them round my neck."

"You are either mortal drunk or in a dream. What water did you cross?"

"The devil take me away, if I know what water it was; but o' my conscience there was a river running, roaring, and tumbling across the step of a road—and so I knew from the sound that it would be after taking me up to the middle—and so I threw off braiches and all, your honour—and so Jardine and I waded across—and by the powers it was no river at all at all."

"The fellow is trifling with us; take his sword from him, and take him likewise into custody; and see that diligent search be made for the part of his clothes, which it is evident he hath secreted."

At this time one of the officers, feeling something entangling his feet, put down his hand to feel what it was, and brought up the fine buckskin breeches of Odogherty, all trampled and abused.—They were searched, and in the pocket was found the gentleman's gold snuff-box. The Captain and all the officers were highly incensed against Odogherty and me, crying out, that we had disgraced them in the eyes of all the country. Odogherty swore by all the saints in the calendar that he was innocent, or that if he had put up the worthy gentlman's box out of which he had snuffed all the evening, it must have been by a very simple and common mistake. "And by Jasus," said he, addressing the captain, "had you but proclaimed the matter, and suffered every man to search his own pockets, the gentleman would have got his box, and the honour of the corps had been preserved."

Every one felt that what the Ensign said was sound sense in this instance. Circumstances, however, were strong against him; and as to my shameful crime, there was nothing to be said in extenuation of it; so, to degrade us as much as possible, we were hand-cuffed and conducted to the guard-house.

We were tried by a court-martial. I was condemned to three months imprisonment, and then to be degraded into the ranks; a most iniquitous sentence for such a trivial affair, but the officers were irritated at me beyond measure.

They asked me if I had any thing to say for myself why this sentence should not be executed?

I said that I would disdain to say a word, but, if there was any honour left among mankind, I should yet be righted.

I said this merely from the irritation of the moment, and without any reference to one circumstance connected with the affair. It was however a lucky phrase, and made some impression on my judges at the time, who looked at one another, as visibly suspecting there might be some trick. I was nevertheless remanded back to prison.

Odogherty was next brought in, and being desired to speak for himself, that the judges might hear what he had to bring forward in his defence, he thus addressed the audience:

"Plaise your honours, the first thing that I must be after spaiking about is not of myself at all at all. I have been told by the mouths of those that conducted me hither, that you have been to pass a sentence, and a hard one enough too, on the other gentleman that was after stealing the poodding. It is all blarney and absoordity together, and your honours must call back the words the moment you have said them; for it was I that put the stooff into his pocket, to be a laugh upon him; and he is as unguilty of the whole affair, as the child that is not after being born."

"Are you positive of what you say?" said the chief judge.

"Positive? by the shoul of Saint Patrick and that I am too. He had taken a beautiful maid from me that night: he had won all my money, and I had cut out of the game; so to amuse myself, and have some little revenge on him, I took the opportunity, when he was busy at play, to stooff his pockets for him; and that is the truth, your honours, to which I am ready to make oath, whenever, and as often as you have a mind."

Now this was all a contrivance of Odogherty's, but it was a generous and good-natured one. There was not a word of it true; but this singular youth had the knack of setting off a lie better than the plain truth; and the manner in which he interested himself in the matter, and expressed his sentiments of it, together with what I had said in court, not only staggered the judges, but convinced them that what he had stated was the fact. The presiding judge however said to him, "Ensign, when once your own character is cleared, we will take your affidavit on this matter. As the case now stands, you cannot be admitted as a witness in this court."

Odogherty's guilt was very doubtful. It was proved that he had stripped to wade an imaginary river, and that in the frolicksome

mood in which he and his associates were, it had never occurred to
his mind to dress himself again, till they were surrounded by the
rest of the officers. There was only one thing against him, and that
was the losing of his breeches at such a convenient time. But on the
other hand, to counterbalance this, it so happened, that as soon as
the box was found, all further search ceased; and it was proven, that
he who had found the *small clothes* never had himself been searched,
so that the box was actually not found in the possession of Odogherty.
After long discussion, a verdict of *not proven* was returned, and the
Ensign was acquitted. For my part, I never know to this day, whether
he stole the box or not. No one could calculate on what Odogherty
might do either good or bad.

My case was again brought under review. The Ensign swore to
all he had said. Some doubts arose on the circumstance of the determined resolution I had manifested not to be searched. "O bless your
honours," said Odogherty, "nothing in the world but sheer drunkenness; he would have fought with a flea that night. I was glad you
all set on him and pummelled him down, or I should have been
forced to fight him myself." The final consequence was, that my
sentence was reversed, and my sword and rank restored to me.

I was perfectly conscious of having pocketted the victuals myself;
and as soon as I was alone with my friend Odogherty, I mentioned
the matter to him, when, to my utter astonishment, he declared to
my face that I did no such thing, and that he put them there for me;
disclaiming, at the same time, any regard for me, but only for *the
truth*. Of all the inconsistencies I had ever seen or heard, this excelled; but as expostulation on my part would have been absurd, I
only observed that "I regarded perjury in a very serious point of
view." "Pough!" said he, "It is nothing at all at all! I would rather
trust myself to the mercy of God than to that of these d——d *connoters*
at any time." I knew not what he meant by this term, nor would he
inform me.

The last winter that I had passed in America was with General
Howe in Philadelphia, where we disgusted the inhabitants very much
by our irregularities. Many of the officers, as well as men, formed
matrimonial connexions, which they never meant to observe any
longer than they remained in that place. Others introduced their
mistresses into respectable families, which at last gave great offence.
Being sick of an ague when I arrived in the city, I boarded Clifford
with an elderly maiden lady in the suburbs, as my sister; and the
lady being very devout and strict in her principles, I thought proper,
by Clifford's advice, to visit there but seldom, and with much cer-

emony and deference to both. The old lady soon grew as fond of Clifford as ever a mother was of a child.

This lady was living in narrow circumstances, but she had a brother that was the richest man in New Jersey, though he seldom paid any regard to her; but seeing a dashing beauty with her every day at church, on whom the eyes of all were constantly turned, his visits to his neglected sister were renewed, after having been discontinued for many years, while at the same time, her circumstances appeared to be bettering every day, as did also those of her lodger, who every week had some new additions to her dress. I grew jealous in the extreme, and determined once more to part with the huzzy, whatever it might cost me; though I was obliged to acknowledge to myself, that of all women I had ever known, I had the least reason to be suspicious of her.

One holiday we were drawn up in files as the company were coming from church, when I perceived the most elegant and splendid creature I had ever seen, coming down the parade among the rest, leaning on the arm of a tall elderly gentleman. She was dressed in green silk, with a plumed bonnet, and veil of the same colour bound with crapes of gold. I was petrified with admiration, but more with astonishment, when, as passing by, she dropt me a low and graceful courtesy. At the same instant she whispered a word to her father, who looked at me, and saluted me with a respectful motion of the head. I could not comprehend it, as I was certain I had never seen either of them before.

I was paralyzed with love, so that my knees shook under me when I saw her turning a corner, where she vanished from my sight. I could not leave my place at that time, for there was no other lieutenant on duty; but my heart was set on discovering her, and from what I had seen, I could not doubt that she was desirous I should. I kept my secret and my situation of mind, however, close from all my brother officers. But being unable to take any dinner, I left the mess at an early hour, and walked up the river towards Burlington, where numbers of people were taking the air; but of my charmer I could see nothing. How my mind yearned to be quit of Clifford—I could not think of her with any degree of patience.

I came back to the town, as it grew late, and was sauntering about the corner, where I last saw this angelic creature, that had so completely turned my brain. A little chubby servant maid came up, who looked in my face, and smiled as if she knew me. I thought I was acquainted with the face, but had not the least recollection where I had seen it. I chucked her under the chin, and asked if she would accompany me to such a place? "Indeed I will do no such thing," replied she.

"But, my dear," said I, "I have something of the greatest importance to say to you."

"Say it here, where we are then," said she, naming me; "there needs not to be any secrets between you and I."

"And who the devil are you, my pretty little dear?" said I; "for though I know you perfectly well, I cannot recollect your name. If you will tell me that, I am ready to make all due acknowledgments."

"I will keep that to myself," returned she, "to learn you to look better about you when among friends. But say what you have to say; for I must not be standing chatting with a gentleman on the street at this time of the evening."

"Then first of all," said I, "before I tell you how much I am in love with yourself, can you tell me who the beautiful lady is, that came down from church to day clad in green silk, and leaning on the arm of her father?"

The urchin dimpled, and eyed me two or three times with a suspicious look; but seeing that I was quite serious, she burst into such a fit of laughter, that I was utterly ashamed, and it was long before I could get another word out of her; but convinced that she knew something of the matter, I would not quit her altogether.

"Are you really quite serious in what you have asked?" inquired she at length, while her eyes were swimming in tears from her excess of merriment. "Upon my honour I am," said I; "there is not any thing on earth I would not give to know who that adorable creature is, and what are her connexions."

After the provoking imp had indulged in another hearty laugh, she came close up to me, and, smirking in my face, said: "Well, captain, in the first place, I have to inform you, that she is reckoned the most beautiful woman that ever was seen in the states of America. In the second place, that it is believed she will be married in a few weeks, to a gentleman of the first rank; and in the third and last place, that she is in love with you, the most imprudent thing perhaps that ever she did in her life, and yet she makes no secret of it. But is it possible, captain, that you do not know that I am her servant, and wait on her, and that you did not see me walking behind her to-day?"

"No, I'll be d——d if I did, my dear," said I; " but the next time that you pass with her, I promise that I shall note you. Nay, I promise that I shall never forget you as long as I live, if you will conduct me directly to the presence of that angelic lady."

"I will not take it upon me to do any such thing," replied she; "as far as I may judge, she is better engaged at present; but if you have any letter or message to send to the lady, I shall be very happy to deliver it."

I showered blessings upon her, shook her by the hand, and desired her to wait for me five minutes; and going into a tavern, I wrote a most flaming epistle of love, and darts, and despair, to this object of my adoration, and vowed everlasting fidelity, craving at the same time to be admitted to her presence. This epistle I gave to the girl, being fully resolved to watch her home; but she perceived my drift, and gave me the slip by going into a mean house, and, as I suppose, out at a door on the other side, for I waited there till it was dark, and saw no more of her.

The next day I received the following letter from the servant in the house where I resided. It was written in a round old fashioned hand, which I had never seen before, and I could not help wondering how such an angelic creature wrote in such a curious antiquated style; but at the contents I wondered still more.

"SIR,—Yours I received. I heard your deeds, and have known you by seeing you longer than mentioned. Inquiries are making to character; if it conform to favour, I shall not say how glad I will be, or what lengths go for your sake; particularly of a certain young lady, I hope it is not true. Be secret; but trust not that I will see you till cleared of that.

Your humble servant, R. Y."

It was plain to me, from this, that the lady was in love with me; but that having heard some suspicious story about Clifford, she was going to make inquiries. I was not afraid of any discoveries being made there, if they came not from my brother officers; for I had behaved always to her as a brother, and a kind one, since we came to that city; but, to make sure of my new flame, I determined to part with her instantly, and accordingly I wrote to her that I could see her no more, and enclosed a note for £50. She waited on me next day in the plain russet dress in which I arrayed her. When she entered my apartment my blood rushed to my head, and I scarcely knew what I did or said; for my heart smote me, and I felt that I had done wrong. She had been kind and faithful to me; had saved my life and honour by preventing me from deserting; had bathed and dressed my wounds, and cheerfully shared all my fortunes. But instead of complaining, she addressed me in the same kind and familiar style as she was wont, and only begged of me, that now since we were to part, we should part good friends. She said, that understanding the regiment was soon to march on a long and perilous enterprise, she rather wished to be left behind; for she was tired of following the camp, and that now since she knew my mind, she was resolved to marry. "Marry! my dear Clifford," said I, "whom do you mean to marry?"

"A very decent worthy man," said she, "who is neither so young nor so rich as I would choose perhaps, but I want to begin an honest and decent life; you cannot imagine how much I begin to enjoy it already. I have only one request to make, that you will give me away as your sister, and behave to me as such on my wedding day; which now, with your permission, shall be the day after to-morrow."

Overjoyed to find that I was like to get so well off, I promised every thing; hoping that now I should enjoy the idol of my affections, the lovely unknown, when this main obstacle was removed. She refused to keep my £50, declaring she had no occasion for it, and I might have much: so I was not hard to persuade to take it again. This was a very shabby mean action. I might have, and ought to have, insisted on her keeping it, as a small marriage portion for the sister of a poor officer; but I took it and put it in my pocket.

On the day appointed for the marriage, a servant came to inform me that the ceremony staid for me; I went reluctantly in my daily dress, knowing that I should be ushered in among a great number of the lower ranks; for not having made any minute inquiries, I took it for granted that Clifford was about to be married to some old doting artizan, or labouring manufacturer. Instead of that, I was ushered into one of the most elegant houses in the town, and to a select party of gentlemen and ladies. Among the rest I was introduced to a Mr Oates, to whom I bowed reservedly, not knowing who he was. The parson was ready, and shortly after the bride and her maidens were ushered in; but I looked in vain for Clifford, and knew not how to calculate on any thing that I saw: for any one may judge of my astonishment, when I perceived that she whom they led in as bride was my beautiful unknown, decked out like a princess, and veiled as before. I knew the air, the shape, the plumes and crapes of gold at first sight, and could not be mistaken. I had nearly fainted. I felt as if I were going to sink through the floor, and wished to do it. Judging that I had come to the wrong wedding, or that they had sent for me there to mock me, I stared all about me, and twice or thrice opened my mouth to speak, without finding any thing to say. At length this angelic being came swimming through the company toward me, and clasping me in her arms, she threw up her veil and kissed me. "My dear brother," said she, "I am so happy to see you here! I was afraid that you would not countenance me in this, nor give your consent to my remaining in a strange land." "My dearest sister," said I, "upon my soul I did not know you: but I never can, and never will, give my consent to part with you—never—never!" "What! did you not give me your word?" said she, "did you not promise that you would give your Clifford in marriage to the man of her choice with all your heart?"

"Yes I did; and I do still; but then I did not know who you were—that is, I did not know who somebody was, that is you—But I am very ill, and know not what I say, and therefore must beg that you will suffer me to retire." She entreated that her dearest brother would remain, and honour her nuptials with his presence; but I felt as if the house and all the wedding guests were wheeling about; so I made off with myself in no very graceful manner. I was duped, confoundedly duped; yet I could hardly tell how: and besides, it was all my own doing, and of my own seeking. I never was so ill in my life, for such an infatuation had seized on me, that I could in nowise regard her whom I had lost as Clifford Mackay, the drunken cooper's daughter of Inverness, but as a new superlative being, who had captivated my heart and affections as by magic.

I could not but see that I had behaved disgracefully to her, and that she had acted prudently and wisely both for herself and me; yet I was eminently unhappy, and kept myself from all company, as much as my duty would allow me, during the short time after that affair that I remained in Philadelphia. Mr Oates, to whom she was married, was a rich and respectable merchant and planter, and doted so much on her, that though he had been possessed of the wealth of America he would have laid it at her feet. He was brother to the lady with whom she lodged; and as I learned afterwards, never discovered that she was not in reality my sister. She had taken my family surname from the time that we first came there. It was a lucky marriage for her, as will soon appear.

We soon received marching orders, and set out on our celebrated western campaign, in which we underwent perils and privations that are not to be named. Our women all either died or left us, and there were some of them carried away by the Indians, and scalped, for any thing that we knew. I was in thirty engagements, in which we lost, by little and little, more than one third of our whole army. We were reduced to live on the flesh of our horses, and all kinds of garbage that we could find; yet for all that, we never once turned our backs on our enemies. We had the better in every engagement on the lakes, and upon land, yet all our brilliant exploits went for nothing.

I was disgusted beyond bearing with our associates, the American Indians; and the very idea of being in affinity with such beasts made every action that we performed loathsome in my eyes. The taking of those horrid savages into our army to destroy our brethren, the men who sprung from the same country, spoke the same language, and worshipped the same God with ourselves, was an unparalleled disgrace. Remorse and pity, with every sensation of tenderness, were entirely extinct in the breasts of those wretches, having given place to the most ferocious and unrelenting cruelty. They often concealed such prisoners as they took, that they might enjoy, without interruption, the diabolical pleasure of tormenting them to death. I never abhorred any beings so much on earth as I did these, and nothing would have pleased me so well in any warlike service as to have cut them all to pieces. I found two of them one evening concealed among some bushes, wrecking their devilish propensity on a poor American girl whom they had taken prisoner. They had her bound hand and foot, and were mincing and slicing off her flesh with the greatest delight. I could not endure the sight, so I cut them both down with my sabre, and set her at liberty; but they had taken out one of her eyes, and otherwise abused her so much that she died. Whenever we were in the greatest danger, they were most remiss; and at the battle of Skensbury, where they should have supported our army, they stood idle spectators of the conflict, and seemed anxiously to desire that both sides should be exterminated. If the German auxiliaries had not come up and supported us, we had been cut off to a man. Their conduct was still more intolerable in St Leger's army, where they mutinied and deserted in a body, but not before they had scalped all their prisoners, and tormented them to death in cold blood. I never expected that we could prosper after our connexion with these hellish wretches.

At the dreadful encounter on the 7th of October, our regiment, that had suffered much before, was quite ruined; General Frazer himself being killed, with a great number of our best men; and the Germans, who supported us, almost totally cut off, so that we were compelled to yield ourselves prisoners of war. I received two bayonet wounds that day, which caused me great pain during our march. When we yielded, it was stipulated that we should be suffered to depart for Britain; but the Congress refused to ratify this, on account, I think, of some suspicion that they took up of the honourableness of our intentions, and we were detained in prison. It was while there in confinement that I saw and took an affectionate leave of Clifford. She had got permission from her husband to visit her dear and beloved brother, and came and staid with me two nights. On her return home she prevailed with her husband to use his influence in my behalf, which he did, and I obtained my liberty, being one of the few that Congress suffered to return home. The worthy old gentleman, after that, had a son that was christened by my name.

I embarked in the Swallow of Leith on the 11th of April. In our passage we suffered a great deal, both from the inclemency of the season and the ignorance of our crew. We were first wrecked in the straits of Bellisle, where we narrowly missed total destruction; and before we got the ship repaired, and reached the coast of Scotland, it was the beginning of October: we were then overtaken by a tremendous storm, and forced to run into a bay called Loch Rog on the west coast of the Isle of Lewis, where we found excellent moorings behind an island. Here I quitted the ship, being heartily sick of the voyage, intending to take a boat across the channel of Lewis, and travel over the Highlands on foot to Edinburgh.

I staid and sauntered about that island a month, and never in my life was in such a curious country, nor among so curious a people. They know all that is to happen by reason of a singular kind of divination called the second sight. They have power over the elements, and can stop the natural progress of them all save the tides. They are a people by themselves, neither Highlanders nor Lowlanders, at least those of Uig are, and have no communication with the rest of the world; but with the beings of another state of existence they have frequent intercourse. I at first laughed at their stories of hobgoblins, and water spirits, but after witnessing a scene that I am going to describe, I never disbelieved an item of any thing I heard afterwards, however far out of the course of nature it might be. I am now about to relate a story which will not be believed. I cannot help it. If it was any optical illusion, let those account for it who can. I shall relate what I saw as nearly as I can recollect, and it was not a scene to be easily forgotten.

On the banks of this Loch Rog there stands a considerably large village, and above that the gentleman's house, who rents all the country around from Lord Seaforth, and lets it off again to numberless small tenants. Between his house and the village there lies a straight green lane, and above the house on a rising ground, stand a great number of tall stones that have been raised in some early age, and appear at a distance like an army of tremendous giants. One day a party of seven from on board the Swallow was invited to dine with this gentleman. We went out a-shooting all the forenoon, and towards evening, on our return, we found all the family in the most dreadful alarm, on account of something that an old maiden lady had seen which they called *Faileas More* (the great shadow), and which they alleged was the herald of terrible things, and the most dismal calamities. The villagers were likewise made acquainted with it, and they were running howling about in consternation.

The family consisted of an old man and his sister; a young man and his wife, and two children: the old man and the two ladies believed the matter throughout, but the young man pretended with us to laugh at it, though I could see he was deeply concerned at what he had heard. The vision was described to us in the following extraordinary manner.

The Great Shadow never comes alone. The next morning after is M'Torquille Dhu's Visit. The loss of all the crops, and a grievous dearth in the island, invariably succeed to these. The apparitions rise sometimes in twelve, sometimes in three years, but always on the appearance of An Faileas More, Todhail Mac Torcill takes place next morning between day-break and the rising of the sun. A dark gigantic shade is seen stalking across the loch in the evening, which vanishes at a certain headland; and from that same place the next morning, at the same degree of lightness, a whole troop of ghosts arise, and with Mac Torcill Dhu (Black M'Torquille) at their head, walk in procession to the standing stones, and there hide themselves again in their ancient graves.

As the one part of this story remained still to be proved, every one of us determined to watch, and see if there was any resemblance of such a thing. But the most extraordinary circumstance attending it was, that it could only be seen from the upper windows of that house, or from the same height in the air, a small space to the eastward of that; and that from no other point on the whole island had it ever been discovered that either of the visions had been seen.

We testified some doubts that the morning might not prove clear, but the old man, and the old maiden lady, both assured us that it would be clear, as the morning of M'Torquille's Visit never was known to be otherwise. Some of us went to bed with our clothes on, but others sat up all night, and at an early hour we were all sitting at the windows, wearying for the break of day. The morning at length broke, and was perfectly clear and serene, as had been predicted. Every eye was strained toward the spot where *the Great Shade* had vanished, and at length the young gentleman of the house said, in a tone expressing great awe, "Yonder they are now." I could not discern any thing for the space of a few seconds, but at length, on looking very narrowly toward the spot, I thought I perceived something like a broad shadow on the shore; and on straining my sight a little more, it really did appear as if divided into small columns like the forms of men. It did not appear like a cloud, but rather like the shadow of a cloud; yet there was not the slightest cloud or vapour to be seen floating in the firmament. We lost sight of it for a very short space, and then beheld it again coming over the heath, above the rocks that overhung the shore. The vision was still very indistinct, but yet it had the appearance of a troop of warriors dressed in greenish tartans with a tinge of red. The headland where the apparition first arose, was distant from us about half a mile,—they appeared to be moving remarkably slow, yet notwithstanding of that, they were close upon us almost instantly. We were told that they would pass in array immediately before the windows, along the green lane between us and the back of the village; and seeing that they actually approached in that direction, Dr Scott, a rough, rash, intrepid fellow, proposed that we should fire at them. I objected to it, deeming that it was a trick, and that they were all fellow creatures; for we saw them now as distinctly as we could see any body of men in the gray of the morning. The young man however assuring us, that it was nothing human that we saw, I agreed to the proposal; and as they passed in array immediately before the windows, we pointed all the eight loaded muskets directly at them, and fired on this mysterious troop all at once: but not one of them paused, or turned round his head. They all of them held on with the same solemn and ghostlike movement, still continuing in appearance to be walking very slow, yet some way they went over the ground with unaccountable celerity; and when they approached near to the group of tall obelisks, they rushed in amongst them, and we saw no more, save a reeling flicker of light that seemed to tremble through the stones for a moment.

They appeared to be a troop of warriors, with plaids and helmets, each having a broad targe on his arm, and a long black lance in the other hand; and they were led on by a tall figure in black armour, that walked considerably a-head of the rest. Some of our people protested that they saw the bare skulls below the helmets, with empty eye sockets, and the nose and lips wanting; but I saw nothing like this. They appeared to me exactly like other men; but the truth is, that I never saw them very distinctly, for they were but a short time near us, and during that time, the smoke issuing from the muskets intervened, and owing to the dead calm of the morning, made us see them much worse. All the people of the village were hid in groups within doors, and engaged in some rite which I did not witness, and cannot describe; but they took great umbrage at our audacity in firing at their unearthly visitors, and I believe there was not one among us, not even the regardless Dr Scott, who was not shocked at what had been done.

I make no pretensions to account for this extraordinary phenomenon, but the singular circumstance of its being visible only from one point, and no other, makes it look like something that might be accounted for. I can well excuse any who do not believe it, for if I had not seen it with my own eyes, I never would have believed it. But of all things I ever beheld for wild sublimity, the march of that troop of apparitions excelled—not a day or a night hath yet passed over my head, on which I have not thought with wonder and awe on *the Visit of M'Torquille.*

From that time forth, as long as I remained in Lewis, I considered myself in the country of the genii, and surrounded with spiritual beings that were ready to start up in some bodily form at my side, whenever they had a mind. Such influence had the vision that I had seen over my mind, and so far was it beyond my comprehension, that I grew like one half crazed about spirits, and could think or speak about nothing else. For a whole week I lingered about the shores to see the mermaid; for I was assured by the people, that they were very frequently to be seen, though they confessed that the male as often appeared as the female. They regarded her as a kind of sea spirit, and ominous, in no ordinary degree, to the boatmen and fishers, but yet they confessed that she was flesh and blood, like other creatures, and that she had long hair, and a face and bosom so beautiful, that their language had no words to describe them. I was actually in love with them, and watched the creeks as anxiously as ever a lover did his mistress's casement; and often when I saw the seals flouncing on the rocks at a distance, I painted them to myself as the most delicate and beautiful mermaids, but on coming near them, was always disappointed, and shocked at the ugly dog's heads that they set up to me; so that after all, I was obliged to give up my search after mermaids.

They told me of one that fell in love with a young man, named Alexander M'Leod, who often met her upon the shore, at a certain place which they showed me, and had amorous dalliance with her; but he soon fell sick and died, and when she came to the shore, and could no more find him, she cried one while, and sung another, in the most plaintive strains that ever were heard. This was the popular account; but there was an old man told me, who heard her one evening, and watched her, from a concealment close beside her, all the time she was on shore, that she made a slight humming noise like that made by a kid, not when it bleats out, but when it is looking round for its dam, and bleating with its mouth shut; and this was all the sound that she made, or that he believed she was able to make. I asked why he did not go to her? but he answered in his own language, that he would not have gone to her for all the lands of *the Mackenzie.*

M'Leod, when on his death-bed, told his friends of all that had passed between them, and grievously regretted having met with her. He said they never met but she clasped her arms around him, and wished to take him into the sea; but that it was from no evil intent, but out of affection, thinking that he could not live more than she, if left upon dry land. When asked if he loved her, he said that she was so beautiful he could not but love her, and would have loved her much better if she had not been so cold; but he added, that he believed she was a wicked creature. If the young man could imagine all this without any foundation, people may imagine after what they list; for my part, I believed every word of it, though disappointed of meeting with her.

I was equally unsuccessful in my endeavours to see the water horse, a monster that inhabited an inland lake, of whom many frightful stories were told to me; but in my next attempt at an intercourse with the spirits that inhabit that dreary country, I had all the success that I could desire.

I was told of an old woman who lived in a lone sheiling, at the head of an arm of the sea, called Loch Kios, to whom a ghost paid a visit every night. I determined to see the place, and to tarry a night with the old woman, if possible. Accordingly, I travelled across the country by a wild and pathless rout, and came to her bothy at the fall of night, and going in, I sat down feigning to be very weary, and unable to move farther. We did not understand a word of each other's language, and consequently no conversation, save by signs, could pass between us. I found a miserable old shrivelled creature, rather neatly dressed for that country, but manifestly deranged somewhat in her intellects.

Before I entered, I heard her singing some coronach or dirge, and when I went in, I found her endeavouring to mend an old mantle, and singing away in a wild unearthly croon; so intent was she on both, that she scarcely lifted her eyes from her work when I went toward her, and when she did, it was not to me that she looked, but to the hole in the roof, or to the door by which I entered. The sight affected me very much, and in all things that affect me I become deeply interested. I heard that she was speaking to herself of me, for I knew the sound of the word that meant *Englishman*; but it was not with any symptoms of fear or displeasure she seemed to talk of me, but merely as a thing that, being before her eyes, her tongue mentioned as by rote.

The story that prevailed of her was, that being left a widow with an only son, then a child at the breast, she nourished him; he became a man; and the love and affection that subsisted between them was of no ordinary nature, as might naturally be supposed. He was an amiable and enterprising young man; but going out to the fishing once with some associates to the Saint's Islands, he never returned, and there were suspicions that he had been foully murdered by his companions, the weather having been so mild that no accident could have been supposed to have happened at sea. There were besides many suspicious circumstances attending it, but no proof could be led. However, the woman hearing that she had lost her darling son, and only stay on earth, set no bounds to her grief, but raved and prayed, and called upon his name; conjuring him by every thing sacred to appear to her, and tell her if he was happy, and all that had befallen to him. These continued conjurations at length moved the dead to return. The spirit of her son appeared to her every night at midnight, and conversed with her about the most mysterious things—about things of life and death—the fates of kingdoms and of men; and of the world that is beyond the grave—she was happy in the communion, and abstracted from all things in this world beside.

Such was the unearthly tale that was told in the country of this rueful old creature, and made me resolve to visit her before I left the island; but I could not procure a man in all the district of Uig to accompany me that could speak both languages; for except the minister and his wife, and one taxman and his family, there was not one in the district, which contained 3000 inhabitants, that could speak the English language, or were book learned. I procured a young lad to be my guide, named Malcolm Morison, but he having gathered something of my intentions before we left the banks of Loch Rog, would on no consideration accompany me into the cot, but left me as soon as we came in sight of it. I no sooner beheld the object of my curiosity, than I thought her crazy, and that the story might have arisen from her ravings. Still she was an interesting object to contemplate; and resolving to do so for the night, I tried by signs to make her understand that I was a traveller fatigued with walking, and wished to repose myself in her cottage until next morning; but she regarded me no more than she would have done a strayed cat or dog that had come in to take shelter with her. There was one sentence which she often repeated, which I afterward understood to be of the following import, "God shield the poor weary Saxon;" but I do not know how to spell it in Earse. I could likewise perceive, that for all the intentness with which she was mending the mantle, she was coming no speed, but was wasting cloth endeavouring to shape a piece suiting to the rent, which she was still making rather worse than better. It was quite visible that either she had no mind, or that it was engaged in something widely different from that at which her hands were employed.

She did not offer me any victuals, nor did she take any herself, but sat shaping and sewing, and always between hands singing slow melancholy airs, having all the wildness of the native airs of that wild and primitive people. Those that she crooned were of a solemn and mournful cast, and seemed to affect her at times very deeply.

Night came on, and still she gave herself no concern at all about me. She made no signs to me either to lie down and rest in the only couch the hovel contained, or to remain, or to go away. The fire sent forth a good deal of smoke, but neither light nor heat; at length, with much delay and fumbling, she put some white shreds of moss into a cruise of oil, and kindled it. This threw a feeble ray of light through the smoke, not much stronger than the light of a glow-worm, making darkness scarcely visible, if I may use the expression.

The woman, who was seated on a dry sod at the side of the fire, not more than a foot from the ground, crossed her arms upon her knees, and laying her head on them fell fast asleep. I wrapt myself in my officer's cloak, and threw myself down on the moss couch, laying myself in such a position that I could watch all her motions as well as looks. About eleven o'clock she awoke, and sat for some time moaning like one about to expire; she then kneeled on the sod seat, and muttered some words, waving her withered arms, and stretching them upward, apparently performing some rite either of necromancy or devotion, which she concluded by uttering three or four feeble howls.

When she was again seated I watched her features and looks, and certainly never before saw any thing more unearthly. The haggard wildness of the features; the anxious and fearful way in which she looked about and about, as if looking for one that she missed away, made such an impression on me that my hairs stood all on end, a feeling that I never experienced before, for I had always been proof against superstitious terrors. But here I could not get the better of them, and wished myself any where else. The dim lamp, shining amidst smoke and darkness, made her features appear as if they had been a dull yellow, and she was altogether rather like a ghastly shade of something that had once been mortal than any thing connected with humanity.

It was apparent from her looks that she expected some one to visit her, and I became firmly persuaded that I should see a ghost, and hear one speak. I was not afraid of any individual of my own species; for, though I had taken good care to conceal them from her for fear of creating alarm, I had two loaded pistols and a short sword under my cloak; and as no one could enter without passing my couch by a very narrow entrance, I was sure to distinguish who or what it was.

I had quitted keeping my eyes upon the woman, and was watching the door, from which I thought I could distinguish voices. I watched still more intensely; but, hearing that the sounds came from the other side, I moved my head slowly round, and saw, apparently, the corpse of her son sitting directly opposite to her. The figure was dressed in dead-clothes; that is, it was wrapt in a coarse white sheet, and had a napkin of the same colour round its head. This was raised up on the brow, as if thrust up recently with the hand, discovering the pale stedfast features, that neither moved eye-lid nor lip, though it spoke in an audible voice again and again. The face was not only pale, but there was a clear glazed whiteness upon it, on which the rays of the lamp falling, shewed a sight that could not be looked on without horror. The winding-sheet fell likewise aside at the knee, and I saw the bare feet and legs of the same bleached hue. The old woman's arms were stretched out towards the figure, and her face thrown upwards, the features meanwhile distorted as with extatic agony. My senses now became so bewildered, that I fell into a stupor, like a trance, without being able to move either hand or foot. I know not how long the apparition staid; for the next thing that I remember was being reluctantly wakened from my trance by a feeble cry which I heard through my slumber repeated several times. I looked, and saw that the old miserable creature had fallen on her face, and was grasping in feeble convulsions the seat where the figure of her dead son had so lately reclined. My compassion overcame my terror; for she seemed on the last verge of life, or rather sliding helplessly from time's slippery precipice, after the thread of existence by which she hung had given way. I lifted her up, and found that all her sufferings were over—the joints were grown supple, and the cold damps of death had settled on her hands and brow. I carried her to the bed from which I had risen, and could scarcely believe that I carried a human body—it being not much heavier than a suit of clothes. After I had laid her down, I brought the lamp near, to see if there was any hope of renovation—she was living, but that was all, and with a resigned though ghastly smile, and a shaking of the head, she expired.

I did not know what to do; for the night was dark as pitch; and I wist not where to fly, knowing the cot to be surrounded by precipitous shores, torrents, and winding bays of the sea; therefore all chance of escape until day light was utterly impossible; so I resolved to trim the lamp, and keep my place, hoping it would not be long till day.

I suppose that I sat about an hour in this dismal place, without moving or changing my attitude, with my brow leaning upon both my hands, and my eyes shut; when I was aroused by hearing a rustling in the bed where the body lay. On looking round, I perceived with horror that the corpse was sitting upright in the bed, shaking its head as it did in the agonies of death, and stretching out its hands towards the hearth. I thought the woman had been vivified, and looked steadily at the face; but I saw that it was the face of a corpse still; for the eye was white, being turned upward and fixed in the socket, the mouth was open, and all the other features immoveably fixed for ever. Seeing that it continued the same motion, I lifted the lamp and looked fearfully round, and there beheld the figure I had so recently seen, sitting on the same seat, in the same attitude, only having its face turned toward the bed.

I could stand this no longer, but fled stumbling out at the door, and ran straight forward. I soon found myself in the sea, and it being ebb tide, I fled along the shore like a deer pursued by the hounds. It was not long till the beach terminated, and I came to an abrupt precipice washed by the sea. I climbed over a ridge on my hands and knees, and found that I was on a rocky point between two narrow friths, and farther progress impracticable.

I had now no choice left me; so, wrapping myself in my cloak, I threw me down in a bush of heath, below an over-hanging cliff, and gave up my whole mind to amazement at what I had witnessed. Astonished as I was, nature yielded to fatigue, and I fell into a sound sleep, from which I did not awake till about the rising of the sun. The scene all around me was frightfully wild and rugged, and I scarce could persuade myself that I was awake, thinking that I was still struggling with a dreadful dream. One would think this was a matter easily settled, but I remember well, it was not so with me that morning. I pulled heath, cut some parts of it off, and chewed them in my mouth;—rose,—walked about, and threw stones into the sea, and still had strong suspicions that I was in a dream. The adventures of the preceding night dawned on my recollection one by one, but these I regarded all as a dream for certain; and it may well be deemed not a little extraordinary, that to this day, if my oath were taken, I declare I could not tell whether I saw these things in a dream, or in reality. My own belief leaned to the former, but every circumstance rather tended to confirm the latter; else, how came I to be in the place where I was.

I scrambled up among the rocks to the westward, and at length came to a small footpath which led from the head of the one bay to the other; and following that, it soon brought me to a straggling hamlet called, I think, Battaline. Here I found a man that had been a soldier, and had a little broken English, and by his help I raised the inhabitants of the village; and getting into a fishing boat, we were soon at the cottage. There we found the body lying stretched, cold and stiff, exactly in the very place and the very position in which I laid it at first on the bed. The house was searched, and, grievous to relate, there was no article either of meat, drink, or clothing in it, save the old mantle which I found her mending the evening before. It appeared to me on reflection, that it had been a settled matter between her and the spirit, that she was to yield up her frail life that night, and join his company; and that I had found her preparing for her change. The cloak she had meant for her winding sheet, having nothing else; and by her little hymns and orgies she had been endeavouring to prepare her soul for the company among whom she knew she was so soon to be. There was a tint of spiritual sublimity in the whole matter.

I have related this story exactly as I remember it. It is possible that the whole might have been a dream, and that I had walked off in my sleep; for I have sometimes been subjected to such vagaries, and have played wonderful pranks in my sleep: but I think the circumstance of the corpse being found in the very way in which I had laid it, or at least, supposed I had laid it, confirms it almost beyond a doubt, that I had looked upon the whole with my natural eyes. Or, perhaps part of it may have been real, and part of it a dream, for the whole, from the first, was so like a vision to me, that I can affirm nothing anent it.

The next adventure that happened me on my way through the

Highlands, was one of a very opposite nature; but as it bore some affinity with sleep-walking, I shall relate it here, for I put no common-place occurrences in these memoirs.

On my way from the upper parts of the country of Loch-Carron, to Strath-Glass in Inverness-shire, I was overtaken by a deluge of rain, which flooded the rivers to such a degree, that the smallest burn was almost impassable. At length I came to a point, at the junction of two rivers that were roaring like the sea, and to proceed a step further was impossible. I had seen no human habitation for several miles, and knew not what I was to do; but perceiving a small footpath that led into the wood, I followed it, and in an instant came to a neat Highland cottage. I went in, and found an elderly decent looking woman at work, together with a plump blowzy red haired maiden, whom I supposed to be her daughter. These were the only inhabitants; they could not speak a word of English; but they rose up, set a seat for me, pulled off my wet stockings, and received me with great kindness, heaping from time to time fir wood on the fire to dry my clothes. They likewise gave me plenty of goat-whey, with coarse bread and cheese to eat, and I never in my life saw two creatures so kind and attentive.

When night came, I saw them making up the only bed in the house with clean blankets, and conceived that they were going to favour me with it for that night, and sit up themselves; accordingly, after getting a sign from the good woman, I threw off my clothes, and lay down. I perceived them next hanging my clothes round the fire to dry; and the bed being clean and comfortable, I stretched myself in the middle of it, and fell sound asleep. I had not long enjoyed my sweet repose, before I was awaked by the maid, who said something to me in Gaelic, bidding me, I suppose, lie farther back, and with the greatest unconcern stretched herself down beside me. "Upon my word," thinks I to myself, "this is carrying kindness to a degree of which I had no conception in the world! This is a degree of easy familiarity, that I never experienced from strangers before!" I was mightily pleased with the simplicity and kind-heartedness of the people, but not so with what immediately followed. There was a torch burning on a shelf at our bed feet, and I wondered that the woman viewed the matter with so little concern, for they appeared both uncommonly decent industrious people; yet I thought I spied a designing roguish look in the face of the old woman, who now likewise came into the bed and lay down at the stock. I was not mistaken; for before she extinguished her torch, she stretched her arm over me, and taking hold of a broad plank that stood up against the back of the bed, and ran on hinges, a thing that I had never noticed before; she brought it down across our bodies, and there being a spring lock on the end of it, she snapt it into the stock, and locked us all three close down to our places till the morning. I tried to compromise matters otherwise, but they only laughed at the predicament of the Sassenach; and the thing was so novel and acute, I was obliged to join in the laugh with all my heart. I was effectually prevented from walking in my sleep for that night, and really felt a great deal of inconveniency in this mode of lying, nevertheless I slept very sound, having been much fatigued the day before. On taking leave of my kind entertainers, after much pressing, I prevailed on the old woman to accept of a crown piece, but the maid positively refused a present of any kind. When we parted she gave me her hand, and with the slyest smile I ever beheld, said something to me about the invidious dale; I did not know what it was, but it made her mother laugh immoderately.

On my arrival at Inverness, I made inquiries concerning Mackay the cooper, and learning that he was still alive, I made the boy at the inn point him out to me. He was a fine looking old Highlander, but in wretched circumstances with regard to apparel; I did not choose to bring him into the house where I lodged, but watching an opportunity, I followed him into a lowly change-house, and found him sitting in a corner, without having called for any thing to drink, and the manner in which his hostess addressed him, bespoke plainly enough how little he was welcome. I called for a pot of whisky, and began to inquire at all about me of the roads that led to the Lowlands, and among other places for the country of the Grants. Here old Mackay spoke up; "If she'll pe after te troving, she'll find te petterest bhaists in Sutherland, and te petterest shentlemans in te whole worlts to pe selling tem from." Thus trying to forward the interest of his clan and chief, of which a Highlander never loses sight for a moment, be his circumstances what they will. But the hostess, who, during this address, had been standing in the middle of the floor with a wooden ladle in her hand, looking sternly and derisively at the speaker, here interposed. "Petter cattles in Sutherland tan Strath-spey, cooper? Fat's te man saying? One of Shemish More Grant's cows wad pe taking in one of Lord Reay's cromachs into within its pody in te inside. And wha will pe saying tat te Mackays are te petterest shentlemans of te Grants in tis house? Wha wad misca' a Gordon on te raws o' Strathbogie? Wha wad come into te Grant's Arms Tavern and Hottle, to tell te Grant's own coosin tat te Mackay's pe te petter shentlemans? Te Mackays forseeth! An te stock shoult pe all like te sample she'll see a fine country of shentlemans forseeth! Tat will eat her neighbour's mhaits and trink him's trinks, an' teil a pawpee to sheath in him's tanks." The cooper, whose old gray eye had begun to kindle at this speech, shrunk from the last sentence. It was rather hitting him on the sore heel. And moreover, the hostess of the Grant's Arms Tavern and Hotel was brandishing her wooden ladle in a way that gave him but little encouragement to proceed with his argument, so he only turned the quid furiously in his mouth; and keeping his gray malignant eye fixed on the lady of the hotel, uttered a kind of low "humph." It was far more provoking than any language he could have uttered. "Fat te deil man, will she pe sitting grumphing like a sow at a porn laty in her own house? Get out of my apodes you auld trunken plackgards;" said the termagant hostess of the Grant's Arms, and so saying, she applied her wooden ladle to the cooper's head and shoulders with very little ceremony. He answered in Gaelic, his native tongue, and was going to make good his retreat, when I desired the hostess to let him remain, as I wished to make some inquiries at him about the country. When he heard that, he ran by her, cowering down his head as if expecting another hearty thwack as he passed, and placed himself up between my chair and the wall. I asked him if he would take share of my beverage, and at the same time handed him a queich filled with good Ferintosh. "And py her faith man and tat she will!— Coot health, sir," said he, with hurried impatience, and drank it off; then fixing his eyes on me, that swam in tears of grateful delight, he added, "Cot pless you, man! Ter has not te like of tat gone up her troat for many a plessed tay." "Aye," said the hostess, "te heat of some's troat has gart teir pottoms kiss te cassick." The cooper eyed her with apparent jealousy; but desirous to keep his station, he only said. "She never was peen sawing Mrs Grant tis way pefore, but her worst wort pe always coming out te first, and she's a coot kint laty after all, and an honest laty too, sir, and she has often peen tooing coot to me and mine."

I conversed for some time with him about general matters, always handing him a little whisky between, which he drank heartily, and soon began to get into high spirits. I then inquired his name, and having heard it, I pretended to ruminate, repeating the name and occupation to myself for some time, and at length asked if he never had a daughter called Clifford? The old man stared at me as if his eyes would rend their sockets, and his head trembled as if some paralytic affection had seized him; but seeing that I still waited for an answer, he held down his head and said with a deep sigh,

"Och! and inteed, and inteed she had!" I asked if he knew that she was still living, or what had become of her? But before he answered this question, with true Highland caution he asked me, "Fat do you ken of my poor misfortunate pairn?" I said I had met with her once, in a country far away, and requested that he would tell me what kind of a girl she had been in her youth, and why she left her native country. The old man was deeply affected, much more than I could have expected one of his dissipated habits to be, and he answered me thus, while the tears were dropping from his eyes: "Alas, alas! my Cliffy was a fary tear pairn; a fary plessed cood disposed pairn as ever were peing porn; but she lost its moter, and ten she pe ill guidit, and worse advised."

"I weet weel, master, te cooper Mackay says right for eence;" said the lady of the Grant's Arms, "for never was ter ane waur eesed breed in nae kintry tan puir Cliffy. De ye ken sir, I hae seen tat auld trunken teek sitting at te fisky a' te neeght, and te peer lassick at heme wi' neither coal nor candle, nor meat nor trink; and gaun climp climping about on te cassick without either stockings or sheen. She was peing a kind affectionfee pairn to him, but was eesed waur tan a peest. Mony's the time and aft tat I hae said, 'Cliffy Mackay will either mak a speen or spill a guid horn',—and sae it turned out, for she was ponny, and left til hersel. But the vagabons that misleedit her has leeved to repent it—pless my heart, I wonder how he can look i' te auld cooper's face! Heaven's ay jeest and rightees, and has paid him heme for traducing ony puir man's pairn—Cot pe wi' us, sir, he's gaun abeet tis town, ye wad pe wae to see him—he gangs twafauld o'er a steeck, and I widnee gie him credit de ye ken for a pot of fisky.—Cot's preath gie tere pe not he jeest coming in; speak o' te teil and he'll appear."

This speech of the lady's of the burning Mountain had almost petrified me, which need not be wondered at, considering how much I was involved in all to which it alluded; but I had not time either to make farther inquiries or observations, ere the identical Lieutenant Colin Frazer entered our hall, (the only tenable apartment that the Grant's Arms Tavern and Hotel contained), in a woeful plight indeed. He was emaciated to skin and bone, and walked quite double, leaning on a staff. Never shall I forget his confounded and mortified looks, when he saw the father of Clifford Mackay and me sitting in close conference together at the side of the fire. He looked as if he would have dropped down, and his very lips turned to a livid whiteness. He had not a word to utter, and none of us spoke to him; but at last our hostess somewhat relieved his embarassment by saying,

"Guide'en, guide'en til ye, captain Frazer." "Coote'en Mustress Grhaunt, coote'en. She pe fary coult tay tat. Any nhews, Mustress Grhant? She pe fary could tay; fary could inteed. Hoh oh oh oh— pooh pooh pooh pooh." And so saying, he left the Grant's Arms faster than he entered.

"Cot bless my heart, fat ails te man?" cried our hostess, "he looks as gin he had seen te ghaist o' his grandmither. Is it te auld cooper's face tat he's sae freihgit for? Ten his kinscience is beguid to barm at last. Teil tat it birst te white middrit o' him."

The cooper now eagerly took up the conversation where we had left off, and inquired about his lost child; and when I told him that she was well, and happy, and married to a rich man that doted on her: that she was the mother of a fine boy, and lived in better style than any lady in Inverness, he seized my hand, and pressing it between his, wet it with a flood of tears; showering all the while his blessings on me, on his Cliffy, her husband, and child promiscuously. I was greatly affected; for, to say the truth, I had felt, ever since we parted, a hankering affection for Clifford, such as I never had for any human being but herself; yet so inconsistent were all my feelings, that the impression she made on my heart, when I did not know who she was, still remained uppermost, keeping all the intimacy and endearments that had passed between us in the shade; and I found myself deeply interested in the old drunken cooper on her account. Being likewise wrought up by the Highland whisky to high and generous sentiments, I made the cooper a present of ten guineas in his daughter's name, assuring him, at the same time, that I would see the same sum paid to him every year.

The lady of the burning Mountain now bustled about, and fearing that the cooper "wadnee hae been birsten wi' his meltith," as she termed it, made him a bowl of wretched tea, and her whole behaviour to him underwent a radical change. I rather repented of this donation; for my finances could but ill afford it; and I dreaded that the lady of the Grant's Arms Tavern and Hotel would soon get it all. However, I did not think of keeping my word with regard to the succeeding years.

It was the middle of winter when I arrived in Edinburgh; and owing to the fatigue I had undergone, I was affected with a scorbutic complaint, and my wounds became very troublesome. This had the effect of getting me established on the half pay list, and I remained totally idle in Edinburgh for the space of three years. During that time I courted, and dangled after, seventeen different ladies, that had, or at least were reported to have, large fortunes; for the greater part of such fortunes amount to nothing more than a report. I was at one time paying my addresses to four with all the ardour I was master of; however, I did not get any of them; and living became very hard, so that I was often driven to my last shift for a dinner, and to keep appearances somewhat fair.

I had my lodgings from a tailor in Nicolson Street, who supplied me with clothes, and with him I soon fell deep in debt; but I took care to keep in most cordial terms with his wife, which helped me on a great deal. When my small pay came in, I went and paid up my grocers in part, and thus procured a little credit for another season, till I could find a fair pretence of being called away on some sudden service, and leaving them all in the lurch. Those who imagine that a half-pay officer lives a life of carelessness and ease, are widely mistaken; there is no business that I know of that requires so much dexterity and exertion. Things were coming to a crisis with me, and I saw the time fast approaching when Edinburgh, and Nicolson Street in particular, would be too hot for my residence. The forage, besides, had completely failed, so that there was an absolute necessity for shifting head quarters, but how to accomplish that was the next great concern.

"A wife I must have!" said I to myself, "either with more or less money, else my credit is gone for ever;" and in order to attain this honourable connexion, never did man court with such fervour as I did at this time. My passion of love rose to the highest possible pitch, and I told several ladies, both old and young ones, that it was impossible I could live without them. This was very true, but there's a kind of coldness about the idea of half pay, that the devil himself cannot warm. They remained unmoved, and took their own way, suffering me to take mine. There was, however, one good thing attending these attacks. Whenever *any* of the besieged were invited to tea, I was sure to be invited too by their gossips; and either with those who invited me, or with such as I conducted home, I generally contrived to *tarry supper*. We are the most useful and convenient of all men for evening parties where not much is going, but worthy citizens seldom choose men of our calibre for their dinner companions.

I was right hard beset now, and at length was obliged to make a great fuss, and tell my landlady that my father was dead, (this was the truth, only he had died four years before,) and that I was obliged to go to the country to attend the funeral, at which I would require all the ready money I had; but on winding up his affairs I would be enabled to settle every thing; and then, embracing the lady of the needle, I bade her adieu for *a few weeks* with much apparent regret.

Straightway I made for my brother's house in Lammer Moor, and resolved to stay there a while at free quarters until my pay ran up; but though my brother was civil, he was no more—he was in easy, but not affluent circumstances, and had a rising family to provide for, and I easily perceived that I was not a very welcome guest. My sister-in-law, in particular, took little pains to conceal her disapprobation, and often let me overhear things not a little mortifying. Nevertheless I kept my ground against every opposition, until found out by my friend the tailor; who having learned that I had not been telling his wife the genuine truth, threatened me with a prosecution for the recovery of the sums I owed him. Others followed his example, and there was no more peace for me there.

I returned to Edinburgh as privately as possible, and took lodgings in a place called Carrubber's Close, from which I never emerged during the day, but continued still to attend the evening parties of my friends the old maids, as well as those of jointured widows. There was a Mrs Rae in Argyle Square, with whom I formed a chance acquaintance on my first arrival from America, that had constantly taken an interest in my affairs of gallantry, though I took care not to inform her of one half of them. She was an intolerable gossip—officious in every one's concerns, and particularly fond of match-making; but seemed to enter into my views and character wonderfully well. It was under the patronage of this illustrious dame that I was first introduced to the house of Dr Robertson, a gentleman who had acquired a considerable fortune in the East, and had an only sister, a maiden lady about forty, who lived with him. Mrs Rae gave me the exact yearly sum settled by the Doctor on this lady, with the assurance that she was his sole heir; and with this fine prospect, I determined on commencing a matrimonial attack on the dame at once. I did so; and had all the success that the most sanguine lover could desire. By the assistance of Mrs Rae, the matter was brought to bear in the course of one month, during which time I had never seen my destined bride, save two or three times always by candle light. Her appearance was not at all amiss; but there was a cold stupid insensibility in her looks, and in every thing that she said or did, that I disliked exceedingly; and notwithstanding the engagements I had entered into, every time that I saw her I disliked her the more; so that when the day appointed for our nuptials arrived, I was never once thinking of performing these engagements, but laying a plan how to get them broken off; when, behold, a simple and natural incident occurred, which determined my choice—a caption

of horning was civilly put into my hand by a messenger at arms. I
had no other resource, so I went away and gave my hand to the
lady, and received hers in return, and we were joined in the holy
bands of wedlock to enjoy all the happiness imaginable. I did not
much relish the joke, and had almost resolved in my own mind that
I would not go to bed with her; but it so chanced, that in endeavouring to keep up my spirits, I became so drunk, that my jovial companions were obliged to undress, and carry me to bed; and I never
knew where my head lay, until the next day that I was awakened by
the bride rising to leave me. I could not recollect in the world where
I was, nor who the beautiful dame was that was dressing at my
bedside; and raising my drumbly head, I uttered some incoherent
sentences, to which my helpmate deigned no reply, but "stately strode
away."

Matters came to my recollection by degrees, and as a man is always unhappy and irritable after drinking to extremity, I cannot
describe how degraded and miserable I felt. The first resolution I
made, was to cut my throat, and thereby to end all my cares, and
griefs, and sorrows at once! and so well pleased was I with the heroic project, that I staggered over the bed to look for some extremely
sharp instrument wherewith to put my design in execution. But coming first to a jug of cold water that stood on the basin-stand, I lifted it
with unsteady hand. "Here's to you captain, and a pleasant journey", said I whimpering, and drank the beverage almost to the bottom. I then stood hanging my head in deep meditation for some
time, always reeling first to the one side and then to the other.

In this space of silent contemplation, it had struck me that drowning would be much better, as well as more handsome and genteel;
and besides, instead of experiencing any pain by being thrown into
the water, I felt from the heat of my body, that it would be excessively delightful. "Captain," said I to myself, "just consider captain,
how it would look—to have all that fine bed—and sheets—and curtains—and carpet—all drenched with blood?—shocking!—shocking!—
shocking! The other plan is far preferable!" At this moment, happening to turn round my eyes, I caught a glimpse of myself in a
mirror, which made such an impression on me, that it rivetted me to
the spot, and the position, for almost a quarter of an hour. Nothing
could be so truly grotesque. I shall never forget it. There was I
standing with looks of the most stupid inebriety, in an attitude intended for one of mature deliberation; my right fore-finger pressed
on the hollow of my left hand, and my head bowed down with a
wise cast to one side; my features the while screwed into groups of

the most demure and pointed calculation, and all to decide on the superior advantages of drowning to the cutting of one's throat.

In the course of a walk which I took down towards the sea to settle the matter, my blood and spirits again grew calm, and after all the reasoning I could make on both sides, it appeared that it was at least as prudent a course that I had taken, as any other of which I had the option; so I determined to be reconciled to my bride, and make an apology.

Well; the Doctor's house being in St James's court, I persuaded my charmer to take a walk with me on the Castle Hill, and as soon as I got her fairly by herself, I began to descant, in general terms, on the indecorous and hateful crime of drunkenness, intending to end it with a humble apology for the mistake I had fallen into, and the insult I had commited: but, to my astonishment, my wife cut me short by a proud disapproving stare, and some most pointed words which I could not comprehend; so I judged it as good to let the matter drop. Now the plain truth of the matter, as I afterwards learned, was this: that on the bridal night my beloved chanced to be fully as much inebriated as I was; but only, having the advantage of me in going earlier to bed, she awakened first; but without knowing of any thing that had passed during the night, either that she had had a drunken bridegroom, or any bridegroom whatsoever by her side.

I had wondered how the Doctor, who seemed a judicious sensible man, had been so willing to part with the lady; and that, without either requiring any settlement on my part, or even deigning to make any inquiry into my circumstances. But it was little wonder that he was glad to get quit of her; for in a few days I found out that she was addicted to the drinking of ardent spirits, to a degree that no consideration could control. I went to him and told him of it. He said his sister was far from being a habitual drunkard, but she was subject to a stomach complaint that often induced her to take more spirits than she was the better of–that I had it, however, in my power to restrain her, by carefully locking up every drop of spirits within my door; and this he charged me to do punctually, assuring me that she was too much of a lady to drink any where else but in her own house.

I promised that I would; and, going home, I locked up every thing, and put the keys into my desk. Contrary to my expectation, my helpmate made no remonstrance. She had perceived my design, and resolved to be even with me. In the course of two days I missed the key of a closet, in which I had a hogshead of brandy locked up; and the next day again it was put upon the ring with the rest. Suspecting that she had been getting one made, I said nothing about it,

but resolved to watch her motions. It was much worse than I expected. Before evening she was in such a state that her old maid
servant desired she might not be disturbed, for that she was taken
suddenly ill. Of course I kept away from her, and slept by myself;
but in spite of all her maid's exertions to restrain her, I heard her at
one time raving and speaking the most extravagant nonsense, at
another singing, and then again thumping the bed-clothes with her
hands, and screaming in convulsions of laughter. Though I liked
my glass as well as any man, I could not help abhorring and despis-
ing my helpmate now; and, as the best revenge I could get on her, I
thought I would humour her, and suffer her to enjoy her glorious
discovery. The door of the closet where the brandy was deposited
was within two steps of her bed-head, and from the time she became
mistress of the secret key, she never left her chamber, but kept herself night and day in a state of delirium. The Doctor, her brother,
came to see her, and told me he believed she had been drinking
spirits; and, considering the high fever she was in, it was death to
her. I said it was impossible; and, taking the keys from my desk, I
opened every press and closet in the house where liquors were
deposited, not forgetting the closet that contained my wife's hidden
treasure. He shook his head, and said he did not know what to
make of it.

From the time that she found herself mistress of this hogshead of
brandy she never tasted meat; and grew every day more intent on
the spirits, till at the last she grew voraciously mad on them; and not
to dwell longer on this disagreeable subject, in three weeks and two
days from the commencement of her drinking campaign, she fairly
drank herself to death; and thus was I deprived of my wife and a
great part of my cask of brandy beside.

I found myself in a curious situation now. None of my former
debts had been discharged; but, my credit having been established
by my marriage, they had no more been insisted on. I had never
received a farthing of my wife's fortune, save my household furniture, which indeed was costly and elegant. No legal contract had
been made, and I found myself little the better of my rich and short
lived connexion. My creditors again began to tease me—I sold part
of my furniture, and at length applied to Dr Robertson, by letter, for
my wife's personal fortune. He answered me by stating, that since
the death of his parents his sister had been solely dependent on
him—that he did intend to have settled his whole property on her,
and her heirs, had she lived; but that since Heaven had decreed it
otherwise, had no farther concern with me, not being satisfied that I

had behaved to his sister exactly as I ought to have done.

I now wished with all my heart that my wife and cask of brandy had been both forthcoming, bad as she was; for here was I again reduced to my miserable half-pay, and all its concomitant evils, shifts, and privations, and was obliged to betake myself to fortune-hunting again, the great business of a half-pay officer's life. I might still have been said to be in my prime, athletic and healthy; and certainly might have thriven in the affections of the fair as well as most heroes of the moiety. But I was in this as in all things else, "unstable as water, and could not excel." I never could stick by one, nor two, nor three, nor any given number. I was a general lover, and as general a wooer; and, if I might be allowed to judge from appearances, which no man ought to do, even in deciding on the quality of an oyster, I was rather a general favourite. The benevolent old maids brightened up at my approach, and the bouncing widows adjusted their kerchiefs and cockernonies, taking care that I should not miss seeing their beautifully turned arms, feet, and ancles, and left the rest to providence.–The blooming maids curtsied and blushed, and every thing looked well. But after all, I found that the ladies uniformly view a half-pay officer in the same light with a tailor; and, let them reason as they will, they look on him only as half a man; while all the time these very excellent fellows think of nothing else, and talk of nothing else save the fair ingrates, and the amount of their fortunes.

It is highly absurd in ladies, if they want a husband, to be shy with a half-pay officer. I have known many of them, who would have been very glad to have had such and such ladies, and I knew well that these would as gladly have had them; yet these same ladies stood out, and grew gray in the service, and died as they had lived, in sincere repentance. They need never think that the sons of the moiety care a farthing for their persons, or have any leisure for constancy, or the most distant thoughts of such a thing; and as it is always a creditable match for a jointured widow or old maid, there is nothing like striking while the iron is hot with such men. But should the ladies presume to differ from one who has had so much experience, and pretend that they do not think such husbands would be a credit to them, I would answer, that they are surely more creditable than none. If ever a soldier is seen dangling after what he denominates a "d——d fine woman," who has no fortune, be sure it is for any other purpose than marriage. It is indeed mostly with the married women that are beautiful that they carry on their amours, that no such idea as that of marriage may have the chance of being entertained, and with the rich and ugly that their matrimonial connexions usually succeed. As I speak from hard experience, and confess all my necessities freely, none of my *half* brethren can possibly take it amiss.

For the space of two years my exertions continued without any abatement, and with as little success, but without a single adventure that is worth recording. I often dressed in full uniform, and went round to all my sweethearts in one day, protesting my violent attachment to each of them, and begging permission to ask them of their friends or guardians; but owing to the absurd customs among the fair, and the equivocal answers they gave me, the day of bliss was always postponed, though, "it was a consummation devoutly to be wished."

I saw that there would be no end of all my labours; and, owing to my thriftless and liberal manner of living, my difficulties increased to a degree that could no longer be withstood.

I therefore was obliged to apply once more to my old friend Mrs Rae, notwithstanding the manner in which she had noosed me before. She had one in her eye ready for me; a rich widow, and a worthy excellent woman rather well looked—so she described her; and shortly after I was introduced. Instead of finding her well looked, she was so ugly I could scarcely bear to look at her. She had gray eyes, shrivelled cheeks, a red nose, and a considerable beard; but every thing about the house had the appearance of plenty, cleanliness, and comfort; matters that weighed mightily with one in my situation; so I was obliged to ask her in marriage, and by the help of Mrs Rae soon overcame all scruples on the part of my fair lady of the mustachio, who seemed quite overjoyed at the prospect of getting such a husband. Our interviews of love were ludicrous beyond any scene ever witnessed. Had any one seen how she ogled, he would have split his sides with laughter. Her thin lips were squeezed into a languishing smile, her gray eyes softly and squintingly turned on me, and the hairs of her beard moved with a kind of muscular motion like the whiskers of a cat. Though my stomach was like to turn at this display of the tender passion, I was obliged to ogle again, and press her to name a day, whereon I was to be made the happiest of men?

"Oh! captain, captain; you are a kind, dear, delightful man!" exclaimed she, "you have stole away my tender heart, and I can no longer *forestand* your *opportunities*. Well then, since you will have it so, let it be at Christmas, when the days are short. Oh! captain!" and saying so, she squeezed my hand in both hers, and lifted up her voice and wept.

The thing that pleased me best in this interview was the receipt of £100 from my now affianced bride to prepare for the wedding, which relieved me a good deal; so that when Christmas came, I was in no hurry for the marriage, but contrived to put it off from day to day. I had a strong impression on my mind that the event was never to happen, though I could divine nothing that was likely to prevent it; but so confident was I of this, that I went on fearlessly till the very last day of my liberty. I had that day, after sitting two hours over my breakfast, thrown myself into an easy chair in a fit of despondence, and was ruminating on all the chequered scenes of my past life, and what was likely to be my future fate with this my whiskered spouse. "Pity me! O ye powers of love, pity me!" I exclaimed, and stretched myself back in one of those silent agonies which regret will sometimes shed over the most careless and dissipated mind. I saw I was going to place myself in a situation in which I would drag out an existence, without having one in the world that cared for me, or one that I loved and could be kind to; and the prospect of such a life of selfishness and insignificance my heart could not brook; never in my life did I experience such bitterness of heart.

While leaning in this languid and sorrowful guise, and just when my grief was at the height, I heard a rap at the door. It was too gentle and timid to be that of a bailiff or creditor, and therefore I took it to be a (still more unwelcome) messenger of love, or perhaps the dame of the mustachio and malmsey nose herself. I strained my organs of hearing to catch the sounds of her disagreeable voice–I heard it– that is, I heard a female voice on the landing place, and I knew it could be no other; and, though I had pledged myself to lead my life with her, my blood revolted from this one private interview, and I sat up in my seat half enraged. The servant opened the door in the quick abrupt manner in which these impertinent rascals always do it. "A lady wishes to speak with you, sir." "Cannot you show her in then, and be d——d to you?" He did so; and there entered–Oh Heaven! not my disasterous dame, but the most lovely, angelic, and splendid creature I had ever seen, who was leading by the hand a comely boy about seven years of age, dressed like a prince. My eyes were dazzled, and my senses so wholly confounded, that I could not speak a word; but, rising from my seat, I made her a low respectful bow. This she did not deign to return, but coming slowly up to me, and looking me full in the face, she stretched out her beautiful hand. "So then I have found you out at last," said she, taking my unresisting hand in hers. It was Clifford Mackay. "My dear Clifford!

My angel, my preserver," said I, "Is it you?" and taking her in my arms, I placed her on my knees in the easy chair, and kissed her lips, her cheek, and chin, a thousand times, in raptures of the most heartfelt delight, till even the little boy, her only son, wept with joy at seeing our happiness. Her husband had died and left this her only son heir to all his wealth, the interest of which was solely at her disposal as long as her son was a minor, for the purpose of his education; and when he became of age she was to have £100 a year as long as she lived. As soon as she found herself in these circumstances, she determined to find me out, and share it with me, to whatever part of the world I had retired, and in whatever condition of life she found me, whether married or unmarried. With this intent, she told the other guardians of her son's property, that she intended going into Scotland, to live for a time with her relations in that country, and to overlook the education of her son, whom she was going to place at the seminaries there. They approved highly of the plan, and furnished her with every means of carrying it into execution; and she having once got a letter from me dated from Edinburgh, as from her brother, she came straight thither, and heard of me at once by applying at the office of the army agent.

I told her of my engagement, and of my determination to break it off, and make her my lawful wife; and she in return acknowledged frankly, that such a connexion was what of all things in the world she most wished, if I could do so with honour; but she added, that were I married a thousand times it could not diminish her interest in me one whit. I assured her there was no fear of getting free of my beloved, and sitting down I wrote a letter to her, stating the impossibility of my fulfilling my engagements with her, as the wife of my youth, whom I had lost among the savages of America more than seven years ago, and had long given up all hopes of ever seeing again, had found her way to this country with my child, to claim her rights, which my conscience would not suffer me to deny; and that she had arrived at my house, and was at that very time sitting with me at the same table.

This intelligence put my gentle bride quite beside herself; for the short days, and long wearisome nights of Christmas had already arrived, and she found that her prospects as well as mine were entirely changed. She wept, raved, tore her hair, and abused me—threatened me with a prosecution, and then fell into hysterics. She was soon after married to a brave old veteran, who had lost a limb, and seen many misfortunes; a match that was brought about by the indefatigable Mrs Rae, and for any thing that I ever heard turned out well enough.

Clifford and I were regularly married, and have now lived together eighteen years as man and wife, and I have always found her a kind, faithful, and good natured companion. It is true we have lived rather a dissipated, confused, irregular sort of life, such as might have been expected from the nature of our first connexion; but this has been wholly owing to my acquired habits, and not to any bias in her disposition towards such a life. She never controlled me in any one thing; and her mind was so soft and gentle, that it was like melted wax, and took the impression at once of the company with which it associated. We lived in affluence till the time that her son became of age, but since that period we feel a good deal of privation, although our wants are mostly artificial; and I believe I have loved her better than I could have loved any other, and as well as my unstaid mind was capable of loving any one.

These last eighteen years of my life have been so regular, or rather so uniformly irregular, that the shortest memorandum of them that I could draw up, would be flat and unprofitable. There has been nothing varied in them—nothing animating; and I am wearing down to the grave, sensible of having spent a long life of insignificance, productive of no rational happiness to myself, nor benefit to my fellow creatures. From these reflections have I been induced to write out this memoir. The exercise has served to amuse me, and may be a source of amusement as well as instruction to others. From the whole of the narrative, these moral axioms may be drawn. That without steadiness in a profession, success in life need not be expected; and without steadiness of principle, we forego our happiness both here and hereafter. It may be deemed by some, that I have treated female imprudence with too great a degree of levity, and represented it as producible of consequences that it does not deserve; but in this, I am only blameable in having adhered to the simple truth. Besides, I would gladly combat the ungenerous and cruel belief, that when a female once steps aside from the paths of rectitude, she is lost for ever. Nothing can be more ungracious than this; yet to act conformably with such a sentiment, is common in the manners of this volatile age, as notorious for its laxity of morals as for its false delicacy. Never yet was there a *young* female seduced from the paths of virtue, who did not grievously repent, and who would not gladly have returned, had an opportunity offered, or had even a possibility been left. How cruel then to shut the only door, on the regaining of which the eternal happiness or misery of a fellow creature depends. I have known many who were timeously

snatched from error, before their *minds* were corrupted, which is not
the work of a day; and who turned out characters more exemplary
for virtue, and every good quality, than in all likelihood they would
have been, had no such misfortune befallen them.

"The rainbow's lovely in the eastern cloud,
  The rose is beauteous on the bended thorn;
Sweet is the evening ray from purple shroud,
  And sweet the orient blushes of the morn;
Sweeter than all the beauties which adorn
  The female form in youth and maiden bloom!
Oh! why should passion ever man suborn
  To work the sweetest flower of nature's doom,
  And cast o'er all her joys a veil of cheerless gloom!

"Oh fragile flower! that blossoms but to fade!—
  One slip recovery or recall defies!—
Thou walk'st the dizzy verge with steps unstaid,
  Fair as the habitants of yonder skies!
Like them thou fallest never more to rise!
  Oh fragile flower! for thee my heart's in pain!—
Haply a world is hid from mortal eyes,
  Where thou may'st smile in purity again,
  And shine in virgin bloom that ever shall remain."

Adam Bell

THIS tale, which may be depended on as in every part true, is singular, for the circumstance of its being insolvable either from the facts that have been discovered relating to it, or by reason: for though events sometimes occur among mankind, which at the time seem inexplicable, yet there being always some individuals acquainted with the primary causes of those events, they seldom fail of being brought to light before all the actors in them, or their confidants, are removed from this state of existence. But the causes which produced the events here related, have never been accounted for in this world; even conjecture is left to wander in a labyrinth, unable to get hold of the thread that leads to the catastrophe.

Mr Bell was a gentleman of Annandale, in Dumfries-shire, in the south of Scotland, the proprietor of a considerable estate in that district, part of which he occupied himself. He lost his father when he was an infant, and his mother dying when he was about 20 years of age, left him the sole proprietor of the estate, besides a large sum of money at interest, for which he was indebted, in a great measure, to his mother's parsimony during his minority. His person was tall, comely, and athletic, and his whole delight was in warlike and violent exercises. He was the best horseman and marksman in the county, and valued himself particularly upon his skill in the broad sword exercise. Of this he often boasted aloud, and regretted that there was not one in the country whose prowess was in some degree equal to his own.

In the autumn of 1745, after being for several days busily and silently employed in preparing for his journey, he left his own house and went for Edinburgh, giving, at the same time, such directions to his servants, as indicated his intention of being absent for some time.

A few days after he had left his home, in the morning, while his house-keeper was putting the house in order for the day, her master, as she thought, entered by the kitchen door, the other being bolted, and passed her in the middle of the floor. He was buttoned in his great coat, which was the same he had on when he went from home; he likewise had the same hat on his head, and the same whip in his hand which he took with him. At sight of him she uttered a shriek, but recovering her surprise, instantly said to him, "You have not staid so long from us, Sir." He made no reply, but went sullenly into his own room, without throwing off his great coat. After a pause

of about five minutes, she followed him into the room—he was standing at his desk with his back towards her—she asked him if he wished
to have a fire kindled? and afterwards if he was well enough? but he
still made no reply to any of these questions. She was astonished,
and returned into the kitchen. After tarrying about other five minutes, he went out at the front door, it being then open, and walked
deliberately towards the bank of the river Kinnel, which was deep
and wooded, and in that he vanished from her sight. The woman
ran out in the utmost consternation to acquaint the men who were
servants belonging to the house; and coming to one of the ploughmen, she told him that their master was come home, and had certainly lost his reason, for that he was wandering about the house
and would not speak. The man loosed his horses from the plough
and came home, listened to the woman's relation, made her repeat
it again and again, and then assured her that she was raving, for
their master's horse was not in the stable, and of course he could
not be come home.—However, as she persisted in her asseveration
with every appearance of sincerity, he went into the linn to see what
was become of his mysterious master. He was neither to be seen
nor heard of in all the country!—It was then concluded that the housekeeper had seen an apparition, and that something had befallen their
master; but on consulting with some old people, skilled in those
matters, they learned, that when a *wraith*, or apparition of a living
person appeared while the sun was up, instead of being a prelude of
instant death, it prognosticated very long life: and, moreover, that it
could not possibly be a ghost that she had seen, for they always
chose the night season for making their visits. In short, though it
was the general topic of conversation among the servants, and the
people in their vicinity, no reasonable conclusion could be formed
on the subject.

The most probable conjecture was, that as Mr Bell was known to
be so fond of arms, and had left his home on the very day that
prince Charles Stuart and his Highlanders defeated General Hawley
on Falkirk moor, he had gone either with him or the Duke of
Cumberland to the north. It was, however, afterwards ascertained,
that he had never joined any of the armies. Week came after week,
and month after month, but no word of Mr Bell. A female cousin
was his nearest living relation; her husband took the management
of his affairs; and, concluding that he had either joined the army,
or drowned himself in the Kinnel when he was seen go into the
linn, made no more inquiries after him.

About this very time, a respectable farmer, whose surname was

M'Millan, and who resided in the neighbourhood of Musselburgh, happened to be in Edinburgh about some business. In the evening he called upon a friend, who lived near Holyrood-house; and being seized with an indisposition, they persuaded him to tarry with them all night. About the middle of the night he grew exceedingly ill, and not being able to find any rest or ease in his bed, imagined he would be the better of a walk. He put on his clothes, and that he might not disturb the family, slipped quietly out at the back door, and walked in St Anthony's garden behind the house. The moon shone so bright that it was almost as light as noon-day, and he had scarcely taken a single turn, until he saw a tall man enter from the other side, buttoned in a drab-coloured great coat. It so happened that at that time M'Millan stood in the shadow of the wall, and perceiving that the stranger did not observe him, a thought struck him that it would not be amiss to keep himself concealed; that he might see what the man was going to be about. He walked backwards and forwards for some time in apparent impatience, looking at his watch every minute, until at length another man came in by the same way, buttoned likewise in a great coat, and having a bonnet on his head. He was remarkably stout made, but considerably lower in stature than the other. They exchanged only a single word; then turning both about, they threw off their great coats, drew their swords, and began a most desperate and well contested combat.

The tall gentleman appeared to have the advantage. He constantly gained ground on the other, and drove him half round the division of the garden in which they fought. Each of them strove to fight with his back towards the moon, so that she might shine full in the face of his opponent; and many rapid wheels were made for the purpose of gaining this position. The engagement was long and obstinate, and by the desperate thrusts that were frequently aimed on both sides, it was evident that they meant one another's destruction. They came at length within a few yards of the place where M'Millan still stood concealed. They were both out of breath, and at that instant a small cloud chancing to overshadow the moon, one of them called out, "Hold, we can't see."—They uncovered their heads—wiped their faces—and as soon as the moon emerged from the cloud, each resumed his guard. Surely that was an awful pause! and short, indeed, was the stage between it and eternity with the one! The tall gentleman made a lounge at the other, who parried and returned it; and as the former sprung back to avoid the thrust, his foot slipped, and he stumbled forward towards his antagonist, who dexterously met his breast in the fall with the point of his sword, and ran him through the body. He made only one feeble convulsive struggle, as if attempting to rise, and expired almost instantaneously.

M'Millan was petrified with horror; but conceiving himself to be in a perilous situation, having stolen out of the house at that dead hour of the night; he had so much presence of mind, as to hold his peace, and to keep from interfering in the smallest degree.

The surviving combatant wiped his sword with great composure;—put on his bonnet—covered the body with one of the great coats—took up the other, and departed; M'Millan returned quietly to his chamber without awakening any of the family. His pains were gone; but his mind was shocked and exceedingly perturbed; and after deliberating until morning, he determined to say nothing of the matter; and to make no living creature acquainted with what he had seen; thinking that suspicion would infallibly rest on him. Accordingly he kept his bed next morning until his friend brought him the tidings, that a gentleman had been murdered at the back of the house during the night. He then arose and examined the body, which was that of a young man; seemingly from the country, having brown hair, and fine manly features. He had neither letter, book, nor signature of any kind about him, that could in the least lead to a discovery of who he was; only a common silver watch was found in his pocket, and an elegant sword was clasped in his cold bloody hand, which had an A. and B. engraved on the hilt. The sword had entered at his breast, and gone out at his back a little below the left shoulder. He had likewise received a slight wound on the sword arm.

The body was carried to the dead-room, where it lay for eight days, and though great numbers inspected it, yet none knew who, or whence the deceased was, and he was at length buried among the strangers in the Grayfriars Churchyard.

Sixteen years elapsed before M'Millan once mentioned the circumstance of his having seen the duel, to any person; but, at that period, being in Annandale receiving some sheep that he had bought, and chancing to hear of the astonishing circumstances of Bell's disappearance, he divulged the whole.—The time, the description of his person, his clothes, and above all, the sword with the initials of his name engraven upon it, confirmed the fact beyond the smallest shadow of doubt that it was Mr Bell whom he had seen killed in the duel behind the Abbey. But who the person was that slew him, how the quarrel commenced, or who it was that appeared to his housekeeper, remains to this day a profound secret, and is likely to remain so, until that day when every deed of darkness shall be brought to light.

Some have even ventured to blame M'Millan for the whole, on account of his long concealment of facts; and likewise in consideration of his uncommon bodily strength, and daring disposition, he being one of the boldest and most enterprising men of the age in which he lived; but all who knew him despised such insinuations, and declared them to be entirely inconsistent with his character, which was most honourable and disinterested; and besides, his tale has every appearance of truth, "Pluris est oculatus testis unus quam auriti decem."

Duncan Campbell

DUNCAN CAMPELL came from the Highlands, when six years of age, to live with an old maiden aunt in Edinburgh, and attend the school. His mother was dead; but his father had supplied her place, by marrying his housekeeper. Duncan did not trouble himself about these matters, nor indeed about any other matters, save a black foal of his father's, and a large sagacious colley, named Oscar, which belonged to one of the shepherds. There being no other boy save Duncan about the house, Oscar and he were constant companions,—with his garter tied round Oscar's neck, and a piece of deal tied to his big bushy tail, Duncan would often lead him about the green, pleased with the idea that he was conducting a horse and cart. Oscar submitted to all this with great cheerfulness, but whenever Duncan mounted to ride on him, he found means instantly to unhorse him, either by galloping, or rolling himself on the green. When Duncan threatened him, he looked submissive and licked his face and hands; when he corrected him with the whip, he cowered at his feet;—matters were soon made up. Oscar would lodge no where during the night but at the door of the room where his young friend slept, and wo be to the man or woman who ventured to enter it at untimely hours.

When Duncan left his native home he thought not of his father, nor any of the servants. He was fond of the ride, and some supposed that he even scarcely thought of the black foal; but when he saw Oscar standing looking him ruefully in the face, the tears immediately blinded both his eyes. He caught him around the neck, hugged and kissed him,—"Good-b'ye Oscar," said he blubbering;—"good-b'ye, God bless you, my dear Oscar;" Duncan mounted before a servant, and rode away—Oscar still followed at a distance, until he reached the top of the hill—he then sat down and howled;—Duncan cried till his little heart was like to burst.—"What ails you?" said the servant. "I will never see my poor honest Oscar again," said Duncan, "an' my heart canna bide it."

Duncan staid a year in Edinburgh, but he did not make great progress in learning. He did not approve highly of attending the school, and his aunt was too indulgent to compel his attendance. She grew extremely ill one day—the maids kept constantly by her, and never regarded Duncan. He was an additional charge to them, and they never loved him, but used him harshly. It was now with great difficulty that he could obtain either meat or drink. In a few days after his aunt was taken ill she died. All was in confusion, and poor Duncan was like to perish with hunger;—he could find no person in the house; but hearing a noise in his aunt's chamber, he went in, and beheld them dressing the corpse of his kind relation;—it was enough.—Duncan was horrified beyond what mortal breast was able to endure;—he hasted down the stair, and ran along the High Street, and South Bridge, as fast as his feet could carry him, crying incessantly all the way. He would not have entered that house again, if the world had been offered him as a reward. Some people stopped him, in order to ask what was the matter; but he could only answer them by exclaiming, "O! dear! O! dear!" and, struggling till he got free, held on his course, careless whither he went, provided he got far enough from the horrid scene he had so lately witnessed. Some have supposed, and I believe Duncan has been heard to confess, that he then imagined he was running for the Highlands, but mistook the direction. However that was, he continued his course until he came to a place where two ways met, a little south of Grange Toll. Here he sat down, and his frenzied passion subsided into a soft melancholy;—he cried no more, but sobbed excessively; fixed his eyes on the ground, and made some strokes in the dust with his finger.

A sight just then appeared, which somewhat cheered, or at least interested, his heavy and forlorn heart—it was a large drove of Highland cattle. They were the only creatures like acquaintances that Duncan had seen for a twelvemonth, and a tender feeling of joy, mixed with regret, thrilled his heart at the sight of their white horns and broad dew-laps. As the van passed him, he thought their looks were particularly gruff and sullen; he soon perceived the cause, they were all in the hands of Englishmen;—poor exiles like himself;—going far away to be killed and eaten, and would never see the Highland hills again!

When they were all gone by, Duncan looked after them and wept anew; but his attention was suddenly called away to something that softly touched his feet;—he looked hastily about—it was a poor hungry lame dog, squatted on the ground, licking his feet, and manifesting the most extravagant joy. Gracious Heaven! it was his own beloved and faithful Oscar! starved, emaciated, and so crippled, that he was scarcely able to walk! He was now doomed to be the slave of a Yorkshire peasant, (who, it seems, had either bought or stolen him at Falkirk,) the generosity and benevolence of whose feelings were as inferior to those of Oscar, as Oscar was inferior to him in strength and power. It is impossible to conceive a more tender meeting than this was; but Duncan soon observed that hunger and misery were painted in his friend's looks, which again pierced his heart with feelings unfelt before. "I have not a crumb to give you, my poor Oscar!" said he—"I have not a crumb to eat myself, but I am not so ill as you are." The peasant whistled aloud. Oscar well knew the sound, and clinging to the boy's bosom, leaned his head upon his thigh, and looked in his face, as if saying, "O Duncan, protect me from yon ruffian." The whistle was repeated accompanied by a loud and surly call. Oscar trembled, but fearing to disobey, he limped away reluctantly after his unfeeling master, who observing him to linger and look back, imagined he wanted to effect his escape, and came running back to meet him. Oscar cowered to the earth in the most submissive and imploring manner, but the peasant laid hold of him by the ear, and uttering many imprecations, struck him with a thick staff till he lay senseless at his feet.

Every possible circumstance seemed combined to wound the feelings of poor Duncan, but this unmerited barbarity shocked him most of all. He hasted to the scene of action, weeping bitterly, and telling the man that he was a cruel brute; and that if ever he himself grew a big man he would certainly kill him. He held up his favourite's head that he might recover his breath, and the man knowing that he could do little without his dog, waited patiently to see what would be the issue. The animal recovered, and stammered away at the heels of his tyrant without daring to look behind him. Duncan stood still, but kept his eyes eagerly fixed upon Oscar, and the farther he went from him, the more strong his desire grew to follow him. He looked the other way, but all there was to him a blank,—he had no desire to stand where he was, so he followed Oscar and the drove of cattle.

The cattle were weary and went slowly, and Duncan, getting a little goad in his hand, assisted the men greatly in driving them. One of the drivers gave him a penny, and another gave him twopence; and the lad who had the charge of the drove, observing how active and pliable he was, and how far he had accompanied him on the way, gave him sixpence; this was a treasure to Duncan, who being extremely hungry, bought three penny rolls as he passed through a town; one of these he ate himself, another he gave to Oscar; and the third he carried below his arm in case of farther necessity. He drove on all the day, and at night the cattle rested upon a height, which, by his description, seems to have been that between Gala Water and Middleton. Duncan went off at a side, in company with Oscar, to eat his roll, and taking shelter behind an old earthen wall, they shared

their dry meal most lovingly between them. Ere it was quite finished, Duncan being fatigued, dropped into a profound slumber,
out of which he did not awake until the next morning was far advanced. Englishmen, cattle, and Oscar, all were gone. Duncan found
himself alone on a wild height, in what country or kingdom he knew
not. He sat for some time in a callous stupor, rubbing his eyes and
scratching his head, but quite irresolute what was farther necessary
for him to do, until he was agreeably surprised by the arrival of
Oscar, who (though he had gone at his master's call in the morning)
had found means to escape and seek the retreat of his young friend
and benefactor. Duncan, without reflecting on the consequences,
rejoiced in the event, and thought of nothing else than furthering his
escape from the ruthless tyrant who now claimed him. For this purpose he thought it would be best to leave the road, and accordingly
he crossed it, in order to go over a waste moor to the westward. He
had not got forty paces from the road, until he beheld the enraged
Englishman running towards him without his coat, and having his
staff heaved over his shoulder. Duncan's heart fainted within him,
knowing it was all over with Oscar, and most likely with himself.
The peasant seemed not to have observed them, as he was running,
and rather looking the other way; and as Duncan quickly lost sight
of him in a hollow place that lay between them, he crept into a bush
of heath, and took Oscar in his bosom;–the heath was so long that it
almost closed above them; the man had observed from whence the
dog started in the morning, and hasted to the place, expecting to find
him sleeping beyond the old earthen dike; he found the nest, but the
birds were flown;–he called aloud; Oscar trembled and clung to
Duncan's breast; Duncan peeped from his purple covert like a heathcock on his native waste, and again beheld the ruffian coming straight
towards them, with his staff still heaved, and fury in his looks;–
when he came within a few yards he stood still and bellowed out;
"Oscar, yho, yho!" Oscar quaked, and crept still closer to Duncan's
breast; Duncan almost sunk in the earth; "D—n him," said the Englishman, "if I had a hold of him I should make both him and the little
thievish rascal dear at a small price; they cannot be far gone,–I think
I hear them;" he then stood listening, but at that instant a farmer
came up on horseback, and having heard him call, asked him if he
had lost his dog? The peasant answered in the affirmative, and added,
that a blackguard boy had stolen him. The farmer said that he met
a boy with a dog about a mile forward. During this dialogue, the
farmer's dog came up to Duncan's den,–smelled upon him, then
upon Oscar,–cocked his tail, walked round them growling, and then

behaved in a very improper and uncivil manner to Duncan, who took all patiently, uncertain whether he was yet discovered. But so intent was the fellow upon the farmer's intelligence, that he took no notice of the discovery made by the dog, but ran off without looking over his shoulder.

Duncan felt this a deliverance so great that all his other distresses vanished; and as soon as the man was out of his sight, he arose from his covert, and ran over the moor, and ere it was long came to a shepherd's house, where he got some whey and bread for his breakfast, which he thought the best meat he had ever tasted, yet shared it with Oscar.

Though I had his history from his own mouth, yet there is a space here which it is impossible to relate with any degree of distinctness or interest. He was a vagabond boy, without any fixed habitation, and wandered about Herriot Moor, from one farm-house to another, for the space of a year; staying from one to twenty nights in each house, according as he found the people kind to him. He seldom resented any indignity offered to himself, but whoever insulted Oscar, or offered any observations on the impropriety of their friendship, lost Duncan's company the next morning. He staid several months at a place called Dewar, which he said was haunted by the ghost of a piper;—that piper had been murdered there many years before, in a manner somewhat mysterious, or at least unaccountable; and there was scarcely a night on which he was not supposed either to be seen or heard about the house. Duncan slept in the cow-house, and was terribly harassed by the piper; he often heard him scratching about the rafters, and sometimes he would groan like a man dying, or a cow that was choaked in the band; but at length he saw him at his side one night, which so discomposed him, that he was obliged to leave the place, after being ill for many days. I shall give this story in Duncan's own words, which I have often heard him repeat without any variation.

"I had been driving some young cattle to the heights of Willenslee—it grew late before I got home—I was thinking, and thinking, how cruel it was to kill the poor piper! to cut out his tongue, and stab him in the back. I thought it was no wonder that his ghost took it extremely ill; when, all on a sudden, I perceived a light before me;—I thought the wand in my hand was all on fire, and threw it away, but I perceived the light glide slowly by my right foot, and burn behind me;—I was nothing afraid, and turned about to look at the light, and there I saw the piper, who was standing hard at my back, and when I turned round, he looked me in the face." "What was he like,

Duncan?" "He was like a dead body! but I got a short view of him; for that moment all around me grew dark as a pit!–I tried to run, but sunk powerless to the earth, and lay in a kind of dream, I do not know how long; when I came to myself, I got up, and endeavoured to run, but fell to the ground every two steps. I was not a hundred yards from the house, and I am sure I fell upwards of a hundred times. Next day I was in a high fever; the servants made me a little bed in the kitchen, to which I was confined by illness many days, during which time I suffered the most dreadful agonies by night, always imagining the piper to be standing over me on the one side or the other. As soon as I was able to walk, I left Dewar, and for a long time durst neither sleep alone during the night, nor stay by myself in the day-time."

The superstitious ideas impressed upon Duncan's mind by this unfortunate encounter with the ghost of the piper, seem never to have been eradicated; a strong instance of the power of early impressions, and a warning how much caution is necessary in modelling the conceptions of the young and tender mind, for, of all men I ever knew, he is the most afraid of meeting with apparitions. So deeply is his imagination tainted with this startling illusion, that even the calm disquisitions of reason have proved quite inadequate to the task of dispelling it. Whenever it wears late, he is always on the look-out for these ideal beings, keeping a jealous eye upon every bush and brake, in case they should be lurking behind them, ready to fly out and surprise him every moment; and the approach of a person in the dark, or any sudden noise, always deprives him of the power of speech for some time.

After leaving Dewar, he again wandered about for a few weeks; and it appears that his youth, beauty, and peculiarly destitute situation, together with his friendship for his faithful Oscar, had interested the most part of the country people in his behalf, for he was generally treated with kindness. He knew his father's name, and the name of his house; but as none of the people he visited had ever before heard of either the one or the other, they gave themselves no trouble about the matter.

He staid nearly two years in a place he called Cowhaur, till a wretch with whom he slept, struck and abused him one day. Duncan, in a rage, flew to the loft, and cut all his Sunday hat, shoes, and coat, in pieces; and, not daring to abide the consequences, decamped that night.

He wandered about for some time longer, among the farmers of Tweed and Yarrow; but this life was now become exceedingly disagreeable to him. He durst not sleep by himself, and the servants did not always choose that a vagrant boy and his great dog should sleep with them.

It was on a rainy night, at the close of harvest, that Duncan came to my father's house. I remember all the circumstances as well as the transactions of yesterday. The whole of his clothing consisted only of one black coat, which, having been made for a full grown man, hung fairly to his heels; the hair of his head was rough, curled, and weather-beaten; but his face was ruddy and beautiful, bespeaking a healthy body, and a sensible feeling heart. Oscar was still nearly as large as himself, had the colour of a fox, with a white stripe down his face, and a ring of the same colour around his neck, and was the most beautiful colley I have ever seen. My heart was knit to Duncan at the first sight, and I wept for joy when I saw my parents so kind to him. My mother, in particular, could scarcely do any thing else than converse with Duncan for several days. I was always of the party, and listened with wonder and admiration; but often have these adventures been repeated to me. My parents, who soon seemed to feel the same concern for him as if he had been their own son, clothed him in blue drugget, and bought him a smart little Highland bonnet; in which dress he looked so charming, that I would not let them have peace until I got one of the same. Indeed, all that Duncan said or did was to me a pattern, for I loved him as my own life. I was, at my own request, which he persuaded me to urge, permitted to be his bed-fellow, and many a happy night and day did I spend with Duncan and Oscar.

As far as I remember, we felt no privation of any kind, and would have been completely happy, if it had not been for the fear of spirits. When the conversation chanced to turn upon the Piper of Dewar, the Maid of Plora, or the Pedlar of Thirlestane Mill, often have we lain with the bed-clothes drawn over our heads until nearly suffocated. We loved the fairies and the brownies, and even felt a little partiality for the mermaids, on account of their beauty and charming songs; we were a little jealous of the water-kelpies, and always kept aloof from the frightsome pools. We hated the devil most heartily, but we were not much afraid of him; but a ghost! oh, dreadful! the names, ghost, spirit, or apparition, sounded in our ears like the knell of destruction, and our hearts sunk within us as if pierced by the cold icy shaft of death. Duncan herded my father's cows all the summer—so did I—we could not live asunder. We grew fishers so expert, that the speckled trout, with all his art, could not elude our machinations; we forced him from his watery cove, admired the beautiful shades and purple drops that were painted on his sleek sides, and forthwith added him to our number without reluctance. We assailed the habitation of the wild bee, and rifled all her accumulated sweets, though not without encountering the most determined resistance. My father's meadows abounded with hives; they were almost in every swath—in every hillock. When the swarm was large, they would beat us off, day after day. In all these desperate engagements, Oscar came to our assistance, and, provided that none of the enemy made a lodgment in his lower defiles, he was always the last combatant of our party on the field. I do not remember of ever being so much diverted by any scene I ever witnessed, or laughing as immoderately as I have done at seeing Oscar involved in a moving cloud of wild bees, wheeling, snapping on all sides, and shaking his ears incessantly.

The sagacity which this animal possessed is almost incredible, while his undaunted spirit and generosity, it would do honour to every servant of our own species to copy. Twice did he save his master's life: at one time when attacked by a furious bull, and at another time when he fell from behind my father off a horse into a flooded river. Oscar had just swimmed across, but instantly plunged in a second time to his master's rescue. He first got hold of his bonnet, but that coming off, he quitted it, and again catching him by the coat, brought him to the side, where my father reached him. He waked Duncan at a certain hour every morning, and would frequently turn the cows of his own will, when he observed them wrong. If Duncan dropped his knife, or any other small article, he would fetch it along in his mouth; and if sent back for a lost thing, would infallibly find it. When sixteen years of age, after being unwell for several days, he died one night below his master's bed. On the evening before, when Duncan came in from the plough, he came from his hiding-place, wagged his tail, licked Duncan's hand, and returned to his death-bed. Duncan and I lamented him with unfeigned sorrow, buried him below the old rowan tree at the back of my father's garden, placing a square stone at his head, which was still standing the last time I was there. With great labour, we composed an epitaph between us, which was once carved on that stone; the metre was good, but the stone was so hard, and the engraving so faint, that the characters, like those of our early joys, are long ago defaced and extinct.

Often have I heard my mother relate with enthusiasm, the manner in which she and my father first discovered the dawnings of goodness and facility of conception in Duncan's mind, though, I confess, dearly as I loved him, these circumstances escaped my observation. It was my father's invariable custom, to pray with the family every night before they retired to rest, to thank the Almighty for his kindness to them during the bygone day, and to beg his protection through the dark and silent watches of the night. I need not inform any of my readers, that that amiable (and now too much neglected and despised) duty, consisted in singing a few stanzas of a psalm, in which all the family joined their voices with my father's, so that the double octaves of the various ages and sexes swelled the simple concert. He then read a chapter from the Bible, going straight on from beginning to end of the Scriptures. The prayer concluded the devotions of each evening, in which the downfall of Antichrist was always strenuously urged, the ministers of the Gospel remembered, nor was any friend or neighbour in distress forgot.

The servants of a family have, in general, liberty either to wait the evening prayers, or retire to bed as they incline, but no consideration whatever could induce Duncan to go one night to rest without the prayers, even though both wet and weary, and intreated by my parents to retire, for fear of catching cold. It seems that I had been of a more complaisant disposition; for I was never very hard to prevail with in this respect; nay, my mother used to say, that I was extremely apt to take a pain about my heart at that time of the night, and was, of course, frequently obliged to betake me to the bed before the worship commenced.

It might be owing to this that Duncan's emotions on these occasions escaped my notice. He sung a treble to the old church tunes most sweetly, for he had a melodious voice; and when my father read the chapter, if it was in any of the historical parts of Scripture, he would lean upon the table, and look him in the face, swallowing every sentence with the utmost avidity. At one time, as my father read the 45th chapter of Genesis, he wept so bitterly, that at the end my father paused, and asked what ailed him? Duncan told him that he did not know.

At another time, the year following, my father, in the course of his evening devotions, had reached the 19th chapter of the book of Judges; when he began reading it, Duncan was seated on the other side of the house, but ere it was half done, he had stolen up close to my father's elbow. "Consider of it, take advice, and speak your minds," said my father, and closed the book. "Go on, go on if you please, Sir," said Duncan—"go on, and let us hear what they said about it." My father looked sternly in Duncan's face, but seeing him abashed on account of his hasty breach of decency, without uttering a word, he again opened the Bible, and read the 20th chapter throughout, notwithstanding of its great length. Next day Duncan was walking about with the Bible below his arm, begging of every body to read it to him again and again. This incident produced a conversation between my parents, on the expenses and utility of education; the consequence of which was, that the week following, Duncan and I were sent to the parish school, and began at the same instant to the study of that most important and fundamental branch of literature, the A, B, C; but my sister Mary, who was older than I, was already an accurate and elegant reader.

This reminds me of another anecdote of Duncan, with regard to family worship, which I have often heard related, and which I myself may well remember. My father happening to be absent over night at a fair, when the usual time of worship arrived, my mother desired a lad, one of the servants, to act as chaplain for that night; the lad declined it, and slunk away to his bed. My mother testified her regret that we should all be obliged to go prayerless to our beds for that night, observing, that she did not remember the time when it had so happened before. Duncan said, he thought we might contrive to manage it amongst us, and instantly proposed to sing the psalm and pray, if Mary would read the chapter. To this my mother with some hesitation agreed, remarking, that if he prayed as he could, with a pure heart, his prayer had as good a chance of being accepted as some others that were *better worded.* Duncan could not then read, but having learned several psalms from Mary by rote, he caused her seek out the place, and sung the 23d Psalm from end to end, with great sweetness and decency. Mary read a chapter in the New Testament, and then (my mother having a child on her knee) we three kneeled in a row, while Duncan prayed thus:–"O Lord, be thou our God, our guide, and our guard unto death, and through death," that was a sentence my father often used in his prayer; Duncan had laid hold of it, and my mother began to think that he had often prayed previous to that time.–"O Lord, thou"–continued Duncan, but his matter was exhausted; a long pause ensued, which I at length broke, by bursting into a loud fit of laughter. Duncan rose hastily, and, without once lifting up his head, went crying to his bed; and as I continued to indulge in laughter, my mother, for my irreverend behaviour, struck me across the shoulders with the tongs; our evening devotions terminated exceedingly ill, I went crying to my bed after Duncan, even louder than he, and abusing him for his *useless prayer,* for which I had been nearly felled.

By the time that we were recalled from school to herd the cows next summer, we could both read the Bible with considerable facility, but Duncan far excelled me in perspicacity; and so fond was he of reading Bible history, that the reading of it was now our constant amusement. Often have Mary, and he, and I, lain under the same plaid by the side of the corn or meadow, and read chapter about on the Bible for hours together, weeping over the failings and fall of good men, and wondering at the inconceivable might of the heroes of antiquity. Never was man so delighted as Duncan was when he came to the history of Samson, and afterwards of David and Goliath; he could not be satisfied until he had read it to every individual with whom he was acquainted, judging it to be as new and as interesting to every one as it was to himself. I have seen him standing by the girls as they were milking the cows, reading to them the feats of Samson; and, in short, harassing every man and woman about the hamlet for audience. On Sundays, my parents accompanied us to the fields, and joined in our delightful exercise.

Time passed away, and so also did our youthful delights! but other cares and other pleasures awaited us. As we advanced in years and strength, we quitted the herding, and bore a hand in the labours of the farm. Mary, too, was often our assistant. She and Duncan were nearly of an age—he was tall, comely, and affable; and if Mary was not the prettiest girl in the parish, at least Duncan and I believed her to be so, which, with us, amounted to the same thing. We often compared the other girls in the parish with one another, as to their beauty and accomplishments, but to think of comparing any of them with Mary, was entirely out of the question. She was, indeed, the emblem of truth, simplicity, and innocence, and if there were few more beautiful, there were still fewer so good and amiable; but still as she advanced in years, she grew fonder and fonder of being near Duncan; and by the time she was nineteen, was so deeply in love, that it affected her manner, her spirits, and her health. At one time she was gay and frisky as a kitten; she would dance, sing, and laugh violently at the most trivial incidents. At other times she was silent and sad, while a languishing softness overspread her features, and added greatly to her charms. The passion was undoubtedly mutual between them; but Duncan, either from a sense of honour, or some other cause, never declared himself farther on the subject, than by the most respectful attention, and tender assiduities. Hope and fear thus alternately swayed the heart of poor Mary, and produced in her deportment that variety of affections, which could not fail of rendering the sentiments of her artless bosom legible to the eye of experience.

In this state matters stood, when an incident occurred which deranged our happiness at once, and the time arrived when the kindest and most affectionate little social band of friends, that ever panted to meet the wishes of each other, were obliged to part.

About forty years ago, the flocks of southern sheep, which have since that period inundated the Highlands, had not found their way over the Grampian mountains; and the native flocks of that sequestered country were so scanty, that it was found necessary to transport small quantities of wool annually to the north, to furnish materials for clothing the inhabitants. During two months of each summer, the hill countries of the Lowlands were inundated by hundreds of women from the Highlands, who bartered small articles of dress, and of domestic import, for wool: these were known by the appellation of *norlan' netties*; and few nights passed, during the wool season, that some of them were not lodged at my father's house. It was from two of these that Duncan learned one day who and what he was; that he was the laird of Glenellich's only son and heir, and that a large sum had been offered to any person that could discover him. My parents certainly rejoiced in Duncan's good fortune, yet they were disconsolate at parting with him; for he had long ago become as a son of their own; and I seriously believe, that from the day they first met, to that on which the two *norlan' netties* came to our house, they never once entertained the idea of parting. For my part, I wished that the netties had never been born, or that they had staid at their own home; for the thoughts of being separated from my dear friend made me sick at heart. All our feelings were, however, nothing, when compared with those of my sister Mary. From the day that the two women left our house, she was no more seen to smile; she had never yet divulged the sentiments of her heart to any one, and imagined her love for Duncan a profound secret—no,

> "She never told her love;
> But let concealment, like a worm i' the bud,
> Feed on her damask cheek;—she pined in thought;
> And, with a green and yellow melancholy,
> She sat, like patience on a monument,
> Smiling at grief."

Our social glee and cheerfulness were now completely clouded; we sat down to our meals, and rose from them in silence. Of the few observations that passed, every one seemed the progeny of embarrassment and discontent, and our general remarks were strained and cold. One day at dinner, after a long and sullen pause, my father said, "I hope you do not intend to leave us very soon, Duncan?" "I am thinking of going away to-morrow, Sir," said Duncan. The knife fell from my mother's hand; she looked him steadily in the face for the space of a minute. "Duncan," said she, her voice faultering, and the tears dropping from her eyes,–"Duncan, I never durst ask you before, but I hope you will not leave us altogether?" Duncan thrust the plate from before him into the middle of the table–took up a book that lay on the window, and looked over the pages–Mary left the room. No answer was returned, nor any further inquiry made; and our little party broke up in silence.

When we met again in the evening, we were still all sullen. My mother tried to speak of indifferent things, but it was apparent that her thoughts had no share in the words that dropped from her tongue. My father at last said, "You will soon forget us, Duncan; but there are some among us who will not so soon forget you." Mary again left the room, and silence ensued, until the family were called together for evening worship. There was one sentence in my father's prayer that night, which I think I yet remember, word for word. It may appear of little importance to those who are nowise interested, but it affected us deeply, and left not a dry cheek in the family. It runs thus: "We are an unworthy little flock, thou seest here kneeling before thee, our God; but few as we are, it is probable we shall never all kneel again together before thee in this world. We have long lived together in peace and happiness, and hoped to have lived so much longer; but since it is thy will that we part, enable us to submit to that will with firmness; and though thou scatter us to the four winds of heaven, may thy Almighty arm still be about us for good, and grant that we may all meet hereafter in another and a better world."

The next morning, after a restless night, Duncan rose early, put on his best suit, and packed up some little articles to carry with him. I lay panting and trembling, but pretended to be fast asleep. When he was ready to depart, he took his bundle below his arm, came up to the side of the bed, and listened if I was sleeping. He then stood long hesitating, looking wistfully to the door, and then to me, alternately; and I saw him three or four times wipe his eyes. At length he shook me gently by the shoulder, and asked if I was awake. I feigned to start, and answered as if half asleep. "I must bid you farewell," said he, groping to get hold of my hand. "Will you not breakfast with us, Duncan?" said I. "No," said he, "I am thinking that it is best to steal away, for it will break my heart to take leave of your parents, and"–"And who, Duncan?" said I. "And you," said he.

"Indeed, but it is not best, Duncan," said I; "we will all breakfast together for the last time, and then take a formal and kind leave of each other." We did breakfast together, and as the conversation turned on former days, it became highly interesting to us all. When my father had returned thanks to Heaven for our meal, we knew what was coming, and began to look at each other. Duncan rose, and after we had all loaded him with our blessings and warmest wishes, he embraced my parents and me.–He turned about.–His eyes said plainly, there is somebody still wanting, but his heart was so full he could not speak. "What is become of Mary?" said my father;–Mary was gone.–We searched the house, the garden, and the houses of all the cottagers, but she was nowhere to be found.–Poor lovelorn forsaken Mary! She had hid herself in the ancient yew that grows in front of the old ruin, that she might see her lover depart, without herself being seen, and might indulge in all the luxury of wo.–Poor Mary! how often have I heard her sigh, and seen her eyes red with weeping; while the smile that played on her languid features, when ought was mentioned to Duncan's recommendation, would have melted a heart of adamant.

I must pass over Duncan's journey to the north Highlands for want of room, but on the evening of the sixth day after leaving my father's house, he reached the mansion-house of Glenellich, which stands in a little beautiful woody strath, commanding a view of the Deu-Caledonian Sea, and part of the Hebrides; every avenue, tree, and rock, was yet familiar to Duncan's recollection; and the feelings of his sensible heart on approaching the abode of his father, whom he had long scarcely thought of, can only be conceived by a heart like his own. He had, without discovering himself, learned from a peasant that his father was still alive, but that he had never overcome the loss of his son, for whom he lamented every day; that his wife and daughter lorded it over him, holding his pleasure at nought, and rendering his age extremely unhappy; that they had expelled all his old farmers and vassals, and introduced the lady's vulgar presumptuous relations, who neither paid him rents, honour, nor obedience.

Old Glenellich was taking his evening walk on the road by which Duncan descended the strath to his dwelling. He was pondering on his own misfortunes, and did not even deign to lift his eyes as the young stranger approached, but seemed counting the number of marks which the horses' hoofs had made on the way. "Good e'en to you, Sir," said Duncan;–the old man started and stared him in the face, but with a look so unsteady and harassed, that he seemed incapable of distinguishing any lineament or feature of it. "Good e'en, good e'en," said he, wiping his brow with his arm, and passing by.–What there was in the voice that struck him so forcibly it is hard to say.–Nature is powerful.–Duncan could not think of ought to detain him; and being desirous of seeing how matters went on about the house, thought it best to remain some days *incog*. He went into the fore-kitchen, conversed freely with the servants, and soon saw his stepmother and sister appear. The former had all the insolence and ignorant pride of vulgarity raised to wealth and eminence; the other seemed naturally of an amiable disposition, but was entirely ruled by her mother, who taught her to disdain her father, all his relations, and whomsoever he loved. On that same evening he came into the kitchen, where she then was chatting with Duncan, to whom she seemed attached at first sight. "Lexy, my dear," said he, "did you see my spectacles?" "Yes," said she, "I think I saw them on your nose to-day at breakfast." "Well, but I have lost them since," said he. "You may take up the next you find then, Sir," said she.– The servants laughed. "I might well have known what information I would get of you," said he, regretfully. "How can you speak in such a style to your father, my dear lady?" said Duncan.–"If I were he I would place you where you should learn better manners.–It ill becomes so pretty a young lady to address an old father thus." "He!" said she, "who minds him? He's a dotard, an old whining, complaining, superannuated being, worse than a child." "But consider his years," said Duncan; "and besides, he may have met with crosses and losses sufficient to sour the temper of a younger man.–You should at all events pity and reverence, but never despise your father." The old lady now joined them. "You have yet heard nothing, young man," said the old laird, "if you saw how my heart is sometimes wrung.– Yes, I have had losses indeed." "You losses!" said his spouse;–"No; you have never had any losses that did not in the end turn out a vast profit."–"Do you then account the loss of a loving wife and a son nothing?" said he–"But have you not got a loving wife and a daughter in their room?" returned she; "the one will not waste your fortune as a prodigal son would have done, and the other will take care of both you and that, when *you* can no longer do either–the loss of your son indeed! it was the greatest blessing you could have received!" "Unfeeling woman," said he; "but Heaven may yet restore that son to protect the gray hairs of his old father, and lay his head in an honoured grave." The old man's spirits were quite gone–he cried like a child–his lady mimicked him–and at this, his daughter and the servants raised a laugh. "Inhuman wretches," said Duncan, starting up, and pushing them aside, "thus to mock the feelings of an old man, even although he were not the lord and master of you all: but take notice—the individual among you all that dares to offer such another insult to him, I'll roast on that fire." The old man clung to him, and looked him ruefully in the face. "You impudent, beggarly vagabond!" said the lady, "do you know to whom you speak?—servants turn that wretch out of the house, and hunt him with all the dogs in the kennel." "Softly, softly, good lady," said Duncan, "take care that I do not turn you out of the house."—"Alas! good youth," said the old laird, "you little know what you are about; for mercy's sake forbear; you are brewing vengeance both for yourself and me." "Fear not," said Duncan, "I will protect you with my life." "Pray, may I ask you what is your name?" said the old man, still looking earnestly at him—"That you may," replied Duncan, "no man has so good a right to ask any thing of me as you have—I am Duncan Campbell, your own son." "*M-m-m-my* son!" exclaimed the old man, and sunk back on a seat with a convulsive moan. Duncan held him in his arms—he soon recovered, and asked many incoherent questions—looked at the two moles on his right leg—kissed him, and then wept on his bosom for joy. "O God of heaven," said he, "it is long since I could thank thee heartily for any thing; now I do thank thee indeed, for I have found my son! my dear and only son!"

Contrary to what might have been expected, Duncan's pretty only sister Alexia rejoiced most of all in his discovery. She was almost wild with joy at finding such a brother.—The old lady, her mother, was said to have wept bitterly in private, but knowing that Duncan would be her master, she behaved to him with civility and respect. Every thing was committed to his management, and he soon discovered, that besides a good clear estate, his father had personal funds to a great amount. The halls and cottages of Glenellich were filled with feasting, joy, and gladness.

It was not so at my father's house. Misfortunes seldom come singly. Scarcely had our feelings overcome the shock which they received by the loss of our beloved Duncan, when a more terrible misfortune overtook us. My father, by the monstrous ingratitude of a friend whom he trusted, lost at once the greater part of his hard-earned fortune. The blow came unexpectedly, and distracted his personal affairs to such a degree, that an arrangement seemed almost totally impracticable. He struggled on with securities for several months; but perceiving that he was drawing his real friends into danger, by their signing of bonds which he might never be able to redeem, he lost heart entirely, and yielded to the torrent. Mary's

mind seemed to gain fresh energy every day. The activity and diligence which she evinced in managing the affairs of the farm, and
even in giving advice with regard to other matters, is quite incredible;—often have I thought what a treasure that inestimable girl would
have been to an industrious man whom she loved. All our efforts
availed nothing; my father received letters of horning on bills to a
large amount, and we expected every day that he would be taken
from us and dragged to a prison.

We were all sitting in our little room one day, consulting what
was best to be done—we could decide upon nothing, for our case
was desperate—we were fallen into a kind of stupor, but the window
being up, a sight appeared that quickly thrilled every heart with the
keenest sensations of anguish. Two men came riding sharply up by
the back of the old school house. "Yonder are the officers of justice
now," said my mother, "what shall we do?" We hurried to the window, and all of us soon discerned that they were no other than some
attorney accompanied by a sheriff's officer. My mother entreated of
my father to escape and hide himself until this first storm was over-
blown, but he would in nowise consent, assuring us that he had
done nothing of which he was ashamed, and that he was determined
to meet every one face to face, and let them do their worst; so finding all our entreaties vain, we could do nothing but sit down and
weep. At length we heard the noise of their horses at the door. "You
had better take the men's horses, James," said my father, "as there is
no other man at hand." "We will stay till they rap, if you please,"
said I. The cautious officer did not however rap, but afraid lest his
debtor should make his escape, he jumped lightly from his horse,
and hasted into the house. When we heard him open the outer door,
and his footsteps approaching along the entry, our hearts fainted
within us—he opened the door and stepped into the room—it was
Duncan! our own dearly beloved Duncan. The women uttered an
involuntary scream of surprise, but my father ran and got hold of
one hand, and I of the other—my mother too soon had him in her
arms, but our embrace was short; for his eyes fixed on Mary, who
stood trembling with joy and wonder in a corner of the room, changing her colour every moment—he snatched her up in his arms and
kissed her lips, and ere ever she was aware, her arms had encircled
his neck. "O my dear Mary," said he, "my heart has been ill at ease
since I left you, but I durst not then tell you a word of my mind, for
I little knew how I was to find affairs in the place where I was going;
but ah! you little elusive rogue, you owe me another for the one you
cheated me out of then;" so saying, he pressed his lips again to her

cheek, and then led her to a seat. Duncan then recounted all his adventures to us, with every circumstance of his good fortune—our hearts were uplifted almost past bearing—all our cares and sorrows were now forgotten, and we were once more the happiest little group that ever perhaps sat together. Before the cloth was laid for dinner, Mary ran out to put on her white gown, and comb her yellow hair, but was surprised at meeting with a smart young gentleman in the kitchen, with a scarlet neck on his coat, and a gold-laced hat. Mary, having never seen so fine a gentleman, made him a low courtesy, and offered to conduct him to the room; but he smiled, and told her he was the squire's servant. We had all of us forgot to ask for the gentleman that came with Duncan.

Duncan and Mary walked for two hours in the garden that evening—we did not know what passed between them, but the next day he asked her in marriage of my parents, and never will I forget the supreme happiness and gratitude that beamed in every face on that happy occasion. I need not tell my readers that my father's affairs were soon retrieved, or that I accompanied my dear Mary a bride to the Highlands, and had the satisfaction of saluting her as Mrs Campbell, and Lady of Glenellich.

An Old Soldier's Tale

"Ye didna use to be sae hard-hearted wi' me, goodwife," said Andrew Gemble to old Margaret, as he rested his meal-pocks on the corner of the table: "If ye'll let me bide a' night I'll tell you a tale." Andrew well knew the way to Margaret's heart. "It's no to be the battle o' Culloden, then, Andrew, ye hae gart me greet owre often about that already." "Weel, weel, good-wife, it sanna be the battle o' Culloden, though I like whiles to crack about the feats o' my young days." "Ah, Andrew! I'll never forgie you for stabbing the young Stuart o' Appin. I wish God may forgie you: but if ye dinna repent o' that, ye'll hae a black account to render again *ae day*." "Aye, but it will maybe be lang till that day; an' I'll just tell ye, goodwife, that I'll *never* repent o' that deed. I wad hae sticket a' the rebel crew, an' their papish prince, the same way, if I could hae laid my neeves on him: repent, quo she!"

"Andrew, ye may gae your ways down to Deephope, we hae nae bed to lay ye in; ye're no gaun to bide here a' night an' the morn the Sabbath day." "There's for ye now! there's for ye! that's the gratitude that an' auld sodger's to expect frae the fock that he has sae often ventured his life for! weel, weel, I'll rather trodge away down to Deephope, auld, an' stiff, an' wearied as I am, ere I'll repent when ony auld witch in the country bids me." "Come your ways into this cozy nook ayont me, Andrew; I'll e'en tak you in for ae night without repentance. We should a' do as we would like to be done to." "The deil tak' ye, goodwife, gin ye' haena spoken a mouthfu' sense for aince; fair fa' your honest heart, you are your father's bairn yet, for a' that's come an' gane." But the unyielding spirit of Andrew never forsook him for a moment. He was no sooner seated, than, laying his meal-pocks aside, and turning his dim eye towards old Margaret, with a malicious grin, he sung the following stanza of an old song, with a hollow and tremulous croon:

> "O the fire, the fire and the smoke
>   That frae our bold British flew,
> When we surrounded the rebels rude,
>   That waefu' popish crew!
> And O the blood o' the rebels rude
>   Alang the field that ran!
> The hurdies bare we turned up there
>   Of many a Highland Clan."

But ere he had done with the last stanza, his antagonist had struck up in a louder and shriller key, "Hey, Johnny Cope, are ye waukin yet," &c. which quite drowned Andrew, and sharpened the acrimony of his temper. He called her "an auld jacobite"—and wished he "had ken'd her in the year forty sax, he wad hae gotten her strappit like a herring." He had, however, given her her cue; she overpowered him with songs on the side of the Highlanders, against whom Andrew had served, all of them so scurrilous and severe, that he was glad to begin his tale that he might get quit of them: it was to the following effect, but were I to tell it in his own dialect, it would be unintelligible to the greater part of readers.

"You will often have heard, goodwife, that the Duke of Cumberland lay long in a state of inaction that year that he pursued the rebels to the north, so long indeed that many had concluded that he durst not follow them into their native fastnesses. The Duke however acted with great prudence, for the roads were bad, and the rivers impassable, and by remaining about Aberdeen until the return of spring, he kept the rebels up among their mountains, and prevented them from committing depredations on the Lowlands.

"I was a sergeant in the Royals then, and was ordered to the westward, along with some of the Campbells, to secure certain passes and fortresses, by which the rebels kept up a communication with the south. We remained two weeks at a little village on the Don, but all was quiet on that road, nor did we ever lay hold of one suspicious character, though we kept a watch at the Bridge-end both night and day. It was about the beginning of March, and the weather was dreadful; the snow was drifting every night; and the roads were so blocked up by wreaths and ice, that to march seemed impossible, although we knew that on the road west from us the Highlanders had established a line of communication; and besides, we could get nothing where we were, either to eat or drink. The gentlemen at head-quarters knew not that the snow lay so deep in the heights of Strath-Don, and we received orders to march directly to the westward, to the next line of road. None of us liked the duty we were engaged in, for besides being half famished with cold and hunger, we had accounts every day of great bodies of rebels that were hovering about the country of the Grants, and Brae-Mar, laying all true subjects under contribution, and taking from the country people whatever they pleased. We were likewise alarmed by a report that John Roy Stuart, accompanied by the Maclauchlans, had cut in pieces all our forces stationed at Keith, which turned out a very trifling matter after all, but it left us, as we supposed, quite exposed to every incursion from the north, and we were highly discontented. Captain Reginald Campbell commanded this flying party, a very brave fellow, and one to whom a soldier might speak as a friend. One day he came up from Lord Kintore's house, and after inspecting the different companies, he took me aside, and asked how I liked the service. 'Faith, Captain,' says I, 'if we stay long here, you will soon have a poor account of us to render; the men are positively dying with hunger and cold. The Campbells make good shift, for they can talk the horrid jargon of the country; but as for us of the Royals, we can not get a morsel: and by G——d, Captain, if these d——d Macintoshes come down upon us, we will not be a mouthful to them. Poor Renwick and Colstan are both dead already; and curse me if I was not afraid that these hungry ragamuffins of the village would eat them.'"

"If ye are gaun to tell us a story, Andrew," said old Margaret, "tell it even on, without mixing it up wi' cursing and swearing. What good can that do to the story? Ye gar a' my heart dirle to hear ye."

"Owther let me tell it in my ain way, gudewife, or else want it."

"Weel, Andrew, I'll rather want it than hear ye tak' *His* name in vain."

"Wha's name? The deil's, I fancy; for the deil another name blew frae my tongue the night. It is a pity, goodwife, that ye sude be sic a great hypocrite! I hate a hypocrite! An' a' you that mak a fike an' a cant about religion, an' grane, an' pray, are hypocrites ilka soul o' ye. Ye are sodgers that haena the mense to do your duty, and then blubber an' whine for fear o' the lash. But I ken ye better than ye ken yoursel; ye wad rather hear nought else but swearing for a month, or ye didna hear out that story. Sae I'll e'en gae on wi't to please mysel; the deil-ma-care whether it please you or no!

"'When men die of cold, sergeant, it is for want of exercise,' said he, 'I must remedy this. Gemble, you are a brave fellow; take ten men with you, and a guide, and proceed into the district of Strathaven; look at the state of the roads, and bring me all the intelligence you can about these rebel clans that are hovering over us.'

"Accordingly I took the men and a guide, and one of the Campbells who could talk Gaelic, and proceeded to the north-west till I came to the Avon, a wild and rapid river; and keeping on its banks, through drift and snow, we turned in rather a southerly direction. We had not travelled long by the side of the stream till I observed that the road had very lately been traversed, either by a large body of men or cattle, yet it was so wholly drifted up that we could in nowise discover which of these it had been. It was moreover all sprinkled with blood, which had an ominous appearance, but none of us could tell what it meant. I observed that the two Highlanders, Campbell and the guide, spoke about it in their own language, in a vehement manner, and from their looks and motions I concluded that they were greatly alarmed; but when I asked them what they meant, or what they were saying, they made me no answer. I asked them what they supposed it to have been that made that track, and left all that blood upon the snow? but they only shook their heads and said, 'they could not pe tehlling her.' Still it appeared to have been shed in larger quantities as we proceeded; the wet snow that was falling had mixed with it, and gorged it up so, that it seemed often as if the road had been covered with hillocks of blood.

"At length we came to a large wood, and by the side of it a small hamlet, where some joiners and sawers resided, and here we commenced our inquiries. My two Highlanders asked plenty for their own information, but they spoke English badly, and were so averse to tell me any thing, that I had nearly lost all patience with them. At length, by dint of threats, and close questioning, I understood that the rebels had fortified two strong Castles to the southward, those of Corgarf and Brae-Mar—that a body of the Mackintoshes had past by that same place about three hours before our arrival, with from twenty to thirty horses, all laden with the carcasses of sheep which they had taken up on the Duke of Gordon's lands, and were carrying to Corgarf, which they were provisioning abundantly. I asked if there were any leaders or gentlemen of the party, and was answered, that Glenfernet and Spital were both with it, and that it was likely that some more, either of the Farquharsons or Mackintoshes, would be passing or repassing there that same night, or next morning. This was an unwelcome piece of news to me; for owing to the fatigue we had undergone, and the fall of snow, which had increased the whole day, we could not again reach Strath-Don that night, nor indeed any place in our rear, for if we had essayed it, the wind and drift would have been straight in our faces. It appeared the most unaccountable circumstance to me I had ever seen, that the country at so short a distance should be completely under the control of the different armies; but it was owing to the lines of road from which there were no cross ones, or these only at great distances from one another.

"Necessity has no law; we were obliged to take up our quarters at this wretched hamlet all night, at the imminent risk of our lives. We could get nothing to eat. There was not meat of any description in these cots that we could find, nor indeed have I ever seen any thing in these Highland bothies, saving sometimes a little milk or wretched cheese. We were obliged to go out a foraging, and at length, after great exertion, got hold of a she-goat, lean, and hard as wood, which we killed and began to roast on a fire of sticks. Ere ever we had tasted it, there came in a woman crying piteously, and pouring forth torrents of Gaelic, of which I could make nothing. I understood, however, that the goat had belonged to her; it had however changed proprietors, and I offered her no redress. I had no trust to put in these savages, so I took them all prisoners, man and woman, and confined them in the same cot with ourselves, lest they might have conveyed intelligence to the clans of our arrival, placing the two Highlanders as sentinels at the door, to prevent all ingress or egress until next morning. We then dried our muskets, loaded them anew, fixed our bayonets, and lay down to rest with our clothes on, wet and weary as we were. The cottagers, with their wives and children, lighted sticks on the fire, and with many wild gestures babbled and spoke Gaelic all the night. I, however, fell sound asleep, and I believe so did all my companions.

"About two in the morning one of the soldiers awaked me from a sound sleep, by shaking me by the shoulder, without speaking a word. It was a good while before I could collect my senses, or remember where I was, but all the while my ears were stunned by the discordant sounds of Gaelic, seemingly issuing from an hundred tongues. 'What is all this, friend?' said I. 'Hush,' said he; 'I suppose it is the Mackintoshes, we are all dead men, *that's all.*' 'Oh! if *that be all,*' returned I, 'that is a matter of small consequence; but d—n the Mackintoshes, if they shall not get as good as they give.' 'Hush!' whispered he again; 'what a loss we cannot understand a word of their language. I think our sentinels are persuading them to pass on.' With that one of our prisoners, an old man, called out and was answered by one of the passengers, who then seemed to be going away. The old man then began a babbling and telling him something aloud, always turning a suspicious glance on me; but while he was yet in the middle of his speech, Campbell turned round, levelled his musket at the old rascal, and shot him dead.

"Such an uproar then commenced as never was before seen in so small a cot—women screaming like a parcel of she-goats; children mewing like cats; and men babbling and crying out in Gaelic, both without and within. Campbell's piece was reloaded in a moment, and need there was for expedition, for they were attacked at the door by the whole party, and at last twenty guns were all fired on them at once. The sod walls, however, sheltered us effectually, while every shot that we could get fired from the door or the holes in the wall, killed or wounded some, and whoever ventured in had two or three bayonets in each side at once. We were in a sad predicament, but it came upon us all in an instant, and we had no shift but to make the best of it we could, which we did without any dismay; and so safe did we find ourselves within our sod walls, that whenever any of them tried to break through the roof, we had such advantage, that we always beat them off at the first assault; and moreover, we saw them distinctly between us and the snow, but within all was darkness, and they could see nothing. That which plagued us most of all was the prisoners that we had within among us, for they were constantly in our way, and we were falling over them, and coming in violent contact with them in every corner; and though we kicked them and flung them from us in great wrath, to make them keep into holes, yet there was so many of them, and the house so small, it was impossible. We had now beat our enemies back from the door, and we took that opportunity of expelling our troublesome guests: our true Highlanders spoke something to them in Gaelic, which made them run out as for bare life. 'Cresorst, cresorst,' cried our guide; they ran still the faster, and were soon all out among the rebels. It was by my own express and hurried order that this was done, and never was any thing so imprudent! the whole party were so overjoyed that they set up a loud and reiterated shout, mixed with a hurra of laughter. What the devil's the matter now? thinks I to myself. I soon found that out to my sad experience. The poor cottagers had been our greatest safeguard, for the rebels no sooner knew that all their countrymen and their families were expelled and safely out, than they immediately set fire to the house on all sides. This was not very easily effected, owing to the wet snow that had fallen; besides, we had opened holes all the way around the heads of the walls, and kept them off as well as we could. It was not long, however, till we found ourselves involved in smoke, and likely to be suffocated. I gave orders instantly to sally out, but the door being triply guarded we could not effect it. In one second we undermined the gable, which falling flat, we sallied forth into the midst of the rebels with fixed bayonets, and bore down all before us. The dogs could not stand our might, but reeled like the withered leaves of a forest that the winds whirl before them. I knew not how the combat terminated, for I soon found myself overpowered, and held fast down by at least half a dozen Highlanders. I swore dreadfully at them, but they only laughed at me, and disarming me, tied my hands behind my back. 'I'm not in a very good way now,' thought I, as they were all keckling and speaking Gaelic around me. Two of them stood as sentinels over me for about the space of an hour, when the troop joined us in a body, and marched away, still keeping by the side of the river, and taking me along with them. It was now the break of day, and I looked about anxiously if I could see any of my companions, but none of them were with us, so I concluded that they were all killed. We came to a large and ugly looking village called Tamantoul, inhabited by a set of the most outlandish ragamuffins that I ever in my life saw; the men were so ragged and rough in their appearance, that they looked rather like savages than creatures of a Christian country; and the women had no shame nor sense of modesty about them, and of this the Highland soldiers seemed quite sensible, and treated them accordingly. Here I was brought in before their commander for examination. He was one of the Farquharsons, a very civil and polite gentleman, but as passionate as a wild bull, and spoke the English language so imperfectly, that I deemed it convenient not to understand a word that he said, lest I should betray some secrets of my commander.

"'Surcheon,' said he, 'you heffing peen tahken caring te harms, tat is te kuns and te sorts, akainst our most plessit sohofrain, and his lennoch more prince Sharles Stehuart, she shoold pe kiffing you ofer to pe shot in te heat wit powter and te pullets of kuns till you pe teat. Not te more, if you will pe cantor of worts to all tat she shall pe asking, akainst te accustoms of war you shall not pe shot wit powter and te pullets of kuns in te heat and prains till she pe teat, put you shall pe hold in free pondage, and peated wit sticks efry tay, and efry night, and efry mhorning, till she pe answering all and mhore.'

"'I beg your pardon, Captain,' says I, 'but really I dinna understand Gaelic, or Earse, or how d'ye ca't; it is sic a blether o' a language that nae living creature can understand it, gin it be na corbies and wullcats.'

"'Cot pe t——ming your improotence, and te hignorant of yourself, tat cannot be tahking town hany ting into your stuhpid prain tat is not peing spohken in te vhile Lowlands prohgue. Hupupup! Cot pe tahking you for a pase repellioner of a Sassenach tief! Finlay Pawn Peg Macalister Monro, you are peing te most least of all my men, pe trawing hout your claymhore, and if you do not pe cutting hoff tat creat Sassenach repel's heat at wan plow, py te shoul of Tonald Farquharson, put yours shall answer for it.'

"'I'm in a waur scrape now than ever,' thinks I to myself; however I pretended to be listening attentively to all that the Captain was saying, and when he had done I shook my head: 'I am really sorry, Captain,' says I, 'that I cannot understand a word that you are saying.'

"'Hu, shay, shay,' said he, 'she'll pe mhaking you to understand petter eneugh.' I was then conducted to the back of the house, with all the men, women, and children in the village about me. The diminutive Finlay Bawn sharped his claymore deliberately upon a stone–the soldiers bared my neck–and I was ordered to lay it flat upon the stump of a tree that they had selected as a convenient block. 'Captain,' says I, 'it is a shame for you to kill your prisoner whom you took fighting in the field for what he supposed to be the right; you are doing the same, and which of us is in the right let Heaven decide. But I'll tell you what it is, Captain, I'll bet you a guinea, and a pint of aquavitae into the bargain, that if none of you lend any assistance to that d—d shabby fellow, he shall not be able to cut off my head in an hour.' The Captain swore a great oath that no one should interfere, and, laughing aloud, he took my bet. My hands only were bound. I stretched myself upon the snow, and laid my neck flat upon the stump. Finlay threw off his jacket, and raised himself to the stroke. I believe the little wretch thought that he would make my head fly away I do not know how far! I however kept a sharp look out from the corner of my eye, and just as his great stroke was descending, I gave my head a sudden jerk to the one side towards his feet, on which he struck his sword several inches into the solid root of the birch tree. He tugged with all his might, but could in nowise extricate it. I lost not a moment; but plaiting my legs around his, I raised myself up against his knees and overthrew him with ease. I had now great need of exertion, for though I was three times as strong and heavy as he, yet my hands being fettered was greatly against me. It happened that, in trying to recover himself as he fell, he alighted with his face downward. I threw myself across his neck, and with my whole strength and weight squeezed his face and head down among the snow. The men and women shouted and clapped their hands until all the Grampian forests of Strathaven rang again. I found I now had him safe, for though he exerted himself with all his power, he could only drag himself backward through the snow, and as I kept my position firm, he was obliged to drag me along with him, so that, not being able to get any breath, his strength soon failed him, and in less than five minutes he could do no more than now and then move a limb, like a frog that is crushed beneath a waggon wheel.

"None of them, however, offered to release their countryman, until I, thinking that he was clean gone, arose from above him of my own accord. I was saluted by all the women, and many of them clasped me in their arms and kissed me; and the prettiest and best dressed one among them took off my bonds and threw them away, at which the Captain seemed nothing offended. I was then conducted back to the inn in triumph, while poor Finlay Bawn Beg Macalister Monro was left lying among the snow, and his sword sticking fast in the stump of the birch tree, and for any thing I know it is sticking there to this day.

"I was loaded with little presents, and treated with the best that the village could afford. The Captain paid his wager; but before we had done drinking our whisky I got as drunk as a boar, and I fear behaved in a very middling way. I had some indistinct remembrance afterwards of travelling over great hills of snow, and by the side of a frozen lake, and of fighting with some Highlanders, and being dreadfully mauled, but all was like a dream; and the next morning when I awoke I found myself lying in a dungeon vault of the Castle of Brae-Mar, on a little withered heath, and all over battered with blood, while every bone of my body was aching with pain. I had some terrible days with these confounded Farquharsons and Mackintoshes, but I got a round amends of them ere all the play was played; it is a long story, but well worth telling, and if you will have patience–"

"Andrew," said old Margaret, "the supper is waiting; when we have got that an' the prayers by, we'll then hae the story out at our ain leisure; an' Andrew, ye sal hae the best i' the house to your supper the night."

"Gudewife, ye're no just sic a fool as I thought you were," said Andrew; "that's twice i' your life ye hae spoken very good sense. I trow we'll e'en take your advice, for ye ken how the auld sang ends,

'Gin ye be for the cock to craw,
Gie him a neivfu' groats, dearie.'"

Highland Adventures

So wonderous wild the whole might seem,
The scenery of a fairy dream.–SCOTT.

SIR,–As every thing that relates to Loch Ketturin and its environs,
that modern classic ground, is become interesting to the public,
I have taken the resolution of sending you a short relation of a
tour which I made through that district near the latter end of March
last; in hopes you will not be displeased at meeting with some account of that romantic and favourite scene, even though by one ill
fitted for such a description, and little acquainted with the rules of
composition.

I went to Stirling in the mail-coach, and riding to Callander that
night, had the peculiar satisfaction of meeting with the old chieftain
of M'Nab, whose name had been familiar to me from my infancy;
and whom I had always been extremely anxious to see. From the
relations that I had heard of his youthful feats and eccentricities, I
expected to find in him a rough imperious old gentleman, who would
scarcely condescend to hold social intercourse with any man, far
less with an inconsiderable wanderer like me; but I found his manners simple and condescending, and his politeness without any affectation. His inexhaustible store of Highland anecdotes, and his
manner of telling them, are extremely amusing. Take him all in all;
his form, manner, and character; and to these add the respect that is
paid to him in the two villages, where he chiefly resides, he is certainly the finest model of an old Highland feudal baron that will
ever again be seen in Scotland. His character evinces a high degree
of obliging condescension, and haughty impatience of control, of the
gentleness of the lamb and the boldness of the lion.

I took the road up Strathgartney on foot, intending to keep on the
south side of the river, until I reached the old bridge a little below
Loch Venachar; but observing, from the road, an artificial mound,
on the level plain between the two rivers, and a small burial ground
enclosed on the top of it, I could not resist the impulse to stem the
water, though rough and deep, for the purpose of viewing it; not
doubting but that it was the tomb of Roderick Dhu. I was rather
disappointed on finding the names of other people recorded on
the tomb; but as it was so nigh to the place of rencounter between
Fitz-James and Roderick, and knowing that our old heroes were
always buried on the fields where they fought, I hoped that the tomb

would be first erected to him, and these other people buried in it afterwards.

I cannot help remarking here, that I think the greatest fault attached to the delightful poem of the *Lady of the Lake*, is, its containing no one fact, on which the mind of the enraptured peruser can rest as the basis of a principle so inherent in the human mind, as is the desire of affixing the stamp of reality on such incidents as interest us. The soul of man thirsts naturally and ardently for truth; and the author that ceases to deceive us with the appearance of it, ceases in a proportional degree to interest our feelings in behalf of the characters which he describes, or the fortunes of the individuals to which these characters are attached. The stories contained in Mr Scott's other poems, are all fairly without the bounds of probability; yet as they relate to some facts of which we are certain, and there being no proof that the most of the events are not founded on facts, which the bard has been pleased to embellish in his own fanciful and peculiar manner, they have the same pleasing effect upon the mind that is produced by an authentic narrative. But in this poem he never once leaves the enchanting field of probability, yet the mind is forced reluctantly to acknowledge, that it has been pursuing an illusion, and interesting itself in a professed fiction. The *possibility* is not even left of attaching the idea of truth to one event, which might have served as a pivot on which the rest would have turned; with which we would gladly have associated every other circumstance, and acquiesced with delight in the delicious deception. I admire the easy and simple majesty of that sweet tale as much as any person can possibly do; but I have never read it without regretting, that it had not been founded on a fact, though ever so trivial; and though my taste may be particular in this matter, I felt the effect rather distressing to reflection on viewing every scene of action referred to in the poem, which causes me to mention it in this place.

The whole of the scenery around Callander and Strathgartney is interesting, and to the man who has traversed the flat extent of the eastern counties of Britain, where the verge of the horizon is always resting on something level with or below his eye, the frowning brows of Ben-Ledi, (the hill of God,) with the broken outline of the mountains, both to the east and the westward, have a peculiarly pleasing effect. Still as you advance, the scenery improves, and in the vicinity of the bridge of Turk, it is highly picturesque, and yields little in variety to the celebrated Trossacks. From the top of Lanrick Mead, the muster place of the Clan-Alpine, which is a small detached hill at the junction of the water of Glen-Finlas with Loch Venachar, the general effect of the view is more noble and better contrasted, than from any other spot I alighted upon in the Strath.

I had here a conversation of considerable length with an old crusty Highlander, with whose remarks I was highly amused. He asked me frankly where I came from? And what my business was in that country? And on my informing him, that I was going to take a view of the Trossacks, he said that I was right to do so, else I would not be in the fashion, but it was a sign I was too idle, and had very little to do at home; but that a Mr Scott had put all the people mad by printing a *lying poem* about a man that never existed,–"What the d— was to be seen about the Trossacks more than in an hundred other places? A few rocks and bushes, nothing else." He gave me the outlines of the story of the Lady of the Lake, with great exactness, and added several improvements of his own. I asked him if there was any truth in it at all; or if it was wholly a fiction? He said, there was once indeed a man who sculked and defended himself in and about Loch-Ketturin; that an old Gaelic song related almost the same story, but that Mr Scott had been quite misled with regard to the names– he was mistaken about them altogether;–he translated some parts of the song into English, which were not much illustrative of any story: He, however, persisted in asserting that the stories were fundamentally the same.

He told me further, that Mr Burrel intended to build a bower in the lonely Isle of Loch-Ketturin, in which he meant to place the prettiest girl that could be found in Edinburgh, during the summer months, to personate *the Lady of the Lake*;–that she was to be splendidly dressed in the Highland Tartans, and ferry the company over to the island;–that Robert Maclean, a weaver at the bridge of Turk, was to be the goblin of Correi-Uriskin, and had already procured the skin of a monstrous shaggy black goat, which was to form a principal part of his dress while in that capacity;–that in fact interest and honour both combined to induce Maclean to turn a goblin this very summer; for in a conversation which he had with two ladies, high in rank, last year, he informed them, with great seriousness, that the goblin actually haunted the den occasionally to this day, at stated periods, and if they were there on such a day, at such an hour, he would forfeit his ears if they did not see him;–they promised to him that they would come, and reward him with a large sum of money if he fulfilled his engagement;–that of course Robert was holding himself in readiness to appear, in case this only surviving brownie, whom they suppose to have been once the king of the whole tribe, should neglect to pay his periodical visit to that lonely seat of his ancient regal court.

After these playful anecdotes, the reader will be a little astonished at hearing, that this man actually believed in the tale of the goblin; and that he had visited Correi-Uriskin, not many years ago, at his usual term; in confirmation of which he related the following story.

"A certain man, who was once the *best shot* in the glen, who is still alive, but whose name I have forgot, went out early one day in winter to shoot wild deer on the ledges of Ben-Venue; and, on the skirts of the hill, near by the den of the ghost, he met with an old man, whose face was wrinkled, his eyes red, and his beard as white as snow, leaning and trembling over a staff—he begged of the lad, whom we shall denominate Duncan, to give him something to eat. Duncan said he had brought very little for himself, but he would share it with him, and gave him some cakes and cheese. The old stranger accepted of the boon with thankfulness, and assured the hunter that he should not have cause to rue what he had done. Immediately after this, Duncan started a fine stag, fired at him, and wounded him, as he thought, mortally. The stag halted exceedingly; yet notwithstanding every exertion on the part of his pursuer, he always eluded his grasp, though the latter was for the most part quite hard upon him. He loaded and fired nine successive times, without being able to make any farther impression upon the stag. He grew quite fatigued—the sun went down—the winter day was drawing fast to a close;—his prey was neither nearer nor more distant than he was in the morning, though he had followed him many a weary mile;—he stopped to load his gun once more with the last shot that he had remaining, when he beheld the stag fall down quite exhausted;—he hasted up to him, and, wonderful to relate! instead of a stag, he found the identical old man lying, whose necessity he had relieved in the morning!—he stood up, and in a menacing mien and voice, addressed him as follows.

"Return, return, Duncan, you have just come far enough; if you come one step further, you shall never return!—mark what I say!—if it had not been for your kindness and beneficence this morning, you should never have seen your friends and family again; but go home, and let the poor remains of my exhausted herd rest in peace; I have but seven now left me in all my wild domain, but these shall never bleed beneath the hand of mortal man." Duncan went home in fear and trembling, and, fond as he was of hunting, has never since that day taken a gun in his hand.

About one o'clock I reached Mr Stuart the guide's house, the name of which I never can either pronounce or spell, and was informed by his mother that he was not at home. I was not in the least sorry on that account, for I wished to lose myself in the Trossacks alone; to have no interruption in my contemplations; but to converse only with nature, please myself with wondering at her wildest picture, and wonder why I was pleased.

After having tasted plentifully of old Mrs Stuart's Highland cheer, I set out with a heart bounding with joy, to put my scheme into execution. I traced every ravin and labyrinth that winded around the rocky pyramids; climbed every insulated mass, and thunder-splintered pinnacle, fantastic as the cones of the gathering thunder-cloud, and huge as the ancient pile that was reared on the valley of Shinar. Mr Scott has superseded the possibility of evermore pleasing, by a second description of the Trossacks, but in so doing he has certainly added to the pleasure arising from a view of them. Whoever goes to survey the Trossacks, let him have the 11th, 12th, and 13th divisions of the first canto of the *Lady of the Lake* in his heart; a little Highland whisky in his head; and then he shall see the most wonderful scene that nature ever produced. If he goes without any of these necessary ingredients, without one verse of poetry in his mind, and "without a drappie in his noodle;" he may as well stay at home; he will see little that will either astonish or delight him, or if it even do the one, will fail of accomplishing the other. The fancy must be aroused, and the imagination and spirits exhilarated, in order that he may enjoy these romantic scenes and groves of wonder with the proper zest. This is no chimera, Sir; I can attest its truth from experience. I once went with a friend to view the Craig of Glen-Whargen in Nithsdale—it was late before we reached it; we were hungry and wearied, having fished all day; it was no rock at all; the Cat-Craig at the back of our house was much more striking;—it was a mere trifle;—we sat down by a well at its base—dined on such provisions as we had,—and, by repeated applications to a bottle full of whisky, emptied it clean out. The rock continued to improve; we drank out of the bottle alternately; and in so doing were obliged to hold up our faces towards the rock of Glen-Whargen; it was so grand and sublime, that it was not without an effort we could ever bring our heads back to their natural position. Still as the whisky diminished the rock of Glen-Whargen increased in size and magnificence; and by the time the bottle was empty, we were fixed to the spot in amazement at that stupendous pile; and both of us agreed that it was such a rock as never was looked upon by man.

The most delightful view of the Trossacks is that which is first seen, I mean the one from the highest part of the road leading from the corner of Loch-Achray to the mouth of the pass; and the most wonderful is that from a rock about mid-way between the pass and Beinnan, where the whole extent of the Trossacks are seen rising behind one another, like the billows of a stormy ocean.

I went next to the top of a cliff, north of the pass, that I might enjoy a view of the setting sun on Loch-Ketturin.–The evening was calm and serene.–There was not the slightest breeze playing on the surface of the water, nor the smallest speck of vapour floating in the firmament over it. It was indeed a delightful scene, and I would have sent you an excellent description of it, had not Mr Scott previously done it for me. But what astonished and delighted me most of all, was the appearance of Roderick Dhu's barge far west on the lake,

> "Which bearing downwards from Glengyle,
> "Steer'd full upon the lonely isle."

She however weathered it, and bore onward to the base of my castle. As the bark approached, I heard a great number of voices from it joining in a Gaelic song, the effect of which on the woods and rocks was truly admirable. I was so transported with the singular coincidence, that I waved my hat and shouted aloud, "Roderick Vich Alpine Dhu, ho eiro," while all the crew waved their bonnets and shouted in return. This chief of the mountains was no other than Mr Stuart, with a boatful of the people of Strathgartney, whom he had that day raised to assist him in clearing away some wood west on the banks of the lake. With him I spent the evening, and we were as happy as Highland cheer and Highland whisky could make us.

> One burnish'd sheet of living gold,
> Loch Katrine lay beneath him roll'd;
> In all her length, far winding lay,
> With promontory, creek, and bay,
> And islands that, empurpled bright,
> Floated amid the livelier light;
> And mountains, that, like giants stand,
> To centinel enchanted land.
>
>   SCOTT

He entertained me with stories of ancient superstition, and anecdotes of sundry great persons who had visited that scene the preceding summer, with their remarks. Of the observations made by the hereditary Prince of Orange, Mrs Stuart seemed to have treasured up every sentence in her memory; his title had impressed her mind deeply with a sense of his importance. Mr Stuart and I got one jug of toddy after another, until we grew such intimate friends, that we could not be satisfied without testifying it by shaking hands every glass, even though at the risk of spilling a part of our beverage. Next morning I arose very early, and hasted to my favourite eminence, which is nearly straight to the west of Mr Stuart's house, from whence I had a delightful prospect of the sun rising on the lake, which was so calm, that there was not even a dimple on its whole surface. The huge bristled bulk of Ben-Venue, whose image, when reflected in the lake, appeared still much larger, while its inverted snowy peak, which seemed as if piercing the centre of the world, had altogether an effect truly grand and totally indescribable.

There was not a breath of wind whispering among the trees, for of green leaves none had yet appeared save those of the holly and woodbine, but the young downy buds of the hazel were hanging in great abundance; and as my impatience had not suffered me to wait the return of the summer months, I was obliged to supply the foliage in idea.

One blackbird only had found his way to the Trossacks at that early though delightful season, who seemed to have chosen for his choir a cluster of tall birches up nigh to the base of Beinan, from which, both morn and even, he poured his wild melody through the woods and spires around him. A number of small birds were, however, trilling their artless notes, and in order to make up the deficiency as well as possible, robin redbreast placed himself upon the very point of the uppermost twig of the tree, immediately over me;– made himself as big a bird as he possibly could, and sung amazingly sweet; and on shifting my situation, he also shifted his, and practised upon another tree still nearer to me.

After breakfast, Mr Stuart again accompanied me through the Trossacks, by the Pass, the entrance into which is amazingly picturesque. In the bosom of a rock, south of the Pass, he told me there was a cave, where an outlaw named Fletcher resided many years; but though tradition was so particular with regard to its situation, as to describe minutely the different views which it commanded, he said he had entirely lost the entrance to it; though he had searched for it with the utmost care.

The Gaelic name *Trossacks*, he said, signified the rough or shaggy place, which is certainly a term very appropriate. Indeed, the Gaelic names of places are in general so highly descriptive of their various appearances and situations, that, if you tell a Highlander the name of a place, he will almost invariably tell you what it is like; that pass in the Trossacks, however, in former ages, had a designation much more terrible, as the pass in those days would certainly itself appear when the wood was all old. It seems to have been called *the Gate of Hell*; for, Mr Stuart assured me that the name Loch Ketturin literally signified *the Loch of the Gate of Hell*. Correi Uriskin signifies *the Brownie's Clough*; but the description given of the spirit that once inhabited it by the Highlanders, must remind every one of the satyrs of old. The only isle of Loch Ketturin is there called *the Rough Island*. It is a likely place for a last retreat, but there is no appearance of any bower or building of any kind ever having been upon it, and we may safely conclude there never has been any, for the foundation being so solid, the remains of the smallest cot would still have continued visible, if stones had at all been used in the structure. The trees are again grown to a considerable height, and the vacant places are all planted.

The day was uncommonly serene, and even warm; and as we sailed up Loch Ketturin, the wild grandeur of the scenery as reflected in the still azure lake, greatly delighted me. Our track on the surface of the water had the appearance of an immense gazoon, of which our boat formed the extreme point; and the gentle swell, rolling from her prow, broke the shadows of the mountains into a thousand fantastic shapes.

About mid-way up the Lake I went on shore, and after taking leave of Mr Stuart, ascended the mountains to the northward, and in about an hour and a half I reached the top of that range which separates the Glen of Loch Ketturin from the braes of Balquhidder. From this height, as the view became more general the effect of any one place was nearly effaced. The most striking image in the landscape, was the huge cloven mountain of Ben-More that towered to the firmament immediately over against me, and high as I knew myself then to be by experience, having climbed incessantly for three half hours, I perceived with astonishment that it was nearly as high again. It was completely covered with prodigious masses of snow, and a little dusky cloud hovered above its top, the only one then to be seen. This seemed to be attracted to it by a sort of magnetic power; for it first pointed towards it at a distance, then took a slender hold of its head by which it hung some time over it, as if keeping its hold with difficulty, and finally settled upon its head in the most striking mural form that can be conceived. The mountain so high, so pyramidal, and so white, with the dark gray crown upon its head, placed there as it were by the hand of Heaven, and descending from the skies in my view, formed, on the whole, such a picture of sublimity as I never before looked upon; and I could not help saying to myself, "robed in the most incontestable insignia of royalty, there stands the king of the Grampians." As the wreathes of snow on the dark sides of the hills were extremely hard, it was not without difficulty that I descended into the valley of Balquhidder. I spent the remainder of that day and the next morning in taking a view of the glen, and slept at a farmer's house.

The braes of Balquhidder form an extent of rich succulent pasture, and are in general green to the very tops. It has the appearance of being a fine pasturing district; but the sheep are said to be subject to many diseases, although they feed exceedingly well. The valley is of considerable extent, and almost a dead level; in consequence of which, it is subjected to frequent inundations by the swelling back of the lakes; for in violent rains and thaws, the torrents pour from the mountains so rapidly, and in such abundance, and the declivity of the valley being so inconsiderable, it becomes as one continued lake. There are two extensive and fine fishing lochs in it, Loch Doine and Loch Voil, signifying the deep Loch, and the shallow Loch. This glen is the northern limits of the country which Mr Scott gives to the Clan-Alpin, and in bringing the fiery cross back from it he commits a simple geographical mistake, by making it come again, "down Strath-Gartney's valley broad," the very track which my kinsman Malise, and young Angus had before traversed.

About an hour before noon I took leave of my hospitable entertainers, and without informing any one of my designs for fear of opposition, I again ascended the mountains to the northward, resolved, if possible, to reach the top of Ben-More. It being in the heat of the day, which was extremely fine, and the sun having softened the snow somewhat, I reached its top without much difficulty, but not without great fatigue; if it had not been for some Highland cakes, cheese, and whisky, which I was easily persuaded to take along with me, I had certainly failed altogether. I however reached the summit of the hill, and of my wishes for the present, where the first thing I did was to drink his Majesty's health, at the same time declaring aloud, as there was no human being to hear me, that I would by no means change situations with him, for that his station in life was extremely low in comparison with that I now occupied.

I believe it is generally allowed, that the depression or elevation of a man's mind is in a great measure conformable to the disposition of his bodily frame; if this holds good in all cases, it is evident that nothing can contribute so much to the elevation of his sentiments, as placing him on the top of a very high hill. I think this might be

demonstratively proved, for, if we consider that the body is the seat
or throne of the mind; that while in this state of existence they cannot subsist asunder; of course, where the body is there must the
mind be also; will any man then venture to deny that mind to be
elevated which is 4000 feet above the level of the sea.

This is only a specimen of Forum reasoning, no one must mind it,
but try if he can for a moment conceive the sublimity of my situation. Conceive a self-important bard sitting in a state of the highest
exultation, on the uppermost pinnacle of the lofty and majestic Ben-
More, whose temples he had, the evening before, seen so solemnly
encircled with the emblems of royalty–above huge masses of eternal snow; above the habitations of the fox and the eagle–above the
cares (and I wish he could say the vanities) of this world. Looking
on the western ocean and isles, the whole range of the Grampian
hills, those stupendous pyramids of nature, and all the south of Scotland spread around him as on a map; while the finest lakes of the
country were lying stretched at rest in their respective vallies, almost immediately below his feet.

The scene was indeed such a one as no imagination can paint
with justice; and what it wanted in softness and verdure, on account
of the early season of the year, it gained in grandeur, by the pure
unsullied robes of snow that enveloped all the mountains from a
certain height upwards.

This was certainly a good criterion for judging of the comparative
heights of these hills, for none of that was new fallen snow, but that
which had been amassed during the winter, and had stood the test of
several regular thaws, one of them the greatest that had been witnessed in that country during the present age; yet, above a certain
height it had taken no visible effect, farther than stiffening the snow
on the return of frost. Ben-Lawers, that rises from the north shore of
Loch Tay, is by all geographers accounted the highest hill in that
bounds; but this is not at all the idea of the inhabitants of the country, whose opinion I account of some weight. They are uniformly of
opinion that Ben-More is the highest, Ben-Leo, that rises between
Strath-fillan and Glen-Orchey, the second, and Ben-Lawers, only
the third. I dare not affirm that this is actually the case, but appearances were at this time rather in favour of the theory; perhaps the
people around the base of the latter may think differently.

I cannot help mentioning here a circumstance, of the truth of which
I have long been convinced: it is, that the highest mountains in Scotland, without exception, are some that are situated in the eastern
division of the Grampian range, and which, as far as I know, no

geographer or tourist has ever mentioned. I do not know the particular names which distinguish each of them, but they rise between the sources of the Dee, the Gairn, the Avin, and Glen-More. Cairn-Gorum is always allowed to be next to Ben-Nevis in height; but there are some to the south-west of it that appear to be much higher, the altitudes of which have never been taken;* I have crossed these mountains both at mid-summer and in April; a great extent of country in that quarter is a complete desert, where no human habitation is to be seen, nor human voice heard for three quarters of the year. Glen-Avin, which belongs to the Duke of Gordon, is nearly twenty miles in length, yet, I dare say, it is not known to above ten persons alive. It is a scene of the most gloomy grandeur, and well calculated to inspire notions of ideal beings, of terror and superstition, which are ascribed by the Highlander to its lonely dells. In its bottom is a fine lake at least ten miles in length, the surface of which is on an elevation of 1700 feet above the level of the sea; yet the mountains around it appear as high from their bases as any other in Scotland; though this is impossible, yet I conceive some of these mountains to be the highest in the kingdom.

I remained in this exalted station as long as the chillness of the atmosphere of that region would suffer me, and I flattered myself that I was in reality as much delighted with the country as any of those could be to whom it belonged; and as a proof of my supposition, concluded that none of them would have climbed Ben-More at such a season to get a view of it. I then began, not without considerable trepidation, to descend, keeping the south-east corner of the hill, the north side being all like a smooth sheet of ice. I soon discovered that the task of getting down from the hill was likely to be a much more arduous one than that of ascending it, for I was obliged to take such short steps, and before I could take them at all, had often to dig holes with my staff wherein to set my feet; so that after toiling an hour, I saw that I had not proceeded a quarter of a mile, I however felt no cold by that time; on the contrary, I never was warmer in my life. At length the steepest part of the hill seemed to be got over; all was white and smooth before me, and I determined to slide down the surface of the snow on my feet, judging myself to be exceedingly adroit in such achievements. The glaring whiteness had, however, deceived me. The hill turned out to be much more steep than I had conceived it to be. For some time I glided on, swiftly

---

* Since the writing of this, the height of these mountains have been measured by Dr Skene, and the highest, Ben-Macdui, found to be 15 feet lower than Ben-Nevis.

indeed, but with great ease; but at length I began to fly with such velocity, that my eyes fell a watering, and I entirely lost sight of my course. In my hurry, not knowing well what to do, I made a sudden lean backward on my staff; in doing which, my feet being posting on at such a rate, went faster than I could follow them, I lost my equilibrium, fell on my back, and darted down the side of Ben-More,

> "As ever ye saw the rain down fa',
> Or yet the arrow gae frae the bow."

My staff, of which I lost the hold when I fell, quite outrun me; my clean shirt, which was tied neatly up in a red handkerchief, came hopping down the hill, sometimes behind and sometimes before me, but my hat took a direction quite different. I struck the snow desperately with my heels, in hopes to stop my career, but all was to no purpose, until I came to a flat shelving part of the hill, where I lay still at once, without being a farthing the worse. The first thing that I did was to raise my eyes towards the top of Ben-More, and was astonished at the distance I had come. As nearly as I could calculate, I had travelled post in that manner upwards of a mile in little more than a quarter of a minute. I indulged in a hearty laugh at my manner of journeying; with some difficulty picked up my scattered travelling accoutrements, my staff, my hat, and my clean shirt tied neatly up in a red handkerchief; and, proceeding on my way, reached Bovain in Glen-Dochart, the house of Robert M'Nab, Esq. about eleven o'clock at night.

I spent two weeks in that house and its neighbourhood, but never mentioned my adventures on Ben-More to any one for fear of being laughed at. I viewed all the varied scenery of Broadalbine, traced all its rivers to their sources, and climbed all the mountains that commanded the most extensive or interesting views of the country, and at length returned to the south by the way of Loch-Earn-head and the pass of Lenny. I would have sent you descriptions of these districts through which I travelled, but I am afraid that I have already drawn out this letter to a ridiculous length.

Halbert of Lyne

So thou'lt not read my Tales, thou say'st, Horatio,
"Because, forsooth, such characters as those
That I have chosen should ne'er be defined,
For when they are,—where's the epitome,
The moral or conclusion? What may man   5
Profit or learn by studying such as these?"

  Wo worth thy shallow, thy insidious wit,
Thy surface-skimming lore, Horatio!
Thou'rt a mere title-page philosopher;
A thing of froth and vapour, formed of all   10
The unsubstantialities of nature,
Nourished by concourse of the elements;
A man of woman born, of woman bred,
Of woman's mind, frame, fashion, and discourse,
A male blue-stocking!—Out upon thee, girl!   15
Nay, do not fume nor wince; for, on my soul,
Let but thy barber smooth that whiskered cheek,
With sterile but well-nourished crop besprent,
Scythe thy mustachio, and by this true hand,
I'll hire thee for a nurse, Horatio.   20

  Dost thou not know, presuming as thou art,
That purest gold in smallest veins is found,
And with most rubbish mixed, which thou must sift,
And sorely dig for?—Treasures of the deep,
The mine, the vale, the mountain—Heaven itself,   25
Man needs must toil for, else he cannot win.
And wilt thou still be fashion's minion,
Reading alone what fashion warrants thee,
The calendar of women?—Wilt thou never
Learn for thyself to judge, and turn thine eye   30
Into that page of life, the human soul,
With all its rays, shades, and dependencies,
For ever varied, and for ever new?

  O if thou dost, be this thy axiom,
Not to despise the slightest, most minute   35

Of all its shades and utterings, if they flow
Warm from the heart but cherish such in thine;
The day may come thou may'st think otherwise
Than thou dost now.—Ah, hast thou never seen,
The kindly flush and genial glow of spring,   40
And summer's flower nipt by the biting blast
Of chill unhealthful gale?—Yes, oft thou hast;
And could'st thou see as well into this breast,
And note the toil and warfare there maintained
By the fond weary sojourner within,   45
That pours this lay, its only anodyne!
Thou could'st not chuse but listen,—it is not
Thy nature to despise my rural lay.

   I would be friends with thee, Horatio,
For I have weaknesses, and foibles too,   50
Worse than thine own, and heavier far to bear!
Then say not thou, by desk or counter placed,
Or haply on the gilded sofa set,
By board of drawing-room, while some fair dame
Stretches her lily hand, with careless mien,   55
To seize my little book—O say not thou,
"This is our friend again; poor man! he is
For ever publishing, and still the same,
The fairy's raide, the witch's embassy,
The spirit's voice, the mountain and the mist."   60
Spare the injurious speech—dost thou not see
That beauteous smirk, and that half-lifted eye,
How they bespeak the comely vacancy,
The void of soul within?—Yet that same dame
Leads and misleads one half of all the town.   65
Dost thou not know, Horatio, that one word,
The first word critical that is pronounced
On any trembling author's valued work,
Nay the first syllable, is like a spark
Set to the mountain, that will flame and spread   70
Even when the breezes rest; working its way,
And none can certify where it may end?
Beware then how thou kindlest such a flame,
To sear a soul and genius in the bloom!

Far rather say—for 'tis as easy said,   75
And haply nigher truth—"Madam, I have
Perused that work, and needs must own to you,
I deemed my time well spent—read it throughout,
Thou wilt not rue it."—This were friendlier far,
And more becoming thee;—but it is not   80
Thy cherished principle, for thou wilt talk
Of egotism, and drawing from one's self,
Chatter of mind, and nerve, and the effect
Of constitution, till the matrons yawn,
And green girls stare at thee—for shame, Horatio;   85

Of "Egotism and drawing from one's self!"
Does this befit thee?—I have heard thee talk
Three hours and thirty minutes by the clock
Of old Saint Giles, and ever of thyself!
Thyself and thine.—Yet thou wilt carp at me,   90
And say that I draw only from myself!
Well, be it so; he who draws otherwise
Than from his feelings never shall draw true.
I know my faults, Horatio, and can laugh
At them and thee, as thou shalt see anon.   95
Read thou the tale before thee—if it please
Not thee I care not; but I pledge my word
My next shall please thee worse—I have a mark
Will better suit,—for it shall be of thee.

There was a time, Horatio—but 'tis gone,   100
Would that we saw't again—when every hind
Of Scotland's southern dales tilled his own field;
When master, dame, and maid, servant and son,
At the same board eat of the same plain meal.
The health and happiness of that repast   105
Made every meal a feast.—In these good days
Of might and hardihood, there lived a man,
A wealthy, worthy, and right honest hind,
Hight John of Manor.—He had ewes and lambs,
Kids and he-goats, more than he well could number,   110
Besides good breeding mares and playful colts,
Heifers and lazy bullocks, many a one.
But John had that, which better fits the song
Of rhyming bard and thee, Horatio,

Than kid or lamb, colt or unwieldy ox;   115
He had five daughters, all of them as fair
As roses in their prime—beshrew that heart
That would not leap and warm at such a sight
As John of Manor's daughters!—At that time
There lived in Lyne a shrewd discerning dame,   120
Who had an only son, Halbert his name.

One day she drew her chair close to the light,
For, ah! her seam was fine, and it was white
As the pure snow, while by her side reclined
Her darling son, just resting from his work.   125
His ruddy cheek was leant upon his hand,
His eyes fixed on the wall, in careless wise,
And all the while he was full earnestly
Whistling a tune, as if it did import
Greatly to him the masterly performance.   130

"Thou never dost remark," said the good dame,
And as she spoke she turned her prying eye
Right o'er the spectacles to look at Hab;
The eyes of glass were still upon the seam,
But the true eye peeped over them—it was   135
A mother's eye! aye fraught with kind concern
When turned on her own offspring!—"Look thou here,
Thou careless thing—thou never dost remark,
What beauteous linen I have bought this year
For my good son—but trow me, it has cost   140
Thy mother a round sum—yet though it has,
I have a meaning in't, which bodes thee well.—
List me, my son. What whillilu is that,
Thou keep'st a trilling at?"—Halbert went on,
Straight with his tune, there was a fall in it   145
He could not lose.—"List what I say, my son;
I'm wearing old and frail, and by the course
Of nature soon must leave thee—we have lived
Full happily and well, but slow decay
Steals on with silent foot, and we must part."   150

"Hush, hush," said Halbert, "talk not of that theme
For many years to come. I'd rather part
With all I have on earth than my dear mother."

She took her spectacles, and wiped them clean,
For a warm tear had dimm'd her aged eye,   155
Then went she on with theme she dearly loved,
Lauding her filial son—who by that time
Had made recovery of his favourite air
On a sweet minor key, and pour'd it forth,
Soft and delightful as a flageolet.   160
"When I have sew'd this sleeve my work is done,
And thou shalt go a-wooing in this shirt;
And, trust me, thou shalt not its marrow meet
In all the lands of Lyne, March, and Montgomery,
So fine, and yet so fair."—Halbert went on   165
Sheer with his tune—it was a lay of love,
An old and plaintive thing, and strangely was
Blent with some nameless feelings of delight,
Which Halbert keenly felt, but little knew
How to account for.—"List to me, my son: 170
Fain would I see thee settled rationally
In life as thee becomes, and fairly join'd
To virtuous daughter of an honest man.
My old acquaintance, John of Manor, has
Five winsome daughters—there is not in all   175
The bounds of Scotland five such lovely maids
As John of Manor's daughters—and he is
A man of wealth, which these fair maids must heir,
For son he hath not.—Would you go, my son,
And chuse a wife from Manor, it would glad   180
The heart of your old mother.—There is Ann,
The eldest born, who likely wilt share most
Of his wide wealth—O such a wife, my son,
As Ann of Manor, would become your house,
Your table head, your right hand at the church,   185
And when the cold long nights of winter come

*   *   *   *

*   *   *   * §

This last description Halbert could not stand;
He gave his tune quite up, which of itself
Long ere that time had nearly died away;
He sigh'd, gave a short yawn, and rising up,   190

§ Some lines wanting here.

Look'd at the linen, praised its snowy hue
And beauteous texture—some inquiry made
What time it would be ready for the wear,
Then sat he down again to hear some more
Of lovely Ann of Manor:—"Ah! my son,   195
She is not one of the light-headed herd,
These gew-gaw, giddy-paced, green-sickly girls,
That mind nought but their gaudery and their glee;
Poor thriftless, shiftless, syrup-lipped shreds
That take men in to ruin.—No, she is   200
A sound man's child, an honest woman born,
And bred up in the paths of decency
And fear of Heaven—and then she is so fair,
So fresh and lovely!—and as sweet, my son,
As field of new-won hay."—Halbert arose,   205
Drew a long breath, stretch'd up his boardly frame
In guise of anxious solicitude,
Look'd at the shirt again, and went away.

That day he thought of Ann, he sung of Ann,
He whistled the sweet air of *Bonny Ann*   210
Along the hay-field, and when came the night,
He lay and dream'd of lovely Ann of Manor.

Next morning Halbert found when he awoke
A fair new shirt, white as the lily's breast,
Well air'd and plaited with neat careful hand,   215
At his bed-head; proudly he put it on,
And in his heart he blest the kindred love
That had prepared it so while others slept.

Hab went away with ardent anxious breast
Across the moor to Manor—as he went,   220
He coned his deep-laid schemes of policy.
I am resolved, said Halbert to himself,
If these fair maidens please me, that I will
Be frank and generous—I'll not sue for dower,
For flock or herd, gelding, or sullen ox.   225
I'll win their favour well, and then I'll trust
To fortune for the rest—With the good-man
I'll talk of farming and the service work;
Of the improven breeds of sheep and wool;

Of crops and servants, and the foolish risk   230
Of selling aught on credit, till he say
When I walk out, "He's a shrewd fellow Hab,
One who knows more than many thrice his age;
Wife, give us of the best the house affords
At dinner-time—you, wenches, get you gone,   235
Put your new kirtles on, and make you clean;
Hab is the son of an old worthy friend,
I love him for his parents' sake as well
As for his own—He's a shrewd fellow Hab!"

   "Then, when a chance occurs, I'll talk apart   240
With the old dame of prudence and of thrift,
The vices and the follies of the age;
I'll talk of sins, of sermons, and of faith,
Of Boston, and Ralph Erskine, and renounce
The slightest atom of dependency   245
Upon my own good works.—"Ah!" she will say,
"He is a sensible good Christian lad
That Halbert!—one who minds the thing that's good!"
Then will she look in her loved daughter's face
With wistful eye, and with a sigh exclaim,   250
"What pity should he throw himself away
On some light worthless jilflirt!—Ah! he is
A sensible good Christian lad that Halbert!"

   "But then the maid, how shall I deal with her?
There lies the difficulty, should they not   255
Once leave us by ourselves—I never can
Ask her in public with as formal face
As I would buy a heifer or a mare.
No, by ourselves we needs must be; and then
O how I'll press, teaze, flatter, and caress her!   260
I'll clasp her waist, and kiss her comely cheek,
Steal by degrees to her soft moisten'd lip—
The sharp reproof will quickly grow more mild
Until it melt away—then will I sigh,
And say that it was cruel in th' extreme   265
To grant so sweet a kiss—for how can man
That has enjoy'd it ever more be happy,
Or live without the owner of such kiss!

Then she'll say to herself as I do now
"I like that Hab—he hath some spirit Hab."   270

  By this time Hab had so wound up his thoughts
With visions of delight, that he had quitted
His common pace, and ran across the moor
Without perceiving it, while shepherds stood
And gazed afar with wonder—dreading sore   275
That Halbert was distraught, or something wrong
With the good folks of Lyne. He came at last
To the hall-door of Manor with a breast
Beating full hard, and little wist he then
What he should say.—Forth came the old goodman   280
With his white hosen and his broad blue bonnet;
Stout and well-framed he was, but in his eye
Lurk'd a discernment Halbert scarce could brook.

  After good-morrow, question, and reply,
With downcast look Hab thus his errand said: 285
"I'm come in search of a much-valued ewe
Which I have lost, and she, it seems, was seen
Coming this way—a beautiful young ewe,
One which I may not and I must not lose."
"What are her marks and whither did she come?"   290
"She came from Lyne." "Ah, do I see the son
Of my old valued friend? Welcome, good youth;
I saw not your lost sheep, but all my flock
I'll put before you; if you find her not,
Chuse one from mine and welcome; you may find   295
Some ewes as young, as beautiful, and good,
As any bred on Lyne."—Halbert look'd down,
Full sore abash'd, but made as fit reply
As he well could.—"My girls are out," said John,
"Milking the ewes, they will be here anon,   300
And they perchance may give you some account
Of your lost ewe. 'Tis hard that a young man
Should lose his ewe—meanwhile let us go in,
See the goodwife, and taste her morning cheer."

  Good ewe-milk whey, thick as the curdled breast   305
Of cauliflower, brose, butter, bread, and cheese,
Furnish'd the breakfast board of John of Manor.

Hard did he press his youthful guest to all,
Whose high resolves had faded into smoke.
He talked not of religion, nor the mode   310
Of farming to advantage, for old John
Failed not at every interval to hint,
With sly demeanour, something of his ewe.
"Who's that," said Halbert, "coming from the bught
With the five maids?"—"I know not," John replied;   315
"He seems a stranger,—some young man perchance
Seeking a ewe.—O these same ewes, my friend,
Are a precarious stock,—they go astray,
And will not stay with one, do as he will."

    At length the maidens, decked all neat and clean,   320
Entered the little parlour one by one.
Ann was not tall, but lively and discreet,
And comely as a cherub,—Halbert weened
No woman ever born so beautiful
As Ann of Manor.—But when entered Jane,   325
Of fair delicious form, round pouting lips,
Cheeks like the damask rose, and liquid eye
That spoke unutterable things, her locks,
Fair as the morning, waving round her brow
Like light clouds curling o'er the rising sun,   330
Or, if you please, the mist-wreaths pale, Horatio.
Soon Halbert saw that all the world beside
Could never once compare with beauteous Jane.
Then came the third, young Douglas, with an eye
Dark and majestic as the eagle's, when   335
She looks down from the cliff.—Her form was tall,
Slender, and elegant, while from her tongue
Flowed such a spirit of melodious breath,
That thrilled the hearer,—not alone they seemed
The language of the soul, her tones and words   340
Were very soul itself.—Halbert was fixed—
Confirmed in this, that never mortal man,
Nor angel, had beheld a female form,
A face, an eye, nor listened to a voice
Like that of lovely Douglas.—Mary came,   345
The modest, diffident, and blushing Mary.
The mild blue eye, the joy of innocence
Beaming through every smile!—O Halbert's heart

Was wholly overpowered; till Barbara came,
The youngest and the loveliest of them all.   350

   Halbert went home,—he went without his ewe,
And heart to boot,—that heart was lost for ever,
To whom he knew not! in the family
That heart had lingered, he wist not with whom.
Such grace, such purity of form and mind,   355
Appeared in all, Halbert was on the rack.
He took to bed, but sleep had flown from thence;
He thought of Ann, and sighed a prayer to Heaven;
Of young and blooming Barbara, and the smile
That shed a radiance o'er the maiden blush   360
Of gentle Mary; then a burning tear,
A tear of sympathy, crept o'er his cheek.
He thought of Jane, and turned him in his bed;
He thought of Douglas, and turned back again.

   Day follow'd day, and week came after week,   365
Years past away, and Halbert all the while
Was wooing hard at Manor—sometimes one,
Sometimes another, as blind chance decreed;
Each of them was so good, so beautiful,
So far surpassing all of womankind,   370
That time, nor chance, nor reason, e'er could frame
A choice determinate; till at the last
Old Manor, in a kind but earnest way,
Enquiry made what his intentions were
That thus he haunted his fair family.   375

   "Sooth, my good friend," said Halbert, "ne'er was man
On earth so hard beset—I love them all
With such a pure esteem and stainless love,
That though I well could give the preference
To any one, yet for my life and soul   380
There is not one of them I can reject.
I give the matter wholly up to you,
I know you wish me well, and all the maids
Alike to you are dear,—Whom shall I chuse?

   John set his bonnet in becoming mode,   385
That well betoken'd deep considerate thought;

One edge of it directed middle way
'Twixt the horizon and the cope of heaven,
And with the one hand in his bosom sheathed,
The other heaving slightly in the air   390
To humour what he said, he utter'd words
Which I desire you note—"My son," said he,
"I've one advice to give you, which through life
I rede you follow—when you make a choice
Of man or woman, beast, farm, fish, or fowl, 395
CHUSE EVER THAT WHICH HAS THE FEWEST FAULTS.
My girls have all their foibles and their faults—
Mary's are FEWEST AND LEAST DANGEROUS.
Take thou my Mary—if she prove to thee
As good a wife as she has ever been   400
A dutiful and loving child to me,
Thou never will repent it."—So it proved,
A happier pair ne'er travell'd through this vale
Of life together, than our Halbert
With his beloved Mary.—Peace to them, 405
And to their ashes!—and may every pair
Of happy lovers in their kindred dale
Cherish their memory, and be blest as they!

Now, dear Horatio, when thou makest choice
Of book, of friend, companion, or of wife, 410
Think of the sage advice of John of Manor;
CHUSE EVER THAT WHICH HAS THE FEWEST FAULTS,
AND THOSE LEAST DANGEROUS.—Take note of this:

All have their faults and foibles—all have too
The feelings that congenial minds will love; 415
And to each other genial minds will cling
Long as this world has being, and the shades
Of nature hold their endless variation.
I say no more, Horatio, but this word:
In time to come, when thronged variety 420
Of books, and men, and women, on thee crowd,
When choice distracts thee, or when spleen misleads,
Think of the sage advice of John of Manor.

The Long Pack

IN the year 1723, Colonel Ridley returned from India, with what, in those days, was accounted an immense fortune, and retired to a country seat on the banks of North Tyne in Northumberland. The house was rebuilt and furnished with every thing elegant and costly; and amongst others, a service of plate supposed to be worth £1000. He went to London annually with his family, during a few of the winter months, and at these times there were but few left at his country house. At the time we treat of, there were only three domestics remained there; a maid servant, whose name was Alice, kept the house, and there were besides, an old man and a boy, the one threshed the corn, and the other took care of some cattle, for the two ploughmen were boarded in houses of their own.

One afternoon as Alice was sitting spinning some yarn for a pair of stockings to herself, a pedlar entered the hall with a comical pack on his back. Alice had seen as long a pack, and as broad a pack; but a pack equally long, broad, and thick, she declared she never saw. It was about the middle of winter, when the days were short, and the nights cold, long, and wearisome. The pedlar was a handsome, well-dressed man, and very likely to be a very agreeable companion for such a maid as Alice, on such a night as that; yet Alice declared, that from the very first she did not like him greatly, and though he introduced himself with a little ribaldry, and a great deal of flattery interlarded, yet when he came to ask a night's lodging, he met with a peremptory refusal; he jested on the subject, said he believed that she was in the right, for that it would scarcely be safe to trust him under the same roof with such a sweet and beautiful creature—Alice was an old maid, and any thing but beautiful—he then took her on his knee, caressed and kissed her, but all would not do. "No, she would not consent to his staying there." "But are you really going to put me away to night?" "Yes." "Indeed, my dear girl, you must not be so unreasonable; I am come straight from Newcastle, where I have been purchasing a fresh stock of goods, which are so heavy, that I cannot travel far with them, and as the people around are all of the poorer sort, I will rather make you a present of the finest shawl in my pack before I go further." At the mentioning of the shawl, the picture of deliberation was pourtrayed in lively colours on Alice's face for a little; but her prudence overcame. "No, she was but a servant, and had orders to harbour no person about the house but such as came on business, nor these either, unless she was well acquainted with them." "What the worst can you, or your master, or any one else be, of suffering me to tarry until the morning?" "I entreat you do not insist, for here you cannot be." "But indeed, I am not able to carry my goods farther to-night." "Then you must leave them, or get a horse to carry them away." "Of all the sweet inflexible beings that ever were made, you certainly are the chief. But I cannot blame you, your resolution is just and right. Well, well, since no better may be, I must leave them, and go search for lodgings myself somewhere else, for, fatigued as I am, it is as much as my life is worth to endeavour carrying them further." Alice was rather taken at her word: she wanted nothing to do with his goods: the man was displeased at her, and might accuse her of stealing some of them; but it was an alternative she had proposed, and against which she could start no plausible objection; so she consented, though with much reluctance. "But the pack will be better out of your way," said he, "and safer, if you will be so kind as lock it by in some room or closet." She then led him into a low parlour, where he placed it carefully on two chairs, and went his way, wishing Alice a good night.

When old Alice and the pack were left together in the large house by themselves, she felt a kind of undefined terror come over her mind about it. "What can be in it," said she to herself, "that makes it so heavy?" Surely when the man carried it this length, he might have carried it farther too—It is a confoundedly queer pack; I'll go and look at it once again, and see what I think is in it; and suppose I should handle it all round, I may then perhaps have a good guess what is in it."

Alice went cautiously and fearfully into the parlour and opened a wall-press—she wanted nothing in the press, indeed she never looked into it, for her eyes were fixed on the pack, and the longer she looked at it, she liked it the worse; and as to handling it, she would not have touched it for all that it contained. She came again into the kitchen and conversed with herself. She thought of the man's earnestness to leave it—of its monstrous shape, and every circumstance connected with it—They were all mysterious, and she was convinced in her own mind, that there was something *uncanny* if not unearthly in the pack.

What surmises will not fear give rise to in the mind of a woman! She lighted a moulded candle, and went again into the parlour, closed the window shutters, and barred them; but before she came out, she set herself upright, held in her breath, and took another steady and scrutinizing look of the pack. God of mercy! She saw it moving, as visibly as she ever saw any thing in her life. Every hair on her head stood upright. Every inch of flesh on her body crept like a nest of pismires. She hasted into the kitchen as fast as she could, for her knees bent under the terror that had overwhelmed the heart of poor Alice. She puffed out the candle, lighted it again, and, not being able to find a candlestick, though a dozen stood on the shelf in the fore kitchen, she set it in a water-jug, and ran out to the barn for old Richard. "Oh Richard! Oh, for mercy, Richard, make haste, and come into the house. Come away Richard." "Why, what is the matter, Alice? what is wrong?" "Oh Richard! a pedlar came into the hall entreating for lodging. Well, I would not let him stay on any account, and behold, he is gone off and left his pack." "And what is the great matter in that?" said Richard. "I will wager a penny he will look after it, before it shall look after him." "But, oh Richard, I tremble to tell you! We are all gone, for it is a living pack." "A living pack!" Said Richard, staring at Alice, and letting his chops fall down. Richard had just lifted his flail over his head to begin threshing a sheaf; but when he heard of a living pack, he dropped one end of the hand-staff to the floor, and leaning on the other, took such a look at Alice. He knew long before that Alice was beautiful; he knew that ten years before, but he never took such a look at her in his life. "A living pack!" said Richard. "Why the woman is mad without all doubt." "Oh, Richard! come away. Heaven knows what is in it! but I saw it moving as plainly as I see you at present. Make haste, and come away Richard." Richard did not stand to expostulate any longer, nor even to put on his coat, but followed Alice into the house, assuring her by the way, that it was nothing but a whim, and of a piece with many of her phantasies. "But," added he, "of all the foolish ideas that ever possessed your brain, this is the most unfeasible, unnatural, and impossible. How can a pack, made up of napkins, and muslins, and corduroy breeches, perhaps, ever become alive? It is even worse than to suppose a horse's hair will turn an eel." So saying, he lifted the candle out of the jug, and turning about, never stopped till he had his hand upon the pack. He felt the deals that surrounded its edges to prevent the goods being rumpled and spoiled by carrying, the cords that bound it, and the canvas in which it was wrapped. "The pack was well enough, he found nought about it that other packs wanted. It was just like other packs made up of the same stuff. He saw nought that ailed it. And a good large pack it was. It would cost the honest man £200, if not more. It would cost him £300 or £350 if the goods were fine. But he would make it all up again by cheating fools like Alice, with his gewgaws." Alice testified some little disappointment at seeing Richard unconvinced, even by ocular proof. She wished she had never seen him or it howsomever; for she was convinced there was something mysterious about it; that they were stolen goods or something that way; and she was terrified to stay in the house with it. But Richard assured her the pack was a right enough pack.

During this conversation, in comes Edward. He was a lad about sixteen years of age, son to a coal-driver on the border—was possessed of a good deal of humour and ingenuity, but somewhat roguish, forward, and commonly very ragged in his apparel. He was about this time wholly intent on shooting the crows and birds of various kinds, that alighted in whole flocks where he foddered the cattle. He had bought a huge old military gun, which he denominated *Copenhagen*, and was continually thundering away at them. He seldom killed any, if ever; but he once or twice knocked off a few feathers, and after much narrow inspection, discovered some drops of blood on the snow. He was at this very moment come in a great haste for *Copenhagen*, having seen a glorious chance of sparrows, and a Robin-red-breast among them, feeding on the site of a corn rick, but hearing them talk of something mysterious, and a living pack, he pricked up his ears, and was all attention. "Faith Alice," said he, "if you will let me, I'll shoot it." "Hold your peace, you fool," said Richard. Edward took the candle from Richard, who still held it in his hand, and, gliding down the passage, edged up the parlour door, and watched the pack attentively for about two minutes. He then came back with a spring, and with looks very different from those which regulated his features as he went down. As sure as he had death to meet with he saw it stirring. "Hold your peace, you fool," said Richard. Edward swore again that he saw it stirring; but whether he really thought so, or only said so, is hard to determine. "Faith, Alice," said he again, "if you will let me, I'll shoot it." "I tell you to hold your peace, you fool," said Richard. "No," said Edward, "in the multitude of counsellors there is safety; and I will maintain this to be our safest plan. Our master's house is consigned to our care, and the wealth that it contains may tempt some people to use stratagems. Now, if we open up this man's pack, he may pursue us for damages to any amount, but if I shoot it what amends can he get of me? If there is any thing that should not be there, Lord how I will pepper it! And if it is lawful goods, he can only make me pay for the few that are damaged, which I will get at valuation; so, if none of you will acquiesce, I will take all the blame upon myself,

and ware a shot upon it." Richard said whatever was the consequence he would be blameless. A half delirious smile rather distorted than beautified Alice's pretty face, but Edward took it for an
assent to what he had been advancing, so, snatching up *Copenhagen*
in one hand, and the candle in the other, he hasted down the passage, and without hesitating one moment, fired at the pack. Gracious Heaven! The blood gushed out upon the floor like a torrent,
and a hideous roar, followed by the groans of death, issued from the
pack. Edward dropped *Copenhagen* upon the ground, and ran into
the kitchen like one distracted. The kitchen was darkish, for he had
left the candle in the parlour; so taking to the door without being
able to utter a word, he ran to the hills like a wild roe, looking over
each shoulder as fast as he could turn his head from the one side to
the other. Alice followed as fast as she could, but lost half the way of
Edward. She was all the way sighing and crying most pitifully. Old
Richard stood for a short space rather in a state of petrification, but,
at length, after some hasty ejaculations, he went into the parlour.
The whole floor flowed with blood. The pack had thrown itself on
the ground; but the groans and cries were ceased, and only a kind of
guttural noise was heard from it. Knowing that then something must
be done, he ran after his companions and called on them to come
back. Though Edward had escaped a good way and was still persevering on, yet, as he never took long time to consider of the utility
of any thing, but acted from immediate impulse, he turned and came
as fast back as he had gone away. Alice also came homeward, but
more slowly, and crying even more bitterly than before. Edward
overtook her, and was holding on his course; but, as he passed, she
turned away her face, and called him a murderer. At the sound of
this epithet Edward made a dead pause, and looked at Alice with a
face much longer than it used to be. He drew in his breath twice, as
if going to speak, but he only swallowed a great mouthful of air, and
held his peace.

They were soon all three in the parlour, and in no little terror
and agitation of mind unloosed the pack, the principal commodity
of which was a stout young man, whom Edward had shot through
the heart, and thus bereaved of existence in a few minutes. To
paint the feelings, or even the appearance, of young Edward
during this scene is impossible; he acted little, spoke less, and appeared in a hopeless stupor; the most of his employment consisted
in gulping down mouthfuls of breath, wiping his eyes, and staring at
his associates.

It is most generally believed, that when Edward fired at the pack, he had not the most distant idea of shooting a man; but seeing Alice so jealous of it he thought the Colonel would approve of his intrepidy, and protect him from being wronged by the pedlar; and besides, he never got a chance of a shot at such a large thing in his life, and was curious to see how many folds of the pedlar's fine haberdashery ware *Copenhagen* would drive the drops through, so that when the stream of blood burst from the pack, accompanied with the dying groans of a human being, Edward was certainly taken by surprise, and quite confounded; he indeed asserted, as long as he lived, that he saw something stirring in the pack, but his eagerness to shoot, and his terror on seeing what he had done, which was no more than what he might have expected, had he been certain he saw the pack moving, makes this asseveration very doubtful. They made all possible speed in extricating the corpse, intending to call medical assistance, but it was too late; the vital spark was gone for ever. "Alas!" said old Richard, heaving a deep sigh, "poor man, 'tis all over with him! I wish he had lived a little longer to have repented of this, for he has surely died in a bad cause. Poor man! he was *somebody's* son, and no doubt dear to them, and nobody can tell how small a crime this hath, by a regular gradation, become the fruits of." Richard came twice across his eyes with the sleeve of his shirt, for he still wanted the coat; a thought of a tender nature shot through his heart. "Alas, if his parents are alive how will their hearts bear this, poor creatures!" said Richard weeping outright, "poor creatures! God pity them!"

The way that he was packed up was artful and curious. His knees were brought up towards his breast, and his feet and legs stuffed in a wooden box; another wooden box, a size larger, and wanting the bottom, made up the vacancy betwixt his face and knees, and there being only one fold of canvass around this, he breathed with the greatest freedom; but it had undoubtedly been the heaving of his breast which had caused the movement noticed by the servants. His right arm was within the box, and to his hand was tied a cutlass, with which he could rip himself from his confinement at once. There were also four loaded pistols secreted with him, and a silver windcall. On coming to the pistols and cutlass, "Villain," said old Richard, "see what he has here. But I should not call him villain," said he again, softening his tone, "for he is now gone to answer at that bar where no false witness, nor loquacious orator, can bias the justice of the sentence pronounced on him. He is now in the true world, and I am in the false one. *We* can judge only from appearances, but thanks to our kind Maker and Preserver, that he was discovered, else it *is*

probable that none of us should have again seen the light of day."
These moral reflections from the mouth of old Richard by degrees
raised the spirits of Edward: he was bewildered in uncertainty, and
had undoubtedly given himself up for lost; but he now began to
discover that he had done a meritorious and manful action, and, for
the first time since he had fired the fatal shot, ventured to speak.
"Faith it was lucky that I shot then," said Edward; but neither of his
companions answered either good or bad. Alice, though rather grown
desperate, behaved and assisted at this bloody affair, better than
might have been expected. Edward surveyed the pistols all round,
two of which were of curious workmanship. "But what do you think
he was going to do with all these?" said Edward. "I think you need
not ask that," Richard answered. "Faith it was a mercy that I shot
after all," said Edward, "for if we *had* loosed him out, we should
have been all dead in a minute. I have given him a devil of a broadside, though. But look ye, Richard, Providence has directed me to
the right spot, for I might as readily have lodged the contents of
Copenhagen in one of these empty boxes." "It has been a deep laid
scheme," said Richard, "to murder us, and rob our master's house;
there must be certainly be more concerned in it than these two."

Ideas beget ideas, often quite different, and then others again in
unspeakable gradation, which run through and shift in the mind
with as much velocity as the streamers around the pole in a frosty
night. On Richard's mentioning more concerned, Edward instantaneously thought of a gang of thieves by night.–How he would break
the leg of one–shoot another through the head–and scatter them
like chaff before the wind. He would rather shoot one robber on his
feet or on horseback than ten lying tied up in packs; and then what
a glorious prey of pistols he would get from the dead rascals–how
he would prime and load and fire away with perfect safety from
within!–how Alice would scream, and Richard would pray, and all
would go on with the noise and rapidity of a windmill, and he would
acquire everlasting fame. So high was the young and ardent mind of
Edward wrought up by this train of ideas, that he was striding up
and down the floor, while his eyes gleamed as with a tint of madness. "Oh! if I had but plenty guns, and nothing ado but to shoot,
how I would pepper the dogs!" said he with great vehemence, to the
no small astonishment of his two associates, who thought him gone
mad. "What can the fool mean?" said old Richard, "What can he ail
at the dogs?" "Oh, it is the robbers that I mean," said Edward. "What
robbers, you young fool?" said Richard. "Why, do not you think
that the pedlar will come back at the dead of the night to the assist-

ance of his friend, and bring plenty of help with him too," said Edward. "There is not a doubt of it," said old Richard. "There is not a doubt of it," said Alice, and both stood up stiff with fear and astonishment. "Oh! merciful Heaven! what is to become of us," said Alice again, "What are we to do?" "Let us trust in the Lord," said old Richard. "I intend, in the first place, to trust in old *Copenhagen*," said Edward, putting down the frizzel, and making it spring up again with a loud snap five or six times, "But, good Lord! what are we thinking about? I'll run and gather in all the guns in the country." The impulse of the moment was Edward's monitor. Off he ran like fire, and warned a few of the Colonel's retainers, who he knew kept guns about them; these again warned others, and at eight o'clock they had twenty-five men in the house and sixteen loaded pieces, including *Copenhagen*, and the four pistols found on the deceased. These were distributed amongst the front windows in the upper stories, and the rest armed with pitch-forks, old swords, and cudgels, kept watch below. Edward had taken care to place himself with a comrade, at a window immediately facing the approach to the house, and now, backed as he was by such a strong party, grew quite impatient for another chance with his redoubted *Copenhagen*. All, however, remained quiet, until an hour past midnight, when it entered into his teeming brain to blow the thief's silver wind-call; so, without warning any of the rest, he set his head out at the window, and blew until all the hills and woods around yelled their echoes. This alarmed the guards, as not knowing the meaning of it; but how were they astonished at hearing it answered by another at no great distance. The state of anxiety into which this sudden and unforeseen circumstance threw our armed peasants, is more easily conceived than described. The fate of their master's great wealth, and even their own fates, was soon to be decided, and none but *he* who surveys and over-rules futurity could tell what was to be the issue. Every breast heaved quicker, every breath was cut short, every gun was cocked and pointed toward the court-gate, every orb of vision was strained to discover the approaching foe, by the dim light of the starry canopy, and every ear expanded to catch the distant sounds as they floated on the slow frosty breeze.

The suspence was not of long continuance. In less than five minutes the trampling of horses was heard, which increased as they approached to the noise of thunder, and in due course, a body of men on horseback, according to the account given by the Colonel's people, exceeding their own number, came up at a brisk trot, and began to enter the court-gate. Edward, unable to restrain himself any longer, fired *Copenhagen* in their faces; one of the foremost dropped, and his horse made a spring towards the hall door. This discharge was rather premature, as the wall still shielded a part of the gang from the windows. It was, however, the watchword to all the rest, and in the course of two seconds, the whole sixteen guns were discharged at them. Before the smoke dispersed they were all fled, no doubt greatly amazed at the reception which they met with. Edward and his comrade ran down stairs to see how matters stood, for it was their opinion that they had shot them every one, and that their horses had taken fright at the noise, and gallopped off without them; but the club below warmly protested against their opening any of the doors till day, so they were obliged to take themselves again to their birth up stairs.

Though our peasants had gathered up a little courage and confidence in themselves, their situation was curious, and to them a dreadful one; they saw and heard a part of their fellow creatures moaning and expiring in agonies in the open air, which was intensely cold, yet durst not go to administer the least relief, for fear of a surprise. An hour or two after this great brush, Edward and his messmate descended again, and begged hard for leave to go and reconnoitre for a few minutes, which after some disputes was granted. They found only four men fallen, who appeared to be all quite dead. One of them was lying within the porch. "Faith," said Edward, "here's the chap that I shot." The other three were without, at a considerable distance from each other. They durst not follow their track farther, as the road entered betwixt groves of trees, but retreated into their posts without touching any thing.

About an hour before day, some of them were alarmed at hearing the sound of horses feet a second time, which, however, was only indistinct and heard at considerable intervals, and nothing of them ever appeared. Not long after this, Edward and his friend were almost frightened out of their wits, at seeing, as they thought, the dead man within the gate, endeavouring to get up and escape. They had seen him dead, lying surrounded by a deluge of congealed blood, and nothing but the ideas of ghosts and hobgoblins entering their brains, they were so indiscreet as never to think of firing, but ran and told the tale of horror to some of their neighbours. The sky was by this time grown so dark, that nothing could be seen with precision, and they all remained in anxious incertitude, until the opening day discovered to them, by degrees, that the corpses were removed, and nothing left but large sheets of frozen blood, and the morning's alarm by the ghost and the noise of horses had been occasioned by some of the friends of the men that had fallen, conveying them away for fear of a discovery.

Next morning the news flew like fire, and the three servants were much incommoded by crowds of idle and officious people that gathered about the house, some inquiring after the smallest particulars, some begging to see the body that lay in the parlour, and others pleased themselves with poring over the sheets of crimson ice, and tracing the drops of blood on the road down the wood. The Colonel had no country factor, nor any particular friend in the neighbourhood, so the affair was not pursued with that speed which was requisite to the discovery of the accomplices, which if it had, would have been productive of some very unpleasant circumstances, by involving sundry respectable families, as it afterwards appeared but too evidently. Dr Herbert, the physician who attended the family occasionally, wrote to the Colonel, by post, concerning the affair, but though he lost no time, it was the fifth day before he arrived. Then indeed advertisements were issued, and posted up in all public places, offering rewards for a discovery of any person killed or wounded of late. All the dead and sick within twenty miles were inspected by medical men, and a most extensive search made, but to no purpose. It was too late; all was secured. Some indeed were missing, but plausible pretences being made for their absence, nothing could be done. But certain it is, sundry of these were never seen any more in the country, though many of the neighbourhood declared they were such people as nobody could suspect.

The body of the unfortunate man who was shot in the pack lay open for inspection a fortnight, but none would ever acknowledge so much as having seen him. The Colonel then caused him to be buried at Bellingham; but it was confidently reported, that his grave was opened and his corpse taken away. In short, not one engaged in this base and bold attempt was ever discovered. A constant watch was kept by night for some time. The Colonel rewarded the defenders of his house liberally. Old Richard remained in the family during the rest of his life, and had a good salary for only saying prayers amongst the servants every night. Alice was married to a tobacconist at Hexham. Edward was made the Colonel's gamekeeper, and had a present of a fine gold mounted gun given him. His master afterwards procured him a commission in a regiment of foot, where he suffered many misfortunes and disappointments. He was shot through the shoulder at the battle of Fontenoy, but recovered, and retiring on half-pay, took a small farm on the Scottish side. His character was that of a brave, but rash officer; kind, generous, and open-hearted in all situations. I have often stood at his knee and listened with wonder and amazement to his stories of battles and sieges, but none of them ever pleased me better than that of the *Long Pack.*

Alas! his fate is fast approaching to us all! he hath many years ago submitted to the conqueror of all mankind. His brave heart is now a clod of the valley, and his gray hairs recline in peace on that pillow from which his head shall be raised only when time shall be no more.

A Peasant's Funeral

On the 10th of April, 1810, I went with my father to the funeral of George Mouncie, who had been removed by a sudden death, from the head of a large family, now left in very narrow circumstances. As he had, however, during his life, been held in high estimation for honesty and simplicity of character, many attended to pay the last sad duty to departed worth. We were shown one by one, as we arrived, into a little hovel where the cows were wont to stand; although it was a pleasant day, and we would have been much more comfortable on the green; but it is held highly indecorous to give the entertainment at a burial without doors, and no one will submit to it.

We got each of us a glass of whisky as we entered, and then sat conversing, sometimes about common topics, but for the most part about our respective parish ministers: what subjects they had of late been handling, and how they had succeeded. Some of them remembered all the texts with the greatest exactness for seasons by-gone, but they could only remark, on many of them, that such a one made much or little of it.

One man said, in the course of some petty argument, "I do not deny it, David, your minister is a very good man, and a very clever man too; he has no fault but one." "What is that?" said David. "It is patronage," said the other. "Patronage," said David, "that cannot be a fault." "Not a fault, Sir? But I say it is a fault; and one that you and every one who encourages it by giving it your countenance will have to answer for. Your minister can never be a good shepherd, for he was not chosen by the flock." "It is a bad simile," said David, "the flock never chooses its own shepherd, but the owner of the flock." The greatest number of the inhabitants of that district being dissenters from the established church, many severe reflections were thrown out against the dangerous system of patronage, while no one ventured to defend it save David; who said, that if one learned man was not capable of making choice for a parish, the populace was much less so; and proved, from scripture, that man's nature was so corrupted, that he was unable to make a wise choice for himself: and maintained, that the inhabitants of this country ought to be thankful that the legislature had taken the task out of their hands.

As a farther proof of the justice of his argument, he asked, whether Jesus of Nazareth or Mahomet was the best preacher? The other answered that none but a reprobate would ask the question. Very well, said David; Mahomet was one of your popular preachers; was followed, and adored by the multitude wherever he went, while he who spoke as never man spake was despised and rejected. Mahomet gained more converts to his religion in his life-time, than has been gained to the true religion in 1800 years. Away with your popular preachers, friend! they are bruised reeds. His antagonist was non-plus'd: he could only answer, "Ah! David, David, ye're on the braid way."

The women are not mixed with the men at these funerals, nor do they accompany the corpse to the place of interment; but in Nithsdale, and Galloway, all the female friends of the family attend at the house, sitting in an apartment by themselves. The servers remark, that in their apartment, the lamentations for the family loss are generally more passionate than in the other.

The widow of the deceased, however, came in amongst us, to see a particular friend, who had travelled far, to honour the memory of his old and intimate acquaintance. He saluted her with great kindness, and every appearance of heart-felt concern for her misfortunes. The dialogue between them interested me; it was the language of nature, and no other spoke a word while it lasted.

"Ah! James," said she, "I did not think, the last time I saw you, that our next meeting would be on so mournful an occasion: we were all cheerful then, and little aware of the troubles awaiting us! I have since that time suffered many hardships and losses, James, but all of them were light to this"—she wept bitterly; James endeavoured to comfort her, but he was nearly as much affected himself. "I do not repine," said she, "since it is the will of Him who orders all things for the best purposes, and to the wisest ends: but, alas! I fear I am ill fitted for the task which Providence has assigned me!" With that she cast a mournful look at two little children who were peeping cautiously into the shiel. "These poor fatherless innocents," said she, "have no other creature to look to but me for any thing; and I have been so little used to manage family affairs, that I scarcely know what I am doing; for he was so careful of us all, so kind! and so good!"—"Yes," said James, wiping his eyes, "if he was not a good man, I know few were so! Did he suffer much in his last illness?" "I knew not what he suffered," returned she, "for he never complained. I now remember all the endearing things that he said to us, though I took little heed to them then, having no thoughts of being so soon separated from him. Little did I think he was so ill! though I might easily have known that he would never murmur or repine at what

Providence appointed him to endure. No, James, he never complained of any thing. Since the time our first great worldly misfortune happened, we two have set down to many a poor meal, but he was ever alike cheerful, and thankful to the Giver.

"He was only ill four days, and was out of his bed every day: whenever I asked him how he did, his answer uniformly was, 'I am not ill now.' On the day preceding the night of his death, he sat on his chair a full hour speaking earnestly all the while to the children. I was busy up and down the house, and did not hear all; but I heard him once saying, that he might soon be taken from them, and then they would have no father but God: but that he would never be taken from them, nor ever would forsake them, if they did not first forsake him. He is a kind indulgent Being, continued he, and feeds the young ravens, and all the little helpless animals that look and cry to him for food, and you may be sure that he will never let the poor orphans who pray to him want.

"Be always dutiful to your mother, and never refuse to do what she bids you on any account; for you may be assured that she has no other aim than your good; confide all your cares and fears in her bosom, for a parent's love is stedfast; misfortune may heighten but cannot cool it.

"When he had finished, he drew his plaid around his head, and went slowly down to the little dell, where he used every day to offer up his morning and evening prayers, and where we have often sat together on Sabbath afternoons, reading verse about with our children in the Bible. I think he was aware of his approaching end, and was gone to recommend us to God; for I looked after him, and saw him on his knees.

"When he returned, I thought he looked extremely ill, and asked him if he was grown worse! He said he was not like to be quite well, and sat down on his chair, looking ruefully at the children, and sometimes at the bed. At length he said feebly, 'Betty, my dear, make down the bed, and help me to it–it will be the last time.' These words went through my head and heart like the knell of death–All grew dark around me, and I knew not what I was doing.

"He spoke very little after that, saving that at night he desired me, in a faint voice, not to go to my bed, but sit up with him; 'for,' said he, 'it is likely you may never need to do it again.' If God had not supported me that night, James, I could not have stood it, for I had much, much to do! A little past midnight my dear husband expired in my arms, without a groan or a struggle, save some convulsive grasps that he gave my hand. Calm resignation marked his behaviour to the last. I had only one acquaintance with me, and she was young—The beds face towards each other, you know, and little John, who was lying awake, was so much shocked by a view which he got of the altered visage of his deceased parent, that he sprung from his bed in a frenzy of horror, and ran naked into the fields, uttering the most piercing and distracted cries. I was obliged to leave the young woman with the corpse and the rest of the children, and pursue the boy; nor was it till after running nearly a mile that I was able to catch him. The young woman had been seized with a super-stitious terror in my absence, and was likewise fled; for, on my re-turn, I found no creature in my dwelling but my dead husband and five sleeping infants. The boy next day was in a burning fever. O James! well may the transactions of that night be engraved on my memory for ever; yet, so bewildered were all the powers of my mind, that on looking back, they appear little otherwise than as a confused undefined shadow of something removed at a great dis-tance."

Her heart was full, and I do not know how long she might have run on, had not one remarked that the company were now all ar-rived, and there was no more time to lose. James then asked a bless-ing, which lasted about ten minutes:—The bread and wine were served plentifully around—the coffin was brought out, covered, and fixed on poles—the widow supported that end of it where the head of her late beloved partner lay, until it passed the gate-way—then she stood looking wistfully after it, while the tears flowed plentifully from her eyes—A turn in the wood soon hid it from her sight for ever—She gave one short look up to Heaven, and returned weeping into her cottage.

Dreadful Story of Macpherson

I RECEIVED yours of the 20th October, intreating me to furnish you with the tale, which you say you have heard me relate, concerning the miraculous death of Major Macpherson and his associates among the Grampian hills. I think the story worthy of being preserved, but I never heard it related save once; and though it then made a considerable impression on my mind, being told by one who was well acquainted both with the scene and the sufferers, yet I fear my memory is not sufficiently accurate, with regard to particulars; and without these the interest of a story is always diminished, and its authenticity rendered liable to be called in question. I will however communicate it exactly as it remains impressed on my memory, without avouching for the particulars relating to it; in these I shall submit to be corrected by such as are better informed.

I have forgot on what year it happened, but I think it was about the year 1805–6, that Major Macpherson and a few gentlemen of his acquaintance, with their attendants, went out to hunt in the middle of that tremendous range of mountains which rise between Athol and Badenoch. Many are the scenes of wild grandeur and rugged deformity which amaze the wanderer in the Grampian deserts; but none of them surpasses this in wildness and still solemnity. No sound salutes the listening ear, but the rushing torrent, or the broken eldrich bleat of the mountain goat. The glens are deep and narrow, and the hills steep and sombre, and so high, that their grizly summits appear to be wrapped in the blue veil that canopies the air. But it is seldom that their tops can be seen; for dark clouds of mist often rest upon them for several weeks together in summer, or wander in detached columns among their cliffs; and during the winter they are abandoned entirely to the storm. Then the flooded torrents and rushing wreaths of accumulated snows spend their fury without doing harm to any living creature; and the howling tempest raves uncontrolled and unregarded.

Into the midst of this sublime solitude did our jovial party wander in search of their game. They were highly successful. The heath cock was interrupted in the middle of his exulting whirr, and dropped lifeless on his native waste; the meek ptarmigan fell fluttering among her gray crusted stones, and the wild-roe foundered in the correi. The noise of the guns, and the cheering cries of the sportsmen, awakened those echoes that had so long slept silent; the fox slid quietly over the hill, and the wild deer bounded away into the forests of Glendee from before the noisy invaders.

In the afternoon they stepped into a little *bothy*, or resting lodge, that stood by the side of a rough mountain stream, and having meat and drink, they abandoned themselves to mirth and jollity.

This Major Macpherson was said to have been guilty of some acts of extreme cruelty and injustice in raising recruits in that country, and was, on that account, held in detestation by the common people. He was otherwise a respectable character, and of honourable connexions, as were also the gentlemen who accompanied him.

When their hilarity was at the highest pitch, ere ever they were aware, a young man stood before them, of a sedate, mysterious appearance, looking sternly at the Major. Their laughter was hushed in a moment, for they had not observed any human being in the glen, save those of their own party, nor did they so much as perceive when their guest entered. Macpherson appeared particularly struck, and somewhat shocked at the sight of him; the stranger beckoned to the Major, who followed him instantly out of the bothy: The curiosity of the party was aroused, and they watched their motions with great punctuality; they walked a short way down by the side of the river, and appeared in earnest conversation for a few minutes, and from some involuntary motions of their bodies, the stranger seemed to be threatening Macpherson, and the latter interceding; they parted, and though then not above twenty yards distant, before the Major got half way back to the bothy, the stranger guest was gone, and they saw no more of him.

> "I cannot tell how the truth may be,
> "I say the tale as 'twas said to me."

But what was certainly extraordinary, after the dreadful catastrophe, though the most strict and extended inquiry was made, neither this stranger, nor his business, could be discovered. The countenance of the Major was so visibly altered on his return, and bore such evident marks of trepidation, that the mirth of the party was marred during the remainder of the excursion, and none of them cared to ask him any questions concerning his visitant, or the errand that he came on.

This was early in the week, and on the Friday immediately following, Macpherson proposed to his companions a second expedition to the mountains. They all objected to it on account of the weather, which was broken and rough; but he persisted in his resolution, and finally told them, that he *must* and *would* go, and those who did not choose to accompany him might tarry at home. The consequence was, that the same party, with the exception of one man, went again to hunt in the forest of Glenmore.

Although none of them returned the first night after their departure, that was little regarded; it being customary for the sportsmen to lodge occasionally in the bothies of the forest; but when Saturday night arrived, and no word from them, their friends became dreadfully alarmed. On Sunday, servants were despatched to all the inns and gentlemen's houses in the bounds, but no accounts of them could be learned. One solitary dog only returned, and he was wounded and maimed. The alarm spread—a number of people rose, and in the utmost consternation went to search for their friends among the mountains. When they reached the fatal bothy—dreadful to relate!— they found the dead bodies of the whole party lying scattered about the place!—Some of them were considerably mangled, and one nearly severed in two.—Others were not marked by any wound, of which number I think it was said the Major was one, who was lying flat on his face. It was a scene of wo, lamentation, and awful astonishment, none being able to account for what had happened; but it was visible that it had not been effected by any human agency. The bothy was torn from its foundations, and scarcely a vestige of it left—its very stones were all scattered about in different directions; there was one huge corner stone in particular, which twelve men could scarcely have raised, that was tossed to a considerable distance, yet no marks of either fire or water were visible. Extraordinary as this story may appear, and an extraordinary story it certainly is, I have not the slightest cause to doubt the certainty of the leading circumstances; with regard to the rest, you have them as I had them. In every mountainous district in Scotland, to this day, a belief in supernatural agency prevails, in a greater or lesser degree. Such an awful dispensation as the above, was likely to re-kindle every lingering spark of it.

Story of Two Highlanders

THERE is perhaps no quality of the mind, in which mankind differ more than in a prompt readiness either to act or answer to the point, in the most imminent and sudden dangers and difficulties; of which the following is a most pleasant instance.

On the banks of the Albany River, which falls into Hudson's Bay, there is, amongst others, a small colony settled, which is mostly made up of emigrants from the Highlands of Scotland. Though the soil of the valleys contiguous to the river is exceedingly rich and fertile, yet the winter being so long and severe, these people do not labour too incessantly in agriculture, but depend for the most part upon their skill in hunting and fishing for their subsistence; there being commonly abundance of both game and fish.

Two young kinsmen, both Macdonalds, went out one day into these boundless woods to hunt, each of them armed with a well-charged gun in his hand, and a *skene-dhu*, or Highland dirk, by his side. They shaped their course towards a small stream, which descends from the mountains to the N. W. of the river; on the banks of which they knew there were still a few wild swine remaining; and of all other creatures they wished most to meet with one of them; little doubting but that they would overcome even a pair of them, if chance would direct them to their lurking places, though they were reported to be so remarkable both for their strength and ferocity. They were not at all successful, having neglected the common game in searching for these animals; and a little before sunset they returned homeward, without having shot any thing save one wild turkey. But when they least expected it, to their infinite joy they discovered a deep pit or cavern, which contained a large litter of fine half-grown pigs, and none of the old ones with them. This was a prize indeed: so, without losing a moment, Donald said to the other, "Mack, you pe te littlest man, creep you in and durk te little sows, and I'll pe keeping vatch at te door." Mack complied without hesitation—gave his gun to Donald—unsheathed his *skene-dhu*, and crept into the cave head foremost; but after he was all out of sight, save the brogues, he stopped short, and called back, "But Lord, Tonald, pe shoor to keep out te ould wans." "Ton't you pe fearing tat, man," said Donald.

The cave was deep, but there was abundance of room in the further end, where Mack, with his sharp *skene-dhu*, now commenced the work of death. He was scarcely well begun, when Donald perceived a monstrous wild boar advancing upon him, roaring, and grinding his tusks, while the fire of rage gleamed from his eyes. Donald said not a word for fear of alarming his friend; besides, the savage was so hard upon him ere ever he was aware, he scarcely had time for any thing: so setting himself firm, and cocking his gun, he took his aim; but, that the shot might prove the more certain death, he suffered the boar to come within a few paces of him before he ventured to fire; he at last drew the fatal trigger, expecting to blow out his eyes, brains and all.–Merciful heaven!–the gun missed fire, or flashed in the pan, I am not sure which. There was no time to lose–Donald dashed the piece in the animal's face, turned his back, and fled with precipitation. The boar pursued him only for a short space, for having heard the cries of his suffering young ones as he passed the mouth of the den, he hasted back to their rescue. Most men would have given all up for lost–It was not so with Donald–Mack's life was at stake.–As soon as he observed the monster return from pursuing him, Donald faced about, and pursued him in his turn; but having, before this, from the horror of being all torn to pieces, run rather too far without looking back, the boar had by that oversight got considerably a-head of him–Donald strained every nerve–uttered some piercing cries–and even for all his haste did not forget to implore assistance from Heaven. His prayer was short, but pithy–"O Lord! puir Mack! puir Mack!" said Donald, in a loud voice, while the tears gushed from his eyes. In spite of all his efforts, the enraged animal reached the mouth of the den before him, and entered!–It was, however, too narrow for him to walk in on all-four; he was obliged to drag himself in as Mack had done before; and, of course, his hind feet lost their hold of the ground. At this important crisis Donald overtook him–laid hold of his large, long tail–wrapped it around both his hands–set his feet to the bank, and held back in the utmost desperation.

Mack, who was all unconscious of what was going on above ground, wondered what way he came to be involved in utter darkness in a moment. He waited a little while, thinking that Donald was only playing a trick upon him, but the most profound obscurity still continuing, he at length bawled out, "Tonald, man, Tonald–phat is it that'll ay pe stopping te light?" Donald was too much engaged, and too breathless, to think of making any reply to Mack's impertinent question, till the latter, having waited in vain a considerable time for an answer, repeated it in a louder cry. Donald's famous laconic answer, which perhaps never was, nor ever will be equalled, has often been heard of–"Tonald man, Tonald,–I say phat is it that'll ay pe stopping te light?" bellowed Mack—"Should te tail preak, you'll fin' tat," said Donald.

Donald continued the struggle, and soon began to entertain hopes of ultimate success. When the boar pulled to get in, Donald held back; and when he struggled to get back again, Donald set his shoulder to his large buttocks and pushed him in: and in this position he kept him, until he got an opportunity of giving him some deadly stabs with his *skene-dhu* behind the short rib, which soon terminated his existence.

Our two young friends by this adventure realised a valuable prize, and secured so much excellent food, that it took them several days to get it conveyed home. During the long winter nights, while the family were regaling themselves on the hams of the great wild boar, often was the above tale related, and as often applauded and laughed at.

Maria's Tale

Written by Herself

SIR,—You have manifested your desire of rendering yourself a useful member of society, by ridiculing the foibles, and branding the crimes of your fellow-citizens. Amidst your ingenious and engaging speculations, can you listen to the voice of the wretched? Even in your endeavours to please, you have hitherto appeared anxious to instruct and to reform; to you, therefore, as the friend of virtue and of man, I beg leave to address the following narrative. It contains nothing wonderful, but it is *true*; and may in some degree serve to warn others against the arts by which I was deceived; it is the relation of a perfidy of which myself was the victim.

I was born in a parish about forty miles distant from Edinburgh. My father was a farmer in that parish, more respectable for his prudence and virtues than for his wealth. As soon as I was old enough, I was sent to the parochial school, where I learned the usual branches of education for one in my station in life; and in the evenings, and on Sunday, I was carefully instructed by my parents in the principles of our holy religion. I was commended as a dutiful and promising child; and was daily reminded that the more cheerfully I obeyed my parents, the more I would be loved. I was taught that the same Almighty Being who caused every flower of the garden to grow, and placed the sun and the moon and all the stars in the sky, created me, and my parents, and all mankind. I was assured that God kept an exact account of every one's words and actions; that he loved the good, and was angry with the wicked; and that he would love me too, and make me for ever happy, if I would obey my parents, and ask his blessing and his love.

As far as the heart was concerned I was sincerely pious, and I felt all the satisfaction of well-doing. Ah! how amiable is the piety of a young and innocent mind! how cheering and sweet the approbation of those we love! With what tenderness I hid my face in the lap of an affectionate mother, and lisped my evening prayer to that God who never slumbers nor sleeps, that he would watch over my repose. When I retired to bed after these simple acts of devotion, I felt a warmer affection for every one I was acquainted with: my little sister, who slept beside me, was dearer than usual; I could not forbear clasping the sleeping infant in my arms, and wishing her awake to share my delightful sensations. Perhaps, Sir, you may think these circumstances trifling, but they are connected with my happiest days, and the recital is pleasing. Miserable and degraded as I now am, the remembrance of early peace sometimes returns to my mind like a dream, and soothes for a time the feelings of shame and remorse.

The frolics of childhood began to be blended with the pursuits of youth, but every one of these pursuits brought me new happiness. I was now in my fifteenth year, and seldom had any thing occurred to ruffle the natural evenness of my temper, or induce a wish which I might not innocently indulge. Under my father's humble roof no temptation assailed me; I knew not what temptation was. My father and mother had been early married, and had gradually acquired each other's sentiments and habits, so that difference of opinion was seldom entertained, and domestic discord was never known.

Most of our family were grown up; as my father's farm was too small to require so many labourers, he determined to let some of us go to service, and I was of that number. I was engaged with a gentleman's family in the neighbourhood that had always expressed great regard for me, and had often solicited my father to let me become one of their servants. To this my father did not agree without considerable reluctance; however, as they had conferred some trifling obligations on him, he did not think it proper to disoblige them, so I entered to their service. I had been there about six months, when the gentleman's youngest son, who was studying medicine in Edinburgh, came to spend the summer with the family. He was a handsome young man, of easy engaging manners, insinuating in his address, and extremely affable to his inferiors. In short, he was both naturally and habitually engaging. His numerous little condescensions could not fail to render him agreeable to those who were beneath him in rank and fortune; and you may easily believe, Sir, that they were peculiarly flattering and dangerous to me, when I tell you, that I was the object of his particular attention. He thought me a sweet innocent girl, and he was too ungenerous to spare that innocence which he admired. He was sufficiently skilled in the female heart, to know that it is not proof against professions of a tender attachment; and that our vanity and self-love too seldom allow us to examine whether such professions are feigned or sincere. My youth and simplicity convinced him that he might easily gain my affections. I had heard many accounts of the falsehood of men, but had always looked upon them as something in which I was nowise interested. I never dreamt that there were men who could profess a sincere affection for me, and, at the same time, resolve deliberately to gratify their passions at the expense of my character and my happiness. I had never loved, but my heart was warm, and I soon experienced that it was susceptible of the fondest regard.

He took every opportunity of conversing with me when alone, followed me to my work and assisted me; and when the other girls were present, always preferred me, and seemed anxious to recommend himself to my esteem. When a party dined at his father's, he left them as soon as possible, and said he was more happy beside me than in the drawing-room. I was flattered by his kindnesses, and in my turn became anxious to please, and show him that I was not ungrateful. I endeavoured to surpass my fellow-servants in dexterity at my work, and in the taste and neatness of my dress; I began to observe and imitate the manners of his sisters, and of such ladies as visited the family; and in short, studied to improve in every thing that I thought could render me more agreeable to him. In all this, however, I had no regard to consequences; I loved him; I followed the dictates of nature; my only aim was to please. His assiduities were multiplied, and my attachment became daily stronger, till my feelings were wound up to the highest pitch.

One morning as I was working alone, he came and sat down beside me, and after remaining for some time silent, and apparently in great agitation, he told me he was soon to set out for Edinburgh, but he feared he should leave his happiness behind him. I blushed, and could not help showing that I understood his meaning. He perceived my confusion, and without giving me time to recollect myself, threw his arms about my neck, and declared, in the most passionate accents, that he loved me, and could not live without my affection.

After I was a little recovered from the delirium into which this declaration had thrown me, I said he surely meant to teaze me, for I was every way unworthy of his notice: he was a gentleman, and could not intend to marry a poor girl like me. He called Heaven to witness that he sincerely intended to marry me, as soon as he had an opportunity; for his birth, he said, he did not value it; he thought me his equal, and his rank should soon be mine.—When I objected that his parents would look down upon me, and be angry with him for forming so mean a connexion, he said, he feared they would be very much displeased, and would perhaps disinherit him; but they could not deprive him of his profession, and he could depend on that for a respectable livelihood. It will easily be perceived what effect this declaration was likely to produce; it was natural for me to be devoted to the man who would renounce his patrimony for my sake, and brave the ridicule of his companions, and the resentment and reproaches of his parents.

Our intimacy had not escaped the observation of his parents, and they had in vain used every art to prevent it. The more they tried to keep us asunder, the more eagerly he sought my company, and studied to elude their vigilance. My own parents, too, had taken notice of our intimacy, and dreaded it more than his; for they justly suspected that he must have designs which he durst not avow. They frequently warned me of the danger of listening to his professions; they entreated me to shun his company; and threatened, in case of disobedience, to remove me from the family. Instead of alarming me, however, their apprehensions appeared altogether groundless; I became tired of their advices, which I thought well-meant, but excessively troublesome; I visited them seldom, and no longer found pleasure in that home where I had so often been happy.

The time of my lover's departure approached, and I looked forward to our marriage as an event that was certain and by no means distant. We agreed that as soon as he was settled, I should leave his father's house privately, and follow him to Edinburgh. For this purpose, he promised to inform me where I should meet him, and to transmit me a sufficient sum of money for defraying the expense of my journey. Such were the promises which I fondly believed, and by which I was decoyed to destruction.

But my crime was soon succeeded by remorse; the consciousness of guilt dissipated the gay visions that had dazzled me, and then, for the first time, I began to fear that he might forget his promises, and leave me to infamy and disgrace. He employed all his art to reassure me, and I affected to be satisfied, and endeavoured to be cheerful, but my peace of mind was gone. My fellow-servants observed my uneasiness, and perhaps guessed the cause; the eyes of every one seemed to be turned on me, and to read my guilt in my countenance. I dreaded the sight of my parents, whose advices I had slighted; and the near prospect of parting with the man I loved aggravated my distress, and made me insensible to every enjoyment. He departed, and I waited month after month in anxious expectation of the promised intelligence, but I waited in vain.

His parents, who had received some hints of my design, were so careful to conceal from me every thing respecting him, that I could scarcely discover in what street he lodged. My parents began to suspect my situation, which I positively denied, until it became too apparent to be longer concealed.

The shame of acknowledging that I had so long persisted in a falsehood, together with the necessity of giving that satisfaction which the church would demand, preyed upon my spirits, and made me form the rash and dangerous resolution of going to throw myself at the feet of the barbarous man who had deceived me, who alone could screen me from ignominy, and in whom I still hoped to find a friend.

In pursuance of this resolution, I rose early in the morning, and tied up a small bundle of clothes, and a few shillings, which was all the money I was mistress of; and having thus prepared for my disconsolate journey, I cast a farewell look on the couch where I had passed a feverish night, and the pillow that was then wet with my tears. Former scenes rushed to my recollection, and nearly overpowered me with anguish. By one imprudent step I saw my peace of mind for ever destroyed. I stole softly out of the house, and after travelling all day with the most painful exertion, which, in the condition I then was, I was ill fitted to bear, I arrived at his lodging late at night, and was informed that he had left Edinburgh, about a week before, to spend the harvest with a relation in one of the northern counties of England. What could I do? I was without a friend and without a home; without money, and unable to work. I rushed into the street in an emotion of anguish and despair, and hurried along without knowing whither I went. I no longer seemed to be the object of Divine care, and, instead of imploring mercy and protection, I thought vengeance was already pursuing me; and, in a transport of passion, raised my eyes to Heaven, and cursed my fate, and the author of all my misfortunes. After wandering about for the greatest part of the night in this distracted state of mind, I entered a house, which I supposed was the haunt of debauchery and vice; for this appeared to be the only abode to which I was entitled now, and the only one where I was likely to be admitted. But never let the wretched despair, or for a moment suppose that the Governor of the universe sports with the miseries of his creatures. Folly may indeed lead them to misery, but misfortune, for the most part, is only a more gentle name for imprudence. That protecting Providence, of which I had just despaired, over-ruled my rash resolution, and directed me into the house of a poor but benevolent woman, who let her mean lodgings to destitute girls that were out of service; but these girls were all virtuous, or at least their hostess believed them to be so, and did every thing in her power to render them comfortable at a small expense. When I went in, I assumed an air of levity, and asked if I could be accommodated with a bed for a few nights. The woman replied that her house was full. I then said that any kind of lodging would please me; that I would rest me by the fire, or any where, for I was a stranger in Edinburgh, and knew of no place where I could go. "You are from the country I see," said she. I answered that I was; and had not yet entered any other house in the town. She then asked if my parents were alive, which I answered in the affirmative. "Why, then, did you leave them?" said she, "and come to a place where there is no one to own you? Believe me you are come to the worst place in the kingdom for a friendless and beautiful girl." I could make no answer but by tears. "I hope, (continued she,) you have not run away from your parents? If you have, what think you they will be suffering on your account?" I sobbed till my heart was like to break—"What! you have then run away from your parents. Pray, what tempted you to do so? Was it some man who persuaded you to take so imprudent a step?"—"Yes," said I; for that was all the answer I could make. "And what is become of him?" said she, "I hope he has not deserted you too." "Yes," said I. The poor woman looked at me with compassion, and I saw a tear glistening in her eye. "Alas! poor girl," said she, "I see how it is with you. I fear somebody has been much to blame; but you are not the first who have been decoyed to folly and ruin by that unrelenting creature man; nor the first whom I have succoured in the same situation. You must not lodge in the street; and any other place in which you could find admittance would still be worse. Endeavour to compose yourself, and stay with me a night or two, until we consider what can be done for you."

The excessive fatigue I had undergone, and the violent agitation of my spirits, brought on premature labour before morning, and I was delivered of a daughter, without any other assistance than such as was afforded by my unfortunate lodgers. I looked upon my helpless infant with a mother's fondness, but had not even the means of providing it with clothes. In wild agony I snatched it to my bosom, and wished in my heart that we might soon be companions in the grave. I asked if it was also accursed for my sake, and doomed, like me, to be the victim of a betrayer? But my anxiety for its fate was of short duration, for it only lived till next morning.

Those who may be least inclined to palliate my crime, would have pitied me had they known what I felt, while I wrapt the body of my child in a napkin, which I had received to keep in remembrance of its father, (for that was the only shroud I could provide), and having laid it in its rude coffin, delivered it to be consigned to the grave of a stranger.

While I was thus expiating my faults, my parents were involved in the deepest affliction. They easily guessed the cause of my departure, and immediately despatched two of my brothers in quest of me; but, notwithstanding the most diligent search, they did not find me till three weeks after the death of my child. Having discharged what debts I had contracted, they conducted me to the house of a relation, a few miles from Edinburgh, where ill health still confines me.

Thus, Sir, you have seen that I possessed all the advantages of a virtuous education, and had given the most promising hopes of future worth and felicity; and you have seen these bright prospects clouded and destroyed by folly and wickedness. You have seen how gradually I proceeded, adding one crime to another, till I was brought into a state of wretchedness and distraction too severe for humanity. I freely forgive the author of my misfortunes, and pray that he may have the pardon of God; nor will I be so harsh as to conclude that he would have pursued his schemes with such cruel perseverance, had he foreseen their fatal consequences. When intoxicated with passion, perhaps, he even believed his promises were sincere. Or is it customary, with the higher orders of your sex, Sir, thus to triumph over virtue and innocence, and take pleasure in the misery of those, who, depending on their honour and integrity, sacrifice every thing to them? It is a gratification so selfish, mean, and ungenerous, that I wonder every delicate and sympathetic affection of the human mind does not recoil from it; from a principle so cruel and so adverse to all the laws of God and man. It is indeed a stain nowise hurtful to the character of a gentleman, and, consequently, may seem a small matter to such as look no farther than the bourne of mortal existence. But let them remember, that they will one day be obliged to answer at that tribunal where there is no respect of persons; and to a Judge who will not suffer the injurer of the meanest of those who bear his image on earth to escape with impunity. And lightly as this vice is treated by the present generation, Sir, there is no other that is so injurious to the cause of morality; so apt to eradicate every tender feeling that nature has shed around the human heart; or the cause of so much wretchedness, misery, and woe.

You see, Sir, that my tale is short and simple, and may appear uninteresting to you, and the greater number of your readers; but it is, nevertheless, highly interesting to me; and I think it does my heart good to relate it, as it recalls to my mind what I once was—what I still might have been—and what I now am. It may, perhaps, be instrumental in warning the young, the gay, and the thoughtless, of my own sex, to steer clear of that whirlpool where all my prospects of happiness have been wrecked, and swallowed up for ever. And that whatever they may suffer, or whatever they may be made to believe, never to part with their virtue; for it is only by preserving that inviolate that they can secure love and esteem from the other sex, respect from their own, the approbation of their own hearts, or the love of their Creator. I am, Sir, your most obedient and wretched

M. M.

Singular Dream

From a Correspondent

THE other night, on my way home, after a fatiguing day, I stumbled into the house of an old acquaintance, on purpose to rest myself, as well as to find amusement in his conversation, until my usual time of going to bed. This friend of mine is a phenomenon of wisdom and foresight. He keeps a weekly, if not a daily register of all the undermining and unmannerly actions practised by the men and women of this metropolis and its environs, as far as his information serves him, and he spares no pains to gain that information; and consequently can, when he pleases, retail all the incidents that have led to the births, marriages, and deaths for twenty years bygone; as well as to all the failures in business, most of which he foresaw and prognosticated with the greatest punctuality. In a short time I was struck with astonishment at the man's amazing discernment, for though we were fellow collegians, and have long been known to one another, we have not been in habits of intimacy; and I did not use to hear him mentioned by associates with half so much defer-ence as it appeared to me he was entitled to. I set him down in my mind as a most useful member of society, and from his extraordi-nary powers of estimating human characters, and human actions aright, one whom it would be wisdom for all men, both high and low, to consult before they formed any permanent connexion, or entered upon any undertaking of moment.

Impelled by a curiosity too natural, of seeing into futurity, I soon began to consult him about the affairs of the nation, and what was most likely to be the result of the present stagnation of trade, and measures of government. My heart thrills with horror to this hour, when I reflect upon the authentic and undeniable information which I received from him. We are all in the very jaws of destruction; our trade, our liberties, our religion, Heaven be our guard! our religion and all are hanging by one slender thread! which the flames of hell have already reached, and will soon singe in two. This was a shocking piece of intelligence for me, who had always cherished the fond idea that we were the most thriving and flourishing people on the face of the whole earth. When I was a young man, the several classes of society in this country were not half so well fed, clothed, or educated as they now are, what could I think but that we were a thriving and happy people? But instead of that, we were ruined bank-rupts, prodigals, depraved reprobates, and the slaves of sin and Satan. Much need have the people of this land to be constantly upon their watch-towers, having their lamps trimmed, and their beacons burning; for indeed there is not one thing as it appears to be. Our liberty is a flam, our riches a supposition, and the Bank notes in fact not worth a halfpenny a piece. Improvements in the arts and sci-ences, or in rural and national economy, are no signs of prosperity, but quite the reverse. And, would you believe it? There are some gentlemen high in office, whom I, and most of the nation, have al-ways regarded as men of the utmost probity—Lord help us, they are nothing better than confounded rascals! O! that we were wise, that we understood this!

Taught thus, by incontrovertible arguments, that the end of all things, at least with respect to Britain, was at hand, I gladly relin-quished the disagreeable topic, and introduced the affairs of this city; yet I confess I did it with a good deal of diffidence, having learned to distrust my own powers of perception altogether, and consequently knew how unfit I was to judge of any thing from ap-pearance. But how shall I ever describe to you the deformed pic-ture, which was now for the first time placed before my astonished view! It is impossible; for it was one huge mass of inconsistence. I was plainly told, that our magistrates are no magistrates, but that they only suppose themselves so: that they are a set of gossipping, gormandizing puppies: that they are fast bringing the city to ruin, which must soon come to the hammer, and be sold to the highest bidder: that our ministers of the gospel are no ministers of the gos-pel—that they are drunkards, wine-bibbers, and friends of publicans and sinners—that there is not one sentence of pure gospel preached amongst them all!—and the holy sacraments are degenerated into a mere mock or matter of form; which those only condescend to ac-cept, who, unable to preserve a character for any thing else, en-deavour to scratch up one for devotion; what a miserable state our church must be in, thought I, when, "the *boar* that from the *forest* comes, doth waste it at his pleasure." I beg your pardon, Sir, I was not meaning you.

In the High Court of Session, too, where I supposed every thing to have been decided with equity and conscience, all is, it seems, conducted by intrigue, and the springs of justice directed by self-interest alone. But that which grieved me most of all was, what he told me of our ladies, those sweet, those amiable creatures, whom I had always fondly viewed as that link in the chain of creation which connected the angelic with the human nature. Alas, Sir! it seems that it is too true that Burns says; "They're a' run w—s and jades thegither;" for my friend assured me, that they are all slaves to the worst of passions; and that they neither think nor act as if they were accountable creatures. He said that none of them ever employed a thought on any thing better, than by what means she might get a husband, or how most to plague one after she had him; and that when they were not ruminating on the one or the other of these, it was sure to be on something worse; and he cited an old foolish Roman in confirmation of his theory, who says, "*mulier quæ sola cogitat, male cogitat.*"

About this time another gentleman entered, who was without doubt come for the same purpose with myself, namely, to learn how mankind were behaving themselves on an average; and as he took up the conversation I remained silent, as indeed I had done for the most part of the time since I entered. My ideas being wound up to the highest pitch of rueful horror, I fell into a profound reverie, and from thence into a sound sleep, in which it seems I continued for nearly half an hour, and might have continued much longer, if they had not awakened me, on perceiving that I was labouring under the most painful sensations. The truth is, though I did not like to tell them all at that time, I had been engaged in a dreadful dream. There is an old Scotch proverb, that "one had better dream of the deil than the minister;" but I dreamed of them both, and mixed them so completely together that they seemed to be one and the same person; but there is no accounting for these vagaries of fancy in the absence of reason.

I thought I was in a country church, where you have often been, Sir, and that I had just taken my seat in the pew where you and I have often sat and sung bass to the old tunes, which our old precentor lilted over to us; when, who should I see mount the pulpit to preach, but the very identical friend who sat discoursing beside me, and who had so lately opened my eyes to our ruined and undone state. He read out a text from the Scriptures with great boldness. I have forgot where he said it was, for indeed I thought he did not name the right book; but I remember some of the words, which run thus: "Because our daughters are haughty, and walk with stretched forth necks, and wanton eyes, walking and mincing as they go, and making a *tripping* with their feet." He read it twice over, and then I heard a tittering noise; when, looking over my shoulder, I saw the church filled with the most beautiful women I had ever beheld in my life!—I wept to think how bad miserable creatures they were all, that so much wickedness should be concealed under so sweet a veil, and that their parents should have been at so much pains bringing up so many pests to society, and objects fitted for destruction. But the more I looked at them, they became the more lovely, and the more I looked at the preacher, he became the more ugly, until I could no longer look at him without terror. At length a tall lady stretched forward her head, and whispered to me that he was the devil. I uttered a loud scream, and hid myself behind the pew, having a peculiar aversion to that august personage, and peeping through a hole, I beheld him change his form gradually from that of a human creature, into a huge black sow. He then stepped down from the pulpit, with some difficulty, and began feeding out of a deep trough. A thought struck me in a moment, that I might easily rid mankind of their greatest enemy, by felling him at one blow, before he observed me, for his head was quite out of sight: so, snatching down a grave-pole, I glided silently away to execute my cowardly purpose. When I came within stroke, I heaved my grave-pole, and collected my whole force for the blow. "I'll do for you now, old boy," said I to myself. At that very moment he lifted up his ugly phiz! and gave me such a look, that I was quite overcome with terror, and fled yelling along the area, and the devil after me. My knees grew extremely weak, and besides, I was so entangled among women and petti-coats, that I sunk powerless to the earth, and Satan got hold of me by the arm. My friend, at that unlucky moment, observing my extraordinary agitation, took hold of my arm, and awaked me. My scattered senses not having got time to collect, I still conceived him to be the devil, and remembering the text, "resist the devil, and he will fly from you," I attacked my astonished friend with the most determined fury, boxing him unmercifully on the face, and uttering the most dreadful imprecations, resolved, it seems, that he should not insult me, or take me away with impunity. The other gentleman interfered, and brought me to my senses. "What do you mean by such a rude and beastly attack, Sir?" said my friend, while the blood poured from his nose. "I most humbly beg your pardon, Sir," said I, "but indeed I thought you was the devil." "Upon my word a very extraordinary excuse," said he; "I know I never had any great share of beauty to boast of, but I am not just so ugly as to be taken for the devil neither; and I am certainly entitled to expect an apology, both for your mad assault, and the whimsical excuse you have made for it." He accompanied this sentence with a look so malicious, and, as I imagined, so like a fiend, that I was utterly disconcerted; and could only add, by way of palliation, that I believed I did not know what I was doing; so, bowing, I walked off rather abruptly, accompanied by the other gentleman, who was ready to burst with laughter, all the way down the stairs.—When we got to the street, "Well" said he, "our friend certainly was to blame, but you have, without doubt, carried the jest rather too far. I believe, after all, that he has been speaking the truth of you, which has caused you to take it so ill." "Speaking the truth of me!" exclaimed I, "what do you mean? I hope he was not assailing my character and foreboding my ruin while I was asleep?" "Aye, that's very good," said he, laughing; "that's very good indeed; so you were indeed sleeping, and did not hear a word that he said?" "Upon my honour, I did not hear a word that he said," returned I. "Oh! that is rather too bad, my dear Sir," said he, continuing to laugh immoderately; "why, what the devil was it then that offended you, and induced you to give him such a drubbing?"—"The devil, I believe it was," said I, and then began a long bungling story about my dream, at which he only laughed the more, being firmly established in the belief that the sleep was a sham, and the assault intentional, or at least that it was the consequence of my having been irritated past bearing, by his injurious reflections.

Now, as this business is soon to be made public, by being discussed in a court of justice, I intreat you to reserve a place in your Book of Tales for this letter, which I declare to you, upon my honour, contains the real and fair statement of the facts as they followed upon one another. I am cited to answer for entering the house of Mr A. T. philosopher, and teacher of the science of chance, without any previous invitation, interpellation, or intimation; but with an intention, as it would appear, of wounding, bruising, maiming, and taking away the life of the foresaid A. T. philosopher, and teacher of the science of chance; and for most feloniously, maliciously, and barbarously, threatening, cursing, and striking the said Mr A. T. philosopher, and teacher of the science of chance, to the effusion of his blood, the damage of his person and clothes, and the endangerment of his life; and that without any provocation on the part of the foresaid A. T. philsopher and foresaid of foresaids. Yet, notwithstanding of all this, and though my counsel assures me, that I will be found liable in expenses to a high amount, I hereby declare to you, and to the world, that I am conscious of no evil intention with regard to my friend the philosopher. I went with an intention of receiving amusement and instruction from his conversation. I believed all that he told me.—I fell asleep,—which was certainly a breach of good manners, but what demon put it into my head, that he was the devil I cannot tell; *certes*, I thought he was; and when a man acts from the best intentions, I do not think he is blame-worthy if the effect should sometimes prove different. It is very hard that a man should be severely fined for resisting the devil, when there are so few that give themselves the trouble to do it.

It is true, that owing to my country education, I am a little inclined to be superstitious; but I cannot help thinking, that the whole of the accident was a kind of judgment inflicted on us both for a dangerous error; on him for abusing so many of the human race behind their backs, who were in all probability better than he; and on me for assenting implicitly to all his injurious insinuations. Nay, I would even fain carry the mystery a little further, by alleging, that a traducer and backbiter is actually a limb or agent of the devil, and that the dream was a whisper conveyed to my fancy by one of those guardian spirits that watch over the affairs of mortal men. The strange combination of ideas which that foolish dream and its concomitant mischiefs have impressed on my mind, have, besides, given me a mortal aversion to the features and looks of my old acquaintance; it has likewise led me often to an examination of the apparent springs of this principle of detraction, and foreboding of evil from every action, whether public or private; and the more I think of it, the more firmly am I persuaded of its impropriety; and that whatever such forseers may pretend, if their inferences point only towards evil, it is a symptom of a bad heart. "Let no such men be trusted."

We can form our opinions of that which we do not know, only by placing it in comparison with something that we do know: whoever therefore is over-run with suspicion, and detects, or pretends to detect artifice, in every proposal, must either have learned the wickedness of mankind by experience, or he must derive his judgment from the consciousness of his own disposition, and impute to others the same inclinations which he feels predominate in himself. Suspicion, however necessary, through ways beset on all sides by fraud and malice, has been always considered, when it exceeds the common measure, as a token of depravity. It is a temper so uneasy and restless, that it is very justly appointed the concomitant of guilt. It is an enemy to virtue and to happiness; for he that is already corrupt, will naturally be suspicious; and he that becomes suspicious will quickly be corrupt.

I was for the space of twenty years intimately acquainted with an old man named Adam Bryden, whose disposition and rule of behaviour, were widely different from those of the philosopher above mentioned, and I fear too many of the inhabitants of this metropolis. It was a maxim with him, which, though never avowed, was easily discovered, that if he could not say well of a person, he said nothing of them at all. Of the characters of the fair sex he was peculiarly tender in this respect, and always defended them against every probability. When the charges became too evident to be longer denied, he framed the kindest and most tender excuses for them, on account of the simplicity of their hearts, and kindness of their natures, which induced them to trust too implicitly to the generosity of others. It was impossible to be long in his company, without conceiving a higher opinion of the goodness of the Almighty, of his love and kindness towards his creatures, and of his wisdom displayed in the government of the universe. On the contrary, it is impossible to be long in the company of Mr A. T. the philosopher, without conceiving that Being who is all goodness, to be a tyrant, who has created man, and woman in particular, for the sole purpose of working mischief, and then of being punished eternally for that very mischievous disposition which is an ingredient in the composition of their natures. It was impossible to be long in company with the former without conceiving a higher opinion of the dignity of human nature, and of the happiness attainable by man, both in this life and that which is to come. It is impossible to be long in the company of the latter, without conceiving ourselves to be in a world of fiends, who have no enjoyment but in the gratification of sensual appetites, nor any hope but in the ruin of others.

Let your readers, then, Sir, consider seriously, which of these two characters appears to be most congenial to a heavenly mind; which of them is most likely to be productive of happiness and contentment in this life; and which of them is most conformable to the precepts left us by our great Lawgiver, in order to fit us for partaking of the blessing of a world to come. Let them weigh all these considerations impartially, and imitate the one or the other, as reason and revelation shall direct; but perhaps those who delight in magnifying the shades in the human character, may, in the end, be subjected to pay as dear, if not dearer, for it, than either Mr A. T. the philosopher, or your humble servant,

J. G.

Love Adventures

of

Mr George Cochrane

"Sans les femmes, les deux extremités de la vie seraient sans secours, et le milieu sans plaisirs." RICH.

IT is well known to all my friends that I am an old bachelor. I must now inform them further, that this situation in life has fallen to me rather by accident than from choice; for though the confession can hardly fail to excite laughter, I frankly acknowledge, that there is nothing I so much regret as the many favourable opportunities which I have suffered to escape me of entering into that state, which every natural and uncontaminated bias of the human soul bears testimony to, as the one our all-wise Creator has ordained for the mutual happiness of his creatures. Never does that day dawn in the east, shedding light and gladness over the universe, nor that night wrap the world in darkness and silence, on which I do not sigh for the want of a kind and beloved bosom friend, whom I might love, trust, and cherish, in every circumstance and situation of life; to whom I might impart every wish and weakness of my heart, and receive hers in return; rejoice in her joy; share her griefs; and weep with her over her own or the misfortunes of others, or the general depravity of human nature; kneel with her at the same footstool of infinite grace, and jointly implore forgiveness for our frailties and failings, and a blessing on our honest endeavours at fulfilling the duties of our station. But as the case now stands with me, I find myself to be an insignificant, selfish creature, unconnected to the world by any ties that can tend to endear it to me, further than the sordid love of life, or the enjoyment of some sensual gratification. I am placed, as it were alone, in the midst of my species; or rather like a cat in a large family of men, women, and children, to whose joys it bears witness, without being able to partake of them; and where no person cares a farthing for it, unless for his own benefit or amusement.

When lying on a bed of sickness, instead of experiencing the tender attention and indulgence which the parent or husband enjoys, I am left to languish alone, without one to bind up my aching head, or supply the cordial or cooling draught to my parched lips. Is not every old bachelor in the same situation? Yes, as Horace says,

"Mutato nomine de te fabula narratur."

Whatever he may be made to believe, he certainly is. If he be a poor man, he is a burden upon his friends, an encumbrance which they would gladly be rid of by any means; if rich, his relations may smile and flatter him, but in their hearts they wish most devoutly for his death.

The married state, it is true, may be entered into with rashness and imprudence, especially in the heat and folly of youth; but in any way, it is more commendable than the selfish and unnatural principle of shunning it altogether. In the worst case that can happen to a man, which is, when his selected partner turns out to be really disagreeable, still the family which she brings him engages his affection; his happiness becomes interwoven with theirs, and if he has been unfortunate in his connubial love, he enjoys the exhilarating sensations of parental affection with the more warmth and delicacy; so that still his family becomes a kind of stay whereon to rest for worldly enjoyments, and the star by which he is directed throughout the dangerous voyage of life.

The argument, that some are unhappy in this state, is of no avail; for there are many people in the world of such refractory and turbulent dispositions, that they will be unhappy in any state, and whose tempers will ever contribute, in a certain degree, to keep every one unhappy who is connected with them. Such people would probably be still more unhappy in any other state than that of wedlock, and such commonly are one, or both of the parties, who thus disagree. These are, however, only the worst cases that can happen; and though I myself am a bachelor, my opinion is fixed with respect to this. I am fully persuaded, that if there is any calm, unruffled felicity, within the grasp of an erring and imperfect creature, subject to so many passions, wants, and infirmities, it is to be found in the married state. That I have missed it, has certainly been my own blame; for I have been many times most desperately in love, and never yet met with an unfavourable reception.

The first time I fell in love was with a pretty girl who lived in our family, when I was scarce seventeen years of age. I never once thought of marrying her, nor even of informing her how much I loved: indeed I did not know myself what I wanted with her; but I could not stay out of her sight if it was possible for me to get into it. I always found some pretext of being where she was, though it had been only to pick a quarrel with her about some trifle. I could not endure to see any other man speak to her, or take the least notice of her whatever, and on every such occurrence wrecked my vengeance upon her.

The next time I fell in love was with one of the most lovely and amiable of the whole sex; but so far above my rank in life, that my cause appeared entirely hopeless. I however took every opportunity of being near to her, and was so overpowered with delight at seeing her, and hearing her speak, that the tears sometimes started to my eyes. I frequented the church every Sunday, and never once looked away from the front of the gallery where she sat. I commonly knew no more of what the parson was talking, than if he had been delivering himself in Greek. Nothing in nature gave me any delight that was not some way connected with her, and every thing that was so was dear to me; I heard with unspeakable delight, that, to the astonishment of the whole neighbourhood, she had positively rejected two gentlemen, each of whom had made her proposals of marriage highly advantageous.

I shall never, while recollection occupies her little tenement amongst the other powers of my mind, forget the day on which I first disclosed my passion to this dear and lovely woman! It was on the 20th of March. The day was sharp; and as I walked towards her father's mansion, I perceived her coming as if to meet me. I was wrapped in my tartan mantle, and was rather warm with walking, yet I was instantly seized with a fit of shivering. She, however, turned off at one side, and passed me at about the distance of twenty paces. She gave me only one look, but that was accompanied by a most bewitching smile, and went into a little summer-house. O how fain would I have followed her—but it was a piece of such monstrous rudeness to intrude upon a lady's privacy, that it quite startled me!— I thought upon the look which she gave me, and the bewitching smile!—Again I concluded that these were given only by chance—as she was always smiling. I spent about ten minutes in the utmost agony, resolving and re-resolving; and still she did not again make her appearance. At length, scarcely sensible, I likewise went into the little summer-house. She was sitting on one of the benches; her lovely cheek leaning on her hand; the train of her gown drawn over her shoulders; a book lay open before her; and the tears were standing in her eyes. I dare say I accosted her with a most sheepish look, saying, I was come in to see what detained her so long in that cold house on such a sharp day. She said, that she had by chance opened that book, which was so engaging that she could not quit it; and that it had cost her some tears. I stepped to the bench, going close up to her, merely to see what book it was—I had no other motive! It was *The Vicar of Wakefield.* It is a charming work, said I, and sat down *to*

read it along with her. I could not see distinctly to read with the ends of
the lines turned towards me; I never could read to any purpose that
way; so I was obliged to sit excessively close to her, before I could
attain the right point of view. We read on—not a single word passed
betwixt us for several pages, save one, which was often repeated, it
was, *Now.* She commonly ran over the pages faster than I could, but
always refrained from turning the leaf until I cried—*Now.* I still could
not see very well, and crept a little closer to her side. I even found it
necessary, in order to *see* with *precision*, to bring my cheek almost
close to her's. What raptures of delight thrilled my whole frame!—
We read on—at least we looked over the words, without taking any
heed to them. This was the case with me, and I believe with her, for
she shed no more tears. We came to the end of a chapter—"*Now*,"
said I; but it seems I had said it in a different way that time, for,
instead of turning the leaf, she closed the book! This little adverb
has many various meanings, all of which are easily distinguished by
the manner of pronouncing it. "I am weary of it," said she. "'Tis
time," said I. I envied not the joys of angels that day! when for the
first time I found myself alone with her whom I loved and valued
above all the rest of the world. I was so electrified with delight, that
for a moment I believed it to be all a dream. I declared my violent
affection for her, in the most respectful manner I was capable of. She
did not receive the information with the smallest degree of surprise,
but as something she was previously well acquainted with. I mentioned that her distinguished and admired personal excellencies,
together with her elevated rank in life, had hitherto restrained me
from making known my love to her; as it also entirely precluded the
least chance of my ever attaining her as my wife. Think how I was
astonished at receiving the following answer:—"The sea, to be sure,
is very deep, but he is a great coward who dares not wade to the
knee in it!"—"What do you say, madam?" said I.—She repeated the
sentence. "But do you say this in earnest?" said I. "Indeed I do,"
said she, firmly, while her eyes were fixed on the ground. I clasped
her to my bosom, and I do not know what extravagant nonsense I
uttered amid the excess of joy with which I was transported.

During the space of three years we were seldom asunder, and
enjoyed all the delights of the most pure and tender affection. I placed
implicit confidence in her; and she received me always with the most
enchanting kindness and good humour; and even, when she once
learned that I had been paying my addresses to another, she did not
in the least resent it, but observed, that it was no more than she
expected; for that she knew me better than I knew myself. I had

long been pressing her most ardently to name a day for our marriage, and at length she condescended to refer it entirely to me. Will any person, even the most dead to every sense of honour, gratitude, or love, believe that I could ever abandon this angel of a woman?– To my everlasting shame and confusion, I acknowledge that I did; and it is a just award of Providence, that I now sigh for that mutual interchange of hearts, which I can no more enjoy. I first fixed on one day for our nuptials–then another–and another. I knew I was sure of her whenever I pleased, and grew more and more careless. Her behaviour to me continued the same, without the smallest abatement of cheerful condescension: never did a single murmur, or a bitter remonstrance escape from her lips, nor one frown of dissatisfaction cloud her brow: and when, at last, my total neglect threw her into the arms of another, who was more deserving of her, still her behaviour remained unchanged; and to this day she receives me as an old friend whom she is glad to see. May Heaven smile on that benign face, which never wore a frown but in contempt of vice or folly; and bestow upon her kind and tender heart that peace and happiness which she so well merits, and to which mine must now ever continue a stranger. I feel my loss the more keenly, by knowing it was once in my power to have enjoyed that happiness which I threw away.

I have, since that period, been several times very deeply in love; sometimes for a fortnight, sometimes for a month, but never exceeding the space of half a year. Some of my adventures with the fair sex have been so whimsical, that I do not think I can divert my readers better, than by relating as many of them as this paper will contain.

I at one time conceived a violent affection for a lady whom I chanced to accompany from Edinburgh in the stage-coach. The marked attention which I paid to her at the stages and by the way, gained so much upon her heart, that she granted me permission to visit her, providing I kept out of her father's sight. This is not an example which I can recommend to my fair readers for their imitation; for indeed, I think, if any of them are admitting of the visits of a lover, of whom they would be ashamed to a father or brother, they would do as well not to admit them at all. But so it was in this instance, and she could not have annexed a condition that pleased me better, as he was a haughty, proud man, and no very warm friend of mine. After many contrivances, we both agreed that the night season was the best and most convenient for us to meet. Perhaps my Edinburgh readers will be startled at this agreement; but it is a fact, that every young woman in the country must be courted by night, or else they will not be courted at all; whatever is said to them on that subject during the day, makes no more impression upon them than stocks or stones, but goes all for nothing, or mere words of course. I was so impatient for this interview, that I got very little rest until I set about it. So one dark winter night, I wrapped myself in my father's chequered plaid, mounted his bay mare, and away I rode to see this new mistress of my heart. I fastened my father's bay mare in a dell, at a distance from the house, which I approached cautiously on foot about eleven at night. As chance directed, the front door was standing open, and as I was necessitated to take some bold step, I slipped off my shoes, took them in my hand, and stole quietly up stairs into her room, where I determined to wait her arrival. It was, however, a place where, in case of a wrong indi-vidual entering, there was not the slightest screen where I could take shelter. I was not altogether at my ease—the people bustled about from one room to another—opened doors, and closed them again, each time with a most terrible noise—every one of them went to my heart like a cannon-shot. In my heart, I wished the people all in the deepest and darkest hollow of—their beds. My terrors in-creased—I durst not sit longer—so again taking my wet shoes in my hand, and my father's chequered plaid below my arm, I slipped quietly up to a garret-room filled with household articles. I was per-fectly safe there, and quite at my ease, as no person slept in it; so, laying my wet shoes on the lid of a large chest, and wrapping my father's chequered plaid around my shoulders, I sat down on an old settee, laden with men's clothes on the back. I had not tarried there above three minutes, until I heard a foot coming lightly up the stair, while the approaching light let me see how thick the rafters stood which supported the roof. I was sure it was the foot of my charming maiden, for it sounded scarcely so loud as a rat's in the ceiling. I flew with joy to meet her, or to enter the room at or near the same time with herself.—O! misery, death, and destruction! Who was it?—No other than the very person, among all the sons of men, whom I dreaded! Yes, it was the young lady's father, coming straight to my garret-room without his hat and shoes, and having a large candle burning in his hand. It was all over with me—to make my escape from the garret-room was impossible; but not having one moment to lose, as a last resource, I jumped in behind the old settee, and coured down as close as I possibly could. I saw him approaching, and marked the most deadly symptoms of revenge in every feature. He took up my wet shoes, turned them round and round in his hand with some marks of astonishment. Now, thought I to myself, what shall I do? or what shall I say? Shall I say I came to rob the house? or steal into his lovely daughter's chamber in the dark?–Any of them is bad enough–so die I must without an alternative!–He turned about–came to the old settee, where I had taken refuge–held over the candle!——O Lord! extend thy–I won't write another word on the subject.–I really meant, when I began, to finish this story; but, I think, I must in all conscience be sunk low enough in the esteem of my readers already; and, will it not do as well to leave the conclusion of the prayer, and the conclusion of the adventure likewise, to the imagination? and then every one will paint the conclusion as best suits his own disposition. It is visible, from my writing of this, that I escaped: so the charitable will suppose me to have escaped unhurt, determining never to engage in the like again; the licentious will suppose me violating every principle of morality, as well as the innate postulate of honour and truth planted in the human breast by the Almighty, as a guard over open, kind, and unsuspecting innocence; and taking an undue advantage over a warm and feeling heart, to make that heart for ever miserable. The malicious will suppose me dragged down stairs–horse-whipped–ducked in the water–and set at liberty. Upon the whole, I find the truth will scarcely be worse than six out of seven among all the constructions that will be put upon it, therefore, on second thoughts, it will be better to go on. The truth then is, (for the whole story is absolute truth) that he held over the candle, and his head too; but it so happened, that either the clothes, or rather I think the beams of the candle, hindered him from seeing me. This was the greatest miracle I ever witnessed, for I was sitting perfectly open, staring him in the face like a hare, and watching, with terror, every motion of his eye. He turned the clothes over and over–selected a coat and over-alls from the heap–went down stairs whistling *Johnny Cope*, and gave me the greatest relief I ever experienced.

The lady came up shortly after–I attended her–was upbraided for my temerity–spent a short space with her in the most harmless and uninteresting chat, mostly about my getting out of the house, which was as absolutely necessary, as it was notoriously dangerous. "It is next to impossible," said she, "for, as you have three bolted doors to open, the dogs will, at the first, be all about you; and if they do not worry you outright, will certainly awaken my father, who will have you by the neck in a moment." "I wish women never had been made," said I; "or that they had not been made so extremely beautiful, for I see they will be my ruin. But, if I were once out"—— She did not let me finish the sentence: "I'll let you out at once," said she; "you always make so much ado about nothing." Then pushing her window gently up, which was straight above the front door, she took hold of my father's chequered plaid, and desired me to let myself down by it, while she would hold by one end until I reached the ground. She wrapped my wet shoes in the end of the plaid next her, to enable her to keep her hold, and set her knee to the wall to be ready. I crawled out, with my feet foremost, requesting her by all means to keep a good hold. "What are you afraid of?" said she; "I'll hold it if you were double the weight that you are." The window had no weights, being kept up by a catch on one side; and as it had been put gently up, the catch had only got a slight hold. What it was that agitated it, I do not know; but at the very moment on which I slid from the window, and had begun to lay my weight to the plaid, down came the window with a crack like a pistol! Whether it struck my charmer's fingers, or only startled her, was a matter of small importance to me, for I was doomed to abide by the bitter consequences either way. In short, the window and I came down precisely at the same time. The thing that I next felt, was the stone stair at the front door, on which my loin and shoulder struck with a dead thump; and at the same instant one of my shoes, which were none of the lightest, hit me on the face, and the other on the breast; for the plaid, having come off with a sudden jerk, brought them down with redoubled velocity. From the stone stair of the front door I tumbled heels-over-head down to the gravel, and took it for granted that I was dead. I was not long, however, in getting to my knees, in which position I remained a long time, considering whether I was killed or not. The dogs barked within the house as if a whole kennel had broken loose. The goodman threatened them loudly, and ordered silence.–The doors now began to open within.–I was fain to get up, bruised as I was, and indeed I was wofully bruised, and taking my wet shoes in my hand, and my father's chequered plaid below my arm, and perceiving, to my astonishment, that all my bones were whole, I never once looked over my shoulder until I reached my father's bay mare. She was standing, capering and cocking her ears, in the dell, where she left a good many indelible marks of her impatience.

The next time I met with the young lady was in a large company, where there was a number of her own sex. After saluting them round, I turned to her–"You little mischief," said I, "what made you let go?" The mentioning of this abruptly in the midst of company, and the ludicrous scene recurring to her imagination, had the effect of throwing her into a convulsion of laughter, out of which she could not recover till obliged to retire. An explanation was asked, but that was impossible to give; and many of the party, I believe, formed conjectures of their own, which, I am sure, were all wide of the truth.

I still continued very bad in love with her; and, as I had reason, from farther experience, to be more and more terrified for her father; therefore I had nothing for it but to use some shifts to see her privately. These were not easily obtained. However, she was fond of variety, and not greatly averse to my schemes. I got a few minutes conversation with her one day, and begged her to name a time when I could call and have a private uninterrupted chat with her. She told me the thing was impossible, and she would consent to no such thing. Besides, there was not a night in the year on which her father staid from home all night, save on *the eve of Lockerbie fair*, when he was obliged to stay from home all night to sell his lambs; but she would not for the world that I should come that night, as there was not a man about *the town* (so we always denominate a farm-steading.) Delighted with this sly prohibition, I shook her hand, and bade her good bye.

O how I longed for the eve of Lockerbie fair! Does any body know what the eve of a fair day, or any other day, means? I wish the reader to settle this in his own mind before he proceeds a sentence farther, and to settle it impartially; for it is a matter that may concern him deeply to understand, and it concerns me particularly that he should understand it.

I did not take my father's bay mare with me that day, but went along the heights, carrying my gun like a fowler, but without any dog. I did not shoot any muirfowl, nor did I wish to shoot any: When I am in love, all kind of noise and disturbance are distressing to me. I love silence and solitude–to be in languor, and think and dream of her that I admire–of all her beauties, sweets, and perfections. Imagination does very much for the women in this way; for I have myself transformed a girl, very little above ordinary, into a being of the most angelic loveliness; and have talked of her with such raptures to others, that they were obliged to view her in the same light; as no one ever disputed my good taste in female beauty. But this girl to whom I was so much attached, excelled every thing. O, she was so clever–so full of animation–had such eyes, such a shape, such a smile!–Good Lord! I wondered how any man, with common feelings of humanity, could live without her! For my part, I found that I could not, and I was determined that I would not live without her, let them all do as they would.

I came at length to the hill opposite to her father's house, where I lay in a bush, and watched the doors and windows with as much anxiety as a devout heathen ever did the rising of the sun. If she would only but take a walk up the side of the river, thought I, I would slide down the back of the hill and meet with her; or if she walked down the river, I would follow her. But, above all, were she to take a walk up the glen, by the side of the planting. O, ye powers of love! to lead the lovely creature into that planting, far from the eyes of all living, and from her surly father's in particular–Then, to see her frown, and hear her chide, and protest that she would not go into the planting with any man on earth, far less with me, and all the while walking faster forward into the thicket than I could keep up with her. What delightful probabilities a lover fancies! She neither walked up the river that I might meet with her, nor down the river that I might follow her, nor up the glen that I might woo her in the planting; for she did not even come out of the house that I could see the whole afternoon. I saw several other females sauntering about in a careless indifferent manner, but they were coarse vulgar creatures, cast in moulds so different from that of my charmer, that they appeared rather like beings of another species. I had no patience with them; and was obliged several times to hide my face among the bent and the heather, that I might not see their round waists, and thick bare ancles as red as carrots, and thereby mar my ideas of the beauty and purity of the sex. I made several love verses while lying on the hill that evening, which I thought very good. One of them, which I made on seeing these vulgar menials going waddling about, run thus:

> "I have looked long, I have looked sore
> For the girl that I do adore;
> But my beloved I cannot see–
> I have found but the draff where the corn should be."

Another, and perhaps a more original verse, ran thus:

> "Oh! an my love were that heather bell
>   That blooms upon the cowe,
> Then I would take her in my arms
>   Like a new clippit yowe;
> And whatsoever we did do,
>   To no man I would tell;
> But I would kiss her rosy lips,
>   As I do that heather bell."

The great art in making poetry, you will observe, is to *round the verse well off*. If the hindmost line sounds well, the verse is safe. I have never known any man who was so much master of that particular knack as myself, of which I could give many instances as well as the above, if I had leisure from more important matters.

It happened to be a particularly long afternoon that on which I lay watching for my charmer. The sun stood still about the same place for several hours, whether on account of any imperative command, or sheer ill-will, I do not know; but it is absurd to suppose that his course is regulated by any stated time. I have seen a very material difference in the celerity of his journeying. If any disbelieve me, let him ask a school boy, whether the afternoon of Friday or Saturday is the longest? Ask the maid-servant, whether the fair day, or the day that she is toiling on the harvest field, wears first or fastest to a close? but, above all, ask the lover who is sitting watching for the fall of night, that he may meet and clasp her whom he admires above all the rest of the world.

After much procrastination, the sun at last went down, and the twilight followed with slow and lingering pace. With a beating heart I again approached the house. "There will be none of these boisterous dogs here to-night," thought I; "the shepherds will be all absent at Lockerbie fair." The thought was barely formed ere I was attacked by two in a most vociferous manner, as I stood by the garden-wall cowering like a bogle. I tried to cajole them in a whisper, pretending to be friends with them. It would not do, they waxed louder and louder. I threw stones at them—they were worse than ever—"Bow—wow—wow. Yough, yough." I was obliged to take to my heels and fly, for the inmates were getting alarmed. The women rushed out; I heard their voices, but could not see them distinctly—my dear angel was among them. "Who can that be?" I heard one saying. "Only some passenger going home from the fair," returned she in a voice sweeter than music. "I hope he means to ca' in," said the other, in a loud giggling, vulgar voice; "he'll surely gie some o' us a bode as he gaes by." "Na, na," cried another gawky, "he hasna sae muckle in him; he's awa wi' his tail atween his legs like Macmillan's messan." My dear angel then called in the dogs, and rebuked them both by name as they passed her; and after desiring her women to keep their jokes within the walls of the house, as they knew not who might hear them, she went in last, and closed the door. Every word that she spoke thrilled my heart with delight; and I was utterly impatient for the hour of meeting—no jealous father to alarm us—no rival to interpose; not even a man-servant about the house; and as for the maids, they had a fellow-feeling for each other; and moreover, she had it in her power to make them do what she pleased.

Urged by this hopeful consideration, I was not long in returning to her window, at which I tapped lightly, my very breath almost clean gone with anxiety. She threw up the sash. I accosted her in a tremulous broken whisper—"My dear, dear Mary," said I, "have I found you alone?" "Bless me, Mr Cochrane," said she aloud, "is it you? Why do you rap at the window rather than the door? Come in, come in; my father, I dare say, will be very glad to see you." I was stupified and speechless. "There is some vile mistake here," thought I. But before I recovered the dear teazing creature opened the door, and bidding me come in, I implicitly obeyed and followed her into the parlour.—"Where have you been, or where are you going so late?" said she. "What need have you to ask," said I, "Mary? You know well enough I am come to bear you company for a little while. Did not you tell me that your father and all the men were to be from home to-night?" "Me!" exclaimed she, "I never told you such a thing! I could not tell you that, for I knew it was impossible. I was afraid you would come last night; for, it being the fair eve, there was not a man about the town—the two maids were away on some business of their own, and here was I for the whole night locked up in the house, without a living soul in it but myself. Positively I do not know what I should have done, if you had come last night."

I am certain there never was another wooer looked so sheepish as I did at this moment. I was chagrined past endurance at myself, at her, and at all mankind. I saw the golden opportunity was past, and that I had run my head into a noose, and consequently I was in a violent querulous humour. She was no less so. "My dear Mary," said I, "surely you will not pretend to assert that the evening of a fair day is not the fair eve!" "Are you so childishly ignorant," returned she, "as not to know that the eve of a festival, holiday, or any particular day whatever, always precedes the day nominally?" I denied the position positively, in all its parts and bearings. She reddened; and added, that she could not help pitying a gentleman who knew so little of the world, and the terms in use among his countrymen—terms with which the meanest hind in the dale was perfectly well acquainted. "Pray, consider," added she, "do you not know that the night before a wedding, the night on which we throw the stocking, is always denominated the wedding eve? All-Hallow eve, the night on which we burn the nuts, pull the kail stocks, and use all our cantrips, is the evening before Hallow-day. St Valentine's eve, and Fasten's eve, are the same. Why then will you set up your own recent system against the sense and understanding of a whole country?"

"Never tell me of your old Popish saws and customs; the whole of your position is founded in absurdity, my love," said I. "This, you know, is the evening of the fair day—the fair is doubtless going on as merrily as ever; this then must either be the fair eve, or else the fair has two eves, which is rather more than either common sense or use and wont will warrant."

I found I had acted very wrong; for by this time anger was depicted on her lovely countenance, and I saw plainly that she had a smithy spark of temper in her constitution.

"I could go farther back, and to higher authority, than old Popish saws, as you call them, for the establishment of my position, if I chose," said she; "I could take the account of the first formation of the day and the night, where you will find it recorded, that 'the *evening* and the morning were the first day;' but as it would be a pity to mortify one by a confutation who is so wise in his own conceit, I therefore give up the argument. You are certainly in the right; and may you always profit in the same way as you have done now, by sticking to your own opinion."

This was a severe one; and in the temper and disposition that I was in, not to be brooked. "Nothing can be more plain," said I, "than that the evening of a day is the evening of that day."

"Nothing can," said she.

"And, moreover," said I, "has not the matter been argued thoroughly by our christian divines?"

"It has," said she.

"And have not they all now agreed, from St Chrysostom down to Ebenezer Erskine, that the Sabbath-day begins in the morning?"

"They have," said she.

"And if the Sabbath begins in the morning, so must also Monday; and so must every day, whether fair day or festival."

"There is no doubt of it at all," said she; "wherefore reason any more about the matter? Here is my father coming, we shall appeal to him, and he will, without doubt, ratify all that you have been saying." Her father now entered; for he had been all the while in the next room settling his fair accounts. His eyes were heavy with fatigue, and his face red with sun-burning and whisky punch—a most ungainly figure he was. "Humph!" said he, as he came in, "wha hae we gotten here?" "It is Mr Cochrane, sir, who stepped in on his way home from the moors to get the news of the fair; but what argument think you he has taken up? he will not let me say that this is the fair eve." "Neither it is, Miss," said he, "any body knows that the night afore the fair is the fair e'en." "I can hardly trow that you are right, sir," said she. "Nor can I, upon my honour," said I. "Ye canna, upon your honour, can ye no? Humph! sic honour! Fine honour, faith! Crocks wad craw and duds wad let them. Ye're unco late asteer, I think, the night, chap.–Whar hae ye been scatterin focks' sheep the day?" I assured him that I had molested no one's sheep, for that my dog had left me, and that I had had very little sport.

"Sport! snuff's o' tobacco!" exclaimed he, "to hear some folk tauk o' sport that it wad suit better to be weeding their minnie's kail-yard, or clouting their ain shoon. Humph! fine sport, faith! Ye surely hae unco little to do at hame."

I could hardly sit all this, but unwilling to break, both with the old gentleman and her I loved so passionately at once, I restrained myself, and answered him in a forced jocular manner. We got some supper; and the young lady proposed that we should drink a jug of toddy together afterwards, but this he positively declined, saying that I would be too late before I got home. This was as broad a hint for me to go about my business as could be given, and I would have been obliged to have taken it, had not sheer good manners compelled the young lady to propose that I should take a bed till the morning. Thinking this offer augured well, and that I would still be favoured with a private conference, I accepted of the proposal; but, without the possibility of getting another private word of her, I was shewn to my bed.

It was on the same floor with that of my charmer; her father's, as is before mentioned, being on the ground floor. I thought it behoved me, after coming so far to see her, to make an attempt at a private interview, and had no doubt but that she intended it, when she urged me to stay, notwithstanding the ill humour we both were in about the fair eve. I only threw off my coat and shoes, and laid me down on my bed; but to think of sleeping, so situated, was out of the question.

I lay till near midnight, when all was quiet, and not so much as a mouse stirring; then rose, put on my coat, and groped my way with great caution to her room, weening that she would have lain down without undressing like myself; but I was mistaken. I waked her– she pretended great astonishment and high displeasure, but always spoke below her breath. She said I was mad–and that it was fine behaviour in sooth–and a great number of such kind of things. I said still a greater number of the most extravagant things that ever were spoke, to all of which she only replied, "go away to your bed, I tell you." "My dear divine Mary," said I, "as you know you are safe from insult in my company at all times, and in all situations, therefore why not suffer me to remain a while with you?"

"Because my father is jealous of us, and your peril, as well as mine, is very great. I must first remove that jealousy, and then you may come as often as you will," she replied.

"O, for Heaven's sake, do remove that jealousy! I'll come every night to see you," said I.

"You must then abide by the consequences," she returned.

"I will abide by any consequences, for the sake of enjoying your sweet company without interruption," said I.

"Well then," she returned, "I intreat that, in the first place, you will behave as you ought to do, and go to your bed. You *shall* go to your bed, I insist on it—you might have come on the fair eve, as a true lover and a man of sense would have done."

"So I have, my dear, I have come on the fair eve;" said I.

I fear this was an unfortunate speech of mine, for, short as it was, it led to very disagreeable consequences. I declare I had no more intention of going into the bed beside the young lady, than I had of again letting myself out at her window. I wanted only to have a private conference, for I loved her to distraction, and the most that I would have ventured would have been to have put my arm round her waist, and perhaps kissed her hand or her cheek. But at this luckless time, my arm happened to be flung over her shoulder above the clothes; at which, being offended, she flung back away from me. Thinking this was all a pretence, and that she wanted to make room for me—what could I do? I certainly did make a lodgement on the foreside of the bed. I was confoundedly mistaken, for at that moment my ears were saluted by a distant tinkling sound; but I thought they themselves were ringing, my spirits being in such commotion, and I paid no attention to the portentous sound. My charmer fled farther away from me, and I followed proportionally, still keeping, however, a due distance. The ill-set creature had a bell-handle at the back of her bed, which I little dreamed of, and far less that she would make any use of such a thing if she had. I had never found it the nature of the fair sex to be ready in exposing the imprudencies of their lovers, if committed for the sake of their own persons; therefore my astonishment may be judged of, when I heard a distant bell ringing fiercely and furiously. "Good God!" said I, "what's that?" She had not time to answer me, when her father entered, half dressed, and apparently only half awake, carrying a lighted candle, before which he held his open hand lest it should go out, and at the same time stared over above it, with open mouth, and his night-cap raised on his brow. "Mary, my dear, what is the matter? what do you want?" said he. "I want you, sir, to show this gentleman back to his bed-room," said she. "He has come here by some mistake, and refuses to go away. He even insists on lying in the same bed with me, a freedom which I *will not* admit of." "Fine behaviour, faith!" said the old savage, but not in particularly bad humour. He seemed pleased with his daughter's intrepidity, whom hitherto I suppose he had trusted but very little in love matters; and not less pleased to find me exposing myself in such a base manner, for which I could have no excuse. "Humph!" continued he, "you did very right, daughter. Fine honour, faith! come awa chap, an' I'll shew you a gate that will set ye better. Humph! my certy! ye're ane indeed." "I hope, my dear sir," said I, "you cannot suspect me of any dishonourable intentions towards your daughter, whom, I declare, I love better than my own life!" "Humph! fine love, faith! Come awa; sic love canna stand words." So saying, the old hound seized me by the collar behind, and began to drag me away. "What do you mean, sir?" said I; "I'll not be handled in this manner—I'll fight you, sir." "O, to be sure you will," returned he. "So will I—I'll fight too; but we maun do ae thing afore another, ye ken." And then, with a ruder grasp, he dragged me down the stair, quite choked by the gripe he had of my collar, and scarcely able to move my limbs. "It is your own house, sir," said I, "else I would beat you most unmercifully—I would beat you like a dog." "Oh, to be sure, you would," said he; "there's nae doubt o't ava." He then pushed me out at the door, giving me a furious kick behind; and then closing the door with a loud clash, he bolted it on the inside.

I was perfectly deranged, at having thus made a fool of myself; and, like all men who make a fool of themselves, I made a still greater fool of myself. I turned in a horrid rage, and ran to his window. "Give me out my clothes, you old dog," I cried. "Give me out my shoes, my hat, my plaid, and my gun, or I'll break every window and door in your house, you old ragamuffin scoundrel that you are!" Clink went one pane of the window—jingle went another—I then heard a step inside, and, on pricking up my ears, I heard these words, "By G— I will give it him." This brought me a little to my senses. I stood aside for a few seconds, and listening, I heard a window of the second flat opened softly, and soon beheld, between me and the sky, the muzzle of a gun coming sliding out. It was needless to bid me take to my heels; so I turned the corner and ran with main speed. The noise I made had wakened the shepherds who slept in the stable, and just as I ran past the door, out sallied two men and four dogs on me. "Seize that rascal, and duck him," cried their master, setting his head out at the window, "he has broken up the house." The two fellows ran after me; but I redoubled my speed; and being ready stripped for the race, I left them a considerable space behind. For some time the chase continued down a level valley, on which I had the heels of them, as the saying is, considerably; but, on leaving that, we came to rough boggy ground interspersed with some sheep-drains. I then heard the panting and blowing of one of the shepherds, who had gained ground, and was coming hard on me. The other was quite behind; and was laughing so immoderately that he could make little speed. I cast a hurried glance behind me, and saw a large brawny rascal within a dozen yards of me, who was bare-headed and bare-legged, and had a huge two-handed staff heaved above his right shoulder. I strained every nerve; and coming to a steep place, I went down it with inconceivable velocity. My pursuer did the same; but either his body came faster down than his feet could keep up with, or, what is as probable, he had set his foot inadvertently, in the height of his speed, into a drain, for down he came with such force, that he actually flew a long way in the air like a meteor before he alighted, and then pitched exactly on his nose and forehead. With such an unwonted force did he fly forward, after losing his equilibrium, that the staff, which he carried above his shoulder, came by me with a swithering noise like that made by a black-cock on the wing at full flight. I suppose he quitted it in his swing, in order to save his face by falling on his hands. Hard as my circumstances were, I could not help laughing at my pursuer's headlong accident; but I lifted the cudgel, and fled as fast as I could. Whether he was hurt or only had his wind cut by his fall, I know not, but I saw no more of him. About a mile farther on I heard their voices behind me, but they were not so near as to alarm me, and besides, I was in possession of the club, which I had resolved to make use of, if attacked.

When out of danger, I deliberated calmly on what had passed. I deemed myself very ill used—most shabbily used! and my first emotions were toward a stern and ample revenge. But when I began to question myself about my motives, and answer these questions strictly according to the dictates of honour and conscience, I found that the answers did not entirely satisfy me; and I was not so sure whether I had received any thing beyond my deserts or not. "What

were you going to do with the girl, George? Did you mean honourably by her?" "Oh, strictly." "That is, you positively intended to
make her your wife?" "No." I searched every crevice of my heart
out and in, and could not say that I did. But then, I could not be
happy out of her company—in short, I loved her. Was not that quite
sufficient? Will said it was—honour said not much about it; but conscience whispered the old father's saying into my heart, "Fine love,
faith!"

"Suppose you had a lovely and beloved daughter, George, and
found a young fellow, of whose principles and honour you did not
much approve, who had stolen clandestinely into her bed-chamber,
and, in spite of remonstrance, was even making his way into her
bed, what would you have done with him? Aye, there's the rub!
That brings the matter home at once! Cut his throat to be sure;
besides stabbing him in different parts of the body. Fine love, faith!"

The thing that chagrined me most of all, was an indistinct recollection, that while the father was dragging me out of the room like a
puppy by the neck, and I was threatening to fight him, I heard my
sweetheart tittering and laughing. This almost drove me mad—it
looked so like a set plan to make a fool of me. Yet I could not believe
but that I had received some proofs of her attachment—proofs that I
had a preference in her esteem, or she must be a very extraordinary girl. "Perhaps," thought I again, "all this shame and obloquy
has sprung from the contradiction I gave her about *Lockerbie fair eve*.
But, say that this is the case, it argues very little for her prudence or
good sense." Upon the whole, I found my admiration of her mixed
with a little bitterness, and I formed some resolutions concerning
her, not the most generous, nor the most commendable in the world.

Next morning I appeared at breakfast with a sullen, dissatisfied
look. "Sauf us! Geordie, what ails ye the day?" said my mother, "ye
look at a' things as ye coudna help it. An' guid forgie us! what hae
ye made o' your hat, that ye are gaun wi' that auld slouch about
your lugs? an' hae ye tint your shoon, that ye maun be strodgin
about i' your boots?" I did not know how to satisfy my mother's
curiosity, far less how to recover my apparel, without exposing myself
and all concerned to both families; so, in the first place, I was obliged
to contrive a manifest lie to pacify my mother. I told her, that while
I was out on the moors, on such and such a height, by came William
Tweedie's hounds hard after a fox; and that, in order to keep up
with them, I had thrown away my plaid, shoes, hat, coat, and gun,
and followed them all the way to Craigmeken Skerrs, where the
hounds lost the foot; but on returning, it was that dark, that I found

it impossible to get my clothes and gun; I had, however, left word
with some of the shepherds, who I trusted would find them.

That same day there was a small packing-box left at the shop near
by, directed to a man in Moffat, with a card for me. It was in these
terms: "M. L.'s comp^{ts} to Mr C., sends the clothes in box. Will hide
the gun till owner calls. No one shall know. Is sorry the consequences
turned out so severe. Jealousy now asleep for ever. Mr C. needs
not be in a hurry in taking advantage of this. When he does, let him
throw a handful or two of gravel against a certain window."

"Woman's an inexplicable thing!" said I to myself; "Is it possible
that the minx has exposed me to this shame and indignity, merely to
lull asleep all jealousy in her father's breast with respect to me, that
we may in future enjoy one another's company without fear or interruption? The thing is beyond my comprehension! She certainly
is an extraordinary, and rather a dangerous girl this! However, I'll
go and see her once more, and if I have such opportunities as I have
had, I shall make better use of them."

I was much pleased with her ingenuity in sending me my clothes;
but the more I studied her, the less I could make of her character;
yet she was a charming girl, nevertheless! It was not long till I again
mounted my father's bay mare at night, and rode away to see her;
and, as she had given me the hint, when all was quiet I went and
threw two handfuls of sand against her bed-room window. It was
not long before she looked out, and, on seeing who it was, she made
a sign with her hand to the door. I threw off my shoes and hid them,
and then went to the door, where soon the dear delightful creature
came, and opened it so softly, that I did not hear it, though standing
at the landing-place, or *door-step*, as they call it there. Without speaking a word, she took me by the hand, pulled me in, and closed the
door, but did not bolt it for fear of noise; then leading me up the
stair, she ushered me darkling into her room, into that room where
I had suffered so severely twice before, and which I did not enter
again without trepidation and some uneasy apprehensions. She was
elegantly dressed in a white night-gown, with a handsome house
cap on her head, garnished with ribbons. I held her by the hand,
and as I looked in her face, by the help of the moon that shone on
her casement, I thought her the handsomest creature on earth. I sat
down on a chair, and took her on my knee, clasping my arms around
her waist. She made no resistance to this arrangement of position,
amorous as it was; and to make it still worse, she leaned her head
on my shoulder. I said many extravagantly fond things, to which
she made no reply. Her behaviour always led me into errors. I

deemed that the position in which we were placed, warranted me in snatching a kiss from those sweet delicious lips that were actually shedding the fragrance of roses and honey-suckle warm on my cheek; so I made the attempt. No—no such liberties could be granted. "I disapprove of kissing altogether," said she; "and cannot tell you how much I admire the substitute resorted to by a certain valued friend of mine. Have you not heard of one, who, in cases of necessity, kissed a heather cowe?" I declared I never had: On which she repeated these two lines, with a softness and pathos that made them more ridiculous than aught I had ever heard:

> "Then I would kiss her rosy lips,
> As I do that heather bell!!!"

"Where the devil did you come by that?" said I. "No matter how I got it," replied she; "I get many things that you are not aware of." "I believe you never said a truer thing in your life," said I; "I always thought you were a witch. But surely you will grant me a kiss of that comely cheek, which is a small boon; after I have come so often and so far to see you, you cannot refuse me when I ask so little?" "O yes!" said she, with a deep feigned sigh,

> "Man wants but little here below
> Nor wants that little long."

"The devil is in this girl!" thought I to myself; "she is quite beyond my depth. I know not what to make of her!" I sat silent for some time, considering what she could mean. At that instant I thought I heard a kind of distant noise in the house, and at the same time, I observed that she was holding in her breath in the act of listening. I was going to ask her what it was; but she prevented me by laying her hand on my mouth, and crying "hush!" I then distinctly heard footsteps on the stair. "Gracious Heaven!" exclaimed she, in a whisper, "there, I believe, is my father! What shall we do? For God's sake hide." The approach of the devil would have been nothing to me in comparison to that of the old desperate ragamuffin, in the situation I then was, so in a moment I was below the bed, where I found things in bad order, and besides, very little room for me. She slid into her bed straight above me, covered herself with the sheets, and fell a sniffing, as if in the most profound sleep. "What a delightful ingenious creature she is," thought I to myself; "now I shall hear how nicely she will bring us off." The door of the room opened; but, as I judged, too softly to be opened by her father, and the steps came over the floor, apparently, with all the caution the walker was mas-

ter of, though his skill was not exquisite in that most necessary acquirement in night-wooing. He came close to the bed-side, and tried,
in vain for a long time, to waken the dear deceitful creature, who at
length was pleased to awake with many smothered exclamations of
astonishment and high resentment. At length I heard her say, "Scott,
is it you?" "Yes, to be sure it is," said he. "For shame!" exclaimed
she; "how have you the impudence to come into a solitary girl's
chamber at this time of night? I assure you, it is a freedom of which
I will not admit; and therefore, if you wish that I should ever speak
to you again, go away this instant without saying another word."
"God save the king, Mary!" said he; "What's the matter w'ye the
night? just as ane was never here afore." "I beg you will take notice
what you say, sir," said she, "and begone instantly, else I'll ring the
bell." "You had better go away, friend," thought I, "and be thankful
she has given you warning—she'll be as good as her word, and ring
the bell with a vengeance." "Suffer me one moment to explain," said
the lover, in a most suppliant tone, for he seemed to know the danger of the ground on which he was treading. "I will not suffer a
word," said she, "from one who treats me in this manner. I'd have
you to know your distance and keep it. If I am consulted, and choose
to admit a gentleman to a private tete-a-tete, that is all very well. I
hope I know what freedoms I should admit of in such cases, and
what not. But I will not have my privacy intruded upon in this manner if you were a prince of the realm; and so, instantly I say, go
about your business."

"Well, upon my word, the girl speaks excellent good sense,"
thought I; "and I hope the fellow will go away. When he does, O
how dearly I will caress the spirited, dear, ingenious creature!" "Well,
I must go away, since you insist on it," said he. "Ay, pray do," said I
to myself; "the sooner the better." "But, as some excuse for my behaviour," continued he, "I must tell you before I go, that, as I set out
for the English market on Monday, and cannot see you again for six
or seven weeks, I came to take leave of you, and bid you good-bye
for a little while. I intended to have wakened you in the way you
prescribed; but finding the hall door open, which is not usual, I
thought I would come in and awake you myself." "Well, you are
very kind," said she, "and I am obliged to you; but you have done
very wrong, therefore, pray, go away, as I have particular reasons
for desiring your absence to-night." "And so have I, sir, if you please,"
thought I. I think that at this time she had put out her arm to push
him away from the side of the bed, for I heard him say, with evident
symptoms of surprise, "Bless me, Mary, you are dressed! In full

dress too!–ruffled at hands and neck! Why are you sleeping with your clothes on? Oh! I see! I see! Yes, you have particular reasons for desiring my absence to-night indeed! You are waiting for some other lover, and have left the door open for him. You need not deny it, for the thing is perfectly evident. But I shall disappoint him for once, for I will not go away to-night." "But, friend," thought I, "could I but reach the handle of the bell at the back of the bed, which perhaps is not impossible from this situation, I should get you a dismissal you are little dreaming of." "And will you indeed presume to stay here without my approval?" said she; "or dictate to me about my lovers? Once you have me under control, you may–leave me instantly." "Well, if you force me to go away, I will watch him at the door." "Watch him where you please, but you may watch in vain–leave the room." "I never saw you so very cross as you are to-night, my beloved Mary, and I am sorry for it, for I had a great many things to talk to you about. But, if you will but suffer me to remain five minutes, I protest I'll ask no more, and I will then go quietly home, and neither watch your door nor window." "Well, as you positively promise to go away at the end of five minutes, I'll indulge you for once; but suffer me to rise, for I do not like to converse with a gentleman in this guise." "I do not see any harm in it." "Perhaps not; nor do I think there is much; but it looks so careless and indelicate that I never can submit to it."

She arose; and as there happened to be only one chair in the room, they were obliged to sit down on the side of the bed. The stock being higher than the matress, it was impossible to sit on it; so, after all, they were obliged to lean across the bed. I heard every word that passed with distinctness, and as the lover declared that he had things of great importance to say to her, I took particular note of them, and shall here give the conversation of a lover who had only five minutes to spend with his mistress, and was not to see her again for two months.

"Well now, after all, we are lying upon the bed; so you might as well have remained where you were."

"I do not think it half so bad to lean across a bed, as to lie at full length upon it."

"A woman's whimsie!"

"Say that it is a whimsie: such whimsies as have no evil tendency you may grant us. But the truth is, that I disapprove of the whole system of wooing by night, and heartily wish it were out of fashion, which I am told it is in every district of the kingdom but this."

"I hope it never will be out of fashion here."

"And why, pray?"

"Because, in the first place, it is always so delightful."

"Not always, friend," thought I; "if you were in my situation, you would feel otherwise."

"And, in the next place, one hears his sweetheart's mind much more explicitly."

"I am not sure of that, Mr Scott," thought I.

"And, in the third and last place, all our fathers courted that way—our mothers were courted that way—every farmer's wife in the three shires has been courted in that way, save a few of a very late date, and I should be sorry to see such a good old established system exploded."

"I have been always told these things, but I do not give credit to them."

"They are, however, true. I have heard the matter disputed by some pretenders to refinement, and to that false delicacy for which the age is notorious; and I have heard it proved to my entire satisfaction, and many curious anecdotes besides, relating to it. Laird K—y of Ch—k—t courted his lady many a night in the hay-mow of her father's cow-house, and she was wont to milk him a jug of sweet milk before he set out on his journey home. The Laird of S—n—e courted his lady in the woods by night, and sometimes among his father's growing corn, who accused him very much of the broadness of the lairs that he made; and he is one of the first landward lairds of the country. The reverend minister of K—m—l courted his wife in her mother's dairy, in the dark; and once in attempting to kiss her, his wig fell into a pail of milk, and was rendered useless. The old woman got a terrible fright with it, when about to skim the milk next morning. All the seven large farmers in the upper part of our parish courted their wives in their own bed-chambers; and I have heard one of them declare, that he found the task so delightful, that he drew it out as long as he could with any degree of decency. My father did the same, and so did yours; ask any of them, and they will tell you. And besides, is it not delightful, the confidence that it displays in the indelible virtue of daughters, sweethearts, &c.?"

"Say rather, the carelessness of their virtue that it displays. I know, from my own experience, that it is impossible for a girl who allows it not to be placed in some very disagreeable dilemmas."

"Oh, you allude to your late adventure with Geordie Cochrane? Upon my word, you served him as he deserved! I never was so much pleased and diverted with any thing that ever I heard in my life."

"Geordie Cochrane's very much obliged to you, neighbour," thought I; "and he may, perhaps, live to be even with you yet."

"Say not a word about Mr Cochrane, sir; for I will not suffer one of my lovers to slander another of them to my face. When he comes back, he may possibly be as much inclined to talk about you."

"Him! He speak of me! If he durst, I would claw the puppy-hide of him! He is as great a skype as I know of."

I heard the little imp like to burst into laughter as he said this, and that all the while she was trying to stop him by holding her hand upon his mouth, for the sentences came out piecemeal and in vollies.

"I would rather see you married on any plowman, or–(bhoo–cease!)–tailor or weaver–(bhoo, give over I tell you) in the country. No man or woman can depend on a word he says, he's the greatest liar (bhoo–oo–oo)"

"D——n the fellow!" said I to myself, "could I but reach the handle of the bell, I would astonish him." I struggled all I could to reach it.

"What is that below the bed?" said he.

"It is our old dog Help, poor fellow, that I often keep with me to bear me company, and be a kind of guardian against intruders like you. Help, go away, you old slyboots; it behoves you well to lie there, and listen to all that passes between my lover and me."

This gave me a little toleration to move, and I struggled more and more to reach the handle of the bell. I was almost smothered to death, while another was lying in the arms of my mistress; so I was determined to suffer the base intruder no longer. But all that I could do, I could not reach the handle of the bell, or rather I could not find it.

"Lie still, Help," cried she, "and be at peace; and I'll let you out in two minutes." I thought I would suffer a little longer for the sake of her dear company; so, wiping my dripping brows, I composed myself to my state of sufferance as well as I could. The important courtship of the lovers terminated here, and I heard, from what they said, that they were greatly alarmed at something they heard below. "Merciful Heaven!" exclaimed the lady; "Who can it be? It is some one speaking to my father in at the window!" I listened as attentively as I could–they did the same–and at length I heard the old farmer say, "watch ye the door, an' I'll gang up an' see what I can see." "Now friend," thought I, "it is your turn come; and if you do not get it I am mistaken." He had just time to spring from the bed, and shut himself into a corner press, before the lady's father entered. Mary had hastily composed her decent form on the bed, and pretended to be sound asleep. He came forward and with some difficulty awaked her; while she seemed to be much frightened and discomposed, and asked what he wanted? "I want," said he, "to see if there is any body with you." "Any body with me, father!–what do you mean? You see there is nobody here." "I dinna understand that, Miss. Aedie, our herd, tells me, that he saw that silly profligate thing, Geordie Cochrane, come riding this way after the gloaming; and that his beast is standing tied at the back of the dike just now."

"It is not likely he would come here after the last reception he got; but take no notice of it, he will be with some of the maids, and he'll go away as he came," said she.

"A fine story, faith! that he would be with ony o' the maids, an' kens the gate here! deil tak' him, gin I catch him here again hingin' o'er my bairn, like a hungry tod o'er a weel nursed lamb, an' I dinna pu' the harrigalds out o' him!" So saying, by a natural impulse, which led him to the only door that was in the room, except the one he entered by, he tried to open the door of the press; but it resisted his pull, although it was not quite close. When he found this, he made it come open with such fury, as if he would have pulled down the house, and there stood his old acquaintance Scott, staring him in the face like a hunted wild cat from its den. "L–d have a care o' us!" said the old farmer; but, before he had time to articulate another word, the lover burst by him, and, running down stairs, made for the door. On the outside of the door there stood the staunch shepherd with his club, who, thinking it was me that was coming on him with such rapidity, determined to have a hearty blow at me, and no sooner did Mr Scott set his head out at the door, than he hit him on the links of the neck with such force, that he was laid flat on the gravel, and the shepherd above him with his knees and elbows. The old farmer followed, and I suspect that between the two Scott got but very rough treatment, for there was a terrible affray before the door for some time, and a great deal of oaths going. He must certainly have been hard put to it, for I heard him saying: "If you won't let wooers come to see your daughter, d—n you, keep her and make a table-post of her. I'm as good as she, or any of her kin,– d—n you; keep her, and make a tea-cannister of her, if you like." "A bonny story, faith!" said the old farmer.

I now began to drag myself out of my hole, anticipating the most delicious morning's courtship with my jewel that ever man enjoyed; but she begged me to lie still until I heard how matters settled, and regretted, as a pernicious business, the discovery made of my horse. I thought the old rascal could never once dream that there was another lover in the chamber, and therefore considered myself as perfectly safe. However, up he came again. "Mary," said he, "the herd assures me that Cochrane is here." And without waiting for any reply, he went to the press, and examined it more minutely; then, kneeling down on his hands and knees, he lifted the curtain and peeped beneath the bed. He did not speak a word on making the joyful discovery; but, observing where my feet lay, he set down the candle, hastened to the end of the bed, and, seizing me by the two feet, soon had me lying on my back in the middle of the floor.

"Deil pike out my een," said he, "gin ever I saw the like o' this sin' my mother bure me! Gude-faith, ye hae been playing at hide-an'-seek here! Chap, what think ye o' yoursel, now?"

"Whatever I may think of myself," said I, "it is apparent that I think more of some one else, that I have ventured so much for her." "Fine government, faith!" said he, while all the time holding me by the feet, with one on each side of him, so that I could not move, but lay on my back, and looked him in the face; and, for the first time, I perceived to my astonishment, that he seemed to watch Mary's eye for the regulation of his behaviour toward me. "What say you to it, Miss? What have you to say for yourself?" "I have nothing to say either for or against myself; but for the gentlemen, I must say that they are both gone mad." "Ay, and waur than mad!" cried he, encouraged by this remark of Mary's. "It is a mischievous madness theirs. Ane creeps into ae corner, an' another into another, to watch a poor bit innocent sleeping lassie, and a' to be her ruin; it can be for nought else. May the ill thief be my landlord, chap, gin I dinna bury my fit in ye up to the instep." I was still lying in the same posture as before–the most awkward one in which a lover could be introduced to his mistress's father, or herself either, and had no power to help or defend myself. Had he given me the kick he meditated, he had finished my course; but Mary raised her hand–which chained him still in a moment! "Hold!" said she, "let Mr Cochrane go; I want to speak with him." He dropped my legs that instant, and I was not long in getting on my feet. "What!" said he, "and leave him here with you?" "If you please, sir." The old farmer, although he was in very bad humour, actually turned round at the first word, on purpose to leave me with his lovely daughter. I never was so much astonished in all my life.

"Humph!" said he, "fine wark, faith! Od, dame, ye coudna stand this an' ye waur made o' bell-metal."

"Speak, my dear father," said she, softly–and he turned about.

"You know, though I am perfectly innocent of their coming here, yet were you to turn out Mr Cochrane now, it would expose me to the servants in a most ridiculous light, and actually ruin me. So, go away and deny that he is here. You surely are not afraid to leave me with any of them?" "I'm nae fear't for ony imprudence, lassie; and I'm nae fear't ye *do* aught that's wrang; but it's your mind that I'm rad for; they'll gie't a wrang swee, thae chaps. Od, they'll pit ye daft! Weel, weel; ye may tak your crack there, sin it maun be sae." And away he went, closed the door, and left us to improve the subject in any way we liked.

"Well, my dear Mary," said I, standing like one petrified, and in the dark, "of all the things I ever witnessed this has surprised me the most; for I always imagined that your father tyrannized over you, and kept you in check, which made you the more willing to over-reach him when opportunity served."

"You never were more deceived in your life, then," said she; "I am frequently obliged to make use of my father to expel those idle young gentlemen who come about me; often merely, as I suspect, to amuse themselves. He is proud of the trust; and often on such occasions assumes very high ground; but my will is his; and he has no wish but mine in such cases. I never expose my lovers to any insult from my father, unless for very good reasons; and I am sometimes driven to shifts to prevent them running their heads together; but I never yet conversed with a lover that I did not inform him of, as well as what I thought of the lover's motives in paying his addresses to me."

"I stand on ticklish ground here," thought I; "therefore must take good care what I say or propose, in a case like this. As the sailor said to his captain, 'No sham here, by G——.'" "Mary," said I, "you astonish me still more! But was it not rather hard to give me such a passport out of the house, as you did that night?"

"No;" said she, "I thought you deserved it. You might have observed, that whenever I desired you to stay all night, my father said no more, but talked to you as a welcome guest; and I thought you were wronging his hospitality, and infringing on the honour of his house, when you left your chamber without leave, and came into that of his daughter."

"You are an extraordinary girl, Mary," said I, "and I can't approach you, even in the dark, but with a kind of fear and trembling. But, the devil! you did not tell him of the drop, surely?"

"Every thing concerning it. He knew you were in the house that night—and that you were in the garret; but did not choose to see you, till he knew if it was by my appointment."

"I think," said I, "you may take for your motto, 'Wha dare meddle wi' me.' Pray, may I ask if it was by chance, or through design, that you gave me such a tumble from the window?"

She was again moved to irresistible laughter. "I beg," said she, "that you will not mention that subject again, for I have many a time laughed at it already till nearly exhausted."

"Upon my word, I'm very much obliged to you, Miss."

"I meant to give you a slight fall; but not by half such a serious one. It was an accident that made me lose my hold at the first, and I was greatly alarmed till I saw you rise and run halting away; then I went to my bed, and laughed almost the remainder of the night. The awkward way that you fell, with your shoes rattling about your head—the astounded and ill-natured manner in which you rolled yourself over and over on the gravel—the length of time you sat considering, and, as I believed, cursing my slim fingers—the noise of dogs and men within doors, and the limping mode in which you made your escape, have altogether left such an impression of the ludicrous on my mind as shall never be erased. Never shall I see any thing so exquisite again! Whenever I am down-hearted, I have only to think of that night to make me merry. I have gained a great deal of credit by it; for whenever I wish to laugh at the stories of any old prosing gentleman, or intolerable dowager, I think of your acute escape from my window, and laugh most unfeignedly, by which I have several times been praised as a most acute sensible girl."

"It is a subject," said I, "on which I never felt any inclination to be merry; and when I furnish you with another divertisement, I sincerely hope it may be by some *less feeling* exhibition. I suspect that you are an exquisite wag."

"I do not think the scene of this present night was much behind the other," said she. "Indeed, it is such a one that I dare not trust myself a moment to think about it; but, once I have the incidents all collated and arranged, I am sure I shall have many a hearty laugh at it. Being very lonely here, I like a little diversion with the fellows now and then."

Afterwards we began a conversing about a Moffat ball that we had both been at, and about the various characters that were there, which served us for a topic of conversation until the time of my dismissal; and thus terminated two night-courtships, without a word of love. I was ashamed of this when I thought of it; for it was a neglect that never used to be the case with me; but I do not know how I was led away from the subject. I believe that girl could have led a man to converse on any subject, or kept him off any, she pleased. I left her with a much higher idea of her character than ever I had before, and was vexed that I had made such a poor use of the time so graciously afforded me.

But I am an unfortunate man; and my love affairs had not been to prosper; for hanging and marrying, they say, go by destiny. One would have thought that the favour shewn me by this lady, and the confidence reposed in me, both by herself and father, bespoke a preference in my favour. I thought so myself, and was very proud of it; not having the least doubt but that I could get my beloved Mary for the asking. How wofully was I mistaken! Just as I was contemplating another journey to see her, I received the following letter.

"Sir,

"I have taken into serious consideration your visiting here clandestinely, and sorely repent me for encouraging it. If I have judged aright of your motives, such visits may lead to evil, but can never lead to good; therefore, I beg that you will discontinue them. To convince you that I am serious, I must tell you, in confidence, that I have now promised my hand to another, who, if he has less merit, has more generosity than you, for he asked it.

"Your most obedient servant,   M. T."

I read the letter twenty times over, and could scarcely believe my eyes. It cut me to the bone. I certainly had never asked her hand in marriage, nor even once mentioned the subject. She had taken it ill; but it was a subject that I never was very rash in proposing; for, in truth, it was not very convenient for me. My father and mother were both living in the same house with myself, and I had no separate establishment. However, I could not think of losing the dear creature, so I wrote a passionate love-letter, proposing marriage off-hand; and, after I had sent it away, I trembled for fear of its being accepted. However, the letter, though it had been opened and read, was returned to me, enclosed in a blank cover; so I found all chance of succeeding in that quarter was gone for ever. She was married to a young farmer on the December following.

The next time that I fell in love was at a Cameronian sacrament, with a tall, lovely, black-eyed girl, the most perfect picture of health and good-nature that I had ever seen. Her dress I could not comprehend, as it was rather too gaudy and fine for a farmer's daughter, and yet the bloom of her cheek bespoke her a country maiden. I watched her the whole day from the time that I first got my eyes upon her, and asked at every one I knew who she was; but no one could tell me. On such occasions, persons often meet whose places of abode are a hundred miles from each other; from such a distance round do they assemble to this striking and original exhibition.–For my own part, I would have enjoyed it very much, had it not been for this bewitching creature, who quite unhinged all my devotional feelings. There was scarcely a young man's eye in the congregation that was not often turned on her, for she had a very striking appearance. I could not help thinking that there was something light in her behaviour; but the liquid enamel of her black eye was irresistible, and I felt that I was fairly in love with I knew not whom. All that I could learn of her was, that some person called her *Jessy*; and I watched which way she went at even. I perceived, likewise, that she lived at a great distance, from the early hour at which she left the meeting. I could not get her out of my mind for days and months. I went to every kirk and market in the bounds toward which she went, but could neither see nor hear of her for upwards of eight months. At length I discovered her at a great hiring fair on the border the spring following.

I watched her the whole day as before, but having scarcely any acquaintances there, I had no means whatever of learning any thing about her rank, her name, or where she lived. About one o'clock, I chanced to meet with a gentleman who had often bought sheep from my father and myself, whose name was Mr John Murray of Baillie-hill, and whose company I loved very much. He proposed that we should dine together, to which I gladly consented. There was a Mr Bell and a Mr Moffat with us, both Eskdale gentlemen, whom I had never seen before; but they were both jolly, good-natured, honest fellows, and we plied the bottle rather freely. I got so much exhilarated by the drink, that I told them of being desperately in love with a girl that was in the fair, whom I did not know–that I had been in close pursuit of her for eight months–that it was in hopes of finding her that I came to the fair–and now that I had found her, I could in no way discover who she was. The gentlemen were highly amused, and every one gave me a different advice. Mr Bell bade me buy her a new gown for a fairing, and ask the direction to put on it. Mr Moffat bade me take time, and be cautious, and make some inquiries. "Ay, d—n thee, Jock!" said the other, "thou'lt take time, and be cautious, and make inquiries till thy head grow gray, an' thou'lt see the upshot." There was a Mr Thomas Laidlaw came in, who gave me the strangest advice of all, but which cannot be repeated. At length my friend Mr Murray said, "I tell thee, Geordie, lad, what I wad de mysale. I wad gae frankly up te the lass, and say, My bonny dow, I's fa'an in love wi' thee; an', feath, thou maun tell me wha thou is, an' I'll gie thee a kiss an' a braw new gown into the bargain." The rest hurra'd, and approved of John's plan; but I said it was impossible to do that, as it might give the young lady offence. "Offence!" said he, "Domm thee, gouk, dost thou think that a woman wul be offendit at a chap for fa'ing in love wi' her? Nay, nay; an' that be a' the skeel thou has, I gie thee up for a bad job. Thou kens naething at a' about women, for that's the very thing of a' ithers that they like best. An' thou offend them wi' that, I little wat what thou'lt please them wi'. Now, gie me thy hand, like a brave lad, an' promise that thou'lt gae and de as I bid thee, an' thou'lt soon fin' out wha she is, thou's tied to de that."

All the rest applauded Mr Murray's plan with loud huzzas; so I gave him my hand, and promised that I would go and do as he had directed. Away I went, half inebriated as I was, to put the scheme in execution, while Mr Moffat cheered me out at the window. I soon found her out; for though love be blind in some respects, he is very sharp-sighted in others.—She had just come out of a house with a party of borderers, utter strangers to me, and who were taking leave of each other. I went boldly into the midst of them, tapped the girl on the shoulder, and when she turned round, said familiarly, "Miss Jessy, I want to speak a word with you—I have a message for you— will you walk this way, if you please?" She followed me without any hesitation into a little area. "You must not be astonished at what I am going to tell you," said I; "for, in the first place, it is simple, honest truth, which always deserves a hearing;—I am in love with you—most violently and passionately in love with you, and have been so for these eight months." I'll never forget the look that she gave me—it was eloquence itself; the eloquence of nature, and in a language that could not be mistaken. It was something between fear and pity, and I am certain she thought I was deranged. "I am not in jest, Jessy," said I again; "I never was more serious in my life: Ever since I saw you at D—f—e sacrament, I have been so overcome by your beauty, that I have neither had rest nor peace of mind, and I humbly beg that, for the future, we may be better acquainted." "Lad, I's rad thou's hardly theesel," said she, in the true border twang; "I never saw thei atween the eyne afore. I disna object nought at a' to thei acquaintance; but we canna be acquainted a' at ance." "If you are free to form an acquaintance with me, and willing to form it, that is all I desire, and all I request at present. Pray, have I your consent to pay you a visit?" "I'se muckil obleyged to thei, sur; I'se shure I should leyke very weil to sey thei, an' seye, I daur say, wod mee

feyther:—but thou canna be nought but jwoking a' this teyme." "I
protest to you again, that I never was more serious in my life, which
I hope to prove; for I am sure such a lovely face must be the index to
a pure exalted mind, and a kind benevolent heart. Will you be so
kind as give me the direction to your father's house? I am
unacquainted with the roads thereabouts, and shall have hard finding it." "Oo! juost ower the sweyer there, and up the waiter till thou
come to the boonmost town; that's auld Tammy Aitchison's. Than
mee feyther's is the neist town ower the hill frey thei; juost speare
for Robie Armstrong's at the Lang-hill-side-gate-end." "O, yes!" said
I; "I know now perfectly well. What, is this the name of old Thomas
Aitchison's farm?" "B—p—a, thou kens," said she; "Tammy an' I's
weel acquaintit; he'll like fine to see thei coming up the Hope." "Well,"
said I, "I'll come and see you in a fortnight, or twenty days at farthest; but come, now, and let me buy your fairing." She accompanied me to a craim, and I bade her choose a fancy gown. She again
took a long, silent, and thoughtful look of me, measuring me from
head to foot; and there was something quite new to me in all this.
She looked at me with as much pride and innocence as a young
colly-dog would look at its master. I could not think her vulgar; for
a face so much indicative of health, love, and joy, I never looked
upon; it was as fresh as a rose, and as delicate; but her frame was
scarcely proportionate, being rather large, and, in some points too
voluptuous. She remained silent, until I again desired her to make a
choice; and then she absolutely declined accepting of any thing beyond the value of a ribbon, or a small buckling-comb, as a keep-
sake. It was in vain that I solicited; so I bought her a roll of ribbon,
with which I presented her; but observing that she cast her eyes
casually on a web of sarsnet, I bought a frock of it, and handed the
merchant a direction where to send it. I perceived by this time that
there were several good-looking, sunburnt, well-dressed, young men
eyeing us all this while with more than ordinary earnestness; and I
likewise observed, that Miss Armstrong was watching some one
with a good deal of triumph in her eye. She was sitting on the end of
the merchant's craim. "Now, my angel, give me a kiss before we
part, as an earnest of better acquaintance," said I. "Ay, that's right,"
said the pedlar. This seemed to be a request that she wished, or at
least expected, should be made, for she instantly turned round her
beauteous face, elevating it with the simplicity of a child, and gave
me what I asked, without either hesitation or confusion, save a slight
blush, that gave her neck a little of the hue of the moss-rose. At that
moment a gentleman came hastily forward, and, taking her by the

hand, he led her away, without taking any notice of me. She made me a courtesy, however, and smiled to me over her shoulder. "Ah, you have made some hearts sair this day!" said the peddling merchant. "Did you see how the chaps were looking?" "So you know Jessy, I see?" said I. "Know her!" said he. "Aye, and her father afore her. She's a sweet gipsy, it maun be confessed!" When I heard that, I looked my watch, and made off as fast as my feet would carry me. I had a mind to have asked a number of things at the pedlar, but when I heard that she was one of the gipsies, that I had been courting and kissing in the open fair, I thought I had heard enough for one time.

Afraid to face my friend, John Murray, and his associates, I sauntered about the street—went and got my father's mare corned, and had some thoughts of riding straight home, without ever looking back to the border again. The merchant observed me passing among the crowd, and beckoned me to him. "Master," said he in a whisper, "tak' care o'yoursel. There was a wheen chaps here speerin after you, an' they're gaun to gie you a leatherin." "A leatherin, friend!" said I, "pray what may that mean?" "'Tis what we ca' threshin' ane's skin i' some places; or, a drubbing, as an Englishman wad ca't," returned he. "They can have no hostility against me?" said I. "Steelity here, steelity there, they're gaun to try't. They think nought o' that here-away. But they'll gie you fair play for your life. They canna bide that ye sude come an' snap away the bonny lass, an' the lass wi' the clink, frae amang them." I understood the meaning of this term well enough. I knew that this girl with whom I was madly in love was beautiful, but now that I heard she had money I looked a little bolder, though how a gipsy should have a fortune I could not see. "Well, well!" said I, "let the blades come on, since that is the case; any one of them may perhaps meet with his man."

"Nay, they'll gie you fair play," said the pedlar. "But gin ye let yoursel' be lickit, nouther the lass nor her father will ever look at ye or hear ye speak; you'll find that I tell you as a friend; an' thae Liddilhead devils are nae canny to cowe haffats wi." I thanked him for his kindness; bade him take no concern about me; and, having got a hint that my captivator was rich, I thought that though she was come of the blood of the Egyptians, I would hie back to Mr Murray and his friends, and acquaint them with the success of my enterprise. At the same time I could not help wondering at what I had heard. I perceived that there was something in Border life, manners, and feeling, quite abstract from any thing I had ever witnessed before.

I found my friend, John Murray of Baillie-hill, and his jovial companions, still over the bowl, and in a high state of elevation. Mr Moffat arose, shook me by both hands–asked of my success, and said, he hoped I had done nothing rashly. As the rest were in a warm debate about the *crocks of Nether Cassway* and *the eild ewes of Billholm*, I sat down beside him, and related all my adventure with the young lady; but I still thought, from the want of speculation in his eye, that he was not taking me very well up; when I had done, I found that he did not comprehend, or rather did not recollect an item of what I had told him; so I was beginning to relate it all over again to him, for I liked the frank, unaffected manners of the gentleman exceedingly; but Mr Murray stopped me; "Cuom, cuom," said he, "hae thee duone lad; Jock's ower far gane to take up thy story the night; an' thou wad tell him till the muorn at day light, thou'lt never make him either the dafter or the wiser." "Heard ye ever the like o' that?" said Moffat, "to say that I canna take up a story? I can take up any story that ever was told in English. But I maun hear it first. I'll defy a man to take up a story before he hears it. Na na–that's impossible–you canna do that mair than I." "Woy dear man thou haurd it aw alraidy," said Mr Bell, "and yet thou disna mind a single sentence o't. I'll bet thee a bowl o' punch that thou disna tell o'er ae sentence of what Mr Cochrane tauld thee juost now about his sweetheart." "Done," said the other, and the wager was taken; but when Moffat came to recite his sentence, he related distinctly enough the history I gave them before going out–his memory retained nothing later, and he vowed he had heard no more.

Murray, who was likewise half-seas-over, gave me the history of my border sweetheart, a subject of great interest to me. Her father was an old shepherd, a man who had been singular in his youth, both for strength and agility; and though only five feet seven in stature, a very diminutive size on the border, there was not one could cope with him, either at running, wrestling, or putting the stane. He added a very amusing anecdote of him, which was as follows.

His master, a Mr Jardine, betted twenty guineas with an English gentleman of the name of Whitaker, who declared that he never had been beat; that Armstrong would beat him at putting the stone; and they set a day on which Whitaker was to call at the shepherd's house, as by chance, along with two witnesses, and try the match. Jardine sent private word to his shepherd of what had taken place, and desired him to be at home on such a day; however, when the English gentleman called, he was not at home–there was none there but Meg Armstrong, his sister, who was busy up and down the house, baking bread, and churning the milk, &c. They asked very particularly about her brother, but Meg assured them he would not be home either that day or next, and begged if she might ask what they wanted with him? Whitaker said it was a matter of no consequence—a mere frolic—That he and his two friends had come off their way a little to see him, having heard so much of his uncommon strength, and that they intended to have tried him at putting the stone, and wrestling. "Ay, ay," said Meg, "Weel I wot, sur, neything wod hae pleysed him better, had he been at heame—he's aftner at theye theyngs nor his beuk. But I trow aye he's neye grit stecks at them eftir aw, for I hae seyne the deye when I cwod hae bett him an Jwock beath, but they hae gwotten queyte aheid o' me for a year or tway bygane, an' I tak it nae that weile out."

Whitaker's friends thought this was high game, and instantly proposed that Meg Armstrong and he should try it, as a specimen of what her brother could do.

"I'll let thee see how fer I can throw it meesail, wi' aw my hairt," said Meg; "an yeance I faund the weight o' thei stane, I'll tell thei till a tryfle whithur thou or Robie will ding."

They went out to an old green turf dike, where it was apparent that much of the business of putting had been going on, as there were choice stones of every dimension lying about, and the ground so beat up, that there was not a blade of grass upon it. Meg bade him choose his stone. He chose one about twenty pounds weight, and threw it carelessly, not thinking it necessary to exert himself to beat a woman. Meg then took up the stone, and throwing it as carelessly, and with as much apparent ease, sent it full two yards beyond him. The Englishmen damned themselves if ever they saw the like of that! and it was not until he stripped off his coat and boots, and threw it six times, that he was able to break ground before Meg, which at last he did. Meg tucked up the sleeves of her short-gown; and, taking up the stone again, threw it with so much art, that it went a foot and a half beyond Whitaker's mark. The latter tried it again twice, but not being able to mend his last throw an inch, he gave in with good humour; but he was quite convinced in his own mind that Meg was a witch. Whitaker was nearly six feet and a half high, and Meg could almost have stood under his arm.

"Thou's naething of a putter," said Meg, "I see by the way thou raises the stane; an thou saw my billy Rwob putt, he wad send it till here. Now, an thou likes, I'll try thee a warstle te; for I comes nearer till him in that nor ony theyng else."

Whitaker would not risk his credit with Meg a second time, as he had no doubt of the issue; but, giving her a guinea, he shook hands with her, and went his way. Shortly after this he enclosed the amount of his wager, and sent it to Mr Jardine in a note, intimating, that he had missed his shepherd when he called; but was fully convinced, from some accounts he had heard of him, that he would have been beat.

The secret never was acknowledged, but every one acquainted with the family knew, that Meg Armstrong, Rob's sister, who was a sprightly handsome girl, fond of dancing and dress, never could wrestle a fall with an ordinary man in her life, or putt a stone; nor did she ever attempt either, save on that occasion. There was therefore no doubt, but that Rob had sent his sister out to the hills to tend the sheep that day, and had dressed himself in her clothes, in order that he might not be affronted if the Englishman beat him, and to humble his antagonist as much as he could.

Mr Murray having told me of this exploit of my intended father-in-law at this time, I thought proper to set it down here, as somewhat illustrative of a character which I had afterwards to do with. Of my border flower he told me, that she was an only daughter by a second marriage; that a maternal uncle of hers, who had been an under-clerk in a counting-house in Liverpool, and by a long life of parsimony had amassed a considerable fortune, had left her his sole heiress, so that the girl had of late been raised to move in a sphere to which she had not been bred; and that her personal beauty, simplicity, with the reports of her great fortune, had brought all the youths on the border to her as wooers. "An' I can juost tell thee, lad," added Mr Murray, "afore thou gets away Jainny, thou'lt hae ilka wight chap to fight atween the head o' Liddal an' the fit of Cannobie." "I have got some short hints of that already," said I; "but tell me, my dear friend, has she got none of the blood of the gipsies in her; for her bright black eyes and long eye-lashes bring me very much in mind of a young Egyptian?" He laughed at me, and said I was raving. "The deil a drap of gipsy blood's in her veins!" said he. "Her mwother was ane o' the Pairks o' the Woofcleuchead, and her feyther's ane o' the true auld border Armstrangs." I then confessed to him, that I heard a merchant at a craim say she was a gipsy. "Oh!" said he, "that's been Pether Willie o' Hawick. A' the women are gipsies wi' him. He never ca's ane o' them by another name. He gies my daughters ney other titles, juost afwore my feace, than gipsy Jean and gipsy Nannie."

At that instant there was a tall raw-boned fellow, with a gray plaid tied round his waist, who opened the door and looked in, without

accosting any of the company; but I perceived that he looked very
eagerly at me, as if examining my features and proportions with
wonderful curiosity. He closed the door quietly, and went away;
but, in about ten minutes afterwards, he opened it again, and inspected the company in the same way as before. "What the devil do
you want, sir?" cried Mr Moffat furiously, who was by this time
nearly whole-seas over. "Ney aill to thei ata', mon; haud thei gollaring
tongue," said the fellow, and closed the door. About two minutes
after, another handsome, athletic, well-dressed borderer opened the
door, and surveyed our party. "What the devil do you want, sir?"
cried Mr Moffat. The man hastened out, and closed the door; but I
overheard him saying to his associates, "That's juost the very mon;
we hae him seafe and snwog." "By G——," said Murray, "these are
the chaps alraidy watching to hae a bellandine wi' thee—an thou tak
nae guod caire, lad, thou's in cwotty Wollie's hands. I ken the faces
o' them weel—they canna leave a fair without some strow, an' they're
makin thee their mark the neyght. Thou maunna steer frae this board;
an' then, when it grows mworning, we'll a' munt an' ride away
thegither." I confess, when I overheard what the fellow said on closing the door, and this suggestion of my friend's, I felt a thrilling
apprehension, which made me very uneasy; however, I pretended
to treat the subject lightly; and, like all other young puppies, my
boastings and threatenings of the other party were proportionate to
my fears of them; for I swore I would make an example of the first
that presumed to intrude his snout into our company again. Mr Moffat
applauded my resolution, and out-swore me, saying that he would
do the same. He even went farther, for he swore that he would fight
them all, one after another.

"Thou'lt fight the devil!" said Mr Bell, who seemed to have a
great friendship for Moffat, and an anxious wish to keep him from
any unwarrantable sally; "thou'lt fight wi' the devil, Jwock! I tell
thee, keep thy seat and be quiet. Thou'lt nae quorrel nor fight wi' a
human creature till thou be that way thou canna stand thy leane, and
then thou wad quorrel wi' the cat an she wod quorrel wi' thee."

Moffat, however, brooding on the insult we had suffered, in being intruded and stared on by blackguards, as he supposed them to
be, proposed to me, by way of retaliation, that we should open their
door thrice, inspecting them in the same manner, and see how they
liked it; and the more his friends disapproved of it, the more intent
he grew of putting his scheme in execution. I could not well refuse
to accompany him, as it was I who began the bragging, though I did
not inwardly approve of the measure, from its being so like seeking

a mischief. However, away we went at last, in spite of all our friends could say to us, and opened the door of a large ball-room, stood in the door, and stared at the company, which consisted of about eight or nine countrymen, who were sitting in one of the corners over a bowl of smoking whisky-toddy. Just as we were going away triumphant, several of the company cheered Mr Moffat as an old welcome acquaintance, and called on him to drink their healths in a glass of toddy before he went. He made no hesitation in complying with this request, for he was in the humour to have done any thing, either good or evil; and, as his arm was linked in mine, we were instantly seated at the table among these wild borderers. "Here's te thei, Mr Moffat," said the tall athletic fellow that first opened our door. I could not help noting him particularly: He had large hands and prodigious wrists—fair lank hair of a bright yellow—a large mouth, and fresh rosy complexion. "I say, here's te thei, Moffat, mon," repeated he. "Thank ye, sir," said Mr Moffat; "but wha am I to thank? for, faith, I hae forgot." "I's Tommy Potts i' the Pease-Gill, disnae thou meynd me?" "O aye, I mind now," said Moffat, "was not it you wha ran at the wedding o' Dews-lees wantin' the breeks?" "Ay, the very seame, Mr Moffat, thei memory's better than thei judgment after a'." Moffat was going to be in a great rage at this compliment, but another diverted his attention by saying, in a kind ardent voice, "Mr Moffat, I's devilish glad to see thy feace, mon; here's te thei very guod health." "Thank ye, sir, thank ye," said Moffat, looking stedfastly across the table; "an' wha the devil are ye, for my memory's never unco clear in a fair-night?" "I's Davie's Will o' Stangerside, mon. I yeance coft thei crocks an' thei paulies, an' tou guidit me like a gentleman, else I had been hard pingled wi' them—Here's to thei, sir." "Here's thei guod health, Mr Moffat," cried a third; "tou'lt hae fargot me too? I's Jock Hogg i' Mangerton." "Ay! Jock, is this you, man? Here's your health. Ye're the saftest chap ever I stude a market wi'." "And, Mr Moffat," continued Jock Hogg, "dis tou meynd Willie Elliot o' Weirhope-Dodd?" "Mind Willie Elliot!" said Moffat, "Ey, my faith, I'll no soon forget him! he's the greatest leear that ever I met wi' o' the race o' Adam." "Woy, this is him on my reyght hand," said Jock Hogg, like to burst with laughter. Moffat never regarded, but went round inquiring all their names; and when he had done, he immediately commenced again. He was so well liked and respected by every body, that no one took offence at what he said, though he certainly gave great occasion.

At length Tommy Potts set his broad-blooming face across the table and accosted me nearly in these terms:

"Sae it seyms tou's coming to teake away Jaissy Armstrang frae amang us, wi' the pockfu' o' auld nails, an' aw thegither? Tou'lt be the lucky chap an' tou gets her. But I's rade, that auld Robie will think tou's hardly beane for her. I can tail thei, that he'll never gie her till a lad that canny carry her through the burn, an' ower the peat-knowe, aneath his oxter, an' she's nae wother-weight nouther. What says tou to that? I doubt tou'lt ne'er be beane for Jainny."

I did not like the homeliness of this address; but, as I had seen a good deal of the same kind of manners during the day, I thought I would parry as good-humouredly as possible; so I said, I did not know the distance which the old man had set for the lover to carry his daughter, but that I certainly would exert my utmost efforts to gain such a lovely girl.

"Ney, ney," said he again; "I's shoor tou's nae beane for Jainny. But, an tou haes a good genteel down-sitting for the lassie, auld Robie woll maybe discount thei a tetherlength or tway. Pray, is nae tou a tailor to thy business?"

"A tailor, sir!" "Ay, to be shoor, a tailor." "A tailor, sir! what do you mean by that?" "I ax your pardon, sir; I was only speerin' if tou was a tailor. I thought by thei dress tou mightst be a Moffat tailor; an' what o' that? I's shoor I hae seen a tailor a better mon than thei."

"I would have you know, sir," said I, "that I am not accustomed to such language as this; and, moreover, if I thought there was a better man in all your country than myself, I would blow out my brains."

"Ney, ney; I ax your pardon, lad; what can a man de mair? I didnae mean to set thei on thei heich horse a' at yeans this geate; but we're noor unco nice o' what we say here, for we're aye content to stand by the consequences."

"And, pray, does the consequence never occur, that a vulgar, impertinent scoundrel, such as you, who takes upon him to insult any stranger that comes into the company, should get himself kicked out of doors?"

"Woy, an the chap be fit to de it, the twother mawn bide by the consequences; there's nae law here but jwost that the thickest skin stands laungest out; and that tou'lt find, or tou taikes Jaissy Armstrang ower Sowerby Hap."

"It is not me you have insulted, you have insulted the company, and your country too, by the manner you have spoken to me. I merely came in as Mr Moffat's friend, in good fellowship, and must insist on your leaving the room."

"Ney, ney, I'll nae leave the room neyther." "But you shall leave the room, sir," said Mr Moffat, who had only heard the last two sentences, the mention of his own name having drawn his attention from a violent dispute he had got into with another man, about some tups, that Moffat averred were half muggs, and which the other man as strenuously denied. Potts, finding that the sentiments of the party, or at least the *voice* of the company in general, were against him for the present, succumbed a little, but apparently in very bad humour.

"Gointlemen, I's very sorry," said he, "for having offended the chop. I dwodna ken but what he could taike a jwoke an' gie a jwoke, like our nain kind o' lads; but I ax his pardon. What can a man de mair? I ax his pardon."

"O, that's quite sufficient," said Mr Moffat and the rest of the party— so Potts and I at length shook hands across the table. Mr Moffat and his opponent again began to their dispute about the breed of Captain Maxwell's tups; the rest fell into committees of a similar nature, according to their various occupations and concerns. Tommy Potts sat for a considerable time silent, leaning his temple upon his hand, and his elbow on the table, while his short upper-lip, which was nearly a span in length from cheek to cheek, seemed curled up almost to his nose, and his white eye-brows sunk fairly in below the arch of the eye, and pointed downwards. He was visibly labouring under a savage displeasure. At length he addressed me again as follows:

"But efter a', mon, I wasna jwoking thei about auld Robie an' his douchter. He was a very straung chop the sel o' him, and he has taukt about it a' his life, and about naithing else; an' it is the only quality that he cares a doit about in a man. If ever tou gaungs to court the lassie, as I hae deune mony a time, tou maun first thraw a' the wooers that are there at a worstle, or the deil a word tou gets o' her. I hae been five times there mysel', an' the shame fa' me an ever I guot a neyght's courting yet; for I was aye turned up, an' obliged to come me weys wi' me finger i' me mouth."

I was so much amused by this picture, and the way in which it was described, that I laughed heartily at it, and again got into free conversation with Potts. He assured me that every word of it was truth; and added many anecdotes of scenes that he had witnessed there and heard of from others. "An' be the bye," added he, "an tou'lt worstle a fa' wi' I, tou sal kean what chaunce tou hess; for I hae found the backsprents o' the maist part of a' the wooers she hes."

I was rather glad of this proposal, for I wanted to give Potts his weight on the floor, and I felt confidently sure of throwing him; for I had the art of giving a trip with the left heel, which I never in my life saw fail with any one that did not know the trick. However, I took care never to wrestle with a man above once or twice; for when my plan was once discovered, it was easily avoided; and, as I trusted solely to it, I run a chance of coming off with the worse. The ballroom, where we were, was remarkably large, so that we had plenty of room; and up we got, in perfect good-humour, apparently, to try a fair wrestle, to the infinite delight of the company. Potts was 'a tremendous fellow for bone. I was afraid I would not be able to bring in his back close enough to get a fair trip at his right foot. But this being a manœuvre that no wrestler ever suspects, in working himself round with his side toward me, he brought himself into the very position I wanted; for he meant to throw me over his right knee. Quite sure of him then, I watched my opportunity; and the next moment, while he was in the act of moving the right foot a little nearer me, I struck it with my heel across before his left one, which brought him down below me with such freedom on the boards (for there was no carpet), that it was some minutes before he could speak. Every one present uttered some exclamation of astonishment, as no one had anticipated the issue but myself. Potts rose, drank off two or three glasses of toddy, changed colour as often, and sat down again much the same man as he was before; surly, savage, and dissatisfied.

"I never saw thei as easily thrawn ower in me life, Tommy," said one. "I trowed he wod hae studden the gentleman a better shake," said another. "He fauldit him like a clout," said Mr Moffat. "Weel, weel, gentlemen," said Potts, "the chop thrawed me, there's ney doubt on't; an' he thrawed me very fairly too; I's nae disputing't; but I'll bet a choppin wi' ony o' ye, that he'll be ney langer wi' the neist he tries than he was wi' mey, if the chop be willing the sel o' him."

I said I was willing to risk a fall with any man, in good fellowship; and never hesitated on such matters. There was no one thought proper to accept my challenge; and, in consequence of my victory over Potts, and this acknowledged superiority, together with the fumes of the whisky-toddy, which high-mettled liquor we had imbibed with considerable liberality, I dare say I assumed rather too much for a stranger, and put on airs that scarcely became me, and which I would not have practised among intimate associates. But thinking I was landed in the company of a set of braggadocios, I resolved to abate no item of my dignity. Potts discovered this; and, still smarting from his late defeat, as well as for having been snubbed by the company before on my account, he made another effort to humble me, taking an opportunity while all the rest were loudly engaged in different disputes, so that no notice might be taken of it. We still filled the seats that we first occupied, straight opposite to each other, on different sides of the narrow board; when, in a half-suppressed voice of the most malevolent accent, he addressed me as follows:

"Tou hess thrawn me, there's nae doubt on't; an' tou's deune it fair eneuch. But what is there in that? tou hess nae right ava to coom into a coontry, an' brag thysel to be the best man in it, as I heard thee de the night; for I can tell thee, that tou's devilishly fer out o' the reckoning, for tou's naething but a dud to mony o' the chops o' this coontry. Thou took't sae ill to be thought a tailor; but, mon, I knows a tailor in this country that wod stap thei neb in a part o' thei—that I's no gaun to neame."

Without answering him a word, I lifted the tumbler of toddy and threw it in his face, sending the glass after it with all my might. This last missile had probably finished the redoubted Tommy Potts for ever, had he not half warded it with his arm, which he dashed to his eyes as they smarted with the warm liquor. It however cut the bridge of his nose, which spouted blood. There was no room for interference now, and none attempted it. Potts loosed his neckcloth, and stripped off his clothes, saying all the while, "Ey, mon, but thou's reather a shairp ane; but meynd the, that's a baptism that we border chops never teakes for neything. Tou maun fallow up the smack wi' something better nor that, or tou had'st better hae keepit it nearer theisel."

I did not strip, being lightly clad, but met my antagonist in the middle of the floor as he advanced, and saluted him with a hearty blow on the left temple, which he returned, and we then instantly closed. I threw him, and gave him his own weight and my own right freely, but instantly jumped up and let him rise again to his feet, which I needed not to have done, for the border laws of war, as I was afterwards told, required no such thing, for 'The thickest skin stand langest out;' and they have no other. I was too late in being aware of this, else I might have saved myself from a great deal of trouble. He was a great deal stronger than I was—clumsy and raw-boned—with longer arms, and a heavier hand, but he was not so agile. Three times, in the heat of our scuffle, we closed, and every time I fell above him. One of these falls cut his wind considerably, for I had fairly the advantage for some time in striking, and mauled and disfigured his face most dreadfully; but he now took care, with his long arms, that we should not come to close gripes. I judged this to be all his aim, and therefore fought fearlessly, though with little science. He was master of a much more deadly art than throwing his antagonist in a struggle, and for that he had till now been watching. It was an open trip with the left foot, followed up by a blow with the right hand on the chest or face; and this he now practised on me so successfully, that I staggered to the further end of the room, and fell with my back against the wall. I felt a little stunned and giddy, but advanced with great rapidity again to the charge. I had now the worst of it; in four seconds he repeated his trip, accompanied with a tremendous blow on the brow, which made me fall freely back, and my head or shoulders striking on one of the forms, I lay in a state of utter insensibility.

It was long before I came to my senses, and then I found myself lying in a bed, with a surgeon and the mistress of the inn standing over me. Mr M–, the surgeon, had bled me copiously in both arms, and for a long time I was in a state that I cannot describe; but felt excessively happy, and always inclined to laugh, yet so weak as not to be able to sit up in the bed. The surgeon left me, and ordered quietness; but what quietness can be had in the inn of a country town on the morning after a fair? About day-light, several of my evening associates came staggering and drowsy into the room, to inquire how I was before they went away, and among the rest, to my utter astonishment, in came Tommy Potts, with his face all patched and blotted, and the blood crusted in dark stripes from his brow to his toes. He came freely forward, and sat down on my bed-side, as if he had been a brother or a most intimate friend, looked anxious like to my face, and addressed me as follows, without ever giving me time to speak a word–fearing, I suppose, that my answers would be ill-natured.

"How is tou now, lad? Guod I's unco glad that tou's come about again, for I was rad that tou had left us awtegeather. I hae nae gatten sickan a gluff sen I was christened, (the first time I mean) an', be me certy, I was reather woshing it had been the sel o' me. Gie me thee hand, mon. I houp thou's nae the woar, an' we'll ay ken ane anwother again. Tou's as guod a chop to thee inches as ever I foregathered wi'. But tou maun never gang to brag a hale country-side again. An' yet after aw, G–, tou fught devilish weel. An' I'll tell Jaissy that tou did. But tou hest crackit thy credit there. But I'll tell her the truth; for, G–, tou did fight *devilish* weel."

And with that Tommy Potts left me, in excellent humour with himself, with me, and with all the world; a state to which victory often influences our minds, while misfortune sours them in a proportionate degree. Mine was so. I was very unhappy, and greatly ashamed of the business; for there were so many who saw it, that it spread like wildfire, and made a great noise among the country gossips. It was some days before I could ride home, and after I got home, it was a good while before I could be seen.

This I did not much regard; for my mind was too much occupied with other matters to feel any regret for the want of the society of my country neighbours. These twenty days form the great era of my *love adventures*, and it was the only period in which I could be said to be *over head and ears in love*. I then cared for nothing else, thought of nothing else, and dreamed of nothing else, save that rural Border flower. It was like witchcraft—a spell by which I was bound I wist not how. I lost my appetite, and all delight in my loved field sports, and became a moping, languid fool, as bad as a green-sick girl. I laugh to this day, when I reflect on the state to which I was reduced. I often caught myself, while repeating her name without intermission, an occupation which I perhaps had been following out with great assiduity for an hour or two—"Jessy Armstrong! Jessy Armstrong! dear, dear, sweet, lovely Jessy Armstrong!"

This is no exaggerated account; for, on the contrary, I felt ten times more than I can possibly describe. To such a loving disposition did this overpowering passion influence me, that I fell in love with other two, besides my adorable borderer. The one was a homely squat servant girl, in the neighbourhood, who chanced to have a cast in her eye that somewhat resembled Miss Armstrong's, or that I fancied resembled it, which amounted to the same thing, and I walked every day to get a blink of this divine creature's eye! The other was an old wife of the same hamlet, who spoke the border dialect in all its primitive broadness and vulgarity, which I thought the sweetest dialect on earth, and that there was a doric softness in the tones that melted the very heart: so I went every day to hear this delightful old wife speak! It must certainly be owing to some feelings that I then imbibed, that, to this day, I like better to hear that language spoken, than any other dialect in Britain.

I had said to this idol of my heart, that I would see her in three weeks at farthest. The time was nearly expired, and away I set on foot, a distance of fifty miles at least, to pay my addresses to her, not only burning and raving with love, but resolved to offer myself as a lover and husband, on any terms she chose. "Give me but the simple, the beautiful, blooming Jessy Armstrong," cried I, "and I ask no more in life!"

The way was long and mountainous, but I took a good part of two days to walk it, being resolved to arrive there in the evening. I liked always night-courting best myself, having been as it were bred to it; and I never had any doubt, whatever some of the women might pretend, but that they too gave it the preference. At all events, I knew that in the sphere in which Miss Armstrong had been bred, in the shepherd's cot, namely, any other time would have been viewed as a practical joke. I asked always the way for B–p–a, the name of Mr Aitchison's farm; but, when I came there about the fall of the evening, I liked very ill to ask the road to Lang-hill-side-gate-end–I could not do it; so I was obliged to guess, and take the hills at random. It grew late–I lost all traces of a road–and was in no doubt but that I had gone astray, and would never reach the Lang-hill-side-gate-end by that route. At length I came to a shepherd's cottage, into which I determined to go and ask the way, whatever shame it might cost me. I never thought any shame to go and court a bonny lass, but I could not endure that people should think I was come so far to catch a girl's fortune. However, in I went to ask the road, and found a group such as is often found in a shepherd's house, sitting round a hearth fire. It consisted of an old man, sitting on a bench made of dried ryegrass divots–his wife, a middle-aged woman, was sitting right opposite to him on the other side, carding fine wool on a pair of singularly long wool-cards–a young man, dressed in his Sunday clothes, with his plaid hung gracefully over the left shoulder, bespeaking him a stranger, sat on a chair before the fire; and a girl leaned with one knee on the hearth beside him, busily employed in lighting birns on the fire, and preparing the family's supper. I addressed them in the usual way, bidding them good-e'en; which was repeated by them in rather a careless indifferent way, very unlike the kind bustle of hospitality that always welcomes a stranger in the house of a Scottish shepherd. I added the common and acute remark, that it was a fine evening. "Aye, I's shure the e'ening's weel eneuch," said the old shepherd. "Are ye gaun a lang gate this wey the neight?" "Upon my word," said I, "that is more than I well know. What may the name of this place be?" "I dosna ken what it may be sometime or wother," said he; "but I kens weel eneuch what it's ca't juost now." "And, pray, what is it called just now?" said I. "It's ca't be a neame that thou canst nae saye; sey thou wadna be ney the better an thou haurd it," said the carl, in a tone, however, in which there was no ill-nature, but rather a kind of homely waggery.

By this time the girl had stirred up the blaze to a bright flame; and, throwing her ringlets back over her left shoulder, turned round her head and looked full at me. Good heavens! who was it, but my dear Jessy Armstrong? I was not only surprised, but perfectly confounded; for, of all things in the world, I least expected to find a lady with a fortune of a thousand pounds, or as some said of five thousand, in a lonely shepherd's cot; and I could not help feeling as if I had got into a scrape. It was so unlike the places to which I had formerly gone a wooing. "Bless me, Miss Armstrong," I exclaimed, "is this you? I just stepped in to inquire the road to your place of residence, not thinking I would have the happiness to get to it so soon." During this short speech, she blushed, turned pale, and blushed again, but made no reply. I had seized her hand, which she still suffered me to hold. "I am so happy to see you again!" continued I; "How do you do? I hope I find you well?"

"Trouth ey, I's weel eneuch. How's tou theesel?" replied she, still looking particularly embarrassed. But after I had replied to this, she plucked up a little confidence, and said, "Say thou hess fund thee way into this coontry? I trowed ay thou wast jucking me; but they say better leate threyve than ne'er de weel. Come thee ways this waye, an' thraw fraebout thee plaid; thou's welcome to the Lang-hill-side-gate-end for aince." So saying, she led me round the hallan—took my plaid from me, and hung it up, at the same time whispering into my ear, "For thee life o' thee, denna tell them who thou is; but ca' theesel some wother neame; an' be sure to man theesel." I could in nowise comprehend the meaning of either of these injunctions; but had not a moment's time to ask the explanation of them, for we were now beside the company, and in a moment she had set a seat for me, which she requested me to occupy. I durst not speak a word, as I had some new character to support, of which I had never thought; and I blamed in my heart the caprices of women, who are always inclined to throw a mystery over every thing, and keep all concerned with them in the dark as far as possible. So there I sat, scratching with my nails at some spots of mud that had jerked on my pantaloons, while the old man surveyed my limbs and muscular frame with considerable attention. The wife looked at me, as if she would have looked me through; and the young shepherd, biting his lip, cast a malicious and prying glance at me occasionally. We were all embarrassed, and no one knew either what to do or say, except the old wife, who again fell to her carding; the young shepherd made figures with the end of his staff among the ashes on the hearth, and Jessy walked about the floor with a most elegant thousand-pound air. The old man was the first to break silence. "Hess thou comed fer the day, lad?" said he. I answered that I had only come from Sorbie. "Ey ey," said he, "dis thou ken Sandy o' Sorbie? he's a gayan' neyce chap, Sandy; I yince herdit to the feyther o'm." "Feyther," said the malicious and incomprehensible beauty, "thou'lt no ken this lad? He an' I's fa'n acqueant at the public pleaces. This is Sandy

Welch o' the Braeside." "Deed I kens noucht about him, Jainny. I
hae seen some o' thae Welches at Staigshawbank mony a time, an'
I's rad there's no that muckle in them; for I never saw ane o' them
owther brik a chop's head, or take him be the neck, aw me days." I
said, that though none of the Welches of *my family* would probably be
the first aggressors in a brawl, yet there were some of them, whose
heads the best men in the kingdom durst not break. "Ey, trouth, that
may be, lad. I should lyke to see them. Hess tou brought ony o' thae
wi' thee?" "No," said I, "I have come by myself. I am one, I believe,
of the weakliest of the name, but I do not think I have seen a man,
since I came from home, that durst break my head." "Ey ey!" said
he, "dost thou say sae? Come, gie me thee hand; thou's a chop o'
some mettle eftir aw. An' is tou come to court our Jainny?" "That is
rather a home question, friend," said I. "Ney, ney, it's a very fair
question," said he. "I's no saying tou's no to court her; thy reyght's
as gwod as anwother's. I's only asking, if thou is come to court." I
was obliged to acknowledge, that I did come with the intention of
paying my addresses to his daughter.

"Then Wullie, lad," said he, with a joyful countenance, and looking to the young shepherd, "thou maun stand to thy taickle again."
The shepherd looked offended, and said, "It is very unfair; now
when I have turned up five already, and got so many strait grips,
can you think there's any justice in bringing a fresh man in on me?
I have set off five *already*; let him wait his day."

I could not comprehend this; and did not yet believe that what
Tommy Potts told me, about the lovers wrestling for the maid's company, had any foundation in truth. The old shepherd, however, soon
explained the matter.

"I dusna ken, Wullie Glendinning," said he; "thou may think it's
hard for thee; but, yince a chop has made a reule, I see ney oose in
brikkin through't. Thou canna beath hae the lass's company at the
seame time, an' I wod reather see her wi' the better chop than wi'
the wauffest o' the tway. I'll tell thee what it is, Sandy Welch: sen
ever my Jainny got a claut o' gear, the lads are like to pu' others
thrapples out about her; an' when twey or threy o' them come in ae
night, as they will ay aw be rinning on a Friday night, an' aw the
saum gate, we juost gar them try a werstle; an' whae-ever coups the
lave, we let him try his hand at the courtin' for a wey, an' the rest
maun jwost strodd their ways. The lassie has walth o' gear to maintain baeth the sel o' her, an' ony chop she likes to marry, and whin
that's the case, I wod reather that she got a man than a bauchle."

"It is a singular way of casting lots for a proper husband, indeed," said I, "and worthy of a Border sheil. But, pray, does Miss Armstrong herself perfectly acquiesce in this plan?"

"Bless the heart o' thee!" said he; "she's the strickest o' the hale twote. She'll no bate a fallow an inch, if he war the son of a luord. Very little wod hae meade my Jainny a man, for she wants neane o' the spirit o' ane."

"I know nothing of the art of wrestling," said I, "but for the sake of your daughter's company, I'll stand the test at that or any thing else."

"Deil a bit, but thou's a lad o' some spunk," said he; "an' thou's better beane than Wullie Glendinning, but he pretends to be a master o' the art. Coom coom, Jainny, lassie, tak thou the bouet an' gie me a candle, I'll haud it i' the bung o' me bonnet, an we'll see some mair fine sport."

Miss Jessy was not slack: she lighted a candle and put it into a lantern, which she called a bouet, and gave another candle to her father, who kept it burning by holding it knowingly in the lee side of his bonnet; and out we went to a beautiful green level, and stripped off our coats and shoes, to wrestle for a night's courting of this beautiful rural heiress. I pretended great ignorance, and made as though I did not even know how to take my hold. Miss Jessy directed us, determined to see fair play, and as soon as we were rightly placed for action, I fell a-struggling, with as much awkwardness as I could assume, until both my antagonist and the old man laughed outright at me, for ever attempting to wrestle. After affording his sweetheart and her parents a little sport, William, to bring the matter to a genteel close, began to work himself round with his right leg toward me, as all good wrestlers do; but, seeing that I made no opposition to this principal manœuvre, he did it in a very careless way, thinking he had to do with a mere novice. Little did he know that this was just what I wanted. He was bringing himself to a position in which it was impossible he could escape me, provided I got the first trip of him, which I took care to take, whipping his right foot in a moment as high as my own knee. This brought him on his back with his full weight, and me above him. The old man uttered three or four exclamations of utter astonishment. "Thou hess gotten thy backbraid for yince, Willie," said Miss Armstrong. "What ailed thee, Willie?" said the wife. "Thou may weel speer, woman," said Robie again; "for, be the saul o' me, I never saw Willie Glendinning sae easily laid on his back aw me lyfe. Ha, ha, Willie, thou jwost fell over as thou had been a corn-seck, or a post set up without ony feet."

"Confound his ignorance!" said Willie; "whae ever thought of his taking the left foot? It was the cleverest trick I ever saw; but if we twa yoke again!" "The present time is only ours," said I; "if that should chance, you will not find me backward."

Glendinning seemed loath to give up the right he had so dearly and so nearly won, and tried again and again to get a private word of Jessy, but did not obtain it. He came in, sat down with us, and joined in the general conversation for about an hour; and all the time eyed the lovely heiress so constantly, that I was persuaded he was as deeply in love as I was. Indeed, I never saw her look so comely, or half so elegant, as in her every-day dress. She was in the dress that the country maidens in the Lowlands of Scotland wear; by far the most becoming dress in the world for setting out the female form in all its lightsome ease and elegance, a circumstance well known to our ingenious countryman, David Wilkie. I cannot describe how much more graceful she looked, in her muslin short-gown and demity petticoat, than in her best dress at the fair, and the solemnity at which I first saw her. I see the dress must always bear a proportion to the polish of the mind; and one woman looks most lovely in a dress in which another would look exceedingly awkward.

Among other topics of conversation, they chanced to fall on one that was not a little irksome to me, and partly explained Jessie's stratagem. "Does tou ken a chap," said Robie, "out amang thy muirs, some gate, that they ca' Geordie Cochrane?" I said I had seen him, but was not intimately acquainted with him. "He gat his skin tightly threshed at the hiring fair, however," said he, "be ane o' our Liddel-head chaps 'at they ca' Tommy Potts. He thought proper to kiss our Jainny, an' gie her her fairing, but he had better hae keepit his kisses and fairings to the sel' o' him, or taen them hame to his muirland lasses an' benty-neckit foresters, for be my certy he gat his dickens." Here the old bully of a borderer scratched his elbow and his ear, and indulged in a hearty laugh, at the circumstance of Potts having *threshed my skin*, as he called it. Glendinning and the wife joined him, and Miss Armstrong laughed the heartiest of all, seeming to enjoy my predicament mightily.

"Had the fool taen the lassie into a house, out o' sight," continued old Robie, chuckling, "he might hae gien her half a score o' kisses, an' then nay man had ony right to pike a hole in his blanket. But, for a stranger to kiss a lass i' the open street, afore a' her sweethearts an' acquaintances, it's bragging them a' to their teeth." "We never look on it in any other light," said Glendinning. "He needs nae come here," said Robie, "an' that ye may tell him, Sandy Welch, frae me;

for the man that first gies a hale coontry-side the brag, an then lets sic a chap as Tommy Potts skelp him till he can nouther gang nor stand, sall never cross haffats wi' a bairn o' mine."

I could not help taking up the cudgels in my own defence; so I said, that I understood my countryman had been provoked beyond sufferance, by vulgar and insulting language; and, moreover, that I had been told there was very little difference in the engagement, by an eye-witness; and that if Cochrane had not been so generous as always to let him up, when he had him under him and at his mercy, the success of the day had been reversed. "I's unco glad, however, that he gat his hide beasted," said Robie. "I likes ay to see a man that brags me coontry come to the woar; and ony chap that wad fling a glass, punch an' aw, in a neighbour's face, deserves aw that Cochrane gat. Be the faith o' me, I never gat sae hard a word frae neay man, but I could hae gien as hard a ane again, rather as be sae belt bursten; he mought hae dung out the chield's herns, an' what wad he hae said for the sel' o' him then? It was a dear kiss to him, Jainny; an' yet thou laughs at it, thou hempy. What's aw this snirtin' an' gigglin the night for? I wat weel this is no Geordie Cochrane the sel' o' him?" "I would not wonder much if it is," said Glendinning. "And now I think on't, I could gay my oath it is no other; the ease with which he threw Tommy Potts, and the trip with the left heel." "Me, sir!" said I, observing how necessary it was to keep up my lovely maid's stratagem—"Me! me Geordie Cochrane?" Glendinning was rather damped, and Jessy was like to die with laughing; but as soon as she recovered breath, she said, "never heed thou what he says, Willie, he's juost Geordie Cochrane—stand to thy point." "The devil's in the wench," thought I, "what is she about now? Is she first going to lay a scheme, and then blow it up in my face for mere diversion?" I was wrong, and she was right. I believe she took the only method, on the emergency, that could have turned them from the right scent. Glendinning looked suspicious; but old Robie, her father, was quite convinced. "Ah! thou pawky elf," said he, "thou's tricking us, and want to set us about the lugs o' ane anowther, to gie thee sport. I'll tell thee what it is, Sandy Welch, thou hast won thysel' a gliff's cracking wi' that skelpie; but an' thou believe aw that she tells thee, thou'lt get few to believe thee."

With that old Robie began to loose his knee buttons and thrust down his hose, which Glendinning took as a signal, and trudged his way in bad humour, and apparently suspecting, that he left the bonny lass, for whom he had wrestled so manfully, in the possession of the detested Geordie Cochrane. Old Robie conversed with me freely

as Sandy Welch, and said, that "he had heard thae Welches about
the head o' Annan war muckle men i' the warld, an' strang i' gear;
but, for his part, he likit strength o' beane an sennin better, for that
Jainny stwood in nay need o' the ane, but the twother might stand
her i' some stead, and might beet a mister meay ways than ane. But
wow, man," continued he, "they hae durty ill-faured sheep! I hae
seen them stannin i' Staigshawbank, wi' great smashis o' ill-bred
tatty things, as black wi' tar as they had been dippit like candle i' the
tar-kitt; but they had some pith i' their spaulds te." The idea of bodily strength was always upmost with Robie; and I conceived, from
the thoughtful mood in which he appeared after he had made the
last remark, that his mind was dwelling on the idea of the success
that the Messrs Welch's black-faced tarry wedders would have had,
in wrestling or running, against the Cheviot and mugg wedders of
the south. At length, he left us abruptly, and went to bed, with this
observation, that, "if I proved as expert at courting as wrestling, he
stood a chance of losing his bit wench."

Not so indifferent was the mother of the young lady. She appeared
dissatisfied, and unwilling to leave her only daughter in the dark
with a stranger. She kept poking about the fire with the tongs, and,
at every word which was said, either by her daughter or me, she
uttered a kind of *hem*, without opening her lips. It sounded to me
like a note of pity, mixed with derision, and I did not like the wife at
all. She did not, however, venture to expostulate for a good while,
seeming afraid of being overheard by her husband; for she was constantly looking over her shoulder toward the bed, in which he had
vanished among good woollen blankets, to dream over the feats of
his youth in running, wrestling, and putting the stone. Robie's breath
began to sound deep—the goodwife's hems became more audible,
and by degrees sounded rather like free groans. I wished her a hundred miles distant, and feared that she would mar all my bliss with
that lovely and delightful creature, for whom my whole vitals had
been so long inflamed with love. "Gae thee ways to thee bed,
mother," said Jessy, who had till now been working up and down
the house. "What's tou sitting graning there for? Mind I hae been
up twae nights this week already."

"Twae nights already!" exclaimed Mrs Armstrong, alias Mary
Park o' the Wolf-cleuch-head, who, having come from the head of
Borthwick Water, did not speak with such a full Border accent as
either her husband or daughter; "twae nights already! H'm, h'm!
bairn, bairn! I hae often tauld thee, that sic watchin's an' wakins, an'
moopins an' mellins wi' ilka ane, can never come to good. But, d'ye

ken, sir, that our Robin's crazed, poor man, about warstling, an' a' sic nonsense. Gude sauf us! I believe he has never thought about aught else a' his days; just as ane could warstle himsel' into heaven. O wad he but mind the ae thing needful! an', instead o' gieing our bairn to the best warstler, gie her at night to him that could pray the best prayer."

"An', be me troth, mwother, I wadna sit five minutes in his company," said Jessie. "Does tou ken what Jamie the poyet's sang says? 'He that prays is ne'er to trust.' I wad reyther trust mysel' wi' a good warstler than wi' a good prayer, ony time. I'm quite o' the poyet's mind."

"H'm! h'm!" said Mary Park, "sic tree, sic fruit! the thing that's bred i' the bane's ill to drive out o' the flesh. Oh! wow me, what this age is come to! I'll tell thee, Mr Welch, the highest part o' my ambition wad be, to see my lassie married on a minister; ane that wad mind the thing that's good, an' keep by his ain wife an' his ain bed; an' that had a snug house, an' a glibe that he could ca' his ain, an' a round sum ilka year, whatever might happen."

"I tell thee sae, now," said Jessie, "I trow there's mony *ae thing needfu'* wi' thee, mwother. But I ne'er saw it otherwise wi' a religious body yet. A' self! a' self! The very dread o' hell, an' their glibeness o' claughtin at heaven, has something selfish in it. But I'm sure I twold thee, mwother, that I had nae objections to a praying man; the oftener on his knees the better, only let me choice the other. Canst tou pray weel, Sandy? I's sure can tou, for I saw thee turnin' up the white o' thy een at Tommy Rewit's sermon. I'se be bound, aften hast tou had thy neb to a lime wa'.'"

"Haud your tongue, ye corky-headit, light-heeled tawpie," said the displeased Mary Park o' the Wolf-cleuch-head; "wad ye rin your head against Heaven, an' your back to the barn wa', at the same time? Sorry wad I be to see it; but I'm sair cheatit gin some o' your warstlers dinna warstle you out o' ony bit virtue an' maidenly mense that ye hae, an' fling a' your bonny gowd guineas to the wind, after they hae ye under their thoom. As the tree fa's, there it maun lie; and, as the maid fa's, sae she maun lie too."

"I ken weel what gate I shall fa', then," said the implacable Miss Armstrong, who evidently wished, by every means in her power, to put a stop to her mother's religious cant, of which, I suppose, she got many a hearty doze; but it would not do.

"H'm! h'm!" said Mary Park, "alak, an' wae's me! but what can I expect? If the good seed be sown among thristles, it will spring among thristles; if it's sown in the flesh, it maun grow in the flesh; if it's sawn among stones, it will rise among stones."

"Hout, fie, mwother," interrupted the maid; "thou's no surely hint-ing that I was sawn in ony o' thae soils? Gin that be Scripture, it's unco hamel made, an' we hae enough o't."

"Carnality's the mother o' invention," said the indefatigable mother. "It is the edder on the hill, that sooks the laverack out o' the lift. It is the raven i' the wilderness, that cries, flesh, flesh, from evening to morning, an' the mair that ye feed her, the louder is her cry. It is the worm that never dieth, an' the fire that is not quenched. But wo be unto her that thirsteth after the manna of life and the waters of unrighteousness! I send ye to the kirk, an' when I expect ye to come hame like a good heavenly-mindit lass, wi' a' the notes o' the sermon, ye come hame wi' half a dozen profane young hempies at your elbow. I send ye to a' the sacraments round, in hopes that ye'll get a draught o' faith; but a' that ye get is another draught o' sense, an' hame ye come wi' another young man after ye. Your ee's like the edder's, it draws a' the carnal and worldly mindit o' this generation to you; an' sair am I fear'd, that a cast o' grace thou'lt never get."

"Indeed, but I will, mwother, an' thou'lt gae to thee bed, Sandy Welch will gie me ane. He gae me ane already, when he threw Willie Glendinning; for ill wad I hae likit to hae sat another night wi' him. But it was nae cast o' grace for poor Willie. But come, come, Sandy, as I'm sure thou didna come fifty miles to hear a sermon on carnality, I trow thou an' I maun e'en make our bed 'low down amang the heather,' for a night."

"Waur an' waur," said Mary Park, "wha can take fire i' their bosom an' no be burnt? I hae tried feathers, I hae tried woo'; I hae tried a bed o' won hay, an' ane o' fleeing bent; but I fand ay the temptations o' Satan harder on a bed o' green heather than a' the lave put thegither. Na, na, an ye will trust yoursel' wi' strangers, keep within your father's door—there's something sacred i' the bigging, an' in the very name. I's e'en gae my ways an' leave ye; my absence will be good company; but, oh! I wish it war *his* will that the days o' warstling an' wooing were ower!' And on saying this, Mary Park, formerly of the Wolfcleuch-head, went groaning to her bed and left us.

I could not help being affected with her words, notwithstanding all the absurdities that she jumbled together. The scriptural style in which her reflections were vented, gave them sometimes a tint of sublimity. I saw that she had fears for her daughter, but wist not well what to fear; and, moreover, that all her ideas were crude and unformed. As for Janet, she was completely her father's child, as the saying is; and actually valued a man principally on his prowess in athletic exercises. No sooner were we left alone, than she lifted my arm, and desired me to hold it up. I obeyed; then, to my astonishment, she clasped her arms round my shoulders and chest, and squeezed me so strait, that I was like to lose my breath. "This," thought I, "is the most amorous girl that ever I met with in my life;" and judging it incumbent on me to return her caresses, I likewise clasped my arms round her, and was going to lay on two or three sound smacks of kisses on her lips; but she repulsed me sharply, saying, at the same time, "Thou did'st nae think, fool, that I was gaun to kiss thee; I was only fathoming thy girth round the shoulders. There's no a lover that I hae, but I ken his poust to a hair. Thinks tou I'll sit wi' a lad till aince I ken whither he's worth the sitting wi' or no?"

She next spanned my wrist, and then, with particular attention, my arm, near the shoulder. "Thou's no the beane o' our border lads," said she; "but there's few o' them better put thegither. I hae nae fund a better shaped, cleaner made arm;" and then she added, with a full sigh, "I wish thou had but lick'd Tommy Potts."

I pretended to hold the matter very light, and said, it was a drunken fray, in which no man could answer for the consequences; but I found that nothing would go down—no pretence or excuse was admissible; I must either *lick Tommy Potts*, or give up all pretensions to her. She even let me know, in plain enough terms, that I was a favourite, and that she regretted the circumstance exceedingly; but that indelible blot on my character rendered it impossible for her either to think of me as a lover or a husband. "What wad my father an' half-brothers say," said she, "if I were to marry a man that loot himsel' be threshed by Tommy Potts, a great supple dugon, wi' a back nae stiffer than a willy-wand? It's nae great matter to settle him. He's gayan' good at arms-length, an' a fleeing trip, but when ane comes to close quarters wi' him, he's but a dugon." I offered to challenge him to fight me with pistols, but that only raised her indignation. She abhorred such mean and cowardly advantages, she said, which was confessing my inferiority in both strength and courage at once, the only two ingredients in a man's character that were of any value. In short, nothing would do, and I was obliged to leave my rural beauty, for whom my heart had been in such pain, without any encouragement. I was, however, greatly amazed with her character; and her personal beauty was such, that I could not help loving her. Her manners were rustic, but not vulgar; and her character, though a perfect anomaly among her sex, was void of affectation. Besides, her fortune was free and unincumbered; no small concern for the son of a poor farmer.

Upon the whole, I thought I could not do less than once more fight Tommy Potts, and either retrieve my lost honour, or die in the skirmish; and with this manful intent, I went to the July fair at Langholm. I soon got my eye upon my antagonist; but who should he be going in close company with, but the identical Willie Glendinning? This was rather an awkward predicament, as I behoved to appear as Sandy Welch to the one, and Geordie Cochrane to the other; so I was obliged to watch them at a distance, and from the way that I saw them looking about, and keeping constantly together, I had no doubt but that they were on some plot against me, either in one of my characters or both.

The day wore to a close, and I saw that they were determined not to separate. I had kept myself sober all the day, that I might have my senses and dexterity in full play; and I was glad to see that Potts seemed to be tippling with great freedom. Resolved not to let the opportunity slip, I got my friend Jock Grieve of Crofthead, a gentleman who feared no man alive, and cared as little either for giving a good threshing, or getting one, as any man I knew of. I took him in, merely on pretence of treating him with a glass before leaving the market, and without apprising him, in the most distant manner, of my intentions of *beginning a rowe*, as it is there called. I knew my mark well; and, in considerable perturbation of mind, led the way into a tent, where sat my two Border antagonists. I chose, as my seat, the form immediately facing theirs, so that when we sat down our noses were almost together. Potts uttered an exclamation of surprise, and instantly held out his hand; but, being determined to stand on no terms with either the one or the other, I refused to shake hands with him. This affronted him greatly; his face grew as red as crimson, and he fell a fretting and growling most furiously. "Sae thou winna sheake hands wo me, wilt tou nae? Gwod, I rues that I offered. I think I cares as little for thee, as thou does for me, an' I think I hess pruven that I needs care as little." I asked what business he, or any low vulgar rascal like him, had ado to interfere with me; and if it was the custom of this country, that two or three friends could not go into a house, or tent, to talk of business, or enjoy themselves, but they must be interrupted by such beastly jargon as his? "I chastised you for your temerity in that already," added I, "and think you should have taken some care before you ventured to do it again."

It is impossible to describe his impatience at hearing this. He fidged and grinned, squeezing his teeth together, and doubling his great fists; and at length, with more readiness than any would have thought he was master of, he answered, "Weal, weal, I's no speak to thee at a'. But tou canna hinder me to speak to my ain neighbour, and tou *sanna* hinder me to speak about what I like. Wullie Glendinning, did'st tou ever hear the like o't, for Geordie Cochrane to say he chasteased me? It is weal known to a' the coontry that I throoshed him till he coodna stand the lane o' him." "And sae thou's Geordie Cochrane after a'?" said Glendinning. Jack Grieve, on seeing that ill blood was getting up, thought it was requisite for him, as my friend, to be angry too. "I beg your pardon, sir," said he; "you're in a small mistake; he is commonly calt *Master* Cochrane; and do you call him aught else, at your peril, in my company." "And thou's Master Grieve, too, I's uphaud; and I's Master Glendinning; and by Gwod, an' thou ca's me aught else the night, I's won thee a good dadd on the tae side o' thee head."

It was needless to blow the coal any hotter between these two; there was defiance in every look that past, and in every word that was uttered between them; so that I was left with Potts to renew our quarrel as we chose. I took care it should not be long, having re-solved before hand to try his mettle once more. I told him, that the manner in which he had talked of me in the country, I was deter-mined not to bear—that he knew I had it in my power to have fin-ished him two or three times in our first encounter, had I chose—that he should now know his master; and if he had the heart of a flea, he could not refuse to give me satisfaction, after the bragging that he had made. Tommy did not flinch a bit; but accepted of my challenge with perfect readiness, and in three minutes we were hard at it on the top of the Langholm-hill, surrounded by a motley crew of Bor-derers, of every age and sex. I was perfectly sober; and Potts, though not intoxicated, had drank a good deal. It was certainly owing to this, that I found such a difference in his prowess from the time of our first combat. He fought with violence, but with little caution; and I felt as if he were nothing in my hands. I guarded against every trip, and warded every blow that he aimed with the greatest ease; but his arms were so long and powerful, that my strokes had little or no effect. I never was a good striker, and I could only strike with the right hand. At length, quite conscious of superiority, and perhaps on that account, I made a break at him, and seized him by the shoulder. He made a desperate exertion to free himself, but I seized him by the hair, and the right ear with the other hand, and, in spite of his struggles, closed with him, tripped the feet from him, and gave him a hearty fall. I then gave him two or three sanguine blows upon the temple and left eye, and sprung again to my feet. He was stunned; and as he attempted to rise, I gave him a blow on the shoulder with the sole of my foot, which tumbled him over again, and always as he attempted to get up I repeated it, kicking him in this way down the Langholm-hill before me. He had not as yet yielded; but must have done so in less than two minutes, for he was quite exhausted. At that moment I was knocked down by a side stroke given me by some one, and it was never known by whom.— The Borderers looked on their honour as being at stake in this encounter, and some one had most unwarrantably taken this method of retrieving the day. Jock Grieve blamed Glendinning, who denied it; and these two fought. However, Grieve beat him, and gave him a severe drubbing; but in a subsequent battle with John Glendinning, William's brother, one of the hardest fought that ever was fought, Grieve had rather the worst of it.

I saw nothing of these, having been led, or rather carried into, the tent from whence we issued. For a while I continued insensible, and had no recollection of any thing that had happened; but, after having drank a glass or two of wine, I believed myself recovered. I was grievously mistaken; for the stroke had been given with a staff, or some thick blunt instrument. My skull was slightly fractured, and though the wound did not bleed, it swelled to an unusual size, and grew all discoloured. I was highly indignant at the foul play I had got, and expressed myself in bitter terms against the borderers in general. Indeed, every one, both friend and foe, were alike violent in their execrations of so base and cowardly an assault. But that which provoked me worst of all, was the word that was brought in to me, that Potts had bragged that he gave the blow himself, although at the very moment I was tossing him with my foot. All that I did afterwards, I did very wrong; for it was done in a rage, and whatever is done in that mood is ill done, and repented of. Had I held myself as I was, I had come off honourably enough, and the base conduct of my adversaries would have been universally reprobated; but I abused Potts, and threatened the utmost vengeance on him, as well as on his accomplice who had knocked me down. There were not wanting some to carry this news to Potts, who was soon found, and as ready either to fight me, or shake hands with me as ever; the former of which I imprudently preferred. Alas, the tables were now fairly turned against me, as the stroke on my head had weakened my whole frame. I had no more strength to fight against a waking assailant than a man sleeping and struggling in a dream, and fell an easy prey to Potts. Still I refused to give in, though I could neither return a blow nor ward one; but the onlookers humanely separated us by force.

It was a twelvemonth before I overcame the effects of this blow, being troubled with a swimming in my head, and great debility; but before the expiry of that time, I had quite forgot my Border darling, or thought on her only as a natural curiosity. I was always a favourite with the girls, but never with their parents or guardian. I lost my first love (regretted to this hour) for never having asked her in marriage at any stated period; but grew careless, and so lost her. I am persuaded I lost the next also, for never having asked her for my wife at all; and I lost the third, the loveliest and richest of them all, the beautiful but unconscionable Jessie Armstrong, because I could not *lick Tommy Potts*.

Thus were the days of my youthful passion worn out. They had their delights; but they were not those delights on which recollection loves to dwell; to which the soul turns with serene satisfaction, as the dawnings of future felicity. They were meteors in the paths of folly, gilding the prospects of youth for a season with rays of the warmest and most brilliant hues; but they dazzled but to deceive, and left the headlong follower mixed in the pursuits, and obliged to pursue his devious course in darkness and uncertainty.

From this time forth, I formed no ardent attachment; I fell into one intrigue after another with my father's servant girls, and afterwards with my own, by some of whom I was much plagued, as well as palpably taken in. But for all those things I had no one to blame but myself; and, to my shame, I confess, that in such kind of courses was the prime of my manhood wasted; and they may say what they will, but every old bachelor has the same crimes to answer for, in a greater or less degree. On account of some of my misdemeanours, I next fell out with the minister and kirk-session of the parish where I resided, because, forsooth, I would not submit to do penance publicly in the church, a foolish and injurious old popish rite, which I despised and abominated; and this misunderstanding caused me to lose a lady of fortune a very few years ago, whom I had courted for conveniency, and who, for conveniency's sake, and, as a last resource in the world of gallantry, had yielded to become my blooming bride. And this anecdote, as it is the last in my love adventures, shall be the last in this narrative.

I was introduced to this young lady of forty-five at Edinburgh, on my annual visit to that city, by a relation of my own. She had been handsome and beautiful, and she still looked very well, but then she was rouged most delicately. This I soon discovered, by observing that her ears and cheeks were of different hues, and I mentioned it to my relation, who smiled at me, and said, "it was better that she should be painted with rouge than with strong liquors, for when a maid of fashion reached a certain period of life, she must paint either with the one or the other." I acquiesced in this sentiment, though I liked the painting very ill; and, as I conceived it impossible for me to be in a state more unsociable than that in which I was, I paid my addresses to her the more briskly, perhaps because I did not care a farthing whether they were accepted or not. She received my addresses with the greatest politeness, and with a manner truly engaging. I liked her the better, and pushed my suit vehemently, in a correspondence that ensued. Her letters to me were filled with the most beautiful and sublime moral sentiments, with sometimes a dash of affected religious enthusiasm, but not a word of love, save that they always began with the endearing and familiar epithet, "My dear sir."

She was a paragon of sanctity and devotion, which I was not fully aware of, as I always suspect very high professions of religion. Her letters contained many hints, that she put the fullest confidence in me; yet, on reviewing all that had past between us, I could not discover when she had ever confided any thing to me. They contained allusions to a supposed change of state, between whom it was not mentioned, but no promises. Such circumspection I had never witnessed before.

> Oh! she was perfect, past all parallel—
>   Of any modern female saint's comparison;
> So far above the cunning powers of hell,
>   Her guardian angel had given up his garrison.

Next summer she came to Moffat, on pretence of drinking the waters; but, in reality, on a reconnoitering expedition to inquire into my character and circumstances. About my fortune she did not care, as she had the means of repairing that; but what she valued as of far greater consequence, the Rev. Mr Johnston and Doctor Singers both spoke well of me. After this my reception was manifestly different, and the cordial shake of the hand, the kind and familiar flirtation, now showed me plainly that the nymph was all my own. I took her hand in mine, and asked her once more to be my wife. "Oh! Mr Cochrane, you are so cruel! You know that I can refuse you nothing; and you are taking advantage of my weakness, to make me change my pure uncontaminated virgin state for one of care and concern. It is not a light matter for an inexperienced creature like me, to venture on becoming the head of a family, and the mother of a blooming offspring, whose souls may be required at my hand." "Hold!" said I, "my dear love; that is a secondary consideration, and I don't think that ever they will." This unlucky expression brought on me a torrent of argumentation, not whether, in the course of nature, my beloved could possibly give birth to a blooming off-spring; oh no! such a thought as a negative to that never entered her brain; but whether or not parents were accountable for the sins of their children. She had the Scripture at her finger-ends, and gave me, verbatim, Thomas Vincent's Exposition on the Duties of Parents to their Children. Finally, however, she consented to become my bride, from an inward belief, as she plainly acknowledged, that it was the will of Heaven, and fore-ordained to be before the moon or stars were created; and that she might act in conformity with the first and great commandment, "Be ye fruitful, and multiply, and re-plenish the earth."

All this was very well: but, unluckily for me, she came to our parish sacrament, as she went to every one in the bounds. I did not like to see her painted face there. An independent fortune is a snug thing for an old bachelor. On the fast-day, when the tokens of admission came to be distributed, I did well enough. I crushed down the stair near the latter end of the crowd, and stood decently in the area, holding my hat in my hand, and waiting as it were my turn. My saintly charmer saw this, and eyed me with looks of heavenly complacency; but when I came opposite to the front door, I slid quietly off, and was never missed. On the Sabbath following, I was not so fortunate when the sacred elements came to be distributed. Until after the first table was served, all went well enough, it having been filled up from the beginning by such of the common people as had not seats of their own. But it was, and is still a custom in our parish, (as absurd a one as can well be) that *the gentry*, as the country people call them, go all into the second table; and there did my charmer go, and there it behoved me to have been also. But there I was not; being obliged, from my disregard of church-discipline, to sit cocking up in the corner of the front gallery all alone. I was not wont to regard this much, as I had some neighbours in the parish, and particularly in the eastern gallery, opposite to me, I could distinctly perceive one in each corner; but I was all by myself, there not being one of the same station near me; and to make the matter worse, the precentor, as he bawled out the following line, looked full at me,—

"Beside thee there is none!"

Sinners are always caught in the net some time or other, which they have themselves prepared. The worst thing of all, my betrothed was so placed at the table, that her eye was fixed on me. She could not lift it but she saw me, and great was the perplexity which that eye manifested. I saw she knew not what to make of it; but, as I suspected, attributed it to the contempt of ordinances. She returned to Moffat in a post-chaise on the Monday evening, and I did not see her till toward the end of the week, when I again visited her. She had not got to the ground of the matter; but, suspecting me of infidelity, she entertained me with a long lecture on the truths of Christianity. I soon convinced her, that I had no doubts to be removed on that subject. "Why then do you not come forward at the sacrament, like other people?" said she. I never was so sore nonplused in my life, and could not answer a word. I did not like to tell a lady the plain truth, and had no tale ready to bring myself off—my face grew red, and I had no other shift but to take out my handkerchief on pretence to wipe it. "Why, me'm," says I, "it is excessively warm in this room; do you not think it would be as well to open one of the windows?" "Certainly, if you wish it, sir," said she. I opened the window, thrust out my head, and said, "Bless me! how empty Moffat is at such a delightful season!" "Mr Cochrane!" exclaimed the lady, "what is the matter with you? Are you raving? I was talking to you of the bread of life, and the water of life, and asking your objections to the partaking of these; and you answer me, 'Bless me, how hot it is! how empty Moffat is!' What does this mean? When the relation in which we stand to one another is considered, I surely have a right to inquire into this most important of all concerns. Good Lord! if such a thing were to be, as that I should give up myself to lie in the arms of a castaway—a child of perdition, to whom it was predestined to go to hell—and then the iniquity of the father visited on my children!—I tremble to think of it. Tell me, then, my dear Mr Cochrane, and tell me truly, what is it that keeps you back from this ordinance?"

"Why, me'm, really, me'm," said I—"Hem—it is rather a delicate subject; but, in truth, me'm, it is the minister and elders who keep me back." She turned up her eyes, and spread her hands towards heaven. "I see it all!—I perceive it all!" cried she, in holy wrath; "you are then an outcast from the visible church—an alien to the commonwealth of Israel—you are groaning under scandal, and sins not wiped away; and to ask my hand while in that state! How could I have set up my face among my religious acquaintances in town? How could I ever have looked the reverend and devout David

D— again in the face, or kneeled at a family ordinance with the Smiths, the Irvings, or the inspired H— G—? And how should I have got my children, my offspring, initiated into the Christian church? To have been obliged to take the vows on myself, and hold up the dear sweet innocents in my own arms! Oh! the snares, the shame, and the participation in iniquity, that I have thus providentially escaped—and all by attending to my religious duties! Let it be a warning to all such as deride them. Mr Cochrane, either go and submit to the censures of your mother church, for your flagrant and gross immoralities, and be again admitted as one of her members, and a partaker of all her divine ordinances, or never see my face again."

"I shall certainly conform to this friendly injunction for your sake, my dear," said I; "though the alternative may be severe, it must nevertheless be complied with. In the mean time, I must bid you a good morning." Then, bowing most respectfully, I left the room, fully determined which side of the alternative to choose.

From that time forth, I never saw my saintly dame any more; but I got one or two long letters from her, apparently intended to renew our acquaintance, as they were filled up with protestations of esteem, and long sentences about the riches of free grace, which I never read. I had got quite enough of her; for, to say the truth, though I believe it is a fault in me, I have an aversion to those ladies who make extravagant pretensions to religion, and am more afraid of them than any set of reformers in the realm.

Being determined that I would not stand up in my native parish church before a whole congregation, to every one of whom I was personally known, not only to be rebuked, but to hear the most gross and indelicate terms mouthed as applying to my character, and that with an assured gravity of deportment, which makes the scene any thing but impressive, save on the organs of risibility, or the more heart-felt inspirations of loathing. And as my nature could not submit to this, I was obliged to forego the blessings of a devout wife and an independent fortune. Thus it was that I lost my fourth and last mistress; namely, because *I would not mount the stool of repentance.*

Whenever I recounted any of these adventures to my social companions, I remarked that they generally amused them in no ordinary degree. It was this that determined me to make a copy of them, as near to the truth of the circumstances as my memory serves me, and to send them to you, as you are so fond of all narratives that tend to illustrate Scottish manners. I have thought it proper to change two or three of the real names; but the adventures are known to so many in the south west of Scotland, that every individual concerned will be readily recollected; for, saving one gentleman, all the rest, as far as I know, are still alive.

Country Dreams and Apparitions
No. I

John Gray o' Middleholm

THERE was once a man of great note, of little wit, some cunning, and inexhaustible good nature, who lived in the wretched village of Middleholm, on the border of Tiviotdale, to whom the strangest lot befell, that ever happened to a poor man before. He was a weaver to his trade, and a feuar; about six feet four inches in height; wore a black coat with horn buttons of the same colour, each of them twice as broad and thick as a modern lady's gold watch. This coat had wide sleeves, but no collar, and was all clouted about the elbows and armpits, and moreover the tails of it met, if not actually over-lapped each other, a little above his knee. He always wore a bonnet, and always the same bonnet, for ought that any one could distin-guish. It was neither a broad nor a round bonnet, a Highland bon-net nor a Lowland bonnet, a large bonnet nor a small bonnet; nev-ertheless, it was a bonnet, and a very singular one too, for it was a *long bonnet*, shaped exactly like a miller's meal-scoop. He was alto-gether a singular figure, and a far more singular man. Who has not heard of John Gray, weaver and feuar in Middleholm?

John had a garden, which was a middling good one, and would have been better, had it been well sorted; he had likewise a cow that was a very little, and a very bad one; but he had a wife that was the worst of all. She was what an author would call a half-witted incon-siderate woman; but the Middleholm wives defined her better, for they called her "a tawpie, and an even-down haverel." Of course John's purse was very light, and it would never throw against the wind; his meals were spare and irregular, and his cheek-bones looked as if they would peep through the face. It is impossible for a man to be in this state without knowing the value of money, or at least re-gretting the want of it. His belly whispers to him every hour of the day, that it would be a good thing to have; and when parched with drought of an evening, and neighbours are going into the alehouse to enjoy their crack and their evening draught, how killing the re-flection, that not one penny is to spare! It even increases a man's thirst, drying the very glands of his mouth to a cinder–It makes him feel more hungry, and creates a sort of void, either in idea or in the stomach, which it is next to impossible to fill up. Such power over the internal feelings has this same emptiness of the purse.

John had all these feelings most keenly in his way; for his sides were so long, and so lank, and enclosed in such a bound of space, that it was no easy matter to fill it up. Now, it being a grand position in philosophy, that no space within the earth's atmosphere can remain a void, owing to the intolerable pressure of air, amounting to the inconceivable weight of fifteen pounds on every square inch, it may well be conceived what an insufferable column pressed constantly on John's spacious tube. Nothing gave John so much uneasiness as the constant suggestions of this invidious column of air.

There was but one thing on earth that could counter-work this pressure of elemental fluid, and keep it up to its proper sphere, and that was money. This was a grand discovery made by John, which Bacon himself never thought on, or thought of only to be completely mistaken. That sage says, "The state of all things here is, to extenuate, and turn things to be more pneumatical and rare; and not to retrograde from pneumatical to that which is dense." How absurd! It is evident that Mr Bacon had never been a feuar in Middleholm.

John's system was exactly the reverse of this, and it was the right one. He conceived, and felt, that the tangible part of the body ought always to prevail over the pneumatical; and then, as to the means of accomplishing this, he discovered that money—money alone, was the equivalent power that could equiponderate in such a case. But as to the means of procuring this great universal anodyne, that puzzled John more than the great discovery itself.

Every man, however, has some prospects, or at least some hopes, of increasing his stock of this material. John had his hopes of doing so too; but no man, or woman either, will guess on what these hopes were founded. It could not possibly be by the profits of his weaving, at least with such a wife as he had; for John's proficiency in that useful art was far short of what was expected of a country weaver in those days. He could work a pair of blankets, or a grey plaid; but beyond that his science reached not. When any customer offered him a linen web, however coarse, or a brace of table-cloths, he modestly declined them, by assuring the goodwife, "that his loom didna answer thae kind o' things, and when fo'k teuk in things that didna answer their looms, they whiles fashed them mair than if they had keepit them out." It could not be by the profits of the miserable feu that he hoped to make money, for the produce of that was annually consumed before it came half to maturity. He had no rich friends; and his live stock consisted of, a small lean cow, two wretched-looking cats, a young one and an old one; six homely half-naked daughters, one son, and his wife, Tibby Stott.

But it is hard for a man to give up the idea of advancing somewhat in life, either by hook or by crook. To stand still, and stagnate as it were, or yield to a retrograde motion, are among the last things that the human mind assents to. John's never assented to any such thing. Notwithstanding all these disadvantages that marshalled against him, he had long-cherished and brilliant hopes of making rich; and that by the simplest and most natural way in the world, namely, by finding a purse, or *a pose*, as he more emphatically called it.

Was not John the true philosopher of nature? What others illustrated by theory, he exemplified in practice; namely, that the mind must grasp at something before. John longed exceedingly to have money—every other method of attaining it seemed fairly out of his reach, save this; and on this he fixed with avidity, and enjoyed the prospect as much as one does who believes he must fall heir to an estate. He knew all the folks in the kingdom that had got forward in life by finding poses; but the greatest curiosity of all was, that he never believed money to be made in any other way. John never saw money made by industry in his life; there was never any made at Middleholm, neither in his days nor those of any other man, and what he had never seen exemplified he could not calculate on: so that, whenever he heard of a man in the neighbourhood who had advanced his fortune rapidly, John uniformly attributed it to his good fortune in having found a pose.

But it was truly amazing, how many of these he believed to be lying hid all over the country, especially in the vicinity of the old abbeys. And John reasoned in this manner: "The monks and the abbots amassed all the money in the country; they had the superiority of all the lands, and all the wealth, and all the rents at their control. Then, on the approach of any marauding army, it was well known that they went always out and hid their enormous wealth in the fields, from whence a great part of it was never again lifted." And then there was all the fields of battle, with which the Border counties abound, concerning which fields John argued in this way: "Suppose now there were 20,000 English and 15,000 Scots met on a field; there might be mony mae, and there might be fewer; but, supposing there were so many, every one of these would hide his purse before he came into the battle, because he kend weel, that if he were either woundit or taen prisoner, he wad soon be strippit o' that. In ony o' thae cases, when it was hidden, he could get it again; whereas, if he was killed, it was o' nae mair use to him, an' was as weel there as in the hands o' his enemies. There was then 35,000 purses, or poses rather, a' hid in a very sma' bounds. An' then, to consider how many great battles war foughten a' o'er the country, an' often too when the tae party was laden wi' spulzie." In short, John believed that all these Border districts were lined with poses, and that we every day walked over immense sums of old sterling coinage.

He had several times visited the fields of Philliphaugh, of Middlestead, and Ancrum Moor; and on each of these he had delved a great deal, looking for poses; but, as he simply and good-naturedly remarked, never chanced to light on the right spot. For all that he was nothing discouraged, but every year grew more and more intent on realizing some of these hidden treasures.

He had heard of a large sum of money that was hid in a castle of Liddesdale, and another at Tamleuchar Cross; and of these two he talked so long, and so intently, that he resolved at last to go and dig, first for the one treasure, and then for the other. So one evening he got some mattocks ready, and prepared for his journey, being resolved to set out the next morning.

But that night he had a singular dream, or rather a vision, that deterred him. The narrative must be given in John's own words, as it has doubtless never been so well told by any other person. No one else could be so affected by the circumstances, and when the heart is affected, the language, however diffuse, has something in it that approximates to nature.

"I was lying in my bed, close yerkit against the stock; for my wife, poor creature! had twae o' the weans in ayont her, an' they war a' sniffin an' sleepin; an' there was I, lying thinking and thinking what I wad do wi' a' my money aince I had it howkit up; when, ere ever I wist, in comes an auld grey-headit man close to my bed-side. He was clad in a grey gown, like the auld monks lang syne; but he had nae cross hingin at his breast; an' he lookit me i' the face, an' says to me,—says he, 'John Gray o' Middleholm, do you ken me?' 'Na, honest man,' quo I; 'how should I ken you?'

"'But I ken you, John Gray; an' I hae often been by your side, an' heard what ye war sayin, an' kend what ye war thinkin, an' seen what ye war doing, when ye didna see me. Ye're a very poor man, John Gray.'

"'Ye needna tell me that, honest man; there needs nae apparition come frae the dead to tell me that.'

"'An' ye hae a very ill wife, John Gray, an' a set o' ill-bred menseless bairns. Now, how many o' them will ye gie me, an' I'll mak ye rich? Will ye gie me Tibby Stott hersel?'

"'Weel I wat, honest man, she wad be better wi' ony body than
me; but I can never gie away auld Tibby Stott, ill as she is, against
her will. She has lien sae lang by my side, an' sleepit i' my bosom,
that she's turned like a second nature to me; an', I trow, we maun
just tak the gude wi' the ill, an' fight thegither as lang as our heads
wag aboon the ground, though mony a sair heart an' hungry wame
she has gart me dree.' He then named o'er a' the bairns to me, ane
by ane, an' pledd an' fleeched me for this an' the tither ane; but,
after a' he could say, an' a' the promises he could make, I wadna
condescend to part wi' ane o' my bairns.'

"'John Gray o' Middleholm,' quo' he, 'ye're a great fool; I kend
ay ye were a fool; an' a' the country kens it as weel as me; but ye're
no just sae ill as I thought you had been. How do you propose to
maintain a' thae tawpies, young an' auld?'

"'Aye, that's the question, friend,' quo I; 'an it's easier to speer
than answer it. But I hae a plan i' my head for that too; yet I dinna
ken how far it may be advisable to tell you a' about it.'

"'O poor daft Jock Gray o' Middleholm!' quo he; 'ye're that lazy
ye winna work, an' ye're that stupid that ye hae married a wife that
canna work, an' ye hae gotten a bike o' gillygawpie weans, that
ye're breedin up like a wheen brute beasts; and the hale o' ye can
neither work nor want; an' ye're gaun away the morn to mine the
auld Castle o' Hermitage, an' carry away the mighty spoils that are
hidden there. An' then ye're gaun away to Tamleuchar Cross,–

> To houk the pots o' goud, that lie
> Atween the wat grund an' the dry,
> Where grows the weirdest an' the warst o' weeds,
> Where the horse never steps, an' the lamb never feeds.

But, John Gray o' Middleholm, you'll never finger a plack o' thae
twa poses, for the deil keeps the taen, an' me the tither.'

"'Eh! gudesooth, friend, an that be the case, I fear I may drink to
them. But wha are ye, an it may be speer'd?'

"'I am ane that kens a' the secrets o' a' the hidden poses in Scotland; an' I'm a great friend to you, John Gray o' Middleholm.'

"'I'm unco glad to hear it, man; troth am I! I'm right blithe to hear
it! Then, there shall be houkin an' shoolin, countin and coupin ower!'

"'Nane where ye trow; for ye're but a short-sightit carle; an' the
warst faut that ye hae–ye're daft, John Gray. But, if ye'll be ruled by
me, I'll tell you where ye'll find a pose that will mak you a rich man
for the langest day ye hae to live. Gang ye away down to the town o'

Kelso, an' tak a line frae the end o' the auld brigg to the north neuk o' the abbey, an' exactly at the middle step you will find a comically shapen stane; raise ye up that when nae body sees, an' there you will find an auld yettlin oon-pan filled fu' o' goud an' siller to the very ee.'

"'But, friend, I never was at Kelso, and I never saw either the brigg or the abbey-kirk; an' how am I to find the stane? an', ower an' aboon a', gin I fa' to an' houk up the fok's streets, what will they say to me?'

"'Weel, weel, tak your ain way, John Gray; I hae tauld ye. But ye're daft, poor man; there, ye're gaun away to mine a' the vaults o' the biggest castle o' Liddesdale, an' then ye're gaun to trench a hale hillside at Tamleuchar, a' upon mere chance. An' here, I tell you where the pose is lying, an' ye'll no be at the pains to gang an' turn ower ae stane an' lift it. Ye're clean daft, John Gray o' Middleholm; but I hae tauld ye, sae tak your ain daft gate.' An' wi' that the auld body elyed away, an' left me. I was sae grieved that he had gane away in a pet, for he was the very kind o' man I wantit, that I hollo'd, an' called after him, as loud as I could, to come back. But, gude sauf us a'! at that moment, my wife, Tibby Stott, poor creature! wakened me; for I was roaring through my sleep, an' the hale had been a dream."

John was terribly puzzled next day, and knew not which way to proceed. He did not like to go to hand-gripes with the devil, after such a warning as he had got, and therefore he judged it as safe to delay storming his Castle of Hermitage, till he considered the matter more maturely. On the other hand, it was rather ungenerous to go and seize on his friend's treasure at the Cross of Tamleuchar, after such a friendly visit; and he feared, likewise, that the finding of it was very uncertain; yet he did not know but this might be some malicious spirit, whose aim was to put him by getting the money. And as to Kelso, he had never thought of it before; and it took such a long time to train his ideas to any subject, that he never once thought of going there: so all the schemes were postponed for some time.

"A while after that," says John, "I was sitting at my loom, an' I was workin an' workin, an' thinkin an' thinkin, how to get ane o' thae hidden poses. 'I maun either hae a pose soon,' says I to mysel, 'or else I maun dee o' hunger; an' Tibby Stott, poor creature! she maun dee o' hunger; an' a' my innocent bairns maun dee o' hunger, afore I get them up to do for theirsels.' Thae war heavy concerns on me, an' I was sair dung down. When, or ever I wist, in comes my auld friend, the grey-headit monk. 'John Gray o' Middleholm,' quo he;

'do you ken me?' 'Ay, that I do, honest man; an' weel too! Right blithe am I to see your face again, for I was unco vexed when ye gaed away an' left me sae cuttily afore.'

"'Yere a daft man, John Gray, that's the truth o' the matter; but ye hae some good points about ye, an' I'm your friend. Ye say, ye dinna ken Kelso, nor the place where the pose is lying: now, if ye'll gang wi' me, I'll let you see the very place, an' the very stane that the money is lying aneath; an' if ye winna be at the pains to turn it ower and take the pose, I'll e'en gie it to some ither body; I hae tauld ye, John Gray o' Middleholm.'

"'Dinna gie it to nae other body, an' it be your will, honest man,' quo' I; I says till him, 'An' I's gang w'ye, fit for fit, when ye like.' Sae up I gets, just as I was workin at the loom, wi' my leather apron on, an' a rash o' loom needles in my cuff; an' it wasna a rap till we were at Kelso, where I soon saw the situation o' the town, an' the brigg, an' the auld abbey. Then he takes me to a stane, a queer three-neukit stane, just like a cockit hat. 'Now,' says he, 'John Gray o' Middleholm, the siller's in aneath this; but it winna be very easily raised; put ye a mark on it, till ye get mattocks an' a convenient time, for I maunna be seen here.' I first thought o' leaving my apron on it, but thinking that wad bring a' the fock o' the town, I took ane o' the loom needles to stick in beside it, thinking naebody wad notice that. Bless me! friend, quo' I, this is the saftest an' the smoothest stane that ever I fand in my life; it is surely made o' chalk; an' wi' that, I rammed ane o' the loom needles down through the middle o' the stane into the very head. But I hadna' weel done that, afore there was sic yells an' cries rase out frae aneath the stane, as gin a' the devils o'hell had been broken loose on me; an' the blood sprang frae the chalk stane; an' it spoutit on my hands, an' it spoutit on my face, till I was frightit out o' my wits! Sae I bang'd up, an' ran for bare life; but sic a fa' as I got! I had almost broken my neck. Where think ye I had been a' the time, but lyin' sound sleepin' i' my bed; an' instead o' rinning the needle into the three-neukit stane, I had rammed it to the head in the haunch o' Tibby Stott, poor creature. Then there was sic a whillibalu as never was heard! An' she threepit, an' insistit on me, that I was ettling to murder her. 'Dear Tibby Stott, woman,' quo' I; 'Tibby,' says I to her, 'If I had been ettling to murder you, wadna' I hae run the loom needle into some other part than where I did? It will be lang or ye murder there, Tibby Stott, especially wi' a loom needle.'

"I had now gotten Kelso sae completely i' my head, that away I sets again, to see, at least, if the town was set the same way as I had seen it in my vision. I fand every thing the same; the brig, the auld abbey, an' the three-neukit stane shapit like a cockit hat, mid-way between them; but I coudna' get it houkit, for the fo'k were a' gaun asteer, an' ay this ane was spying an' looking at me, an' the tither ane was spying an' looking at me. Sae I hides my mattocks in a corner o' the auld abbey-kirk, an' down I gaes to saunter a while about the water side, to see if the Kelso fo'k wad settle within their ain doors, an' mind their ain business. I hadna' been lang at the water side, till I sees a hare sitting sleeping in her den. Now, thinks I, that wad be a good dinner for Tibby an' the bairns, an' me. Sae I slides away very cunningly, never letting wit that I saw her; but I had my ee gledgin' out at the tae side; an' as soon as I wan fornent her, I threw mysel' on aboon her a' my length. Then she waw'd, an' she scream'd, an' she sprawled, till I thought she wad win away frae me; but at length I grippit her by the throat. 'Ye auld bitch, that ye are,' quo' I; 'I's do for ye now. But, wi' that, the hare gae me sic a drive wi' a' her four feet at ance, that she gart me flee aff frae aboon her like a drake into the hard stanes at the water side, till I was amaist fell'd. An' there I lay groaning; an' the hare she lay i' the bit screamin. Pity my case! where had I been a' the time, but sound sleepin' i' my ain bed? An' instead o' catchin' a hare, I had catch'd naething but auld Tibby Stott, poor creature; an' had amaist smoth-ered her an' choakit her into the bargain.

"I was really excessively grieved this time; but what could I help it? I ran an' lightit a candle; an' I thought my heart should hae bro-ken, when the poor thing got up on her bare knees, an' beggit me to spare her life. 'Dear Tibby Stott!' quo' I; 'Tibby, my woman,' I says to her, 'It will be the last thing that ever I'll think of to harm your life, poor creature!' says I.

"'Na, na, but John, I heard ye ca' me an awfu' like name for a man to ca' his wife; an' ye said that ye wad do for me now.'

"'Tibby Stott, my woman,' quo I; 'I'm really sorry for what has happened; but ye maun forgie me, for in faith an' troth I thought ye war a hare.'

"'A hare! Na na, John, that winna gang down—Had ye said ye thought I was a mare, I might hae excused ye. I'm sure there wad hae been far less difference in size wi' the tane as the tither.'

"Tibby Stott's no that far wrang there, thinks I to mysel, horn daft as she is.

"'But, John, what did ye tak me for the ither night, when ye stickit me wi' a loom needle into the bane?'

"'Indeed, Tibby, I'm amaist ashamed to say it; but I thought ye war a three-neukit stane, i' the shape of a cockit hat.'"

When Tibby Stott heard this, she drew quietly to her clothes, and hastened out of the house. She was now quite alarmed, thinking that her husband had lost his reason; and, running to one of the neighbouring cottages, she awakened the family, and related to them her tale of dismay; informing them, that her husband had, in the first place, mistaken her for a three-cornered stone, and had stabbed her through the haunch with a loom needle. This relation only excited their merriment; but when she told them, that a few minutes ago he had mistaken her for a hare, and getting above her, had seized her by the throat, trying to worry her for one, it made them look aghast, and they all acquiesced in the belief, that John had been bitten by a mad dog, and was now seized with the malady; and that, when he tried to worry his wife for a hare, he had believed himself to be a dog, a never failing symptom of the distemper. Their whole concern now was, how to get the poor children out of the house; for they dreaded, that on the return of his fit, he might mistake them all for hares crouching in their dens, and worry every one of them. Two honest weavers therefore volunteered their services to go and reconnoitre, and to try if possible to get out the unfortunate children.

Now it so happened, that John was curiously engaged at the very time that these men went to the window, which was productive of another mistake, and put the villagers into the most dreadful dismay. As soon as he observed that Tibby Stott stayed so long away from her bed, he suspected that she had left the house; and, on rising to search for her, he soon found his conjecture too true. This he regretted, thinking that she would make fools both of herself and him, a thing which John accounted very common for wives to do, as the man had no better experience; and, not doubting but that his presence would be likely to make things worse, he awoke the eldest girl, whose name was *Grace*, (the most unappropriate one that could have been bestowed,) and desired her to go and bring back her mother. At first she refused to move, grumbling excessively, and bidding her father go himself; but John, at last, by dint of expostulation, getting her to comply, she requested him to bring her some clothes, and her stockings and shoes from beyond the fire. John called her a good girl, and ran, naked as he was, to bring her apparel. The clothes he found as she directed him, and hastening to the form beyond the fire to bring her stockings and shoes, he set down the lamp and lifted them. The stockings being tied together by a pair of long red garters, John found that he could not carry them all conveniently, so he took the clothes and the shoes in one hand, the lamp in the other, and the staniraw stockings and red garters, in his hurry, he took in his teeth. In this most equivocal situation was John first discovered by the two men as they peeped in at the window, on which they fled with precipitation, while their breasts were throbbing with horror.

When they returned to the house which they had lately left, they found a number of the villagers assembled, all gaping in dismay at the news, that *the lang weaver*, as they always stiled John Gray, was gone mad, and had tried to worry his wife for a hare. Scarcely had they swallowed this uncommon accident, when the two men entered; and the additional horror of the party may hardly be described, when they told what they had seen. "Mercy on us a', sirs!" cried they, "what will be done? John Gray has worried ane o' the lasses already; an' we saw him wi' our een, rinning up an' down the house naked, wi' her claes a' torn i' the tae hand, an' her heart, liver, and thrapple in his teeth, an' his een glancin' like candles!" The women uttered an involuntary scream; the men groaned in spirit; and the Rev. John Mathews, the Antiburgher minister of the village, who had likewise been called up, and had joined the group, proposed that they should say prayers. The motion was agreed to without a division; the minister became a mouth, as he termed it, to the party, and did not fail to remember the malady of the lang weaver, and the danger to which his children were exposed.

While they were yet in the midst of their devotions, the amiable Grace Gray entered, inquiring for her mother; but, after many interrogations, both by the minister and others, the villagers remained in uncertainty with regard to the state of John's malady until it was day. But then, on his appearance, coming in a hurried manner toward the house to seek his wife and daughter, there was such a dispersion! He ran, and she ran, and there was no one ran faster than the Antiburgher minister, who escaped praying, as he flew, that the Lord would make his feet as the feet of hinds upon the mountains. However, the whole fracas of John's hydrophobia ended without any thing very remarkable, save these: that Tibby Stott asked her daughter with great earnestness, "Whilk o' them it was that was worried? an' hoped in God that it wasna' little Crouchy." This was a poor decrepid, insignificant child, who was however her mother's darling, and whose loss would have been more regretted by her than all the rest of the family put together. The other remarkable circumstance was, that the story had spread so rapidly, that it never could be recalled or again assimilated to the truth, and it is frequently related as a fact over all the south country to this day, among the peasantry. Many a time have I heard it, and shuddered at the story; and I am sure many, into whose hand these tales may fall, have likewise heard the woful relation, that a weaver in Middleholm was once bit by his own terrier, and that five years afterwards, he went mad, and tried to worry his wife, who escaped; but that he suc- ceeded in worrying his daughter, and on the neighbours assembling and breaking into the house, that he was found in the horrible guise in which the two men had described him.

John continued to be eyed with dark and lurking suspicion for some time; but he cared very little about such vulgar mistakes, for his mind was more and more taken up about finding poses. This reiterated vision of the old gray-headed monk, the town of Kelso, the bridge, the abbey, and the three-neukit stane like a cockit hat, had now taken full and ample possession of his brain, that he thought of it all day, and by night again visited it in his dreams. Often had he been there in idea, and, as he believed, in spirit, while his mortal part was lying dormant at the wrong side of Tibby Stott; but, at the long and the last, he resolved to go there in person, and, at all events, to see if the town was the same as had been represented to him in his visions.

Accordingly John set out, one morning early in the spring, on his way to the town of Kelso; but he would neither tell his wife, nor any one about Middleholm, where he was going, or what he was going about. He went as he was, with his staff in his hand, and his long bonnet on his head, without any of his mattocks for digging or heav- ing up broad stones, although he knew that purses were generally hid below them. Therefore John felt as disconsolate by the way, as a parish-minister does who goes from home to preach without a ser- mon in his pocket, or like a warrior going out to battle without his armour or weapons. He had, besides, but very little money in his pocket; only a few halfpence, and these he found could be but ill spared at home; and the only hope he had, was in the great sum of money that lay hid beneath the three-neukit stane like a cocket-hat, which stane, he knew, lay exactly mid-way between the end of the bridge and the north corner of the abbey.

John arrived at the lovely town of Kelso a little before the going down of the sun, and immediately set out about surveying the premises; but, to his great disappointment, he found that nothing was the same as it had been shown to him in his dream. The town and the abbey were both on the wrong side of the river, and he scarcely felt convinced that it was the same place. Moreover, the middle space between the end of the bridge and the abbey it was impossible to fix on, owing to some houses that interrupted the line. However, he looked narrowly and patiently all the way, from the one to the other, for the three-cornered stone, often stopping to scrape away the dust with his hands or feet from the sides of every broad one, to ascertain its exact form. He found many broadish stones, and some that inclined a little to a triangular form, but none of them like the one he had dreamed of; though there were some that he felt a strong inclination to raise up, merely that he might see what was below them.

But the more he looked, the better was he convinced, that the middle space between the abbey and the bridge was occupied by an old low-roofed house, within which the three-cornered stone, and the pose of course, behoved to be. Four or five times, in the course of his investigations, did John draw near to the door of this house, and every time stood hesitating whether or not he should enter; but, as he had resolved to tell his errand to no one living, not for fear of being laughed at, but for fear any one should come between him and the pose, he declined going in.

Not having enough of money to procure himself a night's lodging at an inn, he went and bought a pennyworth of bread at a baker's shop, that he might not be chargeable to any one; and, going down to the side of the river, he made a hearty supper on his roll, drinking a little pure water to it. It was here that John, to his infinite pleasure, first discovered a similarity between his vision and the existing scene. For, be it remembered, that, in one of his dreams, he went down to the side of the River Tweed to while away the time, and there discovered a hare sitting in her form. He now remembered having seen this very scene in his dream, which he now looked on, all in the same arrangement, and thenceforward felt a conviction, that this vision would not go for nothing. He then went into a narrow street that stretched to the eastward, as he described it, and went on till he heard the well-known sound of the jangling of weavers' treadles. As the proverb goes, "Birds of a feather, flock ay thegither;" into that house John went, and asked the privilege of a bed, telling them, he himself was a poor weaver, who had come a long journey, in hopes to recover a large sum of money in the town, but not having as yet been successful, he had not wherewith to pay his night's lodging at an inn. The honest people made him very welcome, for the people of that beautiful town, from the highest to the lowest, are noted for a spirit of benevolence. But they tried in vain to pry into his business, and to learn who the creditor was

from whom he expected to recover the sum of money. John, on the
other hand, was very inquisitive of his host about the old abbey—
what sort of people the monks were—how they were dressed, and if
they had much money—what they did with it on a sudden invasion
by the English? and, in particular, *Where he supposed to be exactly the
middle space between the bridge and the abbey?* The man answered all his
queries civilly; and, though he sometimes suspected his guest of a
little derangement in intellect, gave him what information he could
on these abstruse points; manifesting all the while, however, a disposition rather to enter into a debate about some of the modern
tenets of religion. This John avoided as much as possible; for, though
John was an Antiburgher, he knew little more about the matter, save
that his sect was right and all the rest of the world wrong, which was
quite sufficient for him; but, finding that the Kelso weaver was not
disposed so readily to admit this, he waved the engagement from
time to time, and always introduced the more interesting and not
less mysterious subject, of purses hidden in the earth.

Next morning John was early astir, and busily engaged in search
of the three-cornered stone; but still with the same success; and ever
and anon his investigations brought him to the door of the low-
roofed ancient house before mentioned, which he still surveyed with
a wistful look, as if desirous to enter. The occupier of this old mansion was a cobler, a man stricken in years, who had a stall in the one
end of it, while his wife and daughter kept a small fruit-shop in the
other, and by these means earned a decent livelihood. This cobler,
being a very industrious man, was at his work both late and early,
and had noted all John's motions the evening before, as well as that
morning. Curious to know what were the stranger's motives in prying so much about his door, he went out and accosted him, just as he
was in the act of stooping to clean the dust away from the sides of a
broad stone to see what shape it was. As he spoke, John turned
round his head and looked at him; but he was so amazed at the
figure he saw, that he could not articulate a syllable. "What's the
matter w'ye, friend?" said the cobler; "or what is it you hae lost?"
John still could not speak a word; but there he stuck, with his one
knee leaning on the ground, his muddy hands hanging at a distance
from his body, like a man going to leap, his head turned round, and
his mouth open, gaping on this apparition of a cobler. The latter, at
once conceiving that he had addressed a maniac, stood and gazed at
him in silence and pity. John was the first who broke silence, and
certainly his address had not the effect of removing the cobler's apprehensions. "The warld be a wastle us! friend, is this you?" said

John. "There's nae doubt o't ata', man," returned the cobler; "this is *me*, as sure as that is *you*; but wha either you or me is, I fancy me or you disna very weel ken." "Honest man, do you no ken me?" said John; "tell me honestly, did you never see my face afore?" "Why," said the cobler, "I now think I have seen it before; but where, I do not recollect." "Was it in the night-time or the day-time that you saw me?" said John. "Certainly, never in the night-time," returned the cobler. "Then I fancy I am wrang," said John; "I'm forgetting mysel', an' no thinkin what I'm speakin about; but I aux your pardon." "O there's nae offence, honest friend," quoth the cobler; "no ae grain: It is only a sma' mistake; you thought it was *me*, and I thought it was *you*, an' it seems it turns out to be neither the one nor the other." The cobler's wit was lost upon John, who again sunk into silence and gazed; for he saw that this ancient cobler was the very individual person that had appeared to him in his sleep, and told him of the treasure. And, still to approximate the vision closer to reality, the cobler wore a large three-cocked hat on his head. John was in utter consternation, and knew not what to make of it. He saw that it was not a three-neukit stane which the cobler wore on his head, and though very like one in colour, yet that it had once been felt. Still the hat had such a striking resemblance to the stone which John had so often seen in his vision, that he was satisfied the one was represented by the other. He saw there was something extraordinary in the case, and something that boded him luck; but how to solve this mystery of the three-neukit stane and the cockit hat, John was greatly at a loss. He had no doubt that he had found the cue to the treasure; for he had found this cockit hat exactly mid-way between the bridge and the north corner of the abbey, as nearly as he could judge or measure. It was not indeed a three-neukit stane, but it was very like one; and at any rate, it was the very thing, shape, and size, and all, that he had dreamed about, and under which he had been assured the gold was hid. Above all, here was the very person, in form, voice, size, and feature, whose image had appeared to him in his sleep, and had held repeated conversations with him on the subject of the hidden pose; but then, what was there below the hat save the cobler, and he could not possibly be a pan full of gold and silver? The coincidence was however too striking to be passed over without scrutiny. Even the wisest of men would have been struck with it, and have tried to find out some solution; and curious would I be to know what a wise man, in such a case, would have thought of the matter.

John, as I said, was the philosopher of nature, and always fixed

on the most obvious and simple solutions, in determining on effects
from their general causes. He first asked of the cobler a sight of his
hat; which being granted, he looked inside of it; but perceiving that
there was neither money nor lining of any sort there, he returned it,
saying, it was a curious hat. He then asked the cobler, seriously, if
he had never swallowed any gold. The other said, he had not to his
knowledge. "At least," said John; "you certainly could not swallow
any very large quantity? Very weel, then, frien'; if ye'll be sae gude
as to stand a wee bit back." The cobler did so; and John, marking
the precise spot where he had been standing, and on which he had
first seen him in his real corporeal being, went directly to procure
mattocks to dig with, thinking it would to a certainty be below that
spot, and of course virtually covered by the hat at the time he first
saw its ample and triangular form.

He soon got a pick and spade, and fell to digging on the side of the
narrow street with all expedition, to the great amusement of the old
cobler, who, for fear of incurring blame from his townsmen, went
into his stall, and awaited the issue of this singular adventure.

Poor John was hungry, and the column of air was become so
oppressive on him, that he felt as if his life depended on his success,
and wrought with no ordinary exertion. The pit waxed in its dimen-
sions, and deepened exceedingly. He first came to sand, and then to
loam, at which time his hopes ran very high, for he found two or
three small bones, which he was sure had once formed a part of the
body of some immensely rich abbot; and finally, he came to a stiff,
almost an impenetrable till. Nevertheless he continued to dig, until
the town's people, beginning to move about as the morning advanced,
gathered about him, and asked him what he meant? He desired
them to mind their own business, and let him mind his; and on this
the first comers went away, thinking he was a man employed in
repairing the street; but it was not long ere two town officers arrived, and forced him to desist, threatening, that if he refused to
comply, and to fill up the hole exactly as he found it, they would
carry him to prison, and have him punished. John was forced to
yield, and once more abandon his golden dream. He filled up the
pit with evident marks of chagrin and disappointment, some aver-
ring that they even saw the tears dropping from his eyes, and mixing with the gravel. He had now nothing for it, but to return as he
came, and apply to the wretched loom once more. He even knew
not where he was to procure a breakfast, and still less how Tibby
Stott, poor creature! and the children, were breakfasting at home.
The officers asked him whence he came, and what he wanted; but

he refused to satisfy them; and after he had made the street as it was, and to their satisfaction, they left him.

There was something so whimsical in all that the cobler had witnessed, that he determined, if possible, to find out something of the man's meaning. He dreaded that he was a little deranged in his intellects; still there was a harmless simplicity about the stranger that interested him; and he thought he discerned glimpses of shrewdness that could not possibly be inherent in an ideot. Accordingly, as soon as the crowd had dispersed, and John had lifted his plaid and staff, and blown his nose two or three times, as he took a last look of the bridge and the old abbey, the cobler went out to him, addressed him with kindness, and beseeched him to go in, and take share of his breakfast.

Thankfully did John accept of the invitation, and seldom has a man done more justice to his entertainer's hospitality, than our hero did that morning. After despatching a bowlfull of good oat meal parritch, washed down with a bottle of brisk treacle ale, the cobler's daughter presented them with a large cut of broiled salmon. This rich and solid fare answering John's complaint exceedingly well, he set to it with so much generous avidity, that the cobler restrained himself, and suffered his guest to realize the greater part of it. The delightful sensations excited by this repast raised John's heart a little above his late disappointment, and even before the salmon was finished, he had begun to converse with some spirit. But his sphere of conversation was rather of a circumscribed nature, being confined to one object, namely, that of poses hidden in the earth, with its collateral branches. He asked the cobler what sort of men the monks were, who had lived in that grand abbey—Of the abbots that governed them—The sources of their great riches, and how they disposed of these on any invasion by the English.

There was no subject on which the cobler loved more to converse, having himself come of that race, and, as he assured John, the sixth in descent from the last abbot and a lady of high quality; he, and his forebears so far back, having been the fruits of a Christmas confession; and that, had the establishment still continued, he would in all likelihood have at that day been abbot himself. He showed John an old charter on emblazoned vellum, granted by Malcolm the fourth to the abbey of Kelso, on the removal of the Cistertian Monks from Selkirk to that place; and he talked so long on the customs and usages of the monks, the manner of lives they led, their fasts, holidays, and pilgrimages, that John never thought to be so weary of monachism; no mention having ever been made of their poses, in all this lengthened discourse.

After breakfast, the cobler pledged John in a bumper of brandy, and then handed his guest another, which John took with a blushing smile, and after holding it up between him and the light to enjoy its pure dark colour, he drank to the good health of the cobler; and, as the greatest blessing on earth that he could think of, wished he might find a good pose.

The cobler, thinking he now had his guest in the proper key, asked him to explain to him, if he pleased, the motives of his procedure that morning and last night? John laughed with a sly leer, bit his lip, and looking at the women who were bustling but and ben, at length told his host, that if he was to tell him that, he must tell him by himself; on which they went into the stall, and after John had desired the cobler to shut the door, he addressed him as follows:

"Now, ye see, friend, ye're sic an honest kind man, that I canna refuse to tell you ony thing; an' for that cause, I'll tell you the plain truth; but, as I ken you will think me a great fool, I'll neither tell you my name, nor my wife's name, nor the name o' the place where I bide; but it is a wee bit out o' Kelso; no very far; I can gang hame to my dinner. Ye maun just let that satisfy you on that score. Weel, ye see, disna I dream ae night, that there's an auld oon-pan, fu' o' gold an' silver, hidden aneath a queer shapen stane, exactly mid-way atween the end o' your brig an' the north neuk o' the auld abbey there; an' I dreamed it sae aft, that I could get nae rest; for troth it was like to mislead me, an' pit me by mysel a' thegither. To sickan a height did the fleegary rin in my imagination, (hee, hee, hee! Is the door closs, think ye?) that I mistook the stane that was happin the pose, and, meaning to pit a mark in it to ken it by, (Will naebody hear us, think ye?) disna I rin a lang sharp bodkin into the head i' the wrang side o' my wife, poor creature! till I e'en gart her skirl like a gait, an' was amaist fleyed her out o' her wits. An' there was ae night after that, she ran a greater risk still. Sae, troth, just to prevent me frae fa'ing till her wi' a pick an' a spade some night, an' to see gin it wad help me to ony better blink o' rest, I was fain to come to Kelso yestreen, to see if there was sic a thing or no. An' this morning, when you and I first met, for reasons that I needna an' canna weel explain, I thought I had found the very spot. Now, that's the main truth, an' I daresay you will think me a great fool."

The cobler, who was mightily amused by this statement of facts, answered as follows: "A man, my good friend, may act foolishly at a time, an' yet no be a'thegither a fool. To be a fool, you see, is to—is to—In short, it's to be a fool—a born fool like. But it is a Gallic word that, an' has mony meanings. Now, dreaming disna make a man a fool; but it makes him a fool sae far, that he may play the fool in his dream. He may rise in his sleep, an' play the fool; but if he dinna play the fool after he wakens, he canna just be ca'd an absolute fool. But it is the fool, who, after he has dreamed, takes a' his dreams for reality. At least, it is acting very foolishly to do that." "I thought your speech wad land there," said John. "No, but stay till I explain mysel'," said the cobler. "O, ye needna fash, the thing's plain enough," said John; "I maun think about setting awa' hame." "Stop a wee bit, man," said the cobler, taking hold of John's coat as he was rising, "I hae a queer story to tell you about a purse afore ye gang away, that will explain the matter wi' mair clearness an' precision than a' the learning an' logic that I'm master o'.

"It is ower true, what I maun tell you, honest man, that I am very ill for dreaming mysel, an' mony a wild unsonsy dream I hae had; an' the mair I strave against it, I grew aye the waur. When I was a young child, there was hardly a night that I didna' dream I was a monk, an' confessing some ane or ither o' the bonny lasses an' wives about Kelso. An' sic tales as I thought they tauld me! Then, when I saw them again sittin' i' the kirk, wi' their douse decent faces, I couldna' get their confessions out o' my mind, gude forgie me! an' I had some kind o' inklin' about my heart, that they were a' true. There was the folly o' the thing! Then I had nae sooner closed my een the neist night than I was a monk again, and hard engaged at the auld business. There was ane Bess Kelly, a fine sponkin' lass, that a' the lads were like to gang wudd about; I'm sure I confessed Bess mair nor a hunder times i' my sleep, an' mony was the sin I pardoned till her." John chuckled, and grinned, and made every now and then a long neck by the cobler, to see if the door was close enough shut; but when he reached thus far, John rose, passed him, and felt the latch, and though the door was shut, he gave it a push with his shoulder, to make it, if possible, go a little closer. "Friend, I can tell you," said John; "there may be here that ken, an' here that dinna ken; but that's a very queer story. So you always dreamed you were a monk?" "So often," said the cobler, "that the idea became familiar to me; and even in the day time, I often deemed myself one." "So did I," said John, "it became familiar to me too, and I thought you a monk both by night and by day." The cobler stared at John, and thought him mad in good earnest; but the latter, feeling that he was going to divulge more perhaps than prudence and caution with regard to hidden poses warranted, corrected himself by saying, that he thought he resembled one of that order, in his grave, decent appearance, which was all he meant to say. The cobler then went on.

"Weel, I'm no yet come to the story I was gaun to tell you. I had sic a dream last night, as I hae nae had these twenty years; and, I think, I never had sic a queer dream in my life. An' then it was sae like your ain, too; for it was about a hidden purse." "Aye aye, man!" said John, "Gude sauf us! what was't? but stop a wee till I see if the door be close steekit." John again felt the door, gave it another push, and then sat down, with open mouth and ears, to drink in the story of the cobler's dream.

"I was as usual a monk, and had gane out after vespers to take a walk by the side o' the Tweed; an' as I was gaun down by the boat-pool foot, I sees an ill-faur'd-looking carle, something like yoursel', sitting eating a roll, an' he'd a living hare lying beside him that he had catched in her den."–"Hout, friend!" said John, "but did you really dream that?" "In very deed I did," said the cobler, "why do you doubt it?" "Because, friend," said John, "they may be here that ken, an' here that dinna ken; but that's a very queer dream indeed." "There's nae doubt o't," said the cobler; "but stay till you hear it out. Weel, I says to the carle, (he was very like you,) friend, will you sell your hare? 'Hout na,' quo' he, 'you palmer bodies are a' poor, ye hae nae sae muckle siller atween you an' poverty as wad buy my hare. Ye're a very poor man, monk, for a' the rich confessions ye hae made, an' ye're a daft man, that's waur; but, an' ye wad like to be rich, I can tell you where you will get plenty o' goud an' siller.' I thankit the carle, an' said there were few that wadna' like to be richer than they were, an' I had nae objections at a' to the thing. 'Weel, weel,' quo' he; 'he that hides kens best where to seek; but there was mony ane i' the days o' langsyne, wha haid weel, but never wan back to howk again. Gang ye your ways west the country the morn, an' spier for a place they ca' Middleholm; an' when ye come there, speer for a man they ca' John Gray. Gang ye into his garden, an' ye will find thirteen apple-trees in it, six at the head, an' six at the foot, an' ane in the middle."–"Hout friend!" said John, interrupting him, "but are ye no joking? did you really dream that?" "As sure as yon sun is in the heaven, I did," said the cobler; "why should you doubt it?" "Because ye see, friend," said John, "they are here that ken, an' here that dinna ken; but, let me tell you, that's a very queer dream indeed. Weel, what did the fearsome carle say mair?"

"'Gang ye into that garden,' quo' he, 'an' begin at the auld apple-tree in the middle, an' howk deep in the yird below that tree, an' you will find an auld pan filled fu' o' money to the ee. When ye hae disposed o' that, if ye like to gang back to that man's garden, an' howk weel, you will find a pose o' reid goud aneath every apple-tree that's in it.' Now, wadnae ye hae reckoned me as a fool if I had taen a' this for truth? an' thought I was acting very foolishly, if I had gane away into the west country, asking for a place an' a man that perhaps hae nae existence? To hae gane about, as our school rhyme says, spearing for

> 'The town that ne'er was framed,
> An' the man that ne'er was named,
> The tree that never grew,
> An' the bird that never flew.'"

'O there's nae doubt o' the thing, friend, it wad hae been great non-sense—there's nae doubt o't at a'. But yet, for a' that, its the queerest dream, ae way an' a' ways, that I ever heard i' my life; an' I hae a great mind to gang an' speer after the place an' the man mysel'. If I get as good a breakfast, an' as good a dram, as I did for the last pose I howkit, my labour winna' be lost a' thegither.'"

The cobler laughed, and wished John all manner of success; and the latter parted from him with many professions of esteem; and, in higher spirits than ever he was before, he went straight home to Tibby Stott and Middleholm, and prepared next morning to begin and root up the old apple-tree in the middle of the garden. Now, there were exactly thirteen trees in it, as the cobler said; a circum-stance of which the owner was not aware till that very night when he returned from Kelso.

Poor Tibby Stott was right glad to see her husband again, for the report in the village was, that he had run away mad; and, as the country people were in terrible alarm about that time for mad dogs, and pursuing and killing them every day, Tibby dreaded that poor John would be shot, or sticked with long forks, like the rest. She viewed him at first with a jealous eye; but, on seeing him so good-humoured and kind to the children and herself, she became quite reconciled to him, and wept for joy, poor creature! at getting him back again; for she found she would have been utterly helpless with-out him, although ten times a-day she called him *a cool-the-loom*. John told her how he had travelled to Kelso, and spent a day and a night there on some important business, and had only wared one penny; and, among other things, how he had learned to cultivate his garden so as to make it produce great riches.

Next morning, as soon as it was day, John began a digging at one

side of the old apple-tree, but he was terribly impeded by roots, and
came very ill speed. Some of these he cut, and digged in below
others; for he found, that when they were cut, they impeded his
progress nearly as much as before. By the time the villagers rose,
John had made a large pit; but then the alarm began, and spread like
wild-fire, that the lang weaver was come home again madder than
ever, and had been working all night digging a grave in his garden,
which every one suspected he meant for Tibby Stott. The pit that he
had made, by chance, bore an exact resemblance to a grave, and
great was the buzz in the village of Middleholm that morning. The
people gathered around him, at first looking cautiously over the
garden wall; but at last they came close about him, every man with
his staff in his hand, and asked him how he did, and what he was
engaged in. John said he had been away down the country, inquiring by what means to improve his garden, and he had been instructed
to prune the roots of his apple-trees in place of the branches; for that
they had run to wood below the earth, which had been the cause of
their growing wild and barren. The villagers knew not what to make
of this, it was so unlike any thing that the lang weaver had ever
done before; so they continued to hang over him, and watch his
progress, with all manner of attention. John saw this would never
do, for they would discover all; and then there were so many who
would be for sharing the money along with him, that a small share
might only fall to him; and, moreover, if they told the lord of the
manor, he would claim it altogether.

John had a good deal of low cunning; and, as he had now got very
deep on one side of the tree, in order to mislead the villagers, he
took a wheelbarrow, and hurled a kind of sour dung that had been
accumulating around his cow-house for years, with which he
crammed the pit that he had made below the tree, and, after covering it over with the mould, he tramped it down. His neighbours then
went away and left him, convinced that he had got some new chimera into his head about gardening, which would turn out a piece of
folly at the last. John was now left to prosecute his grand research
quietly; save that Tibby Stott never ceased intreating him "to mind
his loom an' let the trees alane." John answered with great rational-
ity, "sae I will, Tibby, my woman, I will mind the loom; but ye ken
a man maun do ae thing afore anither."

Towards the evening, Mr Mathews, the minister, went into the
garden to *get a crack wi' John*, and see his new scheme of gardening.
John had now got to a considerable depth on the south side of the
tree, and not much regarding the tame moral remarks, or the thread-

bare puns of his pastor, (these two little amiable characteristics of the Calvinistical divine,) was plying at his task with all his might, for still as he grew more hungry his exertions increased; and just at that precious instant, his spade rattled along the surface of a broad stone. "John," said the minister, "What have you got there, John?" "I fancy I'm come to the solid rock now, sir," said John, "I needna' howk nae deeper here." "John, give me the mattock, John," said the minister; "I propine, that it would be nothing inconsistent with prudence and propriety to investigate this matter a little. This garden, as I understand, was planted by four friars of the order of St Benedict, who were the first founders of this village; and these people had sometimes great riches, John. Give me the mattock, John, and if I succeed in raising that stone, I shall claim all that is below it." "I wad maybe contest that point wi' your worship," said John; "for I can tell you what you will find below it." "And pray, what would I find below it, John?" said the Antiburgher minister. "Just yird an' stane to the centre o' the globe," said John; "an' sic a pit wad spoil my bit garden." "Why, you are grown a wit, John," said the divine, "as well as a gardener. That answer is very good; nevertheless, give me the mattock, John."

The minister might as well have asked John's heart's blood. He determined to keep hold of his spade, and likewise the possession of his pit; yet he did not wish to fight the minister. So, turning his face to him, and keeping his spade behind his back, he said to him, "Hout na', sir, ye dinna ken how to handle spades an' shools, gin' it be nae maybe the shool o' the word to delve into our hearts an' souls wi'." "There's more strength than propriety in that remark, John," said the minister. "But I can tell you, sir," continued John, with a readiness that was not customary with him, "the hale secret o' the stane. Thae monk bodies were good gardeners, an' they laid aye a braid stane aneath the roots o' ilka fruit-tree that they plantit, to keep the bits o' tendrils frae gripping down to the cauld till, whilk wad soon spoil the tree." "Why, John, I have heard of such an experiment, indeed; and I suspect you have guessed nearer to the truth than might have been gathered from the tenor of the foregoing chapter of your life, John; it is therefore vain for a man to waste his strength for nought. A good evening to you, John." "Gude e'en, gude e'en to your Reverence," said John, as he turned about in his hole, chuckling and laughing with delight; and when the Antiburgher minister was fairly out at the gate, he nodded his head, and said to himself, "Now, if I hae nae mumpit the minister, my name's no John Gray o' Middleholm. Thae gospel bodies want to hae a finger in

ilka ane's pye, but they manna hae things a' their ain gate neither. O
there's nae set o' men on the face o' the yird, as keen o' siller as the
ministers! Ane wad think, to hear them preach, that they held the
warld quite at the staff's end; but a' the time they're nibblin nibblin
at it just like a trout at a worm, or a hare at a kailstock. He thought
to hae my pose! Let him haud him wi' his steepin'—screw'd as it is
off the backs an' the meltiths o' mony a poor body."

John took hold of a stone hammer, and gave the broad stone a
smash on the one side. As he struck, the stone tottered, and John
heard distinctly, something that jingled below it. The very hairs of
his head stood upright, he was in such agitation! the hammer dropped
from his hand, and he jumped out of the pit, gazed all around him,
and then ran towards the house, impelled by some inward feeling to
communicate his good fortune to his partner; but by the way reflection whispered in his ear, that Tibby Stott, poor creature! was not
the person calculated for keeping such an important secret. This set
him back to his pose; which, in trembling anxiety, he resolved to
survey; and, cleaning all the earth from above the stone, he heaved
it up, and there beheld   *   *   *   *   *   *   *   *

It must not here be told what John beheld.—It would be too much
for the reader's happiness to bear. He must be left to conjecture
what it was that John discovered below that broad stone, and it is
two to one he will guess wrong, for all that he has heard about it,
and for as plain as matters have been made to him. John let the
stone sink down again—took the wheel-barrow and filled the pit full
of wet straw, which he judged better than dung; then, covering it
over with earth, he went into his supper of thin bleared sowins,
amid his confused and noisy family, all quarrelling about their por-
tions; and finally, to his bed with Tibby Stott.

That night, John drew nearer to Tibby than usual, and put his
arm around her neck. "Wow, John, hinny!" quoth she, "what means
a' this kindness the night?" "Tibby Stott, my woman Tibby," said
John, "I hae a secret to tell you; but ye're to promise, an' swear to
me, that ye're never to let it to the tap o' your tongue, as lang as ye
hae life, afore ony body but mysel." Tibby promised all that John
desired her, and she repeated as many oaths after him as he chose,
eager to learn this great secret; and John, after affecting great hesitation and scruples, addressed her as follows:

"Tibby Stott, do ye ken what was the matter wi' me, when I was
last sae unweel?" "Na, John, I didna ken then, nor ken I yet." "But
I kend, Tibby Stott; and there's no anither in this world kens, or
ever maun ken, but yoursel. I was very ill then, Tibby; an' I was in

a very queer way. Ay, I was waur than ony body thought! But do you ken how I got better, Tibby?" "Indeed, I dinna ken that nouther, John." "But I'll tell you, Tibby. I was brought to bed o' twa black birds; an' I hae them keepin concealed i' the house; an' they're twa ill spirits, far waur than cockatrices. Now, if this war kend, I wad be hanged, an' ye wad be burnt at the stake for a witch; therefore, keep the secret as you value both our lives. An' Tibby, ye maun never gang to look for thae twa birds, for if ever ye find them, they'll flee away wi' you to an ill place; an' mind ye an' dinna gang to be telling this to ony living flesh, Tibby Stott."

"Na, na, John; sin' ye bid me, I sall never tak the tale o'er the tap o' my tongue. But, oh! alak! an wae's me! what's to come o' us? Ye hae gart a' my flesh girrel, John; to think that ever my gude-man sude hae been made a mither! an' then to think what he's mither to! Mither o' twa deils! The Lord have a care o' us, John! wad it no be better to let the twa imps flee away, or get Mr Mathews to lair them?"

"But tent me here, Tibby Stott, my woman, Tibby, they're sent for gude luck—"

"It can only be deil's luck, at the best, John; an' his can never be good luck."

"The best o' a' luck, Tibby; for I can tell you, we'll never want as lang as they are in the house. They'll bring me siller when I like, an' what I like; an' a' that ye hae to do, is to haud your tongue, an' ye'll find the good o't; but if ever ye let this secret escape you, we're ruined hip and thigh for ever."

Tibby promised again for the sake of the money; but the next morning before she swept her house, she ran in unto a neighbour-ing gossip, and addressed her as follows:

"Wow, Jean, I hae gotten a screed o' unco news sin' I last saw you! I trow ye didna ken that we had a crying i' this town the tither week?"

"I wat, Tibby, I never heard o' sic a thing afore."

"Aye, but atween you an' me, there's a pair o' braw twins come to the warl, though nane o' the best-hued anes that may be. But they'll be snug-keepit anes, an' weel-tochered anes, and weel keepit out o' sight, as maiden's bairns should be. Aye, Jean, my dow; but an' ye kend wha's the mither o' them, your een wad stand i' back water wi' laughin!"

"What? Hout fie Tibby! I wat weel it isna Bess Bobagain, the Antiburgher minister's housekeeper?"

"Waur nor that yet; an' that wad hae been ill eneuch. But ye see the thing maunna be tauld; or else ye maun swear never to tell it again, as lang as ye live."

"Me tell it again! Nah! It is weel kend I never tauld a secret i' my life. Ane may safely trust me wi' ony thing. My father, honest man, used to say to me, even when I was but a wee toddlin thing, that he had sae muckle to lippen to me, that he could hae trustit me wi' a housefu' o' untelled millstanes. The thing that's bred i' the bane, winna easily ding out o' the flesh. When I was sae trusty then, what should I be now?"

"Aye, to be sure, there's a great deal in that. It says muckle for ane, when ane's pawrent can trust ane, sae as to do as ane likes i' ane's house. My father wad never trust me wi' a boddle; but mony a time he said I wad be a good poor man's wife, for that the best thing ony body could do for a poor man, was to gie him employment, an' I was the ane that wad haud mine busy for the maist part o' the four and twenty hours. But for a' my father's far-seen good sense, I hae had eneuch ado wi' John Gray, for though he's nae bad hand when he's on the loom, it is nae easy matter to keep him at the batt. But that's a' away frae our story. Sin your father could trust you sae far, I think I may trust you too, only ye're to say *as sure as death*, you will never tell it again."

Jane complied, as was most likely, for the sake of this mysterious and scandalous story, as she deemed it to be, and after every precaution on the part of Tibby Stott, her gossip was entrusted with the whole. It would be endless to recount all the promises that were stipulated for, made, and broken at Middleholm, in the course of that day. Suffice it, that before night, every one, both old and young in the village, knew that the lang weaver had been *brought to bed o' twa black craws*.

This was too ridiculous a story to be believed, even by the ignorant inhabitants of that ancient village; and, as John shrewdly anticipated, they only laughed at John Gray's crazy wife. It proved however to him, that it would never do to trust his helpmate with the secret of finding hidden poses, and that whatever money he drew from such funds, it behoved him to ascribe it to the generosity of the two black birds.

So John arose one moonlight night, while others slept, went into his garden, and removing the wet straw, he again lifted up the broad stone, and took from under it the valuable treasure of which he had formerly made discovery. This was neither less nor more than the very thing he had always been told of, both by the vision of the cobler in his dream, and by the cobler himself; namely, an old pan filled with coins, of a date and reign John knew nothing about. Nearly one fourth of the whole bulk was made up of broad pieces of gold, but very thin, enclosed in one side of the pan; the rest was all silver, in a considerable state of decay. There were likewise among the gold, four rude square coins, about a quarter of an inch in thickness, and nearly the weight of a dollar each. John emptied them into a bag, and marched straight to Edinburgh with his treasure; where, after a great deal of manœuvring, he sold the whole for the miserable sum of £213:12:6, being the exact value of the metal (as the man assured him) to a scruple. John got his payment in gold and silver, for he would have nothing to do with bank notes, and brought the whole home with him. He knew nothing about putting money out at interest; and, still in fear lest he should be discovered, he hid it in the corner of his chest, resolved to live well on it till it was done, and then dig up another tree, take the pose from below it, and sell, and spend that in course; and so on: for John knew perfectly well, that he had a dozen of poses more to begin to, when the first was done.

Thenceforward, John's meals became somewhat more plentiful, but improved nothing in quality. He had been so long used to a life of poverty, that parsimony was become natural to him, and it was but seldom that he applied to the two birds for assistance. He could not rest however until he digged below one other tree, that he might have some guess what the extent of his treasure was, and what he had to depend on.

He accordingly began, and digged all round the next, and in beneath it, until the pits on each side met below the stem of the tree at a great depth, so that every one of the downward roots were cut; but for all that he could do, he could find no treasure whatever, and was obliged to give up the scrutiny considerably disappointed. Having, however, discovered, in the former adventure, that the removal of a part of the immense quantity of miry sour dung, from about his cowhouse, had been attended with some conveniences, he likewise filled up this latter pit with a farther portion of that, and again betook himself to his loom and his twa black craws.

The next year, to the astonishment of all, but more particularly to John himself, who had never once calculated on such an event, these two trees, after being literally covered over with healthy blossoms, bore such a load of fruit as never had been witnessed in that country. Almost every branch required a prop to prevent it being torn from the tree, by the increasing weight. John pulled the apples always as they ripened, and sent a quantity down every week by the carrier to his friend, the Cobler of Kelso, whose wife and daughter, it will be remembered, kept a fruit shop in one end of his dwelling. At the close of the year, when John went down to settle with his old friend, and the three-cocked hat, the latter paid him gratefully £7, 10s. for the produce of these two trees, and thanked him for his credit; not forgetting to treat him at breakfast with a cut of broiled salmon and a glass of brandy.

John, perceiving that this was good interest for a few wheel-bar-rows full of sour mire, followed the same mode with all his apple-trees, and planted more, so that in the course of a few years, the cobler paid him annually from 30 to 45 pounds Sterling for fruit, a great sum in those days; and thus was the cobler's extraordinary dream thoroughly fulfilled, not alone with regard to the main pose in the old pan, but that below every tree of the garden.

John now lived comfortably, with his family, all the days of his life, and there were no lasses had such trim and elegant cockernonies in all the Antiburgher meeting-house of Middleholm as the daugh-ters of the lang weaver. But Tibby Stott, poor creature! believed till her dying-day, that their wealth was supplied by the twa mysterious black craws, whose place of concealment she never found out, nor ever sought after.

WINTER EVENING TALES,

COLLECTED AMONG

THE COTTAGERS

IN THE

South of Scotland.

By JAMES HOGG,

AUTHOR OF " THE QUEEN'S WAKE," &c. &c.

IN TWO VOLUMES.
VOL. II.

" In rangles round afore the ingle's lowe,
   Frae Gudame's mouth auld-warld Tales they hear,
O' Warlocks loupin' round the Wirrikow,
   O' Ghaists that won in glen and kirk-yard drear,
Whilk touzles a' their tap, an' gars them shake wi' fear."—*Fergusson.*

EDINBURGH:

PRINTED FOR OLIVER & BOYD, HIGH-STREET; AND
G. & W. B. WHITTAKER, AVE-MARIA-LANE,
LONDON.

1820.

The Bridal of Polmood
Chapter I

LAST autumn, on my return from the Lakes of Cumberland to Edinburgh, I fell in with an old gentleman at the village of Moffat, whose manners and conversation deeply interested me. He was cheerful, unaffected, and loquacious, to a degree which I have not often witnessed; but his loquacity was divested of egotism—his good humour communicated itself to all present, and his narratives were fraught with traditionary knowledge, the information to which, of all others, my heart is most fondly attached. Having learned, in the course of our conversation, that he was bound for Edinburgh, and that he had already been twice disappointed of obtaining a passage by the Dumfries mail, my friend offered to accommodate him with a seat in our carriage; telling him that we had a spare one, and that instead of incommoding us, he would oblige us by his company. He accepted of our proposal, not only with apparent satisfaction, but with an easy and cheerful grace which seemed peculiar to himself; and early next morning we proceeded on our journey.

As we ascended the lofty green mountains which overlook the vale of Annandale, the sun arose, and the scene became inconceivably beautiful and variegated. The dazzling brightness of the distant Solway it was almost impossible to look upon—the high mountains of Queensberry and Lowther, on the west, were all one sheet of burning gold; while the still higher ones to the eastward were wrapt in a solemn shade. In almost any other circumstances I could have contemplated the scene with the highest sensations of delight, and gazed upon it without satiety and without weariness. The shades of the mountains were still lessening as the sun advanced, and those shadows, along the whole of their fantastical outline, seemed to be fringed with a delicate rainbow. This phenomenon I pointed out to our traveller, who said it was common, and occasioned by the first slanting rays of the sun being reflected from the morning dew. On looking more narrowly to the surface of the mountains, I perceived that it was sprinkled with a garnish of silver globules, brighter and more transparent than the purest gem; yet so tiny, that the weight of a thousand scarcely caused the smallest blade of grass to stoop, or bent the web of the gossamer.

The conversation of our new acquaintance, however, almost superseded the possibility of attending to any thing else. Every farmsteading in the valley, every mountain and glen in our way, was either the scene of some ancient exploit, or some way connected with it. His store of anecdotes was inexhaustible—Our time past lightly away—The scenery of the Solway vanished behind us like the setting moon, and ere we were well aware, found that we had crossed the heights of Erickstane, and were descending by the side of the Tweed, which is there an inconsiderable and trifling rivulet working its way among black mountains.

We breakfasted at a good inn by the side of the river; and, on proceeding a little farther, I observed on the opposite bank, an old decayed house standing in a small wood of stately trees, and asked my intelligent companion how it was named? and to whom it belonged? both in a breath. "That is Polmood," said he; "you must often have heard of Polmood." I had never heard of it. "You *must* have heard of it," rejoined he, "though it may have escaped your memory: people do not always retain those things in their minds in which they are not interested; but the antiquity and singularity of the charter by which that estate is held, has become famous throughout the kingdom. It was granted by King Malcom Canmore, to the first Norman Hunter of Polmood, with all above it to heaven, and below it to hell; on condition that he and his heirs should present to the king a bow and a broad arrow whenever he came to hunt on that quarter. This charter has been printed in many histories and collections. But besides that, there have so many remarkable occurrences taken place in that family, that its concerns have never ceased to be a subject of discussion and animadversion, for the space of several ages." I asked of what nature they were? "They are so manifold and so complex," said he, "that I could not relate them all in a week; and if I could they would not attach credit; for, though well authenticated, they are scarcely sanctioned by the stamp of probability. The answer which I must return to your second query, is a striking instance of this. You ask me who is the owner of Polmood? That it seems is a hard question, since all the lawyers and judges in Scotland have not been able to determine it in the course of half a century. It is a positive and lamentable truth, my dear Sir, (I use his own words,) that though it is as apparent to whom the estate of Polmood rightfully belongs, as it is to whom this hand belongs, it has been a subject of litigation, and depending in our Court of Session for these fifty years.

"This is one remarkable circumstance connected with the place, which has rendered it famous of late years; and seems in part to justify an ancient prediction, that the Hunters of Polmood were never more to prosper. This threatening prediction is said to have been delivered at first in a supernatural, or at least an unaccountable manner; and as it is connected with one of the most extraordinary stories that is to be found in the inexhaustible mine of Scottish tradition, for lack of better entertainment, I shall, with your permission, relate to you the leading circumstances of the transaction." As my companion and I both gladly accepted of his proposal, he instantly began the following tale, which, with few interruptions, served us for a topic of conversation during the rest of our journey.

As soon as I reached Edinburgh I wrote it down; and waiting upon the narrator, who is now one of my most intimate friends, I read it over to him, correcting and enlarging it, according to his directions. The general observations and reflections which occur, were all made by himself in course of the narration, and I regret my inability to deliver them in his short and impressive manner. He however testified his hearty approbation of them all, declaring that the ideas were *better brought out* than they would have been by himself. I have retained all his sentiments, and even his expressions, to a degree which the present taste for abstract composition will scarcely justify; and only regret the passive obedience exacted by modern critics to punctilious modes of expression, a conformity to which has obliged me to change others which I was inclined to preserve.

Chapter II

NORMAN HUNTER of Polmood, the ninth of that name, and chief forester to the king of Scotland in all those parts, was a gentleman of high courage and benevolence, much respected by his majesty, and all the nobles of the court who frequented the forests of Frood and Meggat-dale for the purpose of hunting. He had repeatedly entertained the king himself at his little castle of Polmood; and during the harvest months, while the king remained at his hunting seat of Crawmel, Norman of Polmood was never absent from his side; for besides his other qualifications, he was the best marksman then in Scotland; and so well could his eye have measured distances, that when the deer was running at full speed, and the arrows of all the

courtiers flying like meteors, some this way, and some that, whenever Polmood's arrow reached its destination, she was seen to
founder.

While the king and his nobles were enjoying the chase on Meggat-
dale and the mountains of the Lowes, the queen, with her attendants, remained at the castle of Nidpath, where his Majesty went to
visit her once a week; but when the weather was fine, and the mountains of the forest clear, the queen and her maidens frequently made
excursions to the hunting quarters, and spent a few days in diver-
sions with the king and his nobles.

It was during one of those excursions, that the laird of Polmood
fell desperately in love with one of the queen's maidens, a very
young lady, and supposed to have been the greatest beauty of her
time. Her name was Elizabeth Manners; she was of English extraction; having followed the queen of Scots from her native home when
only a little girl. Many of the young courtiers admired the glow of
her opening charms, which were every day ripening into new beauties; and some of them were beginning to tease and flatter her; but
she being an orphan from a strange country, destitute of titles or
inheritance, and dependent on the bounty of the queen, by whom
she was greatly beloved, none of them had the generosity to ask her
in marriage. The principal of these her admirers were the young
Baron Carmichael, and the duke of Rothsay, brother to the king.
They were both goodly knights. Carmichael admired and loved her
with all his heart; but diffidence, or want of opportunity, had prevented him from making his sentiments known to her, otherwise
than by his looks, which he had always flattered himself were returned in a way that bespoke congeniality of feeling. As for Rothsay,
he had no other design than that of gaining her for his mistress, a
scheme on which his heart had for some time been ardently intent.
But no sooner had Norman of Polmood seen her, than he fell violently in love with her, and shortly after asked her of the king and
queen in marriage. Polmood being at that time a man of no small
consequence, both with regard to possessions and respectability,
the royal pair, judging this to be a good offer, and an advantageous
settlement for their beauteous ward, approved readily of the match,
provided that he gained the young lady's consent. The enamoured
forester, having so successfully *started his game*, lost no time in *the
chase*; and by the most determined perseverance, to use his own
expression, *he run her down* in the course of one week. He opened
his proposals in presence of the king and queen, and encouraged
by their approbation, pressed his suit so effectually, that the young

Elizabeth, not being able to offer any plausible reason why she could not consent, and weening that it would be bad manners to give a disinterested lover an absolute refusal, heard him at first in thoughtful silence, and in a few days finally acquiesced, though Polmood was considerably past the bloom of youth.

Every young lady is taught to look forward to marriage as the great and ultimate end of her life. It is that to which she looks forward for happiness, and in which she hopes to rival or excel her associates; and even *the first* to be married in a family, or court, is a matter of no small consideration. These circumstances plead eloquently in favour of the first lover who makes the dear proposal. The female heart is naturally kind and generous—it feels its own weakness, and its inability to encounter singly the snares and troubles of life; and in short, that it must lean upon another, in order to enjoy the delights most congenial to its natural feelings, and the emanation of those tender affections, in the exercise of which, the enjoyments of the female mind chiefly consist. It is thus that the hearts of many young women become by degrees irrevocably fixed on those, whom they were formerly wont to regard with the utmost indifference, if not with contempt; merely from a latent principle of generosity existing in the original frame of their nature; a principle which is absolutely necessary towards the proper balancing of our respective rights and pleasures, as well as the regulation of the conduct of either sex to the other.

It will readily be conjectured, that it was the power of this principle over the heart of young Elizabeth, that caused her to accept with such apparent condescension, the proposal of marriage made to her by the laird of Polmood; and this, without doubt, influenced her conduct in part; but it was only to her mind like the rosy streaks of the morning, that vanish before a brighter day. From the second day after the subject was first proposed to her, Polmood was of all things the least in her mind. She thought of nothing but the gayety and splendour of her approaching nuptials, and the deference and respect that would be paid by all ranks to the lovely bride, and of the mighty conquest that she was about to have over all her titled court associates, every one of whom she was told by the queen would have been blithe to have been the wife of Polmood. Elizabeth had been brought up an eye-witness to the splendour of a court, and learned to emulate, with passionate fondness, every personal qualification, and every ornament of dress, which she had there so often seen admired or envied. Her heart was as yet a stranger to the tender passion. If she felt an impatience for any thing, she knew not

what it was, but believed it to be the attainment of finery and
state; having never previously set her heart upon any thing else,
she believed the void which she began to feel in her heart, was in
consequence of such privations. Of course her bridal ornaments—
the brilliant appearance she would make in them—the distinguished
part that she was to act in the approaching festivity—her incontested
right of taking place of all those court ladies, to whom she had so
long stooped, and even of the queen herself—the honour of leading
the dance in the hall and on the green; as well as the procession to
the chapel of St Mary of the Lowes, and the more distant one to
the shrine of St Bothans. These gay phantoms wrought so powerfully upon the mind of the fair Elizabeth, that it eagerly set aside all
intervening obstacles which placed themselves in array before the
wedding, and the track beyond it vanished from her mind's eye,
or only attracted it occasionally by a transient meteor ray, which,
like the rainbow, retired when she approached it, refusing a nearer
inspection.

Polmood became every day more and more enamoured of his
betrothed bride; and indeed, though she was little more than arrived at woman's estate, it was impossible to converse with her without considering her as a model of all that was lovely and desirable
in woman. She played upon the lute, and sung so exquisitely, that
she ravished the hearts of those that heard her; and it is even reported, that she could charm the wild beasts and birds of the forest,
to gather around her at even-tide. Her air and countenance were
full of grace, and her form was the most elegant symmetry. Her
colour outvied the lily and the damask rose—and the amel of her
eye, when she smiled, it was impossible to look stedfastly on.

Instead of any interchange of fond endearments, or any inquiries
about the mode of life they were in future to lead, in all their short
conversations, she only teased Polmood about such and such articles of dress and necessary equipage; and with proposals for plans
of festivity and pleasure of such a nature, as had never before entered our forester's head. He however yielded to every thing with
cheerful complacency, telling her, that as she had been bred at court,
and understood all those matters; and as the king and court were to
be their guests on that occasion, every thing should be provided and
executed according to her directions. He would then kiss her hand
in the most warm and affectionate manner, while she would in return take her leave with a courtsey, and smile so bewitching, that
Polmood's heart was literally melted with feelings of soft delight,
and he congratulated himself as the happiest of men. At one time, in

the height of his ardour, he attempted to kiss her lips, but was astonished at seeing her shrink involuntarily from his embrace, as if he had been a beast of prey; but as she instantly recovered her gayety, this was no more thought of, and every thing went on as usual.

Chapter III

WHEN the news came to the courtiers' ears, that Elizabeth was instantly to be given away by the king, into the arms of Polmood, they were all a little startled. For even those who had never designed to take any particular notice of her, could not bear the thoughts of seeing such a flower cropped by the hand of a country baron, and removed from their circle for ever. Even the lords who had spouses of their own were heard to say, "that they wished her well, and should rejoice at seeing her married, if it turned out conducive to her happiness; but that indeed they should have been glad of her company for a few years longer, for upon the whole, Polmood could not have taken one from them who would be as much missed." These remarks drew the most sharp retorts from their ladies. They wondered what some people saw about some people—there were some people in the world who were good for nothing but making a flash, and there were others so silly as to admire those people—happy at getting quit of so formidable a rival, the news of her approaching marriage were welcome news to them—they tossed up their heads, and said, "it was the luckiest occurrence that could have happened to her, there was no time to lose.—If Polmood had not taken her from the court in that manner, possibly no other would, and she would in all probability soon have left it in some other way—there were some who knew, and some who did not know about those things."

Alexander, duke of Rothsay, was not at that time along with the court, though he arrived shortly after, else it is conjectured that his violent and enterprising spirit would never have suffered the match to go on. Having had abundance of opportunities, he had frequently flattered and teased Elizabeth, and from her condescending, and, as he judged, easy disposition, he entertained no doubts of gaining his dishonourable purpose. Young Carmichael was with the king; and when he was told, that in a few days his dear Elizabeth was to be given in marriage to his kinsman Polmood, together with the lands of Fingland, Glenbreck, and Kingledoors, as her dowry, it is impossible to describe his sensations. He was pierced to the heart, and actually lost for a time all sense of feeling, and power of motion. On recovering a little, he betook himself to the thickest part of the wood, in order to ponder on the best means of preventing this marriage. Elizabeth had before appeared to his eyes a gem of the first water; but when he heard of the sovereign's favour, and of the jointure lands, which lay contiguous to his own, he then saw too late the value of the jewel he was about to lose. He resolved and re-resolved—formed a thousand desperate schemes, and abandoned them again, as soon as suggested, for others more absurd. From this turmoil of passion and contrivance, he hasted to seek Elizabeth; she was constantly surrounded by the queen and the court ladies; and besides, Polmood was never from her side; therefore, though Carmichael watched every moment, he could not once find an opportunity of imparting his sentiments to her in private, until the very day previous to that which was fixed for the marriage ceremony. About noon that day, he observed her steal privately into the linn, to wash her hands and feet in the brook—sure such hands and such feet were never before, nor since that time, bathed in the Crawmel burn!—Thither Carmichael followed her, trembling with perturbation; and, after begging pardon for his rude intrusion, with the tear rolling in his eye, he declared his passion in the most ardent and moving terms, and concluded by assuring her, that without her it was impossible for him to enjoy any more comfort in this world. The volatile and unconscionable Elizabeth, judging this to be matter of fact, and a very hard case, after eying him from head to foot, observed carelessly, that if he got the king's consent, and would marry her tomorrow, she had no objections. Or, if he chose to carry her off privately that night, she hinted, that she was willing to accompany him. "Either of those modes, my dear Elizabeth," said he, "is utterly impossible. The king cannot and will not revoke his agreement with Polmood; and were it possible to carry you away privately to-night, which it is not, to do so in open defiance of my sovereign, would infallibly procure me the distinguished honour of losing my head in a few days; but you have every thing in your power. Cannot you on some pretence or other delay the wedding? and I promise to make you my own wife, and lady of my extensive domains, as soon as circumstances will permit." Elizabeth turned up her blue eyes, and fixed them on the summit of the dark Clokmore, in a kind of uneasy reverie; she did not like that *permission of circumstances*—the term was rather indefinite, and sounded like something at a distance. Upon the whole, the construction of the sentence was a most unfortunate

one for Carmichael. The wedding had taken such absolute possession of Elizabeth's mind, that she thought of nothing else. The ardent manner and manly beauty of Carmichael had for a moment
struggled for a participation in the movements of her heart, which
even in its then fluctuating state, never lost its hold of the favourite
object. But the mentioning of *the wedding* brought all the cherished
train of delightful images with it at once; and, at the mentioning of it
along with that hated word *delay*—a verb which, of our whole vocabulary, is the most repugnant to every sense and feeling of woman.
The wedding could not be delayed!—All was in readiness, and such
an opportunity of attracting notice and admiration might never again
occur; it was a most repulsive idea; the wedding could not be delayed! such were the fancies that glanced on Elizabeth's mind during
the time that she sat with her feet in the stream, and her lovely eyes
fixed on the verge of the mountain. Then turning them softly on
Carmichael, who waited her decision in breathless impatience, she
drew her feet from the brook, and retiring abruptly, said with considerable emphasis, "I wish you had either spoken of this sooner,
or not at all."

Carmichael was left standing by himself in the linn like a statue;
regret preying on his heart, and that heart the abode of distraction
and suspense. The voice of mirth, and the bustle of preparation,
soon extinguished in the mind of Elizabeth, any anxiety which her
late conversation had excited there; but the case was widely different with regard to Carmichael. The lady's visible indifference for
Polmood, in preference to any other man, while it somewhat astonished him, left him assured that her affections were yet unengaged;
and the possession of her maiden heart appeared now to him an
attainment of such inestimable value, that all other earthly things
faded from the comparison. The equivocal answer with which she
had left him, puzzled him most of all; he could gather nothing from
it unfavourable to himself, but to his hopes every thing, as she went
away seemingly determined to follow the path chalked out to her by
her royal guardians. He stalked up the glen, at every two or three
steps repeating these words, "I wish you had mentioned this sooner,
or not at all." He could decide upon nothing, for his ideas were all in
confusion; and the business was of so delicate a nature that he durst
not break it to any of the courtiers; the resolutions which he framed
were of a hasty and desperate nature; but what will not love urge a
man to encounter.

On his return to the castle, he found the word had been given, to
spend the remainder of the day in such sports as in that country they

were able to practise, by way of celebrating the bridal eve. They first had a round of tilting at the ring, from which king James himself came off victorious, owing, as was said, to the goodness of his charger. Polmood's horse was very untractable, and when it came his turn to engage with Carmichael, the latter unhorsed him in a very rough and ungracious manner. Polmood said he was nothing hurt; but when he arose, the ladies being all on-lookers, his cheek was burning with vexation and anger. There were no plaudits of approbation from the ring, as Carmichael expected there would be, for all the company weened that he had acted rather unhandsomely. He, however, won the race fairly, though there were nine lords and knights started for the prize, and held him at very hard play. Mar, in particular, kept so stoutly by his side, that in the end he lost only by one step. When Carmichael received the prize from the fair hand of Elizabeth, he kissed it, pressed it hard, and, with a speaking eye, pointed to a pass among the mountains of the forest, pronouncing at the same time in a low whisper, the words, "to-night." Elizabeth courtseyed smiling, but in so easy and careless a manner, that he doubted much if she comprehended his meaning.

The sports went on. A number were by this time stripped in order to throw the mall. Each candidate was to have three throws. When the rounds were nearly exhausted, his Majesty continued foremost by a foot only; but Carmichael, by his last throw, broke ground a few inches before his mark. It was then proclaimed, that, if there were no more competitors, Carmichael had gained the prize.

Polmood had declined engaging in the race, though strongly urged to it. He had taken some umbrage at the manner in which Carmichael had used him in the tournament. He likewise refused to enter the lists on this occasion; but when he saw the king beat by Carmichael, and that the latter was about to be proclaimed victor a second time, his blood warmed—he laid hold of the mall—retired in haste to the footing-post, and threw it with such violence that he missed his aim. The mall took a direction exactly on a right angle from the line he intended; flew over the heads of one half of the spectators, and plunged into the river, after having soared to an immense height. The incensed forester, having at the same time, by reason of his exertion, fallen headlong on the ground, the laughing and shouting were so loud that the hills rang again, while some called out to measure the altitude, for that the bridegroom had won. He soon recovered the mall; came again to the footing-post; threw off his blue bonnet; and, with a face redder than crimson, flung it a second time with such inconceivable force, that, to the astonishment of all the beholders, it went about one third further than any of the rest had cast it. Polmood was then proclaimed the victor with loud and reiterated shouts. His heart was a prey to every passion in its fiercest extreme. If he was affronted before, he was no less overwhelmed with pleasure when presented with the prize of honour by his adorable Elizabeth.

But here a ridiculous circumstance occurred, which however it is necessary to relate, as it is in some measure connected with the following events.

The gray stone on which queen Margaret and the beautiful Elizabeth sat, during the celebration of those games, is still to be seen at the bottom of the hill, a small distance to the eastward of the old castle of Crawmel. The rest of the ladies, and such of the nobles as did not choose engaging in those violent exercises, are said to have leaned on a bank below; but the situation which the queen and the bride held, fairly overlooked the field where the sports were. For lack of a better seat, on this stone was placed a small pannel or sack filled with straw. Now it so happened, that the prize for the victor in this exercise, was a love knot of scarlet ribbon, and two beautiful plumes, which branched out like the horns of a deer. When Polmood went up to receive the prize from the hands of his betrothed and adored bride, she, in a most becoming manner, took his blue bonnet from his hand, and fixing the knot and the plumes upon it, in a most showy and tasteful mode, placed it upon his head. Polmood, in the most courtly style he was master of, then kissed her hand, bowed to the queen, and placed Elizabeth by her side on the seat of straw. But when he faced about, the appearance which he made struck every one so forcibly, that the whole company, both men and women, burst out into a roar of laughter; and Carmichael, in whose heart a latent grudge was still gaining ground, valuing himself upon his wit, cried out, "It is rather a singular coincidence, Polmood, that you should place Elizabeth upon the straw, and she a pair of horns on your head at the same instant." The laugh was redoubled— Polmood's cheek burnt to the bone. He could not for shame tear off the ornaments which his darling had so lovingly and so recently placed in his bonnet, but he turned them to one side, at which the laugh was renewed. He was any thing but pleased at Carmichael.

Chapter IV

THE next trial of skill was that of shooting at a mark; but in this the competition was of no avail. Polmood struck the circle in the middle of the board each time with so much exactness, that they were all utterly astonished at his dexterity, and unanimously yielded him the prize. It was a silver arrow, which he also received from the hands of Elizabeth. Carmichael, having been successful in his former philippic, took occasion to break some other jests on that occasion, too coarse to be here repeated, although they were not in those days considered as any breach of good manners.

Sixteen then stripped themselves to try their skill in wrestling, and it having been enacted as a law, that he who won in any one contest, was obliged to begin the next, Polmood was of course one of the number. They all engaged at once, by two and two, and eight of them having been consequently overthrown, the other eight next engaged by two and two, and four of these being cast, two couples only remained.

Some of the nobles engaged were so expert at the exercise, and opposed to others so equal in strength and agility, that the contests were exceedingly equal and amusing. Some of them could not be cast until completely out of breath. It had always been observed, however, that Polmood and Carmichael threw their opponents with so much ease, that it appeared doubtful whether these opponents were serious in their exertions, or only making a sham wrestle; but when it turned out that they two stood the last, all were convinced that they were superior to the rest either in strength or skill. This was the last prize on the field, and on the last throw for that prize the victory of the day depended, which each of the two champions was alike vehemently bent to reave from the grasp of the other. They eyed each other with looks askance, and with visible tokens of jealousy; rested for a minute or two, wiped their brows, and then closed. Carmichael was extremely hard to please of his hold, and caused his antagonist to lose his grip three or four times, and change his position. Polmood was however highly complaisant, although it appeared to every one beside, that Carmichael meant to take him at a disadvantage. At length they fell quiet; set their joints steadily, and began to move in a circular direction, watching each other's motions with great care. Carmichael ventured the first trip, and struck Polmood on the left heel with considerable dexterity. It never moved him; but in returning it, he forced in Carmichael's back with such a squeeze, that the by-standers affirmed they heard his ribs crash;

whipped him lightly up in his arms, and threw him upon the ground with great violence, but seemingly with as much ease as if he had been a boy. The ladies screamed, and even the rest of the nobles doubted if the knight would rise again. He however jumped lightly up, and pretended to smile; but the words he uttered were scarcely articulate; his feelings at that moment may be better conceived than expressed. A squire who waited the king's commands then proclaimed Norman Hunter of Polmood the victor of the day, and consequently entitled, in all sporting parties, to take his place next to the king, until by other competitors deprived of that prerogative. This distinction pleased Elizabeth more than any thing she had yet seen or heard about her intended husband, and she began to regard him as a superior character, and one whom others were likely to value. The ruling passions of her heart seem to have been hitherto levelled only at the attainment of admiration and distinction, an early foible of the sex, but though a foible, one that leads oftener to good than evil. For when a young female is placed in a circle of acquaintances who know how to estimate the qualities of the heart, the graces of a modest deportment and endearing address, how then does this ardent and amiable desire of rendering herself agreeable stimulate to exertions in the way of goodness! But, on the contrary, when she is reared in a circle, where splendour is regarded as the badge of superiority, and title as the compendium of distinction, it is then, as in the case of the beauteous Elizabeth, that this inherent principle "leads to bewilder, and dazzles to blind." The flowers of the forest and garden are not more indicative of the different soils that produce them, than the mind of a young woman is of the company she keeps. It takes its impressions as easily and as true as the wax does from the seal, if these impressions are made while it is heated by the fire of youth; but when that fire cools, the impressions remain, and good or bad remain indelible for ever. With how much caution these impressions ought at first to be made, let parents then consider, when on them depends, not only the happiness or misery of the individual in this life, but in that which is to come; and when thousands of the same stock may be affected by them from generation to generation.

When Polmood went up and received the final prize from the hand of Elizabeth, she delivered it with a smile so gracious and so bewitching, that his heart was almost quite overcome with delight; some even affirmed that they saw the tears of joy trickling from his eyes. Indeed his love was, from the beginning, rather like a frenzy of the mind than a passion founded on esteem, and the queen always remarked, that he loved too well to enjoy true conjugal felicity.

When Carmichael perceived this flood of tenderness and endearment, his bosom was ready to burst, and he tried once more to turn the laugh against Polmood by cutting jests. The prize was a belt with seven silver buckles; and when he received it from Elizabeth, Carmichael cried out, that it was of sufficient length to go about them both; and that Polmood could not do better than make the experiment; and when he once had her buckled fairly in, he would be wise to keep the hold he had, else they would not be one flesh. It would keep her constantly in his view, he said, and it would likewise be a good mark when either of them began to increase in magnitude. There was no one laughed at the jest but himself.

The sports of the evening were closed with a dance on the green, in which the king and queen, and all the nobles joined. The king's old harper was then placed on the gray stone and the sack of straw, and acquitted himself that evening so well, that his strains inspired a hilarity quite unusual. It being so long since such a scene was seen in Scotland, scarcely will it now be believed, that a king and queen, with the lords and ladies of a court, ever danced on the green in the wild remote forest of Meggat-dale; yet the fact is well ascertained, if tradition can be in aught believed. Nay, the sprightly tunes which the king so repeatedly called for that night, *O'er the boggy*, and *Cutty's wedding*, remain, on that account, favourites to this day in that country. Crawmel was then the most favourite hunting retreat of the Scottish court, on account of the excellent sport that its neighbourhood, both in hunting and angling, afforded; and it continued to be the annual retreat of royalty, until the days of the beauteous and unfortunate queen Mary, who was the last sovereign that visited the forest of Meggat, so long famed for the numbers and fleetness of its deer.

James and Elizabeth led the ring and the double octave that evening; and so well did she acquit herself, that all who beheld her were delighted. Polmood made but an indifferent figure in the dance. The field on which he appeared to advantage was overpast, that of Elizabeth's excellence was only commencing. She was dressed in a plain white rail; her pale ringlets were curled and arranged with great care, yet so, that all appeared perfectly natural. Her movements were so graceful, and so easy, that they appeared rather like the motions of a fairy or some celestial being, than those of a mortal composed of flesh and blood. The eyes of the nobles had certainly been dazzled while they looked at her, for they affirmed that they could not convince themselves that the grass bent beneath her toe. The next to her among the court ladies, both in beauty and accomplishments, was one Lady Ann Gray, a great favourite with the king, and of whom it was supposed the queen had good reason to have been jealous; but she being a lady of an easy and unassuming character, never showed any symptoms of suspicion. During the dance, however, it was apparent that the king's eyes were oftener fixed upon her than either his partner or his queen. They continued their frolics on the green till after the setting of the sun, and then, retiring into the pavilion before the castle, they seated themselves promiscuously in a circle, and drank large bumpers to the health of Polmood and Elizabeth, and to other appropriate toasts given by the king—the ladies sung—the lords commended them—and all became one flow of music, mirth, and social glee.

Carmichael alone appeared at times absent and thoughtful, which by the king, and all the rest, was attributed to the defeats he received in the sports of the day; but his intents towards his kinsman Polmood were evil and dangerous, and there was nothing he desired more than an occasion to challenge him, but no such occasion offering, as the mirth and noise still continued to increase, he slipped away to his chamber in the castle without being missed. He lay down on his bed, dressed as he was, and gave himself up to the most poignant and tormenting reflections. The manner in which he had been baffled by Polmood in the sports, hung about his heart, gnawing it in the most tender part, and much he feared that circumstance had lessened him in the eyes of the young Elizabeth, and exalted his more fortunate rival. Polmood had not only baffled and dishonoured him in presence of all the court, but was moreover on the very eve of depriving him of one he believed more dear to him than life—it was too much to be patiently borne. In short, love, envy, revenge, and every passion of the soul were up in arms, exciting him to counteract and baffle his rival, with regard to the possession of Elizabeth. The night was short, it was the last on which she was free, or could with any degree of honour be taken possession of; that opportunity once lost, and she was lost to him for ever. The result of all those reflections was, a resolution to risk every thing, and rather to die than suffer himself to be deprived of her without an effort.

Chapter V

THE castle of Crawmel, besides being on a considerably large scale, was fitted up in such a manner as to accommodate a great number of lodgers. In the uppermost story above were twelve little chambers, all distinct from one another; and in each of these a bed laid with rushes, and above these, by way of matress, a bag filled with a kind of light feathery bent, which they gathered on the hills in abundance, and which made a bed as soft as one of down. When the queen and her attendants visited the hunting quarters, that floor was given wholly up by the gentlemen, who then slept in the pavilion; and each lady had a little chamber to herself, but no curtains to their beds, nor any covering, save one pair of sheets and a rug. The rushes were placed on the floor between a neat seat and the wall, and this was all the furniture that each of these little chambers contained, the beds being only intended for the accommodation of single individuals. The king's chamber was on the second floor. In it there was a good bed, well fitted up, and on the same flat were five other little chambers, in one of which lay Carmichael, with his bosom in a ferment.

Shortly after his retreat from the pavilion, the queen and ladies, judging, from the noise which the wine had excited, that it was proper for them to retire, bade the jolly party good-night. The king, the lord chamberlain, and a few others, having conveyed them to the bottom of the stair-case, they compelled them to return to the rest of the company in the tent, which they knew they would gladly comply with, and proceeded in a body to their attic story.

In the meantime, Carmichael, hearing their voices approach, began to quake with anxiety; and placing his door a little open, he stood by it in such a way that he could both see and hear them without being seen. When they arrived at the door of the king's apartment, which was hard by his own, they halted for a considerable time, giggling and speaking very freely of the gentlemen they had just left; and at the last, when they offered to take leave of the queen for the night, she said, that as his majesty seemed inclined to enjoy himself for some time with his lords, she would leave him his apartment by himself, that he might not be restrained in his mirth, nor have the opportunity of disturbing her. Some of the others rallied her, saying, if they had such a privilege, they would know better what use to make of it. She however went up with the rest to one of the little chambers in the upper story.

Though Carmichael had taken pains previously to ascertain in which of the chambers Elizabeth slept, he nevertheless followed quietly after them, and, from a dark corner, saw her enter it. That was the decisive moment—he had no resource left but to attempt an interview: the adventure was attended with imminent danger, both of shame and disgrace; but he hoped that the ardour of his passion would plead some excuse for his intrusion in the eyes of Elizabeth.

Judging it necessary that he should surprise her before she undressed, though not one of the other ladies was yet gone to sleep, he lifted the latch softly, and entered behind her; for there was not one of the chambers, save the king's, that bolted on the inside. Elizabeth bore no similitude to a number of our ladies, who are so squeamish as to fall into fits when any thing surprises or affects them. On the contrary, she was possessed of an uncommon calmness and equanimity of temper, which sometimes savoured not a little of insensibility; and instead of being startled, and screaming out, when she saw a knight enter her chamber at that time of night, she being busied in putting up her ringlets, did not so much as discontinue her employment, but only reprimanded him in a calm whisper for his temerity, and desired him to withdraw instantly, without any farther noise. But, falling on his knees, he seized both her hands, and, in the most passionate manner, beseeched her by all the endearments of love, and by the estimation in which she held the life of one who adored her, and who was willing to sacrifice his life for her, instantly to elope with him, and become his through life, for good or for evil. "This is the last, and the most favourable moment," said he; "the ladies are gone to their chambers; the king and nobles are drinking themselves drunk; I know all the passes of the forest; we shall easily elude them to-night; if indeed we are once missed, which I do not conceive we will. To-morrow perhaps we may be able to reach a place of safety." Elizabeth was about to reply, but he interrupted her. "Consider, my dearest Elizabeth," continued he, "before you answer me finally; consider that Polmood is nowise worthy of you; his years will outnumber yours three times," added he; "his manners are blunt and uncourtly; and it is well known that his estates, honours, and titles, cannot once be compared with mine."

These were weighty considerations indeed. Elizabeth hesitated, and looked him stedfastly in the face, while a ray of joyful anticipation seemed to play on her lovely countenance. "It will make a great noise," said she; "the ladies will be terribly astonished." "Yes, my dear Elizabeth, they will be all astonished indeed; and some, without doubt, will be highly displeased. But if we can escape to the court of England, or France, until the first fury of the blast is overblown, your kind god-mother the queen will be happy to receive you again into her arms and household, as lady Hyndford."—That title sounded charmingly in Elizabeth's ears—she smiled—Carmichael, observing it, pursued the theme. "Consider," continued he, "which of the two titles is most likely to command respect at court–the plain, common, vulgar designation, Dame Elizabeth Hunter of Polmood; or, lady Carmichael of Hyndford?–The right honourable Countess of Hyndford?" It was all over with Polmood–Elizabeth uttered a sigh of impatience–repeated the title three or four times to herself, and forthwith asked what course he proposed for their procedure. "Come directly with me to my chamber," said he; "I will furnish you with a suit of my clothes–I have a couple of good horses and a trusty squire in readiness–we shall pass the steps of Glendarg before the rising of the sun, and disappoint Polmood, the king, and all his court, of a wedding for once."–"Wedding!–Disappoint the king and all his court of a wedding for once!"–unfortunate and rash expression!–It had no business there. The term *wedding* was itself enough, and too much. It glanced on Elizabeth's mind like electricity, and came not alone, but with all its concatenation of delights. "We shall have no wedding then?" said she,–"Perhaps we may contrive to have one by and by," said Carmichael. Elizabeth sighed deeply, and rested her rosy cheek upon her left shoulder, while the pressure of her chin dimpled the polish of her fair breast.

Whether she was at that time balancing the merits of each side of the alternative which she had in her offer has never yet been thoroughly ascertained; for at that instant they were alarmed by hearing the king tapping at some of the adjoining chamber doors, and asking who slept in each of them; and besides, adding inquiries, in which of them he would find Elizabeth. The door of the apartment in which they stood not being quite close, they were greatly alarmed, as they knew not what was the matter, but, as they had good reason, dreaded the worst–The light and the footsteps were fast approaching; there was not a moment to lose; and if Elizabeth had not been more alert than her lover, they would certainly have been caught in that questionable condition. But the mind of woman is ever fruitful in expedients. It is wonderful to behold with what readiness they will often avert the most sudden and fatal surprises, even before the other sex have leisure to think of their danger. With regard to all love affairs, in particular, if a woman does not fall upon some shift to elude discovery, the exigencies are desperate indeed. This inventive faculty of the fair sex, which is so manifest on all sudden emergencies, is most kindly bestowed by the Creator of the universe and of man. The more we contemplate any of his works, whether these works are displayed in the productions of nature, or the formation of the human soul, the more will we be satisfied of his kind intentions towards all his creatures, of his regards for their happiness, and the provisions he has made for their various natures and habits. The most pure and delicate vesture under heaven, nay the virgin snow itself, is not more easily sullied than female reputation; and when once it is sullied, where is the fountain that will ever wash out the stain? In proportion with the liability of censure to which they are exposed, and the dangerous effects of that censure on their future respectability and moral conduct, is bestowed that superior readiness and activity in managing all the little movements and contingents of life. If it were not for this inventive faculty, many thousands of female characters would be ruined in the eyes of the world, that are fair and unblameable, and which this alone enables the lovely wanderer among snares and toils, to preserve without blemish, till the dangerous era of youth and inexperience is overpast.

There being, as was observed, not a moment to lose, so neither was there a moment lost, from the time that Elizabeth was fully apprized of the danger to which they were both exposed. She flung off her rail, uncovered her bosom, and extinguished the light in her chamber, all ere Carmichael could once move from the spot. Determined to make one effort for the preservation of her honour, and the life of a lover who, at all events, had treated her with respect, she placed herself close behind the door, awaiting the event with firmness and resolution. But here we must leave them for a few minutes, till we explain the cause of this indecorous invasion.

Chapter VI

THE party that conveyed the queen and her ladies from the pavilion to the castle, on the way to their chambers, having returned to the rest, they all, at the king's request, joined in drinking a bumper to the bride's health. Polmood, in return, proposed one to the queen, which was likewise drunk off; the health of all the ladies was next drunk, and afterwards several of them by name, and amongst others the beautiful Madam Gray. By that time the most steady amongst them all were affected by the fumes of the wine, and some of them were become considerably drunk. The battles of the bygone day, in their various sports, were all fought over again, and every man was stouter and swifter in his own estimation than his compeers. Many bets were offered, and as readily accepted, without ever being more thought of; even the lord Chamberlain Hume, who was by no means a strong man, proffered to wrestle with Polmood for 1000 merks.

The latter paid little attention to all these rhodomontades, having entered into a close and humorous argument with his Majesty, who was rallying him most unmercifully about his young wife; and who at length, turning to him with a serious countenance, "Polmood," said he, "you have forgot one particularly important and necessary ceremony, and one which, as far as I know, has never been dispensed with in this realm. It is that of asking the bride, at parting with her on the bridal eve, if she had not rued. Many a bridegroom has been obliged to travel far for that very purpose, and why should you neglect it when living under the same roof?" Polmood acknowledged the justice of the accusation; and likewise the fact that such a custom was prevalent; but excused himself on the grounds, that if she had relented, she had plenty of opportunities to have told him so. His Majesty however persisted in maintaining, that it was an omission of a most serious nature, and one that gave her full liberty to deny him to-morrow even before the priest, which would prove an awkward business; and that therefore he ought, in conformity to the good old custom, to go and ask the question even though the lady was in bed. Polmood objected to this on account that it was a manifest breach of decorum; but that only excited farther raillery against him; for they all cried out, "he dares not, he dares not." Polmood was nettled, and at that instant offered to go, if his Majesty would accompany him as a witness.

Whether or not the king had any sinister motives for this procedure cannot easily be ascertained; but certain it is, that he went cheerfully along with Polmood on the expedition, carrying a lighted torch in his hand, and leading the way. Every chamber door that he came to, he tapped, asking at the same time, who slept there, until he came to that behind which Elizabeth stood with her lover at her back; and observing it not to be quite shut, instead of tapping, he peeped in, holding the torch before him. Elizabeth at that moment put her face and naked bosom by the edge of the door full in his view, and instantly pushed the door in his face, exclaiming, "What does your Majesty mean? I am undressed, you cannot come in now." And having by this manœuvre, as she particularly intended, put out the light, she waited the issue; but instead of being agitated with terror, as most women would have been in the same situation, she could scarcely refrain from indulging in laughter; for the king, instead of returning her any answer, fell a puffing and blowing at the wick of the flambeau, thinking to make it rekindle; but, not being able to succeed, he fell a groping for his companion. "Confound her, Polmood," said he, "she has extinguished our light; what shall we do now?" "We had better ask the question in the dark, if it please your Majesty," said Polmood. "No," said the king, "come along with me, we will try to get it relumined;" then, groping his way along, with Polmood at his back, he tapped at every chamber door he came at around the circle, asking each of the ladies, if she had any light. Several denied, but at length he came to one, below which, on stooping, he espied a little glimmering light, and having by this time learned what lady was in each chamber, he called at that too, but was not a little startled at hearing the voice of her within—It was the queen— but, affecting not to know, he lifted the latch, and pretending great modesty, did not so much as look in, but only held in the torch with the one hand, begging of her to relight it, which she did, and returned it to his hand.

Carmichael, having by these means escaped quietly, and with perfect deliberation, to his own chamber, Elizabeth laid herself down, not a little pleased at the success of her expedient, but somewhat astonished what could have occasioned this extraordinary scrutiny. The two champions returned to Elizabeth's door—the king tapped gently, and asked if she was in undress still. She begged a thousand pardons of his royal Majesty for the trouble which she had caused him, which happened solely from the circumstance of his having surprised her in deshabille, that he might now enter, and let her know what his royal pleasure was with her. James entered cautiously, but took care to keep his flambeau behind him in case of further accidents, and then began by asking pardon in his turn of Elizabeth for his former abrupt entrance; but seeing that her door was not altogether shut, he said, he judged the chamber to be unoccupied— that he had come at her lover's request, in order to be a witness to a question he had to propose to her. He then desired Polmood to proceed, who, stepping forward much abashed, told her bluntly, that all he had to ask was, whether or not she had repented of the promise she had made him of marriage? Elizabeth, not having been previously instructed of any such existing ceremony in Scotland, did not readily comprehend the meaning or drift of this question; or else, thinking it proper to avail herself of it, in order to provide for certain subsequent arrangements which had very lately been proposed to her, answered with perfect good humour, that she understood Polmood had himself relented, and wished to throw the blame upon her. "I therefore tell you, sir," said she, "that I *have* rued our agreement, and that most heartily."—"Bravo!" cried the king, as loud as he could shout, pushing Polmood out at the door before him. He then closed it, and without waiting a moment, ran down the stair laughing, and shouting aloud "hurra! hurra! The bride has rued! the bride has rued! Polmood is undone." He hasted to the pavilion, and communicated the jest to his nobles, who all laughed abundantly at Polmood's expense.

The staircase of the Crawmel castle was in one of the turrets, and from that there were doors which opened to each of the floors. The upper story which contained the twelve chambers in which the queen and ladies were that night lodged, was fitted up so, that it formed a circle. All the chamber doors were at equal distances, and the door which led to the staircase was exactly in the circle with the rest, and in every respect the same. Now Polmood, not being at all satisfied with the answer he had received from Elizabeth, and unwilling to return to the company without some farther explanation, turned round as the king departed, dark as it was, and putting his mouth to the latch hole of the door, began to expostulate on the subject. Elizabeth, perceiving that he was somewhat intoxicated, desired him to withdraw; for that it was highly improper for him to remain there in the dark alone, and added, that she would tell him all about it to-morrow.

Now Polmood was not only half drunk, but he was, beside, greatly stunned with the answer he had received; and moreover, to add to his misfortune, the king had, either in the midst of his frolic, shut the door behind him, or else it had closed of itself. The consequence of all this was, that when Polmood turned about to depart, he soon discovered that it was like to be a very intricate business. By means of going round the circle, with one hand pressed against the wall, he found that the doors were all shut, and that there was no possibility of distinguishing one of them from another. He could easily have opened any of them, because none of them were bolted; but in doing so, he had no assurance that he would not light upon the queen, or some sleeping countess, which might procure him much disgrace and ridicule. He was a modest bashful gentleman, fearful of giving offence, and would not have been guilty of such a piece of rudeness for the world; he knew not what to do; to call was in vain, for the apartment was vaulted below, therefore he could alarm none save the ladies. He had but one chance to find the right door for twelve to go wrong; the odds were too great for him to venture. He would gladly have encroached again upon Elizabeth, but he knew no more of her door than the others.

There is every reason to believe that the fumes of the wine tended greatly to increase Polmood's dilemma; for it is well known how much that impairs the reasoning faculties of some men, and what singular fancies it creates in their minds. Be that as it may, Polmood could think only of one expedient whereby to extricate himself from his whimsical situation, and the idea had no sooner struck him than he proceeded to put it in practice. It was to listen at each door, if there was any person breathing within; and if there was no person breathing within, he thought he might conclude that to be the door he wanted. In order to effect this with more certainty, he kneeled softly on the floor, and laid his ear close to the bottom of each door, creeping always to the next, as soon as he had certified that a lady was within. It was a long time ere he could be satisfied of some, they breathed so softly—he kept an account in his memory of the doors he past, and had nearly got round them all, when he heard, as he thought, a door softly and cautiously opened. No light appearing, Polmood judged that he was overheard; and that this was one of the ladies listening what he was about. He was on the point of speaking to her, and begging for pardon and assistance, when he heard the sound of footsteps approaching behind him. He was resting on his hands and knees at a chamber door, with his head hanging down in the act of listening—he kept his position, pricking up his ears, and scarcely able to hear for the palpitations of his heart; but it was not long ere a man stumbled on his feet, fell above him, and crushed his face against the floor. Polmood swore a loud oath, and being irritated, he laid furiously hold of the stranger's heel, and endeavoured to detain him, but he wrenched it from his grasp, and in a moment was gone. Polmood then judging that it must have been some one of the courtiers stealing to his mistress, and hearing the door close behind him, hasted to his feet, and followed to the sound, hoping to escape after him—opened the same door, as he thought, and rushed forward, but at the third step he foundered over something that interposed his progress; and, to his utter confusion, found that he had alighted with all his weight across a lady in her bed, who was screaming out murder fire and ravishment, in a voice so loud, and so eldrich, that Polmood's ears were deafened, and his joints rendered utterly powerless through vexation and dismay. He tried to get up and escape, but the injured fair laid hold of his coat, pulled it over his head, and as he scorned to hurt her, or resist her frantic violence by violence in return, in that manner she held him fast, continuing all the while her violent outcries. The rest of the ladies awaking, set up one universal yell of murder—sprang from their beds, and endeavoured to escape, some one way and some another, running against each other, and screaming still the louder.—Their cries alarmed the guards, and these the courtiers, who all rushing in promiscuously with lights, beheld one of the most ludicrous scenes that ever was witnessed by man.—A whole circular apartment full of distressed dames, skipping into their holes, as the light appeared, like so many rabbits; and in one apartment, the door of which was shut, but to which they were directed by the cries, the right honourable Lady Hume, holding the worthy bridegroom, the bold, the invincible Norman of Polmood! with his coat drawn over his head, in her own bed-chamber, and abusing him all the while, as a depraved libertine and a ravisher. Polmood was rendered quite speechless, or at least all that he attempted to advance by way of palliation was never once heard, so loud was the mixed noise of laughter, ridicule, and abuse; and the king, with a grave face, observed, that unless he could give security for his future good behaviour, he would be obliged to confine him in the keep until such time as he could be got married, that then perhaps the virtue of other men's wives might be preserved from his outrageous violence.

Chapter VII

THE transactions of that night were not brought to a conclusion, by the unlucky adventure which befel the Laird of Polmood. On the contrary, that was only a prologue to farther mistakes, of greater atrocity, and of consequences more serious.

The king did not again return to the pavilion, but retired to his chamber as they came down stairs. The Earl of Hume, having got extremely drunk, and fallen into an argument with another knight, who was much in the same condition, about some affair of Border chivalry, of which their ideas totally differed, they were both become so warm and so intent upon the subject, that they never once perceived when the late alarm was given, nor when the company left them, in order to succour the distressed ladies. But when they returned with Polmood guarded as a prisoner in jest, and related the circumstances, the earl got into a furious passion, and, right or wrong, insisted on running Polmood through the body. "What, Sir?" said he: "because you cannot get a wife of your own, does that give you a right to go and take violent possession of mine? No, sir! draw out your sword, and I'll give you to know the contrary; I'll carve you, sir, into a great number of pieces, sir."

When the earl was in the height of this passion, and had stripped off a part of his clothes to fight a duel with Polmood by torch light, one of the lords whispered in his ear, that Polmood only *mistook the bed*, that was all; and that lady Hume had acquitted herself in such a manner, by taking him prisoner, that it reflected immortal honour upon her and all her connexions.

This pleased the lord chamberlain so well, that he was never weary of shaking hands with Polmood, and drinking to him; but he did not forget to observe each time, that he thought Polmood would take care in future how he mistook lady Hume for another. The earl grew every minute more and more pleased on account of his lady's resolute and intrepid behaviour, and being a sprightly ingenious gentleman, began singing a song, which he swore was extempore, and which was indeed believed to be so by all present, as none of them had ever heard it before. It is said to be still extant, and to be yet sung in several parts of Scotland, which certainly is not very probable. It began "I hae ane wyffe o' mi ain." In short his enthusiasm and admiration of his lady arose to such a height, that he took up a resolution to go and spend the remainder of the night in her company. A number of his merry associates encouraged this proposal with all the plausible arguments they could suggest, reminding him that the chamber was in sooth his own—that he had only given it up in favour of her ladyship for a few nights, and she could in nowise grudge him a share of it for one night, especially as there was no rest to be had in the tent. Thus encouraged, the earl arose and went towards the castle, singing, with great glee,

> I hae ane wyffe o' mi ain;
> I'll be behadden til nae bodye;
> I'll nowther borey nor lenne,
> Swap nor niffer wi' nae bodye.

The porter and guards at the gate objected strongly to his admission, and began to remonstrate with his lordship on its impropriety: but he drew his sword, and swore he would sacrifice them, every mother's son, if they offered to debar his entrance to his own wife. It was in vain that they reminded him there was no room in her ladyship's apartment for any person beside herself, which they said he himself well knew. He d—d them for liars, and officious knaves, who meddled with matters about which they had no business: said it was his concern to find room, and theirs to obey his orders, or abide the consequences; at the same time, he spit upon his hand and squared, in order forthwith to begin the slaughter of the porters: and as they were afraid of resisting the determined resolution of the lord chamberlain, they suffered him to pass, after leaving his sword behind him, and promising on his honour to make no noise.

The earl, by dint of determined perseverance, found his way, amid utter darkness, to the upper story of the castle, where his beloved lady and her fair associates were all enjoying sweet repose after the sports and merriment of the late day.–He entered with great caution–counted the doors to the right hand with accurate exactness, in order to ascertain his lady's chamber–opened the door softly, and advanced stooping, in search of her lowly but desirable couch–but when he proceeded to clasp her in his arms in a transport of love and admiration–"O horrible! most horrible!" he found that she was already lying fast locked in the arms of a knight, whose cheek was resting upon hers, and his long shaggy beard flowing around her soft neck. It is impossible to conceive the fury into which this discovery threw the enamoured earl. He entertained not the slightest doubt but that it was Polmood; and resolving to make an example of him, he laid hold of him by the beard with one hand, and by the throat with the other, determined to strangle him on the spot. But the desperate inamorato sprung upon his assailant like a tiger from his den–struck the lord chamberlain violently on the head–overturned him on the floor, and forthwith escaped. The earl followed as fast as he was able to the door–gave the alarm with a loud voice, and hastily returned to secure the other accomplice in wickedness and shame. He flung himself upon the bed–laid violent hands upon her–swearing that she too should not escape, and that he would inflict upon her the most condign punishment. The lady bore all with silence and meekness, until she heard the rest of the courtiers approaching, and then she took hold of him by the hair of the head with both hands, held him down thereby, and screamed as loud as she was able.

The waggish lords, who had excited the earl to this expedition, certain that in the state he then was, he was sure to breed some outrage in the castle, were all in waiting without the gate, ready to rush in on the least alarm being given. Consequently, it was not long before they entered with lights, and among the rest the king in his night-gown and slippers. They entered the chamber from which the cries proceeded; and, to their no small astonishment, discovered the lord chamberlain engaged in close combat–not with his own lady, as he had unwarrantably supposed–but with the beauteous lady Ann Gray, who was weeping bitterly, and crying out to revenge her on that wicked and barbarous lord.

The merriment of the party at this discovery would have been without bounds, had not the king appeared to be seriously displeased. He ordered lord Hume to be carried down stairs instantly, and confined in the keep until he should answer for his conduct. The earl attempted to remonstrate, assuring his majesty that he had only *mistaken the bed*; but his ebriety being apparent, that had no effect upon the king, who declared he could not suffer such liberties to be taken with any lady under their royal protection with impunity, and that perhaps the lord chamberlain might have yet to atone for his rudeness and temerity by the loss of his head.

The courtiers were all astonished at this threatening, and at the king's peremptory manner and resentment, as no one could for a moment suppose that the earl had indeed any designs upon the person of lady Ann Gray; and when at length he protested, in mitigation of the crime alleged against him, that he actually caught another man in the chamber with her, the king was still more wroth, asserting that to be impossible, guarded as the castle then was, unless it were himself who was there, which he hoped lord Hume did not mean to insinuate in the presence, or at least in the hearing, of his royal consort—that, as far as he knew, there was not another knight within the walls of the castle, and that such a malicious attempt to asperse the young lady's honour was even worse than the other crime. "Let the castle be instantly searched," cried he, "and if there is no other person found in it, save the ladies, and those now admitted, I shall order the head to be taken from this uncourtly and slanderous earl early in the morning. Was it not enough that he should attempt the violation of a royal ward, of the highest birth and respect, but that, when frustrated, he should endeavour to affix an indelible stain upon her honour, and in the accusation implicate his sovereign, to the lessening of his respectability in the eyes of his queen and his whole nation? Let the castle be searched strictly and instantly."

The earl was confined in the keep—the castle-gate was double guarded—the castle was searched for men throughout, and at last Carmichael was found concealed in his own chamber, and half dressed. No doubt then remained with the courtiers that he was the guilty person with regard to Madam Gray.

The king appeared visibly astonished when Carmichael was discovered, but affecting to be of the same opinion as the rest, he accompanied them down stairs—locked Carmichael in the keep beside the Lord Chamberlain—dismissed the rest to the pavilion, charging them on pain of death not to attempt entering the gate of the castle again, till once they received his orders; and having caused it to be locked, he retired to his apartment.

The displeasure of the king acted like electricity on the minds of the hitherto jovial party. Their organs of sensation were benumbed at once, and their risibility completely quashed. They durst not even speak their minds freely to one another on the subject, afraid of having their remarks overhauled at next day's examination; but they all judged Carmichael to be in a bad predicament, considering how great a favourite lady Ann was with the king. It was then first discovered, that Carmichael had been absent from the pavilion, from the time that the ladies retired, and how long previously to that could not be recollected; consequently, they were all satisfied that they were two lovers, and that the meeting had been preconcerted, although their passion had hitherto been concealed from the eyes of all the court. The whole matter appeared now to them perfectly obvious; whereas there was not a single incident, save one, on which they put a right construction.

A short and profound sleep ushered that group of noble sportsmen into the healthful morning breeze of the mountain, and the beams of the advancing sun, and finished the adventures of that memorable night, but not their consequences. The examination which follows in the next chapter, will assist somewhat in the explication of the one, and the subsequent narrative of the other.

Chapter IX

THE animal spirits have certainly a natural medium level, at which, if suffered to remain, they will continue to flow with a constant and easy motion. But if the spring be drained to the sediment for the supply of a lengthened and frenzied hilarity, it must necessarily remain some time low before it can again collect force sufficient to exert its former energy.

Fair and lovely rose that morning on the forest of Meggat-dale—it was the third of September—the day destined by the king and queen for the marriage of their beloved Elizabeth. The dawning first spread a wavy canopy of scarlet and blue over all the eastern hemisphere; but when the sun mounted from behind the green hills of Yarrow, the fairy curtain was updrawn into the viewless air. The shadows of the mountains were then so beauteously etched, and their natural tints so strongly marked, that it seemed as if the mountains themselves lay cradled in the bosom of the lovely lake—but while the eye yet rested on the adumbrated phenomenon, the spectre hills, with all their inverted woods and rocks, melted away in their dazzling mirror.

It was a scene that might have stirred the most insensate heart to raptures of joy; yet the queen of Scotland and her ladies were demure and sullen, even though their morning walk was over a garnish of small but delicate mountain flowers, belled with the dews of heaven—though fragrance was in every step, and health in every gale that strayed over the purple heath.

The king and his nobles were even more sullen than they—the king took his morning walk by himself—his nobles sauntered about in pairs, but they discoursed only to their hounds, whose gambols and mimic hunts were checked by the unwonted gloom on the brows of their masters. The two aggressors were still lying in the dismal keep, both in the highest chagrin; the one at his disappointment in love, the other at his disgrace. Such are the motley effects of intemperance, and such the importance by the inebriated fancy attached to trifles, which, in moments of calm reflection, would never have been regarded.

The king returning, threw himself into his easy chair; the queen paid her respects to him, and interceded for the imprisoned lords—he ordered them to be brought before him, and summoned all the rest of the nobles to attend. When the news of the examination spread, the ladies came running together, some of them dressed, and some only half-dressed, to hear it. A trial of a delinquent who has come under any suspicions with respect to their sex is to them a most transcendent treat. But the king rising, beseeched them kindly to withdraw, because, in the course of elucidating the matter, some things might be expressed offensive to their modesty. They assured his majesty that there was no danger of such a circumstance occurring; but he persisted in his request, and they were obliged reluctantly to retire.

The king first called on Polmood to give an account of all that befel him in the vault of the twelve chambers; and how he came to make the unmannerly attack on the lady Hume, all which he was required to answer on oath. The speeches which follow are copied literally from the hand-writing of *Archembald Qhitelaw airtshdeiken of Lowden and cekreter to kinge Jemys.* The MSS. are now in the possession of Mr J. Brown, Edin. and fully confirm the authenticity of the story, if any doubts remained of the tradition. The first, as being the most original, is given at full length; it is entitled *Ane speetsh and defenns maide by Normaund Huntyr of Poomoode on ane nyte of royet and lemanrye with Elenir Ladye of Hume.*

"Mucht it pleiz mai sovrayne lege, not to trowe sikkan euil and kittel dooins of yer ain trew cervente, and maist lethfu legeman; nor to lychtlefye myne honer sa that I can ill bruke; by eyndling, that, withoutten dreddour I shulde gaung til broozle ane fayir deme, ane honest mannis wyffe, and mynnie to twa bairnis; and that in the myddis of ane loftful queenes. I boud haife bein dementyde to kicke ane stoure, to the skaithinge of hir preclair pounyis, and hairshillynge myne ayin kewis. Nethynge mai lege was ferder fra myne heid thanne onye sikkan wylld sneckdrawinge and pawkerye. But quhan yer Maigestye jinkyt fra me in the baux, and left me in the darknesse, I was baiss to kum again wi' sikkan ane ancere; and stude summe tyme swutheryng what it avysat me neiste to doo in thilke barbulye. At the launge, I stevellit backe, and lowten downe, set mai nebb to ane gell in the dor, and fleechyt Eleesabett noore to let us torfell in the waretyme of owir raik. But scho skyrit to knuife lownly or siccarlye on thilke sauchning, and heiryne that scho was wilsum and glunchye, I airghit at keuillyng withe hirr in that thraward paughty moode, and baidna langer to haigel. But ben doitrifyed with thilke drynke and sachless and dizzye with lowtyn, and thilke lofte as derke as pick, I tint ilka spunk of ettlyng quhair the dor laye. And thaun I staupyt and gavit about quhille I grewe perfitlye donnarit, and trowit the castil to be snuiffyng and birlyng round; foreby that it was heezing upon the tae syde, and myntyng to whommil me. I had seendil watherit a selwyn raddour, but boddin that I wad coup, that I muchtna gie a dooffe, I hurklit litherlye down, and craup forret alang on myne looffis and myne schynes, herkyng at ilka dorlief gyffe ther was onye ane snifteryng withyn side. Outhir I owirharde, or thocht I owirharde sliepyng soughs ahynte thilk haile, and begoude to kiep sklenderye houpes of wynning out of myne revellet fank unsperkyt with scheme or desgrece. Ben richt laith to rin rashlye, with ane posse, on the kyttes or the chaftis of thilke deir eichil kimmers, that war lying doveryng and snuffyng, and spelderyng, rekelesse and mistrowyns of all harmis, I was eidentlye hotteryng alang with muckle paishens. I was lyinge endslang at ane dor, quhan I harde ane chylde unhaspe thilke sneck, as moothlye as ane snail quhan scho gaungs snowking owir thilk droukyt swaird; but thilk dor gyit ay thilk tother whesk, and thilk tother jerg, and oore I gatt tyme til syne mysel, ane grit man trippyt on myne feit, and fell belly flaught on me with ane dreadful noozle, quhille myne curpin was jermummlyt, and myne grunzie knoityd with ane cranch against thilke lofte. I cursyt him in wraith, and mynding to taigel him, claught haud of his koote whilke I gyit ane hele of ane nibble. Oore I gatt to myne knye he elyit, garryng thilk door clashe ahynt him. I strifflit till thilke samen plesse as gypelye as I culde—puit up thilk samen dor as I thoucht and ran on—but Cryste quhair suld I lichte! but on thilke dafte syde of ane feil madame! Myne heid mellyt thilk biggyng, and I was klien stoundyt and daveryt. Myne ledde sychit and mummlyt, pittyng me in ane dreidfulle fyke; and sae fummylyng til ryse, scho trowit I had bein gumpyng, and sett up sic ane yirlich skrighe that my verie sennyns sloomyt and myne teith chackyt in myne heid. Scho brainzellyt up in ane foorye and dowlicappyd me, and ben richt laithe to lay ane laitless finger on her, I brankyt in myne gram, and laye smooryng quhille ye claum fra the barmykene and redde us. Thys is thilke hale and leil troothe, as I houpe for merse bye ouir blissyt ladye."

The king then asked him if he was certain it was a man that stumbled over him in the dark? Polmood swore he was certain, for that it was weightier and stronger than any three women in the forest, and besides he was farther certified by feeling his clothes and leg. The king still continued to dwell on that subject, as seeming to doubt of it alone; but Polmood, having again sworn to the certainty of the whole, he was dismissed and forgiven, on condition that he asked pardon of Lady Hume, her Majesty, and all the ladies.

The Lord Chamberlain was then called up, and being accused of *"Misleeryt racket and gruesome assault on thilke body of Lady Anne Grey,"* he began as follows:

"Mai maist grashous and soveryne lege, I do humblye beseetsh yer pardonne for myne grit follye and mismainners, and do intrete you til attrybute that haile frolyke to yer Majestye's liberalitye, and no til nae roode and wuckit desyne. I hae nae pley to urge, only that in fayth and troothe I mystuke thilke bed, as myne ayin guid deme, and Lady Grey well baith weil allow; and gin I didna fynde ane man in thilke bed——"

Here it appears the king had interrupted him; for there is no more of this speech in Whitlaw's hand, save some broken sentences which cannot be connected. His majesty is said to have called out angrily, "Hold, hold, no more of that: we have heard enough. Carmichael," continued he, turning about to him, "tell me on your honour, and tell me truly; were you in the room of the twelve chambers last night in the dark, or were you not?" Carmichael answered, with great promptness, that he was. "Was it you who stumbled over Polmood?" "It was indeed." "Then tell me, sir, what was your business there?" Carmichael bowed, and begged to be excused, assuring his majesty, that though he would willingly yield his life for him, that secret he would not yield at that time. "I thank you," said the king, "I know it all. I am glad you have some honour left; had you publicly divulged your motives, you should never have seen the noon of this day. Carmichael! you have been ungrateful, unwary, and presumptuous! I have trusted you near my person for three years, but we must take care that you shall never insult royalty again. Conduct him to the keep, till our farther pleasure is manifested. My Lord Chamberlain, you must ask pardon of Madam Grey, the queen, and all the ladies." The nobles did not comprehend the king's awards, but he knew more and saw farther into the matter than they did.

Chapter X

THE lords having, by desire, retired, the ladies were next sent for, and examined one by one, after being informed that none of them were required to divulge any thing relating to themselves, but only what they heard passing with regard to others.

There was such a flood of mystery and surmise now poured in upon the king, that he felt himself utterly at a loss to distinguish truth from fiction. According to their relations there had been great battles—men cursing and swearing, and occasionally falling down upon the floor with such a shock as if the roof of the castle had fallen in. There were besides whisperings heard, and certain noises which were well described, but left to the judge for interpretation. In a word, it appeared from the relations of the fair enthusiasts, that all the nobles of the court had been there, and the king himself among them; and that every lady in the castle had been engaged with one paramour *at least*–the narrator always excepted. James would gladly have put a stop to this torrent of scandal and insinuation, but, having once begun, he was obliged to hear them all out;

each being alike anxious to vindicate herself by fixing the guilt upon her neighbours.

There was however one circumstance came out, which visibly affected James. It was affirmed by two different ladies, one of whom, at least, he had good reasons for believing, that there was actually one in the chamber with Elizabeth, when he and Polmood came up in their frolic, and when she contrived so artfully to extinguish the light. Several circumstances occurred to his mind at once in confirmation of this accusal, but he affected as much as he was able to receive it with the same indifference that he received the rest. He cast one look at Elizabeth, but he was too much of a gentleman to suffer it to remain–he withdrew his piercing eye in a moment–smiled, and asked questions about something else. When they had done, Elizabeth rose to explain, and had just begun by saying, "My dear lord, it is very very hard indeed, that I cannot pay my evening services to the virgin, but I must be suspected of"——Here she paused, and the lively and petulant Ann Grey, springing up and making a low courtsey, said, in a whimpering tone, "My dear lord! it is very hard indeed, that Carmichael cannot pay his evening services to a virgin but he must be suspected of."——The manner in which she pronounced this, and in particular the emphasis whch she laid upon the concluding preposition, set all the ladies a giggling; and the king, being pleased with the sly humour of his favourite, and seeing Elizabeth put to the blush, he started up, and clasping her in his arms, kissed her, and said, "There is no need of any defence or apology, my dear Elizabeth, I am too well convinced of your purity to regard the insinuations of that volatile imp. We all know whereto her sarcasms tend; she has the Earl of Hume in her mind, and the gentleman who knocked him down last night; she wishes you to be thought like herself, but it will not do. We shall soon see you placed in a situation beyond the power of her wicked biting jests, and of court scandal; while she may continue to sigh and ogle with knights, wreck her disappointment on all her acquaintances, and sigh for that she cannot have." "Heigh-ho!" cried the shrewd minx, in a tone which again set all the party in a titter.

After this, the king, having dismissed them, sent for Carmichael, and said unto him. "Carmichael, I am shocked at your behaviour. The attempt which you have made on a royal ward, on the very eve of her marriage with a man of honour and integrity, whom we esteem, manifests a depravity of mind, and a heart so dead to every sense of gratitude, that I am ashamed at having taken such a knight into my household. Whatever were your motives for this disgraceful and clandestine procedure, whether the seduction of her person or of her affections from the man who adores her, and who has obtained our sanction to her hand, they must have been wrong, and far from that line of respect which, in return for our confidence, it was your bounden duty to pursue. I therefore will, that you quit the society of which you have been an unworthy member for the space of three years, in the course of half an hour; and if at any time within that period you are found within twenty miles of our residence, your life shall answer for it—this I shall cause to be proclaimed to the country at large. I desire to hear no intreaty or excuse."

Carmichael bowed, and retiring from the presence in the utmost trepidation, he and his groom, the only attendant he had, were both ready mounted in less than ten minutes; and being driven, in some degree, to a state of desperation, he rode boldly up to the castle-gate, and desired a word with Elizabeth. This was a most imprudent action, as it in some degree divulged the cause of his expulsion from the court, which it was the king's chief design to conceal, or gloss over with some other pretence.

When the squire in waiting carried up his demand, Elizabeth was sitting between the queen and the lady Hamilton; and acting from the impulse of the moment, as she too often did, she was rising to comply with the request, when a look from the king, which she well knew how to interpret, caused her to sink again into her seat, like a deer that has been aroused by a false alarm. "What answer shall I return?" said the squire, who had only witnessed her spontaneous motion, but received no order; "that Elizabeth has nothing to say to him," said the king. The squire returned down stairs. "Elizabeth has nothing to say to you, my lord." Carmichael turned his horse slowly around, as if not knowing what he did. "Was it she that returned me this answer?" said he; "Yes sir," said the man, walking carelessly back into the castle. That word pierced Carmichael to the heart; he again turned his horse slowly around, and the porter said he seemed as if he had lost sight of the ground. He appeared desirous of leaving some message, but he rode off without uttering another syllable, and instead of shaping his course homeward as was expected, he crossed the Meggat, went round the Breaken Hill, and seemed bound for the border.

Though it is perhaps perfectly well understood, it may not be improper to mention here by way of explanation, that when Carmichael escaped from Elizabeth's chamber in the dark, and had slunk quietly down to his own, in a few minutes he heard the king come running down the stair, laughing, and calling out that the bride had rued; and not having the slightest suspicion that Polmood would remain among the ladies in the dark, he judged him to have gone along with the king. He was extremely happy on hearing the king exclaiming that Elizabeth had taken her word again, not doubting but that it was in consequence of the conversation he had with her; and in order to strengthen her resolution, or prevail upon her instantly to elope with him, he took the opportunity of stealing again to her apartment before any other irruption of the revellers into the castle should take place; but in his way, and when at the very point at which he aimed, he stumbled upon the forlorn Polmood, whose voice and grasp he well knew, and from whom he narrowly escaped.

Carmichael was now gone, and Elizabeth did not believe that any person knew of her amour with him. She thought that the king was merely jealous of him and Lady Ann Gray, yet she could not help considering herself as the cause of the noble youth's disgrace, and for the first time in her life felt her *heart* interested in the person or concerns of another. Perhaps her passion for admiration prompted the feeling, for the circumstance had deprived her of a principal admirer; but it is probable that a sentiment more tender mixed with the regret she felt at his departure.

The king, who perceived well how matters stood, was considerably alarmed for his fair ward, both on account of her bewitching beauty and accomplishments, and her insatiable desire of excelling all others of her sex; but more on account of her rash thoughtless manner of acting. He entertained no doubt of her stainless purity, but he knew that a great deal more was required in order to maintain her character uncontaminated in the eyes of the world—that caution and prudence were as requisite as the others, and that purity of heart, and innocency of intention, instead of proving shields against the aspersions of calumny, often induce to that gayety and freedom of demeanour, which attaches its most poignant and venomous shafts. Of this caution and prudence Elizabeth seemed destitute. Her own word, with that of both her royal guardians, was pledged to Polmood, yet notwithstanding all this, he dreaded that she had admitted a knight into her chamber at midnight, and had artfully effected his escape, within nine hours of the time appointed for her nuptials. He could not judge Carmichael's pretensions to have been honourable from his manner of proceeding, and he trembled for the impressions he might have made upon her inexperienced heart, subversive of honour, faith, and virtue; especially when he considered the answer she had returned to Polmood the very minute after Carmichael had left her.

As for Polmood, he had, as yet, no suspicions of Carmichael nor any man living; but the answer he had received sunk deep into his heart; for he absolutely adored Elizabeth, and feared he had offended her by some part of his behaviour, and that she had actually re-pented of her promise to him on that account. He knew not to whom first to address himself, and wandered about all that morning, with a countenance so rueful that nothing in this age will ever compare with it.

The king put his arm within Elizabeth's, and led her to the bal-cony. The day was clear, and the scene on which they looked around, wild and romantic. The high mountains, the straggling woods, the distant lake, and the limpid river, with its hundred branches, wind-ing through vallies covered with brake and purple heath, whose wild variety of light and shade the plough had never marred.—The kid, the lamb, the leveret, and the young deer, feeding or sporting together in the same green halt, formed altogether a scene of rural simplicity, and peaceful harmony, such as the eye of a Briton shall never again look upon.

"We shall have a sweet day for your wedding, Elizabeth," said the king. Elizabeth cast her eyes towards the brow of the hill, where Carmichael had but a few minutes before vanished, and remained silent. The king was agitated; "yon was an effectual rub you gave the bridegroom last night," continued he; "I owe you a kiss, and a frock of purple silk beside, for it. I would not have missed the jest for an hundred bonnet pieces, and as many merks to boot; you are a most exquisite girl." Never was flattery lost on the ear of a woman! especially if that woman was possessed of youth and beauty. Eliza-beth smiled, and seemed highly pleased with the compliment paid to her ingenuity. "What a loss it is," continued James, "that we can-not push the jest a little farther. Suppose we should try?"

"Oh! by all means!" said Elizabeth, "let us carry the jest a little farther."

"Polmood is in sad taking already," said the king; "were you to persist in your refusal a little longer he would certainly hang him-self." Elizabeth smiled again. "But the worst of it is, he will take it so heinously amiss. I know his proud heart well, that all the world will not persuade him ever to ask you again; and then, if the match is, in our vain humour, broke off, it is irretrievable ruin to you."

"Ruin to me! what does your Majesty mean?"

"Yes, certain ruin to you; for the court and all the kingdom will say that he has slighted and refused you, and you know we cannot help what people say. You know they will say it was because he and

I surprised a man in your chamber at midnight, and much more than that they will say. They know that you could not, and would not resist our will, and therefore they will infallibly regard you as an offcast, and you will be flouted and shunned by the whole court. It would almost break my heart to see those who now envy and imitate you, turning up their noses as you past them."

"But I will inform them; I will swear to them that it was not so," said Elizabeth, almost crying.

"That is the readiest way to make them believe that it was so," said the king. "We shall, besides, lose an excellent and splendid wedding, in which I hoped to see you appear to peculiar advantage, the wonder and admiration of all ranks and degrees; but that is nothing." Elizabeth gave him a glance of restless impatience; "after all, I think we must venture to give Polmood a farther refusal for the joke's sake; even in the worst case I do not know but an old maid is as happy as many a married lady."

These few, seemingly spontaneous sentences, presented to the mind of Elizabeth a picture altogether so repulsive, that she scarcely had patience to listen until the king concluded; and when he had done she remained silent, first turned round the one bracelet, then the other, fetched a slight sigh, and looked the king in the face.

"I think that for the humour of the jest you ought to persist in your refusal," continued James.

"I have often heard your Majesty say, that we should never let the plough stand to kill a mouse," said Elizabeth. "I never saw *long jokes* come to much good."

"Upon my soul I believe you are right after all," returned the king; "you have more sense in your little finger than most ladies have in all. It is not easy to catch you in the wrong; I suppose the wedding must go on?" "I suppose it must," said Elizabeth, pleased with the idea of her acuteness and discernment. She was again turning her eyes toward the brow of the Breaken hill, but the king changed sides with her, linking his left arm in her right, and led her at a sharp walk round the balcony, commending her prudence and discretion as much above her years, and expatiating on the envy and spleen of the court ladies, and the joy they would have manifested if the marriage agreement had been finally dissolved. From that he broke of, and descanted on the amusements and processions in which they were to be engaged, and even on the dresses and jewels in which such and such ladies were likely to appear, until he had winded up Elizabeth's fancy to the highest pitch; for it was always on the wing watching for change of place, and new treasures of vain delight. Without giving her time for any further quiet reflection, he hurried her away to the great hall, where the queen and her attendants remained. "Make haste, make haste, my ladies," said he; "you seem to forget that we have this day to ride to the Maiden chapel, and from thence to the castle of Nidpath, where I have ordered preparations to be made for the ensuing festival. Falgeat is high, and the braes of Hundleshope steep; make haste, my ladies, make haste."

The order of the day seemed hitherto scarcely well understood, but when the king had thus expressed his will, in such apparent haste and good humour, away tripped she, and away tripped she, each lady to her little wardrobe and portable mirror. The king ran down stairs to issue the same orders in the pavilion, where a plentiful breakfast of cakes, venison, and milk was set in order, and where the nobles had begun to assemble; but on his way he perceived Polmood walking rapidly by the side of the burn, with his hands clasped behind his back, and his bonnet over his brow, he heard not, nor saw what was going on. The king accosted him in a hasty careless manner, "Polmood, why are you sauntering there? the ladies are quite ready! the bride is ready for mounting her horse! fy! fy! Polmood, the ladies will all be obliged to wait for you." Polmood ran towards the burn to wash his face; but recollecting something else, he turned, and ran towards the tent; then, stopping short all of a sudden, he turned back again, and ran towards the burn. "I'll be shot to dead with an arrow if I know what to do," said he, as he passed the king this last time with his bonnet on. "And I'll be shot too," said the king, "if you know what you are doing just now—make haste, make haste, Polmood! you have not time to be sauntering and running to and fro in this manner,—fy! fy! that the ladies should be obliged to wait for the bridegroom!"

The king was highly diverted by Polmood's agitation and embarrassment, which he attributed to his violent passion, with its concomitant hopes and fears; and, having thus expelled in one moment his dread of losing Elizabeth, and at the same time, while his senses were all in a flutter, put him into such a terrible hurry, he retired within the door of the tent, and watched his motions for some time without being observed. Polmood washed his hands and face in the stream without delay, and perceiving that he had nothing wherewith to dry them, he tried to do it with the tail of his coat, but that being too short, though he almost doubled himself, he could not bring it in contact with his face. He then ran across the green to the servant's hall, stooping and winking all the way, while the water poured from his beard. In his hurry he left his fine plumed bonnet by the side of the burn, which the king lifted and hid, and afterwards warned his nobles to prepare for the cavalcade; telling them, that the marriage of Polmood with Elizabeth was to be celebrated at Nidpath for several days.

Chapter XI

THE rural breakfast over, our noble party mounted and rode away from the castle of Crawmel. The lightness of the breeze—the presence of so much beauty, royalty, and respect—together with the joyous occasion, completely eradicated from their minds the effects of last night's intemperance and misrule. They were again all in high spirits, and scoured the links of Meggat, so full of mirth and glee, that every earthly care was flung to the wind, in which, too, many a lovely lock and streaming ribbon floated.

If there is any one adventitious circumstance in life which invariably exhilarates the mind, and buoys up the spirits to the highest pitch, it is that of a large party of men and women setting out on an expedition on horseback. Of this party, excluding grooms, pages, and other attendants, there were upwards of forty, the flower of the Scottish nation. The followers scarcely amounted to that number, so little was James afraid of any harm within the realm.

On their way they came to the castle of Pearce Cockburn, who then accompanied the king. He compelled them all to halt and drink wine at his gate; but when the foremost twelve had taken their glasses, and were about to drink to the health of the bride and bridegroom, they looked around in vain for one of them; the bridegroom was lost no one knew how; they were all dumb with astonishment how they had lost Polmood; or how they came to travel so far without missing him; but he was at last discovered, nigh to the rear, sitting silently on his horse, dressed in an old slouch hat, which had lately been cast by one of the grooms. His horse was a good one, his other raiment was costly and elegant, and the ludicrous contrast which the old slouch hat formed to these, with the circumstance of the wearer being a bridegroom, and just going to be married to the most beautiful, elegant, and fashionable lady in the kingdom, altogether struck every one so forcibly, that the whole company burst out in an involuntary shout of laughter. Polmood kept his position without moving a muscle, which added greatly to the humour of the scene. The king, who never till that moment recollected his having hid Polmood's bonnet, was so much tickled, that he was forced to alight from his horse, sit down upon a stone, hold his sides, and laugh.

"What, Polmood!" said he, when he recovered breath to speak. "What, Polmood! do you prefer that courch'e to your own elegant bonnet?"

"No, sire," said Polmood, "but I preferred it to a bare head; for when ready to mount, I found that I had mislaid my bonnet, or lost it some way, I do not know how."

"I have been somewhat to blame in this, Polmood, but no matter; you cannot and shall not appear at your own nuptials in such a cap as that; therefore let us change for a day—no excuses; I insist on it." Polmood then put on his royal master's bonnet, which was beset with plumes, gold, and diamonds. That new honour made him blush deeply, but at the same time he bluntly remarked, that his majesty was the greatest wag in all his dominions. The humour of the party was greatly heightened when they beheld James the fourth of that name, the greatest and the best of all the Stuart line, riding at the head of his nobles, and by the side of his queen, with the old greasy slouched hat on his head. They were mightily diverted, as well as delighted, with the good humour of their sovereign, and his easy condescension.

In a short time they reached the Virgin's chapel, where they were met by the prior, and two monks of St Mary's, dressed in their robes of office. There Polmood was married to the lovely Elizabeth Manners, by the abbot of Inchafferie, chaplain to the king. The king himself gave her in marriage, and during the ceremony Polmood seemed deeply affected, but the fair bride was studious only how to demean herself with proper ease and dignity, which she effected to the admiration of all present. Her beauty was so transcendent, that even the holy brothers were struck with astonishment; and the abbot, in the performance of his office, prayed fervently, as with a prophetic spirit, that that beauty which, as he expressed it, "outvied the dawn of the morning, and dazzled the beholders, might never prove a source of uneasiness, either to her husband or her own breast. May that lovely bloom," said he, "long dwell on the face that now so well becomes it, and blossom again and again in many a future stem. May it never be regarded by the present possessor as a cause of exultation, or self-esteem; but only as a transient engaging varnish, over the more precious beauties of the mind; and may her personal and mental charms be so blended, that her husband may never perceive the decay of the one, save only by the growing beauties of the other." The tear rolled in Polmood's eye. Elizabeth was only intent on the manner in which she stood, and on ordering her downcast looks and blushes aright; she thought not of the petition, but of the compliment paid to her beauty.

Soon were they again on horseback, and ascending the high hill of Falgeat, they dined on its summit, by the side of a crystal spring. From that elevated spot they had an immense and varied prospect, which, on all hands, was intercepted only by the blue haze, in which distance always screens herself from human vision. The whole southern part of the kingdom from sea to sea, lay spread around them as on a map, or rather like one half of a terrestrial globe,–

> Where oceans rolled and rivers ran,
> To bound the aims of sinful man.
>   Man never looked on scene so fair
> As Scotland from the ambient air;
> O'er valleys clouds of vapour rolled,
> While others beamed in burning gold;
> And, stretching far and wide between,
> Were fading shades of fairy green.
> The glossy sea that round her quakes;
> Her thousand isles, and thousand lakes;
> Her mountains frowning o'er the main;
> Her waving fields of golden grain!
> On such a scene, so sweet, so mild,
> The radiant sun-beam never smiled!

But though the vales and frith of Lothian lay stretched like a variegated carpet below his feet on the one side, while the green hills and waving woods of Ettrick Forest formed a contrast so noble on the other, it was remarked, that the king fixed his eyes constantly on the fells of Cheviot, and the eastern borders of England. Did he even then meditate an invasion of that country? or did some invisible power, presiding over the mysteries of elicitation and sympathy, draw his eyes and cogitations irresistibly away to that very spot where his royal and goodly form was so soon to lie in an untimely grave?

Towards the evening, in endeavouring to avoid a morass, the whole party lost their way; and the king, perceiving a young man at a little distance, rode briskly up to him in order to make inquiries. The lad, who was the son of a farmer, and herding his father's sheep, seeing a cavalier with a slouched hat galloping towards him, judged him to be one of a troop of foragers, and throwing away his plaid and brogues, he took to his heels, and fled with precipitation.

It was in vain that the king shouted and called on him to halt; he only fled the faster; and James, who delighted in a frolic, and was under the necessity of having some information concerning the way, seeing no better would, he drew his sword, and pursued him full speed. As the youth ran towards the steepest part of the hill, the king, who soon lost sight of his company, found it no easy matter to come up with him. But at last the hardy mountaineer, perceiving his pursuer hard upon him, and judging that it was all over with him, faced about—heaved his baton, and prepared for a desperate defence.

Whether the king rode briskly up in order to disarm him at once; or whether, as he pretended, he could not manage to stop his horse on the steep, could not be determined, owing to the difference of the relation, when told by the king and the shepherd; but certain it is, that at the first stroke the shepherd stunned the king's Spanish bay, who foundered on the heath, and threw his rider forward among the feet of his antagonist. The shepherd, who deemed himself fighting for life and salvation, plied his blows so thick upon the king's back and shoulders, that, if the former had not previously been quite exhausted by running, he had certainly maimed the king. But James, feeling by experience, that there was no time to parley, sprung upon his assailant, whom he easily overthrew and disarmed, as being completely out of breath. "What does the fool mean?" said the king. "All that I wanted of you, was to put us on our way to Peebles, for we have entirely lost both our path and our aim."

"But you must first tell me who you are," said the youth; "I fear you have no good design on Peebles."

"We are a wedding party going there to make merry. The king and queen are to meet us, and honour us with their company; and if you will go along and direct us the way, you too shall be our guest, and you shall see the king and all his court."

"I can see plenty o' fools without ganging sae far," said the shepherd. "I account that nae great favour; I have often seen the king."

"And would know him perfectly well, I suppose?"

"Oh, yes. I could ken him amang a thousand. But tell me, are you indeed Scotsmen?"

"Indeed we are, did you not see many ladies in company?"

"I am sorry for putting you to sae muckle trouble, sir; but wha the devil ever saw a Scot wear a bonnet like that!"

"Come, mount behind me, and direct us on our way, which seems terribly intricate, and you shall be well rewarded."

The youth mounted, bare legged as he was, behind the stalwart groom, without farther hesitation—they soon came in sight of the company, who were waiting the issue of the pursuit—the king waved his slouched hat, and called on them to follow, and then rode away at a distance before, conversing with his ragged guide. The eminence where the party dined, is called the *King's Seat*; and the glen where they found the shepherd, *the Weddingers' Hope*, to this day.

Chapter XII

THE road which they were now obliged to follow was indeed intricate; it winded among the brakes and woods of Grevington in such a manner, that, if it had not been for the shepherd, the royal party could not have found their way to the town of Peebles or the castle of Nidpath that night. James and the shepherd led the way, the latter being well acquainted with it; and all the rest followed in a string as they could win *their* way. The two foremost being both on the same horse, conversed freely as they went. There being a considerable difference in the relation which the parties gave of the particulars of this conversation, the real truth could not be fully ascertained; but the following is as near a part of it as could be recovered.

King.—"So you know the king well enough by sight, you say?"

Shep. "Perfectly well."

"Pray what is he like?"

"A black-looking thief-like chap, about your ain size, and somewhat like you, but a great deal uglier."

"I should like of all things to see him and hear him speak."

"You would like to see him and hear him speak, would you? Well, if you chance to see him, I will answer for it, you shall soon hear him speak; There's naething in the hale warld he delytes sae muckle in, as to *hear himself* speak—if you are near him, it will gang hard if you hear ony thing else; and if you do not *see* him, it will not be his fault; for he takes every opportunity of showing his *goodly person*."

"So you have no great opinion of your king I perceive."

"I have a *great opinion* that he is a silly fellow; a bad man at heart; and a great rascal."

"I am sorry to hear that, from one who knows him so well, for I have heard, on the contrary, that he is accounted generous, brave, and virtuous."

"Aye, but his generosity is a' ostentation—his bravery has never yet been weel tried; and for his virtue—God mend it."

"Well, shepherd, you know we may here speak the sentiments of our hearts freely, and whatever you say——"

"Whatever I say! I have said nothing which I would not repeat if the king were standing beside me—I only said his courage has not yet been tried—I say sae still—And I said, for his virtue, God mend it. Was that wrong? I say sae still too—I would say as muckle for any person; of you, or even my own father. The truth is, I like James Stuart weel enough as my king, and would fight for him to my last breath against the Englishmen; but I am unco angry at him for a' that, and would as willingly fight *wi'* him. If I had got him amang my feet as I had you lately, mercy! how I would have laid on!"

"The devil you would?"

"That I would! But by the by, what makes you wear an iron chain? you have not killed your father too, have you? Or is it only for the purpose of carrying your master's wallet?"

"No more; only for carrying my master's wallet."

"Aye, but the king wears ane sax times as big as that of yours, man—Was not that a terrible business? How can we expect any blessing or good fortune to attend a king who dethroned and murdered his father? for ye ken it was the same thing as if he had done it wi' his ain hand."

"It is well known that his father was much to blame; and I believe the king was innocent of that, and is besides very sorry for it."

"Though he was to blame, he was still his father—There's nae argument can gang against that; and as to his being sorry, it is easy for him to say sae, and wear a bit chain over his shoulder, as you do: but I firmly believe, if the same temptation, and the same opportunity, were again to recur, he would do the same over again. And then, what a wicked man he is with women! He has a very good queen of his ain, even though she be an Englishwoman, which is certainly wonderful; yet she is a very good queen; yet he is so indifferent about her, that he is barely civil, and delights only in a witching minx, that they ca' Grey—Grey by name and Grey by nature I wad reckon. What a terrible sin and shame it is to gallaunt as they do! I wonder they two never think of hell and purgatory."

"We must allow our king a little liberty in that way."

"Yes; and then he must allow it in others, and they in others again—you little think, what a wicked prince has to answer for."

"Are such things indeed reported of the king?"

"Aye, and in every body's mouth. Fy! fy! what a shame it is! If I were in his place I would 'shu the Heron away,' as the auld song says—Pray did you never hear the song of *the Heron* which one of our shepherds made, a strange chap he is?"

"Never."

"Well, it is the sweetest thing you ever heard, and I will sing it to you when I have time. I would give the best wedder in my father's flock that King James heard it; I am sure he would love our old shepherd, who well deserves his love, for there is no man in Scotland that loves his king and nation so well as he. But to return to our king's faults, the worst of the whole is his negligence in looking after the rights and interests of the common people. It is allowed on all hands, that James is a good-natured and merciful prince; yet, the acts of cruelty and injustice, which every petty lord and laird exercises in his own domain, is beyond all sufferance. If his majesty knew but even the half that I know, he would no more enjoy his humours and pleasures so freely, till once he had rectified those abuses, which it has always been the chief study of his nobles to conceal frae his sight. I could show him some scenes that would convince him what sort of a king he is."

The shepherd, about this time, observing that one of the troop behind them continued to sound a bugle at equal intervals, with a certain peculiar lilt, asked the king what the fellow meant. The king answered, "That he was only warning Mess John and the weddingers, to be ready to receive them. And you will soon see them," continued he, "coming to meet us, and to conduct us into the town." "And will the king indeed be there?" "Yes, the king will indeed be there." "Well, I wish I had my hose, brogues, and Sunday clothes on; but, it is all one, nobody will mind me."

Now it so happened, that James had, a short time previous to that, conferred a grant of the lands of Caidmoor on the town of Peebles, on account of their great attachment and good will towards him; and the news of his approach having been brought there by some of the servants, who had been despatched to provide accommodations at Nidpath, the townsmen had dressed themselves in their best robes, and were all prepared to receive their royal benefactor with every demonstration of joy; and, on hearing the well-known sound of his bugle, they repaired to meet him on a moor south of the river. The king, being still foremost, rode up into the midst of his loyal burgesses without being discovered, and indeed without being regarded or looked at; then, wheeling about his horse, he made a halt until his train came up; the barelegged youth was still riding at his back on the same horse.

The shepherd could perceive no king, nor any thing like one, save Polmood, on whom the eyes of the townsmen were likewise fixed as he approached; yet they could not help thinking their king was transformed.

The courtiers with their attendants soon came up, and after arranging themselves in two rows before the king and the queen, who had now drawn up her horse close by his side, they uncovered their heads, and all bowed themselves at once. The shepherd likewise uncovered his head, without knowing to whom, but he understood some great affair to be going on. "For God sake! neighbour, tak aff that ugly slouched hat of yours, man," said he to his companion; and at the same time pushing it off with one of his arms. The king catched it between his hands as it fell. "To whom should I take it off, sirrah?– to you, I suppose," said he, and put it deliberately on again. This incident discovered his majesty to all present, and a thousand shouts, mixed with a thousand bonnets, scaled the firmament at once.

The dreadful truth now glanced upon the shepherd's mind all at once, like the bolt of heaven that preludes a storm. The station which his companion held in the middle of the ring–the queen by his side– the heads uncovered, and the iron chain, all confirmed it.–He sprung from his seat, as the marten of the Grampians springs from his hold when he smells the fire–darted through an opening in the circle, and ran across the moor with inconceivable swiftness. "Hold that rascal," cried the king, "lay hold of the villain, lay hold of him." The shepherd was pursued by man, horse, and hound, and soon overtaken and secured. Their majesties entered the town amid shouts and acclamations of joy; but the unfortunate shepherd was brought up a prisoner in the rear by four officers of the king's guard, who were highly amused by the different passions that agitated his breast. At one time he was accusing himself bitterly of folly and stupidity– at another, laughing at his mistake, and consoling himself after this manner: "Weel, the king will hang me the morn, there is nae doubt of it; but he canna do it for naething, as he does to mony ane, that is some comfort; by my faith, I gae him a hearty loundering, he never gat sic dadds in his life–let him tak them." Again, when he spoke or thought of his parents, his heart was like to burst. After locking him into the tolbooth of Peebles, they left him to darkness and despair; while all the rest were carousing and making merry, and many of them laughing at his calamity.

The king, whose curiosity had been aroused, made inquiries concerning the name, occupation, and qualities of this youth, and was informed, that his name was Moray (the same it is supposed with

Murray); that he was a great scholar, but an idle, useless fellow; that the old abbot had learned him to sing, for which every one valued him; but that, unfortunately, he had likewise taught him the unprofitable arts of reading and writing, in which alone he delighted; and it was conjectured he would end in becoming a warlock, or studying the black art.

The king, though no profound scholar himself, knew well the value of education, and how to estimate it in others. He was, therefore, desirous of trying the youth a little further, and of being avenged on him for galling him in such a merciless manner, and sent a messenger to him that night, informing him, that he would be brought to the scaffold next day; but that if he had any message or letter to send to his father, the king would despatch a courier with it. The youth replied, that if the king would send a messenger with the letter who could read it to his father, he would certainly write one instantly; but that his father could not read. The messenger, knowing that the king was particularly desirous of seeing the writing and composition of a shepherd, and of comparing it with those of his clerks, promised that such a messenger should be sent with it. The shepherd wrote one without delay, which the man took, and carried straight to the king. This letter is likewise inserted in Mr Brown's book of ancient manuscripts, but it seems to have been written at a much later period than many others that are there; the spelling is somewhat more modern, and the ink scarcely so yellow. The following is a literal copy:–

Dr faythr im to be hangit the morn, for daddinge of the kingis hate; for miskaing him to his fes ahynt his bak; for devering his whors, and layinge on him with ane grit stick. i hope el no be vext, for im no theefe; it was a sayir battil, an a bete him doune wis dran sorde; for i miskent him. if it hadna bin krystis merse, ad kild him. mi muthr l be wae, but ye men pleis her, an il be gled to se ye in at the deth, for i wonte er blissyng. im no feirit, but yit its ane asom thynge; its no deth it feirs me, but the eftir-kum garis my hert girle. if kryste and his muthr dinna do sumthin for me ther, i maye be ill—im er lukles sonne, Villem mora—to Villem mora of kreuksten.

When this letter was read to the king and his courtiers, instead of laughing at it, as might have been expected, they admired it, and wondered at the shepherd's profound erudition; a proof that learning, in those days, was at a very low ebb in Scotland.

The messenger was despatched to his father; and the old man

and his wife, on receiving the news, repaired instantly to Peebles in the utmost consternation. They were however denied access to their son, until such time as he appeared on the scaffold. A great crowd was by that time assembled; for besides the court, all the town people, and those of the country around, were gathered together to see poor William hanged. When his father and mother mounted the steps, he shook each of them by the hand, smiled, and seemed anxious to console them; but they both turned about and wept, and their utterance was for some time quite overpowered. They had been given to understand, that the king would listen to no intercession; for that their son had uttered sentences of a most dangerous and flagrant nature, in which they were likely to be involved, as having instilled such sentiments into his young mind. But when they learned from his own mouth, that he had committed the assault on the person of his majesty under a mistake; and, knowing how justly their son had blamed his conduct and government, they could not help considering it extremely hard, to bring a valuable youth thus to a shameful and public execution for such an offence. The mother cried downright, and the old man with difficulty restrained himself. He did not fall at the king's feet, nor attempt speaking to him, as judging it altogether vain and unprofitable, but he turned on him a look that said more than any words could express: and then, as if hopeless of mercy or justice from that quarter, he turned them to Heaven—uncovered his gray head, and sinking on his knees, invoked the justice and forgiveness of the Almighty in strong and energetic terms. This was the language of nature and of the heart; and when he prayed, there was no cheek in the assembly dry, save those of the king and courtiers. "What hard hearts these great folks have," said the country-people one to another.

The usual ceremonies being all got over, William's face was at length covered—the executioner was just proceeding to do his duty—thousands of burgesses and plebeians were standing around with bare heads and open mouths, holding in their breath in awful suspense—the women had turned their backs to the scaffold, and were holding down their faces, and weeping—the parents of the youth had taken a long farewell of him, when the king sprung forward to the scene of action. "Hold!" said he, "this fellow, traitor as he is, has behaved himself throughout with some degree of spirit, and therefore he shall not die like a common felon—No," continued he, unsheathing his sword, "he shall die by the hand of a king. Kneel down, William, I command you!" William, whose senses were all in confusion, and who felt the same kind of sensations as he sometimes wont to do in a dream, kneeled implicitly down on the boards, and held forward his head, making a long neck that his Majesty might get a fair blow at it. The king, either inadvertently or in a frolic, laid the cold blade of the sword for a moment upon his neck. William imagined his head was off, and fell lifeless upon the scaffold. The king then crossed him with his sword–"Rise up, Sir William Moray," said he; "I here create you a knight, and give to you, and yours, the lands of Crookston and Newley, to hold of me for ever." The old farmer and his wife uttered both an involuntary cry, between a sigh and a shout: it was something like that which a drowning person utters, and they were instantly at the king's feet, clasping his knees. The crowd around hurled their caps into the air, and shouted until the hills rang again; "Long live our gracious king!–long live our good king James!"

When the tumult of joy had somewhat subsided, it was observed that William was lying still upon his face. They unbound his hands, and desired him to rise; but he neither answered nor regarded; and, on lifting him up, they saw with astonishment that he was dead in good earnest. His parents, in the utmost despair, carried him into a house, and for a long time every art to restore suspended animation proved fruitless. When the king laid the cold sword upon his bare neck, it was observed that he gave a violent shiver. The poor youth imagined that his head was then struck off, and to think of living longer in such circumstances was out of the question, so he died with all manner of decorum; and it is believed he would never more have revived, if the most vigorous measures had not been resorted to. King James, who was well versed in every thing relating to the human frame, was the best surgeon, and the most skilful physician then in the realm, succeeded at last in restoring him to life. But even then, so strongly was his fancy impressed with the reality of his dissolution, that he could not be convinced that he was not in a world of spirits; and that all who surrounded him were not ghosts. When he came to understand his real situation, and was informed of the honours and lands conferred on him by the king, he wept out of gratitude, and sagely observed, that, "*after all, the truth told ay best.*"

Chapter XIII

WILLIAM, the shepherd, being now metamorphosed into Sir William Moray, was equipt in proper habiliments, and introduced at court by his new title. He often astonished the courtiers, and put them quite out of countenance, by his blunt and cutting remarks, and of course soon became a great favourite with James, who delighted in that species of entertainment, as all the Stuarts were known to do, but he more than any of them. No sooner had William arisen into favour, than he was on the very point, not only of losing it again, but of incurring the king's serious displeasure.

On the third or fourth evening after their arrival at Nidpath, when the feast and the dance were over, the king reminded William of the song which he had promised to sing to him on their way to Peebles. William hesitated, blushed, and tried to put it off; but, the more averse he seemed to comply, the more clamorous the company grew for his song.

This practice is too frequent even to this day, and it is one which neither betokens generosity nor good sense. It often puts an unoffending youth, or amiable young lady, to the blush, and lays them under the necessity of either making a fool of themselves, or of refusing those whom they wish to oblige, and to appear prudish, when in fact nothing is farther from their hearts. The custom can never be productive of any good; and, in the instance above alluded to, it was the cause of much shame and dissatisfaction; for William, pressed as he was, and unable to hold longer out, began, and with a face glowing with shame, a palpitating heart, and a faultering tongue, sung the following old ballad.

The writer of this tale is particularly happy at having it in his power to present his readers with a genuine and original copy of this celebrated ancient song, save that he cannot answer precisely for having read, or copied, it exactly. He refers them, however, to the original Manuscript in the possession of Mr J. Brown, now living in Richmond Street, the perusal of which they will find no easy matter. It has been quoted by different living authors, or compilers rather, from tradition, and quoted falsely; but the meaning of it, like that of many an ancient allegory, seems never to have been at all understood. It may not be improper here to mention, that the only account that can be obtained of these ancient MSS. is, that they belonged to the house of March, and were found in the castle of Dumlanrig.

The Herone

A Very Ancient Song

LEISHE the hunde on the tassilyt moore!
   Grein growis the birke in the coome se mello!
Strewe the tyme in the greinwude bouir;
   For the dewe fallis sweite in the mune-beim yello!
For owir gude kyngis to the grein-wude gene, &c.
And bonie quene Jeanye lyis hirre lene, &c.
Weil mot scho siche, for scho wetis weil,
He sleipis his lane in the foreste sheile!
   Aleke! and alu! for ouir gude kynge!
He sleipis on the fogge, and drinkis the sprynge!
Ne lorde, ne erl, to be his gyde,
But ane bonnye pege to lye by his syde:
And, O! that pegis weste is slim;
And his ee wad garre the dey looke dim!
And, O! his breiste is rounde and fayir;
And the dymend lurkis in hys revin hayir,
That curlis se sweitlye aboune his brye,
And rounde hys nek of eivorye!
Yet he mene sleipe on a bedde of lynge,
Aleke! and alu! for ouir gude kynge!
Weile mot Quene Jeanye siche and mene,
For scho kennis he sleipis his leiva lane!
   The kreukyt kraine cryis owir the flode,
The capperkayle clukkis in the wode;
The swanne youtis lythelye ouir the lowe;
The bleiter harpis abune the flowe;
The cushey flutis amangis the firris;
And ay the murecokke biks and birris;
And ay the ouirwurde of ther sange,
"What ailis ouir kynge, he lyis se lange."
   Gae hunte the gouke ane uther myle,
Its no the reid eed capperkayle;
Its ne the murekokke birris at morne,
Nor yitte the deire withe hirre breakine horne;
Its nowthir the hunte, nor the murelan game,
Hes brung ouir kynge se ferre fre heme;
The gloomynge gele, norre the danyng dewe,

He is gene to hunte the *Herone* blue.

Ne burde withe hirre mucht evir compaire,
Hirre nekke se tapper, se tall, and fayir!
Hirre breiste se softe, and hirre ee se greye,
Hes stouin ouir gude kyngis herte awaye:
But in that nekke ther is ane linke,
     And in that breiste ther is ane brier,
And in that ee ther is ane blink,
     Will penne the deidis of wae and weir.
But the graffe shall gepe, and the korbe flee;
And the bourik ryse quhair ane kynge sulde bee.

     The *Herone* flewe eist, the *Herone* flewe weste,
The *Herone* flewe to the fayir foryste!
And ther scho sawe ane gudelye bouir,
Was all kledde ouir with the lille flouir:
And in that bouir there was ane bedde,
With silkine scheitis, and weile dune spredde;
And in thilke bed ther laye ane knichte,
Hos oundis did bleide beth day and nicghte:
And by the bedde-syde ther stude ane stene,
And thereon sate ane leil maydene,
Withe silvere nedil, and silkene threde,
Stemmynge the oundis quhan they did blede.

     The *Herone* scho flappyt, the *Herone* scho flewe,
And scho skyrit at bogge quheryn scho grewe.
By leke, or tarne, scho douchtna reste,
Nor bygge on the klofte hirre dowye este;
Scho culdnae see ane fyttyng schedde,
But the lille bouir and the silkene bedde!
And aye scho pifyrit, and aye scho leerit,
And the bonny May scho jaumphit and jeerit;
And aye scho turnit hirre bosim fayir,
And the knichte he luvit to see hirre there;
For, O! hirre quhite and kumlye breiste,
Was softe as the dune of the sulanis neste!

     But the maydene that wachit him nichte and daye,
She shu'd and shu'd the *Herone* awaye;
Leil Virtue was that fayir maydis neme,
And sayir scho gratte for the knichtis bleme!
But the *Herone* scho flappyt, and the *Herone* scho flew,
And scho dabbyt the fayir mayde blak and blewe;
And scho pykkit the fleche fre hirre bonny breiste-bene;

And scho dykkit oute hirre cleir blewe ene;
Till the knichte he douchtna beire to see
The maydene that wonte his meide to bee!
 Swith *Herone*! swith *Herone*! hyde yer heide,
The Herringden haque will be yer deide!
The boue is bente withe ane silkine strynge
And the airrowe fledgit with ane heronis wynge.
O! quhae will werde the wefoue day!
O! quhae will shu the *Herone* awaye!
 Now the blak kokke mootis in his fluthir deipe;
The rowntre rokis the reven to sleipe;
The sei-mawe couris on his glittye stene,
For its greine withe the dewe of the jaupyng maine;
The egill maye gaspe in his yermite riven,
Amiddys the mystis and the raynis of hevin;
The swanne maye sleike hirre breiste of milke,
But the *Herone* sleipis in hirre bedde of silke.
 The gude knichtis wytte is fledde or feye,
By pithe of wyrde and glamurye;
For aye he kissit hirre bille se fayir,
Tho' vennim of eskis and tedis wase there.
He skyrit to trowe bethe dule and payne,
That his hertis blude shulde paye the kene;
But the threidis fre ilka ound scho drewe,
And aye the reide blude runne anewe;
The ether hes leyne in the lyonis laire,
And that blude shall flowe for evermaire.
Now, loose the hunde on the tassilit moore,
 Grein growis the birke in the coome se mello!
And bedde withe rewe the greinwude bouir,
 Quhan the dewe fallis softe in the mune-beime yello.

Chapter XIV

THE youth sung this ballad to a wild melody, that was quite ravishing, though it might be said that he chanted, rather than sung it; but he had proceeded only a short way with the second sentence, which relates to the page, when Madam Grey began to look this way and that way; and to talk flippantly, first to one person, then to another: but seeing that no one answered, or regarded her, and that all were attentive to the song, she rose hastily and retired. The king tipped the wink to William, and made sundry signs for him to desist; but he either did not, or would not understand them, and went on. At length his majesty rose, and commanded, with a loud voice, that the song should be stopped, for that it was evidently offensive. "I am astonished at your majesty," said the queen, "it is the sweetest and most inoffensive song I ever listened to. It is doubtless a moral allegory, to which the bard has been led by a reference to some ancient tale. I beseech your majesty, that our young friend may, at my request, be permitted to go on with it." The queen pretended thus not to understand it, that she might have the pleasure of hearing it out, and of witnessing the triumph of truth and virtue, over a heart subject indeed to weaknesses and wanderings, but whose nature was kind, and whose principles leaned to the side of goodness. Indeed, she hoped that the sly allusions of the bard, and his mysterious predictions of some great impending evil, might finally recall her lord from his wanderings, and reunite his heart to her whose right it was. And, moreover, she did not wish that the courtiers should perceive the poet's aim, although that was too apparent to be easily mistaken.

James, who was a notable judge of the perceptions of others, knew, or at least shrewdly suspected, that the queen understood the song, even couched and warped as it was; but he could not, with a good grace, refuse her request; so he consented, and sat in sullen mood till the song was concluded, when he flung out of the saloon with precipitate steps.

It was several weeks before William was again admitted to the king's presence; but the queen gave him a diamond ring, and many rich presents; and having been informed by him, privately, who was the author of the song, she settled upon the old shepherd 100 merks a-year, which she paid out of the rents of her own dowry-lands.

The king, who was always prone to justice, upon due consideration, and taking a retrospect of all that had passed, became convinced that William wished him particularly well; and that the obstinacy he manifested with regard to the song, in persisting in it, and refusing to leave any part of it out, originated in his good-will, and the hopes he entertained of reclaiming his sovereign to virtue.

The result of those reflections was, that William was one day sent for to his majesty's closet, and admitted to a private conversation with him. The king, without once hinting at any former displeasure or misunderstanding, addressed him to the following purpose: "My worthy and ingenuous young friend, do not you remember, that on the first day of our acquaintance, while on our way to Peebles, you hinted to me, that great injuries were frequently done to the common people under my government, by some of their chieftains and feudal barons? This information has preyed upon my heart ever since; for there is nothing that so much concerns me as the happiness of my people, and I am determined to see them righted. In the meantime, it is necessary that I should have some evidences of the truth of your statement, and for that purpose I have formed a resolution of taking a journey in disguise over a part of the realm, that I may be an eye-witness to the existing grievances of which you complain so bitterly. It is not the first time I have made such excursions, unknown to any of my courtiers; and though it appears that they entertained suspicions that I was otherwise, and worse employed, the consciousness of my own good intentions, and the singular adventures I met with, fully compensated me for their mistaken notions. You little know, Sir William, how the actions of sovereigns are wrested by the malicious and discontented; I am fully persuaded, that the wily insinuations thrown out in the old bard's song of the Heron, are founded on reports, which were then circulated." William would fain have asked him, if he had not a pretty page who travelled in his company; but he feared it would be presuming too much, and touching the king upon the sore heel; so he said nothing, but only looked him in the face, and the king went on.–"Now, as you seem concerned about the welfare of the commonalty, and are conversant in their manners and habits, I purpose to take you as my only attendant and travelling companion. We will visit the halls of the great and the cottages of the poor, and converse freely with all ranks of men, without being known. I have been puzzled in devising what character to assume; but, amongst them all, I am partial to that of a travelling bard, or minstrel." William assured his majesty, there was no character so suitable, as it would secure them a welcome reception both with the rich and poor; "and I can touch the harp and sing," said he; "your majesty sings delightfully, and plays the violin; therefore no other disguise, unless we become fortune-tellers, will answer us so well; and the latter we can assume occasionally as we find circumstances to accord." He was delighted with the project; promised all manner of diligence and secrecy, and extolled his sovereign's ingenuity and concern about his people's welfare.

It would be far too tedious to relate circumstantially all the feasts, revels, and tournaments, which prevailed at Peebles and Nidpath, during the stay of the royal party, and likewise at the castle of Polmood, where the festival and the hunt closed for that season; suffice it, that they were numerous and splendid; and while they continued, the vanity of Elizabeth was fully gratified; for she was the admiration of all who beheld her, both high and low.

It may likewise be necessary to mention in this place, that Alexander, duke of Rosay, having joined the party shortly after their arrival at Nidpath, his attentions to Elizabeth were instantly renewed, and were indeed so marked, that they were obvious to the eyes of all the court. Rosay was a gallant and goodly young man, and full brother to the king; and it was too apparent, that Elizabeth was highly pleased with his attentions and unbounded flattery; and that she never seemed so happy as when he was by her side.

In all their walks and revels about the banks of the Tweed, Polmood was rather like an odd person—like something borrowed, on which no account was set, rather than he who gave the entertainment, and on whose account they were all met. When every lady had her lord or lover by her side, Elizabeth, instead of walking arm in arm with Polmood, as was most fitting, was always to be seen dangling and toying with Rosay. Well could Rosay flatter, and trifle, and talk a great deal about nothing—he could speak of jewels, rings, and laces, their colour, polish, and degrees of value. Polmood cared for none of those things, and knew as little about them. He did not know one gem from another, nor could he distinguish a gold chain or ring from one that was only gilt! What company was he for Elizabeth, in a circle where every one was vieing with another in jewels? To flattery he was an utter stranger, for never had one sentence savouring of that ingredient passed his lips; nor could he in any way testify his love or respect, save by his attention and good offices. Alas! what company was he for Elizabeth? Rosay was a connoisseur in music—he understood the theory so far, that he was able to converse on the subject—knew many of the quaint, borrowed phrases, even to *andante, grazioso,* and *affettuoso!* He hung over Elizabeth while she played and sung, expressing his raptures of delight in the most empassioned terms—sighed, shook his head, and laid both his hands upon his breast at each thrilling melody, and dying fall! Polmood loved a song that contained a tale—farther perceptions of music he had none! Alas! what company was he for Elizabeth? Man is always searching for happiness here below; but, blindfolded by passion, he runs headlong after the gilded shadow, until he either falls into a pit, or sticks so fast in the mire that he is unable to return. Polmood had got a wife, and with her he thought he had got all the world—all that mortal could wish for, or desire! So lovely! so accomplished! so amiable!–and so young! The first week of wedlock–the next–the honey-moon past over–and Polmood did not remember of once having had his heart cheered by a smile from his beloved Elizabeth. In the hall, in the bower, and in the rural excursion, every knight had his consort, or mistress hanging on his arm–sitting on his knee, or toying with him; but Polmood had nobody! He saw his jewel in the possession of another, and was obliged to take himself up with any solitary gentleman like himself, whom he could find, to talk with him about hunting and archery; but even on these subjects his conversation wanted its usual spirit and fervour, and all the court remarked, *that Polmood was become an altered man.*

The season for rural sports drew to a close–the last great hunt was held that year in the forest of Meggat-dale–the tinckell was raised at two in the morning, all the way from Blackdody to Glengaber, and the Dollar-law–upwards of 400 men were gathered that day, to "drive the deer with hound and horn." The circle of gatherers still came closer and closer, until at last some hundreds of deers and roes were surrounded on the green hill behind the castle of Crawmel, which is named the Hunter-hill to this day. Around the skirts of that, the archers were placed at equal distances, with seventy leash of hounds, and one hundred greyhounds. At one sound of the horn the whole dogs were loosed, and the noise, the hurry, and the bustle, was prodigious. Before midday sixty deers were brought in, twenty-four of whom were fine old stags, and the rest yearlings and does.

The royal party then dispersed. The queen retired to Holyrood-house, being constrained to remain in privacy for some time–the courtiers to their respective homes, and King James and William to put their scheme in execution. Elizabeth was left with her husband in his lonely and hereditary castle.

The journey of the king's, before mentioned, being so well authenticated, and as so many curious traditions relating to it are still extant in the several districts through which he travelled, I have been at some pains to collect these, and shall give them in another part of this work.

Chapter XV

THE manner in which Polmood and Elizabeth spent the winter is not generally known. In the remote and lonely castle of Polmood they lived by themselves, without any of the same degree near them, with whom they could associate. In such a scene, it may well be conceived, that Elizabeth rather dragged on existence than enjoyed it. The times were indeed wofully altered with her. Instead of the constant routine of pleasure and festivity in which she had moved at court, there was she placed, in a wilderness, among rocks and mountains, snows and impetuous torrents; and instead of a crowd of gay flatterers, who were constantly testifying their admiration of her fine form, beautiful features, and elegant accomplishments, there was she left to vegetate beside a man who was three times her age, and to whose person she was perfectly indifferent, if not averse. Their manners and habits of life were totally dissimilar, and even in the structure of their minds no congeniality could be traced. She never behaved toward him in a rude or uncivil manner, though uniformly in a way that marked the sentiments of her heart, and therefore it was apparent to all the domestics, that their master enjoyed none of the comforts, delights, or privileges of the married state.

On parting with the queen at Nidpath, Elizabeth had promised to visit her at Holyrood-house during the winter; and the hopes of this visit to the court, where she intended to prolong her stay as long as it was possible, kept up her spirits during the first months of her exile; but this journey Polmood had previously resolved not to permit. He had got enough of courtiers for the present; and he well knew, if he could not engage the affections of Elizabeth, when neither rout, revel nor rival was nigh to attract her mind, he would never gain them by hurrying her again into the midst of licentiousness and dissipation. He perceived that, at the long run, he made rather an awkward figure among King James's voluptuous courtiers; nor could he maintain his consequence among them in any other scene save the mountain sports. He was deemed a most gallant knight among the savage inhabitants of the forest; but, in the polished circle of James's court, he was viewed as little better than a savage himself.

Elizabeth had long been making preparations for her intended journey, and about the close of December, she proposed that they should set out; but Polmood put it off from day to day, on one pretence or other, until the Christmas holidays arrived, when he was urged and entreated by Elizabeth, to accompany her to Edinburgh, or suffer her to go by herself. Though that was the first time Elizabeth had ever deigned to entreat him for any thing, he remained obstinate; and at last gave her a mild, but positive refusal. It was a death-blow to the hopes of Elizabeth—her heart sunk under it; and before the evening she retired to her chamber, which she kept for upwards of a fortnight, seldom rising out of her bed. Polmood testified the greatest uneasiness about her health; but sensible that her principal ailment was chagrin and disappointment, he continued firm to his purpose. When he went to see her, she seldom spoke to him; but when she did so, it was with every appearance of equanimity.

During the remainder of the winter she continued in a state of moping melancholy, and this was the season when her heart first became susceptible of tender impressions. When all gayety, hurry, and bustle, were removed far from her grasp, she began to experience those yearnings of the soul, which mutual endearments only can allay. The source of this feeling Elizabeth had not philosophy sufficient to discover; but it led her insensibly to bestow kindnesses, and to court them in return. She was one week attached to a bird with the most impatient fondness, the next to a tame young doe, and the next to a lamb, or a little spaniel: but from all these her misguided affections again reverted, untenanted and unsatisfied. If there had not been something in her husband's manner repulsive to her very nature, she must at that time have been won; for there is nothing in the world more natural, than two of different sexes, who are for the most part confined together, becoming attached to each other. When this cannot be effected even when desired, it argues a total dissimilarity between the parties in one respect or other. Two or three times did Elizabeth manifest a slight degree of attachment, if not of fondness for her husband; but whenever he began to return these by his homely endearments, her heart shrunk from a closer familiarity, with a feeling of disgust which seems to have been unconquerable. How unfortunate it was, that neither should have reflected on the probability of such a circumstance, until it was too late to retrieve it!

About the turn of the year, there came an idle fellow into that part of the country, who said that his name was Connel, and that he was a native of Galloway. He was constantly lounging about the servant's hall in the castle of Polmood, or in the adjacent cottages. Polmood, having frequently met and conversed with this fellow, found that his answers and observations were always pertinent and sensible, and on that account was induced to take him into the family as his gardener; for Polmood was fond of gardening, and he had observed that Elizabeth seemed to take delight in the various flowers as they sprung.

The appearance of this fellow was whimsical beyond conception; he wore a coarse russet garb, and his red carroty locks hung over his ears and face in a manner that was rather frightful. His beard had a yellowish tint, corresponding with the colour of his hair, both of which seemed unnatural, for his eye and his features were fine, and his form tall and athletic, but he walked with a loutish stoop, that rendered his deportment altogether ludicrous. Elizabeth had often observed him, but she never took any further notice of him than to turn away with a smile.

One day, while sitting in her apartment alone, pensive, and melancholy, she cast her blue eyes around on the dark mountains of Herston—she saw the lambs racing on the gare, and the young deers peeping from the covert of the wood; but this view had no charms for her. The casement was open, and Connel the gardener was busy at work immediately before it—she sat down to her lute, and played one of her favourite and most mournful old airs, accompanying it with her voice. She had begun it merely to amuse herself, and scarcely thought of what she did, till she was surprised at seeing Connel give over working, and lean forward upon his spade, in the attitude of listening attentively. But how much more was she astonished, on perceiving, that when she ceased, he wiped a tear from his eye—turned round, and strode with a hurried pace to the angle of the walk, and then turned and fell again to his work; all the while appearing as if he knew not what he was doing. There is no motive works so powerfully upon the female mind, as the desire of giving delight to others, and thereby exciting their admiration. This marked attention of the humble gardener, encouraged Elizabeth to proceed—she sung and played several other airs with an animation of tone, which had never before been exerted within the walls of Polmood, and which raised her own languid spirits to a degree from which they had long been estranged.—Her curiosity was excited—she flung on a dress that was rather elegant, and before the fall of the evening, went out to walk in the garden, resolved to have some conversation with this awkward but interesting gardener.

When she first entered the walk at a distance, Connel stole some earnest looks at her; but when she approached nigher, he never once looked up, and continued to delve and break the clods with great assiduity. She accosted him in that easy familiar way, which those in power use toward their dependants—commended his skill in gardening, and his treatment of such and such plants—Connel delved away, and gathered the white roots, flinging them into a basket that stood beside him for the purpose, but opened not his mouth.

At length she asked him a question, which he could not avoid answering. He answered it; but without turning his face about, or looking up. When he ceased speaking, Elizabeth found herself in a deep reverie–her mind had wandered, and she felt as if striving to recollect something which her remembrance could not grasp. At considerable intervals she brought him to converse again and again; and, as often did she experience the same sensations, these sensations had something painful as well as pleasing in them; but the most curious thing that attended them was, that they were to her altogether unaccountable.

From that time forward the garden seemed to have become Elizabeth's home; and Connel, the clownish but shrewd gardener, her only companion.–She played and sung every day at her window to delight him, and ceased only on purpose that she might descend into the garden to hear him converse, and commend the works of his hands. She was indeed drawn toward him by an irresistible impulse, that sometimes startled her on reflection; but her heart told her that her motives were not questionable.–Love she was sure it could not be; but whatever it was, she began to experience a faint ray of happiness. Polmood perceived it, and was delighted; while Connel the gardener, on account of his inestimable art in administering pleasure to a desponding beauty, shared of his master's esteem and bounty.

Things passed on in this manner, or with little variety, until the end of summer. On the 14th of August, a guest arrived at the castle of Polmood unexpectedly, and not altogether welcome–welcome indeed to Elizabeth, but not so to her husband, who heard him announced with the most galling vexation.–This was no other than Alexander, duke of Rosay, with his suit, who announced the king's intention of being there by the end of the next week. Elizabeth was literally frantic with joy; she scarcely knew either what she was doing or saying, when Rosay alighted in the court, and saluted her with his own and royal brother's kindest respects. Polmood received the duke as became his high dignity, and his own obligations to the royal family; but in his heart he wished him at the distance of a thousand miles. His discernment of human character was not exquisite, but he foresaw a part of what was likely to ensue, and the precognition foreboded nothing good to any one. He felt so much chagrined at the very first rencounter, that he found he could not behave himself with any degree of propriety; and the consequence was, that Rosay and Elizabeth were soon left by themselves. Her complexion had become a little languid; but the sudden flow of spirits which she experienced, lent a flush to her cheek, a fire to her eye, and a rapid ease and grace to her manner, which were altogether bewitching.

Rosay was a professed libertine, and of course one of those who felt little pleasure in aught, save self-gratification; but he had never in his life been so transported with delight, as he was at beholding Elizabeth's improved charms, and seeming fondness of him; for so he interpreted the feelings of her heart, which gave birth to this charming vivacity—these, however, had their origin from a source quite different from that which he supposed.

As soon as they were left alone, in the first transports of his passion he caught her in his arms, and kissed her hand again and again. She chided him—she was indeed angry with him—but what could she do? Situated as they were, she could not come to a professed and open rupture, on account of any little imprudencies which his passionate admiration had induced him inadvertently to commit; so all was soon forgot and forgiven. But whatever freedoms a man has once taken with one of the other sex, he deems himself at liberty to venture on again whenever occasion serves. A lady ought by all means to be on her guard against a lover's first innovations—the smallest deviation from the path of rectitude is fraught with incalculable danger to her—one imprudence, however slight she may deem it, naturally, and almost invariably, leads to a greater; and when once the tale is begun, there is no mathematical rule by which the final sum may be computed, even though the aggressor should advance in the most imperceptible gradation. The maiden that ventures, in any way, to dally with a known libertine in morals, ventures to play around the hole of the asp, and to lay her hand on the snout of the lion.

The reader must by this time be so well acquainted with the character of Elizabeth, as to perceive, that in this fondness displayed for Rosay, there was no criminality of intention—not a motion of her soul that cherished the idea of guilty love—nor a thought of the heart that such a thing was intended on his part. A thirst for admiration was what had hitherto chiefly ruled all her actions—that passion was now, for a season, likely to be fully gratified in the court circle, whose hostess she would be; and, considering the wearisome season she had passed, was it any wonder that she felt happy at seeing the polished Rosay again, or that his adulations and amorous enticements should, from their novelty, be grateful to her volatile heart?

Polmood viewed the matter in a very different light, and in the worst light which it was possible for a husband to view it. He had long had some faint unformed apprehensions of Elizabeth having been the duke's mistress previous to his marriage with her, and thought it was owing to that circumstance, that the king had got the marriage put suddenly over in the absence of Rosay, and had given him so large a dowry with her. It is easy to conceive how galling such an idea must have been to his proud but honest heart. Their behaviour at Nidpath, immediately after the wedding, first engendered these injurious ideas, and this visit of Rosay's went far to confirm them. That the king and his nobles should come into the forest for a few weeks, to enjoy the hunt, without any other sinister motive, was natural enough; but why, or for what purpose, Rosay should have come a fortnight earlier, he could not divine. Perhaps these suspicions were not without foundation, so far as they regarded Rosay; but they were quite groundless with regard to Elizabeth; yet every part of her conduct and behaviour tended to justify the ungracious surmise. Polmood had felt, with silent regret, her marked coldness and disaffection; but when he saw those smiles and caresses, which he languished for in vain, bestowed so lavishly upon a gay and flippant courtier, his patience was exhausted, and from the hour of Rosay's arrival, the whole frame and disposition of his mind was altered. The seeds of jealousy, which had been early sown in his bosom, had now taken fast root—his vigilance was on the alert to ascertain the dreadful truth, and every pang that shook his frame, whispered to his soul the most deadly revenge on the destroyers of his peace. His conversation and manners were, at best, not very refined; but the mood and temper of mind in which he then was, added to his natural roughness a degree of asperity that was hardly bearable. Polmood's company was of course little courted by Rosay and Elizabeth—he discovered this, and set himself only to keep a strict watch over all their motions, and that with every degree of cunning and diligence that he was master of. They were always together; they toyed, they sung, conversed in the arbour, walked into the wood, and sat by the side of the river. In some of their excursions, Polmood could not follow them with his eyes without being seen by them, and therefore desired Connel the gardener to keep a strict watch over their conduct. He needed not have given him this charge; for Connel was more anxious on the watch than Polmood himself: he perceived the snare into which his young mistress was likely to be led, and trembled to think of the consequences. When they sat in the arbour, he contrived to work at something or other, directly in front of it; when they walked, or sat by the side of the river, he was angling there for fish to the table; and when they re-

tired into the wood, Connel the gardener was there, cutting off twigs
to make baskets, or birches wherewith to dress his garden. He resolved to watch them at all events, and haunted them like their evil
genius. Rosay often cursed him; but Elizabeth seemed always very
glad to see him, and took every occasion of conversing with him, as
she and her gay gallant passed. If Connel ever perceived any improprieties in their conduct, he concealed them; for his report to his
master was always highly favourable, as far as they regarded Elizabeth; but he once or twice ventured to remark, that he did not consider Rosay a character eminently calculated to improve the morals
of any young lady. Polmood bit his lip and continued silent—he was
precisely of the same opinion, but could think of no possible expedient by which they might be separated. His jealousy had increased
his ingenuity; for he had devised means by which he could watch all
their motions in the hall, the parlour, and the arbour, without being
seen. This was rather an undue advantage, for who would wish to
have all their motions and actions subjected to such a scrutiny?

The time of the king's arrival approached, and Polmood, with all
his vigilance, had not hitherto discovered any thing criminal in their
intercourse. He had, however, witnessed some familiarities and
freedoms, on the part of Rosay in particular, which, if they did not
prove, still led him shrewdly to suspect the worst. But now a new
and most unexpected discovery was effected, which enkindled the
ignitable pile of jealousy into the most furious and fatal flame.

Chapter XVI

FROM the time that Rosay arrived, poor Connel the gardener seemed
to labour under some grievous malady, and became thoughtful and
absent. He took pleasure in nothing save herding his fair mistress
and her spark; and it was evident to all the menials, that some great
anxiety preyed upon his mind. Elizabeth, too, had observed this
change in her humble but ingenuous dependant, and had several
times inquired the cause, without being able to draw from him any
definite answer.

One day Elizabeth had left for a while the delightful treat of flip-
pancy, banter, and adulation, for the more sober one of holding a
little rational conversation with Connel, and the following dialogue
past between them: "I have long had a desire to hear your history,
Connel. You once told me that your parents were in good circum-

stances; why, then, did you leave them?" "It was love that occasioned it, madam." This answer threw Elizabeth into a fit of laughter; for the ludicrous idea of his having run away from the object of his affection, together with the appearance of the man, combined in presenting to her mind an image altogether irresistible. "So you really have been seriously in love, Connel?" "Yes, madam, and still am so seriously in love, that I am firmly convinced no living man ever loved so well, or with such unalterable devotion, as I do. Pray, were you ever in love, if it please you, madam?" "A pretty question that, considering the state in which you find me placed." Connel shook his head. "But if you, who are a lover, will describe to me what it is to be in love, I may then be able to answer your question with certainty." "Between two young people of similar dispositions, it is the most delightful of all sensations; all the other generous feelings of the soul are not once to be compared with it—Please, dear madam, did you never see any man of your own age whom you could have loved?" Elizabeth appeared pensive—her mind naturally turned upon the young Baron Carmichael. In her wearisome days and nights she had often thought of him, and of what she might have enjoyed in his company; for, though Elizabeth had little or no foresight, but acted, for the most part, on the impulse of the moment, or as contingent circumstances influenced her, she had nevertheless a clear and distinct memory, and was capable of deep regret. She made no answer to Connel's query, but at length accosted him as follows: "I should like to hear the history of your own love, Connel; that is the chief point at which I aim." "Alas! it is nearly a blank, my dear lady. I love the most sweet, the most lovely creature of her sex; but fate has so ordered it, that she can never be mine." "If you love her so dearly, and she return that love, one would think you might hold fate at defiance." "She did affect me, and, I am convinced, would soon have been won to have loved me with all her heart; but that heart was inexperienced—it was over-ruled by power, and swayed by false argument; and before ever she got leisure to weigh circumstances aright, she was bestowed upon another." "And do you still love her, even when she is the wife of another man?" "Yes, madam, and more dearly than I ever loved her before. I take no delight in any thing with which she is not connected. I love to see her—to hear her speak; and, O! could I but contribute to her happiness, there is nothing on earth that I would not submit to." "Now, you tell me what is impossible; such pure disinterested love does not exist between the sexes as that you pretend to." "Indeed, but it does, madam." "I cannot believe it." "Yes, you will soon believe it; and I can easily convince you of that." On saying this, he loosed a small tie that was behind his neck, and pulling his red beard and wig over his head, there stood Connel, the clownish gardener, transformed into the noble, the accomplished, young Baron Carmichael.

Elizabeth was singular for her cool unmoved temper and presence of mind; but in this instance, she was overcome with astonishment, and for about the space of two minutes, never was statue cast in a mould so striking. Her fine form leaned forward upon the air in a declining posture, like an angel about to take leave of the dwellings of men—her hands upraised, and her eyes fixed upon her lover, who had sunk on his knees at her feet—from him they were raised slowly and gradually up to heaven, while a smile of astonishment played upon her countenance that quite surpassed all description— "Carmichael!" exclaimed she, "Good God of heaven! is it possible!" He attempted to speak and explain his motives, but she interrupted him: "Make haste and resume your impenetrable mask," said she; "for if you are discovered, we are both undone." So saying, she hurried away from him, agitated in such a manner as she had never been before. She posted from one part of the castle to another, tried an hundred different postures and positions, and as often changed them again. She tried to ponder, but she was not used to it—she could reflect on what was past with a hurried restless survey, but no scheme or mode of procedure could she fix on for the future. It was, upon the whole, a sweet morsel; but it was mixed with an intoxicating and pungent ingredient. The adventure had something pleasingly romantic in it; yet she feared—she trembled for some consequence—but did not know what it was that she feared.

In this mood she continued about two hours, shifting from place to place—rising, and as hastily sitting down again, till at last she sunk upon a couch quite exhausted, where she fell into a profound sleep. She had, all this while of restlessness, been endeavouring to form a resolution of banishing Carmichael instantly from her presence, but had not been able to effect it.

There is nothing on which the propriety and justice of any action so much depends, as the temper of mind in which the resolver to do it is framed. And there is, perhaps, no general rule more unexceptionable than this, that when a woman awakens out of a sound and guiltless sleep, her heart is prone to kindness and indulgence. The lover, who had before grieved and wronged her, she will then forgive, and shed a tear at the remembrance of former kindnesses. The child, that had but lately teased and fretted her almost past endurance, she will then hug with the fondest endearment; and even if an inferior animal chance to be nigh, it will then share of her kindness and caresses.

In such a soft and tender mood as this was Elizabeth's resolution formed with regard to her behaviour towards Carmichael. She had dreamed of him in her late sleep, and her fancy had painted him all that was noble, kind, and generous in man–every reflection in which she indulged, terminated favourably for Carmichael–every query that she put to her own mind, was resolved upon the most generous principles, and answered accordingly. The consequence of all this was, that, long before evening, she was again in the garden, and spent at least an hour in the company of the enamoured and delighted gardener.

From that hour forth was Elizabeth estranged from Rosay; for the delineation of his character now formed a principal theme of conversation between her and Carmichael. It was on purpose to prevent her, if possible, from falling into Rosay's snares, that Carmichael had at that time discovered himself; for he saw that her condition and state of mind peculiarly subjected her to danger, if not to utter ruin. Rosay being now deprived of his lovely companion all at once, was left by himself to reflect on the cause, and Polmood and he were frequently left together, although they were not the most social companions in the world. Elizabeth had flowers to examine–she had berries to pull–she had arbours to weave–and, in short, she had occasion to be always in the garden. Polmood perceived this change, and was glad, while Rosay was chagrined beyond measure.

What this sudden and complete change in Elizabeth's behaviour proceeded from, Rosay was utterly at a loss to guess–nor knew he on whom to fix the imputation. Her husband it could not be, for she was less in Polmood's company than in his own. He could not be jealous of the comical red-headed gardener; but he shrewdly suspected, that it was owing to some insinuation of his, that he was thus baulked in his amour, when he conceived the victory as certain as if it had been already won.

Jealousy has many eyes, and is ever on the watch–Rosay learned one day that Elizabeth and her gardener, who were seldom asunder, were to be employed in gathering wood-rasps for a delicate preserve, which she was busied in preparing; and having observed a brake near the castle, where these berries were peculiarly abundant, he was assured they would seek that spot; so he went previously and hid himself in the heart of a bush, in the middle of the thicket, where he heard, without being observed or suspected, a full half hour's conversation between the lovers. He heard his own character very freely treated, and besides, discovered the whole secret; at least he discovered, that Connel, the gardener, was no other than Elizabeth's former lover, the banished Baron Carmichael. Chagrined at his utter disappointment, and full of revenge at hearing his character and motives painted in their true colours, he hasted to apprise Polmood of the circumstance.

When he arrived at the castle, Polmood was gone out; but impatient of delay, and eager for sudden vengeance, he followed to seek him, that he might kindle in his breast a resistless flame, disregarding any other consequences than the hurt it was likely to bring upon his rival. It chanced that they took different directions, and did not meet, until they encountered each other on the green before the castle.

Elizabeth was then sitting at her lattice, and perceiving the unusual eagerness with which Rosay came up and accosted Polmood, she dreaded there was something in the wind. She observed them strictly, and all their gestures tended to confirm it. After they had exchanged a few sentences, Rosay, as if for the sake of privacy, took his host by the hand, and led him to an inner-chamber.

The apartments of these old baronial castles were not ceiled up so close as chambers are now; and, if one set himself to accomplish it, it was not difficult to over-hear any thing that passed in them.

Whether it was fears for her adventurous lover, the natural curiosity inherent in the sex, or an over-ruling providence, that prompted Elizabeth at that time to go and listen, it is needless here to discuss. Yet certainly she did go, and, with trembling limbs and a palpitating heart, heard the secret fully divulged to her husband, with many aggravations, ere it had been many days revealed to herself. Easily foreseeing what would be the immediate consequence, she, hastening back to the garden, warned Carmichael instantly to make his escape, and mentioned a spot where he would find all the necessaries of life by night, provided he thought it safe to hide in the vicinity. Carmichael, expecting from this hint, that he might sometimes meet herself at that spot, without waiting to make any reply, took her advice—slipped into the wood, and continued his flight with all expedition, till he was out of danger of being overtaken. The spot which the baron chose for a hiding-place is well known, and is still pointed out by the shepherds and farmers of *the Muir*; for so that district is called. It is a little den near the top of Herston-hill, from which he could see all that passed about the castle of Polmood; where no one could approach him without being seen at the distance of half a mile, and if danger appeared on either side, he could retire into the other side of the hill with all deliberation, and without the smallest risk of being discovered. Here we will leave him to linger out the day, to weary for the night, and, when that arrived, to haunt the lanes and boor-tree-bush above Polmood, in hopes to meet his lovely misguided Elizabeth, and return to the scenes of violence and mystery at the castle of Polmood.

Chapter XVII

ROSAY had no sooner informed Polmood of the singular circumstance, that Connel the gardener was young Carmichael of Hyndford in disguise, than he formed resolutions of the most signal vengeance on the impostor, on Elizabeth, and on Rosay also. The truth of Rosay's statement he could not doubt, as a thousand things occurred to his mind in testimony of it; but he viewed this anxious and acrimonious act of divulgement merely as the effect of jealousy and rivalship; for with him no doubt remained but that Elizabeth was alike criminal with both. He had, both now and on a former occasion, witnessed her open dalliances with Rosay; and when he considered how long he had been duped by her and another paramour, by his former inveterate rival in disguise, it must be acknowledged, it was not without some reason that he now viewed his wife in the worst light in which it was possible any man could view a wife.

He pretended to treat Rosay's information with high contempt, but the emotions of his heart could not be concealed.—In a short time thereafter, he sallied forth into the garden with a frantic impatient mien, and having his sword drawn in his hand. What might have been the consequences cannot now be positively determined, but it was certainly fortunate for Connel, the gardener, that he was out of the way; as the enraged baron sought every part where he was wont to be employed, and every lane where he used to stray, to no purpose; but having no suspicions of his flight, he hoped to meet with him before the evening, and resolved to restrain his burning rage till then.

On that very evening King James and his nobles arrived at the castle of Polmood, with all their horses, hounds, hawks, and other hunting appurtenances. All was hurry, noise, bustle, and confusion. Polmood received his royal master with all the respect, kindness, and affability, which he was master of at the time; but James, whose discernment of character was unequalled in that age, soon perceived the ferment of his mind.

Elizabeth did all that lay in her power to entertain her guests, and to render them comfortable; and she succeeded to a certain degree. Polmood complained of a severe illness—left the banquet again and again—walked about with his sword in his hand, watching for the base, the unprincipled gardener, resolving to wreck the first effects of his fury on him; but he was no where to be found, nor could any of the menials give the smallest account of him. Elizabeth's gayety and cheerfulness he viewed as the ebullitions of a mind callous to every sense of moral obligement and innate propriety; like one who views a scene with a jaundiced eye, every thing appears with the same blemished tint; so to his distempered fancy a crime was painted in every action of his unwary and careless spouse, however blameless that action might be.

He returned to the hall, sat down, drank several cups of wine in a kind of desperation, and, like a well-bred courtier, laughed at his majesty's jests as well as he could; but he neither listened to them, nor regarded them for all that, because the fury of his heart grew more and more intolerable, and most of all, on learning the arrangements which were made in the castle for the lodging of their guests. These were such, as he deemed the most complete imaginable for preventing him from all command of, or watch over, his faithless spouse while the company remained, and such as appeared the most convenient in the world for an uninterrupted intercourse between her and Rosay. Jealousy reads every thing its own way, and so as to bear always upon one point; although, as in the present instance, that way is generally the one farthest from truth.

Elizabeth never acted from any bad motive: her actions might be fraught with imprudence, for she acted always as nature and feeling directed, without considering farther of the matter. Thoughtless she certainly was, but a mind more chaste and unblemished did not exist. Her chamber was situated in the upper storey, and the best in the castle; but (though with the utmost good humour) she had always declined passing a night in the same chamber with her husband, from the day after their marriage to the present moment, and at the present time she had given up her apartment for the accommodation of two of the royal family. Polmood, who did not know of this circumstance, was appointed to sleep among twelve or fourteen others in temporary beds in the middle flat, and Elizabeth took up her lodging with her waiting-maids, on a flock bed on the ground floor.

Several of the nobles did not undress, of which number Polmood was one, who supposed Elizabeth to be in her own chamber, on the same flat with the king, Rosay, and others of the royal line. Strong as evidences had hitherto been against her, he had never been able to discover her in any very blamable situation; yet he had not the least doubt, but that she was that night sleeping in the arms of the Duke of Rosay. Every thing, he thought, seemed to be so well devised for the accomplishment of this wished-for and wicked purpose—whereas they were only so in the distempered brain of the jealous husband, who was now too visibly in a state of derangement.

Polmood could not sleep, but flounced, groaned, and wandered about like a troubled ghost. The more he pondered on recent discoveries and events, the more he became convinced of his disgrace, and judging that it was highly improper in him to suffer them longer to go on in their wickedness under his own roof, he resolved to be assured of it, and then cut them both off at a blow. He arose from his couch, on which he had lately thrown himself—left the apartment, telling those who were awake, that he was extremely ill, and was obliged to walk out—went straight to the chamber of Elizabeth—opened the door, and entered. The nobles, fatigued with their long journey and mellowed with wine, either did not hear the slight noise he made, or did not regard it, being all wrapped in a profound sleep. He soon discovered that there were two in the bed; that the one next him was a man, whom he judged to be Rosay, and he judged aright; and, in the first transport of rage, he would doubtless have run him through the body, if any weapon had been in his hand. He stood some minutes listening to their breathing, and soon began to suspect, that the other, who breathed uncommonly strong, was not Elizabeth. Determined, however, to ascertain the truth, he put over his hand and felt his bearded chin. It was the Lord Hamilton, the constant companion of Rosay, and as great a rake as himself. On feeling Polmood's hand, he awoke; and thinking it was Rosay who had thrown his arm over him, he pushed it away, bidding him keep his paws nearer to himself, and be d—d to him; and at the same time gave him a hearty box or two with his elbow.

It unfortunately happened, that the amorous Rosay had, at that very moment, been dreaming of Elizabeth; for the first word that he pronounced on waking, was her name. Some, indeed, allege that Rosay was not asleep, and that he understood all that was going on; but that he was chagrined at the reception he had experienced from Polmood, and much more at being frustrated in all his designs upon Elizabeth; and that he studied revenge upon both. This is perhaps the most natural suggestion, for there is none so apt to brag of favours from the fair sex as those who have been disappointed. Be that as it may, when Lord Hamilton threw back Polmood's hand, and began, in jocular mood, to return the salute upon his companion's ribs, Rosay winced, pretending to awake, and said with a languid voice, "Elizabeth, what do you mean, my jewel? Be quiet, I tell you, Elizabeth." "What the d—l," said Hamilton, "is he thinking of? D—n the fellow, I suppose he thinks he is sleeping with Polmood's lady." It would be improper to relate all the conversation that passed between them; suffice it to say, that the confession which Rosay made was untrue, like that of every libertine. He said to Lord Hamilton, that he had but judged too rightly, and lamented he should have unfortunately discovered the amour in his sleep. O! how fain Polmood would have wrested his soul from his body; but he commanded his rage, resolving to give him fair play for his life, and to kill him in open day, with his sword in his hand, rather than in his bed. "Ah! how happy a man you are," said Hamilton; "but thy effrontery outgoes all comment; who else would have attempted the lovely and chaste Elizabeth?" "Not altogether so chaste as you imagine," said Rosay; "besides her husband and myself, she has kept another paramour in disguise ever since her marriage." "The devil she has," returned Hamilton; "then I shall never trust to appearances in woman more."

Polmood groaned in spirit—but unable to contain himself longer, he, hastening down stairs, took down a sword from the armoury, and sallied out, in hopes of meeting the licentious gardener. The ferment of his mind was such, that he did not know what he was about. However, when he got into the fields and open air, he grew better; and roved about at will, uttering his moans and complaints to the trees and the winds, without disturbing any one but himself. But, what he little dreamed of, Carmichael overheard some of his lamentations and threatenings that very night.

The morning came, and the party mounted, and rode forth in high spirits to the hunt. From knowing the miserable night which Polmood had past, the generality of the company supposed that he would decline being of the party that day, but he made no such proposal; on the contrary, he was among the first that appeared, dressed in the uniform which all those who joined the royal party in the chase were obliged to wear—he had other schemes in contemplation than that of lingering and pining at home—schemes of vengeance and of blood. The king asked kindly for his health, and how he had past the night—he thanked his majesty, and said he had been but so so. The king bade him not be cast down, for that the ardour of the chase would soon restore him to his wonted health and cheerfulness. Polmood shook his head, and said, he feared it never would.

Early as it was when they departed, Elizabeth was up, and stirring about, seeing that every one had what necessaries he required. Every one seemed more anxious than another to compliment her, and pay her all manner of attention; while she, on her part, appeared to be exceedingly cheerful and happy. It was not so with Polmood: he was so thoughtful and absent, that when any one spoke to him, he neither heard nor regarded, and his hunting-cap was drawn over his eyes.—When his new liberated hounds fawned upon him, he struck them; and when his hawk perched upon his arm, he flung him again into the air.

The tinckell had been despatched the evening before to the heights around the forest of Frood. The place of rendezvous, to which the deers were to be driven, was a place called the Quarter-hill, somewhere in that neighbourhood, and thither the king and his lords repaired with all expedition. But the tinckell was then but thin, the country not having been sufficiently apprised of the king's arrival; the ground was unmanageable, and the deers shy, and the men found it impossible to circumscribe them. The consequence was, that when the dogs were let loose, it was found that there were not above a dozen of deers on the Quarter-hill. The king himself shot one fine stag as he was endeavouring to make his escape; other two were run down by the dogs at a place called Carter-hope; and these were all the deers that were taken that day, at least all that were gotten. The greater number made their way by a steep rocky hill called the Ericle, where they left both the riders and the dogs far behind. But it being the first day of the chase that year, they were all in high mettle, and the hunt continued with unabated vigour—many new deers were started, which drew off the ardent hounds in every direction, and the chase at last terminated around the heights of a wild uncouth glen, call Gamesope. When the straggling parties came severally to these heights, they found that the deers had taken shelter among rocks and precipices, from which it was not in their power to drive them.

Before they got the hounds called in, it was wearing towards the evening. They were, as I said, greatly scattered—so also were the men, who had followed the sound of the hounds and the echoes, until there scarcely remained above two of them together; and, to add to their confusion, a mist settled down upon the heights; and it was so close, that they could not see one another, even at the distance of a few yards. Long did they sound the bugles—long did they shout and whistle, endeavouring to assemble, but the confusion still grew the greater; and the issue ultimately was, that every one was obliged to find his way back to the castle of Polmood, in the best way he could, where they continued to arrive in twos and threes, until near midnight; others did not appear that night, and some never arrived again.

It was natural enough to suppose, that some of the knights, being strangers on those mountains, would wander in the fog and lose their way; but the company were somewhat startled, when it was reported to them a little before midnight, that Polmood's steed was come home without his master. This had rather a suspicious appearance; for of all men, it was the least likely that Polmood would lose his way, who knew every pass and ford in the forest as well as the walks in his own garden. Elizabeth appearing to be a little alarmed, some of the party went out to the stalls to ascertain the truth. What was their astonishment, when, on a close examination, they found that the steed was wounded with a sword; and, besides, that his bridle, mane, and saddle, were all bathed in blood—from the latter, it appeared that a slight effort seemed to have been made to clean it. When they bore this report into the hall, the company were all in the greatest consternation, and Elizabeth grew pale as death. The king trembled; for his suspicions fixed instantly on his brother, Rosay; yet, after watching him for some time with the greatest attention, he could discover not even the most distant symptoms of guilt in his looks or behaviour, as far as he could judge. The reports of individuals were greatly at variance with regard to the time and place where Polmood was last seen; so also were their proposals with regard to what was most proper to be done. At last, it was agreed to call a muster of all who had left the castle of Polmood in the morning, and who were expected there that night.

On taking the muster, it appeared that other four were wanting besides Polmood. These were—the Lord Hamilton, Lord James Douglas of Dalkeith, Sir Patrick Hepburn, and his friend the Laird of Lamington. Some of those, it was conjectured, might have lost their way; but that Polmood should have lost his there was no probability.

All remained in doubt and perplexity until the morning. When the morning came, a great number of people from all quarters arrived at the castle, in order to assist the king and his nobles in driving the deer; but he told them, that he meant to give his horses and hounds some rest, until he saw what had occasioned the present unaccountable defection; and, in the mean time, ordered that every house in the country adjacent, and every part of the forest, should be searched with all diligence, and every inquiry made concerning the knights who were missing; and, likewise, that the lieshmen should exert themselves in recovering their scattered hounds, many of whom were still missing.

All this was promptly obeyed, and parties of men were sent off in every direction. The two lords, Douglas and Hamilton, were soon found. They had completely lost their way in the mist the evening before, and were conducted by a shepherd to the castle of Hackshaw, on the border of the forest, where they had received a curious entertainment from an old churlish and discourteous knight named Hugh Porteus; but the others they had not seen, nor did they know any thing concerning them.

At length, after much searching to no purpose, one of the parties, in returning homeward, at the very narrowest and most impassable ford of Gamesope, found the bodies of two knights lying together; but the heads were severed from them, and carried away, or so disposed of, that they could not be found. Both their swords were drawn, and one was grasped so firm in a cold bloody hand, that it could scarcely be forced from it; and, from the appearance of the blood upon that sword, it was evident almost to a certainty, that some deadly wounds had been given with it.

All this was perfectly unaccountable; and, as the uniform which the king's party wore was precisely the same on every one, even to the smallest item, they could not distinguish whose bodies they were which had been found; and after they were borne to Polmood, and subjected to the most minute examination, there were not three present who could agree in opinion concerning them. The one, from the slenderness of the form, was judged to be that of Sir Patrick Hepburn; but whether the other was the remains of Norman of Polmood, or Donald of Lamington, no one of the company could possibly determine. At length, when they had almost despaired of determining the matter absolutely, Polmood's page swore to the identity of his master's sword, and likewise his sandals, or hunting brogues, which ended all debates on the subject. The bodies were buried at Drumelzier, as those of Polmood and Sir Patrick Hepburn, and great mourning and lamentation was made for them by all ranks. The Laird of Lamington was blamed for the murder, and a high reward was offered by the king for his apprehension, but all was in vain; he could never be either seen or heard of.

The more this mysterious business was discussed afterwards, the more unaccountable and incredible it appeared. Hepburn and Lamington were known to be relations, the most intimate and loving friends, and no previous contention existed, or was likely to exist, between them; and as to Polmood, Lamington had never before seen him, so that no grudge or animosity could, with any degree of consistency, be supposed to have actuated either of them in such a bloody business, as to seek the life of the other.

In Rosay's heart, no doubt remained but that Carmichael was the perpetrator of this horrid deed; and he secretly rejoiced that it had so fallen out; for he had no doubt but that the sense of his guilt would cause him to abandon the country with all possible speed; and, if he dared to remain in it, his crime would eventually bring him to the block. In either of these cases, all obstruction to his own designs upon Elizabeth was removed. The gaining of her love was now an acquisition of some moment, as she was likely to inherit the extensive and valuable estate of Polmood, as well as her own dowry-lands.

Now that her husband was out of the way, no one living knew of Carmichael having lurked there so long disguised, save Rosay; therefore, in order that he might not affront Elizabeth, and thereby alienate her affections still the more, and, likewise, that the object of his intended conquest might still retain all her value and respectability in the eyes of the world, he judged it proper to keep that circumstance from being made public. But, that the king's vengeance might be pointed aright, and that Carmichael might not escape justice, if he dared to remain in the country, he disclosed the whole to his majesty in confidence.

James, on hearing the particulars of this singular adventure, likewise conceived Carmichael to be the assassin; yet still there was something remaining which required explanation. If Carmichael was the assassin, what had become of the Laird of Lamington? On what account had he absented himself? or how was it that he could neither be found dead nor alive? There was still something inexplicable in this.

From the very first moment that the rumour of this fatal catastrophe reached the castle of Polmood, the suspicions of Elizabeth pointed to Carmichael, and to him alone. She knew he was still lurking in the neighbourhood, for the provisions and the wine, which she had left in the appointed den, had been regularly taken away; and she had likewise found a note there, written with the juice of berries, begging an interview with her, a request which she had even resolved to comply with; but the thoughts that he was a murderer now preyed upon her mind. The more the affair was developed, the more firmly was she convinced that he had slain her husband in hopes of enjoying her love; and she was shocked with horror at the idea.

She went to the den, which she knew he would visit if still in the country, and left a note below the stone to the following purport:

"Wretch! thou hast slain my husband, and I know it. Let me never see thy face again–fly this place, and for what thou hast done, may'st thou be pursued by the curses of Heaven, as thou shalt be by those of the wronged ——!"

She scarcely expected that he would get this letter; for, like Rosay, she imagined he would instantly flee the land; but on examining the spot next day she found that it was gone.

As soon as the funeral was over, the king withdrew with his suit from the castle, that Elizabeth might be suffered to spend the days appointed for mourning, in quietness and peace. But just as they were about to depart, Rosay besought of his royal brother to suffer him to stay and keep Elizabeth company for some time, representing to him, that Elizabeth had many important family concerns to look after, for which she was but ill fitted, and would be much the better of one to assist her. The king did not thoroughly comprehend the nature of Rosay's designs upon Elizabeth; but he judged that her beauty, qualifications, and fortune, now entitled her to the best nobleman's hand in the realm. He was likewise himself an amorous and exceedingly gallant knight, and knew well enough, whatever the women might pretend, that their real joy and happiness were so much connected with the other sex, that without them, they need not be said to exist. On the ground of these considerations, he agreed at once to his brother's request, on condition that Elizabeth joined in it; but not otherwise.

Rosay sought out Elizabeth without delay, and represented to her, in as strong terms as he could, how lonely and frightsome it would be for her to be left by herself, in a place where such foul murders had lately been perpetrated, and where, as was reported, the ghost of the deceased had already been seen: That though it was incumbent on her to stay a while at the castle of Polmood, in order that she might put her late husband's affairs in such a posture, as to enable her to leave them, and live with her natural protectress, the queen, still there was no decorum nor etiquette forbade the retaining of a friend and protector, who had experience in those matters: That he begged of her to accept of his services for that purpose, and he would wait upon her with all due respect, during the time she remained at her castle, and afterwards conduct her to court, where she might he introduced, either as dame Elizabeth Hunter, or as Elizabeth dutchess of Rosay, whichever she had a mind to. Elizabeth did not at first much relish the proposal, but yet was unwilling to be left alone; and Carmichael having forfeited her esteem for ever, by the foulest of murders, she found that her heart was vacant of attachments, and she gave a ready, but cold consent to Rosay's request, there being no other in the land whom, on consideration, she could choose in preference.

Chapter XVIII

ON the day that the king and his suit departed, there came an old palmer to the castle of Polmood, a monk of the order of Saint John of Jerusalem, who craved an asylum in the castle for a few days, with much singularity and abruptness of manner. It was well known, that the reign of James the IV. was not more singular for its gayety than its devotion, and that the court took the lead in the one as well as the other. Pilgrimages to the shrines of different saints were frequent, and all those in holy orders were reverenced and held in high estimation; therefore the request of the old monk was readily complied with, uncouth as his manner seemed; and a little dark chamber, with only one aperture, in the turret of the castle, was assigned to him for a lodging. He was a man of melancholy and gloom, and he shunned, as much as possible, all intercourse with the inhabitants of the castle and places adjacent. He ate little—kept closely shut up in his chamber by day—but in the twilight was often seen walking about the woods; and then, his manner, even at a distance, bespoke a distempered mind. His step was at one time hurried and irregular; at another, slow and feeble, and again all of a sudden he would pause and stand as still as death. He was looked upon as a fanatic in religion; but, as he offered harm to no living, he was pitied, and loved rather than feared. He was often heard conversing with himself, or with some unseen being beside him; but if any one met or approached him, he started like a guilty person, and slunk away into the wood, or among the deep banks of the river.

It is now time to mention, that Carmichael did not fly the country, as Elizabeth expected; but, as no more victuals or wine were deposited in the appointed den, he found that to remain longer there in entire concealment was impracticable, and, therefore, that some new expedient was absolutely necessary. He was by the king's express command, and under the forfeiture of his life, banished twenty miles from court, wherever the court might be, and so long were the miles in those days, that Carmichael durst not approach his own hereditary domains when the court was at Edinburgh; but as the court was now at Crawmel, and within five miles of him, the danger of being discovered at that time was redoubled; besides which, the prejudice of the country was likely to run strongly against him, on account of the late murders. But notwithstanding of all this, so rooted were his affections upon Elizabeth, that maugre all danger and opposition, he determined to remain near her.

Some other disguise being now necessary—he threw away his red wig and beard, and, without any farther mask, equipped himself as a humble shepherd, with a gray plaid about his shoulders, and a broad blue bonnet on his head. He went and offered his services to one of his own tenants, who held the farm of Stenhope, in the immediate vicinity of Polmood.

His conditions were so moderate, that his services were accepted of, and he set about his new occupation with avidity, in hopes of meeting with his beloved Elizabeth—of being again reconciled to her, and perhaps of wrapping her in his gray plaid, in the green woods of Polmood—but wo the while! she had again subjected herself to the guidance and the snares of the unprincipled Rosay.

He watched the woods and walks of Polmood, with more assiduity than his own flock; but so closely was Elizabeth haunted in these walks by Rosay, that he could never once encounter or discover her alone; he nevertheless continued to watch her with increased constancy, for he loved her above every other thing on earth.

Had Rosay been any other person than the king's own brother, he would have challenged him instantly; but, as it was, had he done so, complete ruin to him and his house would have ensued. However, rather than be completely baffled, he seems to have half determined on doing it. It is perhaps unwarrantable to assert, that he really formed such resolution, but it is certain he kept always his broad-sword hid in a hollow tree, at the entrance into the wood of Polmood, and whenever he strayed that way, he took it along with him below his plaid, whatever might happen.

A dreadful sensation was by this time excited about the castle of Polmood. A rumour had circulated, even before the burial of the two murdered chieftains, that the ghost of the late laird had been seen in the environs of the castle; which report was laughed at, and, except by the peasantry, totally disregarded. But, before a week had elapsed, the apparition had been again and again seen, and that by persons whose veracity could not be disputed. The terror became general in the family, particularly over the weaker individuals. It reigned with such despotic sway, that even the stoutest hearts were somewhat appalled. The menials deserted from their service in pairs— horror and sleepless confusion prevailed every night—comments and surmises occupied the day, and to such a height did the perturbation grow, that Elizabeth, and her counsellor Rosay, were obliged to come to the resolution of a sudden departure. A short day was fixed on for the disposing of the costly furniture, or sending it away, and the castle of Polmood was to be locked up, and left desolate and void, for an habitation to the owlets and the spirits of the wilderness.

The report at first originated with the old housekeeper, who averred that she had heard her late master's voice; that he spoke to her distinctly in the dead of the night, and told her of some wonderful circumstance, which she could not remember, from having been so overpowered by fear; but that it was something about her lady. She delivered this relation with apparent seriousness; but there was so much incongruity and contradiction in it, that all who were not notoriously superstitious disbelieved it.

Shortly after this, a young serving man and a maiden, who were lovers, had gone out after the labours of the day into the covert of the wood, to whisper their love-sick tale. They were sitting in a little semi-circular den, more than half surrounded by flowery broom, which had an opening in front to an avenue in the wood; and the maid was leaning upon her lover's bosom, while he was resting against the bank, with his arms around her waist. Often before had they conversed on their little plans of future life, which were unambitious, and circumscribed within a narrow sphere. They were that night recapitulating them; and as much of their dependance had been on the bounty and protection of their late master, they could not dwell long on the subject without mentioning him, which they did with the deepest regret, and with some significant and smothered exclamations. From one thing to another, so serious and regretful was their frame of mind, that it led to the following dialogue, a singular one enough to have taken place between two young lovers, and at that hour of the evening, as the day-light was just hanging with a dying languishment over the verge of the western hill.

"It is a sad thing that I cannot give over dreaming, William," said the fair rustic. "Do you think there is any other person so much troubled with their dreams as I am?" "Your dreams must be always good and sweet, like yourself, Anna." "They are always sweet and delightful when I dream about you, William; but I have had some fearsome dreams of late; heavy, heavy dreams! Ah! such dreams as

I have had! I fear that they bode no good to us. What is it to dream of the dead, William?"

"It generally betokens good to the dreamer, or to those who are dreamed of, Anna." "Ah, William, I fear not! I have heard my mother say, that there was one general rule in dreaming, which might always be depended on. It was this, that dreams never bode good which do not leave grateful and pleasing impressions on the mind;— mine *must* be bad, very bad indeed! How comes it, William, that whenever we dream of the dead, they are always living?" "God knows, Anna! it is a curious reality in the nature of dreaming. We often dream of the living as being dead; but whenever we dream of those that are dead, they are always alive and well." "Aye, it is indeed so, William; and we never then remember that they are departed this life—never once recollect that the grave separates us and them." "All these things have a language of their own, Anna, to those who understand them; but they are above our comprehension, and therefore we ought not to think of them, nor talk of them; for thinking of them leads us into error, and talking of them makes us sad; and to obviate both these, I will reave a kiss from your sweet lips, my Anna, and compel you to change the subject." "O no, William, do not; I love to talk of these things, for I am much concerned about them; and whatever concerns me I love to talk of to you."—"And, pray, what may those dreams have been, which have given my Anna so much concern?"

"I have been dreaming, and dreaming of our late master, William! Ah, such dreams I have had! I fear there has been foul play going on." "Hush, hush, my Anna! we must not say what we think about that; but, for my part, I know not what to think."—"Listen to me, William, but don't be angry, or laugh at me; I believe, that Alice the housekeeper's tale, about the ghost that spoke to her, is every word of it true."—"Do not believe any such thing, my dear Anna; believe me, it is nothing more than the workings of a distempered imagination. Because the late events are wrapt in mystery, the minds of individuals are oppressed by vague conjectures, and surmises of dark and infamous deeds, and in sleep the fancy turns to these images, and is frightened by fantasies of its own creation. I would not have you, nor any woman, to believe in the existence of ghosts."—"Ah, William, I could reason with you on that point for ever, for I must and will always believe in it. That belief gives one a pleasing idea of an over-ruling Providence, of a just God, who will not suffer the guilty and the murderer to escape; nor those of his creatures, who are innocent, to be destroyed. But I know, William, that you will not disbelieve my word, therefore I will tell it to you, though I would not to any other. I said I dreamed of our late master—but, William, I believe as truly as I believe that I am lying in your arms, that I heard him speaking and lamenting last night."—"But that was only in your sleep—it was only through your sleep, my dear Anna, that you heard him."—"No, William; as far as I can judge, I was as fully awake as I am at this moment."—"My dear Anna, you must think no more of dreams and apparitions, there are really no such things in nature as apparitions. I could tell you a tale, that would——"

Here Anna laid her hand upon her lover's mouth to stop him, for she heard something that alarmed her. "Hush!" said she, in a low whisper; "what is that? I hear something coming. Great God! what can it possibly be that is here at this time of night?" They held in their breath and listened, and distinctly heard a slight rustling among the branches, which they at length distinguished to be the sound of something approaching them with soft and gentle steps. It came close to the side of the bush where they lay, and then stood still. They were lying as still as death; but they could see nothing for the broom, while their hearts were beating so, that their repressed breathing was almost cut short. After a considerable pause, it uttered a long deep groan;—terror thrilled their whole frames;—every hair on their heads crept as with life, and their spirits melted within them. Another pause ensued,—after which they heard it utter these words, in a tone of agony, and just loud enough to be distinctly heard:—"Yes, yes! it was she—it was she!—O wicked, wicked Elizabeth!" So saying, it came forward to the opening in the broom, where it stood before their sight. It had one hand upon its breast, and its eyes were fixed on the ground. In that position it remained for about half a minute, and then, in the same voice as before, said, "The torments of hell are slight to this!" On uttering these words, it shook its head with a slow swimming motion, and vanished from their sight. It might have passed into the air—it might have sunk into the earth—it might have stood still where it was, for any thing they knew, as their senses were benumbed, and a darkness, deeper than that of the midnight dungeon, seemed to have fallen upon them.

For a considerable time did they lie panting in each other's arms, without daring to utter a word. William first broke silence: "Great God of heaven!" said he; "what is the meaning of this?"—"Did you see the figure that passed, William?"—"Yes, Anna."—"And did you not know the voice and the stride?" said she.—"Yes, yes! it is needless, it is sinful to deny it! I knew them too well—my mind is mazed and confounded! Eternal God! this is wonderful!"–"Is it not, William? I'm sure we saw him nailed in the coffin and laid in his grave."–"We did, Anna! we did!"–"And we saw him lying a lifeless, headless trunk; and the streams of blood were crusted black upon his arms, and upon his breast! did we not, William?"–"It is true, Anna! it is all true!"–"Yet here he is again, walking in his own real form and manner, and speaking in his own voice." The horror which these reflections occasioned, together with what she had just seen, were too much for the mind of the poor girl to brook: she crept closer and closer to her lover's bosom with a kind of frantic grasp, uttered one or two convulsive moans, and fainted away in his arms.

Agitated as the young man was, his fears for her got the better of his trepidation, or at least gave it a different bias; he sprung up and ran towards the river, which was nigh, to bring her some water. When he came near it, he found he had nothing to carry water in; but, as the only substitute within his reach for such a purpose, by an involuntary impulse, he pulled off his bonnet, and rushed to the side of a pool in order to fill it. But, when he stooped for that purpose, his hurry and agitation were such, that he slipped his foot, and fell headlong into the pool. This accident was not unfortunate, for the sudden immersion brought him better to his senses than any thing else could at that time have done. He soon regained his feet, filled his bonnet with water, and ran towards his beloved Anna. The bonnet would hold no water–so it was all gone in two seconds–however, he ran on, carrying it as if still full to the brim. When he came to her, and found that he could not give her a drink, as the next best resource, he clapped the wet bonnet upon her face, and pressed it to with both his hands. If she had been capable of breathing, he would certainly have suffocated her in a short time; but the streams of water, that ran down her neck and bosom, from the saturated bonnet, soon proved effective in restoring animation.

As soon as she was again able to speak distinctly, they fell both upon their knees, committed themselves to the care and protection of Heaven, and then walked home together, the maiden supported by her affectionate lover.

That very night was the dreadful intelligence circulated among the vassals and menials about the castle, and before noon, next day, it had gained ground exceedingly, and was indeed become a terrible story. It was in every one's mouth, that the ghost of the late laird had appeared to the two lovers in his own natural form and habit; that he had conversed familiarly with them, and told them that he was condemned to hell, and suffering the most dreadful torments;

and that Elizabeth, his own lady, had murdered him.

That their laird should have been condemned to hell astonished the natives very much indeed; for they had always looked upon him as a very good man, and true to his king and country. However, some acknowledged that the spirit had better means of information than they had, and could not possibly be wrong; while others began to make the sage remark, that 'people were ill to know.'

But that Elizabeth should have been the murderer of her lord appeared far more unaccountable, as it was well known that she was at home during the whole of that day on which he was slain, and had spent it in the utmost gayety and bustle, making preparations for the accommodation of her guests in the evening. That she could have suborned the Laird of Lamington to murder him was as improbable; for, saving a slight salute, she had never once exchanged words with him; and it was utterly impossible that she could have held any converse with him, without the rest of the company having known of it.

It would have been blasphemy to have said the ghost was lying; yet, though none durst openly avow it, some went the unwarrantable length of thinking, in their own hearts, that it was misinformed, or had some way taken up the story wrong.

The story reached the ears of Elizabeth. She was far from being naturally superstitious; and had, moreover, associated but little with the country people of Scotland, consequently, was not sufficiently initiated into the truth and mystery of apparitions; nay, she was not even a proselyte to the doctrine, which was a shameful error in her. But, instead of being displeased, as some would have been, at being blamed for the murder of her husband, she only laughed at it, and stated, that she wished the ghost would appear to her, and tell her such a story; that she would walk in the wood every night, in hopes of meeting it, that she might confront, and give it the lie in its teeth.

In this manner did the graceless Elizabeth sport and jeer about the well-attested and sublime truths, so long and so fondly cherished by our forefathers, even after she had heard the two young lovers relate their tale of wonder with the greatest simplicity, and after she had seen the young woman lying ill of a fever, into which her agitation had thrown her.—But mark the consequence:—

On that very night, or the one following, as Elizabeth was lying awake in her chamber, between twelve and one o'clock of the morning, she heard the sound of footsteps coming hastily up the stair. Her heart beat with a strange sensation; but the door of her apartment being locked in the inside, and the key taken out, she therefore knew that it was impossible for any thing to enter there.

However, it came close to her door, where it stopped, and she saw some glimmerings of light, which entered by the keyhole and frame of the door. The door was strong, and the bolt was fast; but, at the very first touch of that mysterious and untimely visitant, the massy lock opened with a loud jerk, and the door flew back to the wall with such violence, that the clash made all the vaults of the castle to resound again;–when, horrid to relate! who should enter but the identical form and figure of her late husband! and in such a guise!–Merciful Heaven! was there ever a female heart, but that of Elizabeth, which could have stood the shock! He was half-naked, with his head and legs quite bare–his colour was pale as death–his hair bristled upon his crown–and his unearthly eyes rolled like those of one in a frenzy, or fit of madness; he had a lighted torch in the one hand and a naked sword in the other, and in this guise he approached the bed where lay, all alone, the beauteous and helpless Elizabeth.

I have often had occasion to mention the cool unmoved temper of Elizabeth's mind; still it was the mind of a woman, and any one will readily suppose that this was too much for the heart of any woman to bear. It was not. Some may term it insensibility, and certainly it bore a resemblance to it occasionally; but it is an old established maxim among the inhabitants of the mountains, that "he who is unconscious of any crime, is incapable of terror;" and such maxims must always be held sacred by the collector of legends. May we not then, in charity, suppose that it was this which steeled the heart of Elizabeth against all sudden surprises and qualms of terror. Some readers may think that Elizabeth's conduct was not quite blameless– grant that it was not, still her heart was so–her errors were errors of nature, not of principle; and on the great basis of self-approval must all actions be weighed; for how can criminality be attached to an action, when by that action no evil whatever was intended? Certainly by no rule in which justice is predominant. Elizabeth was conscious of no guilt, and feared no evil.

When the dreadful spectre approached her bed, she was lying in such an attitude (when her extraordinary personal beauty is considered) as might have made the heart of the most savage fiend relent. Her face was turned towards the door, the bed-clothes were flung a little back, so that her fair neck and bosom, like the most beautiful polished ivory, were partly seen, while one of her arms was lying carelessly outstretched above the coverlet, and the other turned back below her cheek.

Almost any other woman, placed in the same circumstances, would

have swooned away, or raised such an hideous outcry and disturbance, as would have alarmed all within the castle. Elizabeth did
neither—she kept her eyes steadily fixed on the horrid figure, and
did not so much as move, or alter her position, one inch. The apparition likewise kept its looks bent upon her, came onward, and stared
over her in the bed; but in those looks there was no softness, no
love, nor the slightest shade of pity, but a hellish gleam of disappointment, or something resembling it. He approached, turned round,
strode to the other corner of the room, and she heard it pronounce,
with great emphasis, the word "Again!" After which it walked hastily out at the door, which it closed, and left locked as before.

Elizabeth neither arose herself, nor did she call up any of her
household, until it was day, though she lay in a state of the greatest
uneasiness. She was neither terrified nor chilled with dread, but
she was utterly astonished, and what she had seen was to her quite
unaccountable.

Next day she told it to her waiting-maid, who was a great favourite with her, and who implicitly believed it; and she afterwards related the whole to Rosay, who used all his rhetoric in order to persuade her that it was a dream; but she assured him, with the greatest
calmness, that it was not, and requested that both he and the maid
would watch with her in the same chamber the night following. Rosay
consented, but pleaded hard that the company of the maid-servant
might be dispensed with; and though his suit was listened to with
the utmost complacency, it was not granted.

It is necessary, before proceeding farther, to state some particulars of Rosay's behaviour to Elizabeth during the time that had elapsed
of her widowhood; for the motives which induced to such behaviour cannot now be ascertained. He talked now often to her of marriage, as soon as *decency would permit*, and had even gone so far as to
press her to consent, but this was only when she appeared to take
offence at his liberties, and when he could not find aught else to say.
He was nevertheless all the while using his most strenuous endeavours to seduce her morals and gain possession of her person; and,
as the time of their retirement at Polmood was now speedily drawing to a conclusion, he determined to avail himself of every opportunity which his situation afforded, in order to accomplish his selfish purpose. He well knew, that if he could not prevail upon her to
yield to his wishes while they remained in that solitude, and where
Elizabeth had no other person to amuse or attend to her save himself, he could never be able to accomplish it at court, where she
would be surrounded by such a number of admirers. These consid-

erations brought him to the resolution of leaving no art or stratagem unattempted.

The truth is, that Elizabeth seems to have admitted of freedoms and familiarities from Rosay, which she ought not to have admitted; but such being the court fashions in those days, she attributed these freedoms to the great admiration in which he held her person and accomplishments, and not only forgave, but seemed pleased with them. He was accustomed to toy with her, and kiss her hand right frequently; and, indeed, she may be said to have granted him every freedom and indulgence that he could with propriety ask. But either from exalted notions of the dignity of the sex, or out of regard for her exquisite beauty and form, she seems to have hitherto maintained the singular resolution of never subjecting her person to the will of any man living;—if she did so to her late husband, it was more than those who were acquainted with them had reason to suppose. She had always repulsed Rosay sharply when he presumed to use any undue freedoms with her, but with so much apparent gayety and good humour, that the amorous duke knew not what to make of her sentiments. His frequent proposals of marriage she did not much regard or encourage; for perhaps she was aware, that it was only a specious pretence, a piece of courtly gallantry, when he could not find ought better to say. He haunted her evening and morning—led her into the thickest parts of the woods by day, and harrassed her so much every night at parting, that she was always obliged to lock her chamber-door, and refuse every kind of converse after a certain hour. And one evening, having gained admission before it was late, he absolutely refused to go away; on which she rose with much archness as if to seek something—walked off and left him, locking him up fast until the morning. Such was their behaviour to one another, and such their pursuits, when they began to be alarmed with the appearance of the ghost.

It having been agreed, as formerly stated, that Rosay, Elizabeth, and the waiting-maid, should all three watch together in Elizabeth's apartment, on the night following that on which the mysterious guest had first visited her; the scheme was accordingly put in execution. Elizabeth said she believed it would appear again; but Rosay mocked at the idea, and assured her that it would not; for he was convinced Elizabeth had only had a frightful dream. He said, if it had the effrontery to come and face them all three, that, in the first place, he would endeavour to deter it from entering, until it had first declared its errand and business there; and if it did enter without being announced, he should soon make it glad to withdraw. With such a redoubted champion at their head, the women began to muster not a little courage.

Accordingly, they went up all three to the apartment between the hours of ten and eleven at night, and placed themselves in a row at the farthest corner of it, with their faces turned toward the door. Elizabeth was employed in sewing a piece of rich tapestry, which had for a long time engaged her at leisure hours.—She was dressed in her mourning apparel, and the duke sat on one side of her, and her woman on the other.

Some time passed away in unmeaning and inanimate chat, which still grew more and more dull as midnight approached. Clocks were then very rare in Scotland, but the hours by night were rung upon the great bell in the porch; at least this was the custom at the castle of Polmood. The warder had an hour-glass, which he was bound to watch with great punctuality, and tell each hour upon the bell.

The twelfth hour was rung, and still nothing appeared; nor was any thing unusual heard. About half an hour afterwards, they thought they heard a door open at some distance, and with great caution—it was somewhere within the castle, but in what part they could not certainly distinguish—the noise soon ceased, and they heard no more of it. The fire had fallen away, and the embers and pale ashes fairly presided over the few live coals that remained, while the cricket was harping behind them without intermission—the lamps burnt dim, for no one remembered to trim them—all was become sullen and eiry, and the conversation was confined to the eyes alone. The bell rung one! There is something particularly solemn in the tone of that little hour at any time—it is no sooner heard than it is gone—the ear listens to hear further, but the dying sounds alone reach it. That night it was peculiarly solemn, if not awful; for the bell was deep-toned, and the night dark and still. As the last vibrations of the tone were dying away, Elizabeth happened to cast her eyes upon Rosay, and she thought there was something so ghastly in his looks, that she could not forbear smiling. She was proceeding to accost him, when, just as the first sounds passed her lips, she stopped short, and raised herself up on the seat, as in the act of listening; for, at that moment, she heard the footsteps of one who seemed approaching the back of the door with great softness and caution. "There it is now;" said she to Rosay, in a low whisper. Rosay's heart seemed to have started into his throat—he was literally choked with terror—he had, however, so much mind remaining, as to recollect something of his proposed plan of operations, and rising, he stammered to-wards the door, in order to prevent it from entering; but ere he reached the middle of the floor, the door flew open, and the same dreadful being entered, in the very guise in which it had come the preceding night.

It was enough for Rosay—much more than he could bear. He uttered a stifled cry, like that of a person drowning, and fell lifeless at full length upon the floor. The waiting-maid took refuge behind her lady, and howled so incessantly, that she never suffered one shriek to lose hold of another. Elizabeth sat motionless, like a statue, with her eyes fixed upon the apparition. It paused, and gazed at them all with an unsteady and misbelieving look—then advanced forward—stepped over the forlorn duke, and looked at the bed. The bed was neatly spread down, without a fold or wrinkle. It took another look of Elizabeth, but that was a look of rage and despair—and turning to Rosay, it put itself in the attitude of striking—laid the edge of its sword upon his neck, in order to take a surer aim—then rearing the weapon on high, it raised itself to the stroke, as if intent on severing his head from his body at a blow; but just when the stroke was quivering to its descent, the vengeful spright seemed to relent—its arm relaxed, and it turned the sword to the left shoulder—mused for a few seconds, and gave the prostrate duke such a toss with its foot, as heaved him almost to the other side of the room, and, without uttering a word, hastily retired, locking the door behind it.

The loud and reiterated cries of the waiting-woman at length brought all within the castle to the door of the haunted chamber. Elizabeth took down the key, and admitted them with the greatest deliberation; but so wrapt was she in astonishment, and so bewildered in thought, that she did not once open her lips to any of them. She retired again to her seat, where she sat down and leaned her cheek upon her hand, paying no regard to the horror of the group, nor to the bustle they made.

The first thing they did was to lift the forlorn duke, who had already begun to manifest signs of returning animation. When they raised him up, they found that his face and breast were all bathed in blood, and conjectured, with great reason, that some foul and murderous work had been going on. They were for some time confirmed in this suggestion, by the asseverations of the duke, who assured them that he was a dead man, and run through the body in a great number of places. On examining his body all over, however, they could discover no mark or wound whatever; and they all agreed in the conclusion, that he had only been bleeding plentifully at the nose. He complained of grievous hurts and pains about his loins; but as Elizabeth never thought proper to inform him how he came by these hurts when in a state of insensibility, he was almost persuaded of what the vassals were endeavouring to impress upon him, namely, that it was all owing to the effects of fear. Rosay had, however, got enough of watching for ghosts—more than he approved of, and frankly declared off; taking at the same time a solemn oath, that he would never lodge another night within the castle of Polmood. Elizabeth rallied him, and said, that he would surely never abandon her in such an unheard-of dilemma, but continue to sleep in the castle as heretofore—that she was perfectly willing to sleep in her own chamber still, for all that was come and gone, and why might not he as well keep to his, in which he had never been disturbed. But he said, that the spirit seemed to have a particular malevolence against him, and he would on no consideration risk another encounter with it. Alas! the next encounter that he had with it was not far distant, and terminated in a more fatal manner, as will be seen in the sequel.

From that time forth, Rosay mounted his horse every night, and rode to the castle of John Tweedie of Drumelzier, returning always to Polmood in the morning; but he never told that chief the real cause why he changed his lodgings. On the contrary, he said, that he did not judge it altogether consistent with decency and decorum, for him to stay in the castle with the young and beautiful Elizabeth every night, now that she had no husband to protect her—that the tongue of scandal might blast her beauty and future fortunes, and therefore he was resolved that no infamy should attach to her on his account. Drumelzier was much astonished at this instance of self-denial; but, as Rosay continued to persist in the plan, he took no notice of it.

Chapter XIX

ELIZABETH remained in the same state as before, without any seeming alarm. During the time of the spectre's late appearance, she had carefully observed and noted every thing that passed, which no one else had done; and the more she considered of it, the more fully was she convinced, that the apparition was a mortal man, made up of flesh, blood, and bones, like other people. Certain that this disguise was assumed to answer some purpose, her suspicion fell on Carmichael as the author of the whole plot, from knowing how expertly he could assume characters, and how he had lately duped herself, the laird, and all the country, as Connel the gardener, even when they were conversing with him daily face to face. Her husband it could not be! then who could it be else, if it was not Carmichael?—Polmood and he were nearly of the same form and stature—but how he was enabled to counterfeit Polmood's looks so well, she could not comprehend;—still, she thought it was some artifice, and that Carmichael must be at the bottom of it.

She had likewise noticed, that the spectre opened the door with a key, which it left in the lock during the time it remained in the room, and then, on retiring, locked the door and took the key with it. She had thought much of that circumstance since it first appeared, and determined to pay particular attention to it; but, as usual, she kept her thoughts to herself. She knew that, when the laird lived, they had each a key to that chamber, and some other places of importance in the castle; and what was become of these keys now she could not discover. However, she resolved to make trial of the spirit's ingenuity, by a simple expedient, with which she had often balked the laird's designs of entering when alive, and she weened that he could not have gained much additional skill in mechanics, nor muscular strength, since he was consigned to the grave. This expedient was no other than suffering her own key to remain in the lock, and turning it half round, so that no key could possibly enter from without; which she put in practice, and waited the issue without the least emotion; but, from the time that Rosay left the castle by night, the apparition never troubled her more.

Some one or other of the vassals, indeed, was always seeing or hearing it every night; and well did the lower orders thereabouts encourage the belief: it was the pleasantest thing that had ever happened in the country; for the young women were all so dreadfully alarmed, that not one of them durst sleep a night by themselves for twenty miles around; and they soon very sagaciously discovered, that one of their own sex was no safeguard at all in such perilous circumstances.

In this manner did the time pass away for several days. Rosay and Elizabeth met every morning—spent the day together, and separated again at night. The shepherd continued to range the woods of Polmood, asking at every one whom he by accident met, for a strayed sheep that he had lost; but, alas! that fair, that beauteous lamb, could he never see, unless under the care of another shepherd—the old crazy palmer persevered in the same course as before; and the unprofitable menials spent the day in sleep and idleness, and the night in fear and trembling; sometimes half a dozen of them in one bed, and sometimes only two, according as the mode of transposition

suited—but all of them in a state of sufferance and bondage. The
time was at hand when that family was likely to be broken up for
ever.

It happened one day that Rosay had led Elizabeth into the thickest
part of the wood, where there was a natural bower in the midst of a
thicket of copsewood; in that bower they were always wont to rest
themselves, and had one day lately been somewhat surprised by a
noise, like that of a stifled cough; but they could not discover from
whom or from whence it proceeded—yet they did not suppose any
to be in that wood but themselves, yet it seemed to be somewhere
near by them.

Into this bower Rosay wanted to lead Elizabeth as usual, but she
objected to it, and said, he never behaved to her in that bower as
became him, and she was determined never more to go into that
bower in his company. Rosay said, that since she had given him the
hint, he would not presume upon her good nature any more by
amorous freedoms; but added, that he would not be denied that
piece of confidence in his honour, especially as she knew that her
commands were always sufficient to guide his conduct—a mandate
he never dared to disobey, though his passion for her were even
more violent than it had hitherto been, which was impossible. She
said, that might be all true, yet it was as good to give no occasion of
putting that power to the test. However, by dint of raillery, and promises of the most sacred regard to her *increasing delicacy*, he prevailed
upon her to accompany him into the bower, where they leaned them
down upon the sward.

Rosay began as usual to toy and trifle with her, while she, in return, rallied him in a witty and lightsome manner—but his amorous
trifling soon wore to rudeness, and that rudeness began by degrees
to manifest itself in a very unqualified manner. She bore with him,
and kept her temper as long as she could, making several efforts to
rise and leave him, which he always overcame. She uttered no complaint nor reproach, but, on seeing his brutal purpose too fairly
avouched, by a sudden and strenuous exertion, she disengaged herself from his embraces at once—flew away lightly into the wood, and
left him lying in vexation and despair.

They had been watched all the time of this encounter, by one who
ought not to have seen them; and what was worse, who saw indis-
tinctly through the brushwood, and judged of the matter quite otherwise than as it fell out, drawing conclusions the most abstract from
propriety of conduct, and the true character of the fair but thoughtless Elizabeth.

She was not gone above the space of one minute, when Rosay heard the noise of one rushing into the bower; and, lifting up his eyes, he beheld the old maniac, who has sometimes been mentioned, approaching him with rapid strides. "Get thee gone, thou old fanatic," said Rosay; "what seekest *thou* here?" The words were scarcely all pronounced, ere Rosay felt himself seized by a grasp which seemed to have the force of ten men united in it. It was the old palmer alone, who appeared to Rosay at that time to be some infernal giant, or devil incarnate, so far beyond all human comparison was the might of his arm. He dragged the weak effeminate duke from his den, who at first attempted to struggle with him; but his struggles were those of the kid in the paws of the lion. He next essayed to expostulate, and afterwards to cry out; but the superlative monster prevented both, by placing his foot upon the duke's neck, and crushing his face so close to the earth, that he was unable to utter a sound. He then, in the course of a few seconds, bound his hands behind his back, run a cord about his neck, and tucked him up on a bough that bent above them. The maniac never all the while spoke a word, but had sometimes gnashed his teeth over his victim, in token of the most savage satisfaction.

As soon as he had fastened up the unfortunate duke, he ran into the wood to seek Elizabeth, who had gone to the eastward. He soon found her returning by another path to the castle; and laying hold of her in the same savage manner, he dragged her to the fatal spot. She had taken great offence at the late conduct of the duke, and had determined to suffer him no more to come into her presence; but when she saw him hanging in that degraded state, pale and lifeless, she was benumbed with horror. "Thou monster!" said she, "who art thou, who hast dared to perpetrate such an act as this?" "I will soon show thee who I am, poor abandoned, unhappy wretch," said he; on which he threw off his cowl, beard, and gown, and her own husband stood before her. It was no spirit—no phantom of air—no old fanatic palmer—it was the real identical Norman Hunter of Polmood—but in such a guise!—Good God! such features! such looks! it is impossible for man to describe them. "Now, what hast thou to say for thyself?" said he. "That I never yet in my life wronged thee," returned she, firmly.—"Never wronged me! worthless unconscionable minion! were not these charms, which were my right, denied to me, and prostituted to others? For thee have I suffered the torments of the damned, and have delighted in their deeds. Thy scorn and perfidy has driven me to distraction, and now shalt thou reap the fruits of it. Long and patiently have I watched to discover thee prostituting thyself to one or other of thy paramours, that I might glut myself with vengeance; and now I have effected it, you shall hang together till the crows and the eagles devour you piecemeal."

Elizabeth held her peace; for she saw that speech was unavailing, and that his frantic rage was not to be staid—it seemed to redouble every moment, for, without the smallest compunction, he threw her down, bound her hands and feet, and, with paralyzed and shaking hands, knitted the cord about her beauteous neck, and proceeded to hang her up beside her lifeless paramour.

It is impossible for the heart of man to conceive any scene more truly horrible than this was. Polmood seems to have been completely raving mad; for he was all the while crying over her in the most piteous rending agony—he was literally trembling and howling with despair, bellowing like a lion or a bull, yet did he not for a moment stay his fatal purpose.

Elizabeth, when she made her escape from the violence of Rosay in the bower, did not turn homeward, but held her course away to the east, until she came to a small mountain stream that bounded the wood. Carmichael was not at that time in the wood but on the hill above it, when, to his joy and astonishment, he perceived her alone, washing her face in the brook, and adjusting some part of her dress. There were but two paths in the wood, by which it was possible to pass through it from east to west, and one of these paths Carmichael knew she behoved to take in her way homeward.

Now, it happened that the fatal bower was situated exactly at the point where these two paths approached nearest to each other. Toward this point did Carmichael haste with all the speed he could make, in order that he might intercept Elizabeth, whatever path she took, and bring her to an explanation. Judge what his sensations were! when, bolting from a thicket, the unparalleled scene of horror, death, and madness, was disclosed to his view at once. Rosay was hanging quite dead, and already was the cord flung over the bough by which the beauteous Elizabeth was to be drawn up beside him. The inexorable ruffian had even laid hold of it, and begun to apply his sinewy strength, when Carmichael rushed forward with a loud cry of despair, and cut both the ropes by which they were suspended. Ere he had got this effected, Polmood grappled with him—cursed him in wrath, and gave him a tremendous blow with his fist. Carmichael returned the salute so lustily, that his antagonist's mouth and nose gushed blood. Carmichael knew Polmood at first sight, for he was then unmasked; but Polmood did not recognise him through his disguise of a shepherd. He, however, grasped him closer, intent on revenge for his bold interference and emphatic retort. Carmichael well knew with whom he had to do, and how unable any man was to resist the arm of Polmood in a close struggle; therefore, by a sudden and violent exertion, he wrenched himself from his hold—sprung a few paces backward, and drew out his sword from beneath his gray plaid. During this last struggle, Carmichael's bonnet had been knocked off, and, at the next glance, Polmood knew him. All his supposed injuries burst upon his remembrance at once, and this second discovery confirmed the whole of his former suspicions. When he saw it was Carmichael, he uttered a loud howl for joy. "Ah! is it then so!" said he, "the man of all the world whom I wished most to meet! Now shall all my wrongs be revenged at once! Heaven and hell, I thank you both for this!" and with that he gnashed his teeth, and uttered another maniac howl.

He drew his sword, or lifted that which had belonged to Rosay, I am not certain which, and flew to the combat. He was deemed the best archer, the strongest man, and the best swordsman of his day. Carmichael was younger, and more agile, but he wanted experience, consequently the chances were against him.

The onset was inconceivably fierce—the opposition most desperate—and never perhaps was victory better contested—each depended on his own single arm for conquest, and on that alone. Carmichael lost ground, and by degrees gave way faster and faster, while his antagonist pressed him to the last: yet this seemed to have been done intentionally; for when they reached a little lawn where they had fair scope for sword-play, the former remained firm as a rock, and they fought for some minutes, almost foot to foot, with the most determined bravery. Carmichael won the first hit of any consequence. Polmood's fury, and the distracted state of his mind, seem to have given his opponent the advantage over him, for he first wounded him in the shoulder of the sword-arm, and in the very first or second turn thereafter, run him through the body.

Polmood fell, cursing Carmichael, Elizabeth, his wayward fortune, and all mankind; but, when he found his last moments approaching, he grew calm, sighed, and asked if Elizabeth was still alive. Carmichael did not know—"Haste," said he; "go and see; and if she is, I would speak with her—if she is not, I suppose we shall soon meet in circumstances miserable enough." Carmichael hastened to the spot where he had cut the two bodies from the tree, where he found the beauteous Elizabeth, living indeed, but in the most woful and lamentable plight that ever lady was in. She was nothing hurt, for she had never been pulled from the ground. But there was she, lying stretched beside a strangled corpse, with her hands and her feet bound, and a rope tied about her neck.

Carmichael wrapped her in his shepherd's plaid, for her own clothes were torn, and then loosed her in the gentlest manner he could, making use of the most soothing terms all the while. But when he raised her, wrapped her in his plaid, and desired her to go and speak to her dying husband, he found that her senses were wandering, and that she was incapable of talking coherently to any one. He led her to the place where Polmood lay bleeding to death; but this new scene of calamity affected her not, nor did it even appear to draw her attention: her looks were fixed on vacancy, and she spoke neither good nor bad. Carmichael strove all that he could, to convince the dying man of the injustice and ungenerosity of his suspicions with regard to Elizabeth, whose virtue he assured him was unspotted, if any woman's on earth was so; and farther said, that it was the consciousness of that alone, which had led her to indulge in youthful levities, which both her own heart, and the example of the court, had taught her to view as perfectly innocent.

Polmood seemed to admit of this, but not to believe it; he however grasped her hand—bade her farewell, and said that he forgave her.—"If you *are* innocent;" said he, "what a wretch am I!—but there is one who knows the secrets of all hearts, and to his mercy and justice I leave you. For my own part I leave this world without any hope; but things must be as they will—I have now no time for reparation.—If you are innocent, Elizabeth, may you be happier than I could ever make you—happier than I wished to make you, you never can be.—But if you are not innocent, may all the curses of guilt fall on you—may you be miserable in this life, as you have made me; and miserable in the next, as I shall be." She was still incapable of making any consistent reply—she sometimes appeared as forcing herself to listen, but her ideas would not be collected—she uttered some broken sentences, but they were totally unintelligible.

Carmichael then, with some difficulty, gained possession of a few leading circumstances, relating to the two bodies that were found at the straits of Gamesope, one of which was taken for that of Polmood himself. The thread of the tale was not very palpable, for the dying chief could only then express himself in short unfinished sentences; but, as far as could be gathered, the circumstances seem to have been as follows.

Polmood had heard on the night before the hunt, as has been related, a confession of Rosay's guilt from his own mouth. Nay, he had even heard him exult in his conquest, and speak of his host in the most contemptuous terms. This excited his rage and indignation to such a degree, that he resolved to be revenged on the aggressor that day—he had vowed revenge, and deprecated the most potent curses on himself, if Rosay was ever suffered again to return and dishonour him under his own roof, and then brag of his lawless delights.—He watched him all the day of the hunt, but could never find an opportunity to challenge him, except in the midst of a crowd, where his revenge would have been frustrated. As it drew towards the evening, he came to the ford of Gamesope, where he halted; judging, that Rosay and Hamilton must necessarily return by that pass, from the course he saw them take. He had waited but a short time, when he saw two riders approach, whom he conceived for certain to be Rosay and Hamilton, whereas they were in truth, Sir Patrick Hepburn and Donald of Lamington. Sir Patrick not only resembled Rosay much in his personal appearance, but his horse was of the same colour; which Polmood did not know, or did not advert to.—It was wearing late—the mist was dark and thick—the habiliments were in every respect similar. All these combined, misled the blindly passionate and distracted Polmood so completely, that he had actually cleft the scull of the one, and given the other his death wound in self-defence, ere ever he was aware of his error.

Desperate cases suggest desperate remedies.—As the only means of averting instant punishment, and accomplishing dire revenge on the real incendiaries, which swayed him much more than the love of life, he put his own sword in Lamington's hand, which he closed firm upon it, and his own sandals upon his feet: he then cut off the heads from the bodies, and hid them, being certain that no one could distinguish the trunks; and, as he deemed, so it fell out. The place where that fatal affray happened, is called Donald's Cleuch to this day.

Polmood had now no way left of approaching his own castle but in disguise. Intent on executing his great purpose of revenge, with every circumstance of conviction to his own heart of the guilt of the parties, he so effectually concealed himself under the cowl, beard, and weeds of a pilgrim monk, that he was enabled to stay in his own castle, get possession of his own keys, and watch all their motions without being suspected.

The inexplicable mysteries of the ghost, and the murder of the two knights, being thus satisfactorily explained to the world, the soul of the great, the brave, the misguided Norman Hunter of Polmood, forsook its earthly tenement, and left his giant mould a pale disfigured corse in the wood that had so lately been his own.

Carmichael conducted Elizabeth home in the most delicate manner possible—committed her to the care of her women—and caused the two bodies to be brought home and locked up in a chamber of the castle. He then went straight and threw himself at the king's feet, declaring the whole matter, and all the woful devastation Polmood's jealousy had occasioned among his friends and followers. The king was exceedingly grieved for the loss of his brother, and more especially at the disgraceful manner in which he had been cut off; but as none knew the circumstances, save Carmichael and Elizabeth, they schemed to keep it secret, and they effected this in a great measure, by spreading a report that his death had happened in another quarter, to which he had been despatched in haste.

The king was soon convinced, that no blame whatever could be attached to Carmichael, as he had slain his antagonist in his own defence, and in defence of a lady's life; and, after questioning him strictly, with respect to the disguises which he had assumed, he was convinced that his motives throughout had been disinterested, generous, and honourable. In matters that related to gallantry and love, James was an easy and lenient judge, and was graciously pleased to take Sir John Carmichael again into his royal favour and protection.

Elizabeth continued many days in a state of mind in which there seemed a considerable degree of derangement. She sometimes maintained, for whole days together, a dumb callous insensibility; at other times she spoke a good deal, but her speech was inconsistent. From that state, she sunk into a settled melancholy, and often wept bitterly when left alone. It appears that she then began to think much by herself—to reflect on her bypast life; and the more she pondered on it, the more fully was she convinced that she had acted wrong. There was no particular action of her life, with which she could charge herself, that was heinous; but, when these actions had occasioned so much bloodshed and wo, it was evident they had been far amiss. Her conclusion finally was, that the general tenor of her life had been manifestly wrong, and that though the line did not appear crooked or deformed, it had been stretched in a wrong direction.

These workings of the mind were sure preludes to feelings and sensations more tender and delicate than any she had hitherto experienced—more congenial to her nature, and more soothing to the female heart. The heart that reflects seriously, will soon learn to estimate the joys of society aright—will feel that it must depend upon others for its felicity; and that the commixture of mutual joys and sorrows is greatly preferable to the dull monotony of selfish gratification.

Carmichael visited her every day for a whole year, without ever once mentioning love. Before this period had expired, it was needless to mention it; gratitude, the root from which female love springs, if that love is directed as it ought to be, so softened the heart of Elizabeth, and by degrees became so firmly knit to him, that she could not be happy when out of his company. They were at last married, and enjoyed, amid a blooming offspring, as much of happiness and peace as this fleeting and imperfect scene of existence can well be expected to confer.

Some may perhaps say, that this tale is ill-conceived, unnatural, and that the moral of it is not palpable; but let it be duly considered, that he who sits down to write a novel or romance—to produce something that is merely the creation of his own fancy, may be obliged to conform to certain rules and regulations; while he who transmits the traditions of his country to others—does wrong, if he do not transmit them as they are. He may be at liberty to tell them in his own way, but he ought by all means to conform to the incidents as handed down to him; because the greater part of these stories have their foundation in truth. That which is true cannot be unnatural, as the incidents may always be traced from their first principles—the passions and various prejudices of men; and from every important occurrence in human life a moral may with certainty be drawn. And I would ask, if there is any moral with which it is of more importance to impress mankind than this?—That he who ventures upon the married state, without due regard to congeniality of dispositions, feelings, and pursuits, ventures upon a shoreless sea, with neither star nor rudder to direct his course, save unruly and misguided passions, which soon must overwhelm him, or bear him farther and farther from the haven of peace for ever.—Never then was precept more strikingly illustrated by example, than in the incidents recorded in the foregoing tale.

King Gregory

KING Gregory sits in Dunbarton tower,
   He looks far o'er the dale and down;
"What boots it me," said Gregory,
   "That all the land I see's my own?

"Scotland is mine by heritage,   5
   And Erin yields and bows the knee,
And the southron lads they frown afar,
   But they darena' parle again wi' me;

"For they ha'e gotten the meddler's cast,
   Their doughty raids ha'e cost them dear;   10
They'll come nae mair to fair Scotland,
   Or dare her sons to deeds o' weir.

"The shield hangs useless in my hall,
   The sword rusts on the yeoman's thigh,
The hind is whistling o'er the dale,   15
   And here sits sachless Gregory.

"O, I may spread my sails of silk,
   And lightly sweep alang the sea,
And I may mount my milk-white steed,
   And chase the dun deer o'er the lea;   20

"But aye at e'en when I come hame,
   Frae the firth or the muirland hill,
I drink my wine, and I list my fame,
   But there's something a wanting still."–

King Gregory sat in Dunbarton tower,   25
   He looked afar o'er land and sea;
He saw his gray hills round him stand,
   And the vale and the greenwood tree.

He saw the links and the shores of Clyde,
   And the sea that rowed with ceaseless play;   30
It was dyed wi' green, it was dyed wi' red,
   And it tryed to climb the rock so gray,

But aye it fell wi' a grumbling sound,
　And left behind the dewy spray.

It was not the mountain, it was not the dale,   35
　Nor the fairy hues that dyed the sea,
Nor the wave that wrestled wi' the rock,
　That drew King Gregory's wistful e'e;

It was the maidens on Leven side,
　That walked or played with blithesome glee,   40
For they were lythe of lire and limb,
　And O, but they were bright of blee!

King Gregory went into his bower;
　That bower was fair and that bower was wide;
King Gregory went into his hall,   45
　And he strode it o'er from side to side.

King Gregory went to his chamber,
　And looked around with joyful brow;
He looked into his royal bed,
　And he found there was meet room for two.   50

King Gregory called his nobles in:
　"My gallant Knights, pray list to me;
My day of life is past the noon,
　And the gray hairs wave aboon my bree.

"Seek me a may of noble kin,   55
　I reck nought of her dower nor land,
Be she a fair and comely dame,
　As fits the Queen of fair Scotland."

Then every Baron rose with speed,
　Who had fair daughters of his own,   60
And ilk ane roosed the child he loved
　Aboon all maids that e'er were known.

O, they were all sae fair and good,
　King Gregory was in ecstasye;
And every ane that was defined,   65
　King Gregory thought, "that's she for me."

But up spake Douglas of the Dale,
    A grim and stalwart carle was he,
"My liege, I have two maidens young,
    But they're somewhat dark, like you and me;   70

"But John of Erol has a maid,
    For comely maik and courtesye,
Her like ne'er clove the summer gale,
    Since Scotland rose up frae the sea:

"That e'er was bred a form sae fair,   75
    Of earthly life I could not ween;
And ever since I saw her face,
    I deemed her formed to be a Queen."

Then every noble Lord stood dumb,
    And cast at him an angry e'e;   80
But all allowed, in sullen mood,
    That Erol's maid was fair to see.

The King has written a broad letter,
    And sealed it with his signet ring;
And he has sent to Erol's Lord,   85
    To bring his daughter to the King:

"And see that she be robed in silk,
    All fringed wi' the gowden cramasye,
For I have neither spouse nor child,
    And Queen of Scotland she shall be."   90

When Erol looked the letter on,
    A blithe and happy man was he;
But ere the half of it was done,
    There was something glistened in his e'e.

Then Erol turned him round about,   95
    And he stamped, and he cried, "O wo is me!
I have pledged my word to Athol's Lord,
    And a Queen my child must never be.

"O might I live to see the day,
    How blithely would I close my e'en!   100

I've seen enough, could I but see
  My bonny Hay the Scottish Queen.

"Haste to the King, my little page,
  And say, my daughter he shall see;
That she's o'ercome with grateful love—   105
  Say that, and leave the rest to me."

O! but King Gregory was fain,
  The beauteous Hay was all his dream;
And aye he combed his raven locks,
  And aye he bathed him in the stream: 110

And aye he haunted Leven side,
  And bent above the wave so cool;
For there was no mirror in the land,
  But the streamlet or the standing pool.

And King Gregory saw his buirdly form   115
  With pleasure never known before;
And King Gregory thought, his hanging brow
  Of majesty the signal bore.

But the rimy fringe upon his beard,
  O! but it grieved his heart to see;   120
And ill he brooked the silver hairs
  That floated o'er his dark e'e-bree.

But John of Erol he was sad,
  Nor wist he how to win the day;
He feared the pride of Athol's Lord,   125
  And he feared the heart of bonny Hay.

For well he knew he long had wooed
  With fondest love and fervencye,
And rowed her in his Highland plaid,
  When there was ne'er an eye to see: 130

And well he knew that maiden's love,
  Is by such long endearments won;
And much he feared that Athol's Lord,
  Erol and Stormont would o'er-run:

He knew, that should the King assay   135
  To wear him in his Highland glen,
He had much better meet again,
  Canute the Dane, and all his men.

The lovely Hay sat in her bower,
  Her gowden locks the breezes swang;   140
And aye she looked to the Athol hills,
  And aye she lilted and she sang,

"The Highland hills are bonny hills,
  Although they kythe so darkly blue;
The rock-rose nods upon the cliff,   145
  The heather-blooms their brows bedew.

"The braes are steep, and the dells are deep,
  And the water sings unto the tree;
Fair is the face of Lowland dale,
  But dearer far yon hills to me: 150

"For all yon hills will soon be mine,
  Their grizly tops and glens of dew;
And mine shall be the bravest Lord
  That ever gathering bugle blew.

"O! he has rowed me in his plaid,   155
  And he has made my bosom fain;
Which never man has done but he,
  And never man shall do again!"

And aye the southland breeze came bye,
  And blew aside her kirtle green;   160
And aye it kissed her glowing cheek,
  And aye it heaved her bosom's screen.

And sure so light and fair a form
  Was never stretched on Ila's shore;
And sure that moulded lily breast—   165
  Ah! it was ne'er so white before!

Yet, from that fair and comely form,
   The lady raised a startled e'e;
The colour altered on her cheek,
   And the tear-drop fell upon her knee.   170

Her song is past, and gone the blast,
   Up stands her father by her side:
"Rise up, rise up, my daughter dear,
   Thou ne'er canst be Lord Athol's bride;

"Or else my life lies in a wad—   175
   Our royal liege has sent for thee;
He bids me robe you in the silk,
   With gowden gear and cramasye:

"For he has neither spouse nor child,
   And past and signed is this decree;   180
That thou, the fairest of the land,
   Forthwith shalt Queen of Scotland be."

"My faith is pledged, and so is thine;
   No royal bed nor crown for me;
I shall be bride to Athol's Lord,   185
   Or bride on earth I'll never be."

"O! daughter of thy father's house,
   Hast thou no memory nor fear?
And well I ween, the Athol Chief
   Would quit thee for a herd of deer."   190

"He'll sooner brave the King and thee;
   He'll come with all his hardy clan;
And then the King will buy his bride
   With blood of many a Lowland man.

"The Grants, the Frasers, and M'Leods,   195
   And wild M'Phersons, him will join;
The warlike Comyns of the North,
   The Gordon, and the brave Aboyne.

"Oh! ere he win Lord Athol's bride,
   Or brave the lion in his den,   200

Trust me, he'll easier cow again,
   Canute the Dane, and all his men.

"Should Athol's Lord yield up his right,
   And neither love nor wrath bewray,
I'll plight King Gregory my troth,   205
   And blithely, cheerly, trudge away."–

The King walked forth by Leven side,
   His leesome thoughts were all of love;
There he beheld a palmer man,
   That watched his path amid the grove.   210

And, ah! he told him such a tale
   Of danger, brooking no delay!
It was of threatened Northern feud,
   Of Athol's love to bonny Hay.

The King sent out a belted knight   215
   To greet the gallant chief, and say,–
"Lord Athol, thou wert aye the man
   That stood by me in battle fray:

"A hardier wight, or braver knight,
   Ne'er conquered by his sovereign's side;   220
And thee I'll trust, and only thee,
   To bring me home my lovely bride:

"For I have courted Erol's maid,
   And gained her heart right pleasantlye;
Be thou bedight in goodly gear,   225
   My knight and bridesman thou shalt be."

Lord Athol strode into his hall;
   It was too bounded for his grief:
Lord Athol strode into the field,
   In proud resolve to seek relief.   230

He weighed it up, he weighed it down,
   The circumstance and the degree;
He found the King was blameless knight,
   And sighed for woman's treachery.

"Wo that my eye was ever turned 235
    On piece of false and fickle clay!
Wo that my peace was ever set
    Upon that floweret of a day!

"O! she could love, and she could smile!
    And she could sigh, and weep withal! 240
But, ah! that love of selfish wile
    Could not withstand a coronal.

"And she expects, that I will come
    And whine, and talk of broken vow;
And she expects that I will kneel 245
    Beneath her pride and scornful brow.

"But I will show that imp of pride,
    Her hopes of triumph are but vain;
And, though revenge is in my power,
    How easily I can break the chain." 250

The days rolled on. O, they were long!
    Yet, still regretted, passed away;
The nights went bye with weary pace,
    O sleepless nights to lovely Hay!

For every hour she hoped to see 255
    Lord Athol at her father's door;
She longed to see the Highland clans,
    The target, and the broad claymore.

No rescue came!–The day arrived,–
    Oh! cold, cold ran old Erol's blood! 260
There came a loud rap to the gate,
    And at that gate Lord Athol stood,

With seven score clansmen him behind,
    Well mounted, and in bright array;
Old Erol ran into the hall, 265
    Shouting, "To arms, to arms, hurra!

"Haste, warder, to the northern tower,
　　And peal the gathering note amain,
Till every tree bawl forth the sound,
　　From Ila ford to Dunsinnane."　　　　　　　270

O! loud, loud did the maiden laugh,
　　To see old Erol in the gin;
And, loud, loud, was the knock and call;
　　But none would let Lord Athol in.

He heaved the guard-stone from the earth,　　275
　　With strength beyond the wizard's spell;
And dashed it on the iron gate,
　　Till bolts and bars in flinders fell.

Old Erol came into the court,
　　He saw that better might not be;　　　　　280
He touched his bonnet with his hand,
　　Aware of Athol's injury.

"Lord Athol, if thou'rt come to fight,
　　Trust me, thou shalt have routh of weir—
Lord Athol, if thou art come to feast,　　　285
　　There is no knight so welcome here."

A frown hung on Lord Athol's brow;
　　He turned him round upon his heel—
"I come to bear the King his bride;
　　Here is his hand and royal seal."　　　　　290

Old Erol looked the letter on,
　　He scarcely could believe his e'e;
"Our royal Liege is sore misled,
　　I will not yield the maid to thee."

"Then, by my faith, I must her take,　　　　295
　　In spite of all that bars my way;
I bear my order from my King,
　　Which yet I never did gainsay."

He pulled his broadsword from his thigh,
　　It flickered like the meteor's ray;　　　　300

"Lay on them, lads," Lord Athol cried,
　"I long with such to have a fray."

Clash went the swords along the van,
　That onset might not be withstood;
The Highland horse, they were so fierce,　　305
　They bathed their hooves in Lowland blood.

The battle's lost—the bride is won—
　The pipes a merry strain resound;
She weened it was a bold device,
　And to the Highlands they were bound.　　310

O! never was a maiden's look
　So fraught with wonder and dismay!
They did not turn to Ila ford,
　But downward bore upon the Tay.

They plunged into the darksome wave,　　315
　O but the ford was deep and wide!
But they set their faces to the stream,
　And steadily they stemmed the tide.

Away they rode by Almond ford,
　And by the side of silver Earn;　　320
But where they went, or what was meant,
　The bonny Hay had yet to learn.

And aye the bride had something wrong,
　Her veil or scarf was discomposed;
Her bridle twisted on the mane;　　325
　A belt was broke, a band was loosed.

And then her fair and dainty foot
　From out the golden stirrup fell,
And none but Athol might her near;
　But yet no look her doubts dispel.　　330

The live-long day, nor sign of love,
　Nor censure did his looks express;
Oh, his was distant kindness all,
　Attention and obsequiousness.

When they came in by fair Monteith,   335
    She asked a henchman carelesslye,
"Whose land is this?–Has Athol here
    A castle, or a bastailye?"

"No, lady fair, these lands are held
    By Comyn Glas of Barnygill;   340
Lord Athol has no tower nor land
    Besouth the brow of Birnam-hill."

She turned her face back to the north,
    That face grew blenched and pale as clay;
And aye the clear and burning tear   345
    Hung on the cheek of lovely Hay.

Lord Athol turned him round about,
    "Why does the tear stand in your eye?
Say, are you weary of the way,
    Or does your steed bear you too high?   350

"Or does the west wind blirt your cheek?
    Or the sun fa' on your bonny bree?"
She hid her face within her veil,
    "Canst thou such question ask at me?"

"Beshrew my heart, if I can guess,   355
    When honours thus thy path belay;–
Minstrels, play up the music meet,
    And make our royal bride look gay."

As they went down by Endrick side,
    They met our good King Gregory,   360
Who came with all his gallant train,
    And welcomed them right courteouslye.

He kissed his fair and comely bride,
    And placed her on a chariot high;
"Why does Lord Erol stay behind?   365
    Why comes he not to give me joy?"

"My royal liege," Lord Athol said,
    "It fits him not thy face to see;

I showed your order and the seal,
   But he would not yield the maid to me.   370

"I broke his bolts and bars of steel,
   I beat his yeoman on the lea,
I won his towers by dint of weir,
   And here I've brought her safe to thee."

The king looked east, the king looked west,   375
   And asked the maid the truth to tell;
"Sooth, my good lord, the tale is just,
   I nothing wot how it befell."

King Gregory drew a long long breath,
   He pressed his brow, and stroked his beard: 380
"Now, by the rood," King Gregory said,
   "So strange a tale I never heard."

*   *   *   *   *   *   *   *

What ails our fair and comely bride,
   That thus she breathes the broken sigh;
That ever and anon she looks   385
   As if to meet some pitying eye?

No pitying eye, alas! is there;
   Lord Athol jests and looks away;
True love is blighted in the bloom,
   And hope takes leave of bonny Hay.   390

The holy Abbot oped the book,
   The twain arose from royal seat;
The prayer was said, the question put,
   Her tongue refused the answer meet:

But aye she wept and sobbed aloud,   395
   To cheer and comfort her was none;
And aye she glanced to Athol's Lord
   With looks would pierce a heart of stone.

His heart was pierced—he deemed her wronged—
   But now regret could nought avail;   400

O, when her silken glove was drawn,
    He trembled like the aspin pale.

The king he seized her trembling hand,
    And raised it gently from her side,
Then placed it in her lover's grasp,   405
    "Here, Athol, take thy bonny bride.

"These are two hands will better fit,
    Now, Abbot, *here* thy question try."
The Abbot stared, and straight obeyed,
    Ah! it was answered readily!   410

"Then join them, sire, and bless the bond,
    I joy such lovers blest to see,
The one respected sovereign's will,
    The other parent's high decree."

Lord Athol kneeled and clasped his King,   415
    And shed the tears upon his knee;
But the fair bride hung round his neck,
    And kissed his lips in ecstasye.

"Go with thy lover, bonny Hay,
    Thou well befit'st his manly side,   420
And thou shalt have the fairest dower
    That ever went with Highland bride.

"I ne'er saw such a lovely face,
    I never looked on form so fair,
But a foolish thought rose in my breast,   425
    That Athol's child might be my heir.

"Go, my brave Douglas of the Dale,
    And bring your Madeline here to me;
I oft have marked her eagle eye–
    The Queen of Scotland she shall be."   430

Old Douglas bowed and left the hall,
    How proudly waved his locks of gray!
A sound was issuing from his breast,
    Laughing or crying none could say.

O such a double bridal feast,   435
   And such a time of joyful glee,
And such a wise and worthy king,
   Dunbarton never more shall see.

The Shepherd's Calendar

Storms

THESE constitute the various eras of the pastoral life. They are the red lines in the shepherd's manual—the remembrancers of years and ages that are past—the tablets of memory by which the ages of his children, the times of his ancestors, and the rise and downfall of families, are invariably ascertained. Even the progress of improvement in Scots farming can be traced traditionally from these, and the rent of a farm or estate given with precision, before and after such and such a storm, though the narrator be uncertain in what century the said notable storm happened. "Mar's year," and "that year the hielanders raide," are but secondary mementos to *the year nine*, and *the year forty*—these stand in bloody capitals in the annals of the pastoral life, as well as many more that shall hereafter be mentioned.

The most dismal of all those on record is *the thirteen drifty days*. This extraordinary storm, as near as I have been able to trace, must have occurred in the year 1620. The traditionary stories and pictures of desolation that remain of it, are the most dire imaginable; and the mentioning of the thirteen drifty days to an old shepherd, in a stormy winter night, never fails to impress his mind with a sort of religious awe, and often sets him on his knees before that Being who alone can avert such another calamity.

It is said, that for thirteen days and nights the snow-drift never once abated—the ground was covered with frozen snow when it commenced, and during all that time the sheep never broke their fast. The cold was intense to a degree never before remembered; and about the fifth and sixth days of the storm, the young sheep began to fall into a sleepy and torpid state, and all that were so affected in the evening died over night. The intensity of the frost wind often cut them off when in that state quite instantaneously. About the ninth and tenth days, the shepherds began to build up huge semi-circular walls of their dead, in order to afford some shelter for the remainder of the living; but they availed but little, for about the same time they were frequently seen tearing at one another's wool with their teeth.

When the storm abated, on the fourteenth day from its commencement, there was on many a high-lying farm not a living sheep to be seen. Large mishapen walls of dead, surrounding a small prostrate flock likewise all dead, and frozen stiff in their lairs, were all that remained to cheer the forlorn shepherd and his master; and though on low-lying farms, where the snow was not so hard before, numbers of sheep weathered the storm, yet their constitutions received such a shock, that the greater part of them perished afterwards; and the final consequence was, that about nine-tenths of all the sheep in the south of Scotland were destroyed.

In the extensive pastoral district of Eskdale-moor, which maintains upwards of 20,000 sheep, it is said none were left alive, but forty young wedders on one farm, and five old ewes on another. The farm of Phaup remained without a stock and without a tenant for twenty years subsequent to the storm; at length, one very honest and liberal-minded man ventured to take a lease of it, at the annual rent of *a grey coat and a pair of hose*. It is now rented at £500. An extensive glen in Tweedsmuir, belonging to Sir James Montgomery, became a common at that time, to which any man drove his flocks that pleased, and it continued so for nearly a century. On one of Sir Patrick Scott of Thirlestane's farms, that keeps upwards of 900 sheep, they all died save one black ewe, from which the farmer had high hopes of preserving a breed; but some unlucky dogs, that were all laid idle for want of sheep to run at, fell upon this poor solitary remnant of a good stock, and chased her into the lake, where she was drowned. When word of this was brought to John Scott the farmer, commonly called gouffin' Jock, he is reported to have expressed himself as follows: "Ochon, ochon! an' is that the gate o't?– a black beginning maks aye a black end." Then taking down an old rusty sword, he added, "Come thou away, my auld frien', thou an' I maun e'en stock Bourhope-law ance mair. Bessy, my dow, how gaes the auld sang?

> There's walth o' kye i' bonny Braidlees;
>   There's walth o' yowes i' Tine;
> There's walth o' gear i' Gowanburn–
>   An' thae shall a' be thine."

It is a pity that tradition has not preserved any thing farther of the history of gouffin' Jock than this one saying.

The next memorable event of this nature is *the blast o' March*, which happened on the 24th day of that month, in the year 16–, on a Monday's morning; and though it lasted only for one forenoon, it was calculated to have destroyed upwards of a thousand scores of sheep, as well as a number of shepherds. There is one anecdote of this storm that is worthy of being preserved, as it shows with how much attention shepherds, as well as sailors, should observe the appearances of the sky. The Sunday evening before was so warm, that the lasses went home from church barefoot, and the young men threw off their plaids and coats and carried them over their shoulders. A large group of these younkers, going home from the church of Yarrow, equipped in this manner, chanced to pass by an old shepherd on the farm of Newhouse, named Walter Blake, who had all his sheep gathered into the side of a wood. They asked Wattie, who was a very religious man, what could have induced him to gather his sheep on the Sabbath-day? He answered, that he had seen an ill-hued weather-gaw that morning, and was afraid it was going to be a drift. They were so much amused at Wattie's apprehensions, that they clapped their hands, and laughed at him, and one pert girl cried, "Aye, fie tak' care, Wattie; I wadna say but it may be thrapple deep or the morn." Another asked, "if he wasna rather feared for the sun burning the een out o' their heads?" and a third, "if he didna keep a correspondence wi' the thieves, an' kend they were to ride that night." Wattie was obliged to bear all this, for the evening was fine beyond any thing generally seen at that season, and only said to them at parting, "Weel, weel, callans, time will try a'; let him laugh that wins; but slacks will be sleek, a hogg for the howking; we'll a' get horns to tout on the morn." The saying grew proverbial; but Wattie was the only man who saved the whole of his flock in that country.

The years 1709–40, and 72, were all likewise notable years for severity, and for the losses sustained among the flocks of sheep. In the latter, the snow lay from the middle of December until the middle of April, and all the time hard frozen. Partial thaws always kept the farmer's hopes of relief alive, and thus prevented him from removing his sheep to a lower situation, till at length they grew so weak that they could not be removed. There has not been such a general loss in the days of any man living as in that year. It is by these years that all subsequent hard winters have been measured, and, of late by that of 1795; and when the balance turns out in favour of the calculator, there is always a degree of thankfulness expressed, as well as a composed submission to the awards of Divine Providence. The daily feeling naturally impressed on the shepherd's mind, that all his comforts are so entirely in the hand of Him that rules the elements, contributes not a little to that firm spirit of devotion for which the Scottish shepherd is so distinguished. I know of no scene so impressive, as that of a family sequestered in a lone glen during the time of a winter storm; and where is the glen in the kingdom that wants such a habitation? There they are left to the protection of Heaven, and they know and feel it. Throughout all the wild vicissitudes of nature they have no hope of assistance from man, but are conversant with the Almighty alone. Before retiring to rest, the shepherd uniformly goes out to examine the state of the weather, and makes his report to the little dependant group within—nothing is to be seen but the conflict of the elements, nor heard but the raving of the storm—then they all kneel around him, while he recommends them to the protection of Heaven; and though their little hymn of praise can scarcely be heard even by themselves, as it mixes with the roar of the tempest, they never fail to rise from their devotions with their spirits cheered and their confidence renewed, and go to sleep with an exaltation of mind of which kings and conquerors have no share. Often have I been a sharer in such scenes; and never, even in my youngest years, without having my heart deeply impressed by the circumstances. There is a sublimity in the very idea. There we lived, as it were, inmates of the cloud and the storm; but we stood in a relationship to the Ruler of these, that neither time nor eternity could ever cancel. Wo to him that would weaken the bonds with which true Christianity connects us with Heaven and with each other.

But of all the storms that ever Scotland witnessed, or I hope ever will again behold, there is none of them that can once be compared with the memorable 24th of January 1794, which fell with such peculiar violence on that division of the south of Scotland that lies between Crawford-muir and the border. In that bounds there were seventeen shepherds perished, and upwards of thirty carried home insensible, who afterwards recovered; but the number of sheep that were lost far outwent any possibility of calculation. One farmer alone, Mr Thomas Beattie, lost seventy-two scores for his own share—and many others, in the same quarter, from thirty to forty scores each. Whole flocks were overwhelmed with snow, and no one ever knew where they were till the snow was dissolved, that they were all found dead. I myself witnessed one particular instance of this on the farm of Thickside: there were twelve scores of excellent ewes, all one age, that were missing there all the time that the snow lay, which was only a week, and no traces of them could be found; when the snow went away, they were discovered all lying dead, with their heads one way, as if a flock of sheep had dropped dead going from the washing. Many hundreds were driven into waters, burns, and lakes, by the violence of the storm, where they were buried or frozen up, and these the flood carried away, so that they were never

seen or found by the owners at all. The following anecdote somewhat illustrates the confusion and devastation that it bred in the country.–The greater part of the rivers on which the storm was most
deadly, run into the Solway Frith, on which there is a place called *the
Beds of Esk*, where the tide throws out, and leaves whatsoever is
carried into it by the rivers. When the flood after the storm subsided, there were found on that place, and the shores adjacent, 1840
sheep, nine black cattle, three horses, two men, one woman, forty-
five dogs, and one hundred and eighty hares, besides a number of
meaner animals.

To relate all the particular scenes of distress that occurred during
this tremendous hurricane is impossible–a volume would not contain them. I shall, therefore, in order to give a true picture of the
storm, merely relate what I saw, and shall in nothing exaggerate.
But before doing this, I must mention a circumstance, curious in its
nature, and connected with others that afterwards occurred.

Sometime previous to that, a few young shepherds (of whom I
was one, and the youngest, though not the least ambitious of the
number), had formed themselves into a sort of literary society, that
met periodically, at one or other of the houses of its members, where
each read an essay on a subject previously given out; and after that,
every essay was minutely investigated and criticised. We met in the
evening, and continued our important discussions all night. Friday,
the 23d of January, was the day appointed for one of these meetings,
and it was to be held at Entertrony, a wild and remote shieling, at
the very sources of the Ettrick, and now occupied by my own brother.
I had the honour of having been named as preses–so, leaving the
charge of my flock with my master, off I set from Blackhouse, on
Thursday, a very ill day, with a flaming bombastical essay in my
pocket, and my tongue trained to many wise and profound remarks,
to attend this extraordinary meeting, though the place lay at the distance of twenty miles, over the wildest hills in the kingdom, and the
time the depth of winter. I remained that night with my parents at
Ettrick-house, and next day again set out on my journey. I had not,
however, proceeded far, before I perceived, or thought I perceived,
symptoms of an approaching storm, and that of no ordinary nature.
I remember the day well: the wind, which was rough on the preceding day, had subsided into a dead calm; there was a slight fall of
snow, which descended in small thin flakes, that seemed to hover
and reel in the air, as if uncertain whether to go upward or downward–the hills were covered down to the middle in deep folds of
rime, or frost-fog–in the cloughs that was dark, dense, and seemed

as if it were heaped and crushed together—but on the brows of the hills it had a pale and fleecy appearance, and, altogether, I never beheld a day of such gloomy aspect. A thought now began to intrude itself on me, though I strove all that I could to get quit of it, that it would be a wise course in me to return home to my sheep. Inclination urged me on, and I tried to bring reason to her aid, by saying to myself, "I have no reason in the world to be afraid of my sheep, my master took the charge of them cheerfully, there is not a better shepherd in the kingdom, and I cannot doubt his concern in having them right." All would not do: I stood still and contemplated the day, and the more closely I examined it, the more was I impressed that some mischief was a-brewing; so, with a heavy heart, I turned on my heel, and made the best of my way back the road I came; my elaborate essay, and all my wise observations, had come to nothing.

On my way home, I called at a place named the Hopehouse, to see a maternal uncle, whom I loved; he was angry when he saw me, and said it was not like a prudent lad to be running up and down the country in such weather, and at such a season; and urged me to make haste home, for it would be a drift before the morn. He accompanied me to the top of the height called the Black Gate-head, and on parting, he shook his head, and said, "Ah! it is a dangerous looking day! In troth I'm amaist fear'd to look at it;" I said I would not mind it, if any one knew from what quarter the storm would arise; but we might, in all likelihood, gather our sheep to the place where they would be most exposed to danger. He bade me keep a good look out all the way home, and wherever I observed the first opening through the rime, to be assured the wind would rise directly from that point. I did as he desired me, but the clouds continued close set all around, till the fall of evening; and as the snow had been accumulating all day, so as to render walking very unfurthersome, it was that time before I reached home. The first thing I did was to go to my master and inquire where he had left my sheep—he told me—but though I had always the most perfect confidence in his experience, I was not pleased with what he had done— he had left a part of them far too high out on the hills, and the rest were not where I wanted them, and I told him so: he said he had done all for the best, but if there appeared to be any danger, if I would call him up in the morning, he would assist me. We had two beautiful servant girls, and with them I sat chattering till past eleven o'clock, and then I went down to the old tower. What could have taken me to that ruinous habitation of the Black Douglasses at that untimeous hour, I cannot recollect, but it certainly must have been from a supposition that one of the girls would follow me, or else that I would see a hare—both very unlikely events to have taken place on such a night. However, certain it is, that there I was at midnight, and it was while standing on the top of the staircase turret, that I first beheld a bright bore through the clouds, towards the north, which reminded me of my uncle's apophthegm. But at the same time a smart thaw had commenced, and the breeze seemed to be rising from the south, so that I laughed in my heart at his sage rule, and accounted it quite absurd. Short was the time till awful experience told me how true it was.

I then went to my bed in the byre loft, where I slept with a neighbour shepherd, named Borthwick; but though fatigued with walking through the snow, I could not close an eye, so that I heard the first burst of the storm, which commenced between one and two, with a fury that no one can conceive who does not remember of it. Besides, the place where I lived being exposed to two or three gathered winds, as they are called by shepherds, the storm raged there with redoubled ferocity. It began all at once, with such a tremendous roar, that I imagined it was a peal of thunder, until I felt the house trembling to its foundation. In a few minutes I went and thrust my naked arm through a hole in the roof, in order, if possible, to ascertain what was going on without, for not a ray of light could I see. I could not then, nor can I yet, express my astonishment. So completely was the air overloaded with falling and driving snow, that but for the force of the wind, I felt as if I had thrust my arm into a wreath of snow. I deemed it a judgment sent from Heaven upon us, and lay down again in my bed, trembling with agitation. I lay still for about an hour, in hopes that it might prove only a temporary hurricane; but, hearing no abatement of its fury, I awakened Borthwick, and bade him get up, for it was come on such a night or morning, as never blew from the heavens. He was not long in obeying, for as soon as he heard the turmoil, he started from his bed, and in one minute, throwing on his clothes, he hasted down the ladder, and opened the door, where he stood for a good while, uttering exclamations of astonishment. The door where he stood was not above fourteen yards from the door of the dwelling-house, but a wreath was already amassed between them, as high as the walls of the house—and in trying to get round or through this, Borthwick lost himself, and could neither find the house nor his way back to the byre, and about six minutes after, I heard him calling my name, in a shrill desperate tone of voice, at which I could not refrain from laughing immoderately, notwithstanding the dismal prospect that lay before us; for I heard, from his cries, where he was. He had tried to make his way over the top of a large dunghill, but going to the wrong side, had fallen over, and wrestled long among snow, quite over the head. I did not think proper to move to his assistance, but lay still, and shortly after, heard him shouting at the kitchen door for instant admittance; still I kept my bed for about three quarters of an hour longer; and then, on reaching the house with much difficulty, found our master, the ploughman, Borthwick, and the two servant maids, sitting round the kitchen fire, with looks of dismay, I may almost say despair. We all agreed at once, that the sooner we were able to reach the sheep, the better chance we had to save a remnant; and as there were eight hundred excellent ewes, all in one lot, but a long way distant, and the most valuable lot of any on the farm, we resolved to make a bold effort to reach them. Our master made family worship, a duty he never neglected; but that morning, the manner in which we manifested our trust and confidence in Heaven, was particularly affecting. We took our breakfast—stuffed our pockets with bread and cheese—sewed our plaids around us—tied down our hats with napkins coming below our chins—and each taking a strong staff in his hand, we set out on the attempt.

No sooner was the door closed behind us than we lost sight of each other—seeing there was none—it was impossible for a man to see his hand held up before him, and it was still two hours till day. We had no means of keeping together but by following to one another's voices, nor of working our way save by groping with our staves before us. It soon appeared to me a hopeless concern, for, ere ever we got clear of the houses and haystacks, we had to roll ourselves over two or three wreaths which it was impossible to wade through; and all the while the wind and drift were so violent, that every three or four minutes we were obliged to hold our faces down between our knees to recover our breath.

We soon got into an eddying wind that was altogether insufferable, and, at the same time, we were struggling among snow so deep, that our progress in the way we purposed going was indeed very equivocal, for we had, by this time, lost all idea of east, west, north, or south. Still we were as busy as men determined on a business could be, and persevered on we knew not whither, sometimes rolling over the snow, and sometimes weltering in it to the chin. The following instance of our successful exertions marks our progress to a tittle. There was an inclosure around the house to the westward, which we denominated *the park*, as is customary in Scotland. When we went away, we calculated that it was two hours until day—the park did not extend above 300 yards—and we were still engaged in that *park* when day-light appeared.

When we got free of the park, we also got free of the eddy of the wind—it was now straight in our faces—we went in a line before each other, and changed places every three or four minutes, and at length, after great fatigue, we reached a long ridge of a hill, where the snow was thinner, having been blown off it by the force of the wind, and by this time we had hopes of reaching within a short space of the ewes, which were still a mile and a half distant. Our master had taken the lead; I was next him, and soon began to suspect, from the depth of the snow, that he was leading us quite wrong, but as we always trusted implicitly to him that was foremost for the time, I said nothing for a good while, until satisfied that we were going in a direction very nearly right opposite to that we intended. I then tried to expostulate with him, but he did not seem to understand what I said, and, on getting a glimpse of his countenance, I perceived that it was quite altered. Not to alarm the others, nor even himself, I said I was becoming terribly fatigued, and proposed that we should lean on the snow and take each a mouthful of whisky (for I had brought a small bottle in my pocket for fear of the worst), and a bite of bread and cheese. This was unanimously agreed to, and I noted that he swallowed the spirits rather eagerly, a thing not usual with him, and when he tried to eat, it was long before he could swallow any thing. I was convinced that he would fail altogether, but, as it would have been easier to have got him to the shepherd's house before than home again, I made no proposal for him to return. On the contrary, I said if they would trust themselves entirely to me, I would engage to lead them to the ewes without going a foot out of the way—the other two agreed to it, and acknowledged that they knew not where they were, but he never opened his mouth, nor did he speak a word for two hours thereafter. It had only been a temporary exhaustion, however; for after that he recovered, and wrought till night as well as any of us, though he never could recollect a single circumstance that occurred during that part of our way, nor a word that was said, nor of having got any refreshment whatever.

At half an hour after ten, we reached the flock, and just in time to save them; but before that, both Borthwick and the ploughman had lost their hats, notwithstanding all their precautions; and to impede us still farther, I went inadvertently over a precipice, and going down head foremost, between the scaur and the snow, found it impossible to extricate myself; for the more I struggled, I went the deeper. For all our troubles, I heard Borthwick above convulsed with laughter;

he thought he had got the affair of the dunghill paid back. By holding by one another, and letting down a plaid to me, they hauled me up, but I was terribly incommoded by snow that had got inside my clothes.

The ewes were standing in a close body; one half of them were covered over with snow to the depth of ten feet, the rest were jammed against a brae. We knew not what to do for spades to dig them out; but, to our agreeable astonishment, when those before were removed, they had been so close pent together as to be all touching one another, and they walked out from below the snow after their neighbours in a body. If the snow-wreath had not broke, and crumbled down upon a few that were hindmost, we should have got them all out without putting a hand to them. This was effecting a good deal more than I or any of the party expected a few hours before; there were 100 ewes in another place near by, but of these we could only get out a very few, and lost all hopes of saving the rest.

It was now wearing towards mid-day, and there were occasionally short intervals in which we could see about us for perhaps a score of yards; but we got only one momentary glance of the hills around us all that day. I grew quite impatient to be at my own charge, and leaving the rest, I went away to them by myself, that is, I went to the division that was left far out on the hills, while our master and the ploughman volunteered to rescue those that were down on the lower ground. I found mine in miserable circumstances, but making all possible exertion, I got out about one half of them, which I left in a place of safety, and made towards home, for it was beginning to grow dark, and the storm was again raging, without any mitigation, in all its darkness and deformity. I was not the least afraid of losing my way, for I knew all the declivities of the hills so well, that I could have come home with my eyes bound up, and, indeed, long ere I got home, they were of no use to me. I was terrified for the water (Douglas Burn), for in the morning it was flooded and gorged up with snow in a dreadful manner, and I judged that it would be quite impassable. At length I came to a place where I thought the water should be, and fell a boring and groping for it with my long staff. No, I could find no water, and began to dread, that for all my accuracy I had gone wrong. I was greatly astonished, and, standing still to consider, I looked up towards Heaven, I shall not say for what cause, and to my utter amazement thought I beheld trees over my head flourishing abroad over the whole sky. I never had seen such an optical delusion before; it was so like enchantment, that I knew not what to think, but dreaded that some extraordinary thing was coming over me, and that I was deprived of my right senses. I remember I thought the storm was a great judgment sent on us for our sins, and that this strange phantasy was connected with it, an illusion effected by evil spirits. I stood a good while in this painful trance; at length, on making a bold exertion to escape from the fairy vision, I came all at once in contact with the old tower. Never in my life did I experience such a relief; I was not only all at once freed from the fairies, but from the dangers of the gorged river. I had come over it on some mountain of snow, I knew not how nor where, nor do I know to this day. So that, after all, they were trees that I saw, and trees of no great magnitude neither; but their appearance to my eyes it is impossible to describe. I thought they flourished abroad, not for miles, but for hundreds of miles, to the utmost verges of the visible heavens. Such a day and such a night may the eye of a shepherd never again behold.

Chapter II

"That night, a child might understand,
The Deil had business on his hand."

On reaching home, I found our women folk sitting in woful plight. It is well known how wonderfully acute they generally are, either at raising up imaginary evils, or magnifying those that exist; and our's had made out a theory so fraught with misery and distress, that the poor things were quite overwhelmed with grief. "There were none of us ever to see the house again *in life.* There was no possibility of the thing happening, all circumstances considered. There was not a sheep in the country to be saved, nor a single shepherd left alive— nothing but *women!* and there they were left, three poor helpless creatures, and the men lying dead out among the snow, and none to bring them home. Lord help them, what was to become of them!" They perfectly agreed in all this; there was no dissenting voice; and their prospects still continuing to darken with the fall of night, they had no other resource left them, long before my arrival, but to lift up their voices and weep. The group consisted of a young lady, our master's niece, and two servant girls, all of the same age, and beautiful as three spring days, every one of which are mild and sweet, but differ only a little in brightness. No sooner had I entered, than every tongue and every hand was put in motion, the former to pour forth queries faster than six tongues of men could answer them with any degree of precision, and the latter to rid me of the incumbrances of snow and ice with which I was loaded. One slit up the sewing of my frozen plaid, another brushed the icicles from my locks, and a third unloosed my clotted snow-boots; we all arrived within a few minutes of each other, and all shared the same kind offices, and heard the same kind inquiries, and long string of perplexities narrated; even our dogs shared of their caresses and ready assistance in ridding them of the frozen snow, and the dear consistent creatures were six times happier than if no storm or danger had existed. Let no one suppose that, even amid toils and perils, the shepherd's life is destitute of enjoyment.

Borthwick had found his way home without losing his aim in the least. I had deviated but little, save that I lost the river, and remained a short time in the country of the fairies; but the other two had a hard struggle for life. They went off, as I said formerly, in search of seventeen scores of my flock that had been left in a place not far from the house, but being unable to find one of them, in searching for these, they lost themselves, while it was yet early in the afternoon. They supposed that they had gone by the house very near to it, for they had toiled till dark among deep snow in the burn below; and if John Burnet, a neighbouring shepherd, had not heard them calling, and found and conducted them home, it would have stood hard with them indeed, for none of us would have looked for them in that direction. They were both very much exhausted, and the goodman could not speak above his breath that night.

Next morning the sky was clear, but a cold intemperate wind still blew from the north. The face of the country was entirely altered. The form of every hill was changed, and new mountains leaned over every valley. All traces of burns, rivers, and lakes, were obliterated, for the frost had been commensurate with the storm, and such as had never been witnessed in Scotland. Some registers that I have seen, place this storm on the 24th of December, a month too early, but that day was one of the finest winter days I ever saw.

There having been 340 of my flock that had never been found at all during the preceding day, as soon as the morning dawned we set all out to look after them. It was a hideous looking scene—no one could cast his eyes around him and entertain any conception of sheep being saved. It was one picture of desolation. There is a deep glen lies between Blackhouse and Dryhope, called the Hawkshaw Cleuch, which is full of trees. There was not the top of one of them to be seen. This may convey some idea how the country looked; and no one can suspect that I would state circumstances otherwise than they were, when there is so many living that could confute me.

When we came to the ground where these sheep should have been, there was not one of them above the snow. Here and there, at a great distance from each other, we could perceive the head or horns of stragglers appearing, and these were easily got out; but when we had collected these few, we could find no more. They had been all lying abroad in a scattered state when the storm came on, and were covered over just as they had been lying. It was on a kind of slanting ground that lay half beneath the wind, and the snow was uniformly from six to eight feet deep. Under this the hogs were lying scattered over at least 100 acres of heathery ground. It was a very ill looking concern. We went about boring with our long poles, and often did not find one hog in a quarter of an hour. But at length a white shaggy colley, named Sparkie, that belonged to the cow-herd boy, seemed to have comprehended something of our perplexity, for we observed him plying and scraping in the snow with great violence, and always looking over his shoulder to us. On going to the spot, we found that he had marked straight above a sheep. From that he flew to another, and so on to another, as fast as we could dig them out, and ten times faster, for he sometimes had twenty or thirty holes marked before hand.

We got out three hundred of that division before night, and about half as many on the other parts of the farm, in addition to those we had rescued the day before; and the greater part of these would have been lost had it not been for the voluntary exertions of Sparkie. Before the snow went away (which lay only eight days) we had got every sheep on the farm, either dead or alive, except four; and that these were not found was not Sparkie's blame, for though they were buried below a mountain of snow at least fifty feet deep, he had again and again marked on the top of it above them. The sheep were all living when we found them, but those that were buried in the snow to a certain depth, being, I suppose, in a warm, half suffo-cated state, though on being taken out they bounded away like roes, yet the sudden change of atmosphere instantly paralyzed them, and they fell down deprived of all power in their limbs. We had great numbers of these to carry home and feed with the hand, but others that were very deep buried, died outright in a few minutes. We did not however lose above sixty in all, but I am certain Sparkie saved us at least two hundred.

We were for several days utterly ignorant how affairs stood with the country around us, all communication between farms being cut off, at least all communication with such a wild place as that in which

I lived; but John Burnet, a neighbouring shepherd on another farm, was remarkably good at picking up the rumours that were afloat in the country, which he delighted to circulate without abatement. Many people tell their stories by halves, and in a manner so cold and indifferent, that the purport can scarcely be discerned, and if it is, cannot be believed; but that was not the case with John; he gave them with *interest*, and we were very much indebted to him for the intelligence that we daily received that week; for no sooner was the first brunt of the tempest got over, than John made a point of going off at a tangent every day, to learn and bring us word what was going on. The accounts were most dismal; the country was a charnel-house. The first day he brought us tidings of the loss of thousands of sheep, and likewise of the death of Robert Armstrong, a neighbour shepherd, one whom we all well knew, he having but lately left the Blackhouse to herd on another farm. He died not above three hundred paces from a farm-house, while at the same time it was known to them all that he was there. His companion left him at a dike-side, and went in to procure assistance; yet, nigh as it was, they could not reach him, though they attempted it again and again; and at length they were obliged to return, and suffer him to perish at the side of the dike. There were three of my own intimate acquaintances perished that night. There was another shepherd named Watt, the circumstances of whose death were peculiarly affecting. He had been to see his sweetheart on the night before, with whom he had finally agreed and settled every thing about their marriage; but it so happened, in the inscrutable awards of Providence, that at the very time when the banns of his marriage were proclaimed in the church of Moffat, his companions were carrying him home a corpse from the hill.

It may not be amiss here to remark, that it was a received opinion all over the country, that sundry lives were lost, and a great many more endangered, by the administering of ardent spirits to the sufferers while in a state of exhaustion. It was a practice against which I entered my vehement protest, nevertheless the voice of the multitude should never be disregarded. A little bread and sweet milk, or even a little bread and cold water, it was said, proved a much safer restorative in the fields. There is no denying, that there were some who took a glass of spirits that night that never spoke another word, even though they were continuing to walk and converse when their friends found them.

On the other hand, there was one woman who left her children, and followed her husband's dog, who brought her to his master lying in a state of insensibility. He had fallen down bareheaded among the snow, and was all covered over, save one corner of his plaid. She had nothing better to take with her, when she set out, than a bottle of sweet milk and a little oatmeal cake, and yet, with the help of these, she so far recruited his spirits as to get him safe home, though not without long and active perseverance. She took two little vials with her, and in these she heated the milk in her bosom. That man would not be disposed to laugh at the silliness of the fair sex for some time.

It is perfectly unaccountable how easily people died that night. The frost must certainly have been prodigious; so intense as to have seized momentarily on the vitals of those that overheated themselves by wading and toiling too impatiently among the snow, a thing that is very aptly done. I have conversed with five or six that were carried home in a state of insensibility that night, who never would again have moved from the spot where they lay, and were only brought to life by rubbing and warm applications; and they uniformly declared, that they felt no kind of pain or debility, farther than an irresistible desire to sleep. Many fell down while walking and speaking, in a sleep so sound as to resemble torpidity; and there is little doubt that those who perished slept away in the same manner. I knew a man well, whose name was Andrew Murray, that perished in the snow on Minchmoor; and he had taken it so deliberately, that he had buttoned his coat and folded his plaid, which he had laid beneath his head for a bolster.

But it is now time to return to my notable literary society. In spite of the hideous appearances that presented themselves, the fellows actually met, all save myself, in that solitary shieling before mentioned. It is easy to conceive how they were confounded and taken by surprise, when the storm burst forth on them in the middle of the night, while they were in the heat of sublime disputation. There can be little doubt that there was part of loss sustained in their respective flocks, by reason of that meeting; but this was nothing, compared with the obloquy to which they were subjected on another account, and one which will scarcely be believed, even though the most part of the members be yet alive to bear testimony to it.

The storm was altogether an unusual convulsion of nature. Nothing like it had ever been seen or heard of among us before; and it was enough of itself to arouse every spark of superstition that lingered among these mountains. It did so. It was universally viewed as a judgment sent by God for the punishment of some heinous offence, but what that offence was, could not for a while be ascer-

tained; but when it came out, that so many men had been assembled
in a lone unfrequented place, and busily engaged in some mysterious work at the very instant that the blast came on, no doubts were
entertained that all had not been right there, and that some horrible
rite, or correspondence with the powers of darkness, had been going on. It so happened, too, that this shieling of Entertrony was situated in the very vortex of the storm; the devastations made by it
extended all around that to a certain extent, and no farther on any
one quarter than another. This was easily and soon remarked; and,
upon the whole, the first view of the matter had rather an equivocal
appearance to those around who had suffered so severely by it.

But still as the rumour grew, the certainty of the event gained
ground—new corroborative circumstances were every day divulged,
till the whole district was in an uproar, and several of the members
began to meditate a speedy retreat from the country; some of them,
I know, would have fled, if it had not been for the advice of the late
worthy and judicious Mr Bryden of Crosslee. The first intimation
that I had of it was from my friend John Burnet, who gave it me with
his accustomed energy and full assurance. He came over one evening,
and I saw by his face he had some great news. I think I remember,
as I well may, every word that past between us on the subject.

"Weel chap," said he to me, "we hae fund out what has been the
cause of a' this mischief now."

"What do you mean, John?"

"What do I mean?—It seems that a great squad o' birkies that ye
are conneckit wi', had met that night at the herd's house o' Everphaup,
an' had raised the deil amang them."

Every countenance in the kitchen changed; the women gazed at
John, and then at me, and their lips grew white. These kind of feelings are infectious, people may say what they will; fear begets fear
as naturally as light springs from reflection. I reasoned stoutly at
first against the veracity of the report, observing, that it was utter
absurdity, and a shame and disgrace for the country to cherish such
a ridiculous lie.

"Lie!" said John, "it's nae lie; they had him up amang them like a
great rough dog at the very time that the tempest began, and were
glad to draw cuts, and gie him ane o' their number to get quit o' him
again." Lord, how every hair of my head, and inch of my frame
crept at hearing this sentence; for I had a dearly loved brother who
was of the number, several full cousins and intimate acquaintances;
indeed, I looked upon the whole fraternity as my brethren, and
considered myself involved in all their transactions. I could say no

more in defence of the society's proceedings; for, to tell the truth, though I am ashamed to acknowledge it, I suspected that the allegation might be too true.

"Has the deil actually ta'en awa ane o' them bodily?" said Jean. "He has that," returned John, "an' it's thought the skaith wadna hae been grit, had he ta'en twa or three mae o' them. Base villains! that the hale country should hae to suffer for their pranks! But, however, the law's to tak its course on them, an' they'll find, ere a' the play be played, that he has need of a lang spoon that sups wi' the deil."

The next day John brought us word, that it was *only* the servant maid that the *ill thief* had ta'en away; and the next again, that it was actually Bryden of Glenkerry; but, finally, he was obliged to inform us, "That a' was exactly true, as it was first tauld, but only that Jamie Bryden, after being a-wanting for some days, had casten up again."

There has been nothing since that time has caused such a ferment in the country—nought else could be talked of; and grievous was the blame attached to those who had the temerity to raise up the devil to waste the land. If the effects produced by the Chaldee Manuscript had not been fresh in the minds of the present generation, they could have no right conception of the rancour that prevailed against these few individuals; but the two scenes greatly resembled each other, for in that case, as well as the latter one, legal proceedings, it is said, were meditated, and attempted; but lucky it was for the shepherds that they agreed to no reference, for such were the feelings of the country, and the opprobrium in which the act was held, that it is likely it would have fared very ill with them;—at all events, it would have required an arbiter of some decision and uprightness to have dared to oppose them. Two men were sent to come to the house as by chance, and endeavour to learn from the shepherd, and particularly from the servant-maid, what grounds there were for inflicting legal punishments; but before that happened I had the good luck to hear her examined myself, and that in a way by which all suspicions were put to rest, and simplicity and truth left to war with superstition alone. I deemed it very curious at the time, and shall give it verbatim as nearly as I can recollect.

Being all impatience to learn particulars, as soon as the waters abated, so as to become fordable, I hasted over to Ettrick, and the day being fine, I found numbers of people astir on the same errand with myself,—the valley was moving with people, gathered in from the glens around, to hear and relate the dangers and difficulties that were just overpast. Among others, the identical girl who served with the shepherd in whose house the scene of the meeting took place, had come down to Ettrick school-house to see her parents. Her name was Mary Beattie, a beautiful sprightly lass, about twenty years of age; and if the devil had taken her in preference to any one of the shepherds, his good taste could scarcely have been disputed. The first person I met was my friend, the late Mr James Anderson, who was as anxious to hear what had passed at the meeting as I was, so we two contrived a scheme whereby we thought we would hear every thing from the girl's own mouth.

We sent word to the school-house for Mary, to call at my father's house on her return up the water, as there was a parcel to go to Phawhope. She came accordingly, and when we saw her approaching, we went into a little sleeping apartment, where we could hear every thing that passed, leaving directions with my mother how to manage the affair. My mother herself was in perfect horrors about the business, and believed it all; as for my father, he did not say much either the one way or the other, but bit his lip, and remarked, that "fo'k would find it was an ill thing to hae to do wi' *the enemy.*"

My mother would have managed extremely well, had her own early prejudices in favour of the doctrine of all kinds of apparitions not got the better of her. She was very kind to the girl, and talked with her about the storm, and the events that had occurred, till she brought the subject of the meeting forward herself, on which the following dialogue commenced:–

"But dear Mary, my woman, what were the chiels a' met about that night?"

"O, they were just gaun through their papers an' arguing."

"Arguing! what were they arguing about?"

"I have often thought about it sin' syne, but really I canna tell precisely what they were arguing about."

"Were you wi' them a' the time?"

"Yes, a' the time, but the wee while I was milkin' the cow."

"An' did they never bid you gang out?"

"Oo no; they never heedit whether I gaed out or in."

"Its queer that ye canna mind ought ava;–can ye no tell me ae word that ye heard them say?"

"I heard them sayin' something about the fitness o' things."

"Aye, that was a braw subject for them! But, Mary, did ye no hear them sayin nae ill words?"

"No."

"Did ye no hear them speaking naething about the deil?"

"Very little."

"What were they saying about *him?*"

"I thought I aince heard Jamie Fletcher saying there was nae deil ava."

"Ah! the unwordy rascal! How durst he for the life o' him! I wonder he didna think shame."

"I fear aye he's something regardless, Jamie."

"I hope nane that belangs to me will ever join him in sic wickedness! But tell me, Mary, my woman, did ye no see nor hear naething uncanny about the house yoursel' that night?"

"There was something like a plover cried twice i' the peat-neuk, in at the side o' Will's bed."

"A plover! His presence be about us! There was never a plover at this time o' the year. And in the house too! Ah, Mary, I'm feared and concerned about that night's wark! What thought ye it was that cried?"

"I didna ken what it was, it cried just like a plover."

"Did the callans look as they were fear'd when they heard it?"

"They lookit gayan' queer."

"What did they say?"

"Ane cried, 'What is that?' an' another said, 'What can it mean.' 'Hout,' quo Jamie Fletcher, 'its just some bit stray bird that has lost itsel.' 'I dinna ken,' quo your Will, 'I dinna like it unco weel.'"

"Think ye, did nane o' the rest see any thing?"

"I believe there was something seen."

"What was't?" (in a half whisper with manifest alarm.)

"When Will gaed out to try if he could gang to the sheep, he met wi' a great big rough dog, that had very near worn him into a lin in the water."

My mother was now deeply affected, and after two or three smothered exclamations, she fell a whispering; the other followed her example, and shortly after they rose and went out, leaving my friend and me very little wiser than we were, for we had heard both these incidents before with little variation. I accompanied Mary to Phawhope, and met with my brother, who soon convinced me of the falsehood and absurdity of the whole report; but I was grieved to find him so much cast down and distressed about it. None of them durst well shew their faces at either kirk or market for a whole year, and more. The weather continuing fine, we two went together and perambulated Eskdale moor, visiting the principal scenes of carnage among the flocks, where we saw multitudes of men skinning and burying whole droves of sheep, taking with them only the skins and tallow.

I shall now conclude this long account of the storm, and its consequences, by an extract from a poet for whose works I always feel
disposed to have a great partiality; and whoever reads the above
will not doubt on what incident the description is founded, nor yet
deem it greatly overcharged.

*   *   *   *   *   *

"Who was it reared these whelming waves?
  Who scalp'd the brows of old Cairn Gorm,
And scoop'd these ever-yawning caves?
  'Twas I, the Spirit of the Storm!

He waved his sceptre north away,
  The arctic ring was rift asunder;
And through the heaven the startling bray
  Burst louder than the loudest thunder.

The feathery clouds, condensed and furled,
  In columns swept the quaking glen;
Destruction down the dale was hurled,
  O'er bleating flocks and wondering men.

The Grampians groan'd beneath the storm;
  New mountains o'er the correi lean'd;
Ben Nevis shook his shaggy form,
  And wonder'd what his Sovereign mean'd.

Even far on Yarrow's fairy dale,
  The shepherd paused in dumb dismay;
And cries of spirits in the gale
  Lured many a pitying hind away.

The Lowthers felt the tyrant's wrath;
  Proud Hartfell quaked beneath his brand;
And Cheviot heard the cries of death,
  Guarding his loved Northumberland.

But O, as fell that fateful night,
  What horrors Avin wilds deform,
And choak the ghastly lingering light!
  There whirled the vortex of the storm.

Ere morn the wind grew deadly still,
 And dawning in the air updrew
From many a shelve and shining hill,
 Her folding robe of fairy blue.

Then what a smooth and wonderous scene
 Hung o'er Loch Avin's lovely breast!
Not top of tallest pine was seen,
 On which the dazzled eye could rest;

But mitred cliff, and crested fell,
 In lucid curls her brows adorn;
Aloft the radiant crescents swell,
 All pure as robes by angels worn.

Sound sleeps our seer, far from the day,
 Beneath yon sleek and writhed cone;
His spirit steals, unmiss'd, away,
 And dreams across the desart lone.

Sound sleeps our seer!—the tempests rave,
 And cold sheets o'er his bosom fling;
The moldwarp digs his mossy grave;
 His requiem Avin eagles sing."

* * * * * *

Chapter III

LAST autumn, while I was staying a few weeks with my friend, Mr Grumple, minister of the extensive and celebrated parish of *Woolenhorn*, an incident occurred which hath afforded me a great deal of amusement; and as I think it may divert some of your readers, I shall, without further preface, begin the relation.

We had just finished a wearisome debate on the rights of teind, and the claims which every clergyman of the established church of Scotland has for a grass glebe; the china cups were already arranged, and the savoury tea-pot stood basking on the ledge of the grate, when the servant maid entered, and told Mr Grumple that there was one at the door who wanted him.

We immediately heard a debate in the passage,—the parson pressing his guest to *come ben*, which the other stoutly resisted, declaring aloud that "it was a' nonsense thegither, for he was eneuch to fley a' the grand folk out o' the room, an' set the kivering o' the floor a-swoomin." The parlour door was however thrown open, and, to my astonishment, the first guests who presented themselves were two strong honest-looking colleys, or shepherd's dogs, that came bouncing and capering into the room, with a great deal of seeming satisfaction. Their master was shortly after ushered in. He was a tall athletic figure, with a black beard, and dark raven hair hanging over his brow; wore clouted shoes, shod with iron, and faced up with copper; and there was altogether something in his appearance the most homely and uncouth of any exterior I had ever seen.

"This," said the minister, "is Peter Plash, a parishioner of mine, who has brought me in an excellent salmon, and wants a good office at my hand, he says, in return."—"The bit fish is naething, man," said Peter, sleeking down the hair on his brow; "I wish he had been better for your sake—but gin ye had seen the sport that we had wi' him at Pool-Midnight, ye wad hae leughen till ye had burstit." Here the shepherd, observing his two dogs seated comfortably on the hearth-rug, and deeming it an instance of high presumption and very bad manners, broke out with—"Ay, Whitefoot, lad! an' ye're for being a gentleman too? My certy, man, but ye're no blate!—I'm ill eneugh, to be sure, to come into a grand room this way, but yet I wadna set up my impudent nose an' my muckle rough brisket afore the lowe, an' tak a' the fire to mysel—Get aff wi' ye, sir! An' you too, Trimmy, ye limmer! what's your business here?"—So saying, he attempted with the fringe of his plaid to drive them out; but they only ran about the room, eyeing their master with astonishment and concern. They had never, it seemed, been wont to be separated from him either by night or by day, and they could not understand why they should be driven from the parlour, or how they had not as good a right to be there as he. Of course, neither threats nor blows could make them leave him; and it being a scene of life quite new to me, and of which I was resolved to profit as much as possible, at my intercession matters were made up, and the two canine associates were suffered to remain where they were. They were soon seated, one on each side of their master, clinging fondly to his feet, and licking the wet from his dripping trowsers.

Having observed, that when the shepherd entered he had begun to speak with great zest about the sport they had in killing the salmon, I again brought on the subject, and made him describe the diversion to me.—"O man!" said he, and then indulged in a hearty laugh—(*man*

was always the term he used in addressing either of us—*sir* seemed
to be no word in his vocabulary)—"O man, I wish ye had been there!
I'll lay a plack ye wad hae said ye never saw sic sport sin' ever ye
war born. We gat twall fish a' thegither the-day, an' sair broostles
we had wi' some o' them; but a' was naething to the killin o' that ane
at Pool-Midnight. Geordie Otterson, Matthew Ford, an' me, war a'
owr the lugs after him. But ye's hear:—When I came on to the craigs
at the weil o' Pool-Midnight, the sun was shinin' bright, the wind
was lowne, an' wi' the pirl* being away, the pool was as clear as
crystal. I soon saw by the bells coming up, that there was a fish in
the auld hauld; an' I keeks an' I glimes about, till, faith! I sees his
blue murt fin. My teeth war a' waterin to be in him, but I kend
the shank o' my waster§ wasna half length. Sae I cries to Geordie,
'Geordie,' says I, 'aigh man! here's a great chap just lyin steeping
like a aik clog.' Off comes Geordie, shaughle shauglin a' his pith; for
the creature's that greedy o' fish, he wad venture his very saul for
them. I kend brawly what wad be the upshot. 'Now,' says I, 'Geordie, man yoursel for this ae time. Aigh, man! he is a terrible ane for
size—See, yonder he's lying.' The sun was shining sae clear that the
deepness o' the pool was a great cheat. Geordie bait his lip for perfect eagerness, an' his een war stelled in his head—he thought he had
him safe i' the pat; but whenever he put the grains o' the leister into
the water, I could speak nae mair, I kend sae weel what was comin,
for I kend the depth to an inch.—Weel, he airches an' he vizies for a
good while, an' at length made a push down at him wi' his whole
might. Tut!—the leister didna gang to the grund by an ell—an' Geordie gaed into the deepest part o' Pool-Midnight wi' his head foremost! My sennins turned as supple as a dockan, an' I fell just down
i' the bit wi' lauchin—ye might hae bund me wi' a strae. He wad hae
drowned for aught that I could do; for when I saw his heels flingin
up aboon the water as he had been dancin a hornpipe, I lost a'
power thegither; but Matthew Ford harled him into the shallow wi'
his leister.

"Weel, after that we cloddit the pool wi' great stanes, an' aff went
the fish down the gullots, shinin like a rainbow. Then he ran, an' he
ran! an' it was wha to be first in him. Geordie gat the first chance,
an' I thought it was a' owr; but just when he thought he was sure o'
him, down cam Matthew full drive, smashed his grains out through
Geordie's, and gart him miss. It was my chance next; an' I took him
neatly through the gills, though he gaed as fast as a skelldrake.

*Ripple.   § Fish-spear.

"But the sport grew aye better.—Geordie was sae mad at Matthew for taigling him, an' garring him tine the fish—(for he's a greedy dirt), that they had gane to grips in a moment; an' when I lookit back, they war just fightin like twa tarriers in the mids o' the water. The witters o' the twa leisters were fankit in ane anither, an' they couldna get them sindry, else there had been a vast o' bludeshed; but they were knevillin, an' tryin to drown ane anither a' that they could; an' if they hadna been clean forefoughen they wad hae done't; for they were aye gaun out o' sight an' comin howdin up again. Yet after a', when I gaed back to redd them, they were sae inveterate that they wadna part till I was forced to haud them down through the water an' drown them baith."

"But I hope you have not indeed drowned the men," said I. "Ou na, only keepit them down till I took the power fairly frae them—till the bullers gae owr coming up; then I carried them to different sides o' the water, an' laid them down agroof wi' their heads at the inwith; an' after gluthering and spurring a wee while, they came to again. We dinna count muckle of a bit drowning match, us fishers. I wish I could get Geordie as weel doukit ilka day; it wad tak the smeddum frae him—for O, he is a greedy thing! But I fear it will be a while or I see sic glorious sport again."

Mr Grumple remarked, that he thought, by his account, it could not be very good sport to all parties; and that, though he always encouraged these vigorous and healthful exercises among his parishioners, yet he regretted that they could so seldom be concluded in perfect good humour.

"They're nae the waur o' a wee bit splore," said Peter; "they wad turn unco milk-an'-water things, an' dee away a' thegither wantin a broolzie. Ye might as weel think to keep an ale-vat workin wantin barm."

"But, Peter, I hope you have not been breaking the laws of the country by your sport to-day?"

"Na, troth hae we no, man—close-time disna come in till the day after the morn; but atween you an' me, close-time's nae ill time for us. It merely ties up the grit folk's hands, an' thraws a' the sport into ours' thegither. Na, na, we's never complain o' close-time; if it warna for it there wad few fish fa' to poor folk's share."

This was a light in which I had never viewed the laws of the fishing association before; but as this honest hind spoke from experience, I have no doubt that the statement is founded in truth, and that the sole effect of close-time, in all the branches of the principal river, is merely to tie up the hands of every respectable man, and throw the fishing into the hands of poachers. He told me, that in all

the rivers of the extensive parish of *Woolenhorn*, the fish generally
run up during one flood and went away the next; and as the gentlemen and farmers of those parts had no interest in the preservation
of the breeding salmon themselves, nor cared a farthing about the
fishing associations in the great river, whom they viewed as mo-
nopolizers of that to which they had no right, the fish were wholly
abandoned to the poachers, who generally contrived, by burning
lights at the shallows, and spearing the fish by night, and netting the
pools, to annihilate every shoal that came up. This is, however, a
subject that would require an essay by itself.

Our conversation turned on various matters connected with the
country; and I soon found, that though this hind had something in
his manner and address the most uncultivated I had ever seen, yet
his conceptions of such matters as came within the sphere of his
knowledge were pertinent and just. He sung old songs, told us strange
stories of witches and apparitions, and related many anecdotes of
the pastoral life, which I think extremely curious, and wholly unknown to the literary part of the community. But at every observation that he made, he took care to sleek down his black hair over his
brow, as if it were of the utmost consequence to his making a respectable appearance, that it should be equally spread, and as close
pressed down as possible. When desired to join us in drinking tea,
he said "it was a' nonsense thegither, for he hadna the least occasion;" and when pressed to take bread, he persisted in the declaration that "it was great nonsense." He loved to talk of sheep, of dogs,
and of *the lasses*, as he called them; and conversed with his dogs in
the same manner as he did with any of the other guests; nor did the
former ever seem to misunderstand him, unless in his unprecedented
and illiberal attempt to expel them from the company.—"Whitefoot!
haud aff the woman's coat-tails, ye blockhead! Deil hae me gin ye
hae the mense of a miller's horse, man." Whitefoot instantly obeyed.—
"Trimmy! come back aff the fire, dame! Ye're sae wat, ye raise a
reek like a cottar wife's lum—come back, ye limmer!" Trimmy went
behind his chair.

It came out at last that his business with Mr Grumple that day was
to request of him to go over to *Stridekirton* on the Friday following,
and unite him, Peter Plash, in holy wedlock with his sweetheart and
only joe, Jean Windlestrae; and he said, if I "would accompany the
minister, and take share of a haggis wi' them, I wad see some good
lasses, and some good sport too, which was far better." You may be
sure I accepted of the invitation with great cordiality, nor had I any
cause to repent it.

Chapter IV

THE wedding-day at length arrived; and as the bridegroom had charged us to be there at an early hour, we set out on horseback, immediately after breakfast, for the remote hamlet of Stridekirton. We found no regular path, but our way lay through a country which it is impossible to view without soothing emotions. The streams are numerous, clear as crystal, and wind along the glens in many fantastic and irregular curves. The mountains are green to the tops, very high, and form many beautiful soft and shaded outlines. They are, besides, literally speckled with snowy flocks, which, as we passed, were feeding or resting with such appearance of undisturbed repose, that the heart naturally found itself an involuntary sharer in the pastoral tranquillity that pervaded all around.

My good friend, Mr Grumple, could give me no information regarding the names of the romantic glens and mountains that came within our view; he, however, knew who were the proprietors of the land, who the tenants, what rent and stipend each of them paid, and whose teinds were unexhausted; this seemed to be the sum and substance of his knowledge concerning the life, character, and manners of his rural parishioners, save that he could sometimes adduce circumstantial evidence that such and such farmers had made money of their land, and that others had made very little or none.

This district, over which he presides in an ecclesiastical capacity, forms an extensive portion of the Arcadia of Britain. It was likewise, in some late ages, noted for its zeal in the duties of religion, as well as for a thirst after the acquirement of knowledge concerning its doctrines; but under the tuition of such a pastor as my relative appears to be, it is no wonder that practical religion should be losing ground from year to year, and scepticism, the natural consequence of laxity in religious duties, gaining ground in proportion.

It may be deemed, perhaps, rather indecorous, to indulge in such reflections respecting any individual who has the honour to be ranked as a member of a body so generally respectable as our Scottish Clergy, and who, at the same time, maintains a fair *worldly* character; but in a general discussion—in any thing that relates to the common weal of mankind, all such inferior considerations must be laid aside. And the more I consider the simplicity of the people of whom I am now writing—the scenes among which they have been bred—and their lonely and sequestered habits of life, where the workings and phenomena of nature alone appear to attract the eye

or engage the attention,–the more I am convinced that the tempera-
ment of their minds would naturally dispose them to devotional
feelings. If they were but taught to read their Bibles, and only saw
uniformly in the ministers of religion that sanctity of character by
which the profession ought ever to be distinguished, these people
would naturally be such as every well-wisher to the human race
would desire a scattered peasantry to be. But when the most decided variance between example and precept is forced on their observation, what should we, or what can we, expect? Men must see,
hear, feel, and judge accordingly. And certainly in no other instance
is a patron so responsible to his sovereign, his country, and his God,
as in the choice he makes of spiritual pastors.

These were some of the reflections that occupied my mind as I
traversed this beautiful pastoral country with its morose teacher,
and from these I was at length happily aroused by the appearance of
the cottage, or shepherd's steading, to which we were bound. It was
situated in a little valley in the bottom of a wild glen, or *hope*, as it is
there called. It stood all alone; but besides the dwelling-house, there
was a little byre that held the two cows and their young,–a good
stack of hay, another of peats,–a sheep-house, and two homely gardens; and the place had altogether something of a snug, comfortable
appearance. Though this is only an individual picture, I am told it
may be viewed as a general one of almost every shepherd's dwelling in the south of Scotland; and it is only such pictures that, in the
course of these tales, I mean to present to the public.

A number of the young shepherds and country-lasses had already
arrived, impatient for the approaching wedding; others were coming down the green hills in mixed parties all around, leading one
another, and skipping with the agility of lambs. They were all walking barefooted and barelegged, male and female–the men were
dressed much in the ordinary way, only that the texture of their
clothes was somewhat coarse, and the women had black beavers,
white gowns, and "green coats kilted to the knee." When they came
near the house they went into little sequestered hollows, the men
and women apart, "pat on their hose an' shoon, and made themsels
a' trig an' witching," and then came and joined the group with a joy
that could not be restrained by walking,–they ran to mix with their
youthful associates.

Still as they arrived, we saw on our approach, that they drew up
in two rows on the green, and soon found that it was a contest
at leaping. The shepherds were stripped to the shirt and drawers,
and exerting themselves in turn with all their might, while their sweet-

hearts and sisters were looking on with no small share of interest.

We received a kind and hospitable welcome from honest Peter and his father, who was a sagacious-looking old carle, with a broad bonnet and gray locks; but the contest on the green still continuing, I went and joined the circle, delighted to see a pastime so appropriate to the shepherd's life. I was utterly astonished at the agility which the fellows displayed.

They took a short race of about twelve or fourteen paces, which they denominated the *ramrace*, and then rose from the footing-place with such a bound as if they had been going to mount and fly into the air. The crooked guise in which they flew shewed great art—the knees were doubled upward—the body bent forward—and the head thrown somewhat back; so that they alighted on their heels with the greatest ease and safety, their joints being loosened in such a manner that not one of them was straight. If they fell backward on the ground, the leap was not accounted fair. Several of the antagonists took the ramrace with a staff in their hand, which they left at the footing-place as they rose. This I thought unfair, but none of their opponents objected to the custom. I measured the distance, and found that two of them had actually leapt twenty-two feet, on a level plain, at one bound. This may appear extraordinary to those who never witnessed such an exercise, but it is a fact of which I can adduce sufficient proof.

Being delighted as well as astonished at seeing these feats of agility, I took Peter aside, and asked him if I might offer prizes for some other exercises. "Hout na," said Peter; "ye'll affront them; let them just alane; they hae eneuch o' incitement e'now, an' rather owre muckle atween you an' me; forebye the brag o' the thing—as lang as the lasses stand and look at them, they'll ply atween death an' life." What Peter said was true,—instead of getting weary of their sports, their ardour seemed to increase; and always as soon as the superiority of any individual in one particular exercise was manifest, another was instantly resorted to; so that ere long there was one party engaged in wrestling, one in throwing the stone, and another at hop-step-and-leap, all at one and the same time.

This last seems to be rather the favourite amusement. It consists of three succeeding bounds, all with the same race; and as the exertion is greater, and of longer continuance, they can judge with more precision the exact capability of the several competitors. I measured the ground, and found the greatest distance effected in this way to be forty-six feet. I am informed, that whenever two or three young shepherds are gathered together, at fold or bught, moor or market, at all times and seasons, Sundays excepted, one or more of these athletic exercises is uniformly resorted to; and certainly, in a class where hardiness and agility are so requisite, they can never be too much encouraged.

But now all these favourite sports were terminated at once by a loud cry of "Hurra! the broose! the broose!" Not knowing what *the broose* meant, I looked all around with great precipitation, but for some time could see nothing but hills. At length, however, by marking the direction in which the rest looked, I perceived, at a considerable distance down the glen, five horsemen coming at full speed on a determined race, although on such a road, as I believe, a race was never before contested. It was that by which we had lately come, and the only one that led to the house from all the four quarters of the world. For some time it crossed "the crooks of the burn," as they called them; that is, it kept straight up the bottom of the glen, and crossed the burn at every turning. Of course every time that the group crossed this stream, they were for a moment involved in a cloud of spray that almost hid them from view, and the frequent recurrence of this rendered the effect highly comic.

Still, however, they kept apparently close together, till at length the path left the bottom of the narrow valley, and came round the sloping base of a hill that was all interspersed with drains and small irregularities of surface; this producing no abatement of exertion or speed, horses and men were soon foundering, plunging, and tumbling about in all directions. If this was amusing to view, it was still more so to hear the observations of the delighted group that stood round me and beheld it. "Ha, ha, ha! yonder's ane aff! Gude faith! yon's Jock o' the Meer-Cleuch; he has gotten an ill-faur'd flaip.– Holloa! yonder gaes another, down through a lair to the een-holes! Weel done, Aedie o' Aberlosk! Hie till him, Tousy, outher now or never! Lay on, ye deevil, an' hing by the mane! Hurray!"

The women were by this time screaming, and the men literally jumping and clapping their hands for joy at the deray that was going on; and there was one little elderly-looking man whom I could not help noting; he had fallen down on the ground in a convulsion of laughter, and was spurring and laying on it with both hands and feet. One, whom they denominated Davie Scott o' the Ramseycleuch Burn, amid the bay of dogs, and the shouts of men and women, got first to the bridegroom's door, and of course was acknowledged to have won the *broose*; but the attention was soon wholly turned from him to those behind. The man whose horse had sunk in the bog, perceiving that all chance of extricating it again on the instant was out of the question, lost not a moment, but sprung to his feet—threw off his clothes, hat, and shoes, all at one brush—and ran towards the goal with all his might. Jock o' the Meer Cleuch, who was still a good way farther back, and crippled besides with his fall, perceiving this, mounted again—whipped on furiously, and would soon have overhied his pedestrian adversary; but the shepherds are bad horse-men, and, moreover, Jock's horse, which belonged to Gideon of Kirkhope, was unacquainted with the sheep-drains, and terrified at them; consequently, by making a sudden jerk backwards when he should have leapt across one of them, and when Jock supposed that he was just going to do so, he threw his rider a second time. The shouts of laughter were again renewed, and every one was calling out, "Now for the mell! Now for the mell! Deil tak the hindmost now!" These sounds reached Jock's ears; he lost no time in making a last effort, but flew at his horse again—remounted him—and, by urging him to a desperate effort, actually got a-head of his adversary just when within ten yards of the door, and thus escaped the dis-grace of *winning the mell.*

I was afterwards told, that in former ages it was the custom on the Border, when the victor in the race was presented with the prize of honour, the one who came in last was, at the same time, presented with a mallet or large wooden hammer, called a *mell* in the dialect of the country, and that then the rest of the competitors stood in need to be near at hand, and instantly to force the *mell* from him, else he was at liberty to knock as many of them down with it as he could. The mell has now, for many years, been only a nominal prize; but there is often more sport about the gaining of it than the principal one. There was another occurrence which added greatly to the ani-mation of this, which I had not time before fully to relate. About the time when the two unfortunate wights were unhorsed in the bog, those who still kept on were met and attacked, open mouth, by at least twenty frolicsome collies, that seemed fully as intent on sport as their masters. These bit the hind-legs of the horses, snapped at their noses, and raised such an outrage of barking, that the poor animals, forespent as they were, were constrained to lay themselves out almost beyond power. Nor did the fray cease when the race was won. Encouraged by the noise and clamour which then arose about the gaining of the mell, the staunch collies continued the attack, and hunted the racers round and round the houses with great speed, while the horses were all the time wheeling and flinging most furi-ously, and their riders, in desperation, vociferating and cursing their assailants.

All the guests now crowded together, and much humour and blunt wit passed about the gaining of the brooze. Each of the competitors had his difficulties and cross accidents to relate; and each affirmed, that if it had not been such and such hindrances, he would have gained the brooze to a certainty. Davie Scott o' the Ramsey-cleuch-burn, however, assured them, that "he was aye hauding in his yaud wi' the left hand, and gin he had liket to gie her out her head, she wad hae gallopit amaist a third faster."—"That may be," said Aedie o' Aberlosk, "but I hae come better on than I expectit wi' my Cameronian naig. I never saw him streek himsel sae afore—I dare say he thought that Davie was auld Clavers mountit on Hornie. Poor fallow!" continued he, patting him, "he has a good deal o' anti-prelatic dourness in him; but I see he has some spirit, for a' that. I bought him for a powney, but he's turned out a beast."

I next overheard one proposing to the man who left his horse, and exerted himself so manfully on foot, to go and pull his horse out of the quagmire. "Na, na," said he, "let him stick yonder a while, to learn him mair sense than to gang intill an open weel-ee and gar ane get a mell. I saw the gate I was gawn, but I couldna swee him aff; sae I just thought o' Jenny Blythe, and plunged in. I kend weel some-thing was to happen, for I met her first this morning, the ill-hued carlin: but I had need to haud my tongue!—Gudeman, let us see a drap whisky." He was presented with a glass. "Come, here's Jenny Blythe," said Andrew, and drank it off.—"I wad be nae the waur o' a wee drap too," said Aberlosk, taking a glass of whisky in his hand, and looking stedfastly through it. "I think I see Jock the elder here," said he; "ay, it's just him—come, here's *the five kirks o' Eskdale.*" He drank it off. "Gudeman, that's naething but a *Tam-Park* of a glass: if ye'll fill it again, I'll gie a toast ye never heard afore. This is *Bailey's Dictionary*," said Aedie, and drank it off again.—"But when a' your daffin's owre, Aedie," said John, "what hae ye made o' your young friend?"—"Ou! she's safe eneuch," returned he; "the best-man and John the elder are wi' her."

On looking round the corner of the house, we now perceived that the bride and her two attendants were close at hand. They came at a *quick canter.* She managed her horse well, kept her saddle with great ease, and seemed an elegant sprightly girl, of twenty-four or thereabouts. Every cap was instantly waved in the air, and the bride was saluted with three hearty cheers. Old John, well aware of what it behoved him to do, threw off his broad bonnet, and took the bride respectfully from her horse—kissed and welcomed her home. "Ye're welcome hame till us, Jeany, my bonny woman," said he; "may God bless ye, an' mak ye just as good an' as happy as I wish ye." It was a beautiful and affecting sight to see him leading her toward the home that was now to be her own. He held her hand in both his—the wind waved his long gray locks—his features were lengthened considerably the wrong way, and I could perceive a tear glistening on his furrowed cheek.

All seemed to know exactly the parts they had to act; but every thing came on me like magic, and quite by surprise. The bride now stopped short on the threshold, while the old man broke a triangular cake of short-bread over her head, the pieces of which he threw about among the young people. These scrambled for them with great violence and eagerness; and indeed they seemed always to be most in their element when any thing that required strength or activity was presented. For my part, I could not comprehend what the sudden convulsion meant, (for in a moment the crowd was moving like a whirlpool, and tumbling over one another in half dozens) till a little girl, escaping from the vortex, informed me that "they war battling wha first to get a haud o' the bride's bunn." I was still in the dark, till at length I saw the successful candidates presenting their favourites with small pieces of this mystical cake. One beautiful maid, with light locks, blue eyes, and cheeks like the vernal rose, came nimbly up to me, called me familiarly by my name, looked at me with perfect seriousness, and without even a smile on her innocent face, asked me *if I was married.* I could scarcely contain my gravity, while I took her by the hand, and answered in the negative—"An' hae ye no gotten a piece o' the bride's cake?"—"Indeed, my dear, I am sorry I have not."—"O, that's a great shame, that ye hae nae gotten a wee bit! I canna bide to see a stranger guided that gate. Here, sir, I'll gie ye the tae half o' mine, it will ser' us baith; an I wad rather want mysel than as civil a gentleman that's a stranger should want."

So saying, she took a small piece of cake from her lap, and parted it with me, at the same time rolling each of the pieces carefully up in a leaf of an old halfpenny ballad; but the whole of her demeanour showed the utmost seriousness, and of how much import she judged this trivial crumb to be. "Now," continued she, "ye maun lay this aneath your head, sir, when ye gang to your bed, and ye'll dream about the woman ye are to get for your wife. Ye'll just think ye see her plainly an' bodily afore your een; an' ye'll be sae weel acquainted wi' her, that ye'll ken her again when ye see her, if it war amang a thousand. It's a queer thing, but it's perfectly true; sae ye maun *mind no to forget.*"

I promised the most punctual observance of all that she enjoined, and added, that I was sure I would dream of the lovely giver; that indeed I would be sorry were I to dream of any other, as I deemed it impossible to dream of so much innocence and beauty.—"*Now mind no to forget,*" rejoined she, and skipped lightly away to join her youthful associates.

As soon as the bride was led into the house, old Nelly, the bridegroom's mother, went aside to see the beast on which her daughter-in-law had been brought home; and perceiving that it was a mare, she fell a-crying and wringing her hands.—I inquired, with some alarm, what was the matter. "O dear, sir," returned she, "it's for the poor bairnies that'll yet hae to dree this unlucky mischance—Laike-a-day, poor waefu' brats! they'll no lie in a dry bed for a dozen o' years to come!"

"Hout! haud your tongue, Nelly," said the best man, "the thing's but a freat a' thegither. But really we coudna help it: the factor's naig wantit a fore-fit shoe, an' was beckin like a water-craw. If I had ridden five miles to the smiddy wi' him, it is ten to ane but Jock Anderson wad hae been drunk, an' then we wadna hae gotten the bride hame afore twall o'clock at night; sae I thought it was better to let them tak their chance than spoil sae muckle good sport, an' I e'en set her on Wattie Bryden's pownie. The factor has behaved very ill about it, the muckle stoottin gowk! If I had durst, I wad hae gien him a deevil of a thrashin; but he says, 'Faith it's—that—yes, indeed—that—he will send them—yes, faith—it's even a—*a new tikabed* every year.'"

Chapter V

As soon as the marriage ceremony was over, all the company shook hands with the young couple, and wished them every kind of joy and felicity. The rusticity of their benisons amused me, and there were several of them that I have never, to this day, been able to comprehend. As, for instance—one wished them "thumpin luck and fat weans;" another, "a bien rannlebauks, and tight thack and rape o'er their heads;" a third gave them "a routh aumrie and a close nieve;" and the lasses wished them "as mony hiney moons as the family had fingers an' taes." I took notes of these at the time, and many more, and set them down precisely as they were spoken; all of them have doubtless meanings attached to them, but these are perhaps the least mystical.

I expected, now, that we should go quietly to our dinner; but instead of that, they again rushed rapidly away towards the green, crying out, "Now for the broose! now for the broose!"—"The people are unquestionably mad," said I to one that stood beside me; "are they really going to run their horses again among such ravines and bogs as these? they must be dissuaded from it." The man informed me that the race was now to be on foot; that there were always two races—the first on horseback for the bride's napkin, and the second on foot for the bridegroom's spurs. I asked him how it came that they had thus altered the order of things in the appropriation of the prizes, for that the spurs would be the fittest for the riders, as the napkin would for the runners. He admitted this, but could adduce no reason why it was otherwise, save that "it was the gude auld gate, and it would be a pity to alter it." He likewise informed me, that it was customary for some to run on the bride's part, and some on the bridegroom's; and that it was looked on as a great honour to the country, or connexions of either party, to bear the broose away from the other. Accordingly, on our way to the race-ground, the bridegroom was recruiting hard for runners on his part, and, by the time we reached the starting-place, had gained the consent of five. One now asked the *best-man* why he was not recruiting in behalf of the bride. "Never mind," said he; "do ye strip an' mak ready—I'll find them on the bride's part that will do a' the turn." It was instantly rumoured around, that he had brought one all the way from Liddesdale to carry the prize away on the bride's part, and that he was the best runner on all the Border side. The runners, that were all so brisk of late, were now struck dumb; and I marked them going one by one, eyeing the stranger with a jealous curiosity, and measuring him with their eyes from head to foot.—No, not one of them would venture to take the field against him!—"they war only jokin'—they never intendit to rin—they war just jaunderin wi' the bridegroom for fun."—"Come, fling aff your claes, Hobby, an' let them see that ye're ready for them," said the best-man. The stranger obeyed—he was a tall, slender, and handsome youth, with brown hair, prominent features, and a ruddy complexion.—"Come, lads," said the best-man, "Hobby canna stand wanting his claes; if nane of ye are ready to start with him in twa minutes, he shall rin the course himsel, and then I think the folk o' this country are shamed for ever,"—"No sae fast," said a little funny-looking fellow, who instantly began to strip off his stockings and shoes; "no sae fast, lad; he may won, but he sanna won untried." A committee was instantly formed apart, where it was soon agreed, that all the good runners there should, with one accord, start against this stranger; for that, "if naebody ran but Tam the tailor, they wad be a' shamed thegither, for Tam wad never come within a stane-clod o' him."—"Hout, ay—that's something like yoursels, callants," said old John; "try him—he's but a saft feckless-like chiel; I think ye needna be sae feared for him."—"It is a' ye ken," said another; "do nae ye see that he's lingit like a grew—and he'll rin like ane;—they say he rins faster than a horse can gallop."—"I'll try him on my Cameronian whenever he likes," said Aberlosk; "him that beats a Cameronian has but another to beat."

In half a minute after this, seven athletic youths were standing in a row stripped, and panting for the race; and I could note, by the paleness of their faces, how anxious they were about the result—all save Aedie o' Aberlosk, on whom the whisky had made some impression, and who seemed only intent on making fun. At the distance of 500 yards there was a man placed, whom they denominated *the stoop*, and who had his hat raised on the end of his staff, lest another might be mistaken for him. Around this *stoop* they were to run, and return to the starting-place, making in all a heat of only 1000 yards, which I was told is the customary length of a race all over that country. They took all hold of one another's hands—the best-man adjusted the line in which they stood, and then gave the word as follows, with considerable pauses between: *Once—Twice—Thrice,*—and off they flew like lightning, in the most beautiful style I ever beheld. The ground was rough and unequal, but there was no restraint or management practised; every one set out on full speed from the very first. The Borderer took the lead, and had soon distanced them a considerable space—all save Aberlosk, who kept close at his side, straining and twisting his face in a most tremendous manner: at length he got rather before him, but it was an overstretch—Aedie fell flat on his face, nor did he offer to rise, but lay still on the spot, puffing and swearing against the champion of Liddesdale.

Hobby cleared the *stoop* first by about twenty yards;—the rest turned in such a group that I could not discern in what order, but they were all obliged to turn it to the right, or what they called "sun-ways-about," on pain of losing the race. The generality of the "weddingers" were now quite silent, and looked very blank when they saw this stranger still keeping so far a-head. Aberlosk tried to make them all fall one by one, by creeping in before them as they passed; and at length laid hold of the hindmost by the foot, and brought him down.

By this time two of the Borderer's acquaintances had run down the green to meet him, and encourage him on. "Weel done, Hobby!"

they were shouting: "Weel done, Hobby!–Liddesdale for ever!–Let them lick at that!–Let the benty-necks crack now!–Weel done, Hobby!"–I really felt as much interested about the issue, at this time, as it was possible for any of the adverse parties to be. The enthusiasm seemed contagious; for though I knew not one side from the other, yet was I running among the rest, and shouting as they did. A sort of half-animated murmur now began to spread, and gained ground every moment. A little gruff Cossack-looking peasant came running near with a peculiar wildness in his looks, and accosted one of the men that were cheering Hobby. "Dinna be just sae loud an' ye like, Willie Beattie; dinna mak nae mair din than just what's needfu'. Will o' Bellendine! haud till him, sir, or it's day wi' us! Hie, Will, if ever ye ran i' your life!–By Jehu, sir ye're winning every third step!– He has him *dead!* he has him *dead!*" The murmur, which had increased like the rushing of many waters, now terminated in a frantic shout. Hobby had strained too hard at first, in order to turn the stoop before Aberlosk, who never intended turning it at all–the other youth was indeed fast gaining on him, and I saw his lips growing pale, and his knees plaiting as if unable to bear his weight–his breath was quite exhausted, and though within twenty yards of the stoop, Will began to shoulder by him. So anxious was Hobby now to keep his ground, that his body pressed onward faster than his feet could keep up with it, and his face, in consequence, came deliberately against the earth,–he could not be said to fall, for he just ran on till he could get no farther for something that stopped him. Will o' Bellendine won the broose amid clamours of applause, which he seemed fully to appreciate–the rest were over Hobby in a moment; and if it had not been for the wayward freaks of Aberlosk, this redoubted champion would fairly have won the mell.

The lad that Aedie overthrew, in the midst of his career, was very angry with him on account of the outrage–but Aedie cared for no man's anger. "The man's mad," said he; "wad ye attempt to strive wi' the champion of Liddesdale?–Hout, hout! haud your tongue; ye're muckle better as ye are. I sall tak the half o' the mell wi' ye."

On our return to the house, I was anxious to learn something of Aedie, who seemed to be a very singular character. Upon applying to a farmer of his acquaintance, I was told a number of curious and extravagant stories of him, one or two of which I shall insert here, as I profess to be giving anecdotes of the country life.

He once quarrelled with another farmer on the highway, who, getting into a furious rage, rode at Aedie to knock him down. Aedie, who was on foot, fled with all his might to the top of a large dunghill for shelter, where, getting hold of a graip (a three-pronged fork used in agriculture), he attacked his adversary with such an overflow of dung, that his horse took fright, and in spite of all he could do, ran clear off with him, and left Aedie master of the field. The farmer, in high wrath, sent him a challenge to fight with pistols, in a place called Selkith Hope, early in the morning. This is an extremely wild, steep, and narrow glen. Aedie attended, but kept high up on the hill; and when his enemy reached the narrowest part of the Hope, began the attack by rolling great stones at him down from the mountain. Nothing could be more appalling than this—the farmer and his horse were both alike terrified, and, as Aedie expressed it, "he set them baith back the gate they cam, as their heads had been a-lowe."

Another time, in that same Hope of Selkith, he met a stranger, whom he mistook for another man called Jamie Sword; and because the man denied that he was Jamie Sword, Aedie fastened a quarrel on him, insisting on him either being Jamie Sword, or giving some proofs to the contrary. It was very impudent in him, he said, to give any man the lie, when he could produce no evidence of his being wrong. The man gave him his word that he was not Jamie Sword. "O, but that's naething," said Aedie, "I give you my word that you are, and I think my word's as good as yours ony day." Finally, he told the man, that if he would not acknowledge that he was wrong, and confess that he was Jamie Sword, he would fight him.—He did so, and got himself severely thrashed.

The following is a copy of a letter, written by Aedie to a great personage, dated Aberlosk, May 27th, 1806.*

"To George the Third, London."

DEAR SIR,—I went thirty miles on foot yesterday to pay your taxes, and, after all, the bodies would not take them, saying, that I was too late, and that they must now be recovered, with expenses, by regular course of law. I thought if your Majesty was like me, money would never come wrong to you, although it were a few days too late; so I enclose you £27 in notes, and half-a-guinea, which is the amount of what they charge me for last year, and fourpence halfpenny over. You must send me a

---

*Should the reader imagine that this curious epistle is a mere coinage of my own, I can assure him, from undoubted authority, that both Aedie and his letter are faithful transcripts from real and *existing originals.*

receipt when the coach comes back, else they will not believe that I have paid you.

Direct to the care of Andrew Wilson, butcher in Hawick.

I am, dear Sir, your most humble servant. A * * * B * * * *
To the King.

P. S.–This way of taxing the farmers will never do; you will see the upshot."

It has been reported over all that country, that this letter reached its destination, and that a receipt was returned in due course of post; but the truth is (and, for the joke's sake, it is a great pity it should have been so), that the singularity of the address caused some friends to open the letter, and return it, with the money, to the owner; but not before they had taken a copy of it, from which the above is exactly transcribed.

Country Dreams and Apparitions

No. II

Connel of Dee

I.

CONNEL went out by a blink of the moon
　To his light little bower in the deane;
He thought they had gi'en him his supper owr soon,
　And that still it was lang until e'en.
Oh! the air was so sweet, and the sky so serene,　　　　5
　And so high his soft languishment grew—
That visions of happiness danced o'er his mind;
　He longed to leave parent and sisters behind;
For he thought that his Maker to him was unkind,
　For that high were his merits he knew.　　　　10

II.

Sooth, Connel was halesome, and stalwart to see,
　The bloom of fayir yudith he wore;
But the lirk of displeasure hang over his bree,
　Nae glisk of contentment it bore,
He lang'd for a wife with a mailen and store;　　　　15
　He grevit in idless to lie,
Afar from his cottage he wished to remove,
To wassail and waik, and unchided to rove,
And beik in the cordial transports of love
　All under a kindlier sky.　　　　20

III.

O sweet was the fa' of that gloaming to view!
　The day-lighte crap laigh on the doon,
And left its pale borders abeigh on the blue,
　To mix wi' the beams of the moon.
The hill hang its skaddaw the greinwud aboon,　　　　25
　The houf of the bodyng Benshee;
Slow o'er him were sailing the cloudlets of June,
The beetle began his wild airel to tune,
And sang on the wynde with ane eirysome croon,
　Away on the breeze of the Dee!　　　　30

IV.

With haffat on lufe poor Connel lay lorn!
  He languishit for muckle and mair!
His bed of greine hether he eynit to scorn,
    The bygane he doughtna weel bear!
      Atour him the greine leife was fannyng the air,   35
        In noiseless and flychtering play;
The hush of the water fell saft on his ear,
And he fand as gin sleep, wi' her gairies, war near,
Wi' her freaks and her ferlies and phantoms of fear,
      But he eidently wysit her away.   40

V.

Short time had he sped in that sellible strife
  Ere he saw a young maiden stand by,
Who seem'd in the bloom and the bell of her life;
    He wist not that ane was sae nigh!
      But sae sweet was her look, and sae saft was her eye,   45
        That his heart was all quaking with love;
And then there was kythin a dimple sae sly,
At play on her cheek, of the moss-rose's dye,
That kindled the heart of poor Connel on high
      With ravishment deadlye to prove.   50

VI.

He deemed her a beautifull spirit of night,
  And eiry was he to assay;
But he found she was mortal with thrilling delight,
    For her breath was like zephyr of May;
      Her eye was the dew-bell, the beam of the day,   55
        And her arm it was softer than silk;
Her hand was so warm, and her lip was so red,
Her slim taper waiste so enchantingly made!
And some beauties moreover that cannot be said—
      Of bosom far whiter than milk!   60

VII.

Poor Connel was reaved of all power and of speech,
  His frame grew all powerless and weak;
He neither could stir, nor caress her, nor fleech,
    He trembled, but word couldna speak!
      But O, when his lips touched her soft rosy cheek,   65

The channels of feeling ran dry,
He found that like emmets his life-blood it crept,
His liths turned as limber as dud that is steeped,
He streekit his limbs, and he moaned and he wept;
    And for love he was just gaun to die.   70

VIII.

The damsel beheld, and she raised him so kind,
    And she said, "My dear beautiful swain,
Take heart till I tell you the hark of my mind,
    I'm weary of lying my lane;
    I have castles, and lands, and flocks of my ain,   75
      But want ane my gillour to share;
A man that is hale as the hart on the hill,
As stark, and as kind, is the man to my will,
Who has slept on the heather and drank of the rill,
    And, like you, gentle, amorous, and fair.   80

IX.

"I often hae heard, that like you there was nane,
    And I aince gat a glisk of thy face;
Now far have I ridden, and far have I gane,
    In hopes thou wilt nurice the grace,
    To make me thy ain—O come to my embrace!   85
      For I love thee as dear as my life!
I'll make thee a laird of the boonmost degree,
My castles and lands I'll give freely to thee,
Though rich and abundant thine own they shall be,
    If thou wilt but make me thy wife."   90

X.

Oh! never was man sae delighted and fain!
    He bowed a consent to her will,
Kind Providence thankit again and again;
    And 'gan to display his rude skill
    In leifu' endearment, and thought it nae ill   95
      To kiss the sweet lips of the fair,
And press her to lie, in that gloamin sae still,
Adown by his side in the howe of the hill,
For the water flowed sweet, and the sound of the rill
    Would sooth every sorrow and care.   100

XI.

No—she wadna lie by the side of a man
    Till the rites of the marriage were bye.
Away they hae sped; but soon Connel began,
    For his heart it was worn to a sigh,
      To fondle, and simper, and look in her eye,   105
        Oh! direful to bear was his wound!
When on her fair neck fell his fingers sae dun—
It strak thro' his heart like the shot of a gun!
He felt as the sand of existence were run.
      He trembled, and fell to the ground.   110

XII.

O, Connel, dear Connel, be patient a while!
    These wounds of thy bosom will heal,
And thou with thy love may'st walk many a mile
    Nor transport nor passion once feel.
      Thy spirits once broke on electerick wheel,   115
        Cool reason her empire shall gain;
And haply, repentance in dowy array,
And laithly disgust may arise in thy way,
Encumb'ring the night, and o'ercasting the day,
      And turn all those pleasures to pain.   120

XIII.

The mansion is gained, and the bridal is past,
    And the transports of wedlock prevail;
The lot of poor Connel the shepherd is cast
    Mid pleasures that never can fail;
      The balms of Arabia sweeten the gale,   125
        The tables for ever are spread
With damask, and viands, and heart-cheering wine,
Their splendour and elegance fully combine,
His lawns they are ample, his bride is divine,
      And of goud-fringed silk is his bed.   130

XIV.

The transports of love gave rapture, and flew;
    The banquet soon sated and cloyed;
Nae mair they delighted, nae langer were new,
    They could not be ever enjoyed!
      He felt in his bosom a fathomless void,   135

A yearning again to be free;
Than all that voluptuous sickening store,
The wine that he drank and the robes that he wore,
His diet of milk had delighted him more
    Afar on the hills of the Dee.   140

XV.

O oft had he sat by the clear springing well,
    And dined from his wallet full fain!
Then sweet was the scent of the blue heather bell,
    And free was his bosom of pain;
    The laverock was lost in the lift, but her strain   145
    Came trilling so sweetly from far,
To rapture the hour he would wholly resign,
He would listen, and watch, till he saw her decline,
And the sun's yellow beam on her dappled breast shine,
    Like some little musical star.   150

XVI.

And then he wad lay his blue bonnet aside,
    And turn his rapt eyes to the heaven,
And bless his kind Maker who all did provide,
    And beg that he might be forgiven,
    For his sins were like crimson!—all bent and uneven   155
    The path he had wilsomely trode!
Then who the delight of his bosom could tell?
O sweet was that meal by his pure mountain well;
And sweet was its water he drank from the shell,
    And peaceful his moorland abode.   160

XVII.

But now was he deaved and babbled outright,
    By gossips in endless array,
Who thought not of sin, nor of Satan aright,
    Nor the dangers that mankind belay;
    Who joked about heaven, and scorned to pray,   165
    And gloried in that was a shame.
O Connel was troubled at things that befel!
So different from scenes he had once loved so well,
He deem't he was placed on the confines of Hell,
    And fand like the saur of its flame!   170

XVIII.

Of bonds and of law-suits he still was in doubt,
  And old debts coming due every day;
And a thousand odd things he kend naething about
  Kept him in continued dismay.
    At board he was awkward, nor wist what to say,   175
      Nor what his new honours became;
His guests they wad mimic and laugh in their slieve.
He blushed, and he faultered, and scarce dought believe
That men were so base as to smile and deceive;
    Or eynied of him to make game!   180

XIX.

Still franker and freer his gossippers grew,
  And preyed upon him and his dame;
Their jests and their language to Connel were new,
  It was slander, and cursing, and shame!
    He groaned in his heart, and he thought them to blame 185
      For revel and rout without end;
He saw himself destined to pamper and feed
A race whom he hated, a profligate breed,
The scum of existence to vengeance decreed!
    Who laughed at their God and their friend.   190

XX.

He saw that in wickedness all did delight,
  And he kendna what length it might bear;
They drew him to evil by day and by night,
  To scenes that he trembled to share!
    His heart it grew sick and his head it grew sair,   195
      And he thought what he dared not to tell!
He thought of the far distant hills of the Dee!
Of his cake, and his cheese, and his lair on the lea!
Of the laverock that hung on the heaven's ee-bree,
  His prayer and his clear mountain well!   200

XXI.

His breast he durst sparingly trust wi' the thought,
  Of the virtuous days that were fled!
Yet still his kind lady he loved as he ought,
  Or soon from that scene he had fled.
    It now was but rarely she honoured his bed—   205

'Twas modesty, heightening her charms!
A delicate feeling that man cannot ween!
O heaven!—each night from his side she had been—
He found it at length——Nay he saw't with his een,
    She slept in a paramour's arms!!!   210

XXII.

It was the last pang that the spirit could bear!
    Destruction and death was the meed.
For forfeited vows there was nought too severe;
    Even conscience applauded the deed.
        His mind was decided, her doom was decreed;   215
        He led her to chamber apart
To give her to know, of his wrongs he had sense;
To chide and upbraid her in language intense
And kill her, at least, for her heinous offence—
    A crime at which demons would start!   220

XXIII.

With grievous reproaches, in agonized zeal,
    Stern Connel his lecture began,
He mentioned her crime!—She turned on her heel,
    And her mirth to extremity ran.
        "Why that was the fashion!—no sensible man   225
        Could e'er of such freedom complain.
What was it to him? there were maidens enow
Of the loveliest forms, and the loveliest hue,
Who blithely would be his companions, he knew,
    If he wearied of lying his lane."   230

XXIV.

How Connel was shocked!—but his fury still rose,
    He shivered from toe to the crown!
His hair stood like heath on the mountain that grows,
    And each hair had a life of its own!
        "O thou most"—But whereto his passion had flown 235
        No man to this day can declare,
For his dame, with a frown, laid her hand on his mouth,
That hand once as sweet as the breeze of the south!
That hand that gave pleasures and honours and routh,
    And she said, with a dignified air,   240

XXV.

"Peace booby! if life thou regardest beware,
    I have had some fair husbands ere now;
They wooed, and they flattered, they sighed and they sware,
    At length they grew irksome like you.
    Come hither one moment, a sight I will show   245
      That will teach thee some breeding and grace."
She opened a door, and there Connel beheld
A sight that to trembling his spirit impelled,
A man standing chained, who nor 'plained, nor rebelled,
    And that man had a sorrowful face.   250

XXVI.

Down creaked a trap-door, on which he was placed,
    Right softly and slowly it fell;
And the man seemed in terror, and strangely amazed,
    But why Connel could not then tell.
    He sunk and he sunk as the vice did impel;   255
      At length, as far downward he drew,
Good Lord! In a trice, with the pull of a string,
A pair of dread shears, like the thunder-bolt's wing,
Came snap on his neck, with a terrible spring,
    And severed it neatly in two.   260

XXVII.

Adown fell the body—the head lay in sight,
    The lips in a moment grew wan;
The temple just quivered, the eye it grew white,
    And upward the purple threads span!
    The dark crooked streamlets along the boards ran,   265
      Thin pipings of reek could be seen;
Poor Connel was blinded, his lugs how they sung!
He looked once again, and he saw like the tongue,
That motionless out 'twixt the livid lips hung,
    Then mirkness set over his een.   270

XXVIII.

He turned and he dashed his fair lady aside;
    And off like the lightning he broke,
By staircase and gallery, with horrified stride,
    He turned not, he staid not, nor spoke;
    The iron-spiked court-gate he could not unlock   275

His haste was beyond that of man;
He stopp'd not to rap, and he staid not to call,
With ram-race he cleared at a bensil the wall,
And headlong beyond got a grieveous fall,
    But he rose, and he ran, and he ran!   280

XXIX.

As stag of the forest, when fraudfully coiled,
    And mured up in barn for a prey,
Sees his dappled comrades dishonoured and soiled
    In their blood, on some festival day
Bursts all intervention, and hies him away,   285
    Like the wind over holt over lea;
So Connel pressed on, all encumbrance he threw,
Over height, over hollow, he lessened to view,
It may not be said that he ran, for he flew,
    Straight on for the hills of the Dee.   290

XXX.

The contrair of all other runners in life,
    His swiftness increased as he flew,
But be it remembered, he ran from a wife,
    And a trap-door that sunk on a screw.
His prowess he felt and decidedly knew,   295
    So much did his swiftness excel,
That he skimm'd the wild paths like a thing of the mind,
And the stour from each footstep was seen on the wind,
Distinct by itself for a furlong behind,
    Before that it mingled or fell.   300

XXXI.

He came to a hill, the ascent it was steep,
    And much did he fear for his breath;
He halted, he ventured behind him to peep,
    The sight was a vision of death!
His wife and her paramours came on the path,   305
    Well mounted with devilish speed;
O Connel, poor Connel, thy hope is a wreck!
Sir, run for thy life, without stumble or check,
It is thy only stake, the last chance for thy neck,
    Strain Connel, or death is thy meed!   310

XXXII.

O wend to the right, to the woodland betake;
    Gain that, and yet safe thou may'st be;
How fast they are gaining!–O stretch to the brake!
    Poor Connel, 'tis over with thee!
        In the breath of the horses, his yellow locks flee,   315
            The voice of his wife's in the van:
Even that was not needful to heighten his fears,
He sprang o'er the bushes, he dashed thro' the breers,
For he thought of the trap-door and d——ble sheers,
            And he cried to his God, and he ran.   320

XXXIII.

Thro' gallwood and bramble he floundered amain,
    No bar his advancement could stay;
Tho' heels-o'er-head whirled again and again,
    Still faster he gained on his way.
        This moment on swinging bough powerless he lay,   325
            The next he was flying along;
So lightly he scarce made the green leaf to quake,
Impetuous he splashed thro' the bog and the lake,
He rainbowed the hawthorn, he needled the brake,
            With power supernaturally strong.   330

XXXIV.

The riders are foiled, and far lagging behind,
    Poor Connel has leisure to pray,
He hears their dread voices around on the wind,
    Still farther and farther away:
        "O Thou who sit'st throned o'er the fields of the day,   335
            Have pity this once upon me,
Deliver from those that are hunting my life,
From *traps* of the wicked that round me are rife,
And O, above all, from the rage of a wife,
            And guide to the hills of the Dee.   340

XXXV.

And if ever I grumble at Providence more,
    Or scorn my own mountains of heath;
If ever I yearn for that sin-breeding ore,
    Or shape to complaining a breath,
        Then may I be nipt with the scissars of death,"–   345

No farther could Connel proceed,
He thought of the snap that he saw in the nook,
Of the tongue that came out, and the temple that shook,
Of the blood and the reek, and the deadening look;
    He lifted his bonnet and fled. 350

XXXVI.

He wandered and wandered thro' woodlands of gloom,
    And sorely he sobbed and he wept;
At cherk of the pyat, or bee's passing boomb,
    He started, he listened, he leaped.
    With eye and with ear a strick guardship he kept; 355
    No scene could his sorrows beguile.
At length he stood lone by the side of the Dee,
It was placid and deep and as broad as a sea;
O could he get over, how safe he might be,
    And gain his own mountains the while. 360

XXXVII.

'Twas dangerous to turn, but proceeding was worse,
    For the country grew open and bare,
No forest appeared, neither broomwood nor gorse,
    Nor furze that would shelter a hare,
    Ah! could he get over how safe he might fare, 365
    At length he resolved to try.
At worst, 'twas but drowning, and what was a life
Compared to confinement in sin and in strife,
Beside a trap-door, and a scandalous wife?
    'Twas nothing, he'd swim, or he'd die. 370

XXXVIII.

Ah! he could not swim, and was loath to resign
    This life for a world unknown
For he had been sinning, and misery condign
    Would sure be his portion alone.
    How sweetly the sun on the green mountain shone! 375
    And the flocks they were resting in peace,
Or bleating along on each parallel path;
The lambs they were skipping on fringe of the heath,
How different might kythe the lone vallies of death,
    And cheerfulness evermore cease. 380

XXXIX.

All wistful he stood on the brink of the pool,
  And dropt on its surface the tear;
He started at something that boded him dool,
  And his mouth fell wide open with fear,
    The trample of galloppers fell on his ear,   385
      One look was too much for his eye,
For there was his wife, and her paramours twain,
With whip and with spur coming over the plain,
Bent forward, revengeful, they gallopped amain,
    They hasten, they quicken, they fly!   390

XL.

Short time was there now to deliberate, I ween,
  And shortly did Connel decree;
He shut up his mouth, and he closed his een,
  And he pointed his arms like a V,
    And like a scared otter, he dived in the Dee,   395
      His heels pointed up to the sky;
Like bolt from the firmament downward he bears,
The still liquid element startled uprears,
It bubbled and bullered and roared in his ears,
    Like thunder that gallows on high.   400

XLI.

He soon found the symptoms of drowning begin,
  And painful the feeling be sure,
For his breath it gaed out, and the water gaed in,
  With drumble and mudwart impure;
    It was most unpleasant, and hard to endure,   405
      And he struggled its inroads to wear;
But it rushed by his mouth, and it rushed by his nose,
His joints grew benumbed, all his fingers and toes,
And his een turned, they neither would open nor close,
    And he found his departure was near.   410

XLII.

One time he came up, like a porpoise, above,
  He breathed and he lifted his eye,
It was the last glance of the land of his love,
  Of the world, and the beautiful sky;

How bright looked the sun from his window on high,   415
   Through furs of the light golden grain!
O Connel was sad, but he thought with a sigh,
That far above yon peaceful vales of the sky,
In bowers of the morning he shortly might lie,
   Though very unlike it just then.   420

XLIII.

He sunk to the bottom, no more he arose,
The waters for ever his body enclose;
The horse-mussel clasped on his fingers and toes,
   All passive he suffered the scathe.
But O there was one thing his heart could not brook,   425
Even in his last struggles, his spirit it shook,
The eels, with their cursed equivocal look,
   Redoubled the horrors of death.
O aye since the time that he was but a bairn,
When catching his trouts in the Cluny, or Gairn,   430
At sight of an eel he would shudder and darn;
   It almost deprived him of breath.

XLIV.

He died, but he found that he never would be
   So dead to all feeling and smart,
No, not though his flesh were consumed in the Dee,   435
   But that eels would some horror impart.
   With all other fishes he yielded to mart,
   Resistance became not the dead;
The minnow, with gushet sae gouden and braw,
The siller-ribbed perch, and the indolent craw,   440
And the ravenous ged, with his teeth like a saw,
   Came all on poor Connel to feed.

XLV.

They rave and they rugged, he cared not a speal,
   Though they preyed on his vitals alone;
But, lord! when he felt the cold nose of an eel,   445
   A quaking seized every bone;
   Their slid slimy forms lay his bosom upon,
   His mouth that was ope, they came near;

They guddled his loins, and they bored thro' his side,
They warped all his bowels about on the tide,   450
One snapt him on place he no longer would bide.
    It was more than a dead man could bear!

        *   *   *   *   *

XLVI.

Young Connel was missed, and his mother was sad,
    But his sisters consoled her mind;
And said, he was wooing some favourite maid,   455
    For Connel was amorous and kind.
        Ah! little weened they that their Connel reclined
            On a couch that was lothful to see!
'Twas mud!—and the water-bells o'er him did heave,
The lampreys passed thro' him without law or leave,   460
And windowed his frame like a riddle or sieve,
        Afar in the deeps of the Dee!

XLVII.

It was but a night, and a midsummer night,
    And next morning when rose the red sun,
His sisters in haste their fair bodies bedight,   465
    And, ere the day's work was begun,
        They sought for their Connel, for they were undone
            If ought should their brother befall:
And first they went straight to the bower in the dean,
For there he of late had been frequently seen;   470
For nature he loved, and her evening scene,
        To him was the dearest of all.

XLVIII.

And when within view of his bowrak they came,
    It lay in the skaddow so still,
They lift up their voices and called his name,   475
    And their forms they shone white on the hill;
        When trow you that hallo so erlich and shrill
            Arose from those maids on the heath?
It was just as poor Connel most poignant did feel,
As reptiles he loved not of him made a meal,   480
Just when the misleered and unmannerly eel
        Waked him from the slumbers of death.

XLIX.

He opened his eyes, and with wonder beheld
   The sky and the hills once again;
But still he was haunted, for over the field   485
   Two females came running amain.
    No form but his spouse's remained on his brain;
     His sisters to see him were glad;
But he started bolt upright in horror and fear,
He deem't that his wife and her minions were near,   490
He flung off his plaid, and he fled like a deer,
    And they thought their poor brother was mad.

L.

He 'scaped; but he halted on top of the rock;
   And his wonder and pleasure still grew;
For his clothes were not wet, and his skin was unbroke,   495
   But he scarce could believe it was true
    That no eels were within; and too strictly he knew
    He was married and buckled for life.
It could not be a dream; for he slept, and awoke;
Was drunken, and sober; had sung, and had spoke;   500
For months and for days he had dragged in the yoke
    With an unconscientious wife.

LI.

However it was, he was sure he was there,
   On his own native cliffs of the Dee.
O never before looked a morning so fair,   505
   Or the sun-beam so sweet on the lea!
    The song of the merl from her old hawthorn tree,
    And the blackbird's melodious lay,
All sounded to him like an anthem of love,
A song that the spirit of nature did move,   510
A kind little hymn to their Maker above,
    Who gave them the beauties of day.

LII.

So deep the impression was stamped on his brain,
   The image was never defaced;
Whene'er he saw riders that gallopped amain,   515
   He darned in some bush till they passed.
    At kirk or at market sharp glances he cast,

Lest haply his wife might be there;
And once, when the liquor had kindled his ee,
It never was known who or what he did see, 520
But he made a miraculous flight from Dundee,
    The moment he entered the fair.

LIII.

But never again was his bosom estranged,
    From his simple and primitive fare;
No longer his wishes or appetite ranged 525
    With the gay and voluptuous to share.
    He viewed every luxury of life as a snare;
      He drank of his pure mountain spring;
He watched all the flowers of the wild as they sprung;
He blessed his sweet laverock, like fairy that sung, 530
Aloft on the hem of the morning cloud hung,
    Light fanning its down with her wing.

LIV.

And oft on the shelve of the rock he reclined,
    Light carolling humoursome rhyme,
Of his midsummer dream, of his feelings refined, 535
    Or some song of the good olden time.
    And even in age was his spirit in prime.
      Still reverenced on Dee is his name!
His wishes were few, his enjoyments were rife,
He loved and he cherished each thing that had life, 540
With two small exceptions, an eel and a wife,
    Whose commerce he dreaded the same.

Country Dreams and Apparitions

No. III

The Wife of Lochmaben

NOT many years ago, there lived in the ancient royal borough of Lochmaben, an amiable and good christian woman, the wife of a blacksmith, named James Neil, whose death gave rise to a singularly romantic story, and finally to a criminal trial at the Circuit-Court of Dumfries. The story was related to me by a strolling gipsy of the town of Lochmaben, pretty nearly as follows:

The smith's wife had been for several years in a state of great bodily suffering and debility, which she bore with all resignation, and even cheerfulness, although during the period of her illness, she had been utterly neglected by her husband, who was of a loose profligate character, and in every thing the reverse of his wife. Her hours were however greatly cheered by the company of a neighbouring widow, of the same devout and religious cast of mind with herself. These two spent most of their time together, taking great delight in each other's society. The widow attended to all her friend's little wants, and often watched by her bed a good part of the night, reading to her out of the Bible and other religious books, and giving every instance of disinterested kindness and attention.

The gallant blacksmith was all this while consoling himself in the company of another jolly buxom quean, of the tinker breed, who lived in an apartment under the same roof with him and his spouse. He seldom visited the latter; but, on pretence of not disturbing her, both boarded and lodged with his swarthy Egyptian. Nevertheless, whenever the two devout friends said their evening prayers, the blacksmith was not forgotten, but every blessing besought to rest on his head.

One morning, when the widow came in about the usual hour, to visit her friend, she found, to her utter astonishment, that she was gone, though she had been very ill the preceding night. The bed-clothes were cold, the fire on the hearth was gone out, and a part of her daily wearing apparel was lying at the bed side as usual.

She instantly ran and informed the smith. But he hated this widow, and answered her churlishly, without deigning to look up to her, or so much as delaying his work for a moment to listen to her narrative.

There he stood, with his sleeves rolled up to his shoulders, pelting away at his hot iron, and bidding his informant "gang to the devil, for an auld frazing hypocritical jade; an' if she didna find her praying snivelling crony there, to seek her where she saw her last–If she didna ken where she was, how was he to ken?"

The widow alarmed the neighbours, and a general search was instantly set on foot; but, before that time, the body of the lost woman had been discovered floating in the middle of the Loch adjoining the town. Few people paid any attention to the unfortunate circumstance. They knew, or believed, that the woman lived unhappily and in bad terms with her husband, and had no doubt that she had drowned herself in a fit of despair; and, impressed with all the horror that country people naturally have of suicide, they refused her the rights of Christian burial. The body was, in consequence, early next morning, tied between two dales, and carried out to the height, several miles to the westward of the town, where it was consigned to a dishonourable grave; being deep buried precisely in the march, or boundary, between the lands of two different proprietors.

Time passed away, and the gossips of Lochmaben were very free both with the character of the deceased and her surviving husband, not forgetting his jolly Egyptian. The more profligate part of the inhabitants said, "they never saw ony good come o' sae muckle canting an' praying, an' singing o' psalms; an' that for a' the wife's high pretensions to religious zeal, an' faith, an' hope, an' a' the lave o't, there she had gien hersel up to the deil at ae smack." But the more serious part of the community only shook their heads, and said, "alas, it was hard kenning fouk frae outward appearances; for nane wha kend that wife wad hae expectit sic an end as this!"

But the state of the widow's mind after this horrible catastrophe, is not to be described. Her confidence in the mercy of Heaven was shaken; and she began to doubt of its justice. Her faith was stunned, and she felt her heart bewildered in its researches after truth. For several days she was so hardened, that she dared not fall on her knees before the footstool of divine grace. But after casting all about, and finding no other hold or anchor, she again, one evening, in full bitterness of heart, kneeled before her Maker, and poured out her spirit in prayer; begging, that if the tenets she held, were tenets of error, and disapproven of by the fountain of life, she might be forgiven, and directed in the true path to Heaven.

When she had finished, she sat down on her lowly form, leaned her face upon both her hands, and wept bitterly, as she thought on the dismal exit of her beloved friend, with whom she had last prayed.

As she sat thus, she heard the footsteps of one approaching her, and looking up, she beheld her friend whom she supposed to have been dead and buried, standing on the floor, and looking to her with a face of so much mildness and benignity, that the widow, instead of being terrified, was rejoiced to see her. The following dialogue then passed between them, as nearly as I could gather it from the confused narrative of a strolling gipsy, who however knew all the parties.

"God of mercy preserve us, Mary, is that you? Where have you been? We thought it had been you that was found drowned in the Loch."

"And who did you think drowned me?"

"We thought you had drowned yourself."

"Oh, fie! how could *you* do me so much injustice? Would that have been ought in conformity to the life we two have led together, and the sweet heavenly conversation we maintained?"

"What could we say? Or what could we think? The best are sometimes left to themselves. But where have you been, Mary?"

"I have been on a journey far away."

"But why did you go away without informing me?"

"I was hurried away, and had no time."

"But you were so ill, how could you go away?"

"I am better now. I never was so well in my life, no not in the gayest and happiest hour I ever saw. My husband cured me."

"How did he cure you?"

"With a bottle."

"Why then did he not inform us? I cannot comprehend this. Where have you been, Mary?"

"I have been on a journey at a strange place. But you do not know it, my dear friend. You know only the first stage at which I rested on my way, and a cold damp lodging it is. It was at a place called the Crane Moor."

"Heaven defend us! That was the name of the place where they buried the body that was found in the Loch. Tell me implicitly, Mary, were you not dead?"

"How can you ask such a question? Do you not see me alive, and well, and cheerful, and happy?"

"I know and believe that the soul can never die; but strange realities come over my mind. Tell me, was it not your body that was found floating in the Loch, and buried in shame and disgrace on the top of the Crane Moor?"

"You have so far judged right; but I am raised from the dead, as you see, and restored to life, and it is all for your sake; for the faith of the just must not perish. How could *you* believe that I would throw away my precious soul, by taking away my own life? My husband felled me with a bottle on the back part of the head, breaking my skull. He then put my body into a sack, carried it out in the dark, and threw it into the Loch. It was a deed of atrocity and guilt, but he will live to repent it, and it has proved a deed of mercy to me. I am well, and happy; and all that we believed of a Saviour and a future state of existence is true."–

On receiving this extraordinary information, and precisely at this part of the dialogue, the widow fainted; and on recovering from her swoon, she found that her friend was gone; but, conscious of having been in her perfect senses, and remembering every thing that had passed between them, she was convinced that she had seen and conversed with her deceased friend's ghost, or some good benevolent spirit in her likeness.

Accordingly, the next morning, she went to a magistrate, and informed him of the circumstances; but he only laughed her to scorn, and entreated her, for her own sake, never again to mention the matter, else people would account her mad. She offered to make oath before witnesses, to the truth of every particular; but this only increased the chagrin of the man in office, and the worthy widow was dismissed with many bitter reproaches. She next went to the minister, and informed him of what she had seen and heard. He answered her kindly, and with caution; but ultimately strove only to reason her from her belief; assuring her, that it was the effect of a distempered imagination, and occasioned by reflecting too deeply on the unfortunate end of her beloved friend; and his reasoning being too powerful for her to answer, she was obliged to give up the point.

She failed not, however, to publish the matter among her neighbours, relating the circumstances in that firm serious manner in which a person always stands to the truth, thereby making an impression on the minds of every one who heard her. The story was of a nature to take, among such a society as that of which the main bulk of the population of Lochmaben and its vicinity consists. It flew like wildfire. The people blamed their magistrates and ministers; and on the third day after the appearance of the deceased, they rose in a body, and with two ministers, two magistrates, and two surgeons at their head, they marched away to the Crane-moor, and lifted the corpse for inspection.

To the astonishment of all present, it appeared on the very first

examination, that the deceased had been felled by a stroke on the
back part of the head, which had broken her skull, and occasioned
instant death. Little cognizance had been taken of the affair at her
death; but, at any rate, her long hair was folded so carefully over the
wound, and bound with a snood so close to her head, that without a
minute investigation, the fracture could not have been discovered.
Farther still, in confirmation of the words of the apparition, on the
surgeon's opening the head, it appeared plainly from the semi-circular form of the fracture, that it had actually been inflicted by one
side of the bottom of a bottle; and there being hundreds of respectable witnesses to all these things, the body was forthwith carried to
the church-yard, and interred there; the smith was seized, and conveyed to jail; and the inhabitants of Annandale were left to wonder
in the utmost astonishment.

The smith was tried at the ensuing Circuit-court of Dumfries,
where the widow was examined as a principal witness. She told her
story before the judges with firmness, and swore to every circumstance communicated to her by the ghost; and even when cross-
examined by the prisoner's counsel, she was not found to prevari-
cate in the least. The jury appeared to be staggered, and could not
refuse their assent to the truth of this relation. The counsel, however, obviated this proof, on account of its being related at second
hand, and not by an eye-witness of the transaction. He therefore
refused to admit it against his client, unless the ghost appeared personally, and made a verbal accusation; and, being a gentleman of a
sarcastic turn, he was but too successful in turning this part of the
evidence into ridicule, thereby quite, or in a great measure, undoing
the effect that it had made on the minds of the jury.

A material witness being still wanting, the smith was remanded
back to prison until the Autumn circuit, at which time his trial was
concluded. The witness above mentioned having then been found,
he stated to the court, That as he chanced to pass the prisoner's
door, between one and two in the morning of that day on which the
deceased was found in the loch, he heard a noise as of one forcing
his way out; and, wondering who it could be that was in the house at
that hour, he had the curiosity to conceal himself in an adjoining
door, until he saw who came out: That the night being very dark, he
was obliged to cour down almost close to the earth, in order that he
might have the object between him and the sky; and, while sitting in
that posture, he saw a man come out of the smith's house, with
something in a sack upon his back: That he followed the figure for
some time, and intended to have followed farther; but he was seized

with an indescribable terror, and went away home; and that, on the morning, when he heard of the dead body being found in the loch, he entertained not a doubt of the smith having murdered his wife, and then conveyed her in a sack to the loch. On being asked, If he could aver upon oath, that it was the prisoner whom he saw come out of the house bearing the burden—He said he could not, because the burden which he carried, caused the person to stoop, and prevented him from seeing his figure distinctly; but, that it was him, he had no doubt remaining on his mind. On being asked why he had not divulged this sooner and more publicly; he said, that he was afraid the business in which he was engaged that night might have been inquired into, which it was of great consequence to him at that time to keep secret; and, therefore, he was not only obliged to conceal what he had seen, but to escape for a season out of the way, for fear of being examined.

The crime of the prisoner appeared now to be obvious; at least the presumption was strong against him. Nevertheless the judge, in summing up the evidence, considered the proof as defective; expatiated at considerable length on the extraordinary story related by the widow, which it could not be denied had been the occasion of bringing the whole to light, and had been most wonderfully exemplified by corresponding facts; and said he considered himself bound to account for it in a natural way, for the satisfaction of his own mind and the minds of the jury, and could account for it in no other, than by supposing that the witness had discovered the fracture before the body of her friend had been consigned to the grave; and that, on considering leisurely and seriously the various circumstances connected with the fatal catastrophe, she had become convinced of the prisoner's guilt, and had either fancied, or, more probably, dreamed the story, on which she had dwelt so long, that she believed it as a fact.

After all, the jury, by a small majority, returned a verdict of *not proven*; and, after a severe reprehension and suitable exhortations, the smith was dismissed from the bar. I forgot to mention in its proper place, that one of the principal things in his favour was, that of his abandoned inamorata having made oath that he was in her apartment all that night, and never left it.

He was now acquitted in the eye of the law, but not in the eyes of his countrymen; for all those who knew the circumstances, believed him guilty of the murder of his wife. On the very night of his acquittal, he repaired at a late hour to the abode of his beloved Egyptian; but he was suspected, and his motions watched with all due care.

Accordingly, next morning, at break of day, a large mob, who had assembled with all quietness, broke into the house, and dragged both the parties from the same den; and, after making them ride the stang through all the principal streets of the town, threw them into the loch, and gave them a complete ducking, suffering them barely to escape with life. At the same time, on their dismissal, they were informed, that if they continued in the same course of life, the experiment would be very frequently repeated. Shortly after that, the two offending delinquents made a moonlight flitting, and escaped into Cumberland. My informant had not heard more of them, but she assured me they would make a bad end.

Country Dreams and Apparitions
No. IV

Cousin Mattie

AT the lone farm of Finagle, there lived for many years an industrious farmer and his family. Several of his children died, and only one daughter and one son remained to him. He had besides these, a little orphan niece, who was brought into the family, called Matilda; but all her days she went by the familiar name of Cousin Mattie. At the time this simple narrative commences, Alexander, the farmer's son, was six years of age, Mattie was seven, and Flora, the farmer's only daughter, about twelve.

How I do love a little girl about that age! There is nothing in nature so fascinating, so lovely, so innocent; and, at the same time, so full of gayety and playfulness. The tender and delicate affections, to which their natures are moulded, are then beginning unconsciously to form; and every thing beautiful or affecting in nature, claims from them a deep but momentary interest. They have a tear for the weaned lamb, for the drooping flower, and even for the travelling mendicant, though afraid to come near him. But the child of the poor female vagrant is to them, of all others, an object of the deepest interest. How I have seen them look at the little wretch and then at her own parents alternately, the feelings of the soul abundantly conspicuous in every muscle of the face and turn of the eye! Their hearts are like softened wax, and the impressions then made on them remain for ever. Such beings approach nigh to the list where angels stand, and are, in fact, the connecting link that joins us with the inhabitants of a better world. How I do love a well-educated little girl of twelve or thirteen years of age.

At such an age was Flora of Finagle, with a heart moulded to every tender impression, and a memory so retentive, that whatever affected or interested her was engraven there never to be cancelled.

One morning, after her mother had risen and gone to the byre to look after the cows, Flora, who was lying in a bed by herself, heard the following dialogue between the two children, who were lying prattling together in another bed close beside her's.

"Do you ever dream ony, little Sandy?"

"What is't like, cousin Mattie? Sandy no ken what it is til deam."

"It is to think ye do things when you are sleeping, when ye dinna do them at a'."

"O, Sandy deam a geat deal yat way."

"If you will tell me ane o' your dreams, Sandy—I'll tell you ane o' mine that I dreamed last night; and it was about you, Sandy?"

"Sae was mine, cousin. Sandy deamed that he fightit a gaet Englishman, an' it was Yobin Hood; an' Sandy ding'd him's swold out o' him's hand, an' noll'd him on ye face, an' ye back, till him geetit. An' yen thele comed anodel littel despelyate Englishman, an' it was littel John; an' Sandy fightit him till him was dead; an' yen Sandy got on o' ane gyand holse, an' gallompit away."

"But I wish that ye be nae making that dream just e'en now, Sandy?"

"Sandy 'hought it, atweel."

"But were you sleeping when you thought it?"

"Na, Sandy wasna' sleepin', but him was winking."

"O, but that's not a true dream, I'll tell you one that's a true dream. I thought there was a bonny lady came to me, and she held out two roses, a red one and a pale one, and bade me take my choice. I took the white one; and she bade me keep it, and never part with it, for if I gave it away, I would die. But when I came to you, you asked my rose, and I refused to give you it. You then cried for it, and said I did not love you; so I could not refuse you the flower, but wept too, and you took it.

"Then the bonny lady came back to me, and was very angry, and said, 'Did not I tell you to keep your rose? Now the boy that you have given it to will be your murderer. He will kill you; and on this day fortnight, you will be lying in your coffin, and that pale rose upon your breast.'

"I said, 'I could not help it now.' But when I was told that you were to kill me, I liked you aye better and better, and better and better." And with these words, Matilda clasped him to her bosom and wept. Sandy sobbed bitterly too; and said, "She be geat lial, yon lady. Sandy no kill cousin Mattie. When Sandy gows byaw man, an' gets a gyand house, him be vely good till cousin, an' feed hel wi' gingebead, an' yeam, an' tyankil, an' take hel in him's bosy yis way." With that the two children fell silent, and sobbed and wept till they fell sound asleep, clasped in each other's arms.

This artless dialogue made a deep impression on Flora's sensitive heart. It was a part of her mother's creed to rely on dreams, so that it had naturally become Flora's too. She was shocked, and absolutely terrified, when she heard her little ingenious cousin say that Sandy was to murder her; and that on that day fortnight, she should be lying in her coffin; and without informing her mother of what she had overheard, she resolved in her own mind, to avert, if possible, the impending evil. It was on a Sabbath morning, and after little Sandy had got on his clothes, and while Matilda was out, he attempted to tell his mother cousin Mattie's dream, to Flora's great vexation; but he made such a blundering story of it, that it proved altogether incoherent, and his mother took no further notice of it than to bid him hold his tongue; "what was that he was speaking about murdering?"

The next week Flora intreated of her mother, that she would suffer cousin Mattie and herself to pay a visit to their aunt at Kirkmichael; and, though her mother was unwilling, she urged her suit so earnestly, that the worthy dame was fain to consent.

"What's ta'en the gowk lassie the day?" said she; "I think she be gane fey. I never could get her to gang to see her aunt, an' now she has ta'en a tirrovy in her head, that she'll no be keepit. I dinna' like sic absolute freaks, an' sic langings, to come into the heads o' bairns; they're owre often afore something uncannie. Gae your ways an' see your auntie, sin' ye will gang; but ye's no get little cousin w'ye, sae never speak o't. Think ye that I can do wantin' ye baith out o' the house till the Sabbath-day be ower."

"O but, mother, it's sae gousty, an' sae eiry, to lie up in yon loft ane's lane; unless cousin Mattie gang wi' me, I canna' gang ava."

"Then just stay at hame, daughter, an' let us alane o' thae daft nories a' thegither."

Flora now had resource to that expedient which never fails to conquer the opposition of a fond mother: she pretended to cry bitterly. The good dame was quite overcome, and at once yielded, though not with a very good grace. "Saw ever ony body sic a fiegae-to as this? They that will to Cupar maun to Cupar! Gae your ways to Kirkmichael, an' tak the hale town at your tail, gin ye like. What's this that I'm sped wi'?"

"Na, na, mother; I's no gang my foot-length. Ye sanna hae that to flyre about. Ye keep me working frae the tae year's end to the tither, an' winna gie me a day to mysel'. I's no seek to be away again, as lang as I'm aneath your roof."

"Whisht now, an' haud your tongue, my bonny Flora. Ye hae been ower good a bairn to me, no to get your ain way o' ten times mair nor that. Ye ken laith wad your mother be to contrair you i' ought, if she wist it war for your good. I'm right glad that it has come i' your ain side o' the house, to gang an' see your auntie. Gang your ways, an' stay a day or twa; an', if ye dinna like to sleep your lane, take billy Sandy w'ye, an' leave little Cousin wi' me, to help me wi' bits o' turns till ye come back."

This arrangement, suiting Flora's intent equally well with the other, it was readily agreed to, and every thing soon amicably settled between the mother and daughter. The former demurred a little on Sandy's inability to perform the journey; but Flora, being intent on her purpose, overruled this objection, though she knew it was but too well founded.

Accordingly, the couple set out on their journey next morning, but before they were half way, Sandy began to tire, and a short time after gave fairly in. Flora carried him on her back for a space, but finding that would never do, she tried to cajole him into further exertion. No, Sandy would not set a foot to the ground. He was grown drowsy, and would not move. Flora knew not what to do, but at length fell upon an expedient, which an older person would scarcely have thought of. She went to a gate of an enclosure, and, pulling a spoke out of it, she brought that to Sandy, telling him she had now got him a fine horse, and he might ride all the way. Sandy, who was uncommonly fond of horses, swallowed the bait, and, mounting astride on his rung, he took the road at a round pace, and for the last two miles of their journey, Flora could hardly keep in view of him.

She had little pleasure in her visit, farther than the satisfaction, that she was doing what she could to avert a dreadful casualty, which she dreaded to be hanging over the family; and on her return, from the time that she came in view of her father's house, she looked only for the appearance of Mattie running about the door; but no Mattie being seen, Flora's heart began to tremble, and as she advanced nearer, her knees grew so feeble, that they would scarcely support her slender form; for she knew that it was one of the radical principles of a dream to be ambiguous.

"A's unco still about our hame the day, Sandy; I wish ilka ane there may be weel. It's like death."

"Sandy no ken what death *is* like. What *is* like, Sistel Flola?"

"You will maybe see that ower soon. It is death that kills a' living things, Sandy."

"Aye; aih aye! Sandy saw a wee buldie, it could neilel pick, nol flee, nol dab. It was vely ill done o' death! Sistel Flola, didna God make a' living things?"

"Yes; be assured he did."

"Then, what has death ado to kill them? if Sandy wele God, him wad fight him."

"Whisht, whisht, my dear; ye dinna ken what you're sayin. Ye maunna speak about these things."

"Weel, Sandy no speak ony maile about them. But if death should kill cousin Mattie, Oh! Sandy wish him might kill him too!"

"Wha do ye like best i' this world, Sandy?"

"Sandy like sistel Flola best."

"You are learning the art of flattery already; for I heard ye telling Mattie the tither morning, that ye likit her better than a' the rest o' the world put thegither."

"But yan Sandy coudna help yat. Cousin Mattie like Sandy, and what could him say?"

Flora could not answer him for anxiety; for they were now drawing quite near to the house, and still all was quiet. At length Mattie opened the door, and, without returning to tell her aunt the joyful tidings, came running like a little fairy to meet them; gave Flora a hasty kiss; and then, clasping little Sandy about the neck, she exclaimed, in an ecstatic tone, "Aih, Sandy man!" and pressed her cheek to his. Sandy produced a small book of pictures, and a pink rose knot that he had bought for his cousin, and was repaid with another embrace, and a sly compliment to his gallantry.

Matilda was far beyond her years in acuteness. Her mother was an accomplished English lady, though only the daughter of a poor curate, and she had bred her only child with every possible attention. She could read, she could sing, and play some airs on the spinnet; and was altogether a most interesting little nymph. Both her parents came to an untimely end, and to the lone cottage of Finagle was she then removed, where she was still very much caressed. She told Flora all the news of her absence in a breath. There was nothing disastrous had happened. But, so strong was Flora's presentiment of evil, that she could not get quit of it, until she had pressed the hands of both her parents. From that day forth, she suspected that little faith was to be put in dreams. The fourteen days was now fairly over, and no evil nor danger had happened to Matilda, either from the hand of Sandy or otherwise. However, she kept the secret of the dream locked up in her heart, and never either mentioned or forgot it.

Shortly after that, she endeavoured to reason her mother out of her belief in dreams, for she would still gladly have been persuaded in her own mind, that this vision was futile, and of no avail. But she found her mother staunch to her point. She reasoned on the principle, that the Almighty had made nothing in vain, and if dreams had been of no import to man, they would not have been given to him.

And further, she said, we read in the Scriptures that dreams were fulfilled in the days of old; but we didna read in the Scriptures that ever the nature of dreaming was changed. On the contrary, she believed, that since the days of prophecy had departed, and no more warnings of futurity could be derived to man from that, dreaming was of doubly more avail, and ought to be proportionally more attended to, as the only mystical communication remaining between God and man. To this reasoning Flora was obliged to yield. It is no hard matter to conquer, where belief succeeds argument.

Time flew on, and the two children were never asunder. They read together, prayed together, and toyed and caressed without restraint, seeming but to live for one another. But a heavy misfortune at length befel the family. She who had been a kind mother and guardian angel to all the three, was removed by death to a better home. Flora was at that time in her eighteenth year, and the charge of the family then devolved on her. Great was their grief, but their happiness was nothing abated; they lived together in the same kind love and amity as they had done before. The two youngest in particular fondled each other more and more; and this growing fondness, instead of being checked, was constantly encouraged,–Flora still having a lurking dread that some deadly animosity might breed between them.

Matilda and she always slept in the same bed, and very regularly told each other their dreams in the morning,–dreams pure and innocent as their own stainless bosoms. But one morning Flora was surprised by Matilda addressing her as follows, in a tone of great perplexity and distress:

"Ah! my dear cousin, what a dream I have had last night! I thought I saw my aunt, your late worthy mother, who was kind and affectionate to me, as she always wont to be, and more beautiful than I ever saw her. She took me in her arms, and wept over me; and charged me to go and leave this place instantly, and by all means to avoid her son, otherwise he was destined to be my murderer; and on that day seven-night I should be lying in my coffin. She showed me a sight too that I did not know, and cannot give a name to. But the surgeons, with their bloody hands, came between us, and separated us, so that I saw her no more."

Flora trembled and groaned in spirit; nor could she make any answer to Matilda for a long space, save by repeated moans. "Merciful Heaven!" said she at length, "what can such a dream portend? Do not you remember, dear Mattie, of dreaming a dream of the same nature once long ago?"

Mattie had quite forgot of ever having dreamed such a dream; but Flora remembered it well; and thinking that she might formerly have been the mean, under Heaven, of counterworking destiny, she determined to make a farther effort; and, ere ever she arose, advised Matilda to leave the house, and avoid her brother, until the seven days had elapsed. "It can do nae ill, Mattie," said she; "an' mankind hae whiles muckle i' their ain hands to do or no to do; to bring about, or to keep back." Mattie consented, solely to please the amiable Flora; for she was no more afraid of Sandy than she was of one of the flowers of the field. She went to Kirkmichael, staid till the week was expired, came home in safety, and they both laughed at their superstitious fears. Matilda thought of the dream no more, but Flora treasured it up in her memory, though all the coincidence that she could discover between the two dreams was, that they had both happened on a Saturday, and both precisely at the same season of the year; which she well remembered.

At the age of two and twenty, Flora was married to a young farmer, who lived in a distant corner of the same extensive parish, and of course left the charge of her father's household to cousin Mattie, who, with the old farmer, his son, and one maid-servant, managed and did all the work of the farm. Still, as their number was diminished, their affections seemed to be drawn the closer; but Flora scarcely saw them any more, having the concerns of a family to mind at home.

One day, when her husband went to church, he perceived the old beadle standing bent over his staff at the churchyard gate, distributing burial letters to a few as they entered. He held out one to the husband of Flora, and, at the same time, touched the front of his bonnet with the other hand; and, without regarding how the letter affected him who received it, began instantly to look about for others to whom he had letters directed.

The farmer opened the letter, and had almost sunk down on the earth when he read as follows:

> SIR,–The favour of your company, at twelve o'clock, on Tuesday next, to attend the funeral of Matilda A——n, my niece, from this, to the place of interment, in the church-yard of C——r, will much oblige, Sir, your humble servant,
>
> James A——n.
>
> *Finagle, April 12th.*

Think of Flora's amazement and distress, when her husband told her what had happened, and shewed her this letter. She took to her bed on the instant, and wept herself into a fever, for the friend and companion of her youth. Her husband became considerably alarmed on her account, she being in that state in which violent excitement often proves dangerous. Her sickness was however only temporary; but she burned with impatience to learn some particulars of her cousin's death. Her husband could tell her nothing; only, that he heard one say *she died on Saturday.*

This set Flora a calculating, and going over in her mind the reminiscences of their youth; and she soon discovered, to her utter astonishment and even horror, that her cousin Matilda had died precisely on *that day fourteen years* that she first dreamed the ominous dream; and that day seven years that she dreamed it again!

Here was indeed matter of wonder! But her blood ran cold to her heart when she thought what might have been the manner of her death. She dreaded, nay, she almost calculated upon it as certain, that her brother had poisoned, or otherwise made away privately with the deceased, as she was sure such an extraordinary coincidence behoved to be fulfilled in all its parts. She durst no more make any inquiries concerning the circumstances of her cousin's death; but she became moping and unsettled, and her husband feared for her reason.

He went to the funeral; but dreading to leave Flora long by herself, he only met the procession a small space from the church-yard; for his father-in-law's house was distant fourteen miles from his own. On his return, he could still give Flora very little additional information. He said he had asked his father-in-law what had been the nature of the complaint of which she died; but he had given him an equivocal answer, and seemed to avoid entering into any explanation; and that he had then made inquiry at others, who all testified their ignorance of the matter. Flora at length, after long hesitation, ventured to ask *if her brother was at the funeral?* and was told that he was not. This was a death-blow to her lingering hopes, and all but confirmed the hideous catastrophe that she dreaded; and for the remainder of that week she continued in a state of mental agony.

On the Sunday following, she manifested a strong desire to go to church to visit her cousin's grave. Her husband opposed it at first, but at last consenting, in hopes she might be benefited by an overflow of tenderness, he mounted her on a pad, and accompanied her to the church-yard gate, leaving her there to give vent to her feelings.

As she approached the new grave, which was by the side of her mother's, she perceived two aged people whom she knew, sitting beside it busily engaged in conversation about the inhabitant below. Flora drew her hood over her face, and came with a sauntering step toward them, to lull all suspicion that she had any interest or concern in what they were saying; and finally, she leaned herself down on a flat grave-stone close beside them, and made as if she had been busied in deciphering the inscription. There she heard the following dialogue, one may conceive with what sort of feelings.

"An' then she was aye sae kind, an' sae lively, an' sae affable to poor an' rich, an' then sae bonny an' sae young. Oh, but my heart's sair for her! When I saw the morclaith drawn off the coffin, an' saw the silver letters kithe, AGED 21, the tears ran down ower thae auld wizzened cheeks, Janet; an' I said to mysel', 'Wow but that is ae bonny flower cut off i' the bloom!' But, Janet, my joe, warna ye at the corpse-kisting?"

"An' what suppose I was, Matthew? What's your concern wi' that?"

"Because I heard say, that there was nane there but you, an' another that ye ken weel. But canna you tell me, kimmer, what was the corpse like? Was't a' fair, an' bonny, an' nae blueness nor demmish to be seen?"

"An' what wad an auld fool body like you be the better, gin ye kend what the corpse was like? Thae sights are nae for een like yours to see; an' thae subjects are nae fit for tongues like yours to tattle about. What's done canna be undone. The dead will lie still. But oh, what's to come o' the living!"

"Aye, but I'm sure she had been a lusty weel plenished corpse, Janet; for she was a heavy ane; an' a deeper coffin I never saw."

"Haud your auld souple untackit tongue. Gin I hear sic another hint come ower the foul tap o't, it sal be the waur for ye. But lown be it spoken, an little be it said. Weel might the corpse be heavy, an' the coffin deep! ay, weel might the coffin be made deep, Matthew; for there was a stout lad bairn, a poor little pale flower, that hardly ever saw the light o' heaven, was streekit on her breast at the same time wi' hersel'.   *   *   *   *   *   *

    *   *   *   *   *   *   *

Country Dream and Apparitions

No. V

Welldean Hall

"Do you believe this story of the ghost, Gilbert?" "Do I believe this story of the ghost? Such a question as that is now! How many will you answer me in exchange for my ingenious answer to that most exquisite question? You see that tree there. Do you believe that it grew out of the earth? Or do you believe that it is there at all? Secondly, and more particularly. You see me? Good. You see my son at the plow yonder. What do you believe yon boy to be? Do you believe he is a twig of hazel?"

"How can I believe that, old shatterbrains?"

"I'll prove it. What does a hazel twig spring from at first?"

"A nut, or filbert, you may choose to call it."

"Good. Now, which letter of the alphabet begins my name?"

"The seventh."

"Good. Your own sentence. Look at the hornbook. One, two, three, four, five, six, seven. You have it home. My son sprung from a filbert. Satisfied? Ha, ha, ha! Another. Do you believe Old Nick to be a simpleton? A ninny? A higgler for nits and nest-eggs? An even down nose-o'-wax—not possessed of half the sense, foresight, and calculation that's in my one eye? In short, do you believe that both the devil and you are fools, and that Gilbert Falconer is a wise man?"

"There's no speaking seriously to you about any thing, with your low miserable attempts at wit."

"I'll prove it."

"No more of your proofs, else I am off."

"I was coming to the very point which you set out at, if you would have suffered me. I would have come to a direct answer to your question in less than forty minutes. But it is all one. Odds or evens, who of us two shall conform to Solomon's maxim."

"What maxim of Solomon's?"

"*Answer a fool according to his folly.* What say you?"

"Odds."

"I have lost. The wit, the humour, the fire, the spirit, of our afternoon's conversation is at an end. Wit! Wit! Thou art a wreck—a lumber—a spavined jade! Now for a rhyme, and I'm done.

'O Gilbert Falconer!
Thou hast made a hack on her!
For Nick is on the back on her!
Who was't spurr'd her last away?
Bear him, bear him fast away;
Or Nick will be a cast-away!'"

"Is the fit done yet? In the name of all that is rational let us have some respite from that torrent of words, that resemble nothing so much as a water spout, that makes a constant rumbling noise, without any variation or meaning. I wanted to have some serious talk with you about this. The family are getting into the utmost consternation. What can be the meaning of it? Do you believe that such a thing as the apparition of our late master has been seen?"

"Indeed old Nicholas, seriously, I do believe it. How can I believe otherwise?"

"Don't you rather think it is some illusion of the fancy–that the people are deceived, and their senses have imposed on them?"

"A man has nothing but his external senses to depend on in this world. If these may be supposed fallacious, what is to be considered as real that we either hear or see? I conceive, that if a man *believes* that he *does* see an object standing before his eyes, and knows all its features and lineaments, why, he *does* see it, let casuists say what they will. If he hear it pronounce words audibly, who dare challenge the senses that God has given him, and maintain that he heard no such words pronounced? I would account the man a presumptuous fool who would say so, or who would set any limits to the phenomena of nature, knowing in whose hand the universe is balanced, and how little of it he thoroughly understands."

"Why, now, Gilbert, to have heard you speaking the last minute, would any man have believed that such a sentence could have come out of your mouth? That which you have said was certainly very well said; and more to the point than any thing I could have *thought* on the subject for I know not how long. So I find you think a ghost may sometimes be commissioned, or permitted to appear?"

"I have never once doubted it. Superstition has indeed peopled every dell with ideal spectres; but to these I attach no credit. If the senses of men, however, are in ought to be trusted, I cannot doubt that spirits have sometimes walked the earth in the likenesses of men and women that once lived. It is certainly not on any slight or trivial occasion, that such messengers from the dead appear; and, were it not for some great end, I would not believe in it. I conceive it to be only when all natural means are cut off, either of discovering guilt and blood, or of saving life. The idea of this is so pleasant, that I would not for the world misbelieve it. How grand is the conviction, that there is a being on your right hand and your left, that sees the actions of all his creatures, and will not let the innocent suffer, nor the guilty go unpunished!"

"I am so glad to hear you say so, Gilbert; for I had begun to dispute my own senses, and durst not tell what I had seen. I myself saw our late master, face to face, as plainly as I see you at this moment. And that no longer ago than the night before last."

"God have a care of us! Is it even so? Then I fear, old Nicholas, there has been some foul play going on. Where did you see him?"

"In the garden. He went into the house and beckoned me to follow him. I was on the point of complying; for, though I have been deeply troubled at thinking of it, I was not afraid at the time. The deceased had nothing ghostly about him; and I was so used to do all his commands, that I felt very awkward in declining this last one. How I have trembled to think about it! Is it not said and believed, Gilbert, that one who sees a spirit always dies in a very short time after?"

"I believe it is held as an adage."

"O dreadful! Then I shall soon meet him again. How awful a thing it is to go into a world of spirits altogether! And that so soon! Is there no instance of one who has seen a ghost living for any length of time afterwards?"

"No. I believe not."

"I wonder what he had ado in appearing to me? But he never liked me, and had always plenty of malice about him. I am very ill, Gilbert. Oh! oh! Lack-a-day!"

"O fie! Never think about that. You are as well dead as living, if it should be so. Much better."

"And is that all the lamentation you make for your old friend? Ah, Gilbert, life is sweet even to an old man! And though I wish all my friends happy that are gone, yet such happiness is always the last that I wish them. Oh! oh! Good b'ye, Gilbert. Farewell! It is hard to say when you and I may meet again."

"You are not going to leave me that way? Come, sit down, and let us lean our two old backs to this tree, and have some farther conversation about this wonderful occurrence. Tell me seriously, old Nick, or Father Adam, I should rather call you; for you delve a garden like him, and like him have been bilked by a lusty young quean. Tell me, I say, seriously, what you thought of the character of our late master, and what is your opinion of this our present one?"

"I do not think of either of them. Ah! there are many doors to the valley of death, and they stand open day and night! But there are few out of it!"

"A plague on this old fellow, with his valley of death! He thinks of nothing but his worthless carcass. I shall get no more sense out of him. I think, Father Adam, our young master is a wretch; and I now dread our late one has not been much better. Think you the dog can have killed his uncle? I fear he has. And I fear you have been privy to it, since you confess his ghost has appeared to you. Confess that you administered some of your herbs, some simples to him; and that it was not an apoplexy of which he dropt down dead. Eh! I do not wonder that you are afraid of the valley of death, if it is by a noose that you are to enter it."

"Poor fool! poor fool!"

"After all, is it not wonderful, Nicholas? What can have brought our master back from the unseen world? Do you think this nephew of his has had any hand in his death? He has now got possession of all his lands, houses, and wealth, which I well believe never were intended for him; while his younger brother Allan, and his lovely cousin, Swan Sommerville, our late master's chief favourite, are left without a farthing."

"The cause of our master's death was perfectly ascertained by the surgeons. Though the present laird be a man without principle, I do not believe ever he harboured a thought of making away with his uncle."

"How comes it then that his spirit walks even while it is yet twilight, and the sun but shortly gone over the hill? How comes it that his will has not been found? And, if our young laird and his accomplices represent things aright, not one tenth of his great wealth?"

"Heaven knows! It is a grievous and mysterious matter."

"I suppose this mansion will soon be locked up. We must all flit, Nicholas. Is it not conjectured that the laird has himself seen the apparition?"

"It is believed that he encountered it in the library that night on which he grew so ill. He has never slept by himself since that night, and never again re-entered the library. All is to be sold; for the two young people claim their thirds of the moveables; and, as you say, we must all flit. But I need not care! Oh! Oh! Goodb'ye, Gilbert! Oh! Oh! I wonder what the ghost of the old miser—the old world's-worm, had ado to appear to me? To cut me off from the land of the living and the place where repentance may be hoped for! Oh! Oh!

Farewell Gilbert."

Gilbert kept his eye on the bent frame of the old gardener, till a bend in the wood walk hid him from his view, and then he mimicked him for his own amusement, and indulged in a long course of laughter. Gilbert had been bred to the church, but his follies and irregularities drove him from the university. He attempted many things, and at last was engaged as butler and house-steward to the late laird of Welldean; but even there he was disgraced, and became a kind of hanger-on about the mansion, acting occasionally as wood-forester, or rather wood-cleaver; drank as much of the laird's strong beer as he could conveniently get; cracked profane jests with the servants and cottage-dames; talked of agriculture with the farmers; of Homer and Virgil with the school-master; and of ethics with Dr Leadbeater, the parish-minister. Gilbert was every body's body; but cared little for any one, knowing that few cared ought for him. He had nevertheless a good heart, and a mortal abhorrence of every thing tyrannical or unjust, as well as mean and sordid.

Old Welldean had lived a sober retired life, and was exceedingly rich; but was one of those men *who could in no wise part with money*. He had two nephews by a brother, and one niece by a sister. It was known that he had once made a will, which both the writer and one of the witnesses attested; but he had been cut off suddenly, and neither the will, nor his accumulated treasures could be found, though many suspected that the elder nephew, Randal, had concealed the one, and destroyed the other. As heir-at-law, he had seized on the whole property, and his brother Allan, and lovely cousin, Swan Sommerville, two young and amiable lovers, found themselves deprived of that which they had been bred up to regard as their own. They claimed, of course, their share of the moveables, which the heir haughtily proposed to bring to the hammer. These were of considerable value. The library alone was judged to be worth a great sum, as it had descended from father to son, and still been increasing in value for several generations. But from the moment that an inventory began to be taken of the things of the house, which was nearly a year after the old laird's death, the family were driven into the utmost consternation by a visit of an apparition, exactly resembling their late master. It walked not only every night, but was sometimes seen in open day, encountering some with threatening gestures, and beckoning others to follow him.

These circumstances confirmed Randal in his resolution, not only to sell the furniture, but even to dispose of the house and policies, and purchase another place in lieu of it. It was supposed he had got a dreadful fright himself, but this circumstance he judged it proper to conceal, lest advantages might be taken of it by intending purchasers; and he now manifested the utmost impatience to bring the sales about.

Among other interested agents, two wealthy booksellers, Pinchport and Titlepage, were applied to as the best and most conscientious men in the world, to give a fair price for the valuable library. These sent an old book-monger to look over the library, and put down a certain value for every work. The man proceeded with great activity, and no less importance. But one evening, as he approached an oaken bookcase in the middle of a large division, he perceived an old man standing before it, of a most forbidding and threatening aspect. The honest bibliopole bowed low to this mysterious intruder, who regarded him only with a frown, kept his position, and, holding up his right hand, shook it at him, as if daring him to approach nearer to that place.

The man of conscience began to look around him, for he had heard of the ghost, though he disregarded the story. The door was close shut! It was impossible a mouse could have entered without him having perceived it. He looked at the old man again, and thought he discerned the spokes of the bookcase through his body; and, at the same time, there appeared like a lambent flame burning within him.

The valuator of books made toward the door as fast as his loosened and yielding joints could carry him; he even succeeded in opening it; but, in his unparalleled haste to escape, he lost all manner of caution, and fell headlong over the oaken stair. In his fall, he uttered a horrible shriek, which soon brought the servants from the hall to his assistance. When they arrived, he had tumbled all the way to the bottom of the stair; and, though all mangled and bleeding, he was still rolling and floundering onward, in order somewhat to facilitate his escape. They asked him, what was the matter? His answer to them was, "The ghost, the ghost;" and the honest bibliopole spoke not another word that any body could make sense of, for at least two months. One of his jaws was broke, which instantaneously swelling, deprived him of the power of utterance. He was besides much lacerated, and bruised, and fell into a dangerous fever. No explanation having thus been given of the circumstances of the adventure, the story soon spread, and assumed a character highly romantic, and no less uncommon. It was asserted, on the strongest evidence, that the ghost of the late laird had attacked an honest valuator of books in the library, and tossed him down stairs, breaking every bone of his body. The matter began to wear a serious aspect, and the stoutest hearts about the mansion were chilled. A sort of trepidation and uncertainty was apparent in the look, gait, and whole demeanour of every one of the inhabitants. All of them were continually looking around, in the same manner that a man does who is afraid of being taken up for debt. The old housekeeper prayed without ceasing. Nicholas, the gardener, wept night and day, that he had so soon to go to heaven. Dr Leadbeater, the parish-minister, reasoned without end, how "immaterial substances might be imaged forth by the workings of a fancy overheated and bedimmed in its mental vision, until its optics were over-run with opacity; and, that visions thus arose from the discord of colours, springing from the proportions of the vibrations propagated through the fibres of the optic nerves into the brain;" and a thousand other arguments, replete no doubt with deep philosophy, but of which no one knew the bearing of a single point. As for Gibby, the wood-forester, he drank ale and laughed at the whole business, sometimes reasoning on the one side, sometimes on the other, precisely as the whim caught him.

Randal spent little of his time at the mansion. He was engaged running the career of dissipation, to which heirs are generally addicted, and grew every day more impatient to accomplish the sale of his uncle's effects at Welldean. Matters were at a stand. Ever since the misfortune of the bookman, farther proceeding there was none. Most people suspected a trick; but a trick having such serious consequences, was not a safe toy wherewith to dally. Randal lost all temper; and at last yielded to the solicitations of his domestics, to suffer the ghost to be spoken to, that the dead might have rest, as the housekeeper termed it.

Accordingly, he sent for Dr Leadbeater, the great metaphysical minister of the parish; and requested him to watch a night in the library; merely, as he said, to quiet the fears of the domestics, who had taken it into their heads that the house was haunted, and accordingly all order and regularity was at an end among them.

"Why, sir," said Dr Leadbeater, "as to my watching a night, that's nothing. It is not that I would not watch ten nights to benefit your honour, either mainpernorly, laterally, or ultimately; but the sequel of such a vigilancy, would be a thoroughfaring error, that by insidious vermiculation, would work itself into the moral, physical, and mental intestines of those under my charge, in abundant multiformity; so that amaritude or acrimony might be deprehended in choler. But as to the appearance of any thing superhuman, I can assure you, sir, it is nothing more than a penumbra, and proceeds from some obtuse reflection, from a body superficially lustrous; which body must be spherical, or polyedrical, and the protuberant particles cylindrical, elliptical, and irregular; and according to the nature of these, and the situation of the lucid body, the sight of the beholder or beholders, from an angular point, will be affected figuratively and diametrically."

"Why, d——n it, doctor," said Randal, "that, I think, is all excellent philosophical reasoning. But in one word; you pretend to hold your commission from Heaven; and to be set there to watch over the consciences, and all the moral and religious concerns of your parishioners. Now, here is a family, consisting of nearly forty individuals, all thrown into the utmost consternation by what, it seems, according to your theory, is nothing more than *an obtuse reflection.* The people are absolutely in great distress, and on the point of losing their reason. I conceive it therefore your duty, as their spiritual pastor, either to remove this obtuse reflection out of the house, or quiet their apprehensions regarding it. One poor fellow has, I fear, got his death's wounds from this same same peculiar reflection. Certainly the *polyedrical body* might be found out and removed. In one word, doctor, will you be so good as attempt it, or will you not?"

"I have attempted it already, worthy sir," said the doctor; "I have explained the whole nature of the deceptive refraction to you, which you may explain to them, you know."

"Thank you, doctor; I shall. 'It is an obtuse reflection,' you say, 'from a body spiritual, polyedrical, protuberant, cylindrical, elliptical and irregular.' D——n them, if they don't understand that, they deserve to be frightened out of their senses."

"Oh, you're a wag. You are witty. It may be very good, but I like not your wit."

"Like my uncle's ghost, doctor, rather *obtuse.* But faith, doctor, between you and me, I'll give you fifty guineas in a present, and as much good claret as you and an associate can drink, if you will watch a night in the library, and endeavour to find out what this is that disturbs the people of my establishment. But, doctor, it is only on this condition, that whatever you may discover in that library, you are to make it known only to me. My late uncle's hoards of wealth and legal bonds have not been discovered; neither has his will. I have a thought that both may be concealed in that apartment; and that the old miser has had some machinery contrived in his lifetime to guard his treasure. You understand me, doctor? It imports me much; whatever you discover, *I only* must be made privy to it. It is as well that my brother, and his conceited inamorata Swan, should be under my tutelage and direction, as rendered independent of me, and haply raised above me. Doctor, what would you think of a thousand pounds in your hand as the fruits of one night's watching in that library? You are superior I know to any dread of danger from the appearance of a spirit."

"Why, to tell you the truth, squire Randal, as to the amatorculist, and his vertiginous gilt piece of mutability, to such I have nothing to say, and with such I have nothing to do. But to better the fortune of my alderleivest friend, in reciprocation and alternateness with my own, squares as exactly with my views as the contents of an angle; which, in all rectangle triangles is made of the side that subtendeth the right angle, and is equal to the squares which are made of the sides containing the right angle; and this is a perfect definition of my predominant inclination. The discerptibility of fortune is not only admissible, but demonstratively certain, and whatever proves adminicular to its concentration is meritorious."

"I am rather at a loss, Dr Leadbeater."

"Your proposition, squire, as it deserveth, hath met with perfect acceptibility on my part. Only, instead of claret, let the beverage for my friend and me be hock."

"With all my heart, doctor."

"Fifty, at all events, for one night's watching; perhaps a thousand?"

"The precise terms, doctor."

Every thing being thus settled, the doctor sought him out an associate, and fixed on Mr Jinglekirk, an old man who, for want of a patron, had never been able to get a living in the church, though he had been for twenty years what is called a journeyman minister. He had a weak mind, and was addicted to tippling; but had nevertheless an honest and upright heart. The doctor, however, made choice of him, on account of his poverty and simplicity, thinking he could mould him to his will with ease, should any great discovery be made.

The next week, the reverend doctor sent word to Welldean, that he and a friend meant to visit there, to pray with the family, and watch over night, to peruse some books in the library, or rather to make choice of some, previous to the approaching sale. The two divines came; the laird kept purposely out of the way, but left directions with his brother Allan, to receive and attend on them until after supper, and then leave them to themselves.

All the people assembled in the library, and Mr Jinglekirk performed family worship at the request of the doctor. Afterwards a plentiful supper, and various rich wines, were set, of which both the divines partook rather liberally. Allan remained with them during supper, but not perfectly at his ease, for he was at least next to convinced that there was something preternatural about the house;– something unaccountable he was sure there was.

After supper, chancing to lift his eyes to the old bookcase of black oak and glass, that stood exactly opposite to the fireplace, he perceived, or thought he perceived, the form of a hand pointing to a certain pane of glass in the book-case. He grew instantly as pale as ashes; on which both the divines turned their eyes in the same direction, but there was nothing. Even to Allan's eyes, there was nothing. The appearance of the hand was quite gone, and he was convinced it had been an illusion. They asked him, with some symptoms of perturbation, what he saw? But he assured them he saw nothing; only he said, he had not been very well of late, and was subject to sudden qualms–that one of these had seized him, and he would be obliged to wish them a good-night. They intreated him to remain till they finished the bottle, but he begged to be excused, and left them.

As soon as they were alone, the doctor began to sound Jinglekirk with regard to his principles of honesty, and mentioned to him the suspicion and the strong probability that the late old miser's treasures were all concealed in that library; and moreover, that even their host suspected that he had contrived some mechanical trick during his lifetime to guard that treasure, and it was thus that the servants, and even strangers, were frighted out of the apartment.

The reverend John Jinglekirk listened to all this with tacit indifference, filled another glass of old hock, and acquiesced with his learned friend in the strong probability of all that he had advanced. But notwithstanding every hint that the doctor could give, John (as the other familiarly styled him,) would never utter a syllable indicative of a disposition to share the treasure with his liberal friend, or even to understand that such a thing was meant.

The doctor had therefore recourse to another plan, in which he was too sure of success. He toasted one bumper of wine after another, giving first, "the Church of Scotland," and then, some noblemen and gentlemen, particular friends of his, who had plenty of livings in their gift. Then such young ladies as were particularly beautiful, accomplished, and had *the clink*; in short, the very ones for clergyman's ladies. Jinglekirk delighted in these toasts, and was as liberal of them as his friend could wish, drinking deep bumpers to every one of them,

> "Till his een they closed, an' his voice grew low,
> An' his tongue wad hardly gang."

At length he gave one whom he pronounced to be a *divine creature*, drank a huge bumper to her health, and then, leaning forward on the table, his head sank gradually down till it came in contact with his two arms, his tongue now and then pronouncing in a voice scarcely audible, "O, a divine creature! sweet! sweet! sweet! Ha-ha-ha! he-he-he!—Divine creature! Doctor—I shay—Is not she? Eh? O she's lovely and amiable! doctor—I shay—she's the sheaf among ten thousand!" and with that honest Jinglekirk composed himself to a quiet slumber.

The doctor now rose up to reconnoitre; and, walking round and round the library, began to calculate with himself where it was most likely old Welldean would conceal his treasure. His eyes and his contemplations very naturally fixed on the old book-case of black oak. He had previously formed a firm resolution not to be surprised by any sudden appearance; which, he conjectured, might be made by springs to start up on setting his foot on a certain part of the floor, or on opening a folding door. On the contrary, he conceived that any such appearance would be a certain evidence that the treasure was behind that, and in that place his research ought to be doubled.

Accordingly, without more ado, he went up to the old book-case. The upper two leaves were unlocked, as the man of books had left them. There were a few panes of thick, blue, navelled glass in each of them, while the transverse bars were curiously carved, and as black as ebony. "It is an antique and curious cabinet this, and must have many small concealments in it," said the doctor to himself, as he opened the door. He began to remove the books, one by one, from the left hand to the right, not to look at their contents, but to observe if there were any key-holes or concealed drawers behind them. He had only got half way along one shelf. The next three volumes were Latin classics, royal octavo size; in boards, and unproportionally thick. He had just stretched out his hand to remove one of them, when he received from some unseen hand such a blow on some part of his body, he knew not where, but it was as if he had been struck by a thunder-bolt, that made him stagger some paces backward, and fall at full length on the floor. When he received the blow, he uttered the interrogative "What?" as loud as he could bawl; and, as he fell to the floor, he uttered it again; not louder; for that was impossible; but with more emphasis, and an inverted cadence, quite peculiar to a state of inordinate surprise.

These two startling cries, and the rumble that he made when falling, aroused the drowsy John Jinglekirk, not only into a state of sensibility, but perfect accuracy of intellect. The first thing that he saw was his reverend friend raising up his head from the foot of the table, staring wildly about him.

"John—What was that?" said he.

"I had some thought it was your reverence," said Jinglekirk.

"But who was it that knocked me down? John, was it you who had the presumption to strike me down by such a blow as that?"

"Me, doctor? I offer to knock you down? I think you might know I would be the last man in the world who would presume to do such a thing. But simply and honestly, was it not this fellow who did it?" And with that Jinglekirk pointed to the wine bottle; for he believed the doctor had only fallen asleep, and dropt from his chair. "For me, doctor, I was sitting contemplating the beauty and perfections of the divine and delicious Miss Cherrylip! And when I presume to lift a finger against you, doctor, may my right hand forget its cunning! But my Lord, and my God!" exclaimed he, lifting his eyes beyond the doctor, "who is this we have got here?"

The doctor, who had now got upon his knees, hearing this exclamation and question so fraught with surprise, looked around, and beheld in front of the book-case, the exact figure and form of his old intimate friend, the late laird of Welldean. He was clad in his old spotted flannel dressing gown, and a large towel tied round his head like a turban, which he always wore in the house when living. His face was a face of defiance, rage, and torment; and as the doctor looked about, he lifted up his right hand in a threatening manner. As he lifted his hand, his night-gown waved aside, and the doctor and his friend both beheld his loins and his limbs sheathed in red hot burning steel, while a corslet of the same glowing metal enclosed his breast and heart.

It was more than enough for any human eye. The doctor roared louder than a bull, or a lion at bay; and, not taking time, or not able to rise on his legs, he galloped on all four toward the library door; tore it open, and continued the same kangaroo motion, not down the stair, like the hapless bibliopole; but, as providence kindly directed, along an intricate winding gallery that led around a great part of the house, all the while never letting one bellow await another. At the first howl that the doctor uttered, Jinglekirk sprung to his feet to attempt an escape, and would probably have been first out at the door, had he not stumbled on a limb of the table, and fallen flat on his face. Impelled, however, by terror of the tremendous and hellish figure behind, and led onward by the cries before, he made the best of his way that he was able after his routed friend.

The doctor at last came to the end of his journey, running against a double bolted door that impeded his progress. On this he beat with all his might, still continuing his cries of horror. While in this dark and perilous state, he was overtaken by his dismayed friend, the reverend John Jinglekirk, who, not knowing what he did, seized on the doctor behind with a spasmodic grasp. This changed the character of the doctor's cries materially. Before this accident, they were loud cries, and very long cries; but now they became as short as the bark of a dog, and excessively hollow. They were like the last burstings of the heart, "Oh-oh-oh-oh-oh;" for he thought the spirit had hold of him, and was squeezing him to its fiery bosom.

The domestics at length were aroused from their sleep, and arrived in the Bow Gallery, as it was called, in pairs, and groups; but still, at the approach of every one, the doctor renewed his cries, trying to redouble them. He was in a state of utter distraction. They carried him away to what they denominated the safe part of the house, and laid him in a bed, but four men could not hold him; so that before day they had put him in a strait jacket, and had old Gibby Falconer standing over him with a sapling, basting him to make him hold his peace. It was long ere the doctor was himself again, and when he did recover, it was apparent to every one that the fright had deprived him of all his philosophy relating to the physical properties of light, reflection, refraction, the prismatic spectrum, as well as transparency and opacity. These were terms never more mentioned by him, nor did he seem to recollect ought of their existence. It likewise cured him almost entirely of the clerical thirst after money. And all his life, the sight of a man in a flannel dressing-gown, with a white night-cap on his head, threw him into a cold sweat, and rendered him speechless for some time. Jinglekirk was not much the worse; for though he was apparently acute enough at the time, having been aroused by such a sudden surprise, yet, owing to the quantity of old hock he had swilled, he had but imperfect recollections of what had happened next day.

Randal came galloping home next day to learn the issue of the doctor's vigil; and though he could not help laughing till the tears ran down his cheeks, yet was he mightily chagrined and dismayed, not knowing what to do. After cursing the whole concern, and all the ministers of the gospel, and his uncle's restless soul, he galloped off again to the high and important concerns of rout and riot.

Swan had, ever since the death of her mother, lodged with an old maiden lady in the adjoining village. She generally visited her uncle every day, who had always manifested a great attachment to her. Yet, for all that, he had suffered her to run considerably in debt to the lady with whom she lived, for no earthly consideration could make Welldean part with money, as long as he could keep hold of it. Nevertheless, it having been known that his will was regularly made and signed, both Swan and Allan had as much credit as they chose. They were two fond and affectionate lovers, but all their prospects were now blasted; and Randal, finding that they were likely to be dependant on him, had the profligacy and the insolence to make a most dishonourable and degrading proposal to his lovely and virtuous cousin.

How different was Allan's behaviour toward her! True love is ever respectful. His attentions were redoubled; and they condoled together their misfortune, and the dependant state in which they were now left. Allan proposed entering into the army, there being a great demand for officers and men at that period; and, as soon as he had obtained a commission, he said, he would then unite his fate with that of his dear Swan; and, by a life of economy, they would be enabled at least to live independently of others.

Swan felt all the generosity of her lover's scheme, but begged him not to think of marriage for a season. In the mean time, she said, she was resolved to engage in some nobleman or gentleman's family as a governess, for she was resolved, at all events, not to live dependant on his brother's generosity. Allan beseeched her not to think of such a thing, but she continued obstinate. She had never told Allan of his brother's base proposal to her, for fear of embroiling them together, and Randal, finding this to be the case, conceived that her secrecy boded approbation, and forthwith laid a scheme to get her into his power, and gain her to his purposes.

Allan had told his brother, in confidence, of his beloved cousin's simple plan, and besought him to protect her, and keep her in that independent station to which her rank and birth entitled her. Randal said she was such a perverse self-willed girl that Swan, that no one could prevail on her to do ought but what she chose, yet that he would endeavour to contrive something to benefit her.

After this, he ceased not to boast to his associates, that he would soon show them such a flower in his keeping, as never before blossomed within the ports of Edinburgh. Accordingly, he engaged a lady of the town to go out in a coach, in a dashing style, and wait on Swan, and engage her for the family of an Irish Marquis. The terms were so liberal, that the poor girl's heart was elated. She was to go with this civil and polite dame for a few months, that she might be attended by some masters, to complete her education and accomplishments, all which was to be liberally defrayed by the nobleman.

After that, she was to go into the family as an associate, with a salary of £300, an offer too tempting to be refused by one in Swan's situation.

Now, it so happened, that the very night on which the two clergymen watched for the ghost of old Welldean, was that on which this temptress came to Swan's lodging with her proud offer. Both Swan and the old lady with whom she lived were delighted—entertained the woman kindly; and it was agreed that she should tarry there all night, and Swan would depart for Edinburgh with her in the morning. Swan proposed sending for Allan, but to this, both the old dames objected as unnecessary, as well as indelicate. They were both in Randal's interest, and as it afterwards appeared, both knew him.

When Allan left the two ministers, he found his heart so ill at ease that he could not rest. The hand that he had seen upon the wall, haunted his imagination; and he felt as if something portentous were hanging over him. He went out to walk, for the evening was fine, and it was scarcely yet twilight, and naturally went toward the village which contained his heart's whole treasure, and when there, as naturally drew to the house where she resided.

When he went in he found them all in a bustle, preparing for his beloved Swan's departure. The two dames evaded any explanation; but Swan, with whom all deceit and equivocation with Allan was out of the question, took him straightway into her apartment, and made him acquainted with the whole in a few words. He disapproved of every part of the experiment, particularly on account of their total separation. She tried to reason with him, but he remained sullen, absent, and inflexible. His mind was disarranged before this intelligence, which proved an addition it could not bear with any degree of patience. Swan had expected to delight him with the news of her good fortune, and perceiving the effect so different from what she had calculated on, in the bitterness of disappointment she burst into tears.

All his feelings of affection were awakened anew by this. He begged her pardon again and again, pressed her to his bosom, and kissing the tears from her cheek, promised to acquiesce in every thing on which her heart was so much set. "Only, my dear Swan," continued he, "do not enter on such a step with precipitation. Take a little time to inquire into the character of this woman with whom you are to be a lodger, and the connexion in which she stands with this noble family. What if the whole should be a trick to ruin a beautiful and unsuspecting young creature without fortune and friends?"

"How can you suspect such motives as these, Allan? Of that, however, there can be no danger, for I am utterly unknown to any rake of quality that would be guilty of such an action."

"At all events," said he, "take a little time. I am frightened lest something befall you. A preconception of something extraordinary impending over our fates, has for some time pressed itself upon me, and I am afraid lest every step we take may be leading to it. To a friendless girl, so little known, a situation so lucrative and desirable could not be expected to come of itself. Have you ever made inquiry by whose interest it was procured?"

No, Swan had never once thought of making such an inquiry, believing, perhaps, through perfect inexperience of the world, that her own personal merits had been the sole cause. The two lovers returned straight to the parlour to make this necessary inquiry. The wily procuratress, on several pretences, declined answering the question; but Allan, pressing too close for further evasion, she acknowledged that it was all the transaction of the young laird, his brother. The old lady, the owner of the house, was loud in her praises of Randal. Allan likewise professed all his objections to be at an end, and lauded his brother for the kind part he had acted with regard to Swan. But as his eye turned towards the latter, he beheld the most perfect and beautiful statue of amazement that perhaps ever was looked on. Her arms were stretched down by her sides, obtruding only a small degree from perpendicular lines; not hanging loosely, and gently, but fixed as wedges. Her hands were spread horizontally, her lips were asunder, and her eye fixed on vacancy. There was no motion in any muscle of her whole frame, which appeared to have risen up a foot taller than its ordinary size. The women were both speaking to her, but she neither heard nor saw them. Allan watched her in silent astonishment, till her reverie was over. She then gave vent to her suppressed breathing, and uttered, as from her bosom's inmost core, "Ah!—Is it so!" and sitting down on the sofa beside Allan, she seemed to be trying in vain to collect her vagrant ideas. At length she rose hastily up, and retired to her own apartment.

The three now all joined loudly in the praises of laird Randal; and long they conversed, and long they waited, but Swan did not return. Her friend at length went to her, but neither of them returned, until Allan, losing all patience, rung the bell, and desired the servant to tell them that he was going away. Mrs Mayder, the mistress of the house, then re-entered, and appeared flustered and out of humour. "Miss has taken such a mood as I never witnessed in her before," said she; "Pray, dear Allan, go to her, and bring her to reason."

Allan readily obeyed the hint, and found her sitting leaning her cheek on her hand; and, at the very first, she told him that she had changed her mind, and was now determined not to go with that lady, nor to move a step farther in the business. He imputed this to pride, and a feeling averse to lie under any obligations to his brother, and tried to reason her out of it; but it was all in vain; she continued obstinate; and Allan, for the first time in his life, suspected her of something exceedingly cross and perverse of disposition. Yet she chose rather to remain under these suspicions, than be the cause of a quarrel between the two brothers, which she knew would infallibly ensue if she disclosed the truth.

Her lover was about to leave her with evident marks of displeasure; but this she could not brook. She changed the tone of her voice instantly, and said, in the most melting accents, "Are you going to leave me, Allan? If you leave this house to-night, I shall go with you; for there is no one on earth whom I can trust but yourself. I positively will not remain alone with these two women. The one I shall never speak to again, and with the other, who has so long been a kind friend, I shall part to-morrow." Allan stared in silence, doubting that his darling was somewhat deranged in her intellect; and, though he saw the tears rolling in her eyes, he thought in his heart, that she was the most capricious of human beings, and cherished, at that moment, the illiberal suggestion that all women were the same.

"I am an unfortunate girl, Allan;" continued she, "and if I fall under your displeasure, it will indeed crown my misfortune; but I am not what I must appear in your eyes to be at this moment. After what passed a few minutes ago, however, I can no longer be the lodger of Mrs Mayder."

"You are out of humour, my dear Swan, and capricious. I beg you will not make any hasty resolutions while in that humour. Your rejection of that elegant and genteel situation, merely because it was procured for you by my brother, is beyond my comprehension; and, because this worthy woman, your sincere friend, urges you to accept of it, would you throw yourself from under her protection? No earthly motive can ever influence me to forsake you, or to act for a single moment in any other way than as your friend; but I am unwilling to encourage my dear girl in any thing like an unreasonable caprice."

"And will you leave me to-night, when I request and intreat you to stay?"

"Certainly not. At your request I shall sleep here to-night, if Mrs Mayder can supply me with a sleeping apartment. Come, then, and let us join the two ladies in the parlour."

"No. If you please you may go: and I think you should. But I cannot and will not face yon lady again. I have taken a mortal prejudice to her. Allan, you are not to forsake me. Will you become security for what I owe to Mrs Mayder, and board me somewhere else to-morrow?"

Allan stood for some time silent, and looked with pity and concern at the lovely and whimsical creature before him. "Forsake you, Swan!" exclaimed he, "how can your bosom harbour such a doubt? But, pray, explain to me the cause of this so sudden and radical change in all your prospects and ideas?"

"Pardon me; I cannot at this time. At some future period, perhaps, I may; but I cannot, even with certainty, promise that."

"Then I fear that they are groundless or unjust, since you cannot trust me with them."

"I am hard beset, Allan. Pray trust to my own judgment for once. But do not leave this house to-night, for something has occurred which affrights me, and if you leave me here, I know not what may happen."

Allan turned pale, for the sight that he had seen himself recurred to his mind, and a chillness crept over his frame. He had a dread that something portentous impended over him and his beloved Swan.

"I fear I have as good reason to be affrighted," said he; "something unfortunate is certainly soon to overtake you and I; for it appears to me as if our very natures and sentiments had undergone a change."

"I have always anticipated good," returned she, "which is too likely to be fulfilled in evil at present. I do not, however, yield in the least to despair; for I have a very good book that says, 'Never give way to despondency when worldly calamities thicken around you, even though they may drive you to the last goal; for there is one who sees all things, and estimates all aright—who feels for all his creatures, and will not give up the virtuous heart for a prey. Though your sorrows may be multiplied at night, yet joy may arise in the morning.' In this is my hope, and I am light of heart, could I but retain your good opinion. Go and join the two ladies in the parlour, and be sure to rail at me with all the bitterness you are all master of. It will be but reasonable, and it will not affect poor Swan, whose measures are taken."

The trio were indeed right free of their censures on the young lady for her caprice; and Mrs Mayder, who, ever since Allan was left fortuneless, discouraged his addresses by every wile she could devise, hinted broadly enough how much she had often to do to preserve quiet, and to bear from that lady's temper. Allan assured them that it was in vain to think of prevailing on her to go with her kind benefactress at present, whom she declared she would not see again; and that both his friend Mrs Mayder, and himself, had fallen under her high displeasure for endeavouring to sway her resolution. But he assured both, that he intended to use his full interest with his fair cousin, and had no doubt of ultimately bringing her to reason. He never once mentioned what she had said of leaving her old friend, thinking that was only a whim of the moment, which calm reflection would soon allay.

He slept there all night, so that he was not at Welldean when the affray happened with the two parsons. He breakfasted with the two ladies next morning, and finally leading the elegant town dame to her carriage, he took leave of her with many expressions of kindness. Swan continued locked up in her own room until the carriage rolled away from the door. When they returned up stairs, she was come into the parlour, dressed in a plain walking-dress, and appeared quite composed and good-humoured, but somewhat absent in her manner. She fixed once or twice a speaking look on Allan, but unwilling to encourage her in what he judged an unreasonable caprice, he would understand nothing. At length he bade them good-morning, and said he would perhaps call in the evening. She did not open her lips, but, dropping him a slight courtesy, she went into her chamber, and followed him with her eye, as long as he remained in view. She then sat down, and gave vent to a flood of tears. "He even declines becoming my surety for a paltry sum of money!" said she to herself; "whatever it costs me, or whatever shall become of me, which God at this moment only knows, I shall never see him again."

Allan did not return in the evening. The events of the preceding night, and the horrific cries, looks, and madness of the doctor, had thrown the people of the hall into the utmost consternation, and occupied his whole mind. Between ten and eleven at night, he was sent for expressly by Mrs Mayder. Swan was missing, and had not been seen since the morning. Search had been made for her throughout the village, and in the neighbourhood, without effect. No one had seen her, save one girl, who *thought she saw her* walking towards the bank of the river, but was not certain whether it was she or not.

The dismay of Allan cannot be described. He was struck speechless, and appeared for a time bereaved of all his wonted energy of mind; and grievously did he regret his cold and distant behaviour to her that morning. He found Mrs Mayder at one time railing at her for leaving her thus clandestinely, and threatening to have her seized and imprisoned for debt; and at other times weeping and lamenting for her as for her own child. Allan reminded her, never in his hearing to mention the sum owing to her on Swan's account, for that his brother, as their late uncle's heir and executor, was bound for it; and that he himself would voluntarily bind for it likewise, though he had it not in his power to settle it at that instant. Silenced on this score, she now gave herself up wholly to weeping, blaming Swan all the while for ingratitude, and denying positively that she had said one word to her that she could in reason take amiss. Allan knew not what course to take; but that very night, late as it was, he sent off an express to Edinburgh after his brother, informing him of the circumstance, and conjuring him to use every means for the recovery of their dear cousin; adding, that he himself would search the country all round on the ensuing day, but would trust to his dear Randal for Edinburgh, in case she had come that way. Randal rejoiced at the news of her elopement. He had no doubt that she would shape her course toward the metropolis, and as little that he would soon discover her, and have her to himself.

Allan remained at Mrs Mayder's house all that night likewise, having sent up orders for his servant and horses to attend him at an early hour. He slept, through choice, in the chamber which his dear Swan had so long occupied, and continued moaning all night like one at the point of death. Next morning he arose at the break of day; but as he was making ready to mount his horse, having stooped to buckle his spur, as he raised himself up, he was seized with a giddiness, staggered, and fell down in a swoon. The village pharmacopolist was instantly brought, who declared the fit to be from a fabricula in the periosteum or pericranium, and that the gentleman was in a state of great danger as to phrenitis; and therefore, that severe perfrication was requisite, until suspended animation returned, and that then he would instantly phlebotomise him.

To this last operation, Allan's servant objected strongly, observing with great seriousness, that he did not see the necessity of *flaying* any part of his master, merely for a fainting fit, out of which he would soon recover; but if such an operation was necessary, why not rather take the skin of some other part than that he had mentioned, as his master was just about to ride?

Allan recovered from his swoon, but felt great exhaustion. He was again put to bed, blooded, and blistered in the neck; but for all these, before night he was in a raging fever, which affected his head, and appeared pregnant with the worst symptoms. In this deranged and dangerous state he lay for several weeks. Swan was lost, and could not be found either dead or alive. Randal was diligent in his researches, but failed not to console himself in the mean time with the company of such other fine ladies as the town afforded. The ghost of old Welldean kept one part of the house to itself. Mrs Tallowchandler, the fat house-keeper, continued to pray most fervently, but especially when she chanced to take a hearty dram. Nick the gardener did nothing, save preparing himself for another and a better state; and Gilbert the wood-cleaver was harder on the laird's strong beer than ever. Of all wasteful and ruinous stocks in this wasteful and ruinous world, a pack of idle domestics are the most —I'll not write another word on the subject.

This last-mentioned worthy, happening to say to some of his associates, that he would watch a night in the library by himself, for a bottle of brandy, and speak to his old master too, if he presented himself; and this being told to Randal the next time he came out, he instantly ordered the beloved beverage to be provided to Gilbert, and promised moreover, to give him five guineas to drink at the village, when and how he had a mind. There was no more about it, Gilbert took the bait, and actually effected both, if his own word could be believed. It is a great pity that there was nothing but the word of a man mortally drunk, to preserve on record the events of that memorable night. All that can now be done, is to give his relation next morning; for after he had got a sleep, and was recovered from his state of ebriety, the circumstances vanished altogether from his mind.

Randal remained in the house all the night, though not by himself, curious to be a witness of Gilbert's experiment; for every one in the house assured him, that he would be dislodged. Gilbert, however, stood his ground, never making his appearance; and after the rising of the sun, when the laird and a number of his attendants broke in upon him, they found the brandy drunk out, and honest Gilbert lying flat on the floor, sound asleep. With much ado they waked him, and asked if he had seen the ghost?

"The ghost! Oh yes—I remember now—I suppose so. Give me something to drink, will you? Eh! L—d, my throat's on fire! Oh-oh-hone!"

They gave him a jug of small beer, which he drained to the bottom.

"D—d wishy-washy stuff that!—Cooling though.—That brandy has been rather strong for me.—Heh-heh-heh, such a night!"

"Tell me seriously, Mr Falconer," said Randal, "what you saw, and what you heard?"

"What I saw, and what I heard. That's very good! He-he-he! *Very* good indeed! Why, you see, master (*hickups*) I–I saw the ghost–saw your un-(*hick*)nkle–state and form–never saw him better–(*hick*) quite jocular, I assure you."

"Did he indeed speak to you, Gilbert?"

"Speak! To be sure–the whole night.–What did he else?"

"By all means, then, if you can remember, tell us something that he said, if it were but one sentence."

"Remember! Ay, distinctly. Every word. He-he-he-he! 'Gilbert Falconer,' says he; 'Your glass is out.' He-he-he-he! (and all this while Gilbert was speaking in a treble voice, and a tongue so altered with drunkenness, that it was difficult to understand what he said.) 'Your glass is out,' says he–It was true too–there it stood as empty as it is at this moment. 'Gilbert (*hick*) Falconer,' says he, 'Your glass is out.' 'Thank you, sir,'–says I–'Thank you for the hint, sir,' says–I–He-he-he! 'Your glass is out,' says he: 'Thank you kindly, sir,' says I, 'for–the hint–You're quite a gentleman–now,' says I–He-he-he!– 'Quite a gentleman,' says I–'I have seen other days with you,' He-he-he-he!–I said so–I did, upon my honour. For God's sake give me something to drink, will you? Ay; that was the way of it–He-he-he-he!–'Gilbert Falconer,' says he; 'Your'"–(*hick*)–

"The old intoxicated ideot is mocking us," said Randal; "There is nothing to be made of such stuff as that."

"I never knew him tell a lie," said Mrs Tallowchandler; "even at the drunkenest time I ever saw him. Would it please your honour to ask him if that was the first sentence that the apparition spoke to him? If we can bring what passed to his mind by degrees, he will tell us the truth."

Gilbert was still sitting on the floor, rhyming over his story of the glass, and indulging in fits of ideot laughter at it; when Randal again returned to him, and aroused his further attention, by asking him if that was the very first sentence that the ghost spoke to him?

"The first sentence!–No.–Bless your honour, it was the last.–I took the hint and–filled that champaign glass–full to the brim–of brandy.–I thanked him first though–upon my honour, I did.–'Thank you for the hint, sir,' says I–and drank it off. 'Here's a good night's rest to us both,' says I–I saw nae mair of him."

"Did he vanish away just then, Gilbert?"

"I daresay he did; (*hick*) at least, if he was there I did not see him.– If there had been fifty ghosts it would have been the same to old

Gibby.–I think it's time we had both a sleep, if your honour, or your honour's likeness, or whatever you are, be speaking that way. So here's a–"

"In what way do you mean, Gilbert? What was he then speaking about?"

"Did not I tell you?"

"Not that I remarked. Or if you did, it has escaped me."

"Tut! I told you every syllable to the end.–Give me something to drink, will you? And remember I have won my five guineas."

"Well, here they are for you. Only you must first tell me distinctly, all that passed from beginning to end."

"Odd's my life, how often would you hear it? I have told you it word for word ten times.–'Gilbert Falconer,' says he,–'I think you are an honest man.' 'Thank you, sir,' says–I.–'You are come to the right way of thinking at last,'–says I.–'There was no word of that when I lost my butlership,' says I.–'It agreed very well with my constitution–that.' He-he-he! I said so.–He grew very serious then–I knew not what to do.–'I am now in the true world, and you still in the false one,'–said he–'and I have reason to believe you honest at heart; therefore I have a sacred and–important charge to give you–you must read through the Greek and Latin Classics.'–'What?' said I–'Yes,' said he, 'you must go through the classics from beginning to end.'–'I beg your pardon there,'–says I–'Do this for me,' said he, 'else the sand of your existence is run.' 'What?' said I–'Why, the thing is out of my power–if you are speaking that way, it is time we were both gone to sleep.' 'Gilbert Falconer,' says he, 'Your glass is run out.' 'Thank you for the hint, sir,' says I–He-he-he!–That was the best of it all–I thought matters were growing too serious. 'Thank you for the hint, sir,' says I–'I can replenish it'–so I took a bumper to his better rest, that would have given three men up their feet.–I saw no more. He may be standing here yet for ought I know."

"Gilbert, you are endeavouring to amuse us with the mere fumes of a distempered imagination. It is impossible, and altogether unnatural, that one should rise from the grave, and talk to you such flummery as this. Confess honestly, that there is not one word of it true."

"True? By this right hand it is true every word. May I never see the light of heaven, if it is not the downright truth, as near as my memory retains it. A man can answer for no more." As he said this, there was a glow of seriousness in his drumly looks, as well as of anger that his word should have been doubted.

"I will answer for it that it is true," said Mrs Tallowchandler.

"So will I," said old Nicholas.

"But was it not a dream, Gilbert?" inquired Randal.

"No;" said Gilbert, with more steadiness than he had hitherto spoke, "I saw your late uncle with my bodily eyes, in the very likeness in which I have seen him in this apartment a thousand times—just as he wont to be, calm, severe, and stern."

"Were you nothing terrified?"

"Why, I cannot say I was perfectly at my ease. As far as I recollect, I struggled hard to keep my courage up.—I did it.—This was the lad that effected it.—This black bottle.—Come let us go down to the hall, and have something to drink."

These were glorious days for old Gilbert, as long as the five guineas lasted! Every night was spent at a little inn in the village, where he and Andrew Car, game-keeper, more properly game-destroyer, to the laird of Lamington, had many a sappy night. Andrew was the prototype of his jolly master, though only like the shadow to the great original; yet it was agreed by the smith and sutor Fergusson both, that Gilbert's wit predominated, at least, as long as the five guineas lasted, the matter was not to be disputed, and that was not a very short time. At the inn where our old hearty cocks met, strong whisky was sold at three-half-pence a gill, and brandy at twopence. Of course sixpence each was as much as they could carry.

It is a pity that young men should ever drink ardent spirits. They have too much fire in them naturally. But it is a far greater pity that old men should ever want them. Drink reanimates their vital frame; and, as they recount the deeds of their youth, brings back, as it were, a temporary but present enjoyment of these joyous days. It would have done any man's heart good, to have seen the looks of full and perfect satisfaction that glowed in the faces of these notable old men, every time that Gilbert compounded the materials, grateful and inspiring, for a new reeking jug. How each sung his old hackneyed song, heard from night to night, and from year to year, but always commended—How they looked in each other's faces—shook each other's hands, and stroked one another's bald crown. It is a pity such old men should ever want something to drink.

In all these nights of merriment and confidence, however, Gilbert would never converse a word about the apparition. Whenever the subject was mentioned, he grew grave, and pretended to have forgot every circumstance relating to the encounter; and when told what he had said, he only remarked, that he had not known what he was saying: and it is not certain but by this time he had reasoned himself into the belief that the whole was a dream.

After a long, dangerous, and wasting illness, Allan grew better. Gilbert had visited him every day before he went to his carousals, and the attendants were of opinion, that Allan's recovery was more owing to the directions he gave for his treatment, than all that the medical men did for him. During the height of the fever, in the wanderings of his imagination, he was constantly calling on the name of Swan Sommerville, and he generally called every one by her name that came to his bed side. She was still nowhere to be found; even Randal, with all his assiduity, had not been able to trace her. But for nine days running, there were two young ladies came in a coach every day to Mrs Mayder's door, where Allan still lay, and the one went up stairs and saw him, while the other kept still in the coach.

As soon as his reason returned, his first inquiries were about Swan; and, as they were obliged to tell him the truth, it occasioned two or three relapses. At length, the guard of the mail coach flung down a letter. It was directed to Mrs Mayder; but hers was only a blank cover, enclosing one to Allan. His was without date, and simply as follows:

> "I am glad of your recovery, and write this, to entreat you not to distress yourself on my account; for I am well, and situated to my heart's content. Make no inquiries after me; for, in the first place, it is impossible for you to find me out, and moreover, were you to do so, I would not see you. Look to our late uncle's affairs, only in as far as you are yourself concerned. I have engaged another to see justice done to me. If I had not found more kindness and generosity among strangers, than from my relatives and those I trusted, hard indeed, would have been the fate of
>
> SWAN SOMMERVILLE."

Allan read the letter over and over, cried over it like a child; for his nerves were weak and irritable by reason of his late severe illness; and always between hands, thanked Heaven for her health and safety. In the mean time, he planned fifty schemes to find her out, and as many to bring about a reconciliation. "I must have offended her grievously," said he to himself, "but it has cost me dear, and I was so far from doing it intentionally, that at that very time, I would cheerfully have laid down my life for her." He had only one thing to console him; he thought he discerned more acrimony in her letter than was consistent with indifference. He now got better very fast; for his mind was constantly employed on one object, which relieved it of the languor so injurious to one advancing toward a state of convalescence.

In the mean while, Gilbert's drinking money was wearing low, which he found would be an inconvenience for Andrew and him; and the two made it up one night over their jug, that they would watch for the ghost together, for the same sum each that Gilbert had formerly realized. One difficulty occurred, who it was that was to give them this. The laird had not been at Welldean Hall for a long time; and, as for Allan, his finances were so low that he could not spare them so much, though they had no doubt he would gladly have given triple the sum to have this mystery farther explored. At the first proposal of the subject, Andrew Car was averse to it; but as their finances wore nearer and nearer to an end, he listened proportionally with more patience to Gilbert's speculations; and always at their parting, when considerably drunk, they agreed perfectly on the utility of the experiment. It is indeed believed, that Gilbert had anxious and fearful desires of a farther communication with this unearthly visitant, of whose identity and certainty of appearance he had no doubt. Nicholas had once seen it in the twilight, beckoning him from the garden towards the library; and he himself had again at midnight seen and conversed with it face to face; but from all that he could gather, the charges which it then gave him, appeared to have been so whimsical, he could make nothing of their meaning. That a spirit should come from the unseen world, to induce a man of his age to begin a course of studies in Greek and Latin, a study that he always abhorred, was a circumstance only to be laughed at, yet it was impossible he could divest himself of a consciousness of its reality.

On the other hand, he perceived that there was something radically wrong in the appropriation of his late master's effects. His will was lost, or had been fraudulently concealed; and those to whom he was sure the late laird intended leaving the best share of his immense fortune, were thus cut off from any, save a trivial part contained in moveables. It was no wonder that Gilbert, who was a well informed single hearted man, was desirous if possible to see those righted, whom he conceived to have been so grossly wronged, and whom he now saw in very hard circumstances; but, alas, he did not know the worst!

From the time that Allan received the letter from Swan, to that of his complete recovery, he had done nothing but formed schemes how to discover his fair cousin; and after discussing them thoroughly for nights and days together, he pitched on the right one. He knew

there was a young lady in Edinburgh, the only daughter of a reverend professor, with whom Swan had been intimate at the boarding-
school, and still kept up a correspondence. Though Allan had never
seen this young lady, yet, as he knew Swan was shy of her acquaintance, and had so few in the metropolis that she knew any thing
about, he conceived that she must either be living with Miss B——, or
that the latter was well aware of her circumstances, and the place of
her concealment.

He knew that if he applied personally or by letter, he would be
repulsed; and therefore went to Edinburgh, and took private lodgings, with a determination to watch that house day and night rather
than not see who was in it, and to dog Miss B—— wherever she went,
assured that she would visit Miss Sommerville often, if they were
not actually living together. His surmises were right. He soon discovered that Swan was living in this worthy professor's house, and
not very privately neither. She walked abroad with Miss B—— every
good day.

Allan, full of joy, flew to his brother's rooms, and communicated
to him the intelligence of the happy discovery he had made, intending, at the same time, to settle with Randal how they were to act, in
order to regain their cousin's confidence. He found Randal confined to his room, undergoing a course of severe medicines, he having made rather too free with his constitution. He professed great
satisfaction at hearing the news, yet there appeared a confused reserve in his manner that Allan did not comprehend. But the former
was soon relieved from his restraint, by a visit from two of his associates in dissipation. The conversation that then ensued, astounded
Allan not a little, who had led a retired and virtuous life. He never
before had weened that such profligate beings existed. They laughed
at his brother's illness, and seemed to exult in it, telling him they
had taken such and such mistresses off his hand until he got better,
and therefore they hoped he would enjoy his couch for six months
at least. Their language was all of a piece. Allan was disgusted, and
left the house, and then Randal displayed to his honourable associates how he stood with his charming cousin; and how, if it were not
for that whining sweet-milk boy, his brother, whom the foolish girl
affected, he could be in possession of that incomparable rose in a
few days. He told them where she was, within a few doors of him.
One of the bucks had got a sight of her, and declared her the finest
girl that ever bent a busk, and both of them swore she should not
escape their fraternity, were she locked in the seraglio of the grand
Seignior. Long was the consultation, and many proposals highly

honourable were brought forward, but these it is needless to enumerate, as the one adopted will appear in the sequel.

Both Allan and Swan had received charges of horning on debts to a considerable amount, after their uncle's death. Allan applied to his brother, in whom he still placed the most implicit confidence, who promised that he would instantly cause a man of business pay them all up to a fraction. This he actually did; but the man who transacted this for him, was a low specious attorney, quite at his employer's steps. He had plenty of Randal's money in his hand, but these bills were not particularly settled. This was a glorious discovery. Captions were served in the country, the one at Mrs Mayder's, the other at Welldean, as the places of residence of the two debtors, and none of them being there, the time expired. The attorney had got his cue; the unsuspecting lovers were watched apart, and both of them seized and conveyed to jail, but each of them quite unconscious of what had happened to the other. Allan wrote instantly to his brother, expostulating with him on his negligence. He answered him civilly, but carelessly; telling him, that he had neglected to settle with the scoundrelly attorney, having run himself short of cash, but that he would lose no time in getting the affair settled. However, as his health was so bad, he begged of Allan to have a little patience, and not to accept of relief from any other person, else he would be both grieved and affronted. Allan lay still in prison, and waited, but waited in vain.

Swan was seized in the Canongate, at three o'clock, as she was returning with Miss B—, from viewing the palace of Holyrood. The latter was so confounded, that she would have fainted on the street, had she not been supported by some ladies and gentlemen that were passing at the time. Swan suffered herself to be taken into custody in dumb dismay, never opening her lips. One of Randal's worthy and genteel associates was near at hand, to abuse the messenger, the turnkey, and every one connected with the disgraceful affair; and, at the same time, offered to become bound for the whole debt, and take the lady off with him.

This being a business that required some consideration, his proposal was little attended to by the men in office, who regarded it as mere fustian; but poor Swan, in the forlorn and helpless state in which she found herself, could not help being struck with the young stranger's generosity, and thanked him in moving terms; but, at the same time, rejected his kind offer, and assured him she would soon be relieved. He swore he would rather see all Edinburgh burnt to ashes, ere he left such a lady in prison, and if she was determined not to accept of a temporary rescue from him, by G——, he would remain in prison with her, till he saw her relieved in some way more suited to her ideas of decorum. She reminded him, that such a proceeding would be the reverse of all decorum whatsoever, and however much she might value his company, there was a necessity that he should leave her to herself and her own resources. No, no; he would be d——d if he would. She should either go with him or he would remain with her, any of the alternatives she chose. It would be a disgrace to leave a lady in such circumstances, and he disclaimed the idea of it. D——n the rascals, they should not want money. Did they think that he could not pay them the paltry sum of four or five hundred pounds, the confounded puppies? Rot their utensils, if he would think much to dust hell with them!

Swan smiled at the extravagance of the young man; but though it was a smile of pity, it made him still more outrageous. He cursed all lawyers and attorneys, as well as all people to whom ever debts were owing, sending them all to a place of retribution with one sweep. By the Lord Harry! if he were a messenger at arms, if any low-lifed miserable whelp desired him to seize and immure *a lady* in such a place as that in which they sat, d——n him, he would scatter his brains for him. "And such a lady as they have lodged here to-night!" said he, wiping his eyes, "I beg your pardon, madam; but I can easily see that this is some vile plot; for you are born, bred, and educated to other fortune than this. For Heaven's sake, let me disappoint the culprits, and convey you to a place of safety; I have given you my name. I am a gentleman, and a man of honour, I hope–Suffer me to write to some friends, and relieve you forthwith!"

Miss Sommerville positively declined his intervention for the present, and entreated that she might be left to her own thoughts, and her own resources; yet still she did it in that civil and affection-ate way, that the puppy believed, or affected to believe, that she wished him rather to stay. "But are you sure the ragamuffin scoun-drels will do you no harm?" said he, and without waiting for an answer, returned one himself. "D——n them, if I like their looks very well, though. No, no, madam; you must forgive me, but in truth I have not the heart to leave you here by yourself. Suffer me but to write to some friends; d——me, I'll raise all Edinburgh, but I'll have you set at liberty. I'll bring Major Graham, and all the soldiers in the castle, to storm the old hovel, before I leave you here; L——d, how the artillery-men would smatter it down about the ears of the scoundrels! Suffer me to write to my friends, or some of yours; it is all one, provided I get you out here."

Swan continued obstinate; telling him she would write to her own friends herself, if he would be so kind as give her leisure; and as for his agency, she assured him again that she was not at liberty to accept of it. He continued however to wrangle with her on that score, to flatter her one while, and abuse her creditors another, until the arrival of Professor B——, who sent in his name, and asked admission, his daughter having alarmed him, and hurried him away to the prison, without so much as knowing what was the matter. The spark then bowed and made off, as somewhat alarmed, saying, he would call again. The reverend divine and he passed one another immediately within the door of the apartment. The buck bowed, and then cocked up his head again considerably to the leeward of the perpendicular line, while the professor stared him in the face, as striving to recollect him. Both passed on, and the cause of meeting with Miss Sommerville, the place, and the subject they had to converse on, quite banished from the professor's mind to ask who her gay visitor was. This parson came, honest man! with the full intent of relieving Miss Sommerville; but when he heard the amount of the debt, he blenched and turned pale. It was not a sum for a poor clergyman, who had a family of his own, to part with off-hand. Indeed, what man in the same vocation would have done it, for a young lady, almost a stranger, who had run herself into so much debt so early, and whom her natural guardians, it appeared, had not thought it prudent to relieve. He had, besides, heard so much of her sentiments relating to her cousin, the present laird, when he received her into his house, that he had small hopes of being reimbursed there, and that appeared to be the lady's principal dependence. In short, they could come to no conclusion whereby to obtain immediate relief. Miss Sommerville proposed that he should borrow the sum on the security of her share of her uncle's effects; but even there the hero of faith without works discovered that he would be involved, and fought shy: but concluded by observing, that "something behoved to be done immediately."

Before leaving the place, the professor had some conversation with the keeper, who informed him, that the young gentleman, the lady's friend, who was lately gone, had bespoken the best apartment that was unoccupied in that part of the jail appropriated to debtors; and, in case she was detained, every accommodation befitting her rank. He then asked the keeper, who that gentleman was? He named him, name, surname, and title: the divine shook his head, knowing him to be one of the most notorious profligates in the kingdom, and left the prison nothing improved in his estimation of Miss

Sommerville, and almost resolved, whatever his daughter might say, to leave her to shift for herself.

When it was wearing late, Mr M'——, Randal's gallant friend, returned to the prison, sent in his name and compliments to Swan, and after some demur was admitted. What would not youth and innocence grasp at for deliverance, if shut up within the walls of a prison, and the darksome night approaching? Alas! the female heart clings too fondly to proffered kindness, especially in times of danger or distress; without suspecting or endeavouring to weigh the selfish principles from which the apparent generosity springs, the guileless heart judges from its own motions. It had been agreed among the associates that M'——was never to mention Randal's name; else, as the latter alleged, Swan's delicacy in that point would ruin all; and as he was run quite short of ready cash, and in an infirm state of health, M'——was to pay the greater part of Miss Sommerville's debt, on condition that he had the honour of seducing her.

Well, into Swan's apartment he came, bringing £200 with him in notes, and offering his personal bond for the rest, payable in two months with interest. Swan made many objections, but actually wept with gratitude at the disinterested kindness of the gallant young man. The attorney was consulted; but he had got his cue, and after many hems and haws, and repetitions of learned law terms, consented, so that the poor innocent Cygnet was now left fairly in the power of the fox. She had likewise given her consent, with an overflowing heart; but at the last, when every thing was arranged for her departure, some slight demur arose about the place whereto she was to be taken. She insisted on being taken to the house of Professor B——, but this her benevolent guardian angel as violently protested against, declaring that the divine was unworthy of her confidence; a cold hearted, calculating worldling, who had gone off with a few dubious expressions, and left her in the prison without asking any more after her, or coming back even to wish her a good night.

"To what place do you then propose to take me in the mean time?" said Swan.

"I propose to take you to a relation of my own," said he, "who keeps a boarding house for young ladies of quality, where you may either remain for a season, or for a few nights, or weeks, as you feel disposed."

"But will it not look awkward for an utter stranger to go to such a house? How can I expect that the mistress will receive, among young ladies of quality, a girl just relieved from prison, and going to her house at this time of the evening, in company with a gentleman whom she never saw, till a disagreeable circumstance procured her the honour of his friendship this present day?"

"Why, the truth is, that I know no woman on earth who is so particular about the characters of her inmates as my worthy friend is. She must have the most absolute proofs of their capabilities, tempers, and dispositions, and is strict in these matters almost to a proverb. But it so happens, that with her my word or will is a law. I have been a good friend to her house. My purse has been open to her by day and by night, and, in short, my fortune almost at her disposal. Into that house, therefore, you are certain of admittance. There you are perfectly safe, and from thence you can write to your friends, and arrange every thing in future as you shall choose."

"Well, you are so generous, and so candid, that I can never distrust your honour. I will send for Miss B— to your friend's house, and consult with her there, and must trust myself to your protection for the night. What is the name of your friend, to whose house I am going?"

"Mrs M'—, St James' Street."

"Very well."

*　　*　　*　　*　　*　　*　　*　　*

What a dreadful confusion the ghost made at Welldean Hall that night! It was not as if one disturbed sinner had arisen from his grave only, but as if all his warlike progenitors for many ages had returned to that scene of bustle and array during their stern pilgrimage on this sphere. Scarcely had the rubied west lost its summer dyes, and twilight drawn her shadowy veil over the full blown bosom of nature, when the inmates of Welldean heard a noise as if half a score of men had been tearing down the shelves and books of the library, and dashing them on the floor. Nothing like it had ever been heard in the house before. All the domestics, high and low, (for there is no class of people among whom such a subordination of rank is preserved) crowded into the housekeeper's room, huddling one behind another, and testifying, by their looks, the mortal terror and astonishment that overwhelmed their hearts.

Little wonder was it! The noise continued to increase and redouble. It grew, that it was not only as if the old folios had been dashed down in a rage on the floor, but as if the roof and rafters had been plucked down, and put into the hands of infernal giants to smash the building in pieces to its foundations. This turmoil was occasionally accompanied, when at the loudest, by a voice such as man never heard. It was not like any sound produced by art, nor was it precisely like thunder; but they all agreed, that there was nothing in nature to which it bore so strong a resemblance as a flooded roaring cataract uttering human words. Gilbert was down in the village at his cups; but, low as they rated him, in this dilemma he was sent for. The work of devastation above stairs continued and grew. The house-keeper begged of them all to join in prayer. This they were very willing to do, for they saw no other staff on which they could lean; but then there was none to lead them. Mrs Tallowchandler said, though she was a poor, weak, and sinful woman, she would attempt it. Who knew but Heaven would have mercy on them? They all kneeled, and the good woman began; but her sentences were few and disjointed; and she continued repeating and repeating the same thing, till those around her were beginning to lose hold of their gravity. At the first, when they began, and all were devoutly serious, every noise was hushed. The sudden stillness that ensued was in itself awful. Let erring and presumptuous man be assured of this, that the devotion of the heart never fails having influence in heaven, while all lukewarmness and indifference in sacred things is only a mock-ery of the Almighty, and ought but protection may be expected therefrom. At the beginning all was still; and the fiends, of which the house seemed full, appeared to be hushed and quelled, by the sim-ple words of prayer devoutly offered up; but no sooner did the rev-erence due to that Being before whom they professed to be kneeling begin to subside, than the noise began again gradually to increase; and, as Mrs Tallowchandler was continuing her imbecile repetitions, it came rushing nearer and nearer like a speaking whirlwind, till at length it burst open the door of the apartment where they were assembled, and stunned them with a deafening yell. It was a sort of half-howling half-whistling sound; but nothing was seen. Mrs Tallowchandler joined it with a loud scream, and went into hyster-ics. No one regarded her. The female part of the family were all huddled into corners, and all uttering the same kind of shivering moaning sound. The men were sitting on their seats in a half-strap-ping posture, with their shoulders up, their hair standing on end, and their eyes bent fearfully on the door, "May the Lord Almighty preserve us!" cried old Nicholas. "Amen!" cried a hollow tremu-lous voice, at a distance. "And some that are better than you all! amen!"

None durst venture to go out in order to escape; for the inhabit-ants of another world seemed now to be crowding the passages be-tween them and the door: neither durst they throw themselves into the sunk area; for there was a story below them; though every one would gladly have been out, even though kingdoms had been their

ransom. But when the women heard Nicholas, the gardener, pronounce the above sacred and serious words, with the mysterious
response that was added, from a feeling that the wrath of the spirit
was appeased by it, they called on Nicholas with one voice, "Oh!
Nicholas, pray! pray! for God's sake, pray!" Nicholas obeyed without delay; and in the agony of his heart prayed with great fervour.
But in the course of a few sentences, his prayer grew selfish, and he
began to mention his own fears–his own personal safety and well-
being. Such imperfections cling to man's nature! The rest could not
join with him in his petitions, forgetting themselves; and they felt
sorry that the tenor of his words was of that nature that they could
not. The derisions of the spirit was withheld by Heaven no longer
than this principle of self began to develop its cringing, cowardly,
abominable features. A distant laugh of scorn was heard to begin as
if in the library, with a hollow shaking tone like that uttered by the
bittern at midnight; but it increased every moment till it made the
house tremble, and drew nigher and nigher until the chairs on the
floor began to totter. It seemed again approaching to the back of the
door with tenfold violence. The heart of human being could not
stand it. Some of the men that were next to the windows flung them
open, and threw themselves into the area below. It was amazing
with what celerity the rest followed, darting out at the windows head
foremost, as swift as doves from their pigeon-holes, when scared in
their habitation. In half a minute the whole family, consisting of nearly
forty individuals, were weltering in three heaps on the gravel that
bedded the sunk way, and every one escaped as best he could, and
ran for the village.

What a figure they cut when they went there! Every one was
covered with blood; for those who were not cut, and mangled in the
fall, were all blooded over by the rest who were. They looked like
so many demons themselves; and they found that the housekeeper
and two of the maids were missing; on which they rationally concluded, that they having been the greatest sinners, the spirit had got
power over them, and taken them with him. The villagers were
petrified; appearing to be even more confounded, and at their wit's
end, as the saying is, than the fugitives themselves.

While these things which have been narrated were going on at
the hall, Gilbert and Andrew Car, late gamekeeper to the laird of
Lamington, were enjoying themselves at the public house. They were
both right far forward in their evening carousal, when the messenger from the hall arrived, to entreat Gilbert's attendance without a
moment's delay. Gilbert was in no such confounded hurry; he helped

himself to a glass, Andrew Car to another, and the boy to a third.

"Here's for you, Master Rory, my good fellow; take this off to–to help your wind; and then tell us out your s–story at the utmost leisure. It is all buffoonery to be in such a haste. What signifies it to run puffing and–blowing through the world in that guise.–Here's to you, boy.–Your good health I say, Master Rory. Sit down, sirrah, and take time, I tell you. Is it not the best way, Andrew Car?"

Now Andrew had one peculiarity of which I must apprise my readers, that they may understand him aright. He had a very rapid utterance. Many a man speaks quick, but there never was a man in the world spoke half so quick as Andrew Car. A certain printer in Edinburgh, was a mere joke to him; a title-page, or an errata to a volume, as it were; his utterance was ten times more rapid than Mr —'s. Therefore, in going over the part of this dialogue that be-longs to Andrew, the reader must pronounce the words quicker by seventeen degrees than he ever heard a tongue utter them before. Andrew had likewise two keys that he spoke on, C sharp, and G natural, and his voice had no more but these, either intermediate or subordinate. He took the former on all occasions when his passions were ruffled, particularly when he disapproved highly of any thing, and the latter in his ordinary conversation. I shall therefore put down all the sentences adapted by him to the former key in italic charac-ters, that every one may go on with him, and understand him thor-oughly. I hate that my characters, which are all drawn from nature, should not be properly comprehended.

"Should not a man always do a thing leisurely, Andrew Car?–Is it not the best and most eligible way?"

"Ooo-yes-yes-yes-yes-yes–right-Gibby–right-Gibby–Gibby-Gibby-Gibby–right-right-right-right-right–luck-o'-leisure-Gibby–luck-luck-luck-luck-luck-luck–billy-luck-luck."

"I say, Master Rory–my boy–do you–hear–that? Is not that a beautiful specimen–of–Andrew Car's theory and mine? Eh?–He-he-he-he–Eh? Is it not, lad?"

"Oh, Mr Gilbert, I have not time. Mrs Tallowchandler and a' the fowk sent me to gar you come hame directly, an' pray against the ghost. Oh, Gibby, the bogle has been very ill the night, an' we a' suspect it's the deil."

"The deil, Mr Rory! the deil! Did you say it was the deil, lad?–My faith–my man–if it be the deil–that's another thing than a bogle, let me tell you."

"He's layin' about him at an awfu' rate; an' gin ye dinna come an' speak to him, an' lair him, or pray him down, he'll soon hae a' the house about their lugs. When I came alang the ither wauk, rinnin' wi' fright, I heard a kind o' hooning sound, an' I lookit ower my shoulder, an'—Mercy! what d'ye think I saw? I saw the deil i' the shape o' the auld laird, but as heegh as an ordinar tree, standin' on the gavel wa' wi' a great burnin' kipple in his hand; an' he had a' the house daddit down the length o' the third storey. O Gibby, haste an' gang hame, and see if aught can be done."

"What can be done, boy! why, nothing can be done to pacify him, but reading Latin and Greek.—Nothing but going through the classics. We'll go, however. Andrew, you are a scholar, and have the Greek."

"Ooo, no-no-no-no-no—Gibby-Gibby-Gibby—no-Greek, billy—no-Greek—no-Greek—no-Greek—no-no-no-no-no-no."

"Well, but we shall go, howsoever. You know we have now agreed to go together and speak to it. I am in a proper key to go any where— we'll go—it is as well soon as late, when the family is in extremity— we'll be well rewarded—come, let us go."

"*Oooo-no-no-no-no-no—Gibby-Gibby-Gibby—not-the-night—not-the-night—not-the-night*—some-other—some-other—some-other—other-other-other—madness-billy—madness-madness-madness—folly-folly-folly-folly-folly—'nother-gill—'nother-gill—'nother—gill-gill-gill-gill."

"Boy—give my compliments—to Mrs Tallow—chandler, and tell her, that my—friend, Mr Car, dares not come tonight, because the ghost is irritated—and it is dangerous to meddle with him; but—"

"True-Gibby—true-true-true-true—right-billy—right-billy—right-right-right-right—kittle-business—kittle-business—kittle-kittle-kittle—'nother-gill—'nother-gill—'nother-gill—lass-lass-lass-lass-lass—gill-gill-gill-gill-gill."

"But as I was saying—if it is the deil he must have a sacrifice before he lay. They must give him one of their number, which may well be spared."

"Sacrifice? sacrifice—what-Gibby—what-Gibby—what-what-what—sacrifice—sacrifice—fie-fie-fie—no-no-no-no-no."

"It is a literal fact, sir—and well known to all exorcists. They must do it by lot, tell them, boy. Even if Satan should appear when we two watch together, we must cast lots which of us is to be his to appease him. Or, for instance, if I am the speaker, I have the power and right to consign you over to him."

"*Oooo-no-no-no-no-no—Gibby-Gibby-Gibby-Gibby—no-no-no—no-right—no-right—no-right-billy—no-no-no-no-no*—living-soul—living-soul—not-yours—not-yours-billy—not yours—no-no-no-no—soul-soul-soul—soul-billy—not-do—not-do—not-do—no-no-no-no."

"I will reason this matter with you, my worthy friend; suppose you and I make a contract together—to go and watch an incensed spirit, which, to a certainty, makes its appearance—we take our chance together, you know—why, is it not better that one of us should make a sacrifice of the other, than that it should take us both? or, for instance, if you take it on you to address him—"

"No-no-billy—not-address—not-address—not-speak—not-speak—no-no-no-no-no. Too-quick—too-quick—too-quick-quick-wick-wick-wick-wick. 'Stonish-him—'stonish-him—'stonish-him. All-wrang-Gibby—all-wrang—all-wrang—all wrang-wrang-wrang-wrang. Precious-soul-billy—precious soul—precious-soul—precious-soul-soul-soul—Gibby-lad—Gibby-lad—Gibby-lad. Have-you-there—have-you-there—have-you-there—ha-ha-ha-ha-ha-ha! Soul-soul-soul-Gibby-lad—Gibby-lad—ha-ha-ha-ha-ha!"

This sort of argument used by Andrew Car is the worst to answer of all others, because the rest of the company severally join in it, and then the argument is at an end. At this time it was used by Andrew in such a way that it had precisely that effect. Gilbert joined in the laugh, and the gamekeeper chuckled and crowed over his victory.

Another smoking jug having by this time been made, the dilemma of the family at the hall was soon totally forgotten; even the lad Roderick said little more about it, having no wish to return; and there they sat till they were found out and joined by their bloody and half-deranged companions. And then, drunk as the two veterans were, the strangeness of the tale made them serious for a little, though always disposed, in a short time, to forget the subject. Nothing could cheer the hearts of the fugitives in the smallest degree. The horrid scene that they had escaped from, and the loss of their three companions, held their minds chained up in utter dismay. They marvelled what the ghost would do with the three women. Some said he would tear them limb from limb; some that he would take them to a high rock, and throw them headlong down; and some said that he would take them away to hell with him, soul and body; but none thought of attempting a rescue.

It chanced, however, to come into Gilbert's recollection, that he lay under many obligations to the fat housekeeper, for many a scold, and many a glass of strong beer and queich of brandy beside; and he gallantly proposed to go, for one, to the hall, and see if any remains of the women were left. No one would join him, a circumstance that always had the effect of exalting Gilbert's courage, and he persisted in his resolution, advancing many half-intelligible arguments in favour of the measure, which none of them regarded, till he turned his eyes on Andrew, and remarked, that he surely would not desert him, as he was always noted for befriending the fair sex.

"Ha-ha-ha-ha-ha, Gibby-Gibby-Gibby—some-ways-billy—some-ways—some-ways—some-ways—good-at-a-pinch—good-at-a-pinch—good-at-a-pinch,—Gibby-lad—hah-hah-hah-hah!"

"Then you surely will accompany me, Mr Car?—Eh?—hern't you?—you are bound in honour, sir.—Eh?"

"Don't-know-Gibby—don't-know—don't-know-know-know-know. No-joke-this—no-joke—no-joke—no-joke-at-all billy-billy-billy. Long-spoon-sup-wi'-the-deil—long-spoon-sir—long-spoon—long-spoon. Not-safe—not-safe—not-safe—no-no-no-no-no-no."

"Why, Mr Andrew—let—me—tell you, sir—are you a man of honour—and courage, sir, as I always took you for—eh?"

"Ooo-yes-yes-yes-yes—hope-so—hope-so—hope-so-Gibby—hope-so."

"Then what the devil are you afraid of, sir? Eh? I would defy the devil, the world, and the flesh, and despise them."

"*Oooo-no-no-no-no-Gibby-Gibby—no-no-no-no—not-the world-and-the-flesh—not-the-world-and-the-flesh—no-no-no-no*. Nought-behind-at-all-Gibby—nought-behind-at-all—no-no-no-no. Not-do-sir—not-do-billy—not-do—not-do—not-do. Have-you-there—have-you-there—have-you-there—ha-ha-ha-ha-ha."

"Mr Car, I know you to be a man of spirit. Eh?—I will lead the way—Will you go, or will you not? Eh?"

This was a home thrust; there was no evading it. Andrew was obliged to acquiesce, make a virtue of necessity, and value himself on his courage. Accordingly, Gilbert taking a brilliant lanthorn in his left hand, a stout staff in his right, and Andrew Car at his shoulder, staggered away to Welldean Hall as well as he could, well convinced, that though his companion had less drink in his head, he had likewise less courage at his heart, and therefore Gilbert was determined to *show off* that night, and in nowise to manifest fear for any created being. Andrew, though not quite so confident, had yet a certain character of manhood to support, which he judged it quite incumbent on him to retain; he could never otherwise have shewn his face in social circle more. Up the street they went, not keeping exactly the same line of longitude. Gilbert sometimes took a swing, first the one way, and then the other, like a ship beating up against the breeze.

"Come-come-come-Gibby-Gibby-Gibby—straight-straight-straight-

straight. Laugh-at-us-sir—laugh-at-us—laugh-laugh-laugh-laugh-sir—steady-steady-steady-steady-steady."

"Steady—do—you—say—Mr Car?—We'll see—by—and—by—who—is most steady. Come on, my brave fellow."

Forward they went as they best could. The way was well-known to Gilbert. His feet knew it by instinct, for many a hundred nights had they traced it, when their eyes were as completely closed as if they had been tied up with a napkin. The distance from the village to the hall was scarcely a mile and a half through the fields. When they were about half-way, Andrew, whose hearing was more acute than his associate's, began to mumble and speak with more than ordinary velocity, and drew Gilbert always to one side. The latter refused to go in any other direction than that in which he was proceeding, and a few paces onward the cause of Andrew's agitation became apparent. The most dismal groans were heard at about fifty yards distance in the field. As soon as they fell on Gilbert's ears he heaved his lanthorn, and turned off towards the place from whence the sounds proceeded. Andrew instantly took his high key on C sharp, and poured forth such a torrent of speech that no man could take up a distinct sentence of it. They were all terms of decided disapprobation of Gilbert's adventure; but the only sounds that fell on his ear, that he could call language, were some such words as these.

" *Tell-ye-Gibby-Gibby-Gibby—tell-ye-tell-ye-tell-ye-tell-ye. Nooo-no-no-no-no-no. Make-nor-meddle-make-nor-meddle-make-nor-meddle—no-no-no-no. Dogs-lye-dogs-lye-dogs-lye—tell-ye-tell-ye-tell-ye-tell-ye-Gibby-Gibby-Gibby, &c.*"

Gilbert, without regarding this water-spout of human breath, proceeded straight onward to the object of his concern. Andrew was sometimes shouldering away, and sometimes drawing after the light, while the words by degrees died away from his tongue; but the same sound still continued, and became very like the sounds uttered by the bird, called in this country the Heather Bleater, when he wings the air in the gloaming. Gilbert, to his sincere grief, found his old friend and associate, Mrs Tallowchandler, lying stretched on the ground, unable to rise, moaning grievously. She told him, after blessing him for his kind concern, that her leg was broken; on which he called stoutly to Andrew for assistance. Andrew approached, speaking all the way. "Told-ye-told-ye-told-ye," he was saying as he came, half running; and, once he saw who it was, and how grievously she was hurt, it is impossible to describe his manner, and the confusion of ideas that intruded themselves on his imagination; but always between he seemed to blame Gilbert for coming to her, as if that had been the cause of her misfortune. "Told-ye–told-ye–told-ye–told-ye. Would-not-be-told–would-not-be-told–no-no-no-no. Broken-broken-broken-broken? Ooo-no-no-no-no-no–impossible-impossible-impossible-possible-possible. Broken-broken-broken? What-what-what-what-what? Ooo-no-no-no-no-no-no." And so on he went.

Gilbert, in the height of his zeal and friendship, proposed, that Andrew and he should carry the hurt woman to the village; and, setting down his lanthorn, the two essayed the task, unfit even for a Hercules to perform. Andrew lifted her shoulders, and Gilbert her feet; and, having with difficulty heaved her about two inches from the ground, they began to move toward the village, Andrew in a retrograde direction, and Gilbert pushing forward behind. Scarcely had they gained five feet in their progress toward the doctor, when the weight and pressure upon Andrew caused his heels to dip in the soil, and laid him fairly on his back; while Gilbert fell with his full weight above his fair injured friend, who screamed and groaned most piteously. The former of these sounds serving as a pitch-pipe to Andrew, who took his high sharp key–

"Told-ye-told-ye-told-ye-told-ye–body's-mad-body's-mad-body's-mad–hout-hout-hout-out-out-out. Never-do-never-do-never-do-never-do–no-no-no-no-no-no."

"What, did you mean to tumble down there, sir? The man has not the strength of a weazel! But he is drunk," said Gilbert. "Weazel-weazel-weazel-weazel? What-what-what-what-what-d'ye-say-d'ye-say-d'ye-say? Body's-mad-body's-mad-body's-mad–H'm-h'm-h'm-h'm–weazel-weazel-weazel?"

Mrs Tallowchandler put an end to this growing heat and controversy between our two heros, by begging, that in pity they would return to the village, and bring or send a cart. Andrew took the lanthorn and ran back to the village; but Gilbert staid to condole with his old friend, and lend her any kind office he was able until Andrew's return with the cart; and a frightful detail she there gave him of the incidents that had occurred at the hall in the evening, and confirmed the boy's strange asseveration, that the ghost had nearly levelled the building.

A horse and cart soon came, with the doctor and apothecary in attendance, and in it they laid the housekeeper, whose limb the doctor found not to be broken, but sprained, and much swelled. The expedition of our two heroes to the hall was thus broken off, Andrew not having judged it proper to return, and Gilbert totally forgetting it, in the misfortune of his friend, with whom he staid during the remainder of the night, comforting and encouraging her. Indeed, as soon as she found that her leg was not broken, she grew as communicative and whimsically superstitious as ever. Sore she regretted that Gilbert was not there to have spoke to the old laird, when he came in among them, "roaring like a elephant," as she expressed it; and Gilbert rather wished that he had, since matters had come to such a pass, assuring her, in the meantime, that he and his friend Andrew had agreed to sit up in the library a night together, some time or other, to see if they could learn what it was that the old laird had to communicate; and now, since his master's servants were all driven from the house, if she (Mrs Tallowchandler) would countenance the matter, he thought the sooner the better, and he had no objections that it should be the following night. She commended his undaunted and manly spirit; promised that she would see them well rewarded; and moreover, that they should have the keys of the cellar and larder, and want for no entertainment that the hall could afford; and thus, before morning, the matter was finally settled between them.

As soon as the sun arose all the servants hurried up to the mansion-house to witness the devastations of the last night, expecting that there would scarcely be one stone left standing on another. By the way, they discovered that the two young females that were amissing the evening before had both joined the party; but both kept a mysterious silence whither they had been. In the beginning of next year, however, it began to be suspected, that the one had lodged with a journeyman tailor, and the other with the apothecary's apprentice, in their several apartments in the village. Such a dispensation as that they had met with was an excuse for people doing any thing!

At the hall every thing was in its usual style. There was not an item injured or misplaced from the bottom to the top of the house; not a book in the library was altered, nor any one thing that they could discern; all was standing in state and form as they left it, with the doors bolted and the windows barred, all save those out at which they had effected their escape. This was the most wonderful thing of all! People could no more trust their own senses!

It is a difficult matter to tell a story as it should be told; for, after the party separates, it is necessary to fly always from one to another, to bring them forward to the same notch of time. In conformity with this laudable measure, the writer of this notable tale must return to his fair fugitive, whom he left in circumstances more perilous than any of his readers can well suppose, or than any of her connexions, save her uncle's spirit, seemed to be aware of. If they were, they took no concern about the matter. Had Allan known of her danger, how his heart would have been wrung! but he concealed his name and disgrace from every one save his brother, who was in no hurry to relieve him, until the gallant triumvirate had accomplished their purposes with Swan, which the greater part of my readers will remember was wearing but too near to a consummation. These are, I know, quite impatient to get into a detail of all the circumstances; but there are some incidents that it is painful for an author to enumerate, and it is only in adherence to truth that he submits to the ungracious task. Without them, the tale cannot go on, so they must needs be told. The circumstances in the present case were then precisely as follows   *   *   *   *

"Well, I must trust to your protection for this night," said Swan. "What is the name of the lady, your friend, to whose house I am going?"

"Mrs M'— of St James' Street," said he.

"Very well." She took her Indian shawl about her shoulders, and after turning six or seven times round in the apartment, as if looking for something else, she took hold of Mr M'—'s proffered arm, and he led her out. "God bless you!" said she. "Amen, with all my heart," said he, "and the lovely wisher to boot." "And God will bless you," added she, "for this unmerited kindness to a poor friendless orphan."

> "O wad some power the giftie gie us,
> To see oursels as others see us!"

says Burns; but I have often thought this prayer should be reversed; for if we knew the motives and intentions of others, as well as we do our own, how often would we eschew the errors into which we fall! and if Miss Sommerville had known her conductor's intentions at that time, as well as he himself knew them, how far would she have been from blessing him! Yet, poor fellow! he rejoiced in it, and nothing in the world could have made him so happy as taking that lovely and innocent young lady home with him that night, and ruining her. It is a pity there should be gentlemen of such dispositions, but nobody can help it.

"Mrs M'— in St James' Street! Mrs M'— in St James' Street!" In the hurry of departure, Swan could not think or suspect who Mrs M'— of St James' Street was, but repeating it to herself all the way down the stair, just as she came to the door of the coach, it came to her recollection that she had met with that lady before, and not a very great while ago.

"I beg your pardon, sir," said she. "I have forgot something in the apartment that I left: excuse me for a little." "Please step into the coach, madam, I will go up and bring it." "No, you cannot bring it, I must go myself." With that she wrung her arm out of his, and ran up the stairs. When she came to the place she had left, the man was just in the act of locking it up. But when he saw her come thus hastily to the door, he opened it instinctively, and she entered. Instead of looking for ought she had left, she seated herself in the chair, and desired the turnkey to lock her up till to-morrow, and at his peril to let any one enter the door of that apartment till then. The honest man began to expostulate, telling her that the matter was settled, and that neither he nor his captain had any more charge of her; but seeing her so peremptory, he obeyed, and went to consult a higher power, thinking that the lady was a little deranged in her mind.

M'— did not wait long below in the court of the prison, but impatient at the young lady's stay, went likewise up to her apartment, where he was refused admission. At first he began to abuse the turnkey, thinking he had locked her up through mistake; but finding that it was by her own desire, he began to suspect that she had discovered something he wished to conceal, and dared not push the matter much farther at that time. Finding out the under turnkey's ideas of the state of her mental faculties, he said it was but too true, and however disagreeable it might be, there would be a necessity of carrying her away home by force. This he urged strongly as a last resource, and was joined by all the underlings about the prison; but the captain, or principal keeper, would not permit it, for fear of raising an alarm, and making a disturbance at that time of the evening. He undertook however to keep the lady in safe custody until next day, lest any evil might befall her. M'—, by dint of entreaty, got a conversation with her over a half door before he went away, and there was no manner of blandishment, or passionate regret, that he did not use; insomuch that Miss Sommerville was again melted into an affectionate generosity, which she could not repress, yet continued firm in her resolution. He was obliged to go home with a grieved heart, and relate to his associates this first failure of his grand enterprize; on which the rest of the night, or rather morning, was spent by them in devising new schemes more adapted to the characters of those with whom they had to do, and in relating other adventures of the like nature. Every man and woman in the world is engaged in the pursuit of happiness, and though we wonder at one another, yet all continue to pursue it in their own way. Nice young profligate puppies of gentlemen in general believe, that they enjoy life in a most exquisite way. We'll not quarrel with them about that, but we'll force them to admit what all the world sees, that they are of short duration, and generally followed by bitter fruits.

Swan spent a sleepless night, but scarcely were her thoughts ever otherwise employed than on Mr M'——. His kindness and generosity interested her; and if it had not been for the naming of one lady, of whose character she had weighty suspicions, she thought she could have trusted him, and gone with him to any part of the kingdom. So difficult is it for suspicion to find entrance to a guileless heart.

Next morning she sent for the principal keeper, a man well known for probity and honour, and to him she communicated her case, all save two circumstances. The one was the private behaviour of her cousin Randal to her, and the other was the name of the lady to whose house M'—— proposed to have taken her over night. The latter subject was several times at the root of her tongue, but timidity withheld it from being uttered. She had a certain feeling of kindness, or generosity, hankering about her heart for the young gentleman, and she could not bear, with one dash, to run the risk of blotting it out for ever. She therefore asked the keeper only about his name and connexions, and what circle of society he kept? The keeper had heard the name and title of the gentleman, but knew nothing about him farther. He promised, however, in a short time to satisfy her in all these points. "I have a Highland officer about the prison," said he, "principally for the purpose of carrying and bringing messages; I am sure he will either know the gentleman himself, or find those in a few minutes that will give you a list of all his pedigree for forty generations."

The keeper was glad thus to amuse the lady, and reconcile her to what appeared to him to be an inconsistency in her prosecutor. He had during the morning got one letter, and one charge after another, about his prisoner, until he knew not well how to proceed; yet, for his own security, he resolved to detain her. The bucks, terrified that she should get away from under their thumbs, as they termed it, had put the attorney upon different manœuvres to detain her in prison until she was obliged to accept of their relief on their own conditions. They knew too well, that having secured Allan, they had little to fear for the interference of any other. The keeper likewise entered into her scruples, or pretended to do so, of getting so deeply obligated to an utter stranger. "It is not, madam," said he, "what you or I may feel, and know to be the truth, but how the world may view it. A young lady's character is her all, or next to that; and better had you remain a year in this place than owe your liberty to some gentlemen, even though their motives may be unimpeachable. Though it is a truism that things must be as they are, yet their effects are too often modelled by the judgment of the world. I will send for Malcolm, and have this matter cleared up."

Malcolm was sent for, and soon arrived with his bonnet in his hand.

"Malcolm, do you know any thing of the gentleman that came in a coach last night, and waited on this lady?"

"Does the lady not know any thing of him her own self?" said Malcolm, with true Highland caution.

"That is no answer to the question I put to you," said the keeper, sternly.

"Hu, not at hall, your honour—but hersel was peen thinking—that if laidy would pe tahaking in shentlemans—."

"Hold your peace, you Highland rascal! You have no right to form any conjecture of aught that passes here by my authority. I ask you, if you know aught of Mr M'—, who was here last night, or of his connexions, and I desire you to answer me without farther circumlocution?"

"Cot t–n him!" said Malcolm, "has he peen pehaving pad to te dhear lhady?"

Miss Sommerville, never having conversed with a native High-lander, at least with one of Malcolm's rank, before, was so much amused by his shrewd and obstinate caution, as well as his uncouth dialect, that she burst out a laughing at this last question. The keeper also smiled, which, encouraging Malcolm in his petulance, he went on.

"Hu! hope she would only pe some frheedom, lhove? Highland shentlemans pe fery pad for frheedom, lhove—if te lhaidy pe peautifulmost, she pe very pad indheed."

The keeper, finding that nothing would be gotten out of Malcolm, if there was any risk of a Highlander's character being impeached, took a wiser course, and assured him, that so far from behaving ill to the lady, he had acted so nobly, that she was anxious to know a little more of him, to make him some amends, or acknowledgment, at least. Malcolm's eyes gleamed with joy and pride.

"Hu! she might pe shoor of tat! All tat you hafe to do with High-land shentlemans is, to cotinfidence him. Hersel pe fery sorry tat she not kif cood informhation, she know so less of him. But there pe one Maister Ronald Macmurrich, a shairman of the Rhegister, who is full cousin py te creat crhandmhother's side; she pe tell you all and mhore. Had she peen of Clan-Darmachie, or Clan-Stuhart, (all out of Appin) or te long Clan-Khattanich, she could hafe cone through all teir plood."

Here Malcolm was stopped short in his muster-roll, and sent in search of Ronald Macmurrich. In the meantime, the keeper remained conversing with Swan, and advised her strongly to apply to her cousin Randal, who, he said, was her natural guardian, and obliged both in honour and law to pay every farthing that was contracted during the lifetime of her uncle, as it was on his credit that the debt was taken on; and there being a part of her cousin's behaviour which she did not choose to divulge, the keeper wondered at her pride and shyness, and supposed that she had drawn too freely on her cousin's bounty previous to that time.

"This is Mhaster Ronald Macmurrich, sir," said Malcolm, entering briskly with his bonnet in his hand, and bowing with a grace becoming a man of higher rank, "and though I would peen saying it, she pe shentilman that you might pe thependance on hims worts."

"Come away, Mr Ronald, I want to converse with you in this lady's presence for a minute or two. Malcolm, you need not wait. Ronald, do you know any thing of Mr M'— of G–h?–Malcolm, I tell you, you need not wait."

"Hu, it mak fery lhittle dufference to her-nain-sel to whait a few mhinutes to pe oblhiging your honour."

"No, no,–off, off. What the devil are you standing there for, sirrah?"

"I can stand any where that your honour plheases. I can pe sthanding here then."

"Go out at the door, I tell you, and close it."

"Hu, but your honour will soon pe wanting hur ackain; and mhore the less Maister Ronald has peen got a fery pad mhemory, and he'll pe lhosing to forget of mhany things."

"Hu, shay, shay, she pe fery creat of truth all tat Maister Mhawcom has peen to say."

The captain finding that the two cronies were determined to keep together, thought it best to humour them; for he knew if any of them grew obstinate, he might as well contend with a mule.

"So you know the laird of G–h, Ronald?"

"Hu, what then? Pless your honour, she pe full coosin to himself. Mach-Vich-Alaster More Machouston Macmurrich was her crhandmother's fhather; and he was khotten upon a child of Kinloch-Mhulart's."

"And, py my faith, that's all very true that Maister Rhonald says; and she could pe taking her sworn oath to every whord of it."

"What sort of a gentleman is he?"

"Hu! the finest shentilman that's in the whole world. And upon my soul, you would not pe finding such a shentilman if you were to rhide fhifty thousand mhiles."

"Ay, she be all truth and mhore that Maister Rhonald says."

"What sort of moral character does he hold?"

"More-ill? Hu, tamn it, no. He has not cot one single spark of that in his whole pody and souhl."

"No, you may swore that, Maister Macmurrich."

"What? Not one spark of morhality?"

"Morhality?–Ay.–Devil a single scrap of her, I'll pe sworn.–Morality?–What she pe?

Here the captain and Miss Sommerville could not contain their gravity, which staggered Ronald a little, and made him ask the last question.

"That is, perhaps, too general a term to be fully understood," said the keeper; "we shall enter into particulars; and as it is all in good friendship, you may answer me freely. In the first place, then, can you tell me how he has behaved himself in general with regard to women?"

"Oo, ter never was a shentilman pehaved so petter since ta world was made. You know, if ta lhaidy was peing fhery pohnny, and fhery hamiable, and fhery khind, why you know I could not pe answering for myself and far less for him; but I'll take it upon me to pe sworn, that he would not force a child against her own will."

"So you may, so you may, Maister Rhonald."

"What sort of company does he keep? Can you tell me the names of any of the ladies or gentlemen whose houses he visits at?"

"Hu, he goes to the roots of all the lhadies, and all the lhords of ta whoule kingdom; and to ta hadfu cats, and to te grhand mhinisters tat prheach. There is not a shentilman in ta whoule world that is so well taken hould of. I can pe sworn of tat too."

"Indheed so you can, Maister Rhonald, and so can I too."

"He might have peen kitting one hearl's dhaughter last year; and I do know tat tere was mhany traps laid to hould him into her; but there were so very mhany fine lhadies after him, that he would not pe taken."

"Yes, Maister Rhonald, that is vhery troo. And he would have kotten fifty thousand pounds with her, and more; and there was none deserved it so well."

"Hu ay, you may pe saying tat; for it is a kood man, and so khind to the poor at home."

"Is he indeed noted for kindness to the poor?" said Swan, with some degree of warmth.

"Indheed it is, mattam. She pe so much cootness and khindness, that he'll pe koing through his poor fharmers once a year, and when any of them has peen kot a fhery pretty daughter, he takes them off their hands altogether, and pring them to this town to make lhadies of them. And it is fhery khind, for then they would pe trudging at home, and not working like bhaists."

This was rather an equivocal recommendation; but Miss Sommerville, noting that it was given in seriousness, put the best interpretation on it that it could bear; and before they could proceed any farther with their inquiries, Mr M'— arrived, and, sending in his name, was admitted. In this most perilous situation we must again leave poor Swan, like a lamb strayed from the flock, whom three wolves are watching to devour, in order to bring forward our tale. Allan was in the same jail with her, astonished and grieved at the remissness of his brother in relieving him, and concerned about his dear cousin, whom he now found by experience to be dearer to him than life. At this period their circumstances were totally unknown to one another.

After Gilbert had taken a sound sleep, he arose about mid day, and went in search of his friend, Andrew, to whom he imparted his plan, and the agreement he had entered into with the housekeeper, in the absence of all higher concerns of the house; and it being no frightful thing to speak of a ghost, or to think of a ghost in fair day light, Andrew was nothing averse to the plan. Hunger is hard to bide at all times. Thirst is worse; but when fear is absent, it is disregarded; so the two friends had nothing ado but to sip a little brandy and water, and talk over the affair until the evening.

At rather an early hour they repaired to the library, in which they kindled a fire, and, stored with all the good things of this life, intending perhaps to remain there longer than one night, Andrew never seemed to believe that the ghost would really appear. Gilbert firmly believed that it would, and at first proposed that Andrew should speak to it, and that he himself would try to recollect distinctly what it said; but of this Andrew did not approve.

"No-billy-no-no-no-no—not-speak—not-speak—no-no-no-no. Speak-me—speak-me—speak-then—speak-then—speak-then—yes-yes-yes-yes-yes. Not-otherwise—not-otherwise—no-no-no-no."

Gilbert assured him that no spirit had power to speak to a baptized Christian until once it was spoke to, and that it was only permitted to answer such questions as were put to it. For his part, he said, though the world jeered his belief, he was convinced that this was a real apparition, and that it had something to communicate of importance; and he knew that he had not courage, or rather nerve, to speak to it, unless he was the length of a certain stage of inebriety, and then he was afraid of nothing either on earth or in hell. But, on the other hand, as it had once happened before, when he got to that regardless stage, he could remember nothing that passed, so that it served no manner of purpose his speaking to the apparition, unless a sober man were present to take note of every word, sign, and look. He said that there was therefore a necessity that Andrew should refrain, in a great measure, from drinking, till the issue of their night's adventure should be decided, and that he should then have a right to make up his lee-way with double interest. Violent and rapid were Andrew's protestations against this measure, but Gilbert's resolve was not to be shaken, and he possessed a control over the other, which, though never admitted, was daily practised. Andrew's portion of brandy toddy was limited to a small quantity. Gilbert's was to be without measure, otherwise than by the tappit-hen of discretion.

They were both taken rather at unawares. They had never calculated on any disturbance till about midnight, that being the usual time of the ghost's appearance in the library; so they had drawn in the corner of the table between them, and placed themselves, one on each side of the fire, resolved to enjoy themselves as long as they could, and, at all events, let the evil hour come hindmost. Gilbert had only swallowed one glass of strong brandy toddy, and Andrew one much weaker; and while they were yet in keen argument on this contested point, their elocution was cut short by Andrew, who made a sudden bolt across between the fire and table, nearly overturning the latter, and took his station in a cowering posture between his companion and the wall. This was the work of a moment. Gilbert, whose face was turned towards the fire, naturally looked about to see what had affrighted his associate, and there beheld the old laird walking composedly backward and forward before the old black book-case. He appeared to be dressed in his night-gown and slippers, and had, as it were, a white cloth tied round his head. It was so like him that it represented in every part, that it was hardly possible to believe it to be any thing else, save the old laird himself risen from the grave. Gilbert was struck motionless, and almost deprived of sense; and though he had made up his mind to be composed, yet his tongue clave to his mouth, his ears rung, and for a space he could neither be said to speak, hear, nor see. He felt as if falling into a faint, and longed exceedingly to be deprived of all feeling for a time; but it would not do, the strength of his constitution carried him over it; but all that he could do was to sit like a statue, fixed on his seat, and stare at this strange visitant. It appeared as if studious not to alarm them; it had not any of the threatening looks or attitudes that it had assumed towards some, nor did it fix its looks at all on them, but walked with a slow gliding motion, from one side of the room to the other, and again retraced its steps, apparently in a state of patient sufferance.

Andrew, whose tongue was merely a pendulum to his feelings, and wagged of its own accord when the machine was wound up, was the first who broke silence, beginning, it is true, with a prayer, but ending with an injunction that brought every thing to bear. *"O-Lord-God—Lord-God—Lord-God—deliver-deliver-deliver-'liver-'liver-'liver-'liver. Lord Lord-Lord-Lord—save-save-save-save-save-us-is-is-is-is.* Gibby-Gibby-Gibby-Gibby-Gibby—speak-speak-speak-speak-spis-pis-pis-pis. Now-or-never—now-or-never—now-or-never—now-now-now-now. What-want—what-want—what-want—what-what-what-what-what?"

The ghost at this paused, and turned its face toward them; and, though it did not lift its eyes from the floor, made as though it would have come close to them. Andrew instantly took up his sharp key; *"No-no-no-no-no-no—keep-keep-keep-keep-keep. Lord-God—Lord-God—Lord-God—Gibby-Gibby-Gibby-Gibby, &c."*

Unconnected and vehement as these speeches of Andrew's were, they had the effect of bringing Gilbert somewhat to himself, and he pronounced these words, rather down his throat than with his lips: "In the name of God, tell what you have to reveal, and what can be done for your repose."

"I told you already, and wo be to you that you have not done it," said the apparition. "I give you the charge once more; and know, that virtue and life depend on its instant fulfilment."

"If I remember aright," said Gilbert, "the thing that you desired me to do was impossible, or at least would have taken a life-time to have accomplished. In one word, what must I do?"

"Go through these books," said the spirit, pointing at the three huge volumes of Greek and Latin classics, "as you would wish to live and thrive, and never see my face again. It is a charge with which I intrust you; and if you have not patience to turn over every leaf, at least look into the pages marked on the boards. I know you to be honest; therefore, oh do this without delay, for my sake, as well as for your own. If you prove unfaithful, better had it been for you both that you never had been born. Farewell, and may the God of peace and mercy be with you!"

This moment he was standing before them in an earthly form, and speaking to them in an audible voice; the next he was gone, and none of them saw how, or by what place, he departed. They both averred that they believed they were, for the space of two or three seconds, blinded by some supernatural means, and saw nothing. For a good while afterwards, they sat in mute and awful astonishment, Andrew still keeping his hold between Gilbert and the wall. "This is wonderful," said Gilbert, after some minutes had elapsed; "What can be in these books?"

"See-that-billy—see-that-see-that-see-that—see-see-see-see." And so saying he arose from his den, gazing sternly at every corner of the room. "Blest-be-God-blest-be-God," said Andrew, and this he repeated at least a hundred times. Gilbert opened the press, and took down the three volumes, which they inspected narrowly. There was nothing marked on the boards that they could discern. They held them open, with the leaves downward, and shook them, but there was nothing fell out of them. That was, however, little to be wondered at, for they were in boards, and not a leaf of them cut up. They had, therefore, nothing for it but to begin each to a volume, in order to cut them all up and turn over every leaf. They had not gone far on with this task until Andrew, who was again fallen a poring about the boards, discovered some figures on the inside of one of them, made with a pencil, and scarce distinguishable. These, he thought, might refer to some pages, as the apparition had hinted, and, turning to the first numbered on the board, in the double of the octave, which was uncut, he found a note for £1000. Having now discovered the key, in the course of three minutes they had treasure lying on the table, in bonds, bills at interest, &c. to the amount of nearly a plum. But what they reckoned of most value was the late laird's will, regularly signed and witnessed, together with two short codicils in his own holograph. And besides, they found a paper, in which was contained a list of all his funds, small and great. It was almost without end, and puzzled our two heroes not a little. They found that every pound was at the highest legal interest, save in one concealed drawer within the book-case, which was full of gold; and though the shelf was described, yet with all their ingenuity they could not find out the secret. Had the bookseller succeeded in carrying his point, what a bargain some would have gotten of that clumsy collection of classical authors! So heavy and impenetrable had the old laird judged these works to be, that he trusted his dear treasures in them, in preference to any lock or key under which he could secure them. And after this great secret was discovered, it was remembered that he never locked that book-case; it stood always wide open. He found, by experience, how perfectly safe his money was there; and I am told, that a certain wealthy and very worthy gentleman at the Scottish bar, practises the same mode of depositing his bills and cash to this day. I give this hint, as a sincere friend, to officious servants and lacqueys, in hopes they will have the foresight and prudence, at some leisure hour now and then, to cut up and inspect all their masters' neglected books. They may find something there worth their while.

Our two gallant heroes forgetting, and altogether neglecting, the pleasures of the jug, in this notable discovery of theirs, waited not till day; but, locking up the *classics* in a secure place, they packed up their treasures, the will, and the list of the monies, and marched for Edinburgh. Not knowing where to find any of the other members of the family, they of course waited on Randal, whom they found confined to his chamber, emaciated and diseased. Him they informed, that after all the servants had been driven from the house, they had taken their lives in their hands, trusted in Heaven, and watched last night in the library, where they had made some discoveries of great importance, but which they were not at liberty to divulge, except in the presence of his brother Allan, and his cousin Swan Somerville; and therefore they begged that he would, with all haste, expedite such a meeting, accompanied by legal authorities.

Randal rung the bell, and ordered the servant to bring in some brandy and water. "My excellent and worthy friends," said he, "you have laid me under infinite obligations; if it had not been for your courage, my house might have been pillaged, and every thing in it gone to waste. Come, sit down, take a glass with me, and tell me all that you have done, seen, and learned." Fatigued with their journey, both of them blithely accepted of the invitation, sat down, and drank to the better health of the laird; but at first were very shy in communicating the extraordinary intelligence with which their bosoms were charged, but which at the same time was working there like barmy beer in corked bottles, ready to burst. Consequently, by dint of elicitation, Randal, ere long, understood that they had discovered both his late uncle's will, and his concealed hoards. "Why, my most excellent and worthy friends," said Randal, "you know you are both poor men; and it is a pity you should be so; for two more noble, intrepid, fearless hearts, I believe, beat not in Christendom. It is on that I ground the proposal I am going to make. I know you fear none living; indeed, you have none to fear; and you have proven that you fear not the dead; therefore be men; put that will and that list into my hands, to whom they of right belong, and I'll give each of you a thousand pounds, and fifty pounds yearly to drink my health, as long as I live, and you together."

"Either-too-much-too-much-too-much-much-much-much. Else-too-little-billy-too-little-too-little-too-little. Ooo-ay-yes-yes-yes."

"Make your own terms, then, Mr Car, my worthy honourable old buck; but let them be in conscience, you know. In some bounds of conscience between friends."

"Ooo-ay-yes-yes-yes-yes-yes—consh'-consh'-consh'-consh'—be-sure-be-sure-be-sure-what-else-what-else-what-*else?* What-what-what-what-what-*what?*"

The desperate accents laid upon these two monosyllables in italics, made Randal suspect that there was some small spark in Andrew's feelings that was scarcely congenial with his own, and he began to look a little sheepish, or rather scoundrelish, which is a much worse kind of look than a sheep's.

"I think, my friend Andrew," said Gilbert, "the proposal of my master is a noble and liberal proposal, and ought to be duly considered before we go farther. It will perhaps never be in our power again to make so good a bargain. We are both growing old, and it is a dismal thing to have poverty and age staring us in the face at the same time."

"Spoke like yourself, my old trusty servant! Spoke like a man whose spirit rises above being a drudge and a beggar all your days. The world has not been your friend nor the world's law, therefore obey the first law in nature, and stand for yourselves. I do not intend to bereave my brother and cousin of a farthing that is their natural right, only is it not better that they should be somewhat dependent on me? Is it not better in every point of view? For themselves it must be. Put, then, all these papers and documents into my hands, and henceforth you shall be my friends and confidents, and managers of all my concerns."

"What say you to this, my friend Andrew?" said Gilbert.

"What-say-Gibby-what-say-what-say-what-say-what-what-what-what-*what?* Tell-ye-what-say-billy-tell-ye-what-say-tell-ye-tell-ye-tell-ye. Say-hell-billy—hell-hell-hell-hell-hell-hell-*hell.*"

"Stop now and consider, my dear friend," said Randal, "You have been long known as a man of prudence and discernment. You must see that what I request is right and proper, and best for all parties. And moreover, what is it to you who possesses the funds, provided you get so good a share? There is enough for all parties, you know. Therefore just give me the hand of friendship each of you. Put the papers into my hands, and trust my honour."

"Do not you think, Andrew," said Gilbert, "that what my master requests is reasonable, and may be done with all honour and conscience? No one has seen these bills and papers but ourselves."

"Damn'd-soul-Gibby-dam-soul-dam-soul-dam-soul-soul-soul-soul. Heaven-saw-Gibby-heaven-saw-heaven-saw-heaven-heaven-heaven-heaven-God-billy-God-God-God-God."

With that the tears poured over Andrew's furrowed cheeks; his inarticulate utterance entirely failed him; and he stood sobbing and looking ruefully in Gilbert's face, with his arm stretched upward at its full length, and his fore-finger pointed to heaven. Gilbert contemplated this striking position of his friend for a while with apparent delight, then, coming slowly toward him, as if afraid of defacing so fine a statue, he threw his arms about him, and pressed him to his bosom, "My friend and my brother till death," exclaimed he, "I am so glad to see that your honour and integrity are not to be tarnished! Before I would have yielded to the disgraceful request preferred to us, I would have submitted to be hewn in pieces, and I wanted to try you a little, to find if I might depend on you standing by me."

Andrew threw up both his arms, flung his head a cast backward, and pulled up one of his knees as high as his breast, and shouted out, "Hurra-hurra-hurra-hurra-ra-ra-ra-ra-true-man-yet-true-man-yet—true-blue-true-blue-true-blue-trouble-trouble-trouble. Ha-ha-ha-hurra-hurra-hurra," &c.

"Gentlemen," said Randal, "Are you come here to mock me? I think your behaviour testifies as much. But I will show you that I am not to be mocked by such boors and beggarly rascallions as you; and what you refuse to do by fair means, you shall be compelled to do." With that he rung the bell, and ordering the servant to bring a guard of police, he locked the door upon himself and our two heroes.

"Rascallions, Gibby—rascallions-'scallions-'scallions-'scallions. I'll 'nihilate him Gibby—'nihilate-'nihilate-'nihilate."

Gilbert restrained his friend, assuring him that the object of his resentment was neither worthy of being touched nor looked at by a man of honour, like Andrew Car, who would be disgraced by laying a finger on him. This calmed the indignant gamekeeper, who, in all probability, would have subjected himself and friend to a severe punishment by giving the *atomy*, as he called him, a sound drubbing.

The men of office soon arrived. Randal charged the two men with having robbed his house in the country, and taken from thence some papers and documents of value, which they refused to give up. The lieutenant of the guard said it was a most serious charge, and took the two companions forthwith into custody, locking them up in the black-hole till the hour of cause.

They were examined by the sheriff-substitute, and Randal being unable to leave his chamber, his worthy friend, the attorney afore-mentioned, appeared in his stead, and in a laboured harangue, ac-cused the prisoners of "having got clandestinely into the house of Welldean, under pretence of watching for a ghost that they say had disturbed the family, and from an apartment in that house, had sto-len and secreted some papers of great value, of which they refused to give any account to the owner." And forthwith prayed judgment against them, that they might be searched, the papers restored to the rightful owner, and the delinquents committed for trial!

The judge said the charge was of a serious as well as singular nature, but that it bore inconsistency on the very face of it. For how was it supposable, that if the two men had robbed the house only last night of things of so much value, that they should post up to town to the very man whom they had robbed, to inform him what they had done, and lay a statement of the matter before him. He then requested the prisoners to speak for themselves, that he might thereby be enabled to form a judgment according to truth.

Gilbert arose, and in a clear and concise speech of considerable length, related the circumstances precisely as they happened, to the great astonishment of the court; and then proceeded to put into the sheriff's hands, the valuable documents and bonds that he held, say-ing, that he would merely keep a list of them for his own satisfac-tion, and was glad of having this public opportunity of depositing so weighty a charge; it having been because he and his friend refused to give it up privately to his master that they were sent there.

The judge said they had proven that it could not have been de-posited in safer or better hands. But as the papers were of too high value to be carrying about one's person, he would lock it in a place of safety till the legatees and executors could be convened. At the same time he commended, in high terms, the intrepidity, truth, and candour of the two friends; and remarked, that the spirit manifested by the young gentleman, in the demand he made upon them, and afterwards in seizing them as depredators, was disgraceful to the country and to all concerned with him, and ought to be held in the utmost reprobation. He then dismissed them, desiring them to go with all diligence in search of the young gentleman and lady that were co-heirs with the present possessor, and, as it appeared by the will, more favoured than he, of which he hoped they would like-wise be more deserving.

The honest attorney, perceiving how matters were likely to turn about, made a virtue of forwarding that which he could no longer oppose, and conducted our two heroes straight to the Canongate jail, where Allan and Swan lay confined in sorrowful mood, little aware of what fortunes they were now possessed. They had only that morning made a discovery of each other, and that at a most critical period, just as Swan was going finally off with Mr M'—— after many demurs. When she beheld her lover so emaciated by sickness, grief, and misfortune, she melted into tears, and stretched out her hand to him, which he clasped in both his, and pressed to his lips. They found themselves companions in misfortune, as they had been in infancy and youth, and their reconciliation was made up in the heart, and took place naturally, without any effort of the one to refuse, or the other to beg it; and for all the forlorn and neglected state in which they found each other, that was perhaps the sweetest morning ever they had spent in their lives.

On Allan being introduced, Mr M'—— and the keeper withdrew, but the two former bowed to each other slightly, as men slightly acquainted do when they meet. As soon as the two lovers got a little breath from more important matters, Miss Sommerville asked Allan, what he knew of that young gentleman that went out with the captain? "I only saw him once in my brother's lodgings," said he; "he is a constant associate of his; a young man of loose principles, or rather, of no principles at all. He is said to have led my brother into many follies."

"An associate of your brother's?" said she, with something more than ordinary earnestness. "Yes," said he, "they live together."

Swan became fixed like a statue. She saw, as through a glass darkly, the machinations that had been laid for destroying her peace. She thought of the disgraceful proposal that had been broadly made to her by her cousin Randal—of Mrs M'—— in Saint James' Street, the very woman who had tried, in concert with Mrs Mayder, to get her into his power; and she strongly believed, that this imprisonment and proffered relief had all proceeded from the same source. "What a vile heartless wretch that man of fashion, my cousin Randal, is!" thought she to herself; "no matter, he is Allan's brother, and Allan shall never know his true character, if I can prevent it." They were instantly released, on granting the attorney their joint bill for the two sums, and were man and wife in three months thereafter. Randal never left the chamber to which he was then confined, till carried out of it to his grave. He fell, unlamented, the victim of youthful folly and unrestrained libertinism. Gilbert was again constituted house-steward and butler at Welldean Hall, which two *lucrative* posts he maintained as long as he lived. Andrew Car was made game-keeper, and the two friends had a jug or two of brandy toddy together, unrestrained, for many long years. The concealed drawer of gold was at last found out; the ghost of the old laird was never seen any more; and, the year before last, when I was at Welldean Hall, Allan and his lady were both living in great happiness, though far advanced in age.

Country Dreams and Apparitions

No. VI

Tibby Johnston's Wraith

"HOLLOA, Wat, stop till I come up w'ye. Dinna just gallop at sic a rate man, else you'll founder your horse, an' brik your ain neck into the bargain. Whatten a gate o' riding is that? Stop still, I tell you; I have something to say to you."

"What do you want with me? Tell me directly, for I hae nae a moment to wait. Do you not see that I am in a hurry?"

"To be sure I see that, but then you are always in a hurry. Stay till I come up w'ye, an' then I'll tell you what I want. I have something very particular to say to you. What nonsense is it to ride at that rate? I'll tell you what I want w'ye: can you tell me precisely what o'clock it is?"

"D—n the fellow! What do you mean to stop me for sic a trifle as that, an' me riding atween death an' life for the doctor?"

"For the doctor? Hech! wow! Wat, man, but I didna ken that. What is it that's gane wrang w'ye?"

"What's gane wrang! O, bless your heart, man, a's gane wrang thegither. There was never sic a job kend i' this world. Our mistress has seen a wraith; she saw Tibby Johnston's wraith last night, an' she's dead wi' the fright this morning."

"Dead wi' the fright! Wow, Wat, is she really dead?"

"Dead! bless you, sir, she's clean dead. There never was sic a business in this country. My heart's like to break, an' I'm amaist fleyed out o' my wits into a' ither mischiefs. O, bless your heart, man, there never was the like o' this!—Never, never! oh! dead! Bless ye, she's cauld dead, sir!"

"Why then, Wat, it was real true what ye said, that ye war riding atween death an' life; for, gin the wife be dead and the doctor living, there's nae doubt but ye're riding atween them. But, dear Wat, mony a daft thing ye hae done i' your life, but ye never did aught half sae ridiculous as this, to gallop at sic a rate bringing the doctor to a dead wife."

"O, bless your heart, man, what can folk do? Folk are glad to keep a grip o' life as lang as they can, an' even after it flees out at the window, they'll whiles hing by the tail. But it's the fashion now.

Every body sends for the doctor to their wives after they're dead."

"Ay, an' gin a' tales be true, the doctors whiles come to them after they're dead an' buried baith, without being sent for. But truly, Wat, there is something sae far ayont a' ordinary things in this business, that ye maun 'light an' tell me a' about it. Your mistress saw Tibby Johnston's wraith, you say, an' is dead wi' the fright. But what is come o' Tibby Johnston? Is there ought the matter wi' her?"

"O, God bless your heart, sir, Tibby's dead too. There never was sic a job seen! I hardly ken what I'm doing. Of a' the nights that ever was about a town! O, bless you, sir, you never saw the like o't! I maun gae ride, ye see. If the beast should drap dead aneth me there's nae help for it."

"Tak just a wee time, Wat, an' dinna be in sic a fike. What do ye expect that the doctor can do for the dead woman?"

"O, bless your heart, wha kens? It's a' that folk can do. Auld Kilside says he'll maybe open a vain, and gar her refusticate. Hap, woy, beast. For gude sake, get on; fareweel."

"Open a vain an' gar her refusticat! ha, ha, ha! Hap, woy, beast. There goes Wat like a flying eagle! Weel, I canna help laughin' at the gouk, although I'm sorry for the cause o' his confusion an' hurry. If thae twa women really are baith dead, thae haena left ither twa like them i' the parish, an' few i' the hale country. I'll e'en gae up the water a mile or twa, an' try if I can get the particulars."

David went away up the water as he had resolved, and every one that he met with, he stopped to ask what time of the day it was; to make some observations on the weather; and, finally, to inquire if there were any news up the country; knowing, if any of them had heard of the events at Carlshaw, they would inform him; but he got no satisfactory account until he reached the place. It was at the foot of Milseyburn-path that he stopped Wat Scott riding for the doctor, and from that to Carlshaw is at least six miles; so far had he travelled to learn the particulars of that distressing event. David Proudfoot was a very old man, herding cows, when I was a tiny boy at the same occupation. He would often sit with the snuff-mill in his hand, and tell me old tales for hours together; and this was one among the rest. He cared for no tales, unless he had some share in the transactions himself. The story might be told in few words, but it would spoil my early recollections, and I could not endure to see it otherwise than as David told it, with all its interpolations.

"When I wan to Carlshaw, I gaed first into the stable and then into the byre, but there was naebody to be seen. The yauds were standing nickering at the manger, and the kye were rowting ower

the crib. A' isna right here, indeed, quo I to myself, as I sneckit the
door ahint me; for when Mrs Graham was in her ordinary way,
there was nae servant about the house durst neglect their charge
that gate. The plough was standin' idle on the houm, an' the har-
rows lying birstling on the sawn croft. It's e'en a picture o' desolation, quo I to mysel'. Every ane's missed amang their ain; but gae
without the bounds o' the farm, just beyond that dike, an there's no
ane thinkin' o' the loss. I was right. When you an' I slip away to our
lang hame, my man, others will just pop into our places, an' laugh,
and fike, an' mind their ain affairs, an' never ane will think o' us
ava.

"Weel, I didna like to intrude on a family in distress, for I was but
a young man then; sae I thinks that I'll chap away up to Matthew
Hyslop's bit house, and see if it be true that the gouk said; for if he
has lost his wife, Tibby Johnston, says I to mysel', he'll never put the
like o' her in her shoon. When I gaed up near the cot house, they
had nae apartments there to hide themselves in frae the ee o' the
warld; an' there I saw Matthew sitting on the green brae side, an' a'
his five bairns about him; an' he had the muckle Bible open in his
hand, but when he saw me he closed it, and laid it down.

"'How's a' wi' ye the day, Matthew?' quo' I.

"'I canna complain, an' I winna complain, Davie,' said he. 'I am
just as it has been the will o' the Lord to make me. Hale in health,
but broken in heart, Davie. We hae been visited wi' a heavy dispensation here last night.'

"'Wow, Matthew, but I'm wae to hear that,' quo' I. 'Pray, what
has happened i' your family?'

"'It has pleased the Almighty to take thae poor bairns' mother
frae their head last night, David; and here am I left as helpless and
disconsolate a poor man as the sun o' heaven has this day risen on.'

"'It is a heavy trial, Matthew,' quo' I. 'But ye maunna repine. Ye
maun bear it like a man, and a Christian. Your wife has only paid a
debt that she has been awn for these forty years, an' ye maun trust
in Heaven, an' be resigned.'

"'So I am, so I am, David. You have said the truth, and I am
resigned. But our fallen nature is weak, and the human heart maun
be allowed some yearnings ower what it held dearest in life. I hope
my kind Maker and Redeemer will forgive my tears, for my grief's
no out o' my repining at the execution o' his just decrees; but, oh!
David, sic a woman as I hae lost.'

"'She was a good woman, Matthew,' says I. 'If Tibby Johnston
wasna a good woman and a Christian, mony ane may be feared.'

"'There's nane kens what she was but mysel', David. We hae lived thegither for these fifteen years, and I never heard the word o' discontent frae her tongue, nor saw a frown on her brow. She had the true feelings of a wife and a mother; for she only lived in, and for her family. Their happiness was hers; an' a' their pains, an' a' their wants, she felt as her own. But, ower and aboon that, she had a warm heart to a' mankind, and a deep reverence for every sacred thing. Had my dear woman died in my arms, my heart wadna hae been sae sair; but Oh, David! she died out on the hill, wi' no ae friend near, to take her last farewell, to support her head, or to close her ee.'

"I held my tongue, and could make nae answer, for he was sobbing sae hard, that his heart was like to burst. At length he came to himsel', and composed his voice as well as he could.

"'I maun tell ye ower ilka thing as it happened, David,' said he; 'for I hae nae pleasure but in speaking about her whose head's lying low in that house the day. When she waken'd yesterday morning, she says to me, "Bless me, Matthew,"—Ay, she had ay that bit sweet, harmless byword.—Bless me, bairn, or, bless me, Matthew. Mony a time she said it; though I whiles reproved her, and said it was sae like a Papish signing and blessing hersel', that I didna like to hear it. Then she wad gie a bit short laugh—ye mind her good-natured, bashfu' laugh, David?—and say, that she would try to remember no to say't again; but out it came the very next word, and there was nae mair about it; for laith wad I hae been to hae higgled wi' her, an' vex'd her about ony thing! My canny woman! Sae, as I was saying, she says to me, when she waken'd, "Bless me, Matthew, sic a dream as I hae had last night! I dreamed I was gaun away the day to be married to a new bridegroom, an' leave you an' the bairns to shift for yoursel's. How wad ye like that, good-man?" I said something in a joking way, whilk it is needless to repeat, that there was nane wad be sic a fool as to take her aff my hand, but if they did, that I wad soon get a better. "Ay!" quo' she, "it is easy for you to say sae, but weel I ken it's far frae your heart. But, Matthew," continued she, in a graver tone, "does it not bode ill to dream o' marriage? I think I hae heard my auld aunt say, that to dream o' marriage was death." "Daft body," quo' I, "ye trouble aye your head wi' vagaries. Whoever follows freets, freets will follow them." "I saw mony a braw man riding on their horses, but I mysel' gaed i' the fore-end, and was the brawest mountit o' them a'," said she. I thought nae mair about it, and she said nae mair about it; but after we had gotten the breakfast, I sees her unco dinkly dressed, for she was soon made neat and clean. "What are ye after the day, Tibby?" quo' I. "I'm gaun to the market," said she. "I hae three spinles o' sale yarn for auld Tammie, an' I'm gaun to buy barley, an' saut, an' some ither little things for the house wi' the price o't." "Ye're a good creature, an' a thrifty ane," quo' I: "there never was a better about a poor man's house." Then she leugh, an' fikit about putting a' things to rights for the bairns and me through the day; for she likit a bit praise, and whenever I rused her, she was as happy and as light-hearted as when she was nineteen years auld. Then, after settling wi' the bairns what she was to bring ilk ane o' them, she set out wi' her yarn on her back, saying, that she wad be hame about the gloaming; but I wasna to be ony feared for her though she was gayen late, for she had been rather lang o' winning away, and had muckle ado.

"'When the gloaming came, I began to weary, but I couldna get the bairns left, and was obliged to look and listen, and mony lang look and lang listen I took in vain. I put the bairns ane by ane to their beds, and sat up till midnight. But then I could rest nae langer, sae I ran to a neighbour to come and bide i' the house, and aff I set for the market town, expecting at every turn to meet my woman wi' her bit backfu'. I gaed a' the gate to the town without meeting wi' her, and cried the fock out o' their beds that I kend she dealt wi', but she hadna been seen there after three o'clock. At length, after it was day-light, I got some spearings o' her at the holm-head. The weaver's wife there, had seen her and spoken wi' her, and she told her that she was gaun to try the hill road, that she might be hame wi' some hue o' day. I took the hill road as fast as my feet could carry me, and a wild road it is, unfit for a woman wi' a burden to travel. There was but ae sheiling in the hale gate, if she keepit the right track, and I had strong hopes that she had been nightit and staid there until day. When I came to the sheil, and asked for her, the shepherd's wife started to her feet, "What!" said she, holding up both her hands, "did your wife not come home last night?" "No." said I. "Then you will never see her again in life;" said she, with great emotion, "for she left this house after sun-set. She asked a drink of milk, and complained of something about her heart that made her very ill; but nothing would prevail on her to stay." My heart grew as cold as a stone; and, without uttering another word, I took the hill on my way homeward. A wee bit after I came ower the height, and no very far aff the road—no aboon a hunder steps aneath the sand o' the mossy grain——Oh, David, I canna tell ye nae mair! The sight that I saw there will hing about my heart to the day o' my death, an' the sooner that comes the better. She had died at her devotion, whilk was a great comfort to me, for she was in a kneeling posture, and her face on the ground. Her burden was lying beside her. My dear kind woman! there wasna the least bit necessary thing forgotten! There was a play for ilk ane o' the bairns; a whup to Harry; a knife to Jock; and a picture-beuk to little Andrew. She had us a' in her breast; and there's little doubt that her last petition was put up to Heaven for us. I can tell ye nae mair, David, but ye maun come up again Sabbath first, and render the last duty to the best o' women.'

"I promised that I would, and said some words o' comfort to him, that he was a great deal the better o'; but I hadna the heart to tell him what had befallen at Carlshaw; for I thought he coudna thole that. But down I comes mysel', to see if I can make ony farther discoveries about matters. I was mair fortunate this time; an' it's wonderfu' what effect mortality has in making fock devout, for there I finds auld Yiddie, the barnman, who never cared a fig about religion, sitting broggling and spelling at a kittle chapter in Nehemiah, thinkin', I daresay, that he was performing a very devout act. An' Yiddie really had the assurance, when I came to him, to pretend to be in a very religious frame o' mind. But gin ye had but heard Yiddie's sawpient sayings about *the end o' man*, as he ca'd it, really, callant, they wad hae edified ye very muckle. 'Ye're thrang at your beuk, Yiddie,' quo' I. 'O, ay, what can we do? The end o' man's comin on us a'! We maun be preparing lad; for death spares naebody, an' the mair's the pity. He maws them down as the gerse on the field; an' as a thing fa's in time, it maun lie through a' eternity, ye ken. It is a hard compensation this. But it shaws the workings of man, and the end of a things is at hand. We maun e'en be preparing lad, and do the best we can for a good up-pitting.'

"I said something to Yiddie that he was a hantle the better o'. 'Yiddie,' says I, 'Do you expect to mix wi' the auld Jews i' the neist warld?' 'What has put that i' your head?' quo' he. 'Because I dinna see how reading that lang catalogue o' names,' quo' I, 'can prepare ye for death, or for another warld, unless ye expect to meet wi' aw the auld Jews that came back frae Babylon, and wish to be able to name ilka chap by his ain name. I'll tell ye what wad be as wiselike, Yiddie. If ye wad repent o' a' your sins, and beg forgiveness and mercy at the Throne o' Grace, it wad be as likely to gain you acceptance wi' Heaven, as putting on a grave face, and spelling ower a string o' auld warld names. But gie us a' the particulars o' this *hard compensation*, Yiddie. Has the doctor no been able to restore your mistress to life?'

"'Na, na lad, he wad be a wice doctor could do that; an' muckle sale he wad get; an' O sic a benefit he wad be to man!' (I heard Yiddie didna like to die at a'.) 'But as to our mistress that's gane, honest woman! there was nae doctor to be had, an' it was a' ane for that, for she was past redemption. I said there was nae mair hope after she fell into the second fit; an' neither there was; but the goodman wad be hoping against nature an' reason. After a', I dinna wonder muckle at it; for it was an awfu' thing to see a wraith.'

"'Did she indeed see something that coudna be accounted for, Yiddie?' said I, 'and was that the immediate cause of her death?'

"'There's nae doubt but it was the cause o' her death,' said he, 'although the minister is sae daft as to say that she had been affectit wi' the trouble afore, an' that had made her believe that she saw the shape o' her neighbour gaun at her side. But ony body kens that's nonsense. Thae ministers, they will aye pretend to be wicer nor ither fouk, an' the feint a sperk o' sense they ken ava, but just rhaim rhaim rhaiming aye the same thing ower again, like gouks i' June. But as to accounting for the thing, that's what I canna say naething about. She saw Tibby Johnston's wraith; but whether a wraith can be rightly accountit for or no, is mair nor I can persoom.'

"'I can account for it very weel, Yiddie,' says I, 'and I'll do it to set your mind at rest about that, for I hae heard it explained by my ain mother, and several cunning old people. Wraiths are of twa kinds, you see. They appear always immediately before death, or immediately after it. Now, when a wraith is seen before death, that is a spirit sent to conduct the dying person to its new dwelling, in the same way as the Earl o' Hopetoun there, for instance, wad send a servant to conduct a stranger to his house at Rae-hill that had never been there before. These are sometimes good, and sometimes bad spirits, just according to the tenor of the person's life that lies on the bed o' death. And sometimes the deil mistakes himsel', and a spirit o' baith kinds comes: as for instance, when Jean Swinton departit, there was a white dow sat on the ae end o' the house, an' a corby on the ither; but when the death psalm was sung, the corby flew away. Now, when the wraith appears after death, that's the soul o' the deceased, that gets liberty to appear to the ane of a' its acquaintances that is the soonest to follow it; and it does that just afore it leaves this world for the last time; and that's the true doctrine o' wraiths,' says I, 'and we should a' profit by it.'

"'Hech wow man, but that's wonderfu'!' says he, 'How do ye come to ken sicken things sae young? Weel, of a' things i' the world I wad like warst to see a wraith. But your doctrine hauds very fair in this case; for you see our mistress gaed away up to Matthew's house yestreen to see Tibby after she cam hame frae the mercat, for she was to bring her some word that deeply concerned her. Weel, she staid there till the gloaming, and as Tibby wasna like to come hame, she came away, saying, "She wad see her the morn."'

"'Aye, sae she will, Yiddie, sae she will!' says I. 'But little did she ken, when she said sae, that she was to see her in a country sae far away.' 'It is a queer warld this,' said Yiddie. 'Howsomever I'll gang on wi' my story, as I dinna want to dyve into morality eenow. Weel, as I was saying, she comes her ways; but in her road hameward, ere ever she wist, saw Tibby gaun twa or three steps afore her, and at the aff side o' the road, as if she had gaen by without tenting her. She had on her Sunday claes, and appeared to hae a heavy burden on her back, and she was gaun rather like ane dementit. The mistress then cried after her, "Tibby, is that you? I think you're come by your ain house the night." It made nae answer, but postit on; and turned a wee aff the road, and fell down. Our mistress made a' the haste down to the place that she could, still thinking it was Tibby Johnston hersel', and she was gaun to lift her, and see what was the matter; but when she came to the spot there was nothing there, and no living creature to be seen. She was nae frightit that time at a'; but, thinking she hadna seen distinctly, she lookit a' round about her, and cried out several times, "Tibby, what's come o' you? where away are you gane?" or something to that purpose. But, neither seeing nor hearing ought, she came back to the road and held on her way. In less than three minutes after that she saw Tibby gaun before her again, but still mair unsettled and distressed like than she was afore. The mistress didna speak that time, for she thought something was the matter wi' her, but she walked as fast as she could to come up wi' her, and thought aye she was winning some ground. At length she saw her drap down again on her face, and she thought she fell like ane that was never to rise again. On this our mistress gae a loud scream, and ran up to the spot, but there was nobody there.

"'She saw nae mair, but came hame by hersel', and wonderfu' it was how she was able to come hame. As soon as she came in and saw the light she fainted, and gaed out o' ae fainting fit into another the hale night, and was in great distress and horror o' mind. A' the servants o' the house sat up wi' her, and about day she fell into a quiet sleep. When she wakened she was a good deal composed, and we had hopes that she would soon be quite better, and the goodman went to a bed to get some rest. By ill luck, havering Jean

Jinkens came in about nine o'clock to see the mistress, and ere ever ane could prevent her, tauld that Tibby Johnston had died out on the hill the last night; and that her husband had found her this morning lying cauld and lifeless, wi' her burden on her back, and her face on the ground.

"'This intelligence threw Mrs Graham into a stupor, or rather she appeared striving to comprehend something that was beyond the grasp of her mind. She uttered some half-articulate prayers, and then fell into a complete franazy, which increased every minute to a terrible degree, till her strength was clean gane, and she sank back lifeless on the bed. After muckle exertion by her attendants, she revived, but she wasna like hersel; her voice was altered, and her features couldna hae been kend. Her delirium increased, and forced her again to a little bodily exertion, but it soon came to an end, and she fell into that sleep from which a' the attendants and a' the doctors in the warld could not have awaked her again. She's now lying a streekit corpse in her ain bed, and the goodman, I fear, will gang out o' his right mind.'

"Yiddie didna just tell it sae weel, or sae properly as that, but that was the subject matter. I came my way hame right douf an' heavy-hearted, for I had gotten a lesson read to me that I never could forget.

"On the Saturday afore the twa burials, I was down at the road-side afore the sheep as usual, and there I sees Wat Scott coming gallopping faster than ever. When he saw me he laid on his horse, thinking to get by ere I wan on to the road, but I was afore him; and, fearing I couldna stop him otherwise, I brought my coat-tails o'er my head, and cowered afore him on the middle o' the road. Nae horse nor dog in the world will face ane in that guise, and in a moment Wat was gallopping faster up the water than before he was doing down. But, goodness, as he was flyting and banning at me!

"'Wat, just 'light aff your beast feasible like,' says I, 'and lead it down the path, else never a foot ye shall win farther the day.' He was obliged to comply, and I questioned him what was the matter, and if he was riding for the doctor again?

"'Doctor, man! od bless your heart, it's ten times waur than the doctor this. There never was sic a job, sir, sin' this world stood up. Never. I *do not* see, for my part, what's to come o' folk. I think people be infatuate! Bless you, sir, you never knew sic a business in your life. A' things are gawn to utter confusion now.'

"'What is it, Wat, man? What is it?'

"'What is it! Bless my soul, man, did you no hear? you never heard, sir, sic a business *all your* life. What think ye, the confounded idiot of a wright has done, but made our mistress' coffin so short that she canna get a foot into it. There never was sic a job seen in this country. Lord, sir, she'll never look intil't!'

"'It is a very awkward and disagreeable job indeed, Wat,' says I, 'and highly reprehensible; but I should think, by using a little art, it might still answer.'

"'The thing is impossible, sir! perfectly impossible! The man must be a blockhead! Bless your heart, sir, she'll never keek into it. Disagreeable! Ay, there never was ought in the least like it. There, think of it—this is Saturday—the morn's the burial day. I wadna wonder but I hae a coffin to tak hame afore me the night after dark. It's enough to put ony man alive out o' his judgment. I think the folk be a' gane mad and stupid thegither.'

"Wat gallopped away from me, actually crying with perplexity, and exclaiming, that *there never was sic a job kend i' the world.* The burials were baith in the kirk-yard on the Sabbath-day at the same time;— and that is the hale story o' Tibby Johnston's wraith, my little man, sae aften spoken about in this country. When ye come to my time o' life, ye may be telling it to somebody, and, if they should misbelieve it, you may say that you heard it from auld Davie Proudfoot's ain mouth, and he was never kend for a liar."

THE END

Appendix: Hogg's Manuscript of 'The Long Pack'

'The long pack. A Tale. By the Ettrick Shepherd' is the title of a twelve-page manuscript in Hogg's hand in the Houghton Library at Harvard University.[1] The manuscript shows signs of being a fair copy prepared for the printer. Neatly written, with minimal corrections, it includes a header with the author's signature ('By the Ettrick Shepherd'), a rule after the title and again at the end of the text, and carefully numbered pages. What seems to be a printer's mark, 'Vol. XII. N, 97' appears at the top of page 4. The text of the manuscript corresponds to early printings of 'The Long Pack' in miscellanies and chapbooks rather than to the version published in *Winter Evening Tales*. Evidently Hogg revised 'The Long Pack' for inclusion in his book of 'rural and traditionary tales', much as he revised material from *The Spy*, substantially rewriting a couple of passages as well as adjusting details of phrasing and punctuation. The variants are sufficiently extensive and interesting to justify reprinting the earlier version of 'The Long Pack' in this appendix.

In the first printing of the present edition of *Winter Evening Tales* I identified a chapbook, *The Long Pack. A Northumbrian Tale, An hundred years old* (Newcastle: George Angus, 1817), as the earliest extant published version of Hogg's tale. Since then Janette Currie has examined several printings of 'The Long Pack' in English and American magazines which precede the Angus chapbook by up to eight years. The earliest of these, entitled 'The Dead Shot, A Tale. By the Ettrick Shepherd', appeared in two instalments in the *Sporting Magazine*, a London gentleman's miscellany, in September and October 1809.[2] The tale was serialised again the following month, as 'The Long Pack. A Tale. By the Ettrick Shepherd', in the Sherborne *Weekly Entertainer*.[3] Currie reports several American reprintings over the next few years: in the New York *Lady's Weekly Miscellany* of February 1810, where it is headed 'From the London Sporting Magazine', retitled 'The Dead Shot; or, The Long Pack. A Tale, by the Ettrick Shepherd', and lightly bowdlerised for lady readers; in *The Visitor* of Richmond (March 1810), reprinting the *Lady's Weekly Miscellany* version; and in the Philadelphian *Literary Register* (April 1814), restoring the text published in the *Sporting Magazine*.[4] 'The story of the Long Pack is universally popular, and had a circulation in the United

States quite unprecedented', remarked one of Hogg's American editors. 'It was reprinted in newspapers and magazines, and was the principal treasure of the almanacks of the day'.[5] Some of these more ephemeral printings in newspapers and magazines may yet come to light.

Hogg's manuscript is close enough to the British magazine issues to make plausible the conjecture that it served as copytext for the earliest of them. Apart from some minor verbal alterations, the insertion of punctuation, and the regularisation of idiosyncratic spellings, it is reproduced verbatim. The available evidence does not allow us to know for certain, however, whether Hogg originally submitted his tale to the *Sporting Magazine*, where it appeared for the first time, or whether the *Sporting Magazine* reprinted it from an earlier, as yet undiscovered source. The title given in the *Sporting Magazine*, 'The Dead Shot', differs from the title of the manuscript and almost all subsequent printings, including the following month's serialisation in the *Weekly Entertainer* as well as the authorised version in *Winter Evening Tales*.[6] This anomaly may indicate the existence of an earlier publication of 'The Long Pack' for which the manuscript served as printer's copy. The supposed printer's mark, 'Vol. XII. N, 97', does not correspond with any of the known periodical issues. Collation of the versions printed in the *Sporting Magazine* and *Weekly Entertainer* also lends support to the conjecture of an *Ur*-issue, based on Hogg's manuscript, from which both independently derive. While they have textual variants in common, each version also reproduces features of the manuscript not found in the other: for example, the italicisation of words and phrases Hogg underlined for emphasis ('*terrible* queer pack', '*somebody's* son', '*We* can judge [...] it *is* probable', 'if we *had* loosed him', 'the *long pack*') in the *Sporting Magazine*, and the retention of some idiosyncratic spellings and phrasings ('lock it bye', 'turn an eel', 'which appeared', 'Fontenay', 'He hath, now') in the *Weekly Entertainer*. A list of verbal variants between the manuscript and both magazine issues follows the manuscript text in this appendix.

'The Long Pack' was indeed 'universally popular'. Reprints decanted Hogg's tale from middle-class gentlemen's and ladies' miscellanies to the cheapest forms of street literature. Beginning with the 1817 George Angus edition, which prints a lightly corrupted version of the magazine text, chapbooks of 'The Long Pack' proliferated throughout northern England and southern Scotland.[7] Of the various chapbook issues extant in library holdings, several are undated, and several are printed in Newcastle or Durham. These also carry the subtitle 'a Northumbrian Tale', indicating an enthusiastic repatriation of 'The Long Pack' to its regional setting. (If an *Ur*-issue ever comes to light, it may do so in the pages of a northern miscellany.) The specimens I have examined reprint the 1817 Angus version (with varying degrees of corruption) until the 1840s, when chapbooks begin to pick up the *Winter Evening Tales* text.[8]

Many of the variants between the original version of 'The Long Pack' and the version published a dozen years later in *Winter Evening Tales* show Hogg polishing his tale for a more genteel readership. In the revised text he deprives Alice of her youth and beauty, and tones down the pedlar's leering compliment to her: 'it would be impossible for him to keep his own bed and such a sweet creature lying alone under the same roof' (p. 514, ll. 24–25). In 1820 young Edward expresses his panic by 'gulping down mouthfuls of breath' (p. 134, l. 40) instead of 'swallowing his spittle' (p. 518, ll. 32–33). Two passages are extensively rewritten in *Winter Evening Tales*. Hogg gives Alice's broodings on the pack, after the pedlar has left her, a more dramatic and inward rendition, heightening the suspense (p. 131). He replaces Edward's cheerfully sadistic fantasy of blasting away the robbers' brains, jaws, and guts (p. 520, ll. 17–19) with a more elaborate, heroic treatment (p. 136, ll. 25–36). And the final clause undergoes a pious amelioration from 'his gray hairs lie mixed with the cold gravel in the bowels of the earth' (p. 523, ll. 22–23) to 'his gray hairs recline in peace on that pillow from which his head shall be raised only when time shall be no more' (p. 140, ll. 7–9).

Hogg's manuscript is printed here without alteration, except for the following cases. Hogg sometimes forgot to close or open speech marks, and I have regularised these in keeping with usage elsewhere in this edition. Beginning at page 8 of the manuscript Hogg repeats the last word of the preceding page at the start of the next, and I have eliminated these repetitions together with an erroneous repetition of the word 'of' at a line-break (p. 520, l. 8). The binding of the manuscript has obliterated the final characters of a few lines that run into the gutter of the margin, and I have supplied the missing characters in square brackets; in most cases the conjecture is unproblematic, with the readings supported by both magazine and *Winter Evening Tales*. The end-of-line hyphen at p. 517, l. 13 ('Robin-red-breast') should be retained in making a quotation. The text of Hogg's manuscript is followed by a list of verbal variants from the *Sporting Magazine* and *Weekly Entertainer* issues of 1809.

Notes

1. The manuscript of 'The Long Pack' (shelf mark fMS Eng 801 *50M-152 F) is published here by permission of the Houghton Library, Harvard University. It was acquired by Harvard on 5 January 1951 as a gift from Captain John A. Gade of New York, who bought it at a sale of the library of Lucius Wilmerding (Lot 373) on 28 November 1950–see *The Notable Library of the Late Lucius Wilmerding, Part I* (New York, Parke-Bernet Galleries, 1950), p. 94. I thank Dr Gillian Hughes for identifying the manuscript and bringing it to my attention.

2. *The Sporting Magazine; or, Monthly Calendar of the Transactions of the Turf, the Chase, and Every Other Diversion Interesting to the Man of Pleasure, Enterprize, and Spirit*, 34 (September 1809), 261–64 and 35 (October 1809), 17–21.

3. 'The Long Pack. A Tale. By the Ettrick Shepherd', in *The Weekly Entertainer*, 6 and 13 November 1809, pp. 881–84, 924–28 (nos 49 and 50). See Gillian Hughes, 'James Hogg's Fiction and the Periodicals' (unpublished Ph. D. dissertation, 1981), p. 33, and Robert D. Mayo, *The English Novel in the Magazines 1740–1815* (Evanston and London: Northwestern University Press, 1962), p. 546.

4. *The Lady's Weekly Miscellany*, 10 and 17 February 1810, pp. 241–45, 257–62 (nos 16 and 17); *The Visitor*, 3, 10, 17 and 24 March 1810, pp. 18–19, 22–23, 26–27, 30 (nos 4, 5, 6, and 7); *The Literary Register*, 16, 23, and 30 April 1814, pp. 292–93, 300–01, 308 (nos 37, 38, and 39). See Jayne K. Kribbs, *An Annotated Bibliography of American Literary Periodicals, 1741–1850* (Boston: G. K. Hall, 1977).

5. [Simeon De Witt Bloodgood], 'Sketch of the Shepherd's Life', in *Familiar Anecdotes of Sir Walter Scott* (New York: Harper and Brothers, 1834), pp. 7–118 (p. 92).

6. *The Sporting Magazine* (founded in 1792) was 'the first magazine expressly calculated for the Sportsman'–see *Hounds in the Morning, Sundry Sports of Merry England. Selections from the Sporting Magazine, 1792–1836*, ed. by Carl B. Cone (Lexington: University Press of Kentucky, 1981), p. 20. It printed very few original short stories–Janette Currie counts less than ten over the magazine's forty-year run. In a note to the present editor, Dr Currie suggests that *The Sporting Magazine* (wherever it got the tale from) may have changed Hogg's original title to one deemed more suitable to the pages of a sportsman's miscellany. The hybrid title conferred by the American issues appears to acknowledge, at least, that the tale was already known as 'The Long Pack'.

7. The Angus firm was 'one of the most important, if not *the* most important, producer of chapbooks in Newcastle', a major centre of the northern chapbook trade–C. J. Hunt, *The Book Trade in Northumberland and Durham to 1860* (Newcastle: Thorne's Students' Bookshop Ltd., 1975), p. 3. Several library collections hold fine-paper copies of *The Long Pack* printed by George Angus for John Bell (1793–1864), a Newcastle bookseller and important early collector of Northumbrian traditions and antiquities. The Angus chapbook prints a verse epigraph on its title-page (see fascmile on p. 524). I have not been able to identify a source for this quasi-Spenserian stanza, with its evocation of one of Hogg's titles for his projected collection ('Cottage Winter Nights'). 'Cruddling' is a local (northern) dialect usage. Some but not all of the later chapbooks reprint the verses.

9. See the partial list of chapbook printings in Edith C. Batho, *The Ettrick*

Shepherd (Cambridge: Cambridge University Press, 1927), pp. 196–97, and Stephanie Anderson-Currie, *Preliminary Census of Early Hogg Editions in North American Libraries*, South Carolina Working Papers in Scottish Bibliography 3 (Columbia: University of South Carolina, 1993), pp. 4–5. Other chapbooks I have examined include *The long pack. A Northumbrian Tale of 1723* (Durham: George Walker, n. d.); *The long pack. A Northumbrian Tale, an hundred years old* (Barnard Castle: J. Atkinson, *c.* 1830); two separate issues of *The Long Pack, a Northumberland Tale, An Hundred Years Old* (Newcastle: W. & T. Fordyce) respectively printed at the firm's premises on Dean Street (1828–37) and Grey Street (1841–44); and *The long pack; or, The robbers discovered: A Scottish story. By the Ettrick Shepherd* (Glasgow: printed for the booksellers, *c.* 1840). For the dating of the Fordyce issues see Hunt, p. 36. An 1821 chapbook from Kilmarnock continues to reprint the 1817 text; the *Winter Evening Tales* text is adopted in the 1840 Glasgow printing.

The long pack. A Tale.
By the Ettrick Shepherd

In the year 1723 Col. Ridley returned from India, with what in those days was counted an immense fortune, and retired to a country seat on the banks of North Tyne in Northumberland. The house was rebuilt, and furnished with every thing elegant and costly; and amongst others, a service of plate supposed to be worth £10:000. He went to London annually with his family during a few of the winter months, and at these times there were but few left at his country house. At the time we treat of their were only three domestics remained there, a maid servant whose name was Alice kept the house and two men; who threshed the corn and took care of some cattle, for the two plowmen were boarded in houses of their own.

One afternoon as Alice was sitting spinning some yarn for a pair of stockings to herself, a pedlar entered the hall with a comical pack on his back. Alice had seen as long a pack, and as broad a pack; but a pack equally as long, broad, and thick she declared she never saw. It was about the middle of winter when the days were short, and the nights cold, long, and wearisome. The pedlar was a handsome well dressed man, and very likely to be an agreeable companion for such a maid as Alice, on such a night as that: yet Alice declared that from the very beginning she did not like him greatly; and though he introduced himself with a little ribaldry and a great deal of flattery interlarded, yet when he came to ask a nights lodging he met with a peremptory refusal. He jested on the subject; said he believed she was in the right, for that it would be impossible for him to keep his own bed and such a sweet creature lying alone under the same roof. Took her on his knee, and ravished a kiss: but all would not do. "No, she would not consent to his staying there" "But are you really going to put me away to night?" "Yes." "Indeed my dear girl you must not be so unreasonable I am come straight from Newcastle where I have been purchacing a fresh stock of goods, which are so heavy that I cannot travel far with them; and as the people around are all of the poorer sort, I will rather make you a present of th[e] prettiest shawl in my pack before I go further." At the mentioning of the shawl, the picture of deliberation was pourtrayed in lively colours in Alice's face for a little; but her prudence overcame. "No: she was but a servant, and had orders to harbour no person about the house but such as came on business, nor they either unless well acquainted with them" "What the worse can either your master, or you or any other person be of suffering me to tarry until the morning?" "I intreat you do not insist, for here you cannot be." "But indeed I am not able to carry my goods further to night" "Then you must leave them; or get a horse to carry them away." "Of all the inflexible beings ever I saw thou art the first! but I cannot blame you: your resolution is just and right. Well well, since no better may be, I must leave them, and go search for lodgings myself somewhere else; for, fatigued as I am, it is as much as my life is worth to endeavour carrying them further." Alice was rather taken at her word: she wanted nothing to do with his goods: the man was displeased at her, and might accuse her of stealing some of them; but it was an alternative she had proposed, and against which she could start no plausible objection so she rather reluctantly consented. "But the pack will be better out of your way" said he "and safer, if you will be so kind as lock it bye in some room or closet." She then led him into a low parlour, where he placed it carefully on two chairs, and went his way, wishing Alice a good night.

When Alice and the pack were left in the large house by themselves, she could not for her life quit thinking of the pack one moment. What was in it that made it so heavy that its owner could not carry it? She would go and see what was in it. It was a very curious pack. At least she would go and handle it and see what she *thought* was in it—She went into the parlour—opened a wall-press. She wanted nothing in the press. She never so much as looked into it. Her eyes were fixed on the pack.—"It was a very queer pack.—It was square the one way but not square the other way—It was a monstrous queer pack."—It was now wearing late.—She returned from the room in a sort of trepidation.—Sat down to her wheel but could not spin one thread—"It *is* a droll pack yon!—What made the man so very earnest with me to tarry all night? Never was man so importunate.—What in the world has he got in it?—It's a confounded queer pack after all. It's so long and so thick.—It's a *terrible* queer pack."

What surmises will fear not give birth to in the mind of a woman!—She lighted a moulded candle and went again into the parlour—closed the window shutters and barred them: but before she came out, she set herself upright, held in her breath, and took another steady and scrutinizing look of the pack—God of mercy!—she saw it moving as visibly as ever she saw any thing in her life. Every hair on her head stood upright. Every inch of flesh on her body crept like a nest of pismires. She hasted into the kitchen as fast as she could, for her knees bent under the load of terror that had overwhelmed the heart of poor Alice. She puffed out the candle–lighted it again; and not being able to find a candlestick, though a dozen stood on a shelf in the fore kitchen, she set it into a water jugg and ran out to the barn for old Richard. "Oh Richard! Oh for mercy Richard make haste and come into the house. Come away Richard." "Why? what is the matter Alice? What is wrong?" "Oh! Richard, a pedlar came into the hall intreating for lodging. Well, I would not let him stay on any account, and behold he is gone off and left his pack." "And what is the great matter in that" said Richard "I will wager a penny he will look after it before it shall look after him." "But Oh Richard I tremble to tell you! We are all gone, for it is a living pack" "A living pack" said Richard, staring at Alice, and letting his chops fall down. Richard had just lifted the flail over his head to begin threshing a sheaf, but when he heard of a living pack, he dropped one end of the hand-staff to the floor and leaning on the other took such a look of Alice He knew long before that Alice was beautifull–he knew that ten years before, but he never took such a look at her face in his life. "A living pack!" said Richard "Why the woman is mad without all doubts" "Oh Richard! come away! Heaven knows what is in it! but I saw it moving as plainly as I see you at present. Make haste and come away Richard." Richard did not stand to expostulate any longer, nor even to put on his coat, but followed Alice into the house; assuring her by the way, that it was nothing but a whim, and of a piece with many of her phantasies. "But" added he, "of all the foolish ideas that ever posessed thy brain this is the most unfeasible, and un-natural, and impossible. How can a pac[k] made up of napkins, and muslins, and curderoy breeches perhaps, ever become alive? it is even worse than to suppose a horse's hair will turn an eel." So saying he lifted the candle out of the jugg, and turning about, never stopped till he had his hand upon the pack. He felt the dales that surrounded its edges to prevent the goods being runkled and spoiled by carrying the cords that bound it, and the canvass in which it was wrapped.–The pack was well enough–He found nought about it that other packs wanted.–It was just like other packs made up of the same stuff.–He saw nought that ailed it.–And a good large pack it was–It would cost the honest man £200 if not more.–It would cost him more: but he would make it all up again by cheating fools like Alice with his gewgaws. Alice testified some little dissapointment at seeing Richard unconvinced even by ocular proof. She wished she had never seen either him or it howsomever, for she was convinced there was something mysterious about it: that they were stolen goods or something that way; and she was terrified to stay in the house with it. But Richard assured her the pack was right enough.

During this conversation in comes Edward. He was a lad about 16 years of age, son to a coal-driver on the border: was posessed of a good deal of humour and ingenuity, but somewhat roguish, forward and commonly very ragged in his apparel. He was about this time wholly intent on shooting the crows and birds of various kinds that alighted in whole flocks where he foddered the cattle. He had bought a huge old military gun which he denominated Copenhagen and was continually thundering away at them. He seldom killed any if ever, but he once or twice knocked off a few feathers, and after much narrow inspection discovered some drops of blood on the snow. He was at this very moment come in a great haste for Copenhagen, having seen a glorious chance of sparrows and a Robin-red-breast among them feeding on the site of a corn rick, but hearing them talk of something mysterious, and a living pack, he pricked up his ears and became all attention. "Faith Alice" said he "if you will let me I'll shoot it." "Hold your peace fool" said Richard. Edward took the candle from Richard, who still held it in his hand, and gliding down the passage, edged up the parlour door, and watched the pack attentively for about two minutes. He then came back with a spring, and with looks very different from those which regulated his features as he went down.–As sure as he had death to meet with he saw it stirring.–"Hold your peace you fool" said Richard Edward swore again that he saw it stirring; but whether he really thought so or only said so is hard to determine.–"Faith Alice" said he again "if you will let me I'll shoot it" "I tell you to hold your peace you fool" said Richard "No" said Edward "in the multitude of counsellors there is safety: and I will maintain this to be our safest plan. Our masters house is confided to our care, and the wealth that it contains may tempt some people to use stratagems. Now if we open up this mans pack he may pursue us for damages to any amount: but if I shoot at it what amends can he get of me? If there is any thing that should not be there L–d how I will pepper it; and if it is lawful goods he can only make me pay for the few that are damaged which I will get at valuation: so if none of you will acquiesce I will take all the blame myself and ware a shot on it."

Richard said whatever was the consequence he would be blameless. A half delirous smile rather distorted than beautified Alice's pretty face, but Edward took it for an assent to what he had been advancing, so snatching up Copenhagen in one hand, and the candle in the other, he hasted down the passage, and without hesitating a moment fired at the pack. Gracious God! the blood gushed out upon the floor like a torrent, and a heidous roar, followed by the groans of death issued from the pack

Edward dropped Copenhagen upon the ground and ran into the kitchen like one distracted. The kitchen was darkish for he had left the candle in the parlour; so taking to the door without being able to utter a word, he ran to the hills like a wild roe looking over each shoulder as fast as he could turn his head from the one to the other. Alice followed as fast as she could, but lost half the way of Edward: she was all the way sighing and crying most pitifully. Old Richard stood for a short space rather in a state of petrifaction, but at length, after some hasty ejaculations, he went into the parlour. The whole floor flowed with blood. The pack had thrown itself on the ground, but the groans and crys were ceased, and only a kind of gutterel noise was heard from it. Knowing that then something must be done, he run after his companions and called on them to come back. Though Edward had escaped a good way, and was still persevering on; yet as he never took long time to consider of the utility of any thing, but acted from immediate impulse, he turned and came as fast back as he had gone away. Alice also came homeward, but more slowly, and crying even more bitterly than before. Edward overtook her and was holding on his course, but as he passed, she turned away her face and called him a murderer. At the sound of this epithet Edward made a dead pause, and looked at Alice with a face much longer than it used to be. He drew in his breath twice as if going to speak, but he only swallowed his spittle and held his peace.

They were soon all three in the parlour, and in no little terror and agitation of mind loosed the pack; the principal commodity of which was a stout young man, whom Edward had shot through the heart, and thus bereaved of existence in a few minutes. To paint the feelings, or even the appearance of young Edward during this scene is impossible: he acted little, spoke less, and appeared in a hopeless stupor: the most of his employment consisted in swallowing his spittle and staring at his two companions.

It is most generally believed that when Edward fired at the pack he had not the most distant idea of shooting a man but seeing Alice so jealous of it he thought the Colonel would approve of his intrepidity and protect him from being wronged by the pedlar. And besides he had never got a chance of a shot at such a large thing in his life and was curious to see how many folds of the pedlars fine haberdashery ware Copenhagen would drive the drops through: So that when the stream of blood burst from the pack accompanied with the dying groans of a human being Edward was certainly taken by surprise and quite confounded. He indeed asserted as long as he lived that he saw something stirring in the pack but his eagerness to shoot and his terror on seeing what he had done which was no more than what he might have expected had he been certain he saw the pack moving makes this asseveration rather doubtfull. They made all possible expedition in extricating him intending to call medical assistance but it was too late the vital spark was gone for ever "Alas" said old Richard heaving a deep sigh "poor man 'tis all over with him! I wish he had lived a little longer to have repented of this, for he has surely died in a bad cause. Poor man! he was *some*body's son, and no doubt dear to them: and no body can tell how small a crime this hath, by a regular gradation, become the fruits of." Richard came twice across his eyes with the sleeve of his shirt, for he still wanted the coat; a thought of a tender nature shot through his heart "Alas" said he "if his parents are alive how will their hearts bear this! Poor things" said Richard weeping outright "poor things! God pity them"

The way that he was packed up was artfull and curious. His knees were brought up parrallel to his navel and his feet and legs stuffed in a hat-box another hat-box a size larger and wanting the bottom made up the vacancy betwixt his face and knees; and there being only one fold of canvass around this, he breathed with the greatest freedom: but it had undoubtedly been the heaving of his breast which had caused the movement noticed by the servants. His right arm was within the box, and to his hand was tied a cutlass with which he could rip himself from his confinement at once. There were also four loaded pistols secreted with him and a silver wind-call. On coming to the pistols and cutlass "villain!" said old Richard "see what he has here. But I should not call him a villain" said he again softening his tone "for he is now gone to answer at that bar where no false witness nor loquacious orator can biass the justice of the sentence pronounced on him. He is now in the true world and I am in the false one. *We* can judge only from appearance but thanks to our kind maker and preserver that he was discovered, else it *is prob-able* that none of us would have seen the light of a new day" These moral reflections from the mouth of old Richard by degr[ees] raised the spirits of Edward. He was bewildered in uncertainty and ha[d] undoubtedly given himself up for lost, but he now began to discover that he had done a meritorious and manfull action, and for the first since he had fired the fatal shot ventured to speak. "Faith it was lucky that I shot." said Edward, but none of his companions an-swered either good or bad. Alice though rather grown desperate behaved and assisted better at this bloody affair than might have been expected. Edward surveyed the pistols all round, two of which were curious workmanship. "But what do you think he was going to do with all these?" said Edward. "I think you need not ask that," Richard answered. "Faith it was a mercy that I shot after all" said Edward "for if we *had* loosed him out; we would have been all dead in a minute. I have given him a devil of a broadside though.–But look ye Richard; providence has directed me to the right spot, for I might as readily have lodged the contents of Copenhagen in one of these empty boxes." "It has been a deep laid scheme" said Richard "to murder us and rob our masters house: there must certainly be more concerned in it than these two"

Ideas beget ideas often quite different, and these others again in unspeakable gradation, which run through, and shift in the mind with as much ease and velocity as the streamers around the pole in a frosty night. On Richards mentioning more concerned, Edward instantaneously thought of a gang of thieves by night. What devastation he would work amongst them with Copenhagen: how he would make some to lie with their guts in their arms, blow the nether jaws from one, and scatter the brains of another. How Alice would scream, and Richard would pray, and every thing would go on like the work of a wind mill. Oh if he had nothing ado but to shoot! but the plaguy long time he always lost in loading would subject him to a triple disadvantage in the battle. This immediately suggested the necessity of having assistance, two or three others to shoot and keep them at bay while he was loading. The impulse of the moment was Edwards monitor: off he ran like fire and warned a few of the colonels retainers whom he knew kept guns about them; these again warned others, and at eight o clock they had 25 men in the house, and 16 loaded pieces, including Copenhagen and the four pistols found on the deceased. These were distributed amongst the front windows in the upper stories, and the rest, armed with pitch-forks, old swords, and cudgels, kept watch below. Edward had taken care to place himself with a comrade at a window immediately facing the approach to the house; and now backed as he was by such a strong party, grew quite impatient for another chance. All however remained quiet until an hour past midnight, when it entered into his teeming brain to blow the thiefs silver wind-call: so without warning any of the rest, he set himself out at the window, and blew until all the hills and woods around yelled their echoes. This alarmed the guards as not knowing the meaning of it; but how were they astonished at hearing it answered by another at no great distance.

The state of anxiety into which this sudden, and unforeseen circumstance threw our armed peasants is more easily concieved than described. The fate of their masters great wealth, and even their own fates was soon to be decided; and none but he who surveys and overrules futurity could tell what was to be the issue. Every chest heaved quicker; every breath was cut and flustered in the palpitations of an adjoining heart: every gun was cocke[d] and pointed towards the court gate: every orb of vision was strained, to discover the approaching foe by the dim light of the starry canopy; and every ear expanded to catch the distant sounds as they floated on the slow frosty breeze.

The suspence was not of long continuance. In less than five minutes the tramping of horses were heard; which increased as they approached to the noise of thunder; and in due course, a body of men on horseback, according to their account exceeding their own number, came up at a brisk trott, and began to enter the court gate. Edward, unable to restrain himself any longer, fired Copenhagen in their faces; one of the foremost dropped, and his horse made a spring toward the hall door. This discharge was rather premature, as the wall still shielded a part of the gang from the bulk of the windows; it was however the watch-word to all the rest, and in the course of two seconds, the whole 16 guns were discharged at them. Before the smoke dispersed they were all fled like fire, no doubt greatly amazed at the reception which they got.—Edward and his comrade ran down stairs to go and see how matters stood, for it was their opinion that they had shot them every one, and that their horses had taken fright at the noise and galloped off without them; but the club below warmly protested against opening any of the doors until day, so they were obliged to betake themselves again to their birth up stairs.

Though our peasants had now gathered up a little courage and confidence in themselves their situation was curious and to them a dreadfull one. They saw and heard a part of their fellow creatures, moaning and expiring in agonies in the open air, which was intensely cold, yet durst not go to administer the least relief for fear of a surprise. An hour or two after the great brush, Edward and his messmate descended again, and begged hard for leave to go and reconnoitre for a few minutes, which after some disputes was granted. They found only four men fallen, which appeared to them to be all quite dead. One of them was lying within the porch. "Faith" said Edward "here's the gentleman I shot:" the other three were without, at a considerable distance from each other. They durst not follow their track farther, as the road entered betwixt groves of trees, but retreated into their posts without touching any thing.

About an hour before day some of them were alarmed at hearing the sound of horses's feet a second time, which however was only indistinct, and heard at considerable intervals, and nothing of them ever appeared. Not long after this, Edward and his friend were almost frighted out of their wits, at seeing, as they thought, the dead man within side the gate, endeavouring to get up and escape. They had seen him dead, lying surrounded by a deluge of congealed blood, and nothing but the ideas of ghosts and hobgoblins entering their brains, they were so indiscreet as never to think of firing, but ran and told the tale of horror to some of their neighbours. The sky was by this time grown so dark that nothing could be seen with precision; and they all remained in anxious incertitude, until the opening day discovered to them by degrees, that the corpses were all removed, and nothing left but large sheets of frozen blood: and that the mornings alarms, by the ghost and the noise of horses, had been occassioned by some of the friends of the men that had fallen conveying them away for fear of a discovery.

Next morning the news flew like fire, and the three servants were much incommoded by crouds of idle and officious people that gathered about the house; some enquiring after the smallest particulars; some begging to see the body that lay in the parlour; and others pleased themselves with poring over the sheets of crimson ice, and tracing the drops of blood on the road down the wood. The Colonel had no country factor, nor any particular friend in the neighbourhood, so the affair was not pursued with that speed which was requisite to the discovery of the accomplices, which if it had would have been productive of some very unpleasant circumstances, by involving sundry respectable families as it afterward appeared but too evident. Dr. Herbert, the phisician who attended the family occassionally, wrote to the Colonel by post concerning the affair, but though he lost no time, it was the fifth day before he arrived. Then indeed advertisements were issued, and posted up in all public places, offering rewards for a discovery of any person killed, or wounded of late. All the dead and sick within twenty miles were inspected by medical men, and a most extensive search made, but all to no purpose. It was too late; all was secured. Some indeed were missing, but plausible pretences being made for their absence, nothing could be done: but certain it is, sundry of these were never more seen nor heard of in the country, though many of the neighbourhood declared, they were such people as no body could suspect.

The body of the unfortunate man who was shot in the pack lay open for inspection a forthnight, but none would ever acknowledge so much as having seen him. The Colonel then caused him to be buried at Bellenghem, but it was confidently reported that his grave was opened, and his corpse taken away. In short not one concerned in this base and bold attempt was ever discovered.–A constant watch was kept by night for some time. The Colonel rewarded the defenders of his house liberally. Old Richard remained in the family during the rest of his life, and had a good salary for only saying prayers amongst the servants every night. Alice was married to a tobbacconist at Hexam: and Edward was made the Colonels gamekeeper and had a present of a fine gol[d] mounted gun given him. He afterwards procured him a comission in a regiment of foot, where he suffered many misfortunes and dissapointments. He was shot through the shoulder at the battle of Fontenay, but recovered and retiring on half pay took a small farm on the Scottish side. His character was that of a brave, but rash officer: kind, generous, and open hearted in all situations. I have often stood at his knee, and listened with wonder and amazement to his stories of battles and sieges, but none of them ever pleased me better than that of the *long pack*.

Alas! alas! his fate is fast approaching to us all. He hath, now many years ago, submitted to the conqueror of all mankind! his brave heart is now a clod of the valley, and his gray hairs lie mixed with the cold gravel in the bowels of the earth.

THE
LONG PACK.

A
NORTHUMBRIAN TALE,
An Hundred Years old.

In winter nights, when gossips old,
With youthful list'ners, draw around the fire,
　　Who 'tentive hear the legend told,
Of some fell waugh of an old murther'd sire.
　　'Tis then, in anxious hope and fear,
The pelting hail is dreaded as a sprite;
　　And cruddling round, their youthful ear,
Marks to the memory a tale of some poor hapless
　　　　wight.

MDCCCXVII

List of Variants between MS and 1809 Magazine Issues

In the list below, page and line numbers in the preceding text are followed firstly by the reading of Hogg's manuscript, and then, after the first square bracket, by the equivalent passage from *The Sporting Magazine* (September and October 1809), and, lastly, after the second square bracket, by the equivalent passage from *The Weekly Entertainer* (November 1809).

p. 514, l. 1 Col. Ridley] Colonel Ridley] Colonel Ridley

p. 514, l. 5 £10:000] 1000l] 1000l

p. 514, ll. 32–33 th[e] prettiest shawl] the greatest shawl] the greatest shawl

p. 515, l. 23 that made it] which made it] which made it

p. 515, l. 34 give birth to] give rise to] give rise to

p. 515, l. 43 pismires] pigmires] pismires

p. 516, l. 3 into a water jugg] in a water-jug] in a water jug

p. 516, l. 16 of Alice] at Alice] at Alice

p. 516, l. 17 look at her face in] look at her in] look at her in

p. 516, l. 24 phantasies] phantages] phantages

p. 516, l. 26 made up of] made of] made of

p. 516, l. 28 turn an eel] turn to an eel] turn an eel

p. 516, l. 30 dales] bales] bales

p. 516, l. 31 runkled] rumpled] rumpled

p. 517, l. 33 L–d] Lord] Lord

p. 520, l. 12 these others] then others] then others

p. 520, l. 18 guts] guts] entrails

p. 520, l. 21 nothing ado] nothing to do] nothing to do

p. 521, ll. 4–5 Every chest] Every breast] Every breast

p. 521, l. 5 flustered in] fluttered by] flustered by

p. 521, l. 12 tramping of horses were] trampling of horses was] trampling of horses was

p. 521, l. 24 to go and see] to see] to see

p. 522, l. 37 which appeared] who appeared] which appeared

p. 522, l. 28 afterward] afterwards] afterwards

p. 523, l. 20 He hath, now] He hath] He hath, now

Note on the Text

Hogg learnt that his texts were not safe from interference while in the press. After *Winter Evening Tales* came out he complained to George Boyd of 'meddlers' who, among other things, 'made you leave out without asking my leave the dedication to Dr Morris of the Tales, which I meant as an apology for the manners there described and the loss of which was a greater one to the work than the loss of the best tale would have been'.[1] 'Peter Morris' was the pseudonym John Gibson Lockhart had used for his fictionalised anatomy of the Scottish cultural scene, *Peter's Letters to His Kinsfolk* (1819), in the pages of which Hogg himself makes an appearance. Lockhart sets the Ettrick Shepherd among the gallery of 'organic' national figures who will save Scottish culture from the deleterious influence of the *Edinburgh Review* Whigs.[2] Although patronising, Lockhart's portrayal is warmly positive, and no doubt Hogg was flattered by it. The dedication of *Winter Evening Tales* to 'Dr Morris' would have intimated that Hogg was living up to Lockhart's representation of him as a national author, while opening up a more challenging range of voices and genres than Lockhart might have anticipated. In any case, although Boyd apologised for the omission, Hogg evidently did not insist that the dedication be inserted in the second edition, since it does not appear there (and has not survived).

Hogg promised that he would himself correct the second edition. 'Do not begin to print the second edition of the Tales', he instructed Boyd on 6 November 1820, 'till I send you a copy for I will go over them all again with a strick correcting eye'.[3] He wrote again two weeks later: 'I send you in a corrected copy of the first vol. of the tales in which you will find many alterations Let the most scrupulous now find fault if they can In the second vol. I have found nothing worth while therefore you may go on with them both together'.[4] Hogg's claim to have corrected the first but not the second volume of *Winter Evening Tales* is borne out by the posthumous collection of *Tales and Sketches of the Ettrick Shepherd* (1836–37) published by Blackie and Son. Selections from the first volume of *Winter Evening Tales* included in *Tales and Sketches* follow the text of the 1821 second edition, while selections from the second volume follow the uncorrected 1820 first edition–indicating that Hogg supplied Blackie with his own marked-up first edition copy, containing his corrections to the first volume only.

This evidence, then, would seem to make an editor's task straight-forward: the second edition of *Winter Evening Tales* of 1821 repre-sents the author's corrected version, and so should serve as au-thoritative copy-text. But scrutiny of both volumes of 1820 and 1821 reveals a more complicated situation. First of all, the second vol-ume of 1821, although uncorrected by Hogg, carries upwards of 500 variants from 1820. Nearly all of these are minor adjustments of wording and punctuation, presumably made by Oliver and Boyd's compositor or someone at the press. Many of the revisions made to the first volume are of the same kind, which suggests that it too was corrected by the printers as standard house procedure, as well as by Hogg. We have no way of knowing for sure which changes are au-thorial and which are not, although it seems likely that the more extensive kinds of correction in the first volume, not found in the second volume, are Hogg's.

The uncertainty would not matter very much, if it were not for the inconsistency of many of the changes made for 1821. While some obvious errors have been caught, others are left standing. Many alterations seem gratuitous and arbitrary. Worst of all, erroneous changes are made to words and phrases that were perfectly all right in 1820. Examples of errors left unchanged or newly introduced may be found within a few pages of 'Love Adventures of Mr George Cochrane' in the first volume.[5] The clan slogan, 'Wha dare meddle wi' me', (I, 254; pp. 192–93) is garbled as 'middle wi' me' in 1821. 1821 retains an erroneous insertion of speech marks from 1820 (at I, 272; p. 205, l. 32) and perpetrates a further error by removing a first person pronoun (p. 208, l. 10). The comma separating the clauses, 'a tremendous blow on the brow, which made me fall freely back', is turned into a full stop (I, 275; p. 208, l. 7).

The corrections are also unevenly distributed, with dense bursts occurring early (although not at first) in the opening story of the first volume, 'Renowned Adventures of Basil Lee', and then fading away towards the end of the tale. This may or may not reflect the status of 'Basil Lee' as the most heavily rewritten of the pieces originally published in *The Spy*. Some of the later tales (notably those reprinted with little or no revision from *The Spy*) bear minimal correction. Most of the changes are small, if occasionally numerous, adjustments of wording and punctuation. Only in certain passages of 'Basil Lee' are sentences substantially restructured. In these cases the rework-ing of punctuation and syntax may significantly alter the rhythm of Hogg's prose, most drastically perhaps in the brilliant battlefield episode. Here is a representative passage in 1820:

As soon as we set our heads over the verge we began a
sharp fire, and were saluted by a destructive one from their
works: our men fell thick. The two next to me, on my right
hand, both fell at the same time. I made ready for flight. A
bullet struck up a divot of earth exactly between my feet; I
gave a great jump in the air, and escaped unhurt. "The devil's in the men!" thought I, "are they not going to fly yet?"
The reverse was the case. The word *quick march* was given,
and we rushed rapidly forward into a kind of level ground
between the two ridges. Here we halted and kept up a brisk
fire, and I scarcely saw one of our men falling. It was the
best conducted manœuvre of any I ever saw; but this I discovered from after-conversation and reflection, for at that
time I did not know in the least what I was doing. (I, 39; pp.
30–31)

Here is the same passage, in 1821:

As soon as we set our heads over the verge, we began a
sharp fire, which was returned by a destructive one from
their works, and our men fell thick. The two next men to
me, on my right hand, both fell at the same time, and I made
ready for flight. A bullet struck up a divot of earth exactly
between my feet. I gave a great jump in the air, and escaped
unhurt. "The devil's in the men!" thought I, "are they not
going to run yet?" The reverse was the case; for the word
quick march being given, we rushed rapidly forward into a
kind of level ground between two ridges. Here we halted,
still keeping up a brisk fire, and I scarcely saw one of our
men fall. It was the best conducted manœuvre of any I ever
saw; but this I discovered from after-conversation and reflection, for at that time I had not the least knowledge of
what I was doing.

The revision may flow more smoothly, with its grammatically more
complex constructions. But in many ways the roughness of the original, with its rapid, jolting succession of declarative clauses, seems
closer to the experience it represents.

There are very few places where clauses or sentences have been
revised for their content, and these occur in the longer tales 'Basil
Lee' and 'George Cochrane'. If Hogg was responsible for these
changes, and there is no reason to suppose otherwise, they show
him attempting to remove or ameliorate language that polite readers might have found objectionable. The 1821 text of 'Basil Lee'

rewrites the phrase 'twisting his nose, and turning away his face as if he had found a stink' (I, 28; p. 23) as 'turning away his face, twisting his nose as if something had offended it': a miniature allegory of the work of bowdlerisation. Later, as Basil advances reluctantly to the battlefield, looking for a way out, a characteristic detail is lost with the excision of the sentence, 'The calls of nature were very frequent with me' (I, 39; p. 30).

The revision in 'Love Adventures of Mr George Cochrane' is more interesting. 'But I'm sure I twold thee, mwother, that I had nae objections to a praying man', protests Jessie Armstrong; the phrase that follows, 'the oftener on his knees the better, only let me choice the other' (I, 289; p. 217), is cut in 1821, removing the possible disrespect to the act of devotion but also a grain of Jessie's liveliness. Further corrections to the episode dampen the characterisation of Mary Park, Jessie's devout Presbyterian mother. The extraction of precise scriptural allusions from her speech unravels the delicate web of sexual innuendo spun across the conversation. '"Carnality's the mother o' invention," said the indefatigable mother' (I, 289; p. 218) becomes, blandly: '"The want o' religion is the mother of a' evil," said Mary Park'. The words 'flesh, flesh', are excised from, 'It is the raven i' the wilderness, that cries, flesh, flesh, from evening to morning, an' the mair that ye feed her, the louder is her cry' (p. 218)—as is the sentence that follows: 'It is the worm that never dieth, an' the fire that is not quenched'. In the next sentence, the spermatic 'manna of life' (I, 290; p. 218) is replaced with the dull, and unscriptural, 'stolen bread'; further down the page, the deletion of 'on carnality' completes the operation of surgical removal of potentially obscene and blasphemous double-entendres. (A few remain, such as the ingenious triple pun—meshing sexuality, wrestling and religious conversion—on 'cast o' grace'.) The present editor would probably not have detected this pattern of word-play had not the 1821 revision drawn his attention to it.

I think it likely that in making these revisions Hogg was attempting to practise self-censorship in response to the charges of 'coarseness' levelled by his critics. Several of the reviews of *Winter Evening Tales*, in fact, advised him to clean up his text should he have the opportunity in a second edition. 'There is an occasional coarseness— we had almost said grossness—in some of the Tales, which half an hour judiciously spent in correction might have removed', admonished the review that is likely to have carried most weight with Hogg, Wilson's in *Blackwood's*; therefore, 'let our good Shepherd request Oliver and Boyd to leave out all such tid-bits in the second edition, which we prophecy will be called for before midsummer'.[6] The *Monthly Review* expressed a like hope that 'a diligent revisal will enable the author to remove such blemishes' (i.e. Scotticisms and other vulgarisms) in a future edition.[7] The *British Critic* directed Hogg to seek help from his social betters: 'The faults which he displays are such as would easily be cured, if he would only take the advice of any well educated friend, who had been accustomed to more polished society than our author can be supposed to have generally lived in'.[8] More impudently still, *The Scotsman* suggested that the author get married 'before the book again see the public', so that he could read it aloud to his wife 'and strike out every passage which [...] offends her delicacy'.[9] (This may be an in-joke, since Hogg did get married soon after the publication of *Winter Evening Tales*.)

In short, Hogg made these substantive changes, which represent a net loss of piquancy and wit from the 1820 edition, in response to an external pressure of disapproval from his middle-class critics. We know that other works by Hogg were bowdlerised and otherwise disfigured in the press by officious agents, during his lifetime (*Queen Hynde*) as well as after his death (*Private Memoirs and Confessions of a Fanatic* and other titles in the 1836–37 *Tales and Sketches*). The 1821 edition of *Winter Evening Tales* reveals Hogg himself internalising and performing the work of censorship in an attempt to ward off critical displeasure: 'Let the most scrupulous now find fault if they can'. Hogg's complaint about the accusations of indelicacy in his 1821 'Memoir' (see 'Introduction', p. xxxv) expresses his sensitivity at this time to a charge that could seriously depress his sales. (Circulating libraries, which purchased the bulk of the edition of a new novel, would boycott works suspected of indecency.)

For these reasons, I have decided to treat the second edition of *Winter Evening Tales* with caution, rather than relying upon it implicitly as the authoritative expression of Hogg's intentions. I have accepted its revisions only where they have indeed corrected errors and solecisms that might distract the reader in the first edition. Where stylistic revisions were made, in 'Basil Lee', I have preferred the rougher, more vivid version of 1820, and I have retained the coarse passages, in 'Basil Lee' and 'George Cochrane', that were softened or removed in 1821. The resulting text is something of a compromise: the 1820 first edition, corrected conservatively against 1821. I am well aware that such an editorial policy lays itself open to charges of a late-twentieth-century, Neo-Romantic, thoroughly ideological preference for the author's first intentions over the socialising process of publication and revision, and for an 'authentic' roughness and rudeness over a 'compromised' politeness and polish. True, Hogg's attempts to fit in with genteel social and literary standards were as integral to his career as his defiance of those standards, as well as his (less deliberate) failures to meet them. Nevertheless, I believe that a reprint of 1821 would have involved the perpetuation of more inconsistencies and incoherences than the path I have followed, not least because it would have mystified the relationship between the text and authorial intention. For aesthetic reasons, in the last analysis, I judge the present edition to represent the best possible text of *Winter Evening Tales*: it retains the liveliness of 1820, while taking advantage of corrections in 1821. I have made my local choices clear in the Emendation List, which accounts for all divergences from the copy-text.

In the case of those items in *Winter Evening Tales* for which earlier versions exist, I have likewise preferred 1820 as the authoritative text. The versions of tales first published in *The Spy* belong to a distinct and integral work, and so carry no textual authority for *Winter Evening Tales*. Even in cases where alteration is minimal, the piece has been recast by its new context. As for the other pieces written or published elsewhere–'The Long Pack', 'An Old Soldier's Tale', 'Halbert of Lyne', 'King Gregory', 'The Shepherd's Calendar', 'Connel of Dee'–I have examined the earlier texts, but treated them with caution, observing the same editorial principle. Passages from the earlier versions of 'King Gregory' and 'Halbert of Lyne' omitted in *Winter Evening Tales* are printed in the explanatory Notes; I have incorporated a number of corrections of accidentals from the 1814 text of 'King Gregory'. The principle holds even for those few cases in which Hogg's manuscript is available. In returning to the manuscript of 'Storms' in his edition of *The Shepherd's Calendar*, Douglas Mack reprised its original status as copy-text for *Blackwood's Edinburgh Magazine*, in which the *Shepherd's Calendar* series first appeared. I have chosen, once again, to respect the integrity of *Winter Evening Tales* as a collection over the chronological priority of the manuscript, on the grounds that 'Storms' is a different work here, set in a different context.

Hogg's manuscript of 'The Long Pack', which appears to be a fair copy prepared for the printer, corresponds to a text published in magazines eleven years before *Winter Evening Tales*. Hogg revised 'The Long Pack', thoroughly rewriting a couple of passages as well as adjusting details, when he reclaimed it for the 1820 collection. The manuscript thus represents a different version of 'The Long Pack', conceived for a different kind of publication. These differences, like those between texts that appear in both *The Spy* and *Winter Evening Tales*, are sufficiently marked to warrant separate publication in the Stirling / South Carolina Edition. Hogg's manuscript is accordingly reproduced in an appendix to this edition, with a full account of its relation to the earliest known printings (1809).

'Connel of Dee' presents us with the only surviving example of a manuscript that we know for sure was used as printer's copy for *Winter Evening Tales,* even though Hogg had written the poem for another collection. The manuscript shows that the printers followed Hogg's text with fair accuracy, changing or inserting punctuation according to house style, but otherwise (with very few exceptions) reproducing what the author wrote. We cannot know which (if any) of the few lexical variants might have been authorized by Hogg himself at proof stage.[10] If any major changes had been made between the manuscript and printed versions of 'Connel of Dee', or if we possessed manuscripts for the bulk of *Winter Evening Tales*, there would be a clear justification for printing Hogg's original version, as has been done in the case of some other titles in the Stirling / South Carolina Edition. As it is, the very miscellaneousness of *Winter Evening Tales*, comprising the provenance of its constituent parts, requires that the gravitational field of the 1820 first edition be kept intact.[11]

I have not accepted any of the revisions instituted in the edition of Hogg's works published after his death by Blackie. While there is evidence that Hogg revised some individual titles (notably *The Brownie of Bodsbeck*) for *Tales and Sketches of the Ettrick Shepherd*, scholars have concluded that he neither undertook nor oversaw the bulk of the 'final corrections' featured in the edition. (Hogg had given Blackie's corrector, 'whom I know to be a man of genious and good taste[,] the power and charge to alter what he pleases'.)[12] Minor cuts were made to some of the reprinted tales for what seem to be reasons of economy, including the whole of the first, framing chapter of 'The Bridal of Polmood'. The most extensive revisions appear in 'Adventures of Basil Lee', which also bears the most extensive revisions between 1820 and 1821 (as well as from *The Spy* before that). Numerous excisions have been made, from a few sentences here and there to whole paragraphs and even pages. The largest cut removes an episode towards the end of the tale, several pages long, recounting Basil's first marriage to an alcoholic wife who drinks herself to death—even though the cut brings some inconsistencies into the remaining text. Remarkably, the Clifford Mackay plot, although it bore the brunt of reviewers' complaints, remains intact, apart from a few sentences of Clifford's reflecting upon the morals of British army officers. It seems that Hogg took care to present the story as a challenge to middle-class morality, not a lapse from it; and to the very end he refused to alter it.

Notes

1. Hogg to Boyd, 16 October 1820, in NLS Acc. 5000 / 188.
2. See [John Gibson Lockhart], *Peter's Letters to His Kinsfolk*, 3 vols (Edinburgh: Blackwood, 1819), I, 137–42 and III, 141–42.
3. See NLS Acc. 5000 / 140, p. 59 (Letter Book I: Agreements).
4. Hogg to Boyd, 20 November 1820, in NLS Acc. 5000 / 188.
5. The page references which follow are given firstly to the first edition of *Winter Evening Tales* of 1820, and then, for ease of reference, to the present edition.
6. 'Hogg's Tales, &c.', *Blackwood's Edinburgh Magazine*, 7 (May 1820), 148–54 (p. 154).
7. *Monthly Review, or Literary Journal*, new series, 93 (November 1820), 263–67 (p. 264).
8. *British Critic*, new series, 13 (June 1820), 622–31.
9. *The Scotsman*, 29 April 1820, p. 143.
10. David Groves prints the MS version of 'Connel of Dee' in his *James Hogg: Selected Poems and Songs* (Edinburgh: Scottish Academic Press, 1986), pp. 76–89.
11. For a clear and authoritative account of the editorial policy of the S/SC edition in relation to current editorial theory see Douglas S. Mack, 'Editing Different Versions of Romantic Texts', *The Yearbook of English Studies*, 29 (1999), 176–90.
12. Hogg to Blackie, 11 November 1833, in NLS MS 807, fol. 20.

Emendation List

All variants from the 1820 first edition copy-text are listed here, and are taken from the second edition of 1821, unless otherwise noted. The reading of the present edition is listed first, and then the 1820 reading after the bracket. Both the first and second editions are sometimes inconsistent in the application of quotation marks (for example, printing single for double quotation marks), especially within extended passages of speech. I have corrected these silently, standardising according to the following conventions: double quotation marks enclose a speech; single quotation marks enclose a speech within a speech; and opening quotation marks are repeated at the start of a new paragraph within the same speech. In the list which follows 'eol' is an abbreviation for 'end of line'.

The Renowned Adventures of Basil Lee

p. 7, ll. 10–11 and the shepherd's] a shepherd's
p. 7, l. 11 expectations.] expectations;
p. 7, l. 14 exertion,–and, for] exertion, and for
p. 7, l. 16 little minx] minx
p. 8, l. 34 operation!] operation.
p. 9, l. 8 callant,] callant
p. 9, l. 41 and I feared] and feared
p. 9, l. 42 the story] it
p. 12, l. 4 same time,] same, time
p. 13, l. 2 sae] so
p. 13, l. 5 own, which] own which
p. 13, l. 22 which] that
p. 13, l. 22 covet,] coveted
p. 13, l. 39 and thought] but thought
p. 14, l. 16 said he;] said he,
p. 14, l. 22 one;] one,
p. 14, l. 22 the night."] the night?"
p. 15, l. 38 a short time after.] in a short time.
p. 16, l. 36 conclusion. The] conclusion, the
p. 16, ll. 39–40 dispersion. I judged] dispersion, I judged
p. 17, l. 9 resolution;] resolution,
p. 17, l. 10 it. So he] it, so that he
p. 17, l. 11 farm,] farm
p. 17, l. 11 other; and as] other, and

p. 17, l. 12   bargain, he] bargain. He
p. 17, l. 19   something–I] something, I
p. 17, l. 27   are] is
p. 17, l. 36   escape,] escape
p. 18, l. 28   board; but] board, but
p. 18, l. 40   callant] gallant
p. 19, l. 2   py, my] py my
p. 19, l. 9   manner;] manner,
p. 19, l. 25   who at one time was] for at one time he was
p. 19, l. 34   amour;] amour,
p. 20, l. 13   ward and] ward, and
p. 21, l. 5   man and] man, and
p. 21, l. 36   duel with] duel, with
p. 23, l. 23   had now no leisure again] had no leisure ever again
p. 24, l. 1   fall;] fall,
p. 24, l. 7   remember was] remember, was, [Editorial]
p. 24, l. 30   recruits and] recruits, and
p. 24, l. 31   march] March
p. 25, l. 33   who] that
p. 25, l. 42   sister?"] sister."
p. 26, l. 7   do?"] do."
p. 27, l. 11   me to] me, to
p. 27, l. 12   that] the same
p. 27, l. 28   induce] induce,
p. 28, l. 29   me. So, thinking] me; so thinking
p. 28, l. 29   do] do,
p. 28, l. 30   off,] off.
p. 28, l. 33   angry] angry,
p. 28, l. 40   me] me,
p. 29, l. 1   personages] personages,
p. 29, l. 9   quarters] quarters,
p. 30, l. 40   were all,] were,
p. 31, l. 21   sixty] sixty,
p. 34, l. 22   did] *did*
p. 34, l. 26   go] be
p. 35, l. 2   This acquisition] This new acquisition
p. 37, ll. 28–29   gentleman, of great riches] gentleman of great
    riches,
p. 38, ll. 2–3   across the river, which] across, and it
p. 39, l. 21   my pockets.–] my pockets in such a manner.–
p. 39, l. 22   down with him!] down with him.
p. 39, l. 33   about,] about

p. 40, l. 20 which it is] which is
p. 44, l. 9 acknowledgments."] acknowledgments?" [Editorial]
p. 44, ll. 18–19 with a suspicious] with suspicious
p. 44, l. 29 Well,] Well
p. 49, l. 36 Loch Rog] Loch-Rog
p. 50, l. 5 *More*] *More*; [Editorial]
p. 50, l. 5 shadow),] shadow)
p. 53, l. 16 her,] her; [Editorial]
p. 54, l. 4 me,] me; [Editorial]
p. 54, l. 5 *Englishman*;] *Englishman*, [Editorial]
p. 57, ll. 24–25 immoveably] immovebly
p. 63, l. 2 Any nhews, Mustress] Any nhews Mustress [Editorial]
p. 63, l. 13 that] That
p. 63, l. 26 same time,] same, time

Adam Bell

p. 75, l. 7 confidants] confidents
p. 77, l. 20 considerably] conderably

Duncan Campbell

p. 81, l. 2 died. All] died.–All
p. 83, l. 23 heath,] heath
p. 84, l. 38 hand] band
p. 85, l. 33 but as] butas
p. 95, l. 13 man,] man
p. 96, l. 33 too] too,

An Old Soldier's Tale

p. 100, l. 26 an'] and
p. 102, ll. 24–25 *that be all*] *that* be all
p. 105, l. 38 that] tha

Highland Adventures

p. 107, l. 2 public,] public;
p. 109, l. 7 Trossacks,] Trossacks; [Editorial]
p. 111, l. 25 Sir;] Sir,
p. 112, l. 31 that,] that
p. 112, l. 34 centinel] centinal
p. 117, l. 23 and as a proof] and [eol] and as a proof

Halbert of Lyne

p. 121, l. 107 man,] man.
p. 121, l. 109 Manor.–He] Manor–He [Editorial]
p. 124, l. 198 glee;] glee.
p. 124, l. 213 morning] Morning
p. 129, l. 411 John of Manor;] John of manor;
p. 129, l. 412 FAULTS,] FAULTS.
p. 129, l. 419 more,] more

The Long Pack

p. 132, ll. 10–11 matter, Alice?] matter Alice? [Editorial]
p. 132, l. 24 doubt."] doubt"
p. 134, l. 37 appearance,] appearance [Editorial]
p. 134, l. 37 Edward] Edward, [Editorial]
p. 136, l. 5 and,] and
p. 136, l. 6 time] time,
p. 136, l. 6 speak.] speak, [Editorial]
p. 138, l. 29 which,] which
p. 138, l. 42 horses] horses,
p. 139, l. 14 physician] physician,
p. 139, l. 18 places,] places

A Peasant's Funeral

p. 142, l. 13 themselves.] themselves: [Editorial]
p. 142, l. 28 Him] him
p. 143, l. 13 Being] being

Dreadful Story of Macpherson

p. 146, l. 11 highest] higest
p. 146, l. 35 concerning] concerinng

Maria's Tale, written by herself

p. 151, l. 36 clasping] clapsing
p. 154, l. 28 satisfied,] satisfied

Singular Dream, from a Correspondent

p. 160, l. 35 comes,] comes; [Editorial]
p. 160, l. 35 pleasure."] pleasure,"
p. 161, l. 2 a'] a

p. 162, l. 36 he;] he,
p. 163, l. 12 I.] I,

Love Adventures of Mr George Cochrane

p. 176, l. 39 she] he
p. 179, l. 8 focks'] focks [Editorial]
p. 179, l. 13 shoon. Humph!] shoon." [new paragraph] "Humph [Editorial]
p. 179, ll. 14–15 hame." [new paragraph] I] hame." I [Editorial]
p. 180, l. 5 you?"] you."
p. 184, ll. 13–14 interruption?] interruption. [Editorial]
p. 186, l. 8 night?] night.
p. 189, l. 1 you,] you
p. 189, l. 42 asleep] a sleep
p. 190, l. 33 won't] wont
p. 191, l. 3 went] ewnt
p. 192, l. 5 rad] sad
p. 195, l. 15 market in] marketin
p. 198, l. 25 clink,] clink
p. 198, l. 27 love] love,
p. 202, l. 9 borderer] borderer,
p. 203, l. 16 he. "Thank] he; "thank [Editorial]
p. 205, l. 32 I was] "I was [Editorial]
p. 208, l. 13 time I was] time was [Editorial]
p. 208, l. 17 fair?] fair. [Editorial]
p. 210, l. 10 route] rout
p. 210, ll. 19–20 Sunday clothes] sunday-clothes
p. 211, l. 36 thousand-pound] thousand pound
p. 212, l. 5 *family*] *family*,
p. 212, l. 14 question,] question
p. 212, l. 23 me?] me.
p. 212, l. 24 *already*;] *already*,
p. 212, l. 25 believe] believe,
p. 212, l. 33 Welch:] Welch;
p. 213, l. 15 slack:] slack,
p. 213, l. 23 a-struggling] a struggling
p. 213, l. 40 ha,] ha;
p. 213, l. 41 corn-seck] corn seck
p. 214, l. 1 foot?] foot.
p. 214, l. 2 I; "if] I, "If
p. 215, l. 31 method,] method

p. 215, l. 31 emergency,] emergency:
p. 216, l. 9 tar-kitt] tar kitt
p. 216, l. 35 graning] grinning
p. 216, l. 35 for? Mind] for; mind
p. 217, l. 3 himsel'] himsel
p. 217, l. 10 warstler] warstler,
p. 217, l. 29 Wolf-cleuch-head;] Wolf-cleuch-head, [Editorial]
p. 218, l. 4 enough o't."] enough o t."
p. 218, l. 7 lift] lifts
p. 218, l. 20 will,] will
p. 218, l. 28 woo';] woo;
p. 218, l. 30 a'] a
p. 219, l. 16 spanned] spann'd
p. 220, l. 35 hess] has
p. 223, l. 37 conveniency's] conveniences

John Gray o' Middleholm

p. 230, l. 32 was expected] is expected [Editorial]
p. 230, l. 42–p. 231, l. 1 wretched-looking] wretched looking
p. 234, l. 11 gaun] gawn
p. 235, l. 1 Right] right
p. 236, l. 37 tither?] tither" [Editorial]
p. 236, l. 41 bane?] ban e.
p. 238, l. 19 Mathews] Matthews [Editorial]
p. 239, l. 17 and,] and
p. 242, l. 1 ata',] ata'
p. 244, l. 22 repast] repast,
p. 246, l. 34 dinna] disna'
p. 247, l. 2 on.] on
p. 247, l. 18 dinna] disna'
p. 247, l. 38 dinna] disna'
p. 252, l. 28 a neighbouring] a [eol] a neighbouring
p. 253, l. 16 far-seen] far seen

The Bridal of Polmood

p. 259, l. 28 phenomenon] phenomena
p. 260, l. 29 its] it's
p. 260, l. 38 Scotland] Scotland,
p. 262, l. 23 Carmichael,] Carmichael;
p. 263, l. 38 eye-witness] eye witness
p. 266, l. 10 suggested,] suggested

p. 266, l. 19 Crawmel] Cramel
p. 266, l. 33 not,] not;
p. 271, l. 25 bewilder,] bewilder
p. 272, l. 9 view,] view
p. 273, l. 17 occasion] occassion
p. 273, l. 28 borne] born
p. 273, l. 36 considerably] considerable
p. 274, ll. 28–29 considerable] considerahle
p. 274, l. 42 interview:] interview,
p. 275, l. 1 disgrace;] disgrace,
p. 278, l. 10 roof?"] roof."
p. 278, l. 32 by] bye
p. 278, l. 41 companion.] companion,
p. 283, l. 24 glee,] glee [Editorial]
p. 285, l. 3 remonstrate,] remonstrate;
p. 285, l. 29 nation?] nation.
p. 286, l. 5 day's] days
p. 287, l. 41 *nyte*] *wyte* [Editorial]
p. 289, l. 35 that] thatn [Editorial]
p. 290, l. 3 "Hold] "hold
p. 294, ll. 9–10 balcony] Balcony
p. 294, l. 33 king;] king,
p. 295, l. 18 picture] picture,
p. 295, l. 23 refusal,"] refusal;"
p. 295, l. 40 appear,] appear;
p. 296, l. 24 burn.] burn, [Editorial]
p. 297, l. 8 respect–] respect;
p. 297, l. 15 exhilarates] exhilirates
p. 298, l. 10 this,] this
p. 298, l. 23 Virgin's] virgin's [Editorial]
p. 298, ll. 25–26 Manners] Maners
p. 299, l. 41 galloping] gallopping
p. 301, l. 7 *Weddingers' Hope,*] *Weddingers Hope*
p. 301, l. 22 black-looking] black looking
p. 302, l. 17 wallet?"] wallet."
p. 302, ll. 19–20 yours, man] yours man
p. 302, l. 33 yet she] yet, she
p. 302, l. 33 yet he] yet, he
p. 303, l. 3 shepherds] shepherd's
p. 303, l. 27 there."] there?" [Editorial]
p. 303, l. 38 king,] king
p. 304, l. 30 bitterly] bitterly,

p. 304, l. 42 informed,] informed;
p. 305, l. 37 courtiers,] courtiers;
p. 307, ll. 32–33 were not ghosts] were ghosts
p. 314, l. 27 stranger,] stranger;
p. 314, l. 33 *affettuoso*] *affettuosa*
p. 315, l. 14 tinckell] tinkell [Editorial]
p. 316, l. 26 rout,] rout
p. 320, l. 34 part. A] part.–A
p. 321, l. 15 behaviour] behaviour,
p. 322, l. 17 scrutiny?] scrutiny.
p. 329, l. 7 so well] so-well
p. 329, l. 7 wished-for] wished for
p. 334, l. 2 the most intimate] his most intimate [Editorial]
p. 334, l. 4 exist,] exist
p. 337, l. 2 in] on [Editorial]
p. 339, l. 39 must] must,
p. 345, l. 18 good humour] good-humour
p. 350, l. 19 conduct–] conduct;
p. 352, l. 4 unavailing,] unavailable, [Editorial]
p. 354, l. 25 innocent,] innocent
p. 355, l. 14 Hepburn] Hepburn,

King Gregory

p. 362, l. 142 sang,] sang
p. 362, l. 146 heather-blooms] heather blooms [Editorial, as in *Edinburgh Annual Register*]
p. 366, l. 298 Which yet] Which, yet, [Editorial, as in *Edinburgh Annual Register*]

The Shepherd's Calendar

p. 377, l. 41 Douglasses] Danglasses
p. 380, l. 2 day-light] day light
p. 383, l. 4 snow-boots] snow boots
p. 392, l. 30 ledge] lege
p. 395, l. 4 twa] twae
p. 395, l. 5 fankit] frankit [Editorial]
p. 395, l. 29 an ale-vat] a ale-vat
p. 395, l. 33 the morn;] the-morn; [Editorial]
p. 397, ll. 18–19 manners] manners,
p. 404, l. 24 it's] its

The Wife of Lochmaben

p. 428, l. 18 been, Mary?"] been Mary?"
p. 428, l. 41 Moor?"] Moor."

Cousin Mattie

p. 433, l. 17 vagrant] vagrant,
p. 435, l. 32 wi'?"] wi'."
p. 436, l. 26 in view of her father's house] in view of her father
[Editorial]
p. 441, l. 14 corpse-kisting?"] corpse-kisting."

Welldean Hall

p. 443, ll. 6–7 castaway!'" [new paragraph] "Is] castaway!"
[new line] Is [Editorial: change of speaker]
p. 445, l. 33 Nicholas] Nicholson
p. 446, l. 24 suspected] suspected,
p. 446, l. 27 Sommerville] Somerville [Editorial]
p. 449, l. 20 not?"] not."
p. 451, l. 37 ones] one's
p. 453, l. 14 you, doctor] you doctor
p. 464, l. 29 'I can replenish it'] I can replenish it [Editorial]
p. 466, l. 16 hers] her's [Editorial]
p. 468, l. 4 lady,] lady;
p. 468, l. 13 Sommerville] Somerville
p. 473, l. 35 was] wa
p. 476, l. 14 Mr —'s.] Mr —.
p. 477, l. 42 not-do–not-do–not-do] not-do–not [eol] do–not-
do
p. 483, l. 30 him!] him?
p. 485, l. 3 were] was
p. 489, l. 13 are] is
p. 489, l. 15 brother] brother,
p. 491, l. 14 -spis-pis-] -spis [eol] pis- [Editorial]
p. 493, l. 39 beat] beats

Tibby Johnston's Wraith

p. 500, l. 17 woy, beast] woy beast
p. 501, l. 26 quo' I. 'Pray] quo' I. [new paragraph] "Pray [no
new paragraph as in 1821]
p. 501, l. 36 fallen nature] fallin' nature

p. 502, l. 40   a',"]   a", [Editorial]
p. 504, l. 24   spares]   spare's

Hyphenation List

Various words are hyphenated at the ends of lines in this edition of *Winter Evening Tales*. The list below indicates those cases in which hyphens should be retained in making quotations. Each item is referred to by page and line number: as elsewhere, in calculating line numbers headings have been ignored.

p. 7, l. 6 house-maid
p. 12, l. 30 way-side
p. 26, l. 36 to-night
p. 31, l. 10 after-conversation
p. 31, l. 40 flag-staff
p. 52, l. 27 boat-men
p. 59, l. 34 kind-heartedness
p. 76, l. 20 house-keeper
p. 80, l. 26 good-b'ye
p. 83, l. 28 heath-cock
p. 84, l. 25 cow-house
p. 95, l. 36 hard-earned
p. 96, l. 18 over-blown
p. 111, l. 9 thunder-splintered
p. 111, l. 10 thunder-cloud
p. 115, l. 21 Strath-Gartney
p. 116, l. 9 Ben-More
p. 117, l. 3 Cairn-Gorum
p. 117, footnote Ben-Nevis
p. 130, l. 18 well-dressed
p. 135, l. 35 wind-call
p. 148, l. 14 well-charged
p. 160, l. 39 self-interest
p. 162, l. 15 grave-pole
p. 179, l. 12 kail-yard

p. 191, l. 10 hide-an'-seek
p. 194, l. 29 off-hand
p. 195, l. 23 Baillie-hill
p. 201, l. 16 father-in-law
p. 203, l. 26 Stanger-side
p. 206, l. 3 ball-room
p. 207, l. 33 raw-boned
p. 210, l. 9 side-gate-end

p. 211, l. 15 Lang-hill
p. 214, l. 26 Liddel-head
p. 235, l. 16 three-neukit
p. 241, l. 20 low-roofed
p. 247, l. 12 boat-pool
p. 247, l. 41 apple-tree
p. 248, l. 3 apple-tree
p. 248, l. 32 good-humoured
p. 249, l. 42 thread-bare
p. 255, l. 9 apple-trees
p. 260, l. 4 farm-steading
p. 262, l. 4 Meggat-dale
p. 266, l. 27 to-morrow
p. 280, l. 18 to-morrow
p. 292, l. 14 castle-gate
p. 312, l. 31 dowry-lands
p. 315, l. 27 Holyrood-house
p. 334, l. 16 dowry-lands
p. 346, l. 29 deep-toned
p. 374, l. 11 ill-hued
p. 376, l. 8 forty-five
p. 384, l. 14 cow-herd
p. 393, l. 3 a-swoomin
p. 399, l. 34 hop-step-and-leap
p. 402, l. 5 Ramsey-cleuch-burn
p. 402, l. 12 anti-prelatic
p. 404, l. 8 daughter-in-law
p. 404, l. 12 Laike-a-day
p. 405, l. 18 race-ground
p. 406, l. 35 sun-ways-about
p. 426, l. 4 Circuit-Court
p. 426, l. 29 bed-clothes
p. 429, l. 36 wild-fire

p. 430, l. 18 cross-examined

p. 435, l. 29 fie-gae-to

p. 445, l. 40 world's-worm

p. 446, l. 9 wood-forester

p. 452, l. 5 Ha-ha-ha

p. 460, l. 24 good-morning

p. 462, l. 38 Oh-oh-hone

p. 463, l. 17 He-he-he

p. 463, l. 20 He-he-he-he

p. 463, l. 22 He-he-he-he

p. 468, l. 2 boarding-school

p. 475, l. 8 well-being

p. 476, l. 28 Gibby-Gibby

p. 476, l. 32 He-he-he-he

p. 477, l. 12 no-Greek

p. 477, l. 18 *not-the-night*

p. 477, l. 20 folly-folly

p. 477, l. 25 right-right

p. 477, l. 27 gill-gill

p. 477, l. 39 *no-right*

p. 478, l. 7 no-no

p. 478, l. 8 wick-wick

p. 478, l. 9 all-wrang

p. 478, l. 10 soul-billy

p. 478, l. 11 Gibby-lad

p. 478, l. 12 have-you-there

p. 479, l. 5 some-ways

p. 479, l. 11 Long-spoon

p. 479, l. 12 Not-safe

p. 479, l. 16 hope-so

p. 479, l. 42 straight-straight

p. 480, l. 25 *lye-dogs*

p. 481, l. 1 told-ye

p. 481, l. 3 impossible-impossible

p. 481, l. 4 what-what

p. 481, l. 19 body's-mad

p. 481, l. 20 do-never

p. 481, l. 23 Weazel-weazel

p. 481, l. 24 d'ye-say

p. 481, l. 25 h'm-h'm

p. 487, l. 37 Kinloch-Mhulart's

p. 489, l. 35 Speak-me

p. 489, l. 36 yes-yes

p. 491, l. 11 *O-Lord-God*

p. 491, l. 12 *'liver-'liver*

p. 491, l. 13 Gibby-Gibby

p. 491, l. 14 pis-pis

p. 491, l. 15 now-now

p. 491, l. 16 what-what

p. 491, l. 21 *Lord-God*

p. 494, l. 4 too-little

p. 494, l. 9 be-sure

p. 494, l. 10 what-what

p. 494, l. 34 what-what

p. 494, l. 35 tell-ye

p. 495, l. 5 Heaven-saw

p. 495, l. 6 heaven-God

p. 495, l. 22 man-yet

p. 495, l. 23 ha-hurra

p. 496, l. 4 afore-mentioned

p. 507, l. 20 heavy-hearted

p. 507, l. 23 road-side

Notes

In the Notes that follow, page references to prose items include a letter enclosed in brackets: (a) indicates that the passage annotated is to be found in the first quarter of the page, (b) that it is to be found in the second quarter, (c) in the third quarter, and (d) in the fourth. Page references to verse items provide the line number enclosed in brackets. Single words are explained in the Glossary. Quotations from the Bible are from the King James (Authorised) version, with which Hogg and his contemporaries were familiar. Other editions referred to include Robert Burns, *Poems and Songs*, ed. by James Kinsley (Oxford: Oxford University Press, 1969); William Shakespeare, *The Complete Works: Compact Edition*, ed. by Stanley Wells and Gary Taylor (Oxford: Clarendon Press, 1998). References to previous Hogg titles in the Stirling / South Carolina edition (Edinburgh: Edinburgh University Press) are given in the format: editor's name (S/SC, publication date).

Other works cited extensively in these notes are referred to by the following abbreviations:

Confessions: James Hogg, *The Private Memoirs and Confessions of a Justified Sinner*, ed. by P. D. Garside (S/SC, 2001)

Memoir: James Hogg, *Memoir of the Author's Life* and *Familiar Anecdotes of Sir Walter Scott*, ed. by Douglas S. Mack (Edinburgh: Scottish Academic Press, 1972)

Minstrelsy: Walter Scott, *Minstrelsy of the Scottish Border*, second edition, 3 vols (Edinburgh: Constable, 1803)

Mountain Bard: James Hogg, *The Mountain Bard* (Edinburgh: Constable, 1807)

OED: *The Oxford English Dictionary*, second edition, ed. by J. A. Simpson and E. S. C. Weiner, 20 vols (Oxford: Clarendon Press, 1989–)

ODEP: *The Oxford Dictionary of English Proverbs*, third edition, ed. by W. G. Smith and F. P. Wilson (Oxford: Clarendon Press, 1970)

Queen's Wake: James Hogg, *The Queen's Wake* (Edinburgh: George Goldie, 1813)

SND: *The Scottish National Dictionary*, ed. by William Grant and David Murison, 10 vols (Edinburgh: Scottish National Dictionary Association, 1931–76)

Shepherd's Calendar: James Hogg, *The Shepherd's Calendar*, ed. by Douglas S. Mack (S/SC, 1995)

Social Life: Henry Grey Graham, *The Social Life of Scotland in the Eighteenth*

Century (1901; reprinted New York: Benjamin Blom, 1971)

The Spy: James Hogg, *The Spy*, ed. by Gillian Hughes (S/SC, 2000)

Statistical Account: Sir John Sinclair, *The Statistical Account of Scotland*, 21 vols (Edinburgh: W. Creech, 1791–99)

WET: James Hogg, *Winter Evening Tales, Collected among the Cottagers in the South of Scotland*, 2 vols (Edinburgh: Oliver and Boyd, 1820)

Title page
Motto Robert Fergusson, 'The Farmer's Ingle' (1773), ll. 59–63.

The Renowned Adventures of Basil Lee
An early version of 'Basil Lee' was published in *The Spy*, in two parts: 'The Danger of Changing Occupations,–verified in the Life of a Berwick-shire Farmer', No. 3 (15 September 1810), pp. 21–29; 'Story of the Berwick-shire farmer, continued–Description of St. Mary's Lake–Of the War in America,–Of the people on the Western Shore of Lewis', No. 4 (22 September 1810), pp. 32–43. Hogg thoroughly revised and expanded the piece (hereafter referred to as 'Berwick-shire Farmer') for *WET*. 'Berwick-shire Farmer' relates the protagonist's early schooling and his adventures as a ploughman, shepherd, grocer and farmer (expanded in *WET*); his journey across Ettrick Forest to enlist in the army (omitted in *WET*); a brief (two paragraphs long) sketch of his service in Burgoyne's 1777 campaign (massively expanded in *WET*); and ethnographic observations on the Isle of Lewis (substantially rewritten in *WET*). The narrative is abruptly broken off, with an editorial note apologising 'for want of room' to continue. Although the editor's summary of the narrator's subsequent adventures differs in detail from *WET*, it provides an analogue for the later turns of the Clifford Mackay plot: 'He found the woman who was his housekeeper married to a richer and more respectable man than he himself ever was–the man who had taken his farm from his brother amassing a large fortune in it–and a fine boy, who bore his name and lineaments of feature, reared in another man's family' (*The Spy*, p. 43).
3(a) the proverb see Allan Ramsay, *A Collection of Scots Proverbs* (1737), in *The Works of Allan Ramsay: Vol. V*, ed. by A. M. Kinghorn and A. Law (Edinburgh: Blackwood, 1972), p. 64.
3(b) It is on this principle […] I have split Hogg recycles the final clause of the editorial note that closed down 'Berwick-shire Farmer' in *The Spy*: '[He] concludes with expressing a hope, that whoever reads his life will beware of the rock on which he has split, and persevere in the calling to which he is brought up' (*The Spy*, p. 43).
3(c) evil under the sun recurrent phrase in Ecclesiastes: see 4. 3, 5. 13, 6. 1, 9. 3, 10. 5.
3(d) The evil that I complain of here 'Basil Lee' takes up the text (second paragraph) of 'Berwick-shire Farmer' (*The Spy*, p. 21), changing '*instability in a calling*' to '*instability of mind*'.
3(footnote) The original of this extraordinary journal Hogg does not refer elsewhere in *WET* to the provenance of material previously published in *The Spy*.
5(a) Shorter Catechism compare Hogg's account of his schooling: 'I had the honour of standing at the head of a juvenile class, who read the Shorter Catechism and the Proverbs of Solomon' (*Memoir*, p. 5). The Scottish Presbyterian church subscribed to the Larger and Shorter Catechisms drawn up by the Westminster Assembly in 1647–48.

5(b) Cocker's Arithmetic *Cocker's Arithmetick, a plain and familiar method suitable to the meanest capacity* (1678) by Edward Cocker (1631–1675), published after his death by John Hawkins, remained a standard text well into the eighteenth century.

5(b) Rule of Three 'a method of finding a fourth number from three given numbers, of which the first is in the same proportion to the second as the third is to the unknown fourth': *OED* 'Rule', I.8.b.

6(d) celebrated classical employment the *Idylls* of Theocritus and *Eclogues* of Vergil established the European tradition of pastoral poetry: stylised representations of the lives of shepherds, who spend their days making love and music.

7(b) german flute the modern transverse flute (as opposed to the English flute, the recorder).

8(b) the nature of the colley a favourite topic of Hogg's: 'The Author's Address to his Auld Dog Hector', *Mountain Bard*, pp. 183–89; 'Further Anecdotes of the Shepherd's Dog', *Blackwood's Edinburgh Magazine* (hereafter *Blackwood's*), 2 (March 1818), 621–26; 'The Shepherd's Calendar. Class IV. Dogs', *Blackwood's*, 15 (February 1824), 177–83.

8(d) smearing them with tar 'The great use of tar is to kill the vermin, with which sheep are much infested': Hogg, *The Shepherd's Guide* (Edinburgh, 1807), p. 337. In a letter to Scott (23 October 1806) Hogg complains that 'the eident and nauseous business of smearing [...] always makes my hand that I can in nowise handle a pen' (National Library of Scotland (hereafter NLS) MS 865, fols 74–75).

9(c) afore the kirk fornicators were summoned before the Kirk session and ordered to do public penance; see note to p. 155, below, and *Social Life*, pp. 321–24.

10(a) to the great annoyance of the family compare Hogg's account of his attempts to teach himself the violin, to the annoyance of 'the biped part of my neighbours': *Memoir*, p. 7.

10(b) Neil Gow (1727–1807) celebrated Scots violinist and composer of dance music. Burns used many of Gow's airs for his songs; Raeburn painted his portrait.

11(a) Jesuit barks bark of the *Cinchona* tree, a source of quinine, introduced into Europe from the South American Jesuit missions.

11(a) saltpetre [...] glauber salts alkali salts, potassium nitrate and hydrated sodium sulphate, the latter a mild laxative named after the chemist Johann Rudolph Glauber (1604–70).

11(a) "she was te cood;" here as elsewhere Hogg follows a well-established literary tradition for representing Highland speech: voiced consonants are unvoiced ('c' for 'g', 'p' for 'b', 't' for 'd' and 'th', etc.), 'she' is an all-purpose (including first-person) pronoun, 'to be' is added to other verbs. While the first of these reflects Gaelic usage, the others are sheerly conventional. See Mairi Robinson, 'Modern Literary Scots: Fergusson and After', in *Lowland Scots: Papers Presented to an Edinburgh Conference*, ed. by A. J. Aiken, Association for Scottish Literary Studies Occasional Papers 2, (Edinburgh, 1973), pp. 38–55.

12(c) ye are unstable as water, and shall not excel see Genesis 49. 4.

12(d) lang hame grave: see Ecclesiastes 12. 4.

12(d) gray hairs [...] to the grave a phrase used of Jacob's anxiety for his son Benjamin in Genesis 42. 38, 44. 29.

13(b) a rowin' stane never gathers ony fog compare *ODEP*, p. 682: 'A rolling stone gathers no moss'.

13(b) better late thrive than never do weel a variant of the proverb 'better late than never' (*ODEP*, p. 54); see also p. 211.

14(a) Dunse or Duns, market town, about 12 miles west of Berwick.

14(a) Greenlaw Berwickshire county-town, 8 miles southwest of Duns.

14(b) the kail-wife o' Kelso if this is a local or proverbial person, I have not been able to identify her.

14(b) senny leaf senna, used as a purgative; the 'salts' are presumably glauber salts, a laxative (see note to 11 (a)).

16(a) 1s. 6d. per Scots pint the old Scots pint was equal to 3 Imperial (English) pints. Hogg recalled his grandfather selling smuggled French brandy to 'gentlemen and farmers' at 'the enormous rate of a shilling per bottle': *Shepherd's Calendar*, p. 106.

16(d) pregnant proofs the more frankly detailed account of Basil's intrigue with his housekeeper in 'Berwick-shire Farmer' concludes, 'My housekeeper grew nearly double her natural thickness about the waist' (*The Spy*, p. 33). Gillian Hughes notes 'that the tale was supposed in Hogg's lifetime to be based on his own experiences', in particular his years farming in Dumfriesshire between 1805 and 1810; Basil's housekeeper may have been based on Margaret Beattie, who bore Hogg an illegitimate daughter. Hughes cites a contemporary characterisation of 'Berwick-shire Farmer' as 'a *sketch* of [Hogg's] own life up to the time of his coming to Edinburgh—*and a more shameful and indecent paper was never laid so barefacedly before the public*': 'James Hogg and the "Bastard Brood"', *Studies in Hogg and his World* (hereafter *SHW*), 11 (2000), 56–68 (p. 60). Other witnesses commented on the exuberant hospitality at Locherben, Hogg's farm, in the period.

17(a) church anathemas denunciation before the congregation for fornication.

17(a) war was then raging in America in April 1775 fighting broke out between British forces and American colonial militias, leading to the colonists' Declaration of Independence the following year. 'Basil Lee' follows 'Berwick-shire Farmer' in having Basil take part in General John Burgoyne's (1722–92) disastrous invasion of upper New York in 1777. However, Hogg's expansion of the episode rearranges some of the historical chronology. Now Basil joins Burgoyne's earlier campaign to expel the Americans from Canada in the summer and autumn of 1776; he spends the winter in Philadelphia under the occupation of General Howe, brought forward one year from 1777–78; he joins Burgoyne again in the resumption of his campaign in the summer and autumn of 1777; after the British defeat at Saratoga he passes the winter in an American prison, and returns to Scotland in the spring of 1778.

17(b) lower Canada the future province of Québec. Rebel forces occupied Montreal in the autumn of 1775 and besieged Quebec city throughout the winter. The vanguard of the British relief force reached Quebec on 6 May 1776, followed a couple of weeks later by Burgoyne's army. Basil sets out to join one of the six regiments that had sailed from Cork in early April.

18(d) 'Pon my wort [...] attensions see the note on Highland speech to 11(a).

19(b) upper Canada the future province of Ontario. The administrative division between Upper and Lower Canada was not made until 1791.

24(b) nershe 'pehinds' in 1821.

24(d) St Maurice river flowing south into the St Laurence at Trois Rivières, between Quebec and Montreal, presumably the site referred to here. The British advance corps, under the command of Lieutenant-Colonel Simon Fraser (see note to 30(a)), established a base at Trois Rivières after a skirmish with the Americans (4 June), who retreated south to Fort Chambly.

24(d) Ensign Odogherty an in-joke; 'Ensign Morgan Odoherty' was a comic persona in a series of *Blackwood's* articles from February 1818; his friendship with Hogg is celebrated in 3 (April 1818), 51. In his *Memoir* Hogg identifies Thomas Hamilton (a retired Captain, author of *The Youth and Manhood of Cyril Thornton*, 1827) as 'the original O'Dogherty' (p. 78). From 1822 the persona became associated with William Maginn in the *Blackwood's* satirical series 'Noctes Ambrosianae'.

28(a) I bit my lip, and wrote upon the table with my finger an ironical allusion to John 8. 3–11. The scribes and Pharisees bring a woman taken in adultery before Jesus in the temple and invoke the Mosaic law that requires her punishment. 'But

Jesus stooped down, and with his finger wrote on the ground, as though he heard them not'. Eventually he answers: 'Let him who is without sin amongst you, cast the first stone'.

28(d) she must be forgiven according to the Lord's Prayer, Matthew 6. 14–15.

29(d) General Frazer's Simon Fraser (d. 1777), Lieutenant-Colonel of the 24th Foot, promoted to Brigadier-General on 9 June.

30(a) Colonel St Leger's Lieutenant-Colonel Barry St Leger (1737–89), better known for founding the eponymous horse-race than for his part in the American War.

30(a) Americans [...] approaching to Montreal in fact the Americans withdrew from Montreal before the advance of Burgoyne's army in mid-June.

30(c) Fort St John Burgoyne's army continued its advance to Lake Champlain in pursuit of the Americans. They had already evacuated Fort St John, on the Richelieu river just north of the lake, by the time the British got there. No such engagement as is described in the following pages took place until the following year, when Fraser caught up with American troops at Hubbardton, below Lake Champlain (see note to 48 (c)). The British took control of Lake Champlain in October 1776, and then retired to Canada for the winter.

33(d) river Champley the river is the Richelieu; perhaps there is some confusion with Fort Chambly, on the same river north of St John.

37(a) three succeeding years in defiance of the historical chronology, which puts Basil in an American prison one year later and sends him back to Scotland a few months after that.

38(d) their grotesque mistake Robert Chambers tells a similar story in *Traditions of Edinburgh*, 2 vols (Edinburgh: W. & C. Tait, 1825), II, 265.

39(d) *small clothes* (as the ladies now with great indelicacy term them) the term, for breeches, had become current since the event described–*OED* records it from 1796.

42(a) a verdict of *not proven* admissible in Scots but not English law.

42(c) *connoters* obsolete Scots term for notaries (*OED*).

42(d) The last winter [...] General Howe in Philadelphia General William Howe (1729–1814), commander in chief of the British army in North America from 1776, captured Philadelphia in September 1777; the British forces wintered there. Basil's chronology appears to skip forward a year and then back again, since a few pages later we find him at the battle of Saratoga (7 October 1777), after which he passes his 'last winter [...] in America' in captivity.

42(d) our irregularities 'During the winter of 1777–78, Philadelphia has been described as the scene of continual debaucheries and gaming'; General Howe 'gave tacit approval to a festive winter' to keep up his officers' morale: John W. Jackson, *With the British Army in Philadelphia* (San Rafael, CA: Presidio Press, 1979), p. 209.

43(b) green silk [...] gold colours worn by the Fairy Queen in Border tradition: compare 'Mary Burnet' in *Shepherd's Calendar*, pp. 210-11 and *Minstrelsy*, II, 245, 269.

47(d) our celebrated western campaign campaign to occupy the Hudson valley, thus isolating the New England colonies, June–October 1777. Once more Burgoyne marched his army down from Canada via Lake Champlain, with the object of meeting Howe's and St Leger's regiments at Albany, only to be beaten by the rebels at Saratoga.

48(a) American Indians Burgoyne brought 450 Algonquin, Abenakis and Hurons with him from lower Canada; 400 Ottawas joined him at Ticonderoga. Burgoyne exhorted his allies to spare women, children and old men, and take scalps only from dead enemies. Basil's allegations of Indian cruelty reflect contemporary accounts of the campaign, inflamed no doubt by panic and propaganda. The most notorious of the reported atrocities, the murder and scalping of Jane McCrea (27 July), may lie behind the following anecdote of the 'poor American girl'.

48(c) battle of Skensbury the Americans evacuated Ticonderoga (6 July 1777) and fell back to Skenesborough, with Burgoyne's army in hot pursuit. British and German troops under Simon Fraser and Major-General Adolf Friedrich von Riedesel engaged the American rearguard at Hubbardton on the following day. I have not seen any evidence that Indians were present at this particular conflict.

48(c) German auxiliaries Riedesel's support of Fraser's troops, who were severely outnumbered, gained the victory. About 3000 Hessians (2 brigades plus 1 battalion) and Brunswick dragoons took part in the campaign.

48(c) Their conduct [...] in St Leger's army in August 1777 St Leger laid siege to Fort Stanwix, in the Mohawk valley; heavy casualties and (premature) rumours of Burgoyne's defeat drove his Indian allies to mutiny and desert.

48(d) dreadful encounter on the 7th of October decisive defeat of Burgoyne's army at Bemis's Heights, Saratoga. Fraser was killed by a sharpshooter. Burgoyne surrended formally on 17 October.

48(d) Congress refused to ratify this i.e. the articles of the Convention of Saratoga, which would have allowed the defeated army to be sent home. Instead the prisoners were held in Boston, in squalid conditions. Burgoyne and several of his officers were permitted to return to Britain in 1778; Basil appears to have been one of the party.

49(b) straits of Bellisle northernmost opening of the St Lawrence into the Atlantic, between the Canadian mainland and Newfoundland.

49(b) Loch Rog [...] Isle of Lewis Hogg visited 'the extensive and dreary isle of Lewis' in the summer of 1803 (*Mountain Bard*, p. 94). His narrative of the tour takes him as far as Barvas on the west coast, a dozen miles north of Loch Roag ('Unpublished Letters of James Hogg, the Ettrick Shepherd', *Scottish Review*, 12 (July 1888), 1–66 (pp. 57–66)).

49(c) second sight Hogg replaces the ethnographic reportage of 'Berwick-shire Farmer' with a more sensational focus on supernatural phenomena. He does not refer to this kind of material in the narrative of his 1803 visit. In *Familiar Anecdotes of Sir Walter Scott* Hogg recalls Scott telling him: 'I assure you "it's no little that gars auld Donald pegh" but yon Lewis stories of your's frighted me so much that I could not sleep': *Anecdotes of Scott*, ed. by Jill Rubenstein (S/SC, 1999), pp. 55–56. (The quotation is from an earlier episode in 'Basil Lee', p. 11.) The second sight was a stock theme of Highland travel narratives at least since Martin Martin's *Description of the Western Islands of Scotland* (1716).

49(c) neither Highlanders nor Lowlanders descendants of Norse colonists are especially prevalent in the western parish of Uig.

49(d) Lord Seaforth the Mackenzie chief, the island's proprietor.

49(d) tall stones the most spectacular of the Neolithic monuments on Lewis, the constellation of standing stones at Callanish on the shore of E. Loch Roag, 13 miles west of Stornoway. In Hogg's day the megaliths, embedded in peat, reached as high as a man; in 1857 the peat was excavated to reveal their true height.

50(b) M'Torquille Dhu's Visit the Macleods of Lewis styled themselves *Siol Torcuill*, the race of Torquil. They ruled Lewis until 1597, when Torquil Dhu, the last Macleod chief of the island, was betrayed and put to death by Mackenzie of Kintail. The apparition in Hogg's story resembles a tradition of Callanish described by Otta F. Swire: 'when the sun rose on midsummer morning, "Something" came to the Stones, walking down the great avenue heralded by the cuckoo's call': she identifies that 'Something' with an archaic (pre-Celtic) figure called 'the Shining One': *The Outer Hebrides and their Legends* (Edinburgh: Oliver and Boyd, 1966), p. 24.

50(d) no other point [...] had been seen Hogg's interest in 'optical illusion', here and elsewhere in *WET*, is reminiscent of the work of his friend David Brewster (1781–

1868), who contributed articles on optics to early numbers of *Blackwood's* and (much later) wrote a book explaining supernatural phenomena in scientific terms; see note to 448(b). In 1816 Brewster invented the kaleidoscope, which 'requires *a particular position of the eye of the observer, and of the object looked at*, in order to do its effect': *Blackwood's*, 3 (May 1818), 331–37 (p. 335).

52(c) **mermaid** see Hogg's poem 'The Mermaid. A Scottish Ballad', in *Edinburgh Magazine*, 4 (May 1819), 400–01. The idea that mermaids are creatures of flesh and blood also appears in 'Mary Burnet' (*Shepherd's Calendar*, p. 205).

53(a) **the lands of *the Mackenzie*** the Mackenzies of Kintail took over Lewis in 1610–13; the direct male line ceased in 1815 and the island passed out of the family in the 1840s.

53(c) **water horse** or kelpie: see F. Marian McNeill, *The Silver Bough*, 4 vols (Glasgow: Maclellan, 1957–58), I, 124–27. Hogg's guide on his 1803 visit to Lewis refused to go near the banks of Loch Alladale for fear of 'the *Water-Horse*, of which he told me many wonderful stories' (*Mountain Bard*, p. 94).

53(c) **Loch Kios** Loch Keose or Cheois, a fresh-water loch separated by a narrow neck of land from Loch Eireasort, which is an arm of the sea; Hogg may be conflating the two lochs.

54(b) **Saint's Islands** the Flannan Isles or 'Seven Holy Isles'.

54(d) **taxman** or tacksman, a tenant (equivalent to the Irish middleman) who held land directly from the proprietor and leased it to sub-tenants, who comprised most of the population.

54(d) **the English language** *Statistical Account* confirms that Gaelic was the only language spoken in the parish of Uig, except by a few of the tacksmen (XX, 46).

54(d) **Malcolm Morison** on his 1803 visit Hogg hired a 'lad of Stornoway' called Malcolm as his guide and interpreter (*Mountain Bard*, p. 94; 'Unpublished Letters of James Hogg', p. 59).

55(c) **darkness scarcely visible** compare Milton, *Paradise Lost*, I, 63.

57(b) **the corpse was sitting upright in the bed** in *Minstrelsy of the Scottish Border* Scott tells a story illustrative of 'a singular superstition not yet altogether discredited in the wilder parts of Scotland', according to which a spirit will return to its recently evacuated body if the door of the room where the corpse is lying should be left ajar. A married couple lives in a remote Border cottage; one night the husband dies. 'In her confusion and alarm [the wife] accidentally left the door ajar, when the corpse suddenly started up and sat in the bed, frowning and grinning at her frightfully. She sat alone, crying bitterly, unable to avoid the fascination of the dead man's eye and too much terrified to break the sullen silence' ('Young Benjie', III, 251–52). Hogg may have transplanted a similar story to Lewis from Nithsdale. According to his note to 'The Wife of Crowle' in the 1821 edition of *The Mountain Bard*, 'The woman lived at Crowle Chapel in Nithsdale. It is now given at large in "The Winter Evening Tales"' (p. 201).

58(b) **Battaline** perhaps Baile Ailein, a 'straggling hamlet' near the head of Loch Eireasort.

58(c) **orgies** rites in worship of pagan gods.

60(b) **the invidious dale** i.e. 'deal'–the plank drawn across the bed by the old woman to keep her daughter safe from Basil during the night.

60(c) **country of the Grants** Strathspey, southeast of Inverness. Grants had been Sheriffs of Inverness from the 13th century.

60(d) **Lord Reay's cromachs** Lord Reay was hereditary chief of the clan Mackay in Strathnaver, northwest Sutherland. The phrase may carry an echo of Pharaoh's dream of the lean and fat kine in Genesis 41. 1–4, 17–21.

60(d) **misca' a Gordon on te raws o' Strathbogie** proverb: to speak ill of someone on their own ground. See also Hogg, *Tales of the Wars of Montrose*, ed. by Gillian Hughes

(S/SC, 1996), p. 45.

61(a) teil a pawpee to sheath in him's tanks the devil a penny to his credit.

61 (a) Fat te deil What the devil! (exclamation of annoyance or impatience).

61(c) Ferintosh 'the "Ferintosh" of Forbes of Culloden, which paid no duty, was sold cheap, and was so much drunk that "Ferintosh" became a synonym for whisky' in the Highlands—until 1784, when the duty-free privilege was revoked: *Social Life*, p. 529. See also Burns, 'Scotch Drink', ll. 109–14.

62(c) mak a speen or spill a guid horn make a spoon or spoil a good horn: proverbial for 'succeed in an enterprise or botch it'.

62(c) twafauld o'er a steeck i.e., doubled up over a [walking-]stick—as we read in the following paragraph.

62(c) burning Mountain device on the Grant family crest—the 'Grant's Arms'.

63(d) a scorbutic complaint scurvy, caused by vitamin C deficiency—a consequence of the months Basil has spent in prison and at sea.

64(a) Nicolson Street newest of the city's South Side developments.

65(b) Carrubber's Close off the High Street, next to what is now N. Bridge Street. Basil moves into the old city centre, which is losing caste as the quality migrate to the New Town. The Forum, the debating society to which Hogg belonged from 1811 to about 1814, met at St Andrews Chapel in Carruber's Close.

65(b) Argyle Square one of the first of the 18th-century developments (1742) south of the Cowgate, on the site now occupied by the Royal Museum of Scotland; still fashionable in the 1770s, although soon to be eclipsed by the new residential district under construction across the North Loch.

65(d)–66(a) caption of horning Hogg conflates two separate legal writs. A letter of horning charged the recipient to pay his debts on pain of being proclaimed a rebel ('put to the horn'); a caption was a warrant authorizing the seizure of person and property. The former often preceded the latter, as in 'Welldean Hall', p. 469.

66(b) "stately strode away." Michael Bruce, 'Sir James the Ross: An Historical Ballad' (1796), l. 92.

67(a) St James's Court one of the earliest of the New Town developments (1727), off the Lawnmarket (down from Castle Hill).

69(b) in the same light with a tailor allusion to the proverb, 'Nine tailors make a man' (*ODEP*, p. 567).

70(a) a consummation devoutly to be wished *Hamlet*, III. 1. 65–66.

73(b) flat and unprofitable *Hamlet*, I. 2. 133.

74(a–b) "The rainbow's lovely [...] ever shall remain." Hogg's own lines from *Mador of the Moor* (Edinburgh, 1816), Canto II, stanzas 6–7.

Adam Bell

Originally published in *The Spy*, No. 35 (27 April 1811), as 'Dangerous Consequences of the Love of Fame, when ill directed—Exemplified by the remarkable Story of Mr. Bell', pp. 349–54. The first one and a half paragraphs of 'Dangerous Consequences', 'substantially taken from No. 164 of Johnson's *Rambler*' (*The Spy*, p. 610), are omitted from *WET*; as is the penultimate paragraph, with its conjecture that 'some deep laid scheme of villainy' must account for the mystery. Otherwise the tale is reprinted without alteration.

Adam Bell was the name of an outlaw in the Border ballads: see Thomas Percy, *Reliques of Ancient English Poetry* (London: Dodsley, 1765), Book II: 'Adam Bell, Clym o' the Clough, and William of Cloudesly'. As several critics have observed, the moonlit duel anticipates the duel (also fought by moonlight on an Edinburgh green) in which Robert Wringhim kills his brother in *The Private Memoirs and Confessions of a Justified Sinner* (1824). The scene in *Confessions* may have inspired another fratricidal nocturnal duel—this time fought by candlelight rather than moonlight—in Robert Louis

Stevenson's *The Master of Ballantrae: A Winter's Tale* (1889). Stevenson develops the motif, suggested in 'Adam Bell', of a gentleman who mysteriously disappears after leaving his estate to take part in the 1745 campaign, as well as the detail of light dazzling the eyes of one of the combatants.

75(c) **autumn of 1745** Charles Edward Stuart raised his standard at Glenfinnan on 19 August.

76(a) **river Kinnel** descending from the Lowther hills to join the Annan near Lochmaben.

76(c) *wraith* [...] **long life** Compare *OED*, 'Wraith', 1. 'An apparition or spectre of a dead person'; b. 'An immaterial or spectral appearance of a living being, freq. regarded as portending that person's death'. Hogg records that his own wraith was seen during a serious illness (*Memoir*, p. 14).

76(d) **the very day** [...] **on Falkirk Moor** 17 January 1746—several months after 'the autumn of 1745', when Mr Bell is first supposed to have quitted his house.

76(d) **Duke of Cumberland** commander of the King's Army in Scotland. After Falkirk the Jacobite army retreated to Inverness, with Cumberland in pursuit.

77(a) **St Anthony's garden** grounds of the former hermitage of St Anthony, in the King's Park on the north slope of Arthur's Seat; I have found no reference to a formal 'garden' by that name. Compare Chapter 11 of Scott's *The Heart of Mid-Lothian* (1818): 'This sequestered dell, as well as other places of the open pasturage of the King's Park, was, about this time, often the resort of the gallants of the time who had affairs of honour to discuss with the sword'—ed. by Tony Inglis (Harmondsworth: Penguin, 1994), pp. 110–11. George Colwan goes 'by the back of St. Anthony's gardens' on his way up Arthur's Seat in *Confessions*, p. 28.

78(c) **the dead-room** also mentioned in *Confessions* as 'the dead-room in the old Guard-house' (p. 37). The headquarters of the Town Guard was a small building in the middle of the High Street, between the Luckenbooths (alongside St Giles) and the Tron; it was torn down to make way for construction of the South Bridge in 1785. I have not found any historical account of a dead-room there.

78(d) **that day** [...] **brought to light** the day of Judgement; compare I Corinthians 4. 5, 'until the Lord come, who [...] will bring to light the hidden things of darkness'.

79(a) **"Pluris est oculatus testis unus quam auriti decem."** 'one eye-witness is worth more than ten who give hearsay evidence': Plautus, *Truculentus*, II. 6.

Duncan Campbell

Originally published in *The Spy*, in two parts: 'History of the Life of Duncan Campbell, his difficulties, escapes, rencounter with a Ghost and other adventures', No. 49 (3 August 1811), pp. 485–92; 'History of Duncan Campbell, concluded', No. 51 (17 August 1811), pp. 504–13. Reprinted without substantive revision in *WET*. 'Duncan Campbell' was reprinted in chapbook form as late as 1840, and under the title 'Duncan and his Dog' in *The Schoolmaster*, 29 June 1833, pp. 409–15.

Hogg's tale has nothing to do with *The History of the Life and Adventures of Duncan Campbell* by Daniel Defoe (1720), narrating a celebrated case of second sight. Hogg owned a copy of this, but he seems to have acquired it after 1814: see Gordon Willis, 'Hogg's Personal Library: Holdings in Stirling University Library', *SHW*, 3 (1992), 87–88 (p. 88).

80(a) **Oscar** the son of Ossian; the success of *Fingal* (1761) and related poems by James Macpherson made the name popular.

81(b) **Grange Toll** on what is now Mayfield Road, Newington; Duncan is taking the trunk road south from the city (now the A7), towards Galashiels and Selkirk.

81(d) **Falkirk** one of the major towns for trading cattle in Scotland, with a weekly market on Thursdays, several fairs and three trysts every year; see *Statistical Account*, XIX, 83.

82(d) between Gala Water and Middleton Middleton Moor, in the Moorfoot hills, southern Midlothian.

84(b) Herriot Moor between the Lammermuir and Moorfoot hills.

84(d) Willenslee 'I once herded two years on a wild and bare farm called Willenslee, on the border of Mid-Lothian': *Shepherd's Calendar*, p. 96. Hogg worked there *circa* 1788–90; see also *Memoir*, p. 8, and *A Series of Lay Sermons*, ed. by Gillian Hughes (S/SC, 1997), p. 74.

85(d) Cowhaur Colquhar, about 5 miles south of Dewar and 5 miles east of Peebles.

86(c) the Maid of Plora, or the Pedlar of Thirlestane Mill Hogg cites the legend of a little girl abducted by the fairies and found in Plora Wood, near Traquair, as a source for his 'Kilmeny' (*Queen's Wake*, Note XV, pp. 345–46). For the ghost of the murdered pedlar at Thirlestane Mill see Hogg's ballad 'The Pedlar' (*Mountain Bard*, pp. 15–24).

88(c) the 45th chapter of Genesis in which Joseph, made governor of Egypt by the Pharaoh, reveals himself to his brothers. He loads them with gifts and they return to tell their father that he is alive.

88(d) the 19th chapter of the book of Judges a Levite and his concubine, lodging among the children of Benjamin in Gibeah, are attacked by 'certain sons of Belial', who rape the woman. The Levite takes her home, kills and dismembers her, and sends her body-parts 'into all the coasts of Israel' as a sign. The chapter concludes: 'consider of it, take advice, and speak your minds'. The 20th chapter recounts the ensuing war.

89(c) the 23d psalm as given in *The Psalms of David in Metre*, approved by the Church of Scotland in the 17th century, rather than in the King James bible. Hogg learnt most of the metrical psalms by heart in his youth: see *Memoir*, p. 7, and 'A Letter from Yarrow. The Scottish Psalmody Defended', *Edinburgh Literary Journal*, 13 March 1830, pp. 162–63.

90(a) the history of Samson [...] David and Goliath see Judges 13–16, I Samuel 17. Heroic adventures suitable for boyish consumption.

91(a) flocks of southern sheep [...] over the Grampian mountains Blackface moorland sheep began to be introduced into the Highlands in the second half of the 18th century; in the early 19th century some landlords attempted to bring in the Cheviot, which yielded better wool but was less adapted to rugged winter conditions. Hogg himself advocated stocking the Highlands with the hardier 'blackfaced Scottish breed' from the Border hills: *The Shepherd's Guide* (Edinburgh, 1807), p. 283.

91(b) *norlan' netties* *SND* and modern collections of Scottish proverbs cite Hogg's tale for the usage.

91(b) Glenellich's 'Glenegle' in *The Spy* (p. 507); as we find out on p. 93, on the west coast overlooking the Hebrides, no doubt in Argyllshire–Campbell country. Possibly Hogg changed the name to avoid confusion with Glenelg.

91(d) "She never told her love [...] Smiling at grief." *Twelfth Night*, II. 4. 110–15.

93(c) the north Highlands i.e., as opposed to the 'south Highlands', the Borders.

93(c) Deu-Caledonian Sea old name for the sea northwest of Scotland.

95(d) Misfortunes seldom come singly see *ODEP*, p. 535.

96(a) letters of horning see note to 65(d)–66 (a).

An Old Soldier's Tale

First published in the *Clydesdale Magazine*, 1 (July 1818), 106–12. Hogg had offered the tale to *Blackwood's Edinburgh Magazine*, which turned it down. See his letters to William Blackwood of 31 January and [June 1818] (NLS MS 4003, fols 87 and 93–94).

98(a) meal-pocks bags used by beggars to receive alms in the form of meal (*SND*, 'meal', 'mealie'); i.e., the old soldier is a beggar.

98(a) battle o' Culloden bloody defeat of Charles Edward Stuart's Jacobite army by British regiments under the command of the Duke of Cumberland, 16 April 1746.

98(b) Stuart o' Appin Stuart of Appin, the clan chieftain, was a minor, and stayed at home during the Jacobite campaign; the clansmen were led by his tutor, Charles Stewart of Ardshiel, who survived Culloden. See also Hogg's song, 'The Stuarts of Appin', *Songs by the Ettrick Shepherd* (Edinburgh, 1831), pp. 59–62.

98(c) Deephope near Ettrick Kirk and Thirlestane; Hogg's neighbourhood.

98(c) do [...] done to a reference to the Golden Rule in Matthew 7.12.

98(d) an old song Hogg quotes the following lines as 'Fragment, no. III' (air: 'Cowdenknowes') in an appendix, 'Whig Songs', in *Jacobite Relics of Scotland*, Second Series (Edinburgh, 1821), p. 479.

99(a) Johnny Cope famous Jacobite song celebrating the rout of government forces led by Sir John Cope at Prestonpans, 21 September 1745. See *Jacobite Relics of Scotland*, Second Series (Edinburgh, 1821), pp. 111–13.

99(a) forty sax [...] strappit like a herring hung up, like fish to be smoked or roasted (*SND* 'strap', 3). Government soldiers wantonly killed civilians as well as combatants in the pacification of the Highlands that followed Culloden. See Hogg's later treatment in 'Peril Third' of *The Three Perils of Woman: Love, Leasing and Jealousy* (1823).

99(b) until the return of spring Cumberland entered Aberdeen on 27 February and remained there until 8 April, when he marched to attack the Jacobite headquarters at Inverness. He encountered the enemy at Culloden on the way there.

99(b) Royals the Royal Scots regiment.

99(b) Campbells the clan Campbell fought on the side of government in 1715 and 1745.

99(c) the Don [...] Bridge-end in March 'the outposts of the principal armies were extended along the river Spey': Sir Walter Scott, *Tales of a Grandfather: Being Stories from the History of Scotland*, Third Series, 3 vols (Edinburgh: Cadell, 1830), III, 207.

99(d) the country of the Grants, and Brae-Mar i.e. on both sides of the Spey. The Grants supported the government in the 1715 and 1745 risings. Hogg's 'The Adventures of Colonel Peter Aston' takes place in the area, which he had visited in 1802; see *Tales of the Wars of Montrose*, ed. by Gillian Hughes (S/SC, 1996), pp. 99–137.

99(d) John Roy Stuart [...] Keith 'The Highlanders had rather the advantage in this irregular sort of warfare, and in particular, a party of a hundred regulars were surprised at the village of Keith, and entirely slain or made prisoners by John Roy Stewart' (Scott, *Tales of a Grandfather*, III, 208). Stuart, a renegade Hanoverian officer who had fought on the French side against the British at Fontenoy, was one of the most formidable of the Jacobite commanders. His Edinburgh Regiment fought alongside the Maclachlans and the Macleans at Culloden.

101(b) Corgarf and Brae-Mar on the rivers Don and Dee respectively.

101(c) Farquharsons or Mackintoshes the Farquharsons are a sept of the Mackintoshes. Aeneas Mackintosh, the clan chief, was loyal to government, but his wife Anne, an ardent Jacobite, raised the clan against Hanoverian troops during his absence on service in February 1745. See Hogg's treatment of the incident in *The Three Perils of Woman* (S/SC, 1995), pp. 299–332.

103(b) 'Cresorst, cresorst' phonetic rendition of the Gaelic *greas ort*, 'hurry up'.

104(a) Tamantoul Tomintoul. Hogg visited the area on his 1802 Highland tour: see 'The Unpublished Conclusion of James Hogg's 1802 Highland Journey', ed. by Hans de Groot, *SHW*, 6 (1995), 55–66 (pp. 55, 61).

104(b) lennoch more Gaelic *leanabh mor*, 'great child' (*SND*, 'lennochmore').

106(d) 'Gin ye be for the cock to craw, \ Gie him a nievfu' groats, dearie.'" not traced.

Highland Adventures
First published in *The Spy*, in two parts: 'Malise's Journey to the Trossacks', No. 40 (1 June 1811), pp. 397–402; 'Malise's Tour through the Trossacks and Mountains of Bredalbine, concluded', No. 44 (29 June 1811), pp. 437–43. Hogg's satire on the vogue for Highland tourism inspired by *The Lady of the Lake* was no longer quite so fresh as it had been when it first appeared, one year (and nine editions) after the publication of Scott's poem in May 1810. Scott had recently published a yet more sensationally popular Highland romance, *Rob Roy*, in 1818.

107(a) Motto Scott, *The Lady of the Lake*, Canto I, xii, ll. 23–34.

107(a) Loch Ketturin [...] modern classic ground Loch Katrine and the Trossachs, the principal setting of *The Lady of the Lake*. Although lovers of the picturesque had been coming to the Trossachs since the late 18th century, Scott's poem turned the area into one of the most heavily visited tourist sites in Britain.

107(b) old chieftain of M'Nab Francis Macnab (1734–1816), 16th Chief of Macnab. A character. He sired 32 children, although he never married, and his whisky was at one time reputed to be the best in Scotland. Raeburn painted him posing flamboyantly in the uniform of the Royal Breadalbane Volunteers. Macnab died in debt at Callander, where Hogg ate breakfast with him on his 1803 Highland tour: see 'Unpublished Letters of James Hogg, The Ettrick Shepherd', *Scottish Review*, 12 (July 1888), 1–66 (p. 3).

107(d) Roderick Dhu the warlike Highland chief in Scott's poem. For the 'rencounter between Fitz-James and Roderick' see Canto V, xii–xvii. Fitz-James, the disguised King James V, has his men carry the wounded Roderick Dhu to Stirling, where he later dies.

108(b) Mr Scott's other poems [...] the bounds of probability in 1811 Scott's other poems were *The Lay of the Last Minstrel* (1805) and *Marmion* (1808). The former features a 'goblin page' and a magic book retrieved from a wizard's tomb; the latter features a nun walled up alive, ghostly portents, characters in disguise, and other Gothic devices.

108(d) Ben-Ledi, (the hill of God) 'contracted for *Ben-le-dia, the Hill of God*': *Statistical Account*, XI, 580.

108(d) the muster place of the Clan-Alpine see *The Lady of the Lake*, V, xii, l. 5.

109(c) Mr Burrel Gillian Hughes cites a reference to the Hon. Mr Drummond Burrel, a local landowner, in a contemporary guide to the Trossachs: [Margaret Oswald], *A Sketch of the Most Remarkable Scenery near Callander of Mentieth* (Stirling, 1815), p. 26 (*The Spy*, p. 616).

109(c) goblin of Correi-Uriskin for Coir-nan-Uriskin ('Goblin-cave') and 'the *Urisk* [...] a figure between a goat and a man', see Scott's note 41 to *The Lady of the Lake* (Gaelic *uruisg*, a water-goblin).

110(d) Mr Stuart the guide's house 'James Stuart in the nearest house of Ardkenknockan [...] has engaged to attend strangers, to provide them with a boat, to explore both sides of Loch Catherine, to point out the most remarkable places and tell their names, and to gratify the inquisitive with every information': [Margaret Oswald], *A Sketch of the Most Remarkable Scenery near Callander of Mentieth* (Stirling, 1815), pp. 17–18 (cited in *The Spy*, p. 617).

111(a) I traced every ravin [...] valley of Shinar compare *The Lady of the Lake* I, xi, ll. 7–14:

> Where twined the path in shadow hid,
> Round many a rocky pyramid,
> Shooting abruptly from the dell
> Its thunder-splinter'd pinnacle;
> Round many an insulated mass,

The native bulwarks of the pass,
Huge as the tower which builders vain
Presumptuous piled on Shinar's plain.

The tower (Hogg's 'ancient pile') is the tower of Babel: see Genesis 11. 1–9.

111(b) 11th, 12th, and 13th divisions of the first canto describing the 'wondrous wild' mountain scenery discovered by King James.

111(b) "without a drappie in his noodle;" unidentified. Hughes suggests a 'vague reminiscence' of Robert Burns, 'Tam o' Shanter', l. 109 (*The Spy*, p. 617); perhaps also of Burns's song, 'Willie brew'd a peck o' maut', l. 6: 'But just a drappie in our e'e'.

111(c) Craig of Glen-Whargen in Nithsdale 482m above sea-level, according to the Ordnance Survey (*The Spy*, p. 617).

112(b) "Which bearing [...] lonely isle." *The Lady of the Lake*, II, xvi, ll. 5–6.

112(c) "Roderick Vich Alpine Dhu, ho eiro," refrain to the 'Boat Song', *The Lady of the Lake*, II, xix–xx.

112(c–d) One burnish'd sheet [...] enchanted land *The Lady of the Lake*, I, xiv, ll. 9–16.

112(d) hereditary Prince of Orange no doubt, as Hughes suggests (*The Spy*, p. 620), the son of the exiled William VI, Prince of Orange, who became William I of the Netherlands after the defeat of Napoleon. His son settled in England and attended Oxford university; no evidence has come to light that he visited the Trossachs in the summer of 1810.

113(d) *Trossacks* [...] rough or shaggy place 'said to be [Gaelic] for "bristled territory"': James Johnston, *Place-Names in Scotland* (Edinburgh, 1892), p. 239; but from *Na Trosaichean*, 'the cross-hills', according to more recent scholarship; see W. F. H. Nicolaisen, *Scottish Place Names: Their Study and Significance* (London: Batsford, 1976), p. 55.

114(a) *Loch of the Gate of Hell* '[Gaelic] *eath*, "the battle", or as prob. *ceatharch*, "the mist, fog", *urrin* or *uitharn*, "of hell"': Johnston, *Place-Names in Scotland* (p. 142). More recent scholarship derives the name from *ceathairne* ('cateran', bandit).

114(a) Correi Uriskin [...] *Brownie's Clough* see note to 109(c).

114(a) no appearance of any bower i.e. of Ellen's bower in *The Lady of the Lake*, I, xxvi.

114(b) gazoon a word of Hogg's own coinage, according to *OED*, from 'gazon', a wedge-shaped piece of turf used in fortification.

115(c) "down Strath-Gartney's valley broad," *The Lady of the Lake*, III, xxiv, l. 14. Scott's rider goes as far as Lochs Voil and Doine; the Balvaig flows out of the eastern end of Loch Voil into Loch Lubnaig, down Strathyre. This would be the likely southern route taken by a rider, as Malise suggests; the descent along Strathgartney, on the northern bank of Loch Katrine, would require a considerable detour westward.

115(c) my kinsman Malise, and young Angus Roderick Dhu charges his henchman Malise with bearing the fiery cross: *Lady of the Lake*, III, xii: 'my kinsman' since 'Malise' was the supposed author of the version of 'Highland Adventures' first published in *The Spy*. 'Angus, the heir of Duncan's line' receives the cross from Malise and rides to the clan muster, *Lady of the Lake*, III, xviii–xix.

116(a) Forum reasoning another allusion that had lost some of its topical freshness by 1820. Hogg was a member of the Edinburgh Forum, a debating club, from 1811 until around 1814. See *Memoir*, pp. 23–24, and Gillian Hughes, 'James Hogg and the Forum', *SHW*, 1 (1990), 57–70.

116(d) Ben More [...] the third according to *The Times Atlas of the World* (New York, 1990) Ben Lawers is 1214, Ben More 1171, and Ben Lui 1130 metres above sea-level.

117(a) much higher three of the peaks southwest of Cairn Gorm (1245m) are indeed higher: Braeriach (1295m), Cairn Toul (1293m), Ben Macdui (1309m).

117(b) Glen-Avin [...] terror and superstition Hogg visited the area in 1802; see 'The Unpublished Conclusion of James Hogg's 1802 Highland Journey', ed. by H. B. de Groot, *SHW*, 6 (1995), 56–57, and Hogg's note V, 'Glen-Avin', in *The Queen's Wake*: 'My mind, during the whole day, experienced the same sort of sensation as if I had been in a dream; and on returning from the excursion, I did not wonder at the superstition of the neighbouring inhabitants, who believe it to be the summer haunt of innumerable tribes of fairies' (p. 334).

117(footnote) Dr Skene James Skene of Rubislaw (1775–1864), advocate, geologist and antiquary, close friend of Sir Walter Scott. Skene was a member of the Geological Society, London, and the Royal Society of Edinburgh, contributing to their 'Transactions'.

118(a) "As ever ye saw the rain down fa', \ Or yet the arrow gae frae the bow." from the ballad 'The Battle of Bothwell Bridge' (*Minstrelsy*, III, 222); the lines also appear in one of Nanny's songs in Chapter 5 of Hogg's *The Brownie of Bodsbeck* of 1818–see Douglas S. Mack's edition (Edinburgh: Scottish Academic Press, 1976), p. 44.

118(c) Bovain [...] the house of Robert M'Nab, Esq. unidentified. Bovain is about seven miles northeast of Ben More in Glen Dochart, near the southwestern end of Loch Tay.

Halbert of Lyne

An earlier version of this poem appeared as 'Introductory Tale: John of Manor' in R. P. Gillies, *Illustrations of a Poetical Character* (Edinburgh: Alexander Jameson, 1816), pp. 1–31. David Groves records a British Library copy, inscribed by Gillies, which carries a holograph note to the poem: 'supplied by a friend of the Author' (James Hogg, *Selected Poems and Songs*, ed. by David Groves (Edinburgh: Scottish Academic Press, 1986), pp. 215–16.) The 'Introductory Tale' is preceded by a 'Dedicatory Sonnet to James Hogg, Author of the "Queen's Wake," &c. &c. &c.' Gillies remained a lifelong friend of Hogg, and referred to him–without supplying any details–as 'my good old collaborator the Ettrick Shepherd', in *Memoirs of a Literary Veteran*, 3 vols (London: Bentley, 1851), III, 52. It is possible that 'John of Manor' is the fruit of their collaboration. *Illustrations of a Poetical Character* was printed by James Ballantyne. In *Familiar Anecdotes of Sir Walter Scott*, Hogg recalls Scott telling him about a new poem by Gillies that Ballantyne has been reading. Ballantyne thinks the poem is far better than Gillies's usual work. Scott agrees: 'The only thing that I can say [...] is that the former part of the poem is very like the writing of an eunuch and the latter part like that of a man. The stile is altogether unknown to me but Mr Gillies's it cannot be'[.] Hogg interjects: '(I was sorry I durst not inform him it was mine for it had been previously agreed between Mr Gillies and me that no one should know. It was a blank verse poem but I have entirely forgot what it is about. The latter half only was mine)' (*Anecdotes of Scott*, ed. by Jill Rubenstein (S/SC, 1999), p. 62). Scott's phrase 'the writing of an eunuch' echoes lines 13–20 of the present poem. If 'John of Manor' was indeed the 'blank verse poem' on which Gillies and Hogg collaborated, and which Hogg reclaimed in *WET*, this evidence would suggest that Gillies provided the introductory frame (lines 1–99) and Hogg all or most of the narrative; although several lines in the frame appear to allude to or echo writings by Hogg (see notes to p. 120).

In addition to minor lexical variants, 'John of Manor' includes a ten-line passage omitted from 'Halbert of Lyne' (see below). Lyne and Manor are parishes a few miles to the west and southwest of Peebles.

119(1) Horatio generic name for an interlocutor, after the friend of the hero in *Hamlet*. David Groves suggests an allusion to Horace, often cited by Hogg as the model of an urbane satiric style: Hogg, *Selected Poems and Songs*, ed. by David Groves, p. 216.

119(13) A man of woman born compare *Macbeth*, IV. 1. 96 etc.

119(15) blue-stocking (usually hostile) term for a literary or intellectual woman, after Elizabeth Montagu's 'Blue Stocking' assemblies in the 1750s.

120(59–60) The fairy's raide [...] the mountain and the mist topics associated with Hogg's *The Queen's Wake*, especially 'Kilmeny', 'The Witch of Fife', 'Glen-Avin', and 'Old David'.

120(67–72) The first word critical [...] where it may end? compare *Memoir*, p. 25: 'The first report of any work that goes abroad, be it good or bad, spreads like fire set to a hill of heather in a warm spring day, and no one knows where it will stop'.

121(89) old Saint Giles St Giles' Cathedral, on the High Street in Edinburgh.

121(100) There was a time perhaps a reminiscence of the opening lines of Wordsworth's 'Ode: Intimations of Immortality' (1807).

121(104) the same plain meal Hogg discusses the passing of communal meals of this kind in 'On the Changes in the Habits, Amusements and Condition of the Scottish Peasantry', *Quarterly Journal of Agriculture*, 3 (1831–32), 256–63; reprinted in *A Shepherd's Delight: A James Hogg Anthology*, ed. by Judy Steel (Edinburgh: Canongate, 1985), pp. 40–51 (pp. 43–44).

124(210) the sweet air of *Bonny Ann* the song's first stanza is as follows:

> I doutna whiles but I could wale
> A lass wi' mair o' gowd an' lan';
> But no a lass in a' the vale
> I lo'e sae weel as bonnie Ann.
>
> (Alexander Whitelaw, *The Book of Scottish Song* (Glasgow: Blackie, 1867), p. 420.)

124(220) Across the moor to Manor possible echo of the ribald old courting song, 'O'er the Muir to Maggie'; see David Groves's notes on 'The Mistakes of a Night', in Hogg, *Selected Poems and Songs*, p. 209.

125(244) Boston, and Ralph Erskine celebrated Presbyterian clergymen and devotional authors. Thomas Boston (1676–1732), minister of Ettrick, was best known for *Human Nature in its Fourfold State* (1720), Ralph Erskine (1685–1752) for his *Gospel Sonnets* (1726). Both promoted the Calvinist doctrine of salvation by faith rather than by good works.

128(364) turned back again 'John of Manor' inserts ellipses after this line, and a footnote: 'This poem being merely an experiment in a certain species of writing, and widely different from the general descriptions of nature in which the author delights, he has cancelled 100 pages here: they were chiefly descriptive of Halbert's dilemma, and his various courtships with the fair sisters' (p. 26).

129(413) AND THOSE LEAST DANGEROUS several lines from 'John of Manor' are omitted here:

> AND THOSE LEAST DANGEROUS.–Poets all
> Have their main hobby–Byron has his Giaour,
> His gloomy, dark, revengeful ruffian;
> Scott his wild chieftain; Crabbe his mendicant;
> Wordsworth his pedlar sage; Coleridge his dream;
> Campbell his sentiment; Southey the cross;
> Hogg has his witch and fairy of the hill;
> Wilson his ship, sailing by still moonlight;
> And I my poor heart-broken sufferer,
> Too little pitied and too little known! (p. 30)

The references are to Byron's *The Giaour* (1813), Scott's *The Lady of the Lake* (1810), Crabbe's *The Borough* (Letter XXI, 'Abel Keene'; 1810), Wordsworth's *The Excursion* (Book I, 'The Wanderer'; 1814), Coleridge's *Christabel; Kubla Khan, a Vision;*

The Pains of Sleep (1816), Campbell's *The Pleasures of Hope* (1799, 1803), Southey's *Roderick, The Last of the Goths* (1814), Hogg's *The Queen's Wake* (1813), and Wilson's *The Isle of Palms* (1812). If Gillies is co-author, 'my poor broken-hearted sufferer' may refer to his *Childe Alarique: A Poet's Reverie* (1812).

The Long Pack

'The Long Pack' relates a tradition associated with Lee Hall, the home of the Ridley family, on the banks of the North Tyne south of Bellingham, Northumberland. The churchyard of St Cuthbert's at Bellingham is supposed to contain a long stone, shaped like a pedlar's pack and bearing carved images of pistols, cutlass and a silver whistle, which marks the grave of the mysterious robber; for a photograph see Robert Langley, *Walking the Scottish Border* (London: Hale, 1976), between pp. 48–49. According to Roger Leitch, 'Hogg, Pedlars, and the Tale of "The Long Pack"', *SHW*, 12 (2001), 139–42, no printed sources for the tradition have turned up in the Local Studies Department of the Newcastle City Library (p. 141), so it is not clear whether Hogg originated the tale or collected it from local tradition on his visits in the area. Published in British miscellanies as early as 1809, 'The Long Pack' enjoyed great popularity in the United States, where it was often reprinted, as well as in northern England and Lowland Scotland, where numerous chapbook editions appeared throughout the first half of the nineteenth century. Hogg's manuscript of the tale, which survives at the Houghton Library, Harvard University, corresponds with the earliest known printed version in a London magazine of 1809, where it appeared under the title of 'The Dead Shot, A Tale. By the Ettrick Shepherd'–see *Sporting Magazine*, 34 (September 1809), 261–64, and 35 (October 1809), 17–21. Different in several respects from the version published in *WET*, the text of the manuscript is reprinted in an appendix to this volume, with an account of the early magazine and chapbook versions.

'The Long Pack' continued to circulate long after Hogg's death. By the 1840s it had become naturalised north of the Border as 'A Scottish Story, by the Ettrick Shepherd'–see *The Long Pack; or, The Robbers Discovered* (Glasgow: printed for the booksellers, [*c.* 1840]). Elizabeth Gaskell inserts a memorable variant in *Cranford* (1853):

> One of the stories that haunted me for a long time afterwards, was of a girl, who was left in charge of a great house in Cumberland, on some particular fair-day, when the other servants all went off to the gaieties. The family were away in London, and a pedlar came by, and asked to leave his large and heavy pack in the kitchen, saying, he would call for it again at night; and the girl (a game-keeper's daughter) roaming about in search of amusement, chanced to hit upon a gun hanging up in the hall, and took it down to look at the chasing; and it went off through the open kitchen door, hit the pack, and a slow dark thread of blood came oozing out. ((Oxford: Oxford University Press, 1972), p. 92)

The chapbook version was collected by the antiquarian Joseph Crawhall in *Old Tayles Newlye Relayted* (London: Leadenhall Press, 1883), and reprinted at least twice in the next century. *The Long Pack: A Grim Story of Two Centuries Ago. A North Tyne Tragedy* (Hexham: J. Catherall, [*c.* 1950?]) has photographs of the supposed scene of the 'tragedy' and of the gravestone in Bellingham Churchyard. *The Long Pack: A Northumbrian Tale about two hundred and sixty years old* (Newcastle Upon Tyne: Frank Graham, 1968) is reprinted from Crawhall, with illustrations by Frank Varty.

132(d) a horse's hair will turn an eel for the popular belief that a horse's hair, if left in water for nine days, would turn into an eel, see E. Cobham Brewer, *Dictionary of Phrase and Fable* (London, 1894), p. 570.

133(a) ocular proof *Othello*, III. 3. 365.

133(b) *Copenhagen* Gillian Hughes has suggested that this is an anachronistic allusion, as in the name of the Duke of Wellington's horse, to the Copenhagen expedition of 1807.

133(d) in the multitude of counsellors there is safety Proverbs 11. 14.

139(d) Fontenoy battle at which the French defeated the British and their allies in the War of the Austrian Succession in 1745.

A Peasant's Funeral

First published in *The Spy* as 'Description of a Peasant's Funeral, by John Miller', No. 12 (17 November 1810), pp. 122–26. John Miller was the pseudonym for Hogg's shepherd persona in *The Spy*. It is reprinted in *WET* without substantial variants.

141(a) George Mouncie unidentified, although this is a Nithsdale name—Allan Cunningham's brother, Thomas Mouncey Cunningham, was a contributor to Hogg's *The Forest Minstrel* (Edinburgh: Constable, 1810).

141(c) patronage one of the principal bones of contention in church government in 18th-century Scotland. The abolition of patronage in 1690 gave Presbyterian congregations the right to accept or reject candidates for the ministry nominated by the heritors (chief landowners) and elders of the parish. In 1712 a parliamentary act restored lay patronage, allowing landlords to appoint ministers.

142(a) despised and rejected Isaiah 53. 3.

142(a) bruised reeds compare II Kings 18. 21.

142(a) the braid way 'broad is the way, that leadeth to destruction': Matthew 7. 13.

143(b) feeds the young ravens 'He giveth to the beast his food, and to the young ravens which cry': Psalm 147. 9.

Dreadful Story of Macpherson

First published in *The Spy* as 'Dreadful Story of Major Macpherson', No. 13 (24 November 1810), pp. 135–38, and based on an incident reported ten years earlier: 'Major Macpherson of Lorick, and four other gentlemen, unfortunately perished in a storm of snow, when on a shooting party on the Duke of Gordon's grounds in Badenoch.' (*Scots Magazine*, 62 (January 1800), 71.) At Gaick, in the mountains above Dalnacardoch, an avalanche destroyed the stone hut in which retired Captain John Macpherson and his party were sheltering. Hogg seems to have got the story from an oral informant, possibly on his 1802 Highland tour, which took him to the region; see Roger Leitch, 'Hogg, Scott and the Gaick Catastrophe', *SHW*, 1 (1990), 126–28. Scott recounts the story (with variants) in 'On the Supernatural in Fictitious Composition; and particularly on the Works of Ernest Theodore William Hoffmann', *Foreign Quarterly Review*, 1 (1827), 60–98; he gives his source as 'a letter [...] from an amiable and accomplished nobleman some time deceased'. Hogg adapts the tale in Canto I of *Mador of the Moor* (1816).

145(b) the year 1805–6 the accident occurred in the first week of January 1800.

146(c) "I cannot tell [...] 'twas said to me." Scott, *The Lay of the Last Minstrel*, II, xxii, ll. 15–16.

Story of Two Highlanders

First published in *The Spy* as 'Amusing Story of Two Highlanders', No. 17 (22 December 1810), pp. 178–81. Reprinted in *WET* without revision. The tale reappeared in *Johnstone's Edinburgh Magazine* (successor to *The Schoolmaster*), 1 (1833–34), 60, under the title 'The Highlanders and the Boar'.

148(a) the Albany River in Upper Canada (present-day Ontario). Wild swine are not native to the region.

Maria's Tale, Written by herself

First published in *The Spy* as 'Affecting Narrative of a Country Girl–Reflections on the Evils of Seduction', No. 22 (26 January 1811), pp. 223–30. Reprinted in *WET* without revision.

151(d) who never slumbers nor sleeps Compare Psalm 121. 4, in the Church of Scotland metrical version: 'Behold he that keeps Israel, \ he slumbers not, nor sleeps'.

155(a) that satisfaction which the church would demand she would have been obliged to appear before the session and name the father, who would then be summoned in his turn. If he denied the charge the session would investigate the matter further, calling witnesses and gathering evidence. During the service offenders were made to stand on a stool or platform in front of the pulpit and the congregation, wearing a cloak of sackcloth, where they would be rebuked by the minister until he was satisfied of their penitence. This humiliating ritual could last for up to half a year. See *Social Life*, pp. 321–23.

Singular Dream From a Correspondent

First published in *The Spy* as 'Evil Speaking Ridiculed by an Allegorical Dream, &c.– Its Injurious Tendency–Character of Adam Bryden', No. 48 (27 July 1811), pp. 475– 81. Reprinted in *WET* with minor revisions, i.e. the removal of some (but not all) of the traces of original publication, notably the epistolary frame and apostrophes to 'Mr Spy'. In copies of *The Spy* later marked up by him, Hogg attributed a share of authorship to his friend John Gray: see *The Spy*, pp. 624–25. *WET* retains the signature 'J.G.'

159(b) we were fellow collegians one of several signals that the narrator is not the Ettrick Shepherd, but a man with a university education–like the 'Editor' of *The Private Memoirs and Confessions of a Justified Sinner* (*Confessions*, p. 169 and notes).

160(a) upon their watch-towers [...] their lamps trimmed a blend of scriptural motifs enjoining preparedness in a time of impending crisis: compare Isaiah 21. 8, 'I stand continually upon the watchtower'; Matthew 25. 7, 'those virgins arose, and trimmed their lamps'. During the French revolutionary and Napoleonic wars beacons were kept ready around the British coast to be ignited as a warning of invasion.

160(b) O! that we were wise, that we understood this! Deuteronomy 32. 29: 'O that they were wise, that they understood this, that they would consider their latter end!'

160(b) The end of all things [...] was at hand I Peter. 4. 7.

160(c) wine-bibbers, and friends of publicans and sinners compare the Pharisees' accusations against Jesus in Luke 7. 34.

160(d) the *boar* that from the *forest* [...] meaning you compare Psalm 80.13 in the Scottish metrical version: 'The boar who from the forest comes \ doth waste it at his pleasure'. A teasing allusion to the identity of *The Spy*'s anonymous editor, Mr Hogg from Ettrick Forest. A 'hogg' is a yearling sheep, not a pig.

161(a) Burns says in 'The Twa Dogs. A Tale', Burns actually says, 'They're a' rundeils an' jads the gither' (l. 222).

161(a) *mulier quæ sola cogitat, male cogitat* 'the woman who thinks on her own, thinks badly': Publilius Syrus, *Sententiae* (reading 'mulier cum sola [...]').

161(c) an old Scotch proverb not traced.

161(d) our daughters are haughty [...] *tripping* with their feet paraphrase of Isaiah 3. 16 (reading 'tinkling' for 'tripping'). As Hughes notes (*The Spy*, p. 625) Hogg recurs to this text in No. 2, 'Young Women', of his *Lay Sermons*.

162(c) "resist the devil, and he will fly from you" James 4. 7.

163(c) your Book of Tales 'your excellent paper' in *The Spy*, p. 479.

163(c) Mr A. T. Philosopher, and teacher of the science of chance unidentified–if he is a historical person.

164(c) "Let no such men be trusted." *Merchant of Venice*, V. 1. 88.

164(c–d) We can form our opinions [...] quickly be corrupt the paragraph is adapted from Samuel Johnson, *The Rambler*, No. 79. Elsewhere Hogg omits these derivative passages in *The Spy* from *WET.*

164(d) Adam Bryden this seems to be a more serious person than Hogg's old crony Adam Bryden of Aberlosk, featured later in 'The Shepherd's Calendar'—unless the identification is a joke.

165(c) precepts left us by our great Lawgiver e.g. 'Judge not, that ye be not judged', Matthew 7. 1.

Love Adventures of Mr George Cochrane

First published, in part, in *The Spy* as 'Misery of an Old Batchelor—Happiness of the Married State—Two Stories of Love and Courtship', No. 16 (15 December 1810), pp. 165–71. Hogg substantially extended 'Misery of an Old Batchelor', which relates only the first of George's adventures and the first night of his second, for *WET.* Hogg wrote: 'Those who desire to peruse my youthful love adventures will find some of the best of them in those of "George Cochrane"' (*Memoir*, p. 54). The tale is set in Dumfriesshire around Annandale and Eskdale, with a possible excursion into Liddesdale. Hogg farmed in Annandale in 1807–10. The Eskdale setting, with its familiar names (Laidlaw, Hogg) and rough sporting contests in wild surroundings, is reminiscent of Hogg's anecdotes about his maternal grandfather, William Laidlaw; see *Shepherd's Calendar*, pp. 103–17.

166(a) Motto unidentified. Gillian Hughes suggests Richelieu, but has not traced the source. 'Without women, the two extremities of life would be without succour, and the middle without pleasure'.

166(d) Horace says *Satires*, 1. 1. 69–70. 'Change the name and the tale is told about you'.

168(d) *The Vicar of Wakefield* by Oliver Goldsmith (1766). The classic sentimental novel of rural innocence. The scene of amorous reading is conventional; for an early instance see *Inferno*, V. 127–38, in which Francesca tells Dante of her fall into adultery when she and her lover read the romance of Lancelot and Guinevere together. By casting *The Vicar of Wakefield* as the seducing text Hogg makes fun of the censorious theme of books inspiring illicit passion.

171(a) courted by night compare *The Brownie of Bodsbeck*, ed. by Douglas S. Mack (Edinburgh, 1976), p. 5; also 'The Cameronian Preacher's Tale' in James Hogg, *Selected Stories and Sketches*, ed. by Douglas S. Mack (Edinburgh: Scottish Academic Press, 1982), pp. 110–11.

172(c) *Johnny Cope* see note to 99(a).

173(d) marks of her impatience the first version of 'Love Adventures', 'Misery of an Old Batchelor', ends here.

174(b) *Lockerbie fair* held twice a year, at Lammas and Michaelmas. The sale of lambs for the English market took place at Lammas, on 2 August or (if the date fell on a Saturday, Sunday or Monday) the following Tuesday. George's reference to the goodman's obligation to stay out all night hints at the drinking bouts that were customary after the conclusion of business (compare Burns's 'Tam o' Shanter').

175(a) as a devout heathen [...] rising of the sun compare Hogg's treatment of pagan sun worship in *Queen Hynde* (S/SC, 1998), p. 82, ll. 1025–29, and note, p. 264.

175(c) several love verses Hogg no doubt recalls some of his own youthful effusions; see note to 217(a).

176(a–b) The sun stood still [...] the rest of the world see Joshua 10. 12–13, in which God makes the sun and moon stand still while the Israelites slaughter the Amorites—a passage cited in theological arguments about miracles. The rest of the paragraph recalls Rosalind's famous disquisition on the subjectivity of time in *As*

You Like It, III. 2. 296–324.

176(d) awa wi' his tail atween his legs like Macmillan's messan unidentified allusion, although apparently to the famous Cameronian minister John Macmillan (1670–1753). Hogg's tale 'The Wool-gatherer' relates how Macmillan defied a ghost by walking alone through a haunted wood reciting the 109th Psalm: see *The Brownie of Bodsbeck; and Other Tales,* 2 vols (Edinburgh, 1818) II, 131–32. Perhaps this spiritual prowess intimidated Macmillan's dog–or perhaps it was a demonic dog, like Faust's poodle.

177(d) throw the stocking see Allan Ramsay, 'Christ's Kirk on the Green', Canto II (1715), note: 'The practice of throwing the bridegroom or the bride's stocking when they are going to bed, is well known: the person who it lights on is to be next married of the company'. This takes place on the evening of the wedding-day, rather than the evening preceding it; there appears to be some confusion (apt to the context) with the traditional gathering of the bride's unmarried girl friends on the night before the ceremony, when they pull off her stockings, wash her feet, and play games to divine who will be the next to find a husband. For both customs see John Galt, *The Entail,* 3 vols (Edinburgh, 1822), I, Chapters 28 and 30.

177(d) burn the nuts, pull the kail stocks again, popular divination rites. For a description see Burns, 'Halloween', stanzas iv (pulling kail-stalks), vii (burning nuts) and notes.

178(a) Fasten's eve the evening of Shrove Tuesday.

178(b) 'the *evening* and the morning were the first day;' Genesis 1. 5.

178(c) St Chrysostom [...] Ebenezer Erskine St John Chrysostom (*c.* 347–407), Archbishop of Constantinople, one of the Church Fathers. Ebenezer Erskine (1680–1756), Minister of Stirling, founded the Associate Presbytery (1733) in protest against the 1732 Act of Assembly curtailing the popular election of ministers in the Church of Scotland.

179(a) Crocks wad craw and duds wad let them perhaps, as Tony Inglis has suggested to the present editor, a printer's misreading of 'Cocks wad craw and [i.e. if] dugs wad let them'. But Hogg's Scots is rarely garbled in *WET.* Perhaps the phrase means something like, 'Even barren old ewes would show off if they had finery'.

183(d) William Tweedie's hounds a joke: according to James Russell in *Reminiscences of Yarrow* (Edinburgh: William Blackwood, 1886), 'Willie Tweedie' was an eccentric Border beggar 'who went about with fox-hounds, with whom reynard was the one idea; and fancying all he met were on the same outlook, the stereotyped demand was, "Confess you saw him"' (p. 134).

185(c) "Man wants [...] that little long." Oliver Goldsmith, 'Edwin and Angelina' (1765), ll. 31–32.

188(b–c) Laird K—y of Ch–k–t, Laird of S–n–e, minister of K–m–l unidentified, although the last location may be Kirkmichael, about 9 miles north of Dumfries.

192(c) As the sailor said to his captain, 'No sham here, by G—.'" allusion not traced.

192(d)–193(a) "Wha dare meddle wi' me" slogan of the Border clan of the Elliotts.

194(d) Cameronian sacrament a communion service or 'holy fair'. In Scottish usage, 'sacrament' can refer to 'the periodical Communion service of the Presbyterian church' (*SND*). The infrequency of communion in the Presbyterian tradition (two or three times a year) meant that 'Sacrament Sundays' were the highlights of the church calendar, taking the place of the major religious holidays of Christmas and Easter (which were not observed). Services were often held outdoors to accommodate the large number of celebrants, who would come from miles around. For a description of the carnal as well as spiritual business transacted upon these great occasions, including lovers' assignations, see Burns's poem

'The Holy Fair'. A later reference locates the sacrament at 'D–f–e', perhaps Dryfesdale (p. 196).

195(c) John Murray of Baillie-hill if this name (like those of other farmers and countrymen mentioned in the tale) belongs to a historical person, I have not been able to identify him. There is a Bailiehill farm in Eskdale, on the White Esk.

196(d) atween the eyne 'with my own eyes' (*SND*, 'atween' 3 (4)).

197(a) Robie Armstrong's the name and later hints (p. 203) suggest a location near Mangerton, Liddesdale, stronghold of the Armstrongs and site of the Liddesdale games.

198(a) one of the gipsies a community of the Border gipsies lived at Kirk Yetholm, Roxburghshire. But George has misunderstood the colloquial usage of 'gipsy' to mean a sly, fickle girl (*OED* 2. b). Compare 'Basil Lee': 'I was in love with Jessy, one of the servant maids, a little blooming arrogant gypsy', p. 6.

198(c) Steelity here, steelity there, they're gaun to try't compare Edie Ochiltree's phrase, 'Praetorian here, Praetorian there, I mind the bigging o't' in Scott's *The Antiquary*, ed. by David Hewitt (Edinburgh: Edinburgh University Press, 1995), p. 30.

199(a) crocks [...] eild ewes a crock is a ewe that has ceased bearing. 'Eild is a Scotch word to denote a sheep without a lamb': Hogg, *The Shepherd's Guide* (Edinburgh, 1807), p. 258. 'Nether Cassway' is Nether Cassock in Eskdalemuir; see *Shepherd's Calendar*, p. 273.

199(a) want of speculation in his eye like Banquo's ghost: *Macbeth*, III. 4. 93.

200 (a) neye grit stecks at no great shakes at.

201(c) head o' Liddal [...] fit of Cannobie i.e. all Liddesdale; Liddel Water joins the Esk at Canonbie.

202(b) a bellandine a battle-cry, and by extension a fight; slogan of the Scotts of Buccleuch, from Bellendean, the gathering-place of the clan at the head of Borthwick water in Roxburghshire.

204(b) is nae tou a tailor intended as an insult: many passages in Hogg's writings suggest that tailors were held in particularly low esteem by rural Borderers.

204 (c) a' at yeans all at once.

204(d) Sowerby Hap unidentified, although the name suggests a location across the border in Cumbria.

209(c) the border dialect the reflection draws our attention to the virtuosity with which Hogg represents different varieties of Border speech throughout this story.

211(b) better leate [...] ne'er de weel see note to 13(b).

211(d) Sorbie in Wigton, west of Dumfries.

212(a) Staigshawbank Stagshaw Bank, near Corbridge in the Tyne valley, Northumberland; livestock fairs were held there at Whitsun and Midsummer.

214(b) David Wilkie the painter (1785–1841), celebrated for his genre scenes from Scottish popular life, such as 'Pitlessie Fair' (1804) and 'The Penny Wedding' (1819). Scott introduced Hogg to Wilkie in 1817. His admiration for the painter is expressed in three unpublished sketches of 1829, 'The Dorty Wean', 'The History of an Auld Naig', and 'David Wilkie': see *SHW*, 2 (1991), 103–09.

216(b) mugg wedders breed of 'long' or white-faced sheep, like the Cheviot, imported from England for their better yield of wool. They were less hardy than the black-faced ('short') sheep, which thrived on higher ground.

216(d) Wolf-cleuch-head [...] head of Borthwick Water in Craik Forest, between Eskdalemuir and Teviotdale.

217(a) ae thing needful Luke 10. 38–43.

217(a) Jamie the poyet's sang i.e., the youthful James Hogg. 'For several years my compositions consisted wholly of songs and ballads made up for the lasses to sing in chorus; and a proud man I was when I first heard the rosy nymphs chaunting my uncouth strains, and jeering me by the still dear appellation of "Jamie the poeter"' (*Memoir*, p. 10). 'He that prays is ne'er to trust' is a line from Hogg's song 'The Laird o' Lamington', printed in *A Border Garland* (Edinburgh, 1819), p. 19.

217(b) sic tree, sic fruit see Matthew 7. 17: 'Even so every good tree bringeth forth good fruit; but a corrupt tree bringeth forth evil fruit'.

217(b) bred i' the bane [...] out o' the flesh see *ODEP*, p. 83.

217(c) Tommy Rewit's sermon perhaps a punning reference ('rue it') to Thomas Rowatt (1768–1832), Cameronian minister of Penpont from 1796. Hogg alludes to 'Penpunt' as famous for Cameronian piety in *Confessions* (p. 133) and 'The Barber of Duncow', *Fraser's Magazine*, 3 (March 1831), 174–80.

217(d) As the tree fa's, there it maun lie compare Ecclesiastes 11. 3: 'in the place where the tree falleth, there it shall be'.

217(d)–218(a) If the good seed [...] among stones see Matthew 13. 18–23.

218(a) "Carnality's the mother o' invention," compare *ODEP*, p. 558: 'Necessity's the mother of invention'.

218(a) the edder on the hill, that sooks the laverack out o' the lift 'the adder on the hill, that sucks the lark out of the sky': alluding to the archetypal serpent in Eden (Genesis 3), as well as to the powers of fascination popularly attributed to snakes.

218(a) the raven [...] flesh, flesh compare the biblical account of ravens feeding the prophet Elijah: 'the ravens brought him bread and flesh in the morning, and bread and flesh in the evening' (I Kings 17. 6).

218(a) the worm that never dieth, an' the fire that is not quenched Mark 9. 44, 46, 48.

218(b) manna of life [...] waters of unrighteousness a mixture of scriptural phrases ('manna', 'of life', 'unrighteousness') rather than a quoted passage. Mary is rebuking her daughter for appetites that do not conform to Christ's teaching in Matthew 5. 6: 'Blessed are they which do hunger and thirst after righteousness, for they shall be filled'.

218(b) Your ee's like the edder's see note to 218(a); 'And the woman said, The serpent beguiled me' (Genesis 3. 13).

218(b) cast o' grace religious conversion (*SND*, 'cast', n. phrases, 3).

218(c) 'low down amang the heather,' unidentified, but similar phrases occur in many poems and songs, e.g. Burns, 'Tam Samson's Elegy': 'amang the heather [...] low he lies' (ll. 69, 73). For 'Low down i' the Brume' see Alexander Whitelaw, *The Book of Scottish Song* (Glasgow: Blackie, 1867), p. 35.

218(c) wha can take fire i' their bosom an' no be burnt? Proverbs 6. 27.

220(a) July fair at Langholm 'the greatest fair for lambs in Scotland', held on 26 July: *Statistical Account*, XIII, 611.

223(d) penance publicly in the church Hogg himself, like Burns before him, had been obliged to stand in penance before the Presbyterian congregation for amorous intrigues. He sired two illegitimate daughters while farming in Dumfriesshire in 1807 and 1810. See Gillian Hughes, 'James Hogg and the "Bastard Brood"', *SHW*, 11 (2000), 56–68.

224(c–d) Oh! she was perfect [...] given up his garrison Byron, *Don Juan*, I, xvii.

224(d) Rev. Mr Johnston and Doctor Singers if these are historical figures, 'Doctor Singers' is probably William Singer, D. D. (1765–1850), Minister of Wamphray (from 1794) and Kirkpatrick-Juxta and Dungree, Annandale (from 1799); he wrote the account of Moffat, as well as of his own parish, for the *Statistical Account of Scotland*, and his daughter married John Bennet, Minister of Ettrick, in 1821. Among several Johnstons, the likeliest candidate would appear to be Alexander Johnston (1769–1851), Minister of Cranshaws (from 1792) and Moffat (from 1801).

225(b) Thomas Vincent's Exposition on the Duties of Parents to their Children in

Thomas Vincent, *An Explicatory Catechism, or an Explanation of the Assembly's Shorter Catechism* (London, 1673), reprinted throughout the 18th century.

225 (b) **"Be ye fruitful [...] replenish the earth."** Genesis 1. 28.

225 (b) **parish sacrament** 'At communion the people [...] sat on the forms at the long table, the elements being handed round from person to person. "Tickets," or "tokens," were given out to communicants, and the tables were "fenced," debarring the unworthy': *Social Life*, p. 279.

225 (c) **fast-day** a day in the week preceding the annual or twice-yearly Presbyterian communion, set aside for fasting in preparation for taking the sacrament.

226 (a) **"Beside thee there is none!"** Psalm 73. 25, in the Scottish metrical version: 'Whom have I in the heavens high \ but thee, O Lord, alone? \ And in the earth whom I desire \ besides thee there is none'. In the Presbyterian service the precentor would sing out each line separately and the congregation repeat it after him.

226 (d) **the iniquity of the father visited on my children!** compare Exodus 20. 5.

226 (d)–227 (a) **reverend and devout David D—** [...] **inspired H— G—** if these are Ministers of the Church of Scotland in Edinburgh, 'David D—' may be David Dickson (1754–1820), Minister at several Edinburgh parishes from 1795, including West St Giles from 1801; he published a set of his sermons in 1818. 'H— G—' may be Henry Grey (1778–1859), ordained in 1801, Minister at St Cuthbert's Chapel-of-Ease, and author of several works of an Evangelical tendency in the years preceding *WET* (including *The Veil of Moses Done Away in Christ*, 1820); he would join the Free Church after the Disruption.

John Gray o' Middleholm

Published for the first time in *WET*. The tale combines several traditional motifs. Robert Chambers relates a version of the story associated with Dundonald Castle in Ayrshire: 'Donald, the builder, was originally a poor man, but had the faculty of dreaming lucky dreams. Upon one occasion he dreamed, thrice in one night, that if he were to go to London Bridge, he would become a wealthy man. He went accordingly, saw a man looking over the parapet of the bridge, whom he accosted courteously, and, after a little conversation, intrusted with the secret of his occasion of visiting London Bridge. The stranger told him that he had made a very foolish errand, for he himself had once had a similar vision, which directed him to go to a certain spot in Ayrshire, in Scotland, where he would find a vast treasure, and, for his part, he had never once thought of obeying the injunction. From his description of the spot, the sly Scotsman at once perceived that the treasure in question must be concealed in no other place than his own humble *kail-yard* at home, to which he immediately repaired, in full expectation of finding it. Nor was he disappointed; for, after destroying many good and promising cabbages, and completely cracking credit with his wife, who esteemed him mad, he found a large potful of gold coin, with the proceeds of which he built a stout castle for himself, and became the founder of a flourishing family': Robert Chambers, *Popular Rhymes of Scotland* (London: W. & R. Chambers, 1870), pp. 237–38. Chambers adds that the 'story is localised in almost every part of Scotland' (p. 238), and records several variants, including one in which the treasure is supposed to be buried under a broad stone (pp. 242–43). An almost identical tradition is associated with the church of Swaffham in Norfolk; see Francis White, *Gazetteer and Directory of Norfolk* (1854), pp. 739–40.

For the end of the tale, compare the parable Jesus relates in Luke 13. 6–9: 'A certain man had a fig tree planted in his vineyard; and he came and sought fruit thereon, but found none. Then said he to the dresser of his vineyard, Behold, these three years I come seeking fruit on this fig tree, and find none; cut it down; why cumbereth it the ground? And he answering said unto him, Lord, let it alone this year also, till I shall dig about it, and dung it: And if it bear fruit, well; and if not, then after that thou shalt cut it down'.

229(a) Middleholm on the Esk, a couple of miles south of Langholm.

230(a) fifteen pounds on every square inch atmospheric pressure at sea-level is 14.7 lb per square inch.

230(b) "The state of all things [...] that which is dense." Francis Bacon, *Sylva Sylvarum: or A Natural History*, I. 29 (1627) (slightly misquoted).

231(a) Stott i.e. bullock.

232(a) immense sums of old sterling coinage 'finds of coins of all dates are by no means rare in the Scottish border countries [...] Coins, in greater or less number, are continually turning up in all sorts of unlikely spots': Andrew Lang and John Lang, *Highways and Byways in the Border* (London: Macmillan, 1913), pp. 12–13.

232(a) the fields of Philliphaugh, of Middlestead, and Ancrum Moor these Border battles took place in 1645 (Philiphaugh) and 1545 (Ancrum); Middlestead is unidentified. Hogg transmitted a tradition that the Earl of Traquair had thrown a bag of gold into a pond in his flight from Philiphaugh: see *Minstrelsy*, III, 170 (citing Hogg as informant) and 'Wat Pringle o' the Yair' in Hogg's *Tales of the Wars of Montrose*, ed. by Gillian Hughes (S/SC, 1996), pp. 202–03.

232(b) a castle of Liddesdale [...] Tamleuchar Cross 'In the south of Scotland, it is the popular belief that vast treasures are concealed beneath the ruins of Hermitage Castle [in Liddesdale]; but being in the keeping of the Evil One, they are considered beyond redemption. [...] it is also believed that there is concealed at Tamleuchar Cross, in Selkirkshire, a valuable treasure' (Chambers, *Popular Rhymes of Scotland*, p. 240).

233(c) To houk the pots o' goud [...] lamb never feeds variant of the popular rhyme on the treasure of Tamleuchar Cross, recorded by Robert Chambers: 'Atween the wat grund and the dry, \ The gowd o' Tamleuchar doth lie' (*Popular Rhymes of Scotland*, p. 240).

234(a) Kelso [...] the auld brigg the bridge of 1754, swept away by a flood in 1797; a splendid replacement was built in 1800–03.

236(d) a mare allusion to the proverb, 'the grey mare is the better horse' (i.e. the wife rules the husband): *ODEP*, p. 338.

238(b) Antiburgher Presbyterian Seceder minister belonging to the General Associate, or Anti-Burgher, Synod, formed in April 1747 in protest against the religious clause in the oath sworn by burgesses. The Seceders had withdrawn from the Church of Scotland in 1733.

238(c) He ran, and she ran perhaps an echo of 'The Battle of Sherrifmuir', Song I in Hogg's *Jacobite Relics of Scotland*, Second Series (Edinburgh, 1821): 'And we ran, and they ran, and they ran, and we ran' (pp. 1–5).

238(d) as the feet of hinds upon the mountains compare II Samuel 22. 34, 'He maketh my feet like hinds' feet; and setteth me upon my high places', quoted in Psalm 18. 33.

240(d) Birds of a feather, flock ay thegither *ODEP*, p. 60.

241 (d) The warld be a wastle us! may worldly cares be far from us.

244(d) Cistertian Monks from Selkirk Kelso Abbey was founded in 1128 by David I, who transferred a colony of Tironensian (Benedictine) monks there from Selkirk, where they had settled in 1113. Building continued through the reign of Malcolm IV, David's successor and grandson.

245(d) fool [...] a Gallic word the Gaelic *fuil* is a loan-word from the English; more usual terms are *amadan* or *burraidh*.

248(a) The town that ne'er was framed [...] the bird that never flew variant of a traditional rhyme describing the coat of arms of the city of Glasgow (from the seals of the Bishop of Glasgow): 'This is the tree that never grew; \ This is the bird that never flew; \ This is the bell that never rang; \ And this the fish that never swam' (Chambers, *Popular Rhymes of Scotland*, p. 396).

252(c) hip and thigh Judges 15. 8.

252(d) your een wad stand i' back water 'you would be reduced to helplessness' (*SND*, 'back-water').

253(a) bred i' the bane [...] out o' the flesh see *ODEP*, p. 83.

The Bridal of Polmood

Published for the first time in *WET*, where it opens the second volume. 'The Bridal of Polmood' was among the 'Cottage tales' Hogg offered to Blackwood in 1817, and it may have been part of the set he offered to Constable in 1813: see 'Introduction'. In the opening chapter Hogg refers to the notorious Hunter law case, disputing the Polmood inheritance (see note to 261(a)). The topicality of the case between 1810 and 1814 lends support to some form of the story having been written by 1813. The story, set late in the reign of James IV, does not so much depart from the historical record as defy it. In a note to the present editor, Douglas Mack suggests that Hogg is attempting to represent 'the view of James IV and his court preserved in Ettrick popular oral tradition from Ettrick's time as royal hunting forest', in conscientious opposition to Scott's account of the era of Flodden in *Marmion* (1808). Once more, Hogg chooses a topographical setting–upper Tweeddale and Meggatdale–that he knew intimately.

259(a) LAST autumn, on my return from the Lakes of Cumberland this introductory, framing chapter may be based on Hogg's first meeting with James Gray (1770–1830) on a stage-coach journey to Dumfriesshire in 1808. The two men conversed about 'Border scenery and lore, and the Ettrick Shepherd's poetry'; Gray became Hogg's 'intimate friend', and Hogg married his first wife's sister, Margaret Phillips, in 1820. See *The Spy*, pp. 562–63, and 'G.', 'Some Particulars Relative to the Ettrick Shepherd', *New Monthly Magazine*, 46 (February 1836), 194–203 (pp. 201–02). If this is so, it lends support to the theory that Hogg had written a version of 'Polmood' by 1813. Hogg also visited John Wilson in the Lake District around 1814.

260(a) the web of the gossamer see note to 50(d). Hogg reprises these optical effects, more memorably, in the Arthur's Seat episode of *Confessions*, pp. 29–30, 34.

260(a) by the side of the Tweed the old Carlisle-Dumfries-Edinburgh coach road runs up Annandale through Moffat, across Erickstanebrae ('the heights of Erickstane') and along the upper reaches of the Tweed, before descending to Yarrow and St Mary's Loch.

260(b) a good inn the Crook Inn, near Tweedsmuir; see Andrew and John Lang, *Highways and Byways in the Border* (London: Macmillan, 1913), pp. 357–59.

260(b) That is Polmood the estate 'lies along the north side of the Polmood burn, which runs to the Tweed down a deep narrow glen, and is bounded on the north by Stanhope, on the south by Hearthstane (Tweedsmuir), and on the west by Kingledoors': J. W. Buchan and Rev. H. Paton, *A History of Peeblesshire*, 3 vols (Glasgow, 1925–27), III, 451.

260(c) printed in many histories and collections Hogg is most likely referring to Alexander Pennecuik's *Description of Tweeddale* (1715), reprinted in *The Works of Alexander Pennecuik, Esq., of New-Hall, M.D.* (Leith: A. Allardice, 1815), p. 251. Buchan and Paton reproduce a copy of the charter (p. 452), 'said to have been made in 1790' from an unknown original, and quote the version of the text given by Pennecuik: 'Tradition records that King Malcolm Canmore, in or about 1057, gave to Hunter the lands of Polmood, and in proof of this the fantastic rhyming charter so well known in connection with the origin of this family is quoted: "I, Malcolm Kenmure, King, the first of my reign, gives [*sic*] to thee, Norman Hunter of Powmood, the Hope, up and down, above the earth to heaven, and below the earth to hell, as free to thee and thine as ever God gave it to me and mine, and that for a bow and a broad arrow, when I come to hunt in Yarrow; and for the mair suith I byte the white wax with my tooth, before thir witnesses three, May, Maud and Marjorie"' (*A History of Peeblesshire*, III, 451). Buchan and Paton suggest that although the charter has evidently been 'manufactured to uphold a family tradition', 'there is no reason to throw aside the tradition itself, as it is quite a probability that Polmood may have been given by one of the early Scottish kings for some signal service to one of his hunters called Norman. [...] The earliest reference to Polmood shows that in the fifteenth century it was part of the barony of Oliver Castle, and held of the Flemings and afterwards of the Hays of Yester as superiors' (III, 451–52).

261(a) **for these fifty years** Buchan and Paton, *A History of Peeblesshire*, give a detailed account of the famous—and immensely complicated—Hunter law case, with the relevant genealogy (III, 457–61). Beginning in 1780 Adam Hunter, tenant of Alterstone, brought a series of actions to establish his right as heir to Thomas Hunter of Polmood, the last of the old line (d. 1765). In 1802 a Peebles jury granted the claim, but three years later it was annulled on technical grounds by the Edinburgh Court of Session. Hunter brought another action in 1810, and again in 1811; the Court finally refused his appeal in 1814, leaving Elizabeth Hunter, Lady Forbes (1775–1830) in possession of the estate. The case would have been highly topical in 1813, when Hogg first offered his collection of 'Cottage Winter Nights' to Constable.

261(d) **the ninth of that name** Hogg's invention. Edward Hunter of Polmood was killed by Gilbert Tweedie *c.* 1502; his successor, Walter Hunter, survived the Battle of Flodden (1513), which postdates the events of the present tale.

261(d) **the king of Scotland** James IV (1473–1513).

261(d) **the forests of Frood and Meggat-dale** the tale is set in the wild hill country between the upper Tweed and Yarrow, south of Peebles and north of St Mary's Loch. This part of Ettrick Forest was a royal hunting-ground until the reign of Queen Mary.

261(d) **Crawmel** Cramalt Tower is near Blackhouse, where Hogg worked as a shepherd in his youth. '*Crammel* [...] seems to have been an old hunting-house of our kings' (*The Works of Alexander Pennecuik*, p. 248).

262(a) **Nidpath** Neidpath Castle, then owned by the Hays of Yester, overlooking Peebles.

262(b) **English extraction** King James married Margaret Tudor, daughter of the English King Henry VII, in 1503; she brought her retinue of English servants and ladies-in-waiting with her to Scotland. Elizabeth Manners does not appear to be historical.

262(c) **Baron Carmichael [...] duke of Rothsay** historical figures, although Hogg's treatment is fictional. Carmichael would be William Carmichael of Carmichael, 6th Baron, who succeeded to the title in 1507 and died in 1530. Duke of Rothesay is the traditional title for the eldest son of the King of Scotland; in case of the eldest son's decease, the title passed to the king's next surviving son. Hogg's use of it (later rendered phonetically as 'Rosay') for the king's younger brother is incongruous, although one of James IV's brothers was Duke of Ross (and Archbishop of St Andrews, 1476–1504).

264(a) **St Mary of the Lowes [...] St Bothans** the ruined chapel on the hillside above St Mary's Loch, commemorated in poems by Scott and Hogg; the former convent of Abbey St Bathans in the Lammermuirs.

266(d) **the dark Clokmore** hill above Cramalt.

268(a) **king James himself came off victorious** James IV's reign was famous throughout Europe for the splendour of its games and tournaments, in which the king himself would compete.

268(b) throw the mall 'a mallet or large wooden hammer': for a description see p. 401. Hogg mixes chivalric tournament (tilting, archery) with traditional Border games (throwing the hammer, wrestling). The St Ronan's Border Games, founded by Hogg in 1827 and still flourishing, include an archery contest.

269(d) upon the straw [...] a pair of horns on your head variant of 'in the straw', i.e. in childbed (*OED* 'straw', 2.b); horns are a traditional emblem of cuckoldry.

271(c) "leads to bewilder, and dazzles to blind." James Beattie, *The Hermit* (1776), l. 34.

271(c) The flowers of the forest and garden a favourite topos of Hogg's for the distinction between nature and art, as in the concluding lines of Book 1 of *Queen Hynde*: 'Let those who list, the garden chuse, \ Where flowers are regular and profuse', etc. (S/SC 1998), p. 31, ll. 1108–15. The phrase 'the flowers of the forest' echoes (with particular aptness in this story) the celebrated 18th-century lyric by Jean Elliott (based on a traditional song), 'The Flowers of the Forest', a lament for the generation of young men of Ettrick Forest wiped out defending James IV at Flodden: see *The Poetry of Scotland*, ed. by Roderick Watson (Edinburgh: Edinburgh University Press, 1995), p. 414.

271(d) loved too well compare *Othello*, V. 2. 353.

272(b) a dance on the green an allusion, perhaps, to the archetypal Scots poem of popular festivity, 'Christ's Kirk on the Green', variously attributed (in Hogg's day) to James I and James V.

272(c) O'er the boggy, and Cutty's wedding popular songs associated with 'irregular or runaway marriages': see Alexander Whitelaw, *The Book of Scottish Song* (Glasgow: Blackie, 1867), p. 311 ('Cuttie's Wedding') and p. 503 ('Ower Bogie'). See also Hogg's *Songs by the Ettrick Shepherd* (Edinburgh, 1831), p. 94: 'Our forefathers had cried down songs, which all men and women were strictly prohibited from singing, such as "O'er Boggie" and "The wee Cock Chicken," &c., because Auld Nick was a proficient at playing them on the pipes'.

272(c) queen Mary [...] Meggat in August 1566 Mary and her husband, Henry Darnley, came to Cramalt to hunt; disappointed by the scarcity of game, the queen issued an edict forbidding hunting in Ettrick Forest.

272(c) ring and the double octave dance formations; *OED* cites this usage, 'Octave', 4a.

273(a) Lady Ann Gray, a great favourite with the king the King had numerous mistresses, including Marion Boyd, Janet Kennedy, Margaret Drummond and Isabel Stuart, who all bore him illegitimate children. This Lady Ann Gray appears to be Hogg's invention, although the name may be taken from Lady Grey, daughter of the Countess of Surrey.

275(d) lady Hyndford the title of Earl of Hyndford was not created until 1701 (and became extinct in 1817).

276(a) steps of Glendarg Glendearg in Eskdale (heading south towards England) rather than Glendearg near Galashiels, described in Chapter 2 of Scott's *The Monastery* (1820). Hogg features 'the Steps of Glen-dearg' as a haunt of the gypsy clan of the Fas in 'A Genuine Border Story', ed. by Gillian Hughes, *SHW*, 3 (1992), 95–145 (p. 113).

277(d) lord Chamberlain Hume Alexander, 3rd Baron Home, who succeeded his father in 1506, and was executed by James V in 1516. As Lord High Chamberlain and Warden of the Borders he was the most powerful man in the south of Scotland. His raid into Northumberland in 1513 precipitated the king's fatal invasion the same year. Home's name was remembered with real hostility in Ettrick tradition due to the conduct of his followers at Flodden—they abandoned the field, leaving the men of Selkirk to die defending the king. See *Shepherd's Calendar*, p.

268, note to 126(d).

283(c) I hae ane wyffe o' mi ain 'antique' version of Robert Burns's song, 'I hae a wife o' my ain' (*Poems and Songs*, no. 361): 'I hae a wife o' my ain, \ I'll partake wi' naebody; \ I'll tak Cuckold frae nane, \ I'll gie Cuckold to naebody.' Hogg's third and fourth lines adapt Burns's second verse: 'I hae naething to lend, \ I'll borrow frae naebody.'

284(a) O horrible! most horrible! *Hamlet*, I. 5. 80.

284(c) condign punishment legal phrase, originating in Tudor statutes; compare *2 Henry VI*, III. 1. 130.

287(d) MSS. [...] Mr J. Brown, Edin. This gentleman and the pastiche that follows seem to be figments of Hogg's own imagination.

288(a)–289(b) "Mucht it pleiz [...] ouir blissyt ladye." a full translation of this speech into modern English is given at the end of the Notes, on pp. 586–87.

294(c) bonnet pieces a minor anachronism: gold coins of the reign of James V, in which the king is shown wearing a bonnet.

295(c) never let the plough stand to kill a mouse *ODEP* (p. 635) records a variant of this proverb from the 17th century.

296(a) the Maiden chapel that of St Mary of the Lowes.

296(a) Falgeat [...] braes of Hundleshope the heights above Manor Water, which flows into the Tweed above Peebles.

297(c) castle of Pearce Cockburn Henderland Tower, where James's son, James V, would hang the Border reiver Peres Cockburn at his own gate, according to an inaccurate tradition transmitted in *Minstrelsy of the Scottish Border* ('Lament of the Border Widow', III, 80–82) and repeated by Hogg in Note XVII to *The Queen's Wake*, pp. 349–50.

298(a) courch'e obsolete form of Scots *curch*, head-covering.

298(c) abbot of Inchafferie this would be Laurence Oliphant, killed at Flodden (1513). Inchaffray, an Augustinian foundation established under David I, was then at the height of its influence.

299(b–c) Where oceans rolled [...] sun-beam never smiled! The first couplet comes from Hogg's modern-spelling version of 'Kilmeny' (ll. 234–35) in the sixth edition of *The Queen's Wake* (Edinburgh: Blackwood, 1819), p. 188; the lines that follow appear to be improvised from an earlier passage in the poem (ll. 179–94).

299(d) an untimely grave a prolepsis of the disastrous Battle of Flodden. The peace between England and Scotland sealed with James's marriage did not survive the death of Henry VII. James joined the French alliance against Henry VIII, and was induced to mount an invasion. The Scottish and English armies met at Flodden, on the English side of the Border, on 9 September 1513. The king and most of the Scots nobility perished on the field. Scott's *Marmion* (1808), vaguely in the background here, is 'A Tale of Flodden Field'.

301(a) King's Seat [...] Weddingers' Hope unidentified; perhaps Hogg's invention, after the *Lady's Seat* and *King's Road*, associated with Henderland and Peres Cockburn; see *Minstrelsy*, III, 81.

301(b) James and the shepherd although James IV was reputed to have gone among his subjects incognito, such exploits are traditionally associated with his son, James V, who would walk abroad disguised as 'the Goodman of Ballengeich'. See Scott, *The Lady of the Lake*. This is a common motif in folklore and literature: compare Haroun Al-Raschid in the *Arabian Nights Entertainments*, 'a little touch of Harry in the night' in the Chorus introducing Act 4 of Shakespeare's *Henry V*, etc.

302(b) an iron chain James, as Duke of Rothsay, rode with the army of mutinous nobles that overthrew his father, James III, at the battle of Sauchieburn in June 1488. The king was killed in mysterious circumstances after he fled the field; James is supposed to have worn an iron belt as penance for the remainder of his life.

302(d) **Grey by name and Grey by nature** perhaps an allusion to one or both of the proverbs, 'A' Cats are gray in the dark' (Ramsay, *A Collection of Scots Proverbs*, p. 66), 'The grey mare is the better horse' (see note to 236 (d)).

303(a) **'shu the Heron away'** in 1511 John Heron the Bastard, half-brother of William Heron of Ford, murdered the warden of the Middle Marches, Sir Robert Ker, and fled to England; his residence there was one of the chief grievances King James held against Henry VIII. James imprisoned Heron of Ford as a hostage; according to a now discredited tradition, an intrigue with Heron's wife delayed James on his fatal march into England. Hogg is no doubt thinking of the liberty Scott took with the historical record, bringing Lady Heron to the Scottish court to carry on a royal flirtation, in *Marmion*, V. x: 'O'er James's heart, the courtiers say, \ Sir Hugh [*sic*] the Heron's wife held sway: \ To Scotland's court she came, \ To be a hostage for her lord'. In 'The Bridal of Polmood' her role is taken by Lady Anne Grey.

303(a) **the song of *the Heron*** see pp. 309–11.

303(c) **Mess John** generic name for a priest.

303(d) **a grant of the lands of Caidmoor** Cademuir hill, on the SW side of Peebles, was given to the townspeople around the time of David II; confirmatory charters were issued by James II and (on 25 July 1506) by James IV. I thank Jean Moffat for this information.

304(b) **discovered his majesty to all present** the detail of the king's being recognised for keeping his hat on appears in an anecdote of James V as 'the goodman of Ballengeich': see Scott, *Tales of a Grandfather: Being Stories from the History of Scotland*, 3 vols (Edinburgh: Cadell, 1828), III, 61.

305(d) **learning [...] at a very low ebb in Scotland** although the vast majority of the population was illiterate, this was actually a golden age of Scottish letters. James IV passed an education act for the sons of landowners; founded a third Scottish university, King's College in Aberdeen, the Royal College of Surgeons in Edinburgh, and St Leonard's College, St Andrews; and issued a royal patent for the first Scottish printing-press. Scholars and poets flourished at James's court, including the great makars William Dunbar and Gavin Douglas.

307(a) **Sir William Moray** there were no baronets until James VI and I and the Union of Crowns. James IV conferred the vacant earldom of Moray upon his natural son by Janet Kennedy (1501). Perhaps, as Gillian Hughes has suggested to the editor, Hogg is drawing on traditions associated with the Murrays of Philiphaugh. See Scott's note to 'The Sang of the Outlaw Murray': 'by a charter from James IV, dated 30 November 1509 John Murray of Philiphaugh is vested with the dignity of heritable sheriff of Ettrick Forest, an office held by his descendants until the final abolition of such jurisdictions [in 1747]' (*Minstrelsy*, I, 2).

307(c) **the best surgeon, and the most skilful physician** early historians (e.g. Robert Lindsay of Pitscottie) credit James with medical skill. The king supported research in alchemy and medicine; under his auspices a separate medical faculty was established at King's College, Aberdeen, and he issued an edict regulating the surgeons and barbers of Edinburgh.

308(d) **Richmond Street** on Edinburgh's south side, developed in the later 18th century.

308(d)–309(a) **March [...] Dumlanrig** Drumlanrig Castle was the seat of the Dukes of Queensberry, who held the title Earl of March until 1810. Hogg farmed land near there in 1808.

309(a) **A Very Ancient Song** an exercise in Hogg's 'ancient stile', characterised by Peter Garside as 'a combination of ballad phraseology, the rhetoric of the late medieval Scottish "makars", [...] and more modern idiomatic expression' (James Hogg, *A Queer Book*, ed. by P. D. Garside (S/SC, 1995), p. xv). This modern antique style of Scots poetry was inaugurated by Allan Ramsay in 'The Vision' (1724).

310(b) **The *Herone* flewe eist** the following lines are adapted from 'a beautiful old rhyme which I have often heard my mother repeat, but of which she knows no tradition':

> The heron flew east, the heron flew west,
> The heron flew to the fair forest [...]
> For there she saw a lovely bower,
> Was a' clad o'er wi' lilly-flower;
> And in the bower there was a bed
> With silken sheets, and weel down spread;
> And in the bed there lay a knight,
> Whose wounds did bleed both day and night;
> And by the bed there stood a stane,
> And there was set a leal maiden,
> With silver needle and silken thread,
> Stemming the wounds when they did bleed—
> (*Mountain Bard*, pp. 13–14).

Edith Batho discusses several analogues for these lines in traditional songs and carols, none of which was collected until later in the 19th century: *The Ettrick Shepherd*, pp. 32–36. The most notable of them is reprinted in *Songs, Carols, and other Miscellaneous Poems from the Balliol MS 352, Richard Hill's Commonplace Book*, ed. by Roman Dyboski (London: Early English Text Society, 1907), p. 86.

314(d) ***andante, grazioso*, and *affetuoso*** these expressive terms are not recorded in Scots or English before the 18th century; nor would Italian music have been current at a Scottish court in the period. Hogg draws on a post-Union convention lamenting the displacement of native airs by pretentious foreign styles: compare Robert Fergusson, 'Elegy, On the Death of Scots Music' (1773): 'Now foreign sonnets bear the gree, \ And crabbit queer variety \ Of sound fresh sprung from Italy, \ A bastard breed!' Hogg keeps up the tradition in his preface to *The Forest Minstrel* (Edinburgh: Constable, 1810), inveighing against 'Italian tirlie-whirlies' (p. ix).

315(b) **the tinckell** circle of beaters (Gaelic, *timchioll*): see the description of a hunt at Braemar by John Taylor the Water Poet (1630), quoted by Scott in note 21 to *Marmion*. Hogg is also recalling Robert Lindsay of Pitscottie's account of the great hunt held by James V in 'Meggitland' in 1528 (*History of Scotland from 1436 to 1565* (1778), p. 143), cited in the same note.

315(b) **"drive the deer with hound and horn"** from 'Chevy Chase', stanza 2, in the version cited by Joseph Addison in *The Spectator* (25 May 1711): 'To drive the Deer with Hound and Horn \ Earl Piercy took his Way'. Hogg cites the lines as a motto to the first part of *Mador of the Moor* (Edinburgh, 1816).

315(c) **Holyrood-house** James IV began a palatial extension to the Abbey at Holyrood for Queen Margaret.

315(d) **in another part of this work** while Hogg does not recur to the adventures of James IV incognito in *WET*, he features another king (based on Robert II, the first Stuart king) going about in disguise in *Mador of the Moor*.

317(d) **a native of Galloway** 'mock-derogatory comments against Galloway are something of a running joke in Hogg'–*A Queer Book*, ed. by P. D. Garside (S/SC, 1995), p. 247.

320(c) **to play around the hole of the asp, and to lay her hand on the snout of the lion** compare Isaiah 11. 6–8, held in Christian tradition to predict the coming Kingdom of Christ: 'The wolf also shall dwell with the lamb, and the leopard shall lie down with the kid; and the calf and the young lion and the fatling together; and a little child shall lead them. [...] And the sucking child shall play on the hole of the asp, and the weaned child shall put his hand on the cockatrice' den'. The lion rampant appeared on the royal standard of Scotland–hence Rosay.

323(c) **a blank, my dear lady** compare *Twelfth Night*, II. 4. 110: 'A blank, my lord. She never told her love'.

331(d) **Gamesope** also a setting (Gemsop) in *The Brownie of Bodsbeck*: 'the wildest and most picturesque [glen] in Peeblesshire', according to W. R. Crockett, *The Scott Country* (London: A. & C. Black, 1905), p. 236.

332(d) **Lord James Douglas of Dalkeith** a mischievous mixing-up of the rival Border families of Scott and Douglas–'Earl of Dalkeith' is the traditional title of the heir of the Duke of Buccleuch.

332(d) **Sir Patrick Hepburn [...] Laird of Lamington** more apocryphal persons. This Sir Patrick Hepburn does not sound much like his historical namesake, the 3rd Baron Hailes and 1st Earl of Bothwell (d. 1508). Hogg's song 'The Laird of Lamington', quoted in 'Love Adventures of Mr George Cochrane', celebrates the Laird as a carousing good fellow. Andrew Car is identified as the Laird of Lamington's gamekeeper in 'Welldean Hall' (p. 465).

333(a) **Hackshaw [...] Hugh Porteus** the current Porteous of Hackshaw, near Tweedsmuir, would have been Patrick, who succeeded his turbulent father Thomas in 1507. A later Porteous of Hackshaw won local fame for cutting off sixteen of Cromwell's troopers at Falla Moss in 1650.

336(a) **an old palmer** 'A *Palmer*, opposed to a *Pilgrim*, was one who made it his sole business to visit holy shrines; travelling incessantly and subsisting by charity' (Scott, *Marmion*, note 18).The lost lord or heir who returns disguised as a palmer is an old romance convention, which Scott revived in *Marmion* (Hogg's likely source here) and *Ivanhoe* (1820). The 'order of Saint John of Jerusalem' is the famous crusading order of the Knights Hospitallers.

337(a) **so long were the miles in those days** the pre-Union Scots mile was longer than the English Imperial mile–1984 to 1760 yards, respectively.

348(b) **John Tweedie of Drumelzier** laird since 1490. Drumelzier was the Tweedie stronghold until 1623, when the property passed into the hands of the Hays of Yester.

351(b) **the unfortunate duke** the catastrophe, although not historical, is perhaps a reminiscence of the death of the most notorious Duke of Rothesay, the son of Robert III, who led a life of debauchery and was widely believed to have been murdered by his uncle, the Duke of Albany, in 1402; see Scott's treatment in *St Valentine's Day, or The Fair Maid of Perth* (1827).

355(c) **Donald's Cleuch** up Gameshope burn, above Loch Skene. According to Lang (and as Hogg would have known perfectly well) it is named after the famous Covenanting minister Donald Cargill (1619–81), who sought refuge there in the 'Killing Time' (*Highways and Byways in the Border* (London: Macmillan, 1913), pp. 368–69).

King Gregory

First published as 'The Ballad of King Gregory' in the *Edinburgh Annual Register for 1812* (Edinburgh, 1814), pp. i–xii. *WET* omits one stanza from the 1814 version, expands a later stanza into two stanzas, and revises the last line of the poem (see below for details); there are numerous variants in punctuation and some in spelling. Formally 'King Gregory' is an imitation of the traditional Lowland ballad, with echoes, in particular, of 'Sir Patrick Spens'. The setting of Hogg's poem, however, is the quasi-mythical Celtic past revisited by Hogg in *Queen Hynde* (1824). Based on the historical Giric, or Grig, king of Strathclyde (d. 898), Gregory was one of the legendary kings of Scotland, a Caledonian counterpart of Alfred the Great. According to George Buchanan he fought off the Danes under Hardnute (Harduntus) and secured a glorious peace before his death in 892 (*The History of Scotland*, trans. by J. Aikman, 4 vols (Glasgow: Blackie, 1827), I, 281–84; see also Raphael Holinshed, *Chronicles of England, Scotland and Ireland*, 6 vols (London: Longman, 1808), V, 218–25). In its new setting the poem represents an honourable corrective to the disasters of 'The Bridal of Polmood'. Hogg may have got the germ of his story from Holinshed: '[Gregorie] was never married, but continued in chastitie all his life time' (*Chronicles*, V, 218).

358(1) KING **Gregory sits in Dunbarton tower** compare the opening line of 'Sir Patrick Spens': 'The king sits in Dunfermline town' (*Minstrelsy*, III, 64). The king in the ballad, who recklessly sends his subjects to their deaths in his zeal for a bride, provides a foil for the more responsible conduct of Hogg's Gregory.

358(6–7) **Erin [...] frown afar** according to Buchanan Gregory followed up his victory over the Danes with a conquest of Ireland, meanwhile keeping the Britons at bay in Northumbria.

358(9) **meddler's cast** perhaps (Gillian Hughes has suggested to the editor) a variant of 'the redder's straik', i.e. a nasty blow got by the person who tries to intervene in a fight.

359(39) **Leven side** Dumbarton Castle stands at the mouth of the River Leven where it flows from Loch Lomond into the Clyde.

359(50) **meet room for two** following this stanza 'The Ballad of King Gregory' includes a stanza omitted in *WET*:

> And sore he wondered that so long
> Something awanting he should ken;
> Something he lacked of happiness,
> But knew not what it was till then.

360(70) **somewhat dark, like you and me** perhaps a reference to the Black Douglases (see note to 377(d), below) and to the dark-haired Stuarts (hence a suggestion that Scottish kings were usually dark).

360(71) **John de Erol** the name of Erol's daughter, 'Hay', suggests that Hogg might have had in mind the claim of the Hays of Erroll to be descended from a peasant called Hay, ennobled by Kenneth III for his part in defeating the Danes at the Battle of Luncarty in 990. Here 'King Gregory' shares territory with *Mador of the Moor* (1816)—the environs of the River Tay, above (Athol) and below (Errol) Perth.

360(83–84) **The King has written a broad letter, \ And sealed it with his signet ring** compare 'Sir Patrick Spens', stanza 3: 'Our King has written a braid letter, \ And seal'd it with his hand'.

362(138) **Canute the Dane** a paronomasic chain converts Buchanan's obscure 'Hardnute' into the celebrated Canute (d. 1035), Danish king of England, via (presumably) Canute's successor Hardicanute (d. 1042).

366(270) **Dunsinnane** Tayside setting associated with Macbeth, as also in *Mador of the Moor*. See also 'Birnam-hill', l. 342.

367(319–20) **Almond [...] Earn** rivers that flow into the Tay near Perth.

368(335) **Monteith** the Lake of Menteith, west of Stirling, marking the descent from the Highlands.

370(403–10) **The king he seized [...] answered readily!** *WET* expands and clarifies a single stanza in 'The Ballad of King Gregory':

> The king put her fair hand in his!
> "Now, abbot, *here* thy question try."
> The abbot stared and straight obeyed,
> Ah, it was answered readily!

371(438) **Dunbarton never more shall see** the last line of 'The Ballad of King Gregory' reads: 'Dumbarton town shall never see'.

The Shepherd's Calendar
First published, in two separate series, in *Blackwood's Edinburgh Magazine*. Chapters III–V appeared in *Blackwood's*, 1 (April 1817), 22–25, (May 1817), 143–47, and (June 1817), 247–50, under the title 'Tales and Anecdotes of the Pastoral Life'. Chapters I–II appeared in *Blackwood's*, 5 (April 1819), 75–81, and (May 1819), 210–16, under the title 'The Shepherd's Calendar. Storms'. 'Storms' was also reprinted in Hogg, *The Shepherd's Calendar*, 2 vols (Edinburgh: Blackwood, 1829), II, 254–92, along with other tales and sketches that appeared under that title in *Blackwood's* throughout the 1820s. The manuscript of 'Storms' survives in the Blackwood archive in the National Library of Scotland; Douglas Mack uses it as copy-text for the Stirling\South Carolina edition of *The Shepherd's Calendar* (S/SC, 1995), pp. 1–21 and note on pp. 257–58. *WET* reprints the *Blackwood's* text substantially without alteration (omitting the final paragraphs of chapters III and IV). The two series, combined in *WET*, follow different conventions. Chapters III–V, written earlier, reproduce the kind of 'pastoral anecdote' typical of an earlier periodical literature, with its narration by a polite stranger and stylized names such as 'Grumple' and 'Peter Plash'; while the Ettrick Shepherd is clearly the narrator of chapters I–II, featuring actual persons and events, as well as of the later 'Shepherd's Calendar' contributions to *Blackwood's*.

372(a) **tablets of memory** compare *Hamlet*, I. 5. 98: 'the table of my memory'.

372(b) **"Mar's year,"** 1715, when the Earl of Mar led the first great Jacobite rising.

372(b) **"that year the hielanders raide,"** the 1745 Jacobite rising.

372(b) **the year nine, and the year forty** on these terrible years of bad weather, crop failure and famine throughout Scotland see *Social Life*, pp. 151, 170.

372(b) **thirteen drifty days** [...] 1620 *Statistical Account*, 'Eskdale', gives a different date: 'In 1674, there were 13 drifty days in the end of February and beginning of March, O.S., which proved fatal to most of the sheep in this parish': XII, 610.

373(b) **Phaup** a farm (Phawhope) at the head of the Ettrick valley, on the edge of Eskdalemuir; the home of Hogg's maternal grandfather, William Laidlaw.

373(b) **Sir James Montgomery** Sir James Montgomery, Bart. (1776–1839) of Stanhope, Peeblesshire, who became 2nd Baronet in 1803.

373(b) **Sir Patrick Scott of Thirlestane's** Patrick Scott (d. 1666) bought up the wadsets (mortgages) to the Thirlestane property, in Ettrick, from the senior branch of the family. The current proprietor was Captain William John Napier, whom Hogg knew well; the Scotts of Thirlestane had acquired the title Napier through marriage in 1699. See W. J. Napier, *A Treatise on Practical Store-Farming* (Edinburgh, 1822) and Hogg's review, 'The Hon. Captain Napier and Ettrick Forest', *Blackwood's*, 13 (February 1823), 175–88.

373(c) **Bourhope-law** farm on the Thirlestane estate, the home of Hogg's friend Alexander Laidlaw (d. 1842), who contributed an account of the 1794 storm to Captain Napier's book.

373(d) **There's walth o' kye** [...] **An' thae shall a' be thine** unidentified.

373(d) **the blast o' March** [...] **16–** possibly during the years of blight and famine from 1696; see *Social Life*, pp. 146–51.

375(c) **24th of January 1794** Hogg's account of the great storm is corroborated by that of the Rev. William Brown, Minister of Eskdalemuir, in *The New Statistical Account of Scotland*, 15 vols (Edinburgh: Blackwood, 1845), IV, 414–15. Working up 'a memorandum taken at the time', Brown comments on the unseasonable mildness of the weather until 'the fatal 25th January 1794', when rain that had begun falling the previous day turned to 'the most dreadful [snowstorm] ever known in this place'.

375(c) **Mr Thomas Beattie** Beattie's journal, which survives in private ownership, 'emphasizes the significance of the storm in the country at large and supports Hogg's testimony about the date of the storm and the fairness of the winter until the storm broke': Elaine E. Petrie, 'James Hogg: A Study in the Transition from Folk Tradition to Literature' (unpublished Ph.D. thesis, University of Stirling, 1980), p. 178.

376(c) **Entertrony** where Hogg's grandfather, Will o' Phaup, once saw the fairies: *Shepherd's Calendar*, p. 109.

376(c) **my own brother** Hogg had three brothers; since the eldest, William (baptised 1767), had been living in Tweedsmuir parish, Peeblesshire, from 1815, this is likelier to be Robert or David (b. 1773), who was in Yarrow in 1819.

376(c) **my master [...] Blackhouse** Hogg worked for James Laidlaw at Blackhouse farm in Yarrow from 1790 to 1800; see *Memoir*, p. 9. His son William Laidlaw was Hogg's lifelong friend and the steward and amanuensis of Walter Scott.

377(b) **Hopehouse [...] maternal uncle** almost certainly Robert Laidlaw, whose gravestone in Ettrick Kirkyard reads: 'In memory of ROBERT LAIDLAW who died at Hopehouse June 29th 1800 aged 72'.

377(d) **ruinous habitation of the Black Douglasses** Blackhope, with the ruined keep of the 'Good Sir James' Douglas, and the adjacent Douglas Burn, a tributary of Yarrow, are the site of events recounted in the ballad 'The Douglas Tragedy': *Minstrelsy*, III, 243–44. The famous Border clan were nicknamed 'Black Douglas' to distinguish them from the 'Red Douglas' of Angus.

382(c) **motto** Robert Burns, 'Tam o' Shanter', ll. 77–78.

387(b) **Mr Bryden of Crosslee** Walter Bryden of Crosslee (d. 1799), an early friend and benefactor of the Hogg family; he leased Ettrickhouse and placed Hogg's father there as shepherd after his ruin. See *Memoir*, pp. 4–5. Hogg's poem 'Dialogue in a Country Churchyard' (*Scottish Pastorals*, 1801) was written on the occasion of Bryden's death.

387(d) **get quit o' him again** compare Robert Burns, 'Address to the Deil', ll. 79–84: 'When MASONS' mystic *word* an' *grip*, \ In storms an' tempests raise you up, \ Some cock, or cat, your rage maun stop, \ Or, strange to tell! \ The *youngest brother* ye wad whip \ Aff straught to *H–ll*.' See also 'Welldean Hall', p. 477, for the detail of necromancers giving the devil one of their number to get rid of him. John MacQueen surmises that 'a more or less secret meeting of young agricultural labourers' might well have included freemasons or radicals in Scotland in 1794: *The Rise of the Historical Novel* (Edinburgh: Scottish Academic Press, 1989), pp. 207–08.

387(d) **a dearly loved brother** as we learn below, Hogg's elder brother William.

388(a) **he has need of a lang spoon that sups wi' the deil** proverbial (*ODEP*, pp. 480–81).

388(a) **ill thief** for the epithet see Burns, '[To Dr Blacklock]': "The *Ill-thief* blaw the *Heron* south!'

388(b) **Chaldee Manuscript** 'Translation from an Ancient Chaldee Manuscript', a satire of the Edinburgh literary scene written in a burlesque biblical style, was composed by Hogg in collaboration with John Wilson and John Gibson Lockhart, and published in *Blackwood's*, 2 (October 1817), 89–96. Threats of prosecution forced Blackwood to withdraw the offending article, while its authors went into hiding.

389(a) **Mary Beattie** daughter of the Ettrick schoolmaster, John Beattie, who married Hogg's elder brother William on 28 December 1798 (Ettrick OPR).

389(a) **the late Mr James Anderson** perhaps the proprietor of Ettrickhall and Phaup, which Hogg's father and grandfather leased as shepherds.

391(a) **a poet [...] great partiality** in the verses that follow Hogg quotes his own 'Glen-Avin' (omitting two stanzas following the first stanza quoted here): *Queen's Wake*, pp. 100–03.

392(d) **Woolenhorn** apparently a fictitious setting.

NOTES 581

392(d) rights of teind [...] grass glebe at the Reformation the *Book of Discipline* stipulated that ministers of the Church of Scotland were to be provided with 'manses and glebes and adequate stipends' from teinds (tithes); but the teinds were never a sufficient resource for payment of the ministry, which remained an ongoing problem: see J. H. S. Burleigh, *A Church History of Scotland* (London, 1960), pp. 175–76, 211.

394(c) leister three-pronged spear. For a description of this traditional mode of salmon-fishing, see Scott's *Guy Mannering* (1815), volume II, Chapter 5. Hogg recalls Scott, James Skene and himself 'leistering kippers in Tweed' in *Anecdotes of Scott*, ed. by Jill Rubenstein (S/SC, 1999) p. 41.

395(d) close-time season when it is illegal to take certain fish or game.

396(d) Stridekirton again, apparently fictitious.

396(d) Jean Windlestrae 'windlestrae' is a tall, thin, withered stalk of grass; thus, someone easily blown about, feeble, delicate (*SND*).

397(c) zeal in the duties of religion [...] its doctrines in his article 'Statistics of Selkirkshire' Hogg attributes the superior intelligence and religious knowledge of the shepherds of Ettrick to the ministry of the Rev. Thomas Boston: *Prize Essays and Transactions of the Highland Society of Scotland*, second series, III (1832), 281–306 (pp. 303–04). Grumple appears to be a Moderate, a member of the party in the 18th-century Kirk opposed to Boston's heirs, the Evangelicals. The Moderates tended to carry the gentry's seal of approval, while the Evangelicals enjoyed popular support.

398(a) a patron see note on patronage to 141(c).

398(d) "green coats kilted to the knee." James Hogg, *The Pilgrims of the Sun* (Edinburgh and London, 1815), Part First, l. 4.

400(c) Aedie o' Aberlosk Adam Bryden of Aberlosk (1766–1850), Hogg's former boon companion and partner in the ill-fated lease of Locherben farm, Dumfriesshire, in 1807. In his letter of 7 March [1821] Hogg wrote to Blackwood, 'He is much fallen off, indeed quite doited by worldly misfortune now, but he was the greatest original I ever saw' (NLS MS 4719, fols 154–55). Aberlosk is in the wild hills of Eskdalemuir, south of Ettrick.

402(a) Clavers mountit on Hornie John Graham of Claverhouse, Viscount Dundee (1648–89), riding the black steed supplied him by his master Satan. Hogg depicts the fiendish 'Clavers' of Border tradition, detested for his persecution of the Covenanters, in *The Brownie of Bodsbeck* (1818).

402(c) the five kirks o' Eskdale in 1537 James V 'gifted the lands comprehended under the name of the Five Kirks of Eskdale to Lord Maxwell': *The New Statistical Account of Scotland*, 15 vols (Edinburgh: Blackwood, 1845), IV, 400. In Hogg's day the five parishes were Westerkirk, Eskdalemuir, Staplegorton, Wauchope and Ewes.

402(c) Tam-Park citing the present passage (under 'Tam'), *SND* glosses: 'A small drinking glass. The origin of the name is not traced'. A local reference, perhaps—Tam may have been notorious for serving his guests (or customers) short measure.

402(c) Bailey's Dictionary Nathan Bailey, *An Universal Etymological Dictionary* (1721), reprinted throughout the 18th century. Hogg may be alluding to a local joke: 'I found myself much in the same predicament with the man of Eskdalemuir, who had borrowed Bailey's Dictionary from his neighbour. On returning it, the lender asked him what he thought of it. "I dinna ken, man," replied he; "I have read it all through, but canna say that I understand it; it is the most confused book that ever I saw in my life!"' (*Memoir*, p. 9)

406(a) Tam the tailor perhaps (Gillian Hughes has suggested) Hogg's cousin, Thomas Hogg, a source for airs in R. A. Smith's *The Scotish Minstrel* (1824). He is featured as 'Hogg the celebrated Ettrick tailor' in 'Letter from the Ettrick Shepherd', *Blackwood's*, 6 (March 1820), 630–32.

406(d) "sun-ways-about," propitious ceremony (Gaelic, *deiseal*) in which one walks around a person or building in the direction of the sun to ward off bad luck. See Scott, *Waverley*, ed. by Claire Lamont (Oxford: Oxford University Press, 1986), p. 118.

Connel of Dee

Composed for an unpublished collection of poems, *Midsummer Night Dreams*, in 1814. Hogg's friend James Park persuaded him that 'The Pilgrims of the Sun', the longest piece in the set, merited publication on its own; it appeared in 1815 together with another poem, 'Superstition', but without 'Connel of Dee' (*Memoir*, pp. 32–33). Hogg reunited all three poems under their original rubric in the second volume of *The Poetical Works of James Hogg*, 4 vols (Edinburgh: Constable, 1822). The manuscript of 'Connel of Dee' survives at the Alexander Turnbull Library, New Zealand (MS Papers 42, Item 16, 'Country dreams and apparitions, No. 2: Connel of Dee'). The manuscript carries a note: 'This tale to be inserted in the second vol. after the Shepherd's Callander and proofs put to me J. H.' Printer's marks (indicating new gatherings at '205 Vol II' and '217 vol 2') confirm that the manuscript was used as copy for *WET*. Numerous scorings out and alterations suggest that it is a working draft, pressed into service as printer's copy, rather than one of Hogg's fair copy manuscripts, carefully prepared for the printer—hence the request to check proofs. As usual, the printer supplied punctuation according to house style; in addition there are several minor lexical variants between manuscript and printed text. The 1822 *Poetical Works* text (II, 117–49) omits the last two lines of stanza 45, no doubt for propriety's sake.

The manuscript shows that Hogg drafted the poem in 9-line stanzas with a rhyme scheme ABABBCDDC, until he got to stanza 31, when the stanza expands to 10 lines. Hogg went back and inserted an extra line (usually the penultimate), turning the couplet (DD) into a triad (DDD). 'Connel of Dee' is one of the strangest items in *WET*, with its combination of Hogg's 'ancient style' and Gothic psychosexual fantasy. The domestic guillotine and the hallucination of being drowned and eaten by fishes recall the 'tales of terror' published in *Blackwood's*: see R. Morrison and C. Baldick, *Tales of Terror from Blackwood's Magazine* (Oxford: World's Classics, 1995). Kate McGrail argues that 'Connel of Dee' reworks an anti-marriage dream poem by William Dunbar, 'Tretis of the Tua Mariit Wemen and the Wedo': 'Hogg subtly reveals and hides the traditional "vision" theme of a discontented and naive subject enlightened eventually by an allegorical vision': 'Re-Making the Fire: James Hogg and the Makars', *SHW*, 7 (1996), 26–36 (pp. 30–31).

419(338) From the *traps* of the wicked reminiscent of prayers for deliverance in Psalms 140 and 141.

421(406) wear variant spelling of Scots 'weir', to guard against, deny entry to (*SND*).

422(430) Cluny, or Gairn Clunie Water and the River Gairn are Aberdeenshire tributaries of the Dee.

423(463) a midsummer night 'in traditional lore, midsummer night is a night devoted to lovers, and is also a night (like Halloween) when spirits and supernatural beings are abroad. A certain W. Shakespeare draws on these traditions in his play *A Midsummer Night's Dream*, and Hogg doubtless had all this in mind when he planned his projected collection *Midsummer Night Dreams*. For this collection, "Connel" and "Pilgrims of the Sun" were to present a matched and contrasting pair of midsummer night dreams, one of heaven and one of hell.' (Note by Douglas Mack).

The Wife of Lochmaben

Originally published in *The Spy* as 'Story of the Ghost of Lochmaben, by John Miller', No. 18 (29 December 1810), pp. 191–93. While retaining the original outline of events, the story is considerably expanded in *WET*.

426(a) Lochmaben about ten miles NE of Dumfries.

426(a) Circuit-Court of Dumfries since Dumfries is the county town, the High Court of Justiciary would sit regularly there on circuit.

426(c) tinker breed [...] swarthy Egyptian i.e. (derogatorily) a gypsy.

427(b) between the lands of two different proprietors tradition forbade the interment of suicides in consecrated ground. The most famous allusion to the rural custom of burying suicides on the boundary between properties occurs in *The Private Memoirs and Confessions of a Justified Sinner*. Peter Garside cites the case of Tibbie Tamson, who killed herself after being accused of a petty theft and was buried 'at the junction of three lairds' lands' near Hawick, *c.* 1790: *Confessions*, p. 252.

427(d) fountain of life Revelation 21. 6, 'the fountain of the water of life'.

429(d) on the third day [...] they rose in a body to do God's work, as the echo of various gospel passages (e.g. Matthew 20. 19) suggests.

431(d) a verdict of *not proven* see note to 42(a).

432(a) ride the stang as Hughes says (*The Spy*, p. 598), a popular ceremony of public shaming, like the skimmington-ride depicted by Thomas Hardy in Chapter 39 of *The Mayor of Casterbridge*. Offenders against the community were mounted on a rough pole or tree-trunk (the stang) and paraded through the streets.

Cousin Mattie

Published for the first time in *WET*. Although the narrative of a 'superstitious' omen coming to pass is conventional, Hogg's treatment is remarkable for the interruptions that delay fulfilment. The intervening periods of seven years echo (with variation) the prophecy of the astrologer in Scott's *Guy Mannering* (1815): 'three periods would be particularly hazardous–his *fifth*–his *tenth*–his *twenty-first* year'–see P. D. Garside's edition (Edinburgh: Edinburgh University Press, 1999), p. 20.

433(a) Finagle not identified.

435(a) Kirkmichael near Lochmaben, Dumfriesshire.

435(c) They that will to Cupar maun to Cupar proverbial expression of obstinacy. Cupar is a royal burgh in Fife.

438(a) dreams were fulfilled in the days of old as in Genesis 37. 40–1, and in the Book of Daniel.

441(b) corpse-kisting preparation of the corpse in its coffin; for a description of the ritual, see Valentina Bold, 'Traditional Narrative Elements in *The Three Perils of Woman*', *SHW*, 3 (1992), 42–56 (pp. 48–49).

441(c) What's done canna be undone proverb (*ODEP*, p. 199) quoted in *Macbeth*, V. 1. 65.

Welldean Hall

Published for the first time in *WET*. Hogg returned to this material (re-casting it substantially) in his 'Shepherd's Calendar' tale 'Smithy Cracks', first published in *Blackwood's* for July 1827 (see *Shepherd's Calendar*, pp. 163–78). M. R. James adapted 'Welldean Hall' in 'The Tractate Middoth' (1911): the ghost of a clergyman haunts the library where his will is concealed in an 18th-century Talmud, and thwarts an attempt by his nephew to defraud his niece of the inheritance: M. R. James, *Collected Ghost Stories* (London: E. Arnold, 1931), pp. 209–34.

442(d) Solomon's maxim Proverbs 26. 5: 'Answer a fool according to his folly, lest he be wise in his own conceit'. Solomon was traditionally supposed to have been the author of the book of Proverbs.

443(a) "O Gilbert Falconer! [...] Nick will be a cast-away! lines apparently by Hogg.

444(a) saving life a belief cited elsewhere in Hogg's fiction, e.g. 'The Wool-Gatherer' in *The Brownie of Bodsbeck; and Other Tales*, 2 vols (Edinburgh, 1818), II, 89–228 (p. 140): 'The Border Chronicler' in *Literary Souvenir* (1826), pp. 257–79 (p. 276).

444(a) on your right hand and your left where God bides as a protector, e.g. Psalm 16. 8.

445(a) there are many doors to the valley of death [...] few out of it compare the famous lines from Vergil, *Aeneid* VI. 126–29: 'facilis descensus Auerno: \ noctes atque dies patet atri ianua Ditis; \ sed reuocare gradum superasque euadere ad auras, \ hoc opus, hoc labor est' (easy is the descent to the underworld; dark Dis's door stands open night and day; but to retrace your steps, to escape to the upper air–that is the task, that the labour). Hogg also used Vergil's lines as motto to No. 27 of *The Spy* (p. 273)–the nether regions being the Canongate Jail, which features later in the present story. Here the allusion initiates a running joke about '[reading] through the Greek and Latin classics'.

445(d) their thirds of the moveables invoking the legal distinction between heritable property (land and buildings), which would go to the heir at law, and moveables (furniture, assets), which would be divided among the family members.

446(b) cared little for any one [...] few cared ought for him compare the 18th-century English folksong, 'The Miller of Dee', ll. 7–8: 'I care for nobody, no, not I, \ If nobody cares for me'.

447(c) loosened and yielding joints a pun: technical terms for the condition of old books offered for sale.

448(b) "immaterial substances [...] into the brain;" Dr Leadbeater's explanation of spectral apparitions by appealing to optical science anticipates David Brewster's *Letters on Natural Magic* (1832), although Brewster's style is clear and straightforward, in contrast to the bombastic jargon mocked here. See also note to 50(d).

450(b) the right angle a sonorous citation of Pythagoras's theorem.

451(d) "Till his een they closed [...] his tongue wad hardly gang." lines from Hogg's 'The Witch of Fife', ll. 233–34, in *The Queen's Wake*.

453(b) may my right hand forget its cunning Psalm 137. 5.

456(a) a salary of £300 'an outrageously high salary for a governess. Miss Violet Smith in Conan Doyle's "The Solitary Cyclist" (1905) considered £100 p.a. "splendid pay", while Charlotte Brontë's heroine in *Jane Eyre* (1847) was only paid £30 p.a. by Mr Rochester, and that was double what she got as a teacher at Lowood.' (Gillian Hughes's note).

459(c–d) a very good book [...] joy may arise in the morning i.e., the Bible. Swan paraphrases Psalm 30. 5: 'weeping may endure for a night, but joy cometh in the morning'.

461(d) phlebotomise [...] *flaying* any part of his master compare Francis Grose, *A Dictionary of Buckish Slang, University Wit, and Pickpocket Eloquence* (1811): 'Flaybottomist. A bum-brusher, or schoolmaster', *The 1811 Dictionary of the Vulgar Tongue* (reprinted London: Studio Editions, 1994).

465(b) the laird of Lamington celebrated for his conviviality in Hogg's eponymous song, printed in *A Border Garland* (Edinburgh, 1819); see notes to 217(a) and 332(d).

468(d) the grand Seignior the Ottoman Sultan.

469(a) charges of horning [...] Captions see note to 65(d)–66(a).

469(c) siezed in the Canongate [...] Holyrood Swan is arrested as she leaves the bounds of the ruined Abbey of Holyrood, within which debtors had the legal right of sanctuary. See Walter Scott, *Chronicles of the Canongate*, ed. by Claire Lamont

(Edinburgh: Edinburgh University Press, 2000), p. 15 and note, pp. 385–86. Swan is conveyed to the Canongate Tolbooth (see p. 497); for a description of conditions there see *The Spy*, pp. 234–38, 274–78.

470(d) Major Graham unidentified.

471(c) the hero of faith without works ironical allusion to the long-running Presbyterian controversy about the means of salvation, which receives spectacular treatment in *The Private Memoirs and Confessions of a Justified Sinner*. The (popular) Evangelical party was associated with the doctrine of faith without works (i.e. justification by grace alone), while the (genteel) Moderates, of whom Professor B— is presumably a representative, held that salvation could be earned by good works. 'Hogg's winter evening tale, that is to say, reflects the widely-held popular / anti-gentry view by slyly suggesting that good works in practice might well be more likely to be done by a good and sincere popular preacher of justification by faith, such as [Rev. Thomas] Boston, rather than by an eminently respectable Moderate gentleman-preacher of justification by works' (Douglas Mack).

473(b) St James' Street by St James's Square in the New Town, on the site now occupied by the St James Centre; apparently a respectable address.

474(b) lukewarmness and indifference in sacred things the popular view of the Moderates.

476(b) A certain printer in Edinburgh unidentified. J. G. Lockhart quotes a description of Scott's famously excitable associate John Ballantyne (1774–1821): 'John's tone in singing was a sharp treble—in conversation something between a croak and a squeak': *Memoirs of the Life of Sir Walter Scott, Bart.*, 10 vols (Edinburgh: Cadell, 1839), III, 120. But it is unlikely that Hogg would have referred to John as a 'printer'. A printer named Linton, 'a flippant unstable being', makes a brief appearance in *Confessions*; Hogg gives him speech mannerisms similar to Andrew's, although less pronounced (pp. 151–52).

479(a) Long-spoon-sup-wi'-the-deil for the proverb see note to 388(a).

479(b) the devil, the world, and the flesh from the Baptism service in the traditional (16th-century) Anglican Book of Common Prayer.

480(c) *Dogs-lye* the proverb 'let sleeping dogs lie'.

480(d) Heather Bleater snipe. Richard Rickleton is nicknamed 'heather bleater' on account of his obstreperous laugh—see James Hogg, *The Three Perils of Woman*, ed. by David Groves, Antony Hasler, and Douglas S. Mack (S/SC, 1995), pp. 59–71.

483(c) "O wad some power [...] as others see us!" Burns, 'To a Louse', ll. 43–44.

485(a) bitter fruits Matthew 7. 15–20.

488(a) More-ill Ronald misunderstands 'moral' as '*mhor* [Gaelic, great] ill'.

488(c) hadfu cats i.e. advocates.

491(d) better [...] you never had been born compare Jesus's words at the last supper, Matthew 26. 24: 'woe unto that man by whom the Son of man is betrayed! it had been good for that man if he had not been born'.

492(b) in boards [...] cut up i.e. as they have come from the printers: not yet leather-bound, the pages uncut.

492(c) in the double of the octave i.e. tucked into a double fold in an uncut sheet of octavo; some leaves would be joined only at the head of the book, others also at the fore-edge.

492(c) a plum i.e. £100,000.

494(c) The world has not been your friend nor the world's law compare *Romeo and Juliet*, V. 1. 72: 'The world is not thy friend, nor the world's law'.

495(d) *atomy* pigmy or midget; or 'anatomy', miserable specimen.

497(c) through a glass darkly I Corinthians 13. 12.

Tibby Johnston's Wraith

Published for the first time in *WET*. The names 'Tibby' and 'Hyslop' recur in Hogg's tale 'Tibby Hyslop's Dream', published in the 'Shepherd's Calendar' series in *Blackwood's*, 21 (June 1827), 664–76.

500(a) doctors whiles come to them after they're dead an' buried baith allusion to the 'Resurrectionists', criminal entrepreneurs who would exhume the recently dead and sell them to anatomists for dissection. Scandals about grave-robbery were rife in the years preceding the Burke and Hare case (1827–29) and the Anatomy Act (1832). In January 1820 the Provost of Peebles complained to the town council that 'melancholy and extensive depredations [...] had been committed in the Churchyard, and [...] many bodies had been carried off': Buchan and Paton, *History of Peeblesshire*, II, 137.

500(c) Milseyburn-path the Milsey Burn flows near Gamescleugh hill, Ettrick–Hogg's neighbourhood. 'Carlshaw' has not been traced.

500(d) David Proudfoot perhaps a real person, but I have not been able to identify him.

502(d) Whoever follows freets, freets will follow them proverb: see *SND*, 'freit', noun, 3 (first and third quotations).

504(b) a kittle chapter in Nehemiah chapter 7, which contains the 'lang catalogue o' names' of 'the auld Jews that came back frae Babylon' specified in the next paragraph.

504(b) *the end o' man* a Biblical commonplace, although not found in Nehemiah; compare Ecclesiastes 7. 2, 'the end of all men'. Or perhaps a reference to the Shorter Catechism (see note to 5 (a)), the first question of which is, 'What is the chief end of man?', and the answer, 'The chief end of man is to glorify God, and to enjoy him for ever'.

504(c) the gerse on the field compare the Metrical version of Psalm 37. 2: 'For, even like unto the grass, soon be cut down shall they'.

504(c) a hard compensation malapropism for 'dispensation'.

504(c) the end of a things is at hand I Peter 4. 7.

505(c) Wraiths are of twa kinds see 'Adam Bell', p. 76 and note to 76(c).

505(c) Earl o' Hopetoun [...] Rae-hill *Statistical Account* mentions 'the new and elegant palace belonging to Lord Hopetoun at Raehills on the Annandale estate' (IX, 430). John, 2nd Earl of Hopetoun (d. 1781) was appointed curator of the estate on behalf of his mentally incompetent uncle, the 3rd Marquis of Annandale; James, 3rd Earl of Hopetoun (d. 1816) inherited the property at the Marquis's death in 1792.

Ane speetsh and defenns maide by Normaund Huntyr of Poomoode
[Translated from 'The Bridal of Polmood', pp. 288–89]

Much may it please my sovereign liege, not to believe such wicked and untrustworthy doings of your own true servant, and most loyal liegeman; nor so to belittle my honour that I can ill brook, by presuming that I should recklessly go to trouble a fair dame, an honest man's wife, and mother to two children; and that in the midst of a loft full of wenches. I would have been mad to have kicked up such a row–ruffling those gorgeous guineafowl and harrying my own cattle. Nothing, my liege, was further from my head than any such wild roguery and trickery. But when your Majesty dodged away from me in the loft, and left me in utter darkness, I was ashamed to come back with such an answer; and stood for some time hesitating what I should be advised next to do in that quandary. After a while, I stumbled back, and bowed down, set my nose to a chink in the door, and coaxed Elizabeth, saying we should never waste our ardour in the springtime of our life's journey. But she shied away from our having a snug, quiet chat together to settle the matter; finding her bashful and sullen, I was reluctant to wrangle with her in that perverse and saucy mood, and stayed no longer to argue. But being stupefied with drink, and senseless and dizzy with bending over, and the loft being dark as pitch, I lost all glimmer of any sense of where the door was. And then I stooped and went about until I grew perfectly dazed, and thought the castle was twirling and spinning around; and besides that it was rising up on one side of me and threatening to bowl me over. I have seldom weathered such a dreadful predicament, but fearing that I would fall over, and so as not to make a thump, I relaxed my joints and crouched down, and crept forward along on my shins and elbows, listening at each door whether there was anyone snoring within. Either I overheard, or thought I overheard, sleeping sighs behind them all, and I began to entertain slender hopes of winning my way out of this tangled snare unspotted with shame or disgrace. Being very reluctant to run rashly and press down upon the bellies or cheeks of those sweet enticing girlfriends, who were lying dozing and snoring and sprawling, heedless and unsuspicious of any harm, I was tottering cautiously along with a great deal of patience. I was lying at full length at one door, when I heard a knight unhasp the catch, as softly as a snail when she goes creeping over the wet turf; but the door gave a wheeze one way and a creak the other, and before I had time to right myself, a big man tripped over my feet, and fell belly flat on me with a dreadful buffet, so that my rump was squashed, and my snout rapped with a crunch against the loft. I cursed him in wrath, and intending to hold him back, I grabbed hold of his coat and got a heel of a noble. Before I got to my knees he disappeared, making the door clash behind him. I shuffled to the same place as eagerly as I could—opened the same door, as I thought, and ran forward—but Christ, where should I alight! but on the giddy side of a cosy madame! My head slammed against the building, and I was clean stunned and dazed. My lady sighed and murmured, putting me in a dreadful bother; and as I was fumbling to rise, she thought I was fondling her, and set up such an unearthly shriek that my very senses swooned and my teeth chattered in my head. She reared up in a rage and seized me with grievous violence, and being right loath to lay a guiltless finger on her, I curbed my wrath, and lay choking until you came groping your way from the tower and parted us. This is the whole and faithful truth, as I hope for mercy by our blessed Lady.

Glossary

This Glossary sets out to provide a convenient guide to Scots, English, and other words in *Winter Evening Tales* which may be unfamiliar to some readers. It is greatly indebted to the *Oxford English Dictionary*, to the *Scottish National Dictionary*, and to the *Concise Scots Dictionary*, ed. by Mairi Robinson (Aberdeen: Aberdeen University Press, 1985), to which the reader requiring more information should refer. The Glossary concentrates on single words, and guidance on phrases, idioms, and expressions involving more than one word will normally be found in the explanatory Notes.

a': all
abeigh: apart, aloof
aboon: above
adminicular: helpful, auxiliary, corroborative
ae, ae': one, every
aff: off
aftner: more often
agroof: with face downward, prone
aik: oak, oaken, wooden
ain: own
aince: once
airches: takes aim
airel: payment as a token of engagement
alderleivest: dearest of all, most beloved
a-low: ablaze
amain: in full force; without delay
amaist: almost
amang: among
amaritude: bitterness
amatorculist: a trifling sweetheart, a general lover
amel: enamel (of the eye)
ance: once
ane: one
assilyt: forgiven, absolved

asteer: astir
a-swooming: flooded, awash
a'thegither: altogether
atour: around
atweel: indeed, for sure
atween: in between; between times
auld: old
aumrie: cupboard, repository for keeping domestic utensils
ava: of all, at all
ax, axe: ask
ay, aye: still, always, ever
ayont: beyond

backbraid: the breadth of the back
backsprents: backbones
baeth: both
bairn, bairnie: child
baith: both
banning: cursing
barm: yeast, ferment
barmy: fermented
bastailye: fortified tower
bate: beat
batt: position, situation; beat
bauchle: clumsy, useless person
bawbee: coin, worth six pence

Scots

beadle: church officer; gravedigger

beane: bone

beath: both

beckin: bowing, bending

beguid: began

behodden: beholden

beik: bask

bellandine: battle cry, brawl

bell-handle: handle for pulling a bell-rope or bell-wire

ben, ben-: inside; towards the inner part of a house or building

Benshee: Banshee; female spirit of ill omen

bensil: force, rush, sudden movement

bent: open country, heath

benty-necks, benty-neckit: crooked-necked; weak

besprent: scattered; besprinkled

beuk: book, especially the Bible

bibber: frequent drinker, a tippler

bien: in good condition, well-to-do, comfortable, pleasant

bigging: building

bike: swarm

billy: brother, fellow

birke: birch

birkies: lads

birns: scorched heather-stems

birris: whirring sound (as made by a partridge)

birst: burst

birstling: bristling, broiling

bit: small portion

bits: affectionate, pitying, or contemptuous expression to indicate smallness, diminu-

tiveness, insignificance

blarney: flattering talk

blate: modest, bashful, sheepish

blather: foolish, long-winded talk

bleared: thin, watery

blear-eyed: dim-sighted, short-sighted, blinded

blee: blow

bleiter: snipe

blether: foolish, long-winded talk

blink: glance fondly at

blirt: cry, weep; gust of wind or rain

boddle: small copper coin, worth twopence Scots

bode: portend, foretell

bogle: goblin

bonny: pretty, pleasant-looking

boonmost: highest, uppermost

boor-tree-bush: bourtree, or elder-tree

bothy: rough hut or resting lodge

bouet: lantern

bourick, bourock, bowrack: cairn, mound; hovel, small hut

bowe: bowl

brae: bank, hillside, or steeply-rising piece of ground

brag: challenge

braid: broad

braw: fine, handsome, splendid

bray: bank, hillside, or steeply-rising piece of ground

break: fall or deposit of snow

bree: brow

breeks: trousers

brier: eyelashes or brows

brig, brigg: bridge

brik: break, broken

brisket: breast

broad-sword: cutting sword with a broad blade

broggling: doing work clumsily; failing to do a task

brogues: shoes of untanned leather

broolzie: fight, turmoil

broose: race on horse or foot at a wedding

broostles: bout of hard struggle

brose: oatmeal or pease-meal mixed with boiling water or milk

brosey-mou'd: slow of speech; stupid

brownie: elemental spirit

brulzie: fight, turmoil

buckling-comb: comb for curling the hair

bught: pen for confining ewes at milking; sheepfold

buirdly: burly, stalwart, well-built

buller: bubble; gurgle

bumper: glass of wine or spirits

bure: bore

burn: brook or stream

bygane: bygone

bygge: build

ca': drive (sheep or cattle)

cairn: pile of stones, landmark on mountain-top

caitiff: despicable wretch, villain

callan, callant: boy, youth

canna: cannot

cannie, canny: careful, skilful; good, kind

cantrip: charm, spell; trick

capperkayle: capercaillie, the wood-grouse

carena: don't care

carle: man, fellow; old man

carlin: witch; old woman

cassick: causeway

cauld: cold

cauny: careful, skilful; good, kind

certes: certainly, assuredly

chap, chop: strike, knock

chapman: itinerant merchant, pedlar

chiel, chield: young man, fellow

chop: carry on, jog along

choppin: liquid measure, equal to half a Scots pint

claes: clothes

claughtin: clutching

claymore: Highlander's large two-edged sword

cleuch, -cleuch: narrow glen with high sides

clink: money, coins

clout: cloth or rag; to patch, to mend; to strike

cockernonies: women's starched caps

cockit: cocked (of a hat)

coft: bought

condign: fitting, appropriate

cool-the-loom: lazy worker

coome: wood

cope: vault (of heaven)

corbie, corby: raven

corky-headit: light-headed, giddy

corn rick: stack of corn

coronach: dirge

coronal: garland for the head

correi: hollow on a mountainside

cot: cottage

cottar: peasant, tenant farmer

coup: turn over, upset

courch'e: kerchief, head covering

cowe: twig, stem

cowhouse: cowshed

crack: gossip, chat

craim: merchant's booth or stall

cramasye: crimson cloth

crap: crept

craw: crow

crock: old ewe, past bearing lambs

croft: smallholding

cromach: cow

cushey: dove

cutty, cwotty: short, stumpy

dadd: blow or strike

daffin: jest, frolic

daft: foolish, crazy

dale: deal, i.e. wooden plank or board

danyng: dawning, early morning

darn: thread one's way in and out of

daur: dare

deave: deafen, bother, annoy

dee: die

deil: devil

deil hae't: 'devil take it', exclamation of disgust

demmish: damage, injury

deprehended: caught in the act

deshabille: partly undressed

deune: done

dever: stun, knock out

dew-bell: a flower, the lady's mantle (*Alchemilla pratensis*)

ding: strike hard, knock down, beat

dinkly: neatly, sprucely

dirle: thrill, tingle with emotion

dirt: mean, worthless person

dirk: short dagger worn in the belt by Highlanders

discerptibility: capacity for being plucked asunder; divisibility

dochter: daughter

docken: dock-leaf

doit: copper coin of low value

doon: down

douf: dull, stupid, melancholy

douse, douce: sober, quiet, well-behaved

dow: dove, dear one; to thrive, prosper; to fade away

dowkit: ducked

down-sitting: action of settling in a place

dowye: sad, dreary, dull

drappie: small drop

dree: suffer, endure

drugget: woollen cloth

drumble: sluggard, inert person

dry: thirsty

dud: cloth, article of clothing

duds: clothes

dugon: worthless person

dule: dole, sorrow, pain

dung: struck

durk: short dagger worn in the belt by Highlanders

dyve: argue

ebriety: drunkenness

edder: adder

ee, een: eye, eyes

e'e-bree: eyebrow

eesed: used

egress: going out, issuing forth

eidently: industriously, conscientiously, carefully

eild: barren old ewe

eiry: eerie

eirysome: fearsome

eldritch: weird, unearthly,

frightful

elyed: went away, disappeared

emmets: ants

eneuch: enough

erlich: elf-like; weird, ghostly

eskis: newts

ether: adder

ettle: intend, project; attempt; aim

ey, eyne: eye, eyes

eynied, eynit: presumed, thought fit

fa': fall, befall

fabricula: the vapours, neurasthenia; chronic fatigue syndrome

fain: willing, content; gladly

fairing: gift bought at a fair

falderal: trifle, idle fancy, fuss

falderall: business

fankit: entangled

fash: bother, vex

faud: favour, good looks

fauldit: folded

feint o': no, nothing, none

ferlies: marvels, wonders

ferrar, ferrer: further

feuar: person who holds land under feudal duty of a payment in cash or kind

feye: fey; fated; behaving strangely, as though bewitched

fike: fidget, twitch; vex, trouble, bother

firth: estuary

fisky: whisky

fit: foot

flageolet: small flute

flaip: heavy fall, thud

flee: fly

fleech: coax, cajole, entreat

fleegary: gewgaw, trifle; finery in dress

fley: frighten

flummery: humbug, flattery

flushir: boggy ground

flychtering: fluttering

flyting: scolding, railing

fock: folk

fog: moss

fore-fit: forefoot

forebye: besides

forefoughen: exhausted, worn out

fornent: opposite, in front of, against

fouk: folk

fraebout: from about

franazy: frenzy

frazing: phrasing; making elaborate speech or wordy fuss

freaks: tricks

freat, freet: superstition; omen

frith: firth, estuary

frizzel: hammer of flintlock gun

frizzle: frizzled hair; short crisp curl

furze: spiny evergreen shrub with yellow flowers

fustian: coarse cotton cloth

gaed: went

gairie: streaked, variegated, gaudy; whim or fancy

gait: way

gane: mouth

gang: go

gar, garre: make, cause (something to be done)

gare: strip of fresh grass

gart: caused, made

gat: got

gate: way

gaun: going

gavel: end wall of upper part of building

gayan': rather, very

gear: property, goods, herds

geate: mad, insane

ged: pike

gepe: gape

gerse: grass

gie: give

gill: one fourth of a standard pint

gillour: manservant

gillygawpie: foolish, giddy person

gin: if, whether

gin: snare, trap

girl(e): thrill

girrel: eat and drink intemperately

glamarye: magic, enchantment

glebe: plot of cultivated land

gledge: squint

glen: mountain valley

glibe: glebe, field

glibeness: sharpness, slyness

gliff: moment, instant, short while; shock, scare

glime: look slyly, squint, peer

glisk: glimpse, gleam

gloaming: twilight

gluff: shock, scare

gluther: gurgle

gollaring: roaring, shouting; gurgling

goodman: husband, farmer, male head of household

goodwife: farmer's wife, female head of household

gorse: prickly shrub (*Ulex europaeus*)

goud: gold

gouffin': striking with open hand

gouk: cuckoo; fool, simpleton

gousty: dreary, eerie

gowan, gown: daisy

gowd: gold

graffe: grave

grains: tines, points

graip: farmyard fork

grane: groan

gratte: wept, cried

grave-pole: pole for transporting coffin to grave-side

greet: weep

grew, grewe: shudder, shiver

grit: great

groat: small coin, four pence Scots

groats: hulled oats

grumph: grunt, snore

grunstane: grindstone

guddle: tickle; catch fish by groping with hands

gude: good; God

gullet, gullot: narrow, deep channel

gushet: ornamental pattern, like stitching; flexible part between joints or scales

hae: have

haffat(s): side of face, temples

haggis: pudding made of the heart, lungs, and liver of a sheep

hairt: hart, male deer

hale: whole, healthy

halesome: wholesome

hallan: partition dividing interior of cottage between door and hearth, or living-room and byre

hame: home

hamel: home-made

hantle: large quantity, a great deal

haque: a kind of short gun

hark: listen

harl: drag

harns: brains

harrigalds: animal's pluck

haud: hold

haverel: foolish, garrulous person

havering: gossiping, garrulous; talking nonsense

hay-mow: hay-rick

heather-blooter: snipe

hech, heich: exclamation of sorrow, surprise, contempt

hempy: wild, mischievous person, rogue

herns: brains

hess: has

higgle: sell, trade

hing: hang

hinny: honey

hogshead: large cask for liquids

holm: stretch of low-lying ground by river or stream

hooning: loitering, lingering

hope, -hope: small enclosed upland valley or hollow

hottle: inn or hotel

houdy: midwife

houf: haunt

houk, howk: dig

houm: stretch of low-lying ground by river or stream

hout: exclamation (dismissive of another's opinion)

howdin: act as midwife; sway, lurch from side to side

howe: hollow, low-lying patch of ground

hurdies: buttocks, hips, haunches

huzza: shout of exultation or applause

huzzy: frivolous woman or servant-girl

ilka: each, every, same

ill-faur'd: ill-favoured, ugly

Indians: Indies

ingress: flowing into

intil: into

inwith: inner side

I's, I'se: I shall; I am

ither: other

jade: worn-out nag; term of abuse for horse or woman

jaumphit: mocked, jeered

jaunder: talk foolishly or jokingly

jaupying: splashing

jeerit: jeered

jilflirt: wanton or giddy young woman

jink: dodge, skip, move nimbly

joe: sweetheart

jointure: provide with a dowry

juck, jwock: joke

kail: cabbage

kail stock, kailstock: cabbage stalk

kail-wife: woman who sells greens

kail-yard: cabbage-garden, kitchen-garden

kean: payment in kind

keek: peer, peep

kelpie: water-horse, lake-dwelling monster or demon

ken: know

kene: payment in kind

kimmer: woman friend, gossip

kipple: one of a pair of rafters

or beams

kirk: church, particularly the presbyterian Church of Scotland

kirtle: woman's gown

kithe, kythe: show, display; appear

kittle: tricky, sly, deceitful; ticklish, uncertain, difficult (of a situation)

kivering: covering

knevillin: punching, pummelling

kye: kine, cattle

lacquey: footman

laigh: low

laike-a-day: alas

lair: boggy patch, mire

lair: lay

laird: landed proprietor

laith: loath

laithly: loathsome, foul

lane: alone; (by) himself or yourself

lang: long

lang hame: the grave

lang syne, langsyne: long ago

lassick, lassock: little girl

lauchin: laugh at, ridicule

lave: rest, remainder

laverack, laverock: skylark

law, -law: cone-shaped hill

lawn: linen

leane: alone; by (him)self or (your)self

leatherin': thrashing

leear: liar

leerit: taught

leesome: pleasant, agreeable

leesome lane: utterly alone

leifu': sympathetic, amiable, lovely

leil: honest, faithful

leister: three-pronged fishing spear

leiva lane: all alone

lene: conceal, keep silent

lennoch more: son

leughen: laughed

lift: sky

likit: liked

limmer: idle hussy

lin, linn: waterfall; ravine

ling: heather

lingit: strode (briskly); flexible, pliant

links: joints, vertebrae

lippen: trust, rely on

lire: flesh, muscle

lirk: fold or wrinkle; frown

liths: limbs, joints

loch: lake

loot: let

loundering: thrashing

lowe: flame, blaze

lown, lowne: soft, quiet; softly, quietly; hushed

lufe: palm; outstretched hand

lugs: ears

lum: chimney

lynge: ling, heather

mae: more

maik: figure, form; resemblance

maile: rent; farm

mailen: small-holding; piece of arable land held on lease

mainpernorly: giving surety for the accused's appearance in a court of law

mair: more, bigger, more generous

maist: most

mak: make

manna: mustn't

mattock: spade for loosening hard ground

maugre: despite

maun: must

may: maid, young lady

mell: mallet

mellin: consorting

meltith: a meal or repast

mence, mense: honour, credit, respect; common sense

merk: sum of money equal to two-thirds of a pound

merl: blackbird

messan: small house-dog, cur

middrit: midriff; diaphragm; belly

mind: remember, intend

minnie: mother

misleered: mistaken, misguided; unmannerly

mither: mother

moldwarp: mole

monachism: mode of rule in the monastic system

mony: many

moopin: kissing

moorfowl, muirfowl: red grouse

mootis: moults

morclaith: pall, covering for a coffin

morn: next day

muckle: large, big; much

mudwart: pondweed

mug, mugg: breed of long-woolled, white-faced sheep

mumpit: cheated, deceived

munt: low, tree-covered hill

murecokke: red grouse

murt: second (large) dorsal fin

nae: no

nain: own

navelled: knobbed, with a boss in the centre

neb: nose

neeve: hand, fist

neist: next

neivfu': handful

nershe: arse

nettie: woman who goes about the country gathering wool

neuk: corner

neukit: cornered

neive: hand, fist

nightit: benighted

noozle: nose

nor: than

nories: whims, fancies, caprices

norlan': northern

nurice: to nourish; a nurse, especially a wet-nurse

ochon, ohon: alas

ony: any

oon-pan: large, shallow pan used for baking bread

or: before

orgies: secret rites or ceremonies

ouirwurde: burden

oundis: wounds

outher: either, or

ower, owr: too (much), excessively

oxter: armpit

pack: bag, pouch

palmer: professional pilgrim

parle: speech, language

parritch: porridge

pat: pot

paulie: undersized, ailing lamb

pawky: tricky, artful, sly

pawpee: bawbee, a coin worth six pence Scots

peat-knowe: peat-knoll, stack of

dried peats kept outside for
fuel

peat-neuk: corner where peat is
kept inside for fuel

peck: measure of capacity used
for dried goods

peer: puir, poor

pegh: gasp, pant

pericranium: membrane envel-
oping the skull

periosteum: dense fibro-vascular
membrane which envelopes
the bones

phiz: face, countenance

phlebotomise: let blood from

phrenitis: inflammation of the
brain or of its membranes

pifyrit: trembled, shivered

pike: peck, pick

pill: peel

pingle: strive, exert force

pirl: ripple

pismire: ant

pit: put

pith: strength, vigour

plack: small copper coin, worth
four pence Scots

pled: plaid

pleugh: plough

ply: strive, work hard; fold

pock: bag, small sack

polyedrical: many-sided

poust: strength, vigour, force

powney: pony

poyet: poet

prooder: prouder

puir: poor

putting the stane: contest much
like shot putting

pyat: magpie

quat: quit

quean: familiar term for a

young woman

queich: drinking cup

quhair: where

rad: afraid, worried

rade: rode

ragamuffian: rough, good-for-
nothing man or boy

rail: woman's short-sleeved
front or over-bodice

rallying: making fun of

ramrace: headlong race or
charge

rannlebauks: bar across the
chimney for suspending
cooking utensils

rape: rope

raws: mountain-ridges

redd: interpret, explain

reek: smoke

refusticat: resuscitate

rhodomontade: vainglorious
brag or boast

rinnin': running

rood: cross

roosed: stirred up, provoked

roup: public auction

routh: plenty, abundance

row: roll, wrap

rowntre: rowan-tree

rowt: bellow

rugged: pulled vigorously,
tugged

rused: stirred up, provoked

sachless: feeble, useless

sae: so

sair: sore

sanna: shall not

sarsnet: fine silken material

sauf: save

saur: smell, savour

sawn: sown

sax: six

sayir: sore, sorely

scaur: rock, crag, precipice

schedde: strip of land

screed: fragment, scrap; long discourse, harangue

screen: shawl, scarf

sei-mawe: seamew, seagull

sel, sell (o't, o' him): self, (it)self, (him)self

sellible: blessed, fortunate, happy

sennins: sinews

senny leaf: senna, a purgative

shatterbrain: thoughtless, giddy person

shaugle, shauglin: stumbling, shambling along

sheen: shoes

sheile, shiel: shepherd's hut

shilly shally: wishy-washy, feeble

shoal, shool: shovel

shoon: shoes

shurf: worthless person

sic, sickan, sicken: such; of such a kind

sickerly: thus

siller: silver, money

sin': since

sindry: apart

skaddaw, skaddow: shadow

skaith: harm

skeel: (medical) skill

skelldrake: sheldrake, a wild duck

skelp: strike, slap

skelpie: hussy

skene-dhu: Highland dirk or dagger

skirl: screech, wail

skype: mean rogue; low, ill-mannered person

skyrit: shunned, avoided, turned away from

slack: old ewe past breeding age, fattened for slaughter

slaes: sloes

slubber: slobber

slyboots: sly, cunning, or crafty person

small clothes: breeches

small sword: light sword with tapering blade, used in fencing

smeddum: spirit, energy, vigorous resourcefulness

smiddy: smithy

sneckit: latched

snipiltin': chasing after (used contemptuously)

snirtin': sniggering; snoring

sodger: soldier

souple: smooth, fluent, prattling

sowins: oatmeal steeped and fermented in water

span: distance from the tip of the thumb to the tip of the little finger

spaulds: shoulders, limbs

spavined: worn-out

speal: particle, something of little or no value

spearings: news

sped wi': fared with

speen: wean

speer: ask, make enquiries

splore: quarrel, hubbub, excitement

sponkin: sparkling, twinkling, flashing

spulzie: rob, plunder; spoil or booty

stand to: stand by, support

stane: stone

stane-clod: stone's throw

staniraw: reddish dye from lichen
steek: shut, make fast
steep: soak
steepin': clergyman's stipend
steer: stir, disturb, interfere
stelled: fixed (of eyes), staring
stick: botch, break off, fail
stock: outer edge of box-bed
stootin: stuttering, stammering
stour: dust-cloud; uproar, fuss, haste, disorder
straik: blow, stroke
strap: hang up
strath: stretch of flat land by waterside
streek: stretch out
strodgin: strutting, striding
strow: squabble, quarrel, confusion
studden: stood; stopped to consider
suborned: obtained by corrupt means
sude: should
sulanis: solan's, gannet's
swee: sway, move from side to side
sweyer, swire: steep pass
swith: go away, be off (exclamation)
syne: ago

tae: the one
taes: toes
taigling: grabbing, holding back
tak: take
tane: the one
tap: top or tip
tar-kitt: tub or pail containing tar
tassylit: tufted

tawpie: foolish, slovenly girl
tedis: toads
teil: deil, devil
teind: tithe
tetherlength: rope's length
teuk: took
thack: thatch
thilke: the same
thole: endure, suffer
thrang: busy
thrapple: throat, windpipe
threep: strongly held belief; superstition; argue obstinately
threyve: thrive
tikabed: mattress
til, till: to
till: stiff clay, impervious to water, forming unproductive subsoil
tinckell: circle of beaters
tine: lose
tint: lost, strayed
tirrovy: tantrum, fit
tither: the other
tocher: bride's dowry; to supply with a dowry
tod: fox
toddy: beverage made of whisky with hot water and sugar
town: farm buildings
trig: neat, spruce
tripping: moving quickly and lightly
troth: truth
trouth: pledged word or promise
trow: believe
tup: ram
twall: twelve

unco: very; extraordinary; uncanny

unsonsy: unlucky

untackit: not stitched down; unbound, loose

untelled: untold, uncounted

vellum: fine variety of parchment made from calfskin

vitriol: sulphuric acid

vizies: takes aim

wad, wadna: would, wouldn't

waefu': woeful, grieved

waik: wake, vigil

walth: plenty

wame: stomach, belly

wan: won; reach, find one's way to a destination

wark: work; fuss, business

warld: world

warstle: wrestle

wassail: carousal, merrymaking

waster: fish spear

wastle: keep away from

wat: know

wat: wet

water-bells: bubbles in water

water-kelpies: sea or lake demons

wauffest: weakest, feeblest, most worthless

wauk: wake, awake

waukin': awake

waur: worse

wean: child, infant

wear: ward off, keep out

wedder: wether, castrated male sheep

weel: well

weel-ee: water-logged place in bog whence spring arises

weel-tochered: provided with a large dowry

wefoue: woeful

weil: deep pool in stream or river

weir: war

weird: baneful

werde: prophesy, foretell

wetis: knows

wha: who

wheen: several, a few

whelp: cub; unmannerly youth

whiles: sometimes, at times

whilk: which

whillibalu: uproar, hullabaloo

whillilu: melody, air

whup: whip

widnee, wadnee: wouldn't

wight: person, human being

willy-wand: willow wand

wilsomely: wilfully

wist: know, knew

witters: barbs (of fishing spear)

wod: mad

won: deliver, drive home (of a blow); dried for storage by exposure to sun and air

wood-rasp: wild raspberry

wother-weight: counter-weight, counter-balance

wraith: apparition of a living or recently dead person

wrang: wrong

wudd: crazy

wudward: woodward, or forest keeper

wullcat: wild cat

wyrde: fate

yaud: jade, old horse

yerkit: jerked, cramped

yermite: hermit

yestreen: yesterday evening
yettlin: made of cast-iron
yince: once
yird: earth

younkers: children
youtis: screams
yowe: ewe
yudith: youth